CAPE REFUGE

TWO BOOKS IN ONE

SOUTHERN STORM

Books by Terri Blackstock

Emerald Windows

Cape Refuge Series

1 | *Cape Refuge*
2 | *Southern Storm*
3 | *River's Edge*
4 | *Breaker's Reef*

Newpointe 911

1 | *Private Justice*
2 | *Shadow of Doubt*
3 | *Word of Honor*
4 | *Trial by Fire*
5 | *Line of Duty*

Sun Coast Chronicles

1 | *Evidence of Mercy*
2 | *Justifiable Means*
3 | *Ulterior Motives*
4 | *Presumption of Guilt*

Second Chances

1 | *Never Again Good-bye*
2 | *When Dreams Cross*
3 | *Blind Trust*
4 | *Broken Wings*

With Beverly LaHaye

1 | *Seasons Under Heaven*
2 | *Showers in Season*
3 | *Times and Seasons*
4 | *Season of Blessing*

Novellas

Seaside

CAPE REFUGE

TWO BOOKS IN ONE

SOUTHERN STORM

Terri Blackstock

ZONDERVAN™

GRAND RAPIDS, MICHIGAN 49530 USA

ZONDERVAN.COM/
AUTHOR**TRACKER**

ZONDERVAN™

Cape Refuge/Southern Storm
Copyright © 2006 by Terri Blackstock

Cape Refuge
Copyright © 2002 by Terri Blackstock

Southern Storm
Copyright © 2003 by Terri Blackstock

Requests for information should be addressed to:

Zondervan, *Grand Rapids, Michigan 49530*

ISBN-10: 0-310-60535-0 (softcover)
ISBN-13: 978-0-310-60535-5 (softcover)

Published in association with the literary agency of Alive Communications, Inc., 7680 Goddard Street, Suite 200, Colorado Springs, CO 80920.

Interior design by Beth Shagene

Printed in the United States of America

06 07 08 09 10 11 12 • 10 9 8 7 6 5 4 3 2 1

CAPE REFUGE

*This book is lovingly dedicated
to the Nazarene.*

ACKNOWLEDGMENTS

*P*eople often ask me if I base my characters on real people. My answer is usually no. In writing *Cape Refuge,* however, I depart slightly from that policy. Thelma and Wayne Owens are based on two very close friends of mine—Nicki and Dick Benz, who created Buried Treasures Ministry in Jackson, Mississippi. Buried Treasures Ministry got its name when Nicki began visiting the women in the Hinds County Detention Center, and started every meeting by blessing each woman individually, looking into their eyes and telling them that they are God's treasures. These are women who have been treated like trash for much of their lives, and they have treated *themselves* like trash. Many have horrible pasts. Their futures look grim. But the truth of their worth in Jesus Christ brings them to tears. Then they listen to the message that Nicki and the others with Buried Treasures bring to them and their children through Bible studies, parenting classes, a Girl Scout troop, and ongoing ministry when they are released.

But the battle is not easy, and the Enemy fights viciously for them when they are back in the world. In many cases, they are released without enough money to support them for a week, and they return to the boyfriends, families, friends, pimps, and drug dealers who led them down the wrong path. Often, they fall back into their old habits and eventually wind up back in jail.

For this reason, the Lord put the Buried Treasures Home on Nicki and Dick's heart. When it is built, Buried Treasures Home will be a transitional place for women to recover, learn, and begin new lives in Christ for a year or longer. Like Hanover House in this book, it will be a place of refuge. However, the Buried Treasures Home will be a much more structured place where residents can complete their educations, study the Bible extensively, learn to be good parents, develop new careers, and develop the strength in Christ that will enable them to stand against evil when they are on their own. The first home will be in Mississippi, but their dream is to eventually have homes like it all across the country.

Unlike Thelma and Wayne, Nicki and Dick are very much alive, and I have learned much from them about bearing fruit for Christ's kingdom, about loving with Christ's love, and about doing Christ's work.

For more information about this precious ministry, or to contribute to the building of the first Buried Treasures Home, please write to Buried Treasures Home, P. O. Box 497, Clinton, Mississippi 39056–0497.

PREFACE

*C*ape Refuge is a fictitious island which I set just east of Savannah, Georgia, on the Atlantic Coast. To research it, I spent time on Tybee Island, a lovely little beachside community outside of Savannah. Many of my ideas for life in Cape Refuge came from there.

There's another island just south of Tybee called Little Tybee Island, an uninhabited marshland and wildlife refuge. For this novel, I turned Little Tybee into Cape Refuge, after a few alterations to the terrain and the coastline. I hope the kind people of Georgia's coast will forgive me.

I owe a big thanks to J. R. Roseberry, editor and publisher of the *Tybee News,* for his help in my research.

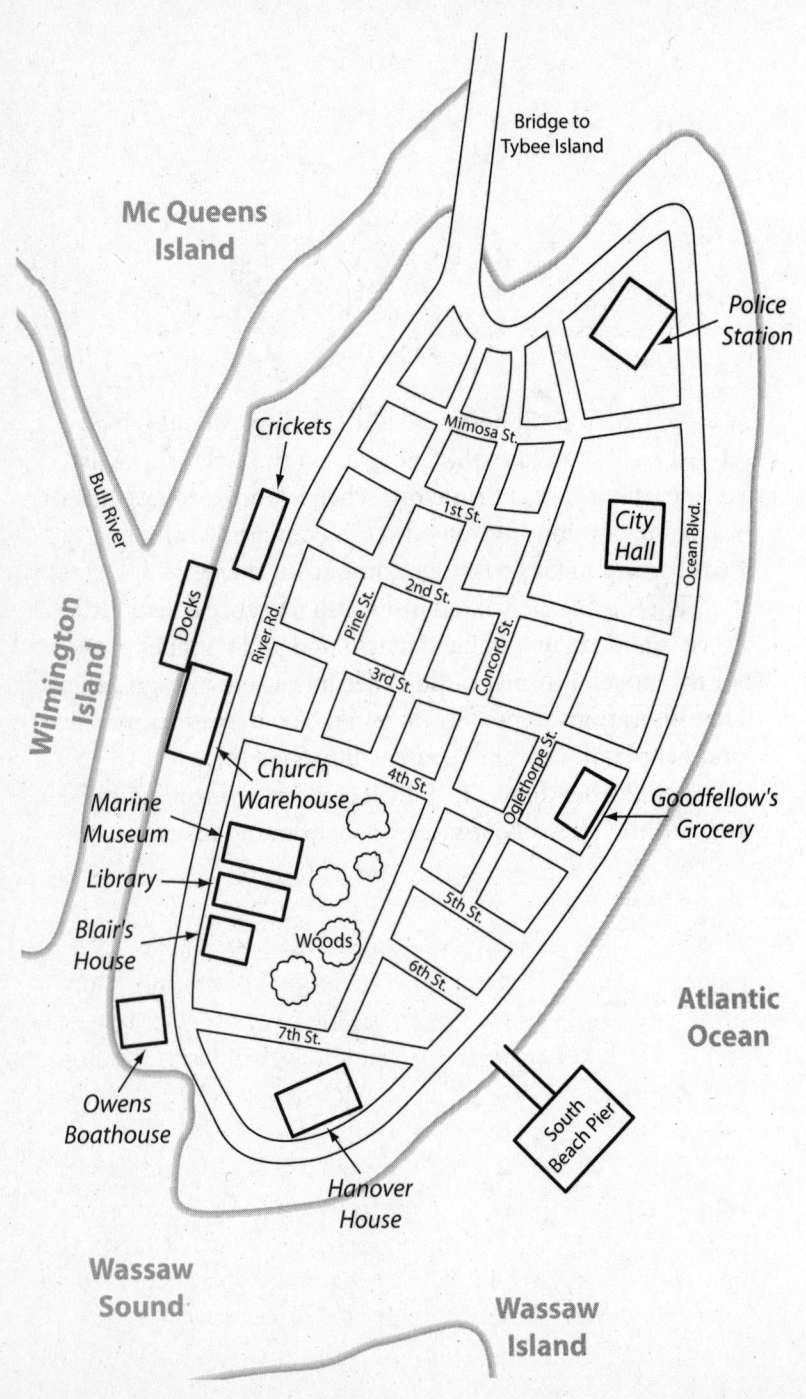

CHAPTER

1

*T*he air conditioner was broken at City Hall, and the smell of warm salt air drifted through the windows from the beach across the street. Morgan Cleary fanned herself and wished she hadn't dressed up. She might have known that no one else would. The mayor sat in shorts and a T-shirt that advertised his favorite beer. One of the city councilmen wore a Panama hat and flip-flops. Sarah Williford, the newest member of the Cape Refuge City Council, looked as if she'd come in from a day of surfing and hadn't even bothered to stop by the shower. She wore a spandex top that looked like a bathing suit and a pair of cutoff jeans. Her long hair could have used a brush.

The council members sat with relaxed arrogance, rocking back and forth in the executive chairs they'd spent too much money on. Their critics—which included almost everyone in town—thought they should have used that money to fix the potholes in the roads that threaded through the island. But Morgan was glad the council was comfortable. She didn't want them irritable when her parents spoke.

The mayor's nasal drone moved to the next item on the agenda. "I was going to suggest jellyfish warning signs at some of the more popular sites on the beach, but Doc Spencer tells me he ain't seen too many patients from stings in the last week or so—"

"Wait, Fred," Sarah interrupted without the microphone. "Just because they're not stinging this week doesn't mean they won't be stinging next week. My sign shop would give the city a good price on a design for a logo of some kind to put up on *all* the beaches, warning people of possible jellyfish attacks."

"Jellyfish don't attack," the mayor said, his amplified voice giving everyone a start.

"Well, I can see you never got stung by one."

"How you gonna draw a picture of 'em when you can't hardly see 'em?"

Everyone laughed, and Sarah threw back some comment that couldn't be heard over the noise.

Morgan leaned over Jonathan, her husband, and nudged her sister. "Blair, what should we do?" she whispered. "We're coming up on the agenda. Where are Mama and Pop?"

Blair tore her amused eyes from the sight at the front of the room and checked her watch. "Somebody needs to go check on them," she whispered. "Do you believe these people? I'm so proud to have them serving as my elected officials."

"This is a waste of time," Jonathan said. He'd been angry and stewing all day, mostly at Morgan's parents, but also at her. His leather-tanned face was sunburned from the day's fishing, but he was clean and freshly shaven. He hadn't slept much last night, and the fatigue showed in the lines of his face.

"Just wait," she said, stroking his arm. "When Mama and Pop get here, it'll be worth it."

He set his hand over hers—a silent affirmation that he was putting the angry morning behind him—and got to his feet. "I'm going to find them."

"Good idea," Morgan said. "Tell them to hurry."

"They don't need to hurry," Blair whispered. "We've got lots of stuff to cover before they talk about shutting down our bed-and-breakfast. Shoot, there's that stop sign down at Pine and Mimosa. And Goodfellows Grocery has a lightbulb out in their parking lot."

"Now, before we move on," Fred Hutchins, the mayor, said, studying his notes as if broaching a matter of extreme importance, "I'd like to mention that Chief Cade of the Cape Refuge Police Department tells me he has several leads on the person or persons who dumped that pile of gravel in my parking spot."

A chuckle rippled over the room, and the mayor scowled. "The perpetrator will be prosecuted."

Blair spat out her suppressed laughter, and Morgan slapped her arm. "Shhh," Morgan tried not to grin, "you're going to make him mad."

"I'm just picturing a statewide search for the fugitive with the dump truck," Blair said, "on a gravel-dumping spree across the whole state of Georgia."

Morgan saw the mayor's eyes fasten on her, and she punched her sister again. Blair drew in a quick breath and tried to straighten up.

"The Owenses still ain't here?" he asked.

While Morgan glanced back at the door, Blair shot to her feet. "No, Fred, they're not here. Why don't you just move this off the agenda and save it until next week? I'm sure something's come up."

"Maybe they don't intend to come," the mayor said.

"Don't you wish," Blair fired back. "You're threatening to shut down their business. They'll be here, all right."

"Well, I'm tired of waiting," the mayor said into the microphone, causing feedback to squeal across the room. Everybody covered their ears until Jason Manford got down on his knees and fiddled with the knob. "We've moved it down the agenda twice already tonight," the mayor went on. "If we ever want to get out of here, I think we need to start arguin' this right now."

Morgan got up. "Mayor, there must be something wrong. Jonathan went to see if he could find them. Please, if we could just have a few more minutes."

"We're not waitin' any longer. Now if anybody from your camp has somethin' to say . . ."

"What are you gonna do, Mayor?" Blair asked, pushing up her sleeves and shuffling past the knees and feet on her row. "Shut us down without a hearing? That's not even legal. You could find yourself slapped with a lawsuit, and then you wouldn't even have time to worry about jellyfish and gravel. Where would that leave the town?"

She marched defiantly past the standing-room-only crowd against the wall to the microphone at the front of the room.

Morgan got a queasy feeling in her stomach. Blair wasn't the most diplomatic of the Owens family. She was an impatient intellectual who found her greatest fulfillment in the books of the library she ran. People were something of a nuisance to her, and she found their pettiness unforgivable.

Blair set her hands on her hips. "I've been wanting to give you a piece of my mind for a long time now, Fred."

The people erupted into loud chatter, and the mayor banged his gavel to silence them. "As you know, young lady, the city council members and I have agreed that the publicity from the 20/20 show about Hanover House a few months ago brought a whole new element to this town. The show portrayed your folks as willin' to take in any ol' Joe with a past and even exposed some things about one of your current tenants that made the people of this town uncomfortable and afraid. We want to be a family-friendly tourist town, not a refuge for every ex-con with a proba-tion officer. For that reason, we believe Hanover House is a danger to this town and that it's in the city's best interest to close it down under Zoning Ordinance number 503."

Blair waited patiently through the mayor's speech, her arms crossed. "Before we address the absurdity of your pathetic attempts to shut down Hanover House just because my parents refused to help campaign for you—" Cheers rose again, and Blair forged on.

"Maybe I should remind you that Cape Refuge got its name because of the work of the Hanovers who had that bed-and-breakfast before my parents did. It was a refuge for those who were hurting and had no place else to go. I think we have a whole lot more to fear from an ex-con released from jail with a pocketful of change and no prospects for a job or a home, than we do from the ones who have jobs and housing and the support of people who care about them."

Morgan couldn't believe she was hearing these words come out of her sister's mouth. Blair had never sympathized with her parents' calling to help the needy, and she had little to do with the bed-and-breakfast. To hear her talk now, one would think she was on the frontlines in her parents' war against hopelessness.

"Hanover House is one of the oldest homes on this island, and it's part of our heritage," Blair went on. "And I find it real interesting that you'd be all offended by what they do there out in the open, when Betty Jean's *secret* playhouse for men is still operating without a hitch."

Again the crowd roared. Horrified, Morgan stood up. Quickly trying to scoot out of her row, she whispered to those around her, "I'm sorry, I'm so sorry, I didn't know she was going to say that. She didn't mean it, she just says whatever comes to her mind—"

"Incidentally, Fred," Blair shouted, "I've noticed that you don't have any trouble finding a parking spot at *her* place!" Blair added.

The mayor came out of his seat, his mouth hanging open with stunned indignation. Morgan stepped on three feet, trying to get to her sister. She fully expected Fred to find Blair in contempt—if mayors did that sort of thing in city council meetings—and order the Hanover House bulldozed before nightfall.

"She didn't mean that!" Morgan shouted over the crowd, pushing toward the front. "I'm sure she's never seen your car at Betty Jean's, have you, Blair? Mayor, please, if I may say a few words . . ." She finally got to the front, her eyes rebuking Blair.

Blair wouldn't surrender the microphone. "And I might add, Mayor, that your own parents were on this island because of Joe and Miranda Hanover and that bed-and-breakfast. If I remember, your daddy killed a man accidentally and came here to stay while he was awaiting trial."

The veins in Fred's neck protruded, and his face was so red that Morgan feared the top of his head would shoot right off. "My daddy was never convicted!" he shouted. "And if you're suggesting that he was the same type of criminal that flocks to Hanover House, you are *sadly* mistaken!"

Morgan reached for the microphone again, her mind already composing a damage-control speech, but her sister's grip was strong.

"After my parents inherited the bed-and-breakfast from the Hanovers," Blair said, "they continued their policy of never harboring anybody illegally. You know that my father works with these people while they're still in prison, and he only agrees to house the ones he trusts, who are trying to turn their lives around. Hanover House gives those people an opportunity to become good people who can contribute to society . . . unlike some of those serving on our city council."

Again, there was applause and laughter, and Morgan grabbed Blair's arm and covered the microphone. "You're turning this into a joke!" she whispered through her teeth. "Mama and Pop are going to be mortified! You are not helping our cause!"

"I can handle this," Blair said, jerking it back.

Morgan forced herself between Blair and the microphone. "Your honor . . . uh . . . Mr. Mayor . . . council members . . . I am so sorry for my sister's outbursts. Really, I had no idea she would say such things."

Blair stepped to her side, glaring at her as if she'd just betrayed her.

"But I think we've gotten a little off track here. The fact is that Hanover House doesn't *just* house those who've gotten out of jail. It also houses others who have no place to go."

Art Russell grabbed the mayor's microphone, sending feedback reverberating over the room. "I don't think Cape Refuge is very well served by a bunch of people who have no place else to go."

"Well, that's not up to you, is it, Art?" Blair asked, her voice carrying over the speakers.

"If I may," Morgan said, trying to make her soft voice sound steady, "the question here is whether there's something illegal going on at Hanover House. And unless there is, you have no grounds for closing us down."

The crowd applauded again, but Sarah, the swimsuit-clad councilwoman, dragged the microphone across the table. The cord wasn't quite long enough, so she leaned in. "If there aren't any dangerous people staying at the bed-and-breakfast, then how come *20/20* said Gus Hampton served time for armed robbery and didn't even complete his sentence? And how come your husband was at the dock fighting with your parents just this morning, complaining about Hampton? I heard it myself. Jonathan didn't want you working there around Hampton, and he said it loud and clear."

Blair's eyes pierced Morgan. "Why didn't you tell me this?" she whispered.

"It wasn't relevant," Morgan hissed back, "since I didn't think you'd be the one speaking for us."

The council members all came to attention, their rocking stopped, and they waited for an answer. "If there isn't any danger at Hanover House," Sarah repeated, "then how come your own family's fighting over it?"

Blair tried to rally. "Well, Sarah, when Jonathan gets back here, you can ask him. But meanwhile, the question is simple. Do you have the right to shut down Hanover House, and if you do try to close it, are you financially able to handle the lawsuit that's going to be leveled at this town . . . and maybe even at each of you individually?"

"They can't file a lawsuit," Fred said, his face still red.

"Watch us," she bit out. "And the chances of your reelection would be slim at best, since the people of this town love my parents. Most everybody in this town has benefited from their kindness in one way or another."

The crowd applauded again, and cheers and whoops backed up her words. But Morgan realized that it wasn't the cries of the people that would decide the fate of Hanover House. It was those angry members of the city council, sitting there with their hackles up because Blair had insulted them.

"Some call that kindness, others call it naivete," the mayor said. "They'll believe anything anybody tells them. Just because some convict claims he wants to change, doesn't mean he will."

"Thank goodness they believed your daddy," Blair said, "or you might not be sitting on this island in some overpriced chair!"

As the crowd expressed their enjoyment again, Morgan pressed her fingertips against her temples and wondered where her parents were. If they would just rush in right now and take over the microphone, she knew they could turn this around.

While the mayor tried to get control of the crowd again, Morgan looked fully at Blair, pleading for her to surrender the mike and not do any more harm. But Blair's scathing look told Morgan that her sister was in this to the end. The burn scar on the right side of Blair's face was as red as the mayor's face. It always got that way when she was upset, reminding Morgan of her sister's one vulnerability. It was that imperfect half of her face that kept her unmarried and alone—and it had a lot to do with the hair-trigger temper she was displaying now.

"Order, now! Come on, people—*order!*" the mayor bellowed, banging his gavel as if he were hammering a nail.

The sound of sirens rose over the crowd's noise, cutting across the mayor's words and quieting the crowd. Those on the east side of the building, where Morgan and Blair stood, craned their necks to see out the open window, trying to figure out where the fire trucks and police cars were heading. As one after another went by, sirens wailing and lights flashing, Morgan realized that something big must have happened. The island was small, and the sound of sirens was not an everyday occurrence. But now the sound of several at once could not be ignored.

When the front doors of the room swung open, everyone turned expectantly. Police Chief Matthew Cade—whom friends called simply "Cade"—stood scanning the faces, his skin pale against his dark, windblown hair.

His eyes fell on the sisters at the front of the crowd. "Blair, Morgan, I need to see both of you right away."

Morgan's eyes locked with her sister's for a second, terrors storming through her mind.

"What is it, Cade?" Blair asked.

He cleared his throat and swallowed hard. "We need to hurry," he said, then pushed the door open wider and stood beside it, watching them, clearly expecting them to accompany him.

Whatever it was, Morgan realized, he couldn't or wouldn't say it in front of all these people. Something horrible had happened.

Melba Jefferson, their mother's closest friend, stood and touched Morgan's back. "Oh, honey."

Morgan took Blair's hand, and the now-silent crowd parted as they made their way out. Cade escorted them into the fading sunlight and his waiting squad car.

Jonathan Cleary pulled his truck onto the gravel driveway at Hanover House and parked in the shade of the wax myrtles that reached up to the cloudless sky. The front door to the big yellow house usually sat open, and from the driveway one could see through the glass storm door into the welcoming front room.

He glanced toward the side of the house, to the three red cedars where Thelma and Wayne always parked their old Buick Regal. It wasn't there now, and neither was the old black pickup that Gus Hampton drove, or the little Honda in which Rick Morrison scooted around town.

He took the porch steps two at a time and rushed through the storm door.

"Thelma! Wayne!" he called as he stepped into the front room. There was no answer, so he went halfway up the staircase and peered up to the second floor. Thelma and Wayne's bedroom looked empty from there.

They were probably already at City Hall, making their speech—undoubtedly glossing over the risks taken in this house each day. He went further up the steps and glanced into his own bedroom. Morgan had left the door open, after he'd asked her repeatedly to keep it closed and locked. He didn't like the idea of his private things being open for anyone to steal. It wasn't as if the tenants around here didn't have clouded histories. At any given time, there was likely to be someone staying here who'd served time for armed robbery. Morgan's trust level in the tenants' "changed lives" bordered on naive. But he supposed she'd come by it honestly. Her parents had spent years instilling that in her.

He closed and locked the bedroom door, then gave a cursory glance around the hallway at the tenants' locked doors. They weren't nearly as trusting of each other as Morgan or her parents were.

He hurried back down the stairs and looked around the phone for a note or message of some kind, but there was none.

He left the house again, this time locking the front door behind him. It was a rule in the house that the last one to leave should lock it, but that rule was seldom enforced even by the Owens themselves. But Jonathan never forgot.

He stepped out onto the porch. From here he could see the beach across the street, with a clear view of Wassaw Sound. Just to the left, the sound opened into the Atlantic. It had always been Jonathan's opinion that Hanover House occupied the best spot on this small barrier island east of Savannah. No wonder the city council wanted to close them down. The council's hope, as far as Jonathan could figure, was that, without tenants, Thelma and Wayne couldn't afford to keep the house. If it ever went on the market, there would be some fierce competition to buy it and turn it into condominiums or a high-priced hotel. As much as Jonathan meant what he'd told Thelma and Wayne this morning about moving, part of him wished he hadn't made that vow. He'd grown to love this huge old house; it had so much more personality than the old two-bedroom home he'd grown up in.

The chairs on the beach that belonged to Hanover House were empty. The tide was low, so the chairs seemed far back from where the waves slapped at the shore, teasing and reaching, then fleeing back out into the Atlantic and chasing back again.

He got into his truck and sat for a moment, thinking. He could drive back to City Hall and see if Thelma and Wayne had made it yet. On the way, he could swing by the dock and see if they had gone by the warehouse where they held church services on Sunday. It would be just like them to find some wayward soul waiting there. They left the door to the building unlocked for that very purpose. Jonathan expected the piano to disappear any day now, along with the carved wooden pulpit that sat at the front of the room.

But you couldn't tell them anything. They were as hardheaded and stubborn as anyone who'd ever put their stamp on this island. And he'd said as much to their faces this morning, in front of God, the breakfast patrons of Crickets who sat listening through screen windows, and his deckhand preparing to take his rig out.

He supposed he owed Thelma and Wayne an apology for the public attack. He should have waited until later when they were alone, but he hadn't wanted to explode in front of Morgan. She had asked him to trust her judgment, and he knew better than to tell her he couldn't. Her faith in their tenants was blinding her to the risks. It was a hard thing to ask a newly married man to stop worrying about his bride's well-being.

He had still been stewing when he'd arrived at the dock that morning and begun preparing his boat for his morning tour. The heat index had already hit record highs, and even at that early hour, humidity rode thick over the Bull River, just a couple of miles from where it joined the Atlantic. A few of the tourists who had hired him to take them saltwater fishing were already waiting near the boat.

He had seen Thelma and Wayne go into Crickets, the hole-in-the-wall restaurant and bar that looked like a rotten screened porch. Crickets did its best business in the early morning or late night hours, when the breeze was cooler as it swept through the place.

Thelma and Wayne often showed up there as the sun came up, hoping to build relationships with the fishermen and dockworkers who took their meals there. Many of them wound up joining the little warehouse church, and some of them became temporary residents of Hanover House.

Jonathan wished his in-laws would just eat breakfast at home with Morgan and stop beating the bushes for ex-cons and strays who had wandered in from nowhere. The sight of them going into Crickets had levered his anger up a notch, so he had decided to confront them right then and there.

He had told his deck hand that he'd be back in a minute, and he'd crossed the pier to the screen door of the old restaurant.

His mother-in-law, dressed in a yellow blouse too bright for this time of morning, was sipping coffee when she spotted him, and her eyes lit up in that way she had, as if he was just the one she'd been waiting to see. But he knew she made everyone feel that way. "Jonathan, have you had breakfast yet? Sit down and let the Colonel fix you some bacon and eggs. Colonel!" she called to the proprietor, "get Jonathan here—"

"I ate," he said, cutting her off.

Wayne grinned up at him. "I swanny, I think he's the only fisherman on this island who gets up and shaves in the morning."

"Oh, hush," Thelma told her husband. "It pays to look nice, doesn't it, Jonathan? And it's good for business. People have more trust in a clean-cut fellow." She reached out for Jonathan's hand. "Come on, honey, sit down and have some coffee."

Jonathan shoved his rough hands through his sandy, wind-blown hair. "I don't want to sit down," he said. "I wanted to talk to you about Gus Hampton. I'm worried about Morgan being in that house alone with him."

Thelma's face twisted in weariness, and she expelled a sigh. "Jonathan, not that again. Gus is a good man, and you don't have to worry about him."

"Are you willing to bet your daughter's life on it?" Jonathan asked her.

She met her husband's eyes, and Wayne got up to face Jonathan. He was a big man, at least as tall as Jonathan, who stood six foot three. "Jonathan, what's the matter with you?" His voice was gruff and way too loud, to compensate for his poor hearing. "Now, I'm proud to call you my son-in-law, and I feel real secure that Morgan has you looking out for her. That's the way it's supposed to be. I know that whatever happens to me, you'll always take care of her. So I don't fault you for your concern. But you knew where she lived and that she helped us at Hanover House before you ever started dating her. You didn't seem to care who lived in our house when you were coming over every night for supper. You got along just fine with everybody then."

"But I see things now that I didn't see then," he said in a low voice, hoping Wayne would take his cue and lower his as well. "And there's something about Gus Hampton that I don't trust."

"Just because he's Jamaican and has an accent—"

"It's not that!" Jonathan said.

"Is it because he's black?" Thelma asked. "Because if it is, Jonathan, I have to say that I'm disappointed in you—"

"No, it's not because he's black! It's because he's as big as a football lineman and sneaks around like a prowler and looks at my wife—"

"Sneaks around?" Wayne boomed. "When does he sneak around?"

"Last night," Jonathan said. "I couldn't sleep. I got up about two-thirty. I was going to go downstairs and read, and here he came up the stairs, walking so quiet you wouldn't have even known he was in the house."

"For heaven's sake," Thelma said. "Jonathan, he was being considerate. Trying not to wake us up!"

"I don't trust him!" he said. "And neither does anybody else on this island, which is exactly why the city council wants to close us down."

"That's not going to happen," Wayne said. "We found out a few things that we're going to bring out tonight at the council meeting, and I guarantee you, those council members will get off our backs."

"What, so you can just keep inviting criminals and rapists and murderers to come and live in the house with my wife?" Now *he* was talking too loudly, and the other patrons were silent, undoubtedly tuning in to every word he and Wayne said.

Thelma sprang out of her seat and grabbed Jonathan by the arm. She was only five feet five, and three inches of that was the curly gray hair that padded her head. But she had a way of making a big man seem small. "Outside, Jonathan," she said through her teeth. "You're about to make me mad."

"*I'm* gonna make *you* mad?" he asked as she escorted him through the screen door. Wayne stalked behind them, his heavy boots clomping on the hollow floor. The door bounced shut behind them.

"Now you look here!" Thelma said, turning him to face her when they were out of earshot of the crowd in Crickets. "We have enough problems in this town with people spreading lies about our tenants and the work we do. But it will not come from our own family. Do you hear me?"

"Why won't you listen to me? I can't sleep nights. I have nightmares about that man hurting Morgan—"

"We can't help your nightmares," Wayne said, loud enough for everyone inside to hear him anyway. Even the tourists waiting at Jonathan's boat seemed to be listening now. "All we can tell you is what we know. I don't invite anybody to live in our house unless I've worked with them for a long time and I know their character."

"Worked with them in jail, you mean!" Jonathan said. "Some of them are con artists. They're going to show you whatever you want to see, if they know you're the one who can get them a job and a place to live when they get out. But what if they're not rehabilitated? What if it's just an act?"

"Jonathan," Thelma said, "those people are saved by the blood of Christ just like you were. Gus Hampton was a drug addict who stole to support his habit, and he's been clean for five years."

"Only because he's been locked up, Thelma." Jonathan shook his head and took a few steps away from her, then turned back. "Are you both telling me that you don't even think it's possible that someone could pull the wool over your eyes? That someone might pretend to have cleaned up his act just to get out of jail?"

"We have to have faith that God will work it all out, Jonathan," Wayne said.

Jonathan's voice rose again. "What if there were clear signs that this guy was bad news? What would it take for you to throw him out?"

"A lot."

"Your daughter's rape? Her murder?"

Thelma grabbed his shoulders and shook him, her eyes flashing lightning. "That will not happen, Jonathan. Do you think you love my daughter more than I do? I have seen that man on his knees, weeping his heart out over gratitude for Christ's redemption," she said. "We would no more throw him out than we would throw *you* out, Jonathan."

"I asked you a question," he bit out. "What would it take?"

Wayne finally stepped between them, as if he feared Thelma might hurt him. "Jonathan, we screen every applicant from the jail who wants to stay in our home very carefully. We don't take all of them. They have to promise a lot of things to stay there. Hours a day of Bible study, a full-time, steady job, work around our house to keep things going, community service, church attendance. They're basically under my thumb while they live there, and you know that I don't let 'em off the hook. Not everybody wants to live by those rules, but Gus did. And he's followed them to a T. He hasn't done anything to deserve your accusations."

"So Morgan doesn't matter?"

"Of course she matters," Wayne bellowed. "If I had an inkling that any of our tenants was going to hurt either of my daughters, they'd be out in a minute."

Jonathan shook away from him and started to his boat. "I get it," he said. "He'll have to hurt somebody before you'll throw him out."

"Jonathan!" Wayne bellowed.

Jonathan swung around. "You people are crazy!" he shouted, not caring anymore who heard. "You think you're brave because you trust people—but you're not brave, you're reckless! And I hope to God that Morgan doesn't have to pay for that!"

He stepped into his boat—only then aware of the gaping tourists watching the drama unfold. He turned back to Thelma and Wayne. "We're moving," he said. "As soon as we can find another place to live, I'm taking my wife and we're moving out."

"Jonathan!" Thelma shouted. "Don't say that. That's her home."

"I mean it!" he yelled. "If you won't do something about it, I will."

He had gone down into his boat's galley then, and Thelma and Wayne had walked over to the warehouse church to lick their wounds.

Jonathan had run that conversation through his mind at least five hundred times today, each time wishing it had turned out better. He should have tried to talk to them in private, should have stayed calm, should have included Morgan in the discussion. As the day wore on, his anger had faded, and remorse had taken its place.

Still, he didn't plan to back down now. He'd made himself clear, and he intended to stick to it. If they didn't ask Gus Hampton to leave Hanover House, then Jonathan would do everything in his power to persuade Morgan to move out and find another job.

He drove around the southernmost point of the island, then up toward the dock at the mouth of Bull River. By now, Thelma and Wayne had probably made it to the meeting and laid all their cards on the table, and the council members were voting to keep Hanover House open and send engraved invitations to the inmates of every jail in Georgia. His in-laws just had that effect on people.

He heard sirens out the window and looked in his rearview mirror for the flashing lights. Some tourist probably had a fender bender. A squad car came up behind him, then whipped past him and hurried off toward the dock.

As the warehouse came into view, he saw that the police cars and fire trucks congregated in the parking lot just outside the building.

In the center of it all sat Thelma and Wayne's twenty-year-old Regal.

Something was wrong.

He started to turn into the gravel parking lot, but a horn and screeching tires made him slam on his brakes. The car passed, and he tried again, stopping his car among the squad cars and fire trucks rumbling out their impatience. Billy Caldwell, one of the rookie cops on the force, broke into a trot and headed toward the warehouse door.

"Billy!" Jonathan called, leaving his car on the street and getting out. The young man turned around.

"What's going on?" Jonathan asked.

Billy looked as if he'd been caught at something. His sunburned face went blank, and he dropped his hands helplessly to his side. His mouth moved as if he couldn't quite get his lips to form the answer.

Jonathan crossed the parking lot and reached him. "Billy, what is it?"

"It's . . . Thelma and Wayne," he said. Jonathan stared at him for a moment, trying to make sense of Billy's simple statement. He started toward the door.

"Jonathan, you don't want to go in there," Billy said.

But he had already opened the door and bolted into the big room.

The place had been turned from a place of worship to a crime scene. Four police officers stood taking pictures and dusting the piano and doors for prints, while others spilled out the side door onto the boardwalk that went down to the dock and Crickets.

Joe McCormick, the detective on the police force, stood at the southwest corner of the makeshift chapel. He was sweating and looked shaken. Jonathan started toward him, but Joe saw him and held out a hand to stop him. "Jonathan, this is no place for you right now. Somebody get him out of here."

But Jonathan hurried around the pews, getting closer . . .

Between the uniformed legs that blocked his view, a body lay on the floor. He caught a glimpse of the bright yellow sleeve on the small, limp arm ...

"Thelma!" he shouted and bolted forward.

Joe caught him and tried to hold him back. "Jonathan, you can't get any closer. This is a crime scene."

"Let me go!" He wrestled his way out of Joe's grip and pushed someone out of his way. Then he saw them, Thelma and Wayne both, lying lifeless on the bloodstained floor.

His body went limp and he stopped fighting. Billy, the young cop with a more compassionate touch, pulled him back away from the scene and walked him out the side door. He felt dizzy, like he might pass out. His heart seemed inadequate to do its job, and his eyes stung. "How ... how did this happen?" he asked, grabbing Billy's arm. "They were supposed to be at the meeting ... they were on the agenda...." Even as he spoke, he recognized the absurdity of his statement, as if they'd had no right to die when they'd had other commitments.

"*Who did this?*" he screamed. Chess Springer, the old fisherman who had taught him most of what he knew about making a living on the sea, crossed the boardwalk and put his arm around Jonathan's shoulder.

"Come in Crickets and sit down," Chess said in his raspy, smoke-ravaged voice. "I'll get you some water."

Jonathan shook free. "I don't need water, Chess. I need answers!"

The old man rubbed his wizened face. "I saw their car and came over to shoot the breeze," he said. "Found them just like that. Nobody around here heard gunshots or nothing."

"So they were *shot?*" he asked.

"Seems so, though I didn't look too long. I ran to Crickets and called the police."

Jonathan turned back to the scene, his mouth open with the silent wail of gut-wrenching anguish. "My wife. How will I tell my wife?" He brought both hands to his head. "I fought with them this morning! I said things ..."

Horror too deep to voice muted him. Who could have murdered the two kindest people on the island of Cape Refuge? Was it someone they had taken in, a soul so twisted that he would kill the very people who gave him a place to sleep and food to eat, helped him find work, and offered him a reason to live? How many people had they helped over the years? How many lives had they changed? How many hearts had been saved? How much hope had they offered?

And now someone had come in here and murdered them? Cruelly, brutally, cold-bloodedly . . . *murdered* them? It didn't make sense.

He stood on the pier, gaping through that door, wondering when they would stop taking pictures and get Thelma and Wayne off the floor. He couldn't let Morgan know until they did. He couldn't let her see them like this.

He heard a new siren coming and the squad car's wheels on the gravel parking lot. He wished they'd turn the noise off before a crowd formed, before Morgan heard it from City Hall.

He wanted to be the one to tell his wife. Just as soon as he could breathe. . . .

But it was too late.

Through the door, he saw Morgan burst through the front entrance of the warehouse. It was clear from her face that she'd already been told. Two cops tried to hold her back, but she was determined to get to Thelma and Wayne.

"No!" she screamed as she saw the policemen clustered near the front of the makeshift sanctuary. "Aw, no!"

Jonathan bolted back into the warehouse, pulled her into his arms, and tried to hold her.

"They can't be dead!" The torment ripped from her chest, shook her body, emptied her. She fell against him, weak and unsteady, just as he'd been moments before. But her need gave him back his strength, and he concentrated that strength on trying to hold her together.

*B*lair didn't have enough information to accept the deaths as fact. She sat in the front seat of Cade's squad car, staring at a chip on his windshield. He was saying something about the time of death, the murder weapon, the lack of witnesses.

They would know more, he said, when they finished doing the perimeter search for evidence and could examine the bodies.

The thought of her parents lying murdered on the floor of that warehouse short-circuited her mind, and she found herself looking out at the schooners docked at slips nearby, with their masts tall and bare, and scant activity on board some of them. The smell of salt water fish drifted on the warm breeze.

She didn't move, but inside her, emotional troops lined up for battle.

"You okay?" he asked.

The words came soft and unhurried, and she thought of telling Cade that he didn't have to baby-sit her. She just

needed to sit here for a minute. Just needed to get her brain working again.

"You're shaking," he said, and took her hand. "You can't go
in the warehouse . . . but I can take you around to the boardwalk.
Or you can just sit here, or I can take you home. Whatever you
want."

Her mouth was dry, and she found it hard to swallow. His
hand was big and warm over the ice cold of hers. "I don't know
how to do this," she whispered finally.

He didn't ask her what she didn't know how to do. "None
of us does, Blair."

She wished she had her computer with her, that she could
pound on the keys and do a quick search of the Internet and come
up with answers. . . . But she wouldn't even know the questions
until she got out of this car.

She reached for the door handle, and Cade let her hand go
and got out. He came around before she got the door open, and
opened it for her.

She thought of some unnamed killer walking across this
parking lot, going into that building, killing her parents . . . and
rage like a nuclear bomb exploded inside her.

"Cade, why aren't you hunting him down? Why haven't you
caught him?"

"We're trying, Blair. I need to be in there right now, working
the scene."

"Then go," she said through her teeth. "Stop worrying about
me and go. Find him, Cade, before he gets away."

"I'll find him, Blair. You can count on it."

He started into the building but stopped when he saw that
she was following. "Blair, you can't come in here."

She trudged forward until she was face-to-face with him, and
a slow, defiant, desperate agony rose in her chest like a scream.
"Get out of my way, Cade."

He caught her arm. "Blair, you can't. For your own good.
You can see them later, when they've been cleaned up. But right
now—"

She jerked past him and went into the building. An odd thought struck her: she'd never been here when they weren't here too. It was as if the building was an extension of them, a floor built beneath them, walls built around, a roof covering them.

Cade took her arm again. "Blair, please. Don't do this."

"I have to see them," she said, feeling a throbbing beginning in her temple, on the side where the flesh was coarse and scarred.

She heard her sister wailing on the boardwalk outside the door, heard Joe McCormick urging Cade to keep Blair out. But she walked toward them, intent on seeing what some maniac had done to her parents.

Cade took her arm gently, no longer trying to hold her back. His voice broke as he said, "Blair, if you see this, it will be stamped on your mind for the rest of your life. Let me take you outside."

She suddenly went weak, and Cade turned her and walked her to the side door, where Jonathan and Morgan clung together. The room seemed to tip, and shadows shifted on the walls. She was going to faint, she thought. Like some prissy little thing who couldn't stand the sight of blood. . . .

As Cade got her onto the pier and lowered her to a bench, she heard her sister wailing with gut-emptying anguish. She thought of her mother lying on the floor there, with people gawking and probing her. Thelma had a thing about clean clothes. She hated for anyone to see her with a stain. There was bound to be a lot of blood, which meant stains on her mother's clothes and skin. . . . "Their clothes," Blair said to no one in particular. "I have to get them a change of clothes."

She started off the pier and back toward the parking lot, wondering what her mother would want her to bring. "She'll need a dry pair of slacks and a blouse, maybe the pink one, and some clean socks and another pair of shoes . . . underwear too. And a hairbrush . . ."

Someone touched her arm, and she turned. She hadn't known Cade was still with her, but there he was, looking down at her with worried eyes as his hands gripped her shoulders. "Blair, you sure you're all right?"

"I'll be back as soon as I get them, Cade," she whispered.

"Blair."

She swallowed back the panic rising in her throat. "I have to hurry," she said, moving away from him and only then realizing that she had left her car at City Hall.

"They don't need clothes, Blair." His voice was gentle, patient, pulling her back to reality.

She stopped in the parking lot and looked helplessly around. A van with the words WSAV-TV pulled in, and a crew jumped out. The familiar anchor, dressed in a white shirt and tie, with sweat rings under his arms, was trying to hook up his microphone as he headed toward her.

"You can't go in there," Cade said. "It's a crime scene."

"Can you tell us what happened?"

"Not at this time," Cade said, turning Blair back toward the pier.

But Blair resisted. "Don't you take their pictures," she told a man emerging from the truck with a television camera. "Don't you dare. You get back in that van and you leave. Cade, tell them—"

"*Chief* Cade?" the anchor asked. "Chief, could you please confirm the names of the victims? We heard on the scanner that it was Thelma and Wayne Owens."

"Excuse me," he said and firmly escorted Blair away from them.

"Stop them, Cade," she said. "Don't let them put my parents on the news. Not like that."

Cade left her at the bench where she had sat moments before, but she couldn't stay put; she followed him, a few steps behind, as he went through the side door of the warehouse again. Her eyes swept the room—the pews she had squirmed on as a child, writing notes to her sister, then swearing to her father that they were notes on his sermons. Her gaze locked on the piano on which their mother had taught Morgan and her to play. Blair had hated to practice, and eventually Thelma had given up and let her quit. But

Morgan, always the dutiful daughter, had become almost as good at the keyboard as their mother.

Blair wished now that she hadn't quit playing. It had meant so much to her mother for her to learn. She looked at the keys—and at the bare rectangle at the center of the piano above the keys, where an old mirror had once hung, for who knows what reason. Her mother had taken it off when Blair had started to play, because the sight of her own reflection was too distracting to Blair. Mirrors had never been her friends, and her mother had helped her avoid them.

The front door opened, and the Chatham County medical examiner came into the room. She watched as he walked toward the crowd of officers across the room. They stepped away from the body as the man stooped next to them . . .

. . . and as she caught the first glimpse of their lifeless bodies, her stomach lurched. She stumbled to the edge of the boardwalk and threw up into the water.

CHAPTER

*C*ade wiped the sweat from his brow and tried to remain objective as the medical examiner studied Thelma Owens's wound. Her head rolled back; her chin and neck and chest were covered with blood, and her eyes were open, frozen in some silent horror. He couldn't be emotional now. He had to stay focused.

A metal pin protruded from the back of her neck, straight out her throat. "That's a bulletnose point," Cade said. "From a speargun."

The examiner nodded. "Looks like it. Hit him from the front." He started to turn Wayne over, and Cade turned away. He needed some air, he thought. He walked to the side door, opposite the one where Jonathan, Morgan, and Blair had been sitting, and stepped out onto the wharf.

Billy followed him out. "You okay, Chief?"

"Yeah," he said. "Look, I need to get somebody out to confiscate all the spearguns on the island, so we can determine if they were the murder weapon. There're thirty members in the diving club, including me." He swallowed, tried to steady his breathing. "Only about five who spearfish."

"Know who they are off the top of your head?" Billy asked.

Cade nodded. "I'm one. Also Jonathan, Sam Sullivan, Marty Roberts, and Cliff Cash. There may be others, but those are the ones I know about. Go get Sam, Marty, and Cliff, and collect their spearguns. Treat them as evidence. See if there's blood on any of them, if any are missing, what kind of points they use. Bring those guys to the station for questioning."

"Yes, sir." Billy headed out, and Cade wiped his face on his sleeve. He looked out over the water, trying to think through the men he'd just named. They were all good friends, and two or three times a year they headed down to the Florida Keys and went diving and fishing together. None of those men could have killed Thelma and Wayne.

But it was all he had.

Something clicked against the post beneath his feet, and he looked down through the boards. Something that looked like a brown pole floated in the water there. He got down on his stomach and looked under the wharf.

He recognized it immediately. It wasn't a pole, it was a speargun.

He pulled a handkerchief from his pocket and used it to grab the narrow end of it and pull it out. "McCormick!" he yelled.

Joe came through the door, then froze at the sight of the gun dripping in Cade's hands. "The murder weapon," he said.

"That's it," Cade said and got back up. "It's a Magnum Blue Water." The words lodged in his throat as he realized what that meant. There was only one person he knew who had a Blue Water gun.

"The killer must have panicked and gotten rid of it," Joe said. "May have even had to swim away to avoid being seen."

Cade looked through the door across the building. Blair had bent over the water and was throwing up, and Jonathan had gone to help her.

"I have Billy going to round up everybody who spearfishes," he said. "He's collecting their guns."

"Well, if one of them is missing, we've got our man."

Cade wished he could turn the clock back two hours, when his biggest concern was the car that had been stolen from the Goodfellows parking lot. His mouth was dry, but he managed to get the words out. "I know whose gun this is. I recognize it. I was with him when he bought it."

"Who?" Joe asked.

Cade's eyes were fixed on the three just outside the warehouse. Jonathan had lowered Blair to her knees and was holding her hair back as she retched into the river.

"Cade, tell me whose it is."

Cade tore his eyes from the scene and looked hard at his balding colleague. "This gun belongs to Jonathan Cleary," he said.

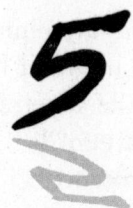

*J*onathan sat back as Morgan fell to Blair's side and pulled her into a hug. The two women clung to each other.

"Jonathan," a voice called. Jonathan looked up. Cade was standing in the door to the warehouse. "I need to talk to you," Cade said. "You may want to come out front."

"No!" Morgan let go of her sister and looked up at him. "I want to hear. Talk to him right here."

Cade looked down. His black hair flapped in the breeze over a face tight with strain. "I came by Crickets for breakfast this morning after you'd had your fight with Thelma and Wayne. Everybody was talking about it."

Jonathan wished he had the morning to do over. He wished he hadn't left on an angry note, wished he hadn't threatened to take their daughter and leave. . . .

"Were you here this afternoon? Did you come by here before going home?"

"No," he said.

"Did you notice if their car was here then?"

"It wasn't. I looked for it, because I wanted to talk to them. They weren't home, either."

"And did you go straight home when you left your boat?"

"Yes, straight home. I had the meeting to go to, and Morgan was waiting."

Cade looked even more somber than he had when he brought Morgan and Blair here. He set his foot up on the empty bench. Rubbing the sun creases in his face, he said, "Jonathan, where's your speargun?"

Jonathan frowned. This wasn't the time to talk about spearfishing, so he knew that Cade had a purpose for asking. "In the toolshed behind the house," he said. "Why?"

"Because I just found a Magnum Blue Water gun floating in the water on the other side of the warehouse."

"*What?*" Jonathan gasped. "Was that the murder weapon?"

Cade looked down at Blair, who gaped up at him, one side of her face pale, the other dark pink. "Jonathan, let's talk out front," he said.

"Answer him, Cade," Blair said, getting back to her feet. "Were my parents killed with a speargun?"

He rubbed his face and looked away. "They were each hit with a bulletnose point to the neck or throat, which explains why no one heard gunshots."

"The throat?" Morgan choked out. "Oh, dear God . . ."

Jonathan's face twisted, and he took a step toward Cade. "Who besides me has a Blue Water gun?"

Cade shook his head and kept his eyes on Jonathan's face. "You're the only one in our diving group, Jonathan."

Jonathan stood there a moment, staring at his old friend. "There could be others," he said. "Tourists, or someone not in our group. They're not that expensive."

"I'm just asking you where it is," Cade said.

Jonathan let go of Morgan. She looked up at Cade, waiting for the point to his question. Her face was wet, and mascara ran under her eyes. "It's in the storage shed behind the house where

I've always kept it," Jonathan said. "Come with me and I'll show you."

"I'll send McCormick to get it," he said. "Got a key?"

Jonathan nodded and pulled his key chain out. His hands were still trembling as he worked the toolshed key off the chain.

"Tell me about your fight this morning," Cade said.

Jonathan tried to shift gears and think, but the memory crushed him. His mouth trembled with the force of his emotion. "Man, I wish I could take it all back."

"Take what back?" Cade asked.

"The fight. I lost my temper, said things I shouldn't have said. . . . It ended badly. If I'd known it was going to be the last time I saw them . . ."

"What was the fight about, Jonathan?" Blair demanded. "Everybody on this island seems to know but me."

"It was about Gus Hampton. I don't trust him, and I didn't want Morgan around him."

He watched Blair get up, her eyes intense as she grabbed Cade's arm. "Cade, maybe Gus did it. Maybe he's the one. Maybe *he* did this to Mama and Pop." Her voice quivered as her body straightened with purpose. "If he did, so help me, I'll kill him myself. I'm gonna go find out." She started toward the parking lot again.

"Where are you going?" Cade asked.

"To talk to Gus Hampton," she said. The color was starting to return to her face.

"No, you can't go," Cade said. "Blair, you need to stay here."

"Why?" she asked, swinging around. "Am I under arrest?"

"Of course not," he said. "But you're interfering with an investigation. I already have officers looking for Gus. He shouldn't be that hard to find. But when they find him, *they'll* be interviewing him, not you." He caught up to her, touched her shoulder, and leaned down to look into her face. "Blair, I promise you, we're going to find who did this. But you'll have to let us do it, without getting in our way."

"Well, I don't let things rest, Cade," she said.

"I know you don't," he said.

Jonathan put his arm around Morgan. "Cade, I want to see that gun."

"I'm sorry, Jonathan. It's evidence in a homicide case."

"Well, then I'm going with McCormick to show him where mine is. I'll take Morgan with me."

"You can't go, Jonathan," Cade said.

Jonathan gaped at him. "What do you mean, I can't go?"

"I need you here," he said. "We may need to ask you more questions."

"You know where to find me," Jonathan told him. "You can call me at home and ask me."

"Jonathan, you're not going anywhere."

"Why not?" Jonathan asked again. "Cade, what're you saying?"

Cade stood eye to eye with him, unmoving. "I'm saying that if you try to leave, I'll have to arrest you."

He went back into the warehouse, and Jonathan stood there, his mouth open—feeling as if nothing in his world made sense any more.

It wasn't long before McCormick was back at the warehouse with the news. The door to the toolshed was wide open, and Jonathan Cleary's speargun wasn't there.

That wasn't what Cade wanted to hear. He had hoped McCormick would tell him that the gun was right where Jonathan kept it. He'd already heard back from Billy Caldwell, who was at the station with the other three spearfishermen. He'd found each of their guns and brought them in with them. Another officer had checked with every sports store in town. Only one sold spearguns, mostly through catalog orders. He hadn't sold any Blue Water Magnums.

Jonathan's was still the only one they knew of on the island.

"Want me to read him his rights?" McCormick asked.

Cade couldn't conceive of locking up his friend. He tried to think through the possibilities. Someone had taken the gun out of the shed and used it to kill Thelma and Wayne. Then they had left it at the scene so the police would find it. Maybe they wanted it to look like Jonathan had done it.

Or maybe there was someone else on the island who had one, or one of the transient seamen, or a psychotic tourist. . . .

Maybe Jonathan had just misplaced his gun. . . .

Or maybe the most obvious possibility was the truth—that Jonathan had gotten so angry at them that he had acted in a fit of rage, hardly knowing what he was doing. . . .

But Cade had known Jonathan for years, had grown up with him, played baseball and football with him. They had gone to college together, and Cade had been best man in Jonathan's wedding. He knew his friend to be a good person, one who didn't have murder in his heart. Could some set of circumstances have conspired to push Jonathan into a lethal rage?

If there was a possibility, even a remote one, that Jonathan might have done this, Cade had to lock him up. He had no choice.

For the first time since his uncle, the mayor, had appointed him chief of police, he wished he had found another vocation.

"Tell me what to do, and I'll do it," McCormick said.

"I'll take care of it," Cade said. He looked across the warehouse to the open door. Through it, he could see Blair, sitting out on that bench, looking so strong and angry, when inside he knew she was falling apart. And sweet Morgan, still clinging to her husband, shivering from the shock. She would accuse Cade of using Jonathan as a scapegoat. She would claim that he was trying to look effective by making an arrest—any arrest—so the people of the town wouldn't panic. Would she be right?

But Jonathan owned the murder weapon, and he'd had that fight with his in-laws earlier that day. He was a hothead, always had been. He flew off the handle at the slightest thing. Maybe today he'd gotten too angry . . . gone too far . . .

If he could just get Jonathan away from Morgan and Blair, maybe he could soften the blow for them. Maybe Jonathan would come willingly and wouldn't make him cuff him. Or even better, maybe he'd have an explanation for everything, one that made sense and cleared him as a suspect.

He crossed the warehouse, his steps shaking the hardwood floor. Jonathan met his eyes as he stepped outside. "Jonathan, your speargun wasn't in the toolshed."

Jonathan seemed to process that for a moment, and his face changed. "Gus. He ... or any of the other tenants ... could have gotten it out. The key is hanging right there on a hook in the kitchen."

"I have somebody still looking for Gus," he said. "But meanwhile, I'm going to have to take you in."

"Now?"

"Now." Cade looked out over the water. It looked like a storm was brewing in the south, and the water on the river was growing restless. He wished he could get into his boat, ride the river out to the sea, and watch that angry sky open up around him. It would be better to face that storm than the one raging inside him.

Jonathan gaped at him, confused. "Cade, you don't have to take me to the station to talk to me. I don't want to leave my wife right now. She needs me. I have to take her home." He pulled Morgan up and put his arms around her shoulders. "When you get through here, you can come over to Hanover House, and we'll check out the toolshed. If my gun is gone, then that's a crime scene too. There might be evidence there."

"I intend to check out the toolshed," Cade said. "McCormick put one of my men on it. But in the meantime, Jonathan, I got to tell you—you're the prime suspect. And as I see it, I have no choice but to arrest you for the murder of Thelma and Wayne Owens."

"What?" Morgan asked, her voice hollow with grief. She was shivering so badly that she needed a blanket. "Cade, you can't!" she cried. "This is crazy."

Jonathan got that wild look in his eyes, the one he used to get when their team was behind. "My family has just been gutted, and you're arresting me? What are you? Crazy?"

"I'm doing my job, Jonathan," Cade said. "You have the right to remain silent—"

"Well, you can do your job on somebody else!"

"You have the right to an attorney . . ." Cade pulled the cuffs off his belt as he spoke, but Jonathan backed away.

"Cade, don't be stupid. People don't take you seriously as it is. They're really going to mock you when they hear about this. They'll ride you out of town."

"Jonathan, I'm asking you to come willingly, without the cuffs. I don't want to make this ugly."

Morgan cried out and clung harder to her husband. "Please, Cade. No! Not now."

Cade had to turn away and look out over that water again. His eyes stung, and a lifetime of history reeled in fast-forward through his mind. His friendship with Jonathan, his affection for Morgan, his love for her parents . . .

And Blair.

He forced himself to look at her. Blair was staring at Jonathan, her face twisted and stunned. "Jonathan, how did your gun kill Mama and Pop?"

"I want to know that too," Jonathan said. "Cade, you're not taking me anywhere. I'm taking my wife home, and I'm going to look in that toolshed, and I'm going to get right in the face of every one of our tenants. I'll see it in their eyes if one of them did this. And when I do, you can arrest me then, because that's when I'll be guilty of murder."

Cade snapped a cuff on Jonathan's wrist. Jonathan tried to pull away from him, but Cade wrestled him to the ground.

Sobbing, Morgan threw herself at Cade. *What are you doing? Cade, stop it!*"

Cade snapped the other cuff and pulled Jonathan up. He kept the thought of those bleeding bodies at the forefront of his mind as he forced Jonathan across the parking lot and into the back of his squad car.

CHAPTER

*A*n hour later, when he could finally leave the crime scene, Cade pulled away from the warehouse with Jonathan still cuffed in the backseat.

Blair hadn't shed a tear yet. Instead, she stood on the gravel that filled the parking area, between an ambulance and the hearse where her parents' bodies lay, feeling as if she had nothing to do with this scene or this circumstance. She was some detached soul, watching from outside the glass bubble that was her life, filing facts in her mind, filtering them, and coming up with answers.

Only none of them fit. There were more questions for every answer, different answers for every question. It was as if someone had mixed up a couple of intricate jigsaw puzzles and she was trying to fit the wrong pieces into the holes left empty.

Morgan, standing nearby, had a blanket around her now, but she was still shivering so hard that Blair thought she needed medical attention. "He didn't do it," Morgan said as the car pulled out of sight.

"Morgan, we don't know *who* did it."

"My husband did not kill Mama and Pop!" Morgan bit out again.

"He fought with them this morning, Morgan. It was his gun."

Morgan started walking toward Jonathan's truck, which he had left parked haphazardly at the edge of the parking lot. "Where are you going?" Blair asked.

"Away from here," her sister said.

Blair tried to shake herself out of her morbid detachment and think. She had all her faculties—her heart was still beating, her lungs still took in air, her mind still processed the things that were happening. She had to think and act. She had to do what needed to be done. "Don't go home," she said. "You ought to stay away from Hanover House."

"Why?" Morgan turned around. "There are people there who need to know."

"*They* might be the killers!" Blair shouted.

"How can *they* be if Jonathan is?" Morgan screamed back. "Make up your mind, Blair."

"*Somebody* did this, Morgan. We have to be careful. We don't know who it was. Or why."

"We know who it was *not*," Morgan rasped. "It was not Jonathan." She turned around and shook her head, running her fingers through her hair. "I've got to get him out," she said. "I've got to go down there and convince them that he didn't do it. Oh, where are my keys?"

One of the cops who had just come out of the building walked toward her. "Morgan, are you all right?"

She opened the door to Jonathan's truck, and the bell began to ring. Jonathan had left the keys in the ignition.

"Don't let her drive, Doug," Blair said. "She's in no shape to drive."

Morgan was sobbing when she turned back to her sister. "Just tell me one thing, Blair. He's your brother-in-law. You know him. Okay, so you don't get along that well. But you were my maid of honor just a few months ago. You were right there beside me when I married him. How could you give us your blessing and be so happy for us and now turn around and think he could have done this?"

"I didn't think *anybody* could have done this," Blair said. "But somebody did. And the evidence is pointing toward him."

Morgan just shook her head and got into the truck.

Blair stepped up to the window, touched it with her fingertips. "I'll go with you," she said.

But Morgan started the truck and pulled out into the street.

Blair watched her drive away as a smothering sense of aloneness washed over her. Standing here, between the vehicles that held her parents' white-cloaked bodies, she felt like a dot at the center of a massive mountain range, so small and insignificant that some little breeze could blow her off the earth like a flake of dust.

The crowd that had formed outside Crickets couldn't help her now. The police, still working the scene, had other things on their minds. The God to whom her parents had been so devoted seemed distant and far away, too busy with other matters to waste his time with her.

She didn't know what to do or where to go. Taking action seemed as abhorrent as standing idle. But her thoughts were too fragmented, and her organs didn't seem to be working in tandem. Her body was a cage for this tornado that had ravaged her life.

And any moment now, it would all go flying apart.

CHAPTER

7

The Greyhound bus held an odd combination of smells that made Sadie Caruso feel slightly sick. The woman behind her had been eating oranges since they had left Atlanta, and the man next to her who had slept the whole way snored in her direction, his bad breath sending up a cloud that was almost visible in the fading light. The man in front of her had a fierce case of body odor that spoke of disease and perhaps homelessness, but she had no room to talk—now, she was just as homeless.

She cradled her left arm across her stomach and wished she had enough money to spare to buy a bottle of Tylenol to ease the pain. The bone was broken; she had no doubt. Her forearm was swollen, discolored and disfigured. But there was nothing she could do about it until she found safety. For that reason, she kept it under her shirt. When people saw it, they inevitably gasped in shock and insisted she get medical help. There would be time for that later, she told herself. When she had gone as far as the forty-two-dollar ticket would carry her, then she would see to herself.

Her eyes drifted out the window to the highway, and she scanned the cars, making sure Jack hadn't followed her. She didn't see his car, but that didn't mean he wasn't back there somewhere, waiting to pounce the moment she stepped off the bus. It had happened before. She had once believed she was home free in St. Louis, but he had been standing there just inside the bus station, waiting to descend on her the moment she got off. That time he had broken three ribs and given her a concussion.

She closed her eyes and leaned her head back on the dirty seat. With her right hand, she fished through her bag for a mirror. She couldn't look like a runaway when she got off this bus. She needed to look older, full of purpose, like she knew where she was going, even if she didn't. But the huge black bruise under her eye would attract attention. And the blonde, wispy hair that feathered around her face gave her the look of a fourteen-year-old. That would never do. She would be seventeen next month, but she had to look at least eighteen so she could get a job and support herself while she hid.

With one hand she tried to scrape her hair up into a ponytail, then tried to flip it around so that it looked like some kind of well-planned updo—something a professional woman might wear. Or at least a sorority sister. But Sadie knew better than that. She had never even known a sorority girl. And she wasn't the type to be college-bound, not with a ninth-grade education, a broken arm, and thirty-three dollars to her name.

Abandoning her hair, she threw the mirror back into her backpack and fished around for the thin wallet at the bottom. She opened it, found the picture of little Caleb, only nine months old. In the picture she held, the light hadn't gone out of his eyes just yet, and fragile laughter still rose from that open mouth. His hands were poised as if to clap. He loved to clap.

She closed the wallet and buried it deep beneath her few belongings. She would go back for him soon enough, and then things would change. The bus engine changed its pitch, and she looked out the window again and saw the station up ahead. It was the end of the line, as far east as Greyhound would take her. Savannah, Georgia. Judging from the map on the wall in the Greyhound station, the Atlantic Ocean was just a few miles east from here. Then she would have to decide whether to stay put or go north or south. West was simply too treacherous.

The man next to her grunted awake and turned his smelly mouth away from her. He got out of his seat and she followed, standing in the aisle waiting to get off. Through the window she could see people milling around just outside the station waiting for loved ones . . . or not-so-loved ones. She felt alone and cold, but she straightened her shoulders, pulled her bag over her shoulder, and cradled that arm against her stomach.

The passengers began to file off one by one, and as she stepped down onto the hot pavement, she looked around helplessly.

"Hey, baby. Need a ride?"

She turned and saw a scruffy man with dreadlocks, a scraggly beard, and a lusty, amused look in his eyes. She knew that look, and she'd been around enough to know that he was not her answer.

"No," she said, lifting her chin. "I've got it under control."

"'Cause I can fix you up real nice," the man said, "give you a place to stay, even some money. And if you use—"

"I don't use," she snapped back, "and I don't need a place to stay, and I don't need a ride."

She started to go inside but realized that was where Jack had been waiting in the St. Louis station. This time she turned and took off across the street. When she was half a block away, she glanced back over her shoulder. No one had followed her, thankfully, but she wasn't dumb enough to take that for granted. Walking fast, as if she knew exactly where she was headed, she made her way into downtown Savannah.

CHAPTER

Cade pulled the squad car into the parking lot in front of the police station, still running murder scenarios through his brain. Someone had thought it through. They had deliberately used a weapon that wouldn't make noise, so they wouldn't draw attention from the people at Crickets or on the dock.

Did that ruin the theory that Jonathan could have lost his temper and acted out of rage?

For the life of him, Cade couldn't conceive of Jonathan *deciding* to kill them, plotting the murders, taking out his speargun, going back to the warehouse, and looking them in the eye. . . .

He had known Jonathan too long. It wasn't like him.

But what if he had had the gun in his car for some reason and in his anger had grabbed it and reacted?

It was a brutal way to die. The spear could kill a large fish at a range of twenty-four feet. When they'd hunted off the Florida Keys, Jonathan had caught a forty-seven-pound amberjack with that gun. At closer range, the point could easily kill a human. But would *Jonathan* do such a thing? Maybe he would scream and yell, maybe even shove Wayne. But raise a speargun to their throats and fire?

No way.

Still, he couldn't base his actions as police chief on gut feelings or on the years of history between him and Jonathan. He had to be objective. And objectively, he knew that the evidence pointed to Jonathan.

"This is just a formality, right?" Jonathan asked from the backseat. "You just want everybody to know you're a big man doing your job, right? You really don't mean to parade me in there in handcuffs and lock me behind bars."

Cade looked over the seat. "Jonathan, what am I supposed to do? It was your gun. There are two people dead on this island. I have no choice."

He slammed out of the car. But before he opened the door to get Jonathan out, Cade stood for a moment on the gravel. Looking back toward the beach across the street, he saw that people had converged—no doubt to talk about what had happened. Word was spreading like a barely controlled fire across the island. There had been two murders. Jonathan Cleary had been arrested. He took a deep breath and opened the back door, helped Jonathan out of the car.

Jonathan met his eyes. "I thought you were my friend."

"I've got to do my job, Jonathan."

"Your job is to find the killer," Jonathan said, "not to go locking up the victims. They were like my own parents, you know." His voice broke off and his mouth trembled. "I loved those people. I *lived* with them."

"But everybody knows about your temper, Jonathan," he said and started toward the door. "Everybody knows that you get raging mad at them sometimes. Until I'm sure what happened, until I sort out what happened with that gun, I've got to bring you in."

Jonathan looked around as if wondering who was witnessing this. Cade didn't even want to know how many across the

street were taking pictures, noting every detail for later gossip. He
hoped he had done the right thing.

He ushered Jonathan into the small station, converted from
an old Laundromat. Three officers sat at their desks in the front
room, making the phone calls to track down the information that
Cade and Joe McCormick had asked for. The police force was
small—only twelve uniformed officers who worked four to a shift,
two office workers, three dispatchers (one per shift), and him and
McCormick. The twelve lifeguards on the island were under his
jurisdiction as well. Under ordinary circumstances, there were no
more than five or six people working at the station, but today, all
of the uniforms had been called to work to help with this investigation, and the phones were ringing as the cops working the town
called in information for Cade and McCormick to process.

Cade put Jonathan in an interview room that had served as
a closet in the building's former life. It was only ten by ten, just
enough room for a table and a few chairs. Jonathan plopped
down, his hands still cuffed.

"You can undo these, Cade. I'm not going to break and run."

Cade leaned toward him and unhooked the handcuffs.

"So much for you blocking for me on the football team,"
Jonathan said. "When I ran the ball, I always knew you were
going to be clearing a path for me. If I'd known someday you'd
be arresting me for murder, I wouldn't have saved your life when
you were drowning in that lake at scout camp in fifth grade."

"I wasn't drowning," Cade said. "I was faking it. It was a joke."

"It didn't look like a joke," Jonathan said, "when I dragged
you out of there and Mr. Martin had to do mouth-to-mouth. And
that time I had tickets to the Super Bowl, I wouldn't have taken you."

"That's enough, Jonathan," Cade said quietly. "This is hard
for me too. I have a job to do on this island and I intend to do it."

"You have something to prove," Jonathan said, "and you're
using me to do it. You want to prove that you're not some light-
weight the mayor hired because you were related."

Cade didn't react. He had heard enough of that from every
resident of the island who got a ticket or a fine. They all claimed

he had gotten the job because his uncle was mayor. No one ever considered the fact that Cade had a degree in criminal justice and ten years on the Savannah police force. At thirty-three, he might be a little young to head up a police force, but he wouldn't have taken the job if he hadn't been qualified.

He started toward the door.

"Where you going?" Jonathan asked. "You're not going to just leave me here, are you?"

"It's your choice," Cade said. "I can leave you here or put you in a cell. I'm just going to get a stenographer, and then we're going to get started answering some questions."

"Fine," Jonathan said, "let's get on with it. I'm ready to get this over and get out of here. My wife needs me. There are two funerals to plan."

Cade stopped at the door and slowly turned back. Jonathan had his hands over his face and was rubbing it roughly. "Those are going to be tough funerals," Cade said, letting out a long, sad sigh as he leaned back against the door casing. "I'm going to figure out who did this, and if it's you, I don't care if we *were* in scouts together. If it's you, Jonathan, I'm going to make sure you pay. And if it's not, you'll go free, and somebody else will fry."

He closed the door and locked it before he lost control of his own emotions. He stood outside it for a moment, swallowing his grief. Then, drawing a long breath, he went out to one of the desks in the front room and picked up the phone. He dialed the stenographer's number, and as the phone rang, he closed his eyes and saw those bodies again. He would see them tonight when he tried to sleep. He imagined he would see them for a long time to come.

After telling the stenographer to come to the station, Cade gathered the information that had come in over the last few minutes. Gus Hampton was still at large; the other tenants were all being questioned at Hanover House; his officers had gotten the manifests of every boat that had come in or gone out from that dock today; they had found two others on the island who owned spearguns; they had done background checks on all of the spearfishermen, and none of them had records.

His mind wandered to the eclectic group of church members who met in the warehouse on Sunday mornings. Many of them *did* have records. Some were drifters, hard to trace.

He rubbed the tense muscles of his neck. What would they do about church services without Thelma and Wayne there to lead things? Would the church just fall apart and scatter? Half the people there would never be welcome at other churches. Some of them were only in town while their boats docked; others hadn't had a bath since they'd gone out to sea. No, they'd never fit in at the other churches in the area.

And what of Hanover House? For so long it had been a fixture on Cape Refuge. Even lately, with the city council threatening to close it down, Cade couldn't picture the island without it. It was why this island was known to be warm and friendly and welcoming, even to the most lost and rootless soul. No—Hanover House wasn't the reason. Thelma and Wayne were the reason.

He got up, telling himself that maybe he should let his old friend go. Maybe he should just tell people he had brought Jonathan in for questioning, then had let him get back to Morgan and Blair to comfort them and do what needed to be done. Cade honestly didn't know the right thing to do.

One of the squad cars pulled up in the parking lot. It was Joe McCormick, his best and only detective. Cade met him at the door.

"Jack wanted me to tell you that the coroner put their time of death at five this afternoon."

"Five," Cade said, raking his hands through his hair. What did that tell him? "Have them check to see what time Jonathan's rig came in."

"I already did, Chief. It came in about four-thirty."

Cade closed his eyes. "He was at the six o'clock meeting tonight. He had showered and shaved. Would he have had time to kill them, shower and shave, and still get to the meeting?"

"Depends," Joe said in a slow southern drawl. "Rage goes fast sometimes. Don't take long to snap. But it seems like somebody would have seen the killer going into the building or coming out. Nobody saw anything."

Cade heard another car in the parking lot and looked out. Melinda Jane, the stenographer, was just pulling in.

"Well, looks like we can get started questioning Jonathan," he said. "Where are the three guys you brought in earlier?"

"The jail was empty, so I put 'em into a cell for now. I have Jim Henry guarding them, with the door open so they can't come back with unlawful imprisonment. We were very clear that we just wanted to question them."

Cade walked to the plateglass window on the front of the building and stared out at the passing traffic.

"You okay, Chief?"

Cade tried to shake off his emotions. He had work to do. "Yeah, I'm fine."

"You want me to do the interview?" Joe asked. "I don't have a history with him. Might be harder for you."

"I'd appreciate that," Cade said. "I'll jump in where I need to."

The door swung open, and Melinda Jane rushed in. "Oh, Cade, it isn't true, is it?" the chubby woman asked. "About Thelma and Wayne? Melba called cryin' so hard I couldn't hardly understand a word. Oh, it's just terrible!"

He swallowed and tried to look unmoved. "Melinda Jane, do you think you can do this objectively and confidentially?"

She dabbed at her eyes and straightened her shift. "Well, yes, of course. I'm a professional, Cade. Are you interrogating the killer?"

"We're interviewing Jonathan Cleary," he said.

"*Jonathan Cleary?* Not Jonathan! Oh, Cade! He's the one fixed my roof last month when it was leakin'. Did it for free, just because I'm a widow and on a tight budget. Well, he wouldn't hurt a fly." She dug into her purse for a tissue, then dabbed at the tears in her eyes. "Oh, that poor man. And Blair and Morgan . . . I just don't know what they're gonna do."

Cade wondered whether Melinda Jane would make it through the interview as he followed her back to where Jonathan waited.

CHAPTER 9

*M*organ's car seemed to be on automatic pilot. She didn't remember driving to the police station or pulling into the parking spot in front. But here she was, still behind the wheel, trying to direct her thinking, trying to remember ...

She should have seen something coming. She should have changed just one thing in the afternoon's routine, something, anything—maybe discouraged her parents from leaving the house. She should have sensed the evil waiting. She should have asked more questions about where her parents were going, who they were seeing.

But she had been too self-absorbed, worrying about her fight with Jonathan that morning.

If only she'd paid closer attention.

She thought back a few hours, to the last time she'd seen her parents. They had been in the small office off the kitchen at Hanover House, and she'd been helping them, hurrying to prepare a mailing to the donors who helped support their ministry.

Her father had been stuffing envelopes while Morgan applied the address labels and Thelma stuck on the postage. They had just told her about Jonathan's fight with them that morning.

"I don't want to move," she said. "That's ridiculous. What if he insists on it?"

"Then you'll have to do it," Thelma said. "He's your husband."

"But what if he's wrong?"

"He *is* wrong," Wayne said. "But you've got to keep peace with your husband."

"But if he makes us move out, he's also going to want me to quit working here."

"We'd have to get along without you."

"But what would I do? I don't want to leave, Mama. This is who I am." She stacked the letters she had finished, passed them to Thelma. "It might not matter, anyway. They might close us down tonight."

"Where's your faith, little gal?" Wayne asked her. "The Lord didn't bring us this far to abandon us now."

"Hanover House Ministries was his idea, not ours," Thelma said. "It's been his all along, and he'll take care of it. Those folks at the city council aren't putting one over on God. He's still in control."

"But things do happen, Mama. Sometimes people like that win."

"Well, the Lord would have a purpose for that too. We have to trust him, honey. He does have a plan."

Wayne got up and stretched out his stiffness. "We'd better run if we're going to get these to the post office before it closes. Then we can go by the church for our meeting before we head over to City Hall."

"What meeting?" Morgan asked.

Her mother grabbed her purse off of the hook on the wall. "We'll tell you about it later. We'd better run now. Be praying."

That was it. No good-bye, no farewell hug, no premonition that she would never see them alive again. Now she pressed her forehead against the hot steering wheel, groping for the tissue she had dropped on the seat next to her. She blew her nose, wondering when—and if—there would be an end to these tears.

She had sometimes wondered whether people who died suddenly left clues. Whether there was some subconscious preparation, some hastily scrawled note, a conversation that, when remembered, gave peace and comfort to those left behind.

But there had been nothing like that this morning. Just another few moments in their busy lives, a frustrated exchange, a rushing out the door.

And there was so much unfinished business. Didn't God know that? Didn't he understand?

She forced herself out of the car. Wiping her face, she tried to summon some strength, but she found she was still shaking. If she could just get Jonathan released, she could lean on him—and then she could fall apart, knowing that he would be there to help gather the scattered pieces.

She stepped in the front door and felt the whish of air-conditioning blowing her hair back from her face. She didn't know why they kept it so cold in here. It wasn't as if the police department on Cape Refuge had that much to do. There weren't car chases, foot pursuits, or adrenaline jolts keeping them hot. Not until today.

The few other times she had come in here she had seen police officers with feet propped up on their desks, reading the newspaper. Today, however, every police officer on the island had been called in, and she knew that most of them were working the scene. This would go down as one of the busiest days in Cape Refuge police history.

The day Thelma and Wayne Owens were murdered.

She imagined the residents using this day as a marker. *Where were you when you heard about the murders?* They would each have their own story. The trauma would spread over the island and linger for years.

Her parents never did anything small.

She swallowed a lump in her throat and let the glass door close behind her. She saw Cade standing over a fax machine.

"Where's my husband?" she demanded.

He looked up at her, and she saw the strain on his face. "We're about to question him," Cade said. "You can't go in."

"This is cruel!" she managed to say. "They're my parents, Cade. He is my husband. Why in the world would he want to kill them? You're wasting time when you could be out there looking for the person who did it."

His face changed, and for a moment he was the man who sat on the second row, middle pew, every Sunday, sometimes shedding tears as he praised the Lord. "Morgan, I wouldn't do anything to hurt you for the world. I loved your parents too. You know that."

"Then let their son-in-law go!" she said, surprised at the volume and force behind her words. "Let him out so he can help me get through this. Don't you understand? I'm afraid to go home. I don't think I can do this alone." She covered her mouth and collapsed into a chair. "I'm afraid to do anything, Cade. What if they're after me too? And Blair? What if they're after Jonathan and he's sitting in there like a target?"

"He's not a target," Cade said. "There's nobody in here but us."

"And that's supposed to make me feel better?" Morgan asked. "Who's in there with him?"

"Joe McCormick," he said.

"I went to high school with Joe McCormick," she said. "He has more skeletons in his closet than the tenants at Hanover House. Why does he have the right and I don't?"

"He's got the right because he's a police officer," Cade said calmly. "Morgan, you can sit here and wait. I'll get you something to drink. You can put your feet up."

"Don't coddle me," she bit out. "I have things to do. My parents are dead." Her voice broke off, and grief assaulted her again. She hated to cry in front of other people.

Cade reached out to comfort her. She shook him off.

"Morgan," he said in a quiet voice. "I can promise you we won't hold him any longer than we have to. It made me sick to my stomach when I had to put those cuffs on him. He's the last person in the world I'd want to arrest. But there are two people I cared a lot about who are dead, and somebody murdered them. And he had a fight with them this morning . . . a real public fight. It was his gun that killed them. Can you explain that?"

"No, I can't explain it," she cried. "I can't explain anything. My head feels like it's just been clobbered with a baseball bat. You want me to explain things? Then let me explain what it feels like to know that my parents were the two most cherished people on this island, that they did something for just about everybody who lives here. People loved them. And I can't imagine why anyone would want to see them dead."

Cade straightened up, raked his fingers through his hair. He seemed to struggle with his own pain. Then that hard, professional look returned to his face. He went to the watercooler, got her a cone-shaped cup of water, and brought it back to her.

Staring down at it, she said, "I want to see my husband, Cade."

"Later, Morgan. But I can't let you right now." He backed away and started toward the interview room, which she knew was a converted broom closet. No two-way mirrors, no hidden microphones. This was definitely a no-frills police department. How would they ever be able to find the real killer?

When Cade opened the door, Morgan saw her husband sitting behind the table, hands over his face. Joe McCormick stood in front of him, foot propped on a chair like some television cop.

Jonathan caught her eye and got up. "Honey, are you okay?" he called.

"I'm fine. Just go ahead. Answer their stupid questions so you can get out of here."

The door closed behind Cade, and Morgan sank back into her chair. Anguish overtook her as she recalled the sight of her parents, covered with white sheets, being carried out to the hearse.

People had warned them to be more careful in their ministry, but they had always been completely sold out to Christ, going where others feared to go, loving those who were patently unlovable.

In God I have put my trust, they'd always quoted. *I shall not be afraid. What can man do to me?*

Yet man had killed them ... brutally, horribly ...

She grabbed two Kleenexes from a box on someone's desk, wadded them, and pressed them against her eyes. *Where are you, God?*

The question drilled through her soul, leaving a void that she doubted would ever be filled again.

CHAPTER

10

*S*adie made her way up West Oglethorpe, then crossed the street at Montgomery, and walked the block to Liberty Square. It was a charming little park in the middle of the city, one with a statue of someone she didn't know in the center of it, and little park benches placed here and there under massive oaks. She smiled in spite of herself. It was just as she had pictured it.

She adjusted her backpack and headed up West York Street past a parking garage and groomed strips of grass until she reached another park. She had heard that Savannah had been designed and built around parks, each representing some famous part of their history. She had always wanted to visit this city and see for herself, but today she was tired and hungry. She could come back and see it another day. Right now she had to find a place to stay before dark. On thirty-three dollars, it wouldn't be easy.

She saw a diner across from Telfair Square and started toward it. She hadn't eaten since yesterday, before Jack had come home and blown a gasket. She had wound up spending the night in her neighbor's car, hunkered down so he couldn't find her. This morning there hadn't been time to eat. She shoved back her blonde hair and went into the old diner.

She took a stool at the bar and set her backpack down on the one next to her.

"Can I help you, honey?"

A waitress stood across the bar from her. The woman's blonde hair was a little too teased, and she desperately needed to have her roots done. But she had kind eyes even if they were caked with eyeliner and half a tube of mascara. Her lips were red and outlined a little bigger than they really were. Her fingernails, tapping nervously on the Formica countertop, were painted bright red too, with little stars embedded in the center of each. She popped on a piece of gum. "Want to hear the special?"

Sadie shook her head and absently brought her right hand to cradle her left, still tucked under her shirt.

"I'd just like a hamburger," she said, "and a glass of water."

The waitress pulled the pencil from its place over her ear and, chomping on her gum, wrote on a slip of paper as if she couldn't remember the order. "Anything else, honey? A piece of pie maybe?"

"No, thank you," she said.

The woman went on her way and in a few moments came back with a plate bearing an open hamburger and a tall glass of water.

She set the check down next to the plate. Sadie picked it up. "I'll pay now, if that's all right," she said.

"Sure, honey. I'll take it."

Awkwardly, Sadie reached into her backpack with that one good hand and groped around until she came to her wallet again. She pulled out a five-dollar bill and laid it on the counter.

"Who won?" the waitress asked. "If you don't mind my asking."

Sadie glanced up at her. "Won what?"

"The fight you were in, honey." The waitress leaned down conspiratorially on the counter. "That's an impressive-looking shiner, if you don't mind my saying so. And it looks like your arm might be even worse. So who won?"

Sadie lowered her gaze to the countertop. "I fell," she said.

"Fell." The waitress laughed. "Yeah, I've heard that before. Said it myself." Again she bent across the counter and whispered. "Never met a girl yet who fell on her eye. So what's the matter with the arm? Is it broke?"

Sadie cradled it again. "I don't know," she said. "I don't think so. Probably just bruised." She knew better. She could see where the bone had separated, and the pain had been unbearable all night and most of the day.

The waitress came around the counter. "Let me see, hon," she said.

"I'm okay," Sadie said. "Really."

The waitress drew a deep, laborious sigh, then straightened up. "Okay, I got you. All you have to say is, 'Tammy, mind your own business.' They say it around here all the time. Never hurt me yet."

Sadie smiled.

"Eat your hamburger," the woman said, "and if you're still hungry after, I'll throw in a piece of pie, no charge."

Sadie watched her as she pranced away, her too-tight waitress uniform straining to cover her hips. Sadie devoured the hamburger and felt the energy seeping back into her.

Tammy put a piece of pie in front of her as the door jingled. Still on the alert for Jack, Sadie glanced back. It was the man with the dreadlocks who had been waiting at the bus station, the one who had offered her money and a place to live. He spotted Sadie and smiled. She hadn't seen him following her from the bus station, but surely it was no coincidence that he had shown up here. She quickly turned away, but he came and took the stool next to her backpack.

"You again," he said with a smile. "Thought you said you had a ride and a place to stay."

She tried to ignore him and turned her body away. Tammy was there in a moment, popping on her gum and pulling that pencil out from behind her ear.

"May I help you?"

"Just coffee," he said, then he turned back to Sadie. "You don't have to be afraid of me, you know. I saw you get off that bus and look around like you didn't know a soul in town. And you wouldn't be eating in a diner if you had any place to go."

"Slick, you're not trying to bother my cousin, are you?" Tammy asked, leaning on the counter. "Because I get real protective when men come around here hitting on her."

He looked up at her, surprised. "Your cousin?"

"Yeah, my cousin," she said. "You got a problem with that?"

He looked slowly from Tammy to Sadie a time or two, then got back to his feet. "Cancel the coffee," he said. He strolled to the door, glancing one last time at Sadie as he started out.

"Come again," Tammy shouted cheerfully across the room.

Sadie grinned up at her when he was gone. "Thank you. I appreciate it. I don't know him, and he keeps trying to get me to go home with him."

"He wants you to do more than go home with him," Tammy said. "He wants to put you to work. He spends a lot of time over at the bus station waiting for runaways. You ain't a runaway, are you?"

Sadie shook her head hard. "No. Of course not. I'm eighteen. I can go anywhere I want."

Tammy nodded. "Eighteen, huh? Yeah, and I'm twenty-two."

The woman was at least thirty-five.

"Eat your pie," she said. "It's on me."

"I can pay," Sadie said.

"I know you can, honey, but if my intuition is telling me right, you need to keep every penny you got. Just accept it as a goodwill offering welcoming you to the big city of Savannah."

Sadie buried her fork into it. "I'm actually not staying here," she said. "It's just as far as Greyhound would take me. I'm headed east."

Tammy laughed. "Well, not far east. Tybee Island is only fifteen minutes away, and then you're right smack-dab at the Atlantic Ocean. No farther east to go unless you get on a boat or swim. Few minutes south of that and you're on Cape Refuge."

"Cape Refuge?" Sadie asked. The name sounded inviting. "How do you get there?"

"Out Highway 80," she said, "on the Island Expressway. It takes you to the bridge that goes to the Cape."

Sadie had pictured herself at the Atlantic Ocean, sleeping on the beach where no one would bother her, listening to the sound of the waves against the shore. She had only seen that on television, had never experienced it for herself. It sounded romantic and hopeful. How could anyone ever be unsafe on a peaceful beach? And in a beach town she could probably find a job working in a restaurant or a deli or in a souvenir shop of some kind. No high school diploma needed. No college degree.

"Honey, level with me," Tammy said, meeting her eyes across the counter. "It's one thing to lie to old Dreadlocks about having a place to stay, but give it to me straight. You're on your own, aren't you? You don't know the slightest soul here, do you?"

Sadie averted her eyes again.

"That's what I thought," Tammy said. She pulled out her writing pad, jotted something down, then tore off the page and handed it to Sadie.

Sadie looked at the piece of paper Tammy had given her. "'Thelma and Wayne Owens,'" she read aloud. "'Hanover House.' Who're these people?"

"People who'll take you in," Tammy said. "They're known around this area for collecting strays, if you know what I mean."

Sadie didn't like the sound of that. She wasn't a stray. She had a purpose, even though she didn't know what it was.

"They put people up all the time. Mostly, they take people just out of jail, who don't have jobs or places to live, and they help them get on their feet. They have this real cute little bed-and-breakfast on the island. They'll take you in, all right, if you can get there. And let me tell you something. You could do worse than hooking up with Thelma and Wayne Owens and sleeping in that precious place."

Sadie sat straighter. "But I don't have enough money for a bed-and-breakfast."

"You find Thelma and Wayne and you don't have to worry about the money, at least not for a while. They'll give you time to get a job and get set up. Yes, sir, if I had just blown into town on a Greyhound bus, that's the first place I'd go."

Sadie felt a faint sense of hope. "Okay," she said, "I'll look into it. Thanks."

She finished the pie, then got to her feet and slid the backpack onto one shoulder. Reluctantly, she started out of the diner, wishing she didn't have to leave her new friend, but knowing that she had to get wherever she was going before it got dark, so that neither Jack nor Dreadlocks could catch up to her.

CHAPTER

So tell me again why you were at the dock this morning fighting with your in-laws?" Joe McCormick asked Jonathan when the door closed.

Jonathan watched the detective smooth his hand over his shaved head. He had his foot propped on a chair and was looking down his nose at him. A little power was a dangerous thing, Jonathan thought.

"I told you," he said. "We've been all through this. Melinda Jane can read it back to you."

Melinda Jane wiped her nose with a wadded tissue. "Want me to, Joe?"

"That won't be necessary," Cade said.

"The rumor is that you gave them an ultimatum," McCormick said, dropping his foot to the floor and pacing to the window. "What was that ultimatum?"

"I told them that either Gus had to go or Morgan was quitting and we were moving out."

Cade, who sat on a folding chair in the corner of the room, lifted one eyebrow. "Would she have done that?"

Jonathan rubbed his face. "I don't know. It was half bluff. I figured I'd worry about that later. I was hoping they'd just ask him to leave. But they said no, they weren't going to let Gus go. I couldn't believe it."

"And then it escalated into a yelling fight," Cade said. "One witness said you yelled that if they didn't take care of it, you would. What did you mean by that?"

"Just what I said. That I'd take Morgan and move out."

"So you got pretty mad at them," McCormick said. "Were there any blows thrown?"

Jonathan looked up at him like he was crazy. "No, there were no blows thrown. I raised my voice a little, that's all. Several people heard it and got all bug-eyed like they'd just witnessed something real important. And I stormed down the pier and got on my rig."

McCormick's eyes narrowed. "Jonathan, tell us what happened when you brought your rig back."

"Well, we cleaned up, got the boat put to bed," Jonathan said. "And then I had to rush to shower and shave before the city council meeting."

Cade slid his chair closer to the table and leaned on his elbows. "So you were at the city council meeting when they started talking about Hanover House?"

"Right," Jonathan said, "only Thelma and Wayne weren't there. So I took off looking for them."

"Where did you go first?" Cade asked.

"Well, I went by the house, but no one was there."

"Did you go out to the toolshed?"

"No. I haven't been out there for several days." He slapped his hands on the table. "Look, I know I'm a hothead. I lost my temper this morning. I yelled a little too loud. It's my wife we're talking about. I didn't want her around some ex-con who claims he's found God. I was afraid of what he might do. Maybe I was wrong to do and say what I did, but you can't arrest me for that." He stood and leaned across the table, his eyes fixed on McCormick's. "And think about it. Why would I use my own speargun if I was going to kill them? And why would I be so stupid as to toss the gun into the water before I left?"

"Maybe you panicked. Not thinking," McCormick said.

Jonathan turned to Cade. "You can't seriously think I'm capable of this."

"Jonathan," Cade said, "you've been known to have a violent temper before. I remember once before you married Morgan, when you kicked Thelma and Wayne's toolshed until the thing toppled over."

"I was mad because they wanted her to wait a few months before marrying me. Hey, I rebuilt it, okay? It was a building, not a person. I've never been violent with people."

"You've put your fist through walls," Cade added. "Did that at camp. Almost got sent home."

"I was fourteen! Give me a break! What are you gonna do? Haul me into court and tell them you think I killed my in-laws because I lost my temper in eighth grade and tore up a shed once?"

"I don't see how we can release you," Cade said.

"You're going to *lock me up?* Cade, don't you realize my wife just lost her parents? She needs me. If you've ever cared anything about the Owens—"

"I have to do my job," Cade said. "I don't like it, Jonathan, but I can't take any chances right now."

"I did *not* kill them," he said. "Ask my deckhand. I was in a bad mood this morning, but I got over it. I didn't have blood on my mind when I went out this morning or when I came back. I've had fights with Thelma and Wayne, but we've always gotten over it. There were a lot of things about them I didn't understand, and they weren't always willing to explain. But I loved them just the same," he said. "They were good to me and good to my wife. And they wound up with the best-built shed in town, and you know it."

Despite his efforts to hold his emotions back, Jonathan's mouth trembled. "What's this town going to do without them?"

"What's going to happen to Hanover House? The whole island is going to change. Not to mention the fact that there's a killer running around. And if you ask me, his name is Gus Hampton. You're going to at least question him, aren't you, Cade?"

"Of course we're going to question him, Jonathan. We're going to question everybody. But meanwhile, we're going to hold you here."

"Cade, you can't. You can't put me in jail and give my wife something else to grieve over."

"Morgan has Blair," Cade said. "She can help her through it."

"And who's going to help Blair?" Jonathan asked.

"Blair Owens is the strongest woman I know," Cade said.

"Oh, yeah?" Jonathan asked. "See if *you* don't have nightmares tonight, and then ask yourself what it would be like to see your own parents that way."

Cade looked down at his hands. "Come on," he said. "I'm going to have to book you and put you in a cell."

"And suppose the real guy gets arrested. Suppose somebody finds out who really did it. You've only got two cells back there, Cade. What are you going to do? Don't you have any drunks or shoplifters in there?"

"Nope. Just some temporary residents waiting to be questioned."

Slowly, Cade got to his feet.

Jonathan wanted to kick the chair over, head-butt his old football buddy, put both fists through this particular wall. Instead he got up, seething quietly, and followed Cade out of the room.

*M*organ thought they might be letting Jonathan go when they brought him out of the interview closet. "They're locking me up," he whispered. "Honey, I'm so sorry."

"No," she wailed. "Cade, what are you trying to do?" She stepped back and looked at the chief. "I'll bail him out," she said. "How much?"

Cade shook his head. "I can't set bail, Morgan. Only the judge can do that, and it's after hours. He's not in his office."

"Then I'll call him at home." There was only one judge on the island of Cape Refuge—a forty-eight-year-old ex-hippie who still wore his gray hair in a ponytail. His name was Randy Simmons, and she knew him well.

She grabbed the phone book and flipped through until she came to the name *Simmons.* Quickly she dialed his number.

"Nancy," she said when his wife answered. "Nancy, it's Morgan Cleary. I need to speak to Randy."

"Morgan," his wife said, "I heard about your parents. Oh, honey, you must be just upside down with grief." Nancy sounded sweet as honey, but Morgan knew she was only after something to run in the newspaper she published, the *Cape Refuge Journal*.

"I need to speak to Randy," she said again. "Please. Put him on the phone."

"He's not here right now," Nancy said. "Are you all right?"

"Where is he?" Morgan shouted.

"Well, he's at soccer practice. He coaches Jimmy's team, you know. And they're over at the soccer field down by the school."

"I need to talk to him real bad," Morgan said. "Nancy, do you think you can get in touch with him?"

"Well, I guess I could drive over to the field and tell him to call you."

"Does he have a cell phone with him?"

"No, honey, I'm afraid not," she said. "You know how it is out here. You can't get a signal no matter what you do. He's thinking about getting one of those satellite phones, but he hasn't done it yet."

"Then, yes, would you please drive over and get him? I really need to talk to him. It's an emergency."

"Well, where can he reach you, hon?"

She closed her eyes and tried to think. She couldn't stay here. She had to go to Hanover House and tell the tenants in case they hadn't heard already. She had to go back to the scene and sort through everything. She had to find out what they were doing with her parents' bodies.

"I don't know," she said. "I'm at the police station right now. Look, Nancy, just tell him that I need for him to set bail so I can get Jonathan out. They're holding him for no reason. He did not kill my parents."

"Oh, my," Nancy said, in that southern drawl that sounded so innocent but packed such punch. "They've arrested Jonathan?"

"When you publish that in your newspaper," Morgan said too loudly, "tell them he didn't do it. He's innocent—they were just looking for somebody to blame. But meanwhile, they'd better realize that there's a killer running loose on this island."

Morgan slammed the phone down. Cade had already taken Jonathan back to lock him up. She felt so helpless that she wanted to break something.

She heard the cell door bang shut and echo throughout the building, then Cade reemerged.

"He'll be all right, Morgan. Just have faith."

"I do have faith, Matthew Cade," she spat out. "Where's *your* faith? You know Jonathan is a Christian, that he could never kill anybody. You're members of the same church. You worship together, pray together. How can you lock up your Christian brother like that?"

"It's not easy," Cade said. He came toward her and put his hands on her shoulders. This time she didn't shake him off.

"Don't worry about him," he said. "He's going to be all right. But Morgan, while you're here, I need you to answer a few questions too."

"Me? You suspect me too?" she threw back.

"No, of course not. But we need to retrace their steps. I need to know what they were doing today, who they talked to, what they said the last time you saw them."

"All right," she said. "I'll tell you whatever I know."

He took her into the interview room, where Melinda Jane still sat with her stenotype machine. She was dabbing at her eyes with her tissue, and Morgan wondered whether she was crying over how they were treating Jonathan or over the death of her parents.

Cade had barely closed the door when she started talking. "They had a regular day, Cade, like any other day. Except that Pop said something about meeting with somebody before going over to City Hall. They said they'd tell me about it later. I should have demanded to know."

"Oh, honey," Melinda Jane said. "You didn't know. How could you know?"

"Melinda Jane," Cade warned, and she got back to her work.

"Morgan," Joe McCormick asked, "what do you think about Gus Hampton? Is Jonathan right about him?"

She leaned back. All she had to do was tell Joe something negative about Gus, something that would cast him in a bad light and get Jonathan out of trouble. But she couldn't. It wouldn't be true.

"My parents knew Gus was an ex-con. They weren't harboring him illegally at all. He came here, a broken soul trying to start over, and they gave him a place. I've seen them do wonders with him," she said. "I've seen him transformed. I don't think he killed my parents, but I don't know who did. All I know, Cade, is that you won't find him by sitting in this building."

"We're looking," Cade said. "As soon as we find him, we'll bring him in."

He questioned her further about her parents' activities of the day: people they called, places they had gone, things they had said. When she had told him everything she knew, he finally walked her back out to the front door.

"I appreciate your help."

She wiped her eyes. "I want you to find the killer," she said. "I'll cooperate in any way I can. But I want my husband out of here."

"I know you do," he said. "Morgan, you just go do what you need to do, take care of yourself and Blair, and let me take care of this."

"Right," she said, and turned away from him. She started to the front door, opened it, and stood at the threshold. "My parents would want me to forgive you," she said, "but it's going to be hard when this is all over."

"I know it is," Cade said. "I'd have trouble too. Believe me, Morgan. This is the hardest thing I've ever had to do."

She pointed at Cade, her finger trembling. "You protect my husband. Whoever did this, whoever stole his speargun and set him up, might have it in for him too. So help me, you'd better protect him, Cade."

Sobbing into her hand, she headed back out to her car.

CHAPTER

13

*A*cross Cape Refuge, Blair stood in front of the warehouse, fighting nausea. Someone had brought her car over from City Hall, so she got into it and sat behind the wheel.

Alex Johnson, one of the police rookies, came to her window. "You okay, ma'am? Sure you can drive?"

"I'm fine," she said. "I'm going to follow the hearse and see that my parents get there safely."

The absurdity of her words struck her, and she looked away, fighting despair. What could happen? Could the hearse run into a tree and kill her parents all over again?

She started her car and pulled off the gravel, following the hearse back across the bridge to Tybee Island, then to the causeway that led into Savannah.

Morgan would say that her parents were in heaven, that their souls had ascended instantly, that they would never be unsafe again. But Blair couldn't buy it. She had trouble buying into anything that she couldn't see and feel and taste. If it couldn't be explained with physics and chemistry, if you couldn't look it up on the Internet or find it in a book, spelled out all nice and neat with foolproof formulas and definitive explanations, then she couldn't accept it.

But that created a problem. That meant that her parents were no more, that she would never see them again, that the last time she had seen them, sometime yesterday, had been a farewell and she hadn't even known it. What good had it done them to be so spiritual and so godly, only to have their lives end so cruelly?

She didn't cry, didn't even blink back tears, as she followed the hearse into town. Even so, sorrow crushed her with such heaviness that she almost couldn't breathe. There were too many things her parents had left unsaid, too many equations that hadn't yet been solved.

She had known for years that she hadn't been told the whole story about those red, hideous scars on the side of her face, which repulsed the men who were attracted to her other side. Her parents had insisted as long as she could remember that she had been burned as a baby when a grease fire erupted in their kitchen. The story had made sense when she was a child, but as she'd grown older, she had begun to recognize their evasions about the fire and their reluctance to talk about it even when she'd pleaded for details. She had had screaming arguments with her parents, demanding to know the truth, but they had insisted they had told her everything there was to know. She had left home in a fit of anger, taken the job as the town librarian, and set up her own house. Eventually, she had gotten over that anger, trying to convince herself that her parents would never lie to her.

Her mother had once told her she was lucky to have the scars, that the man who finally fell for her would see her inner beauty and the outside wouldn't matter. Her mother hadn't meant it in a cruel way, but it had felt cruel to Blair.

Even so, Blair agreed with her mother. She was *glad* she hadn't been caught in the whirlwind of dates and dances to which Morgan, with her delicate beauty and gentle spirit, had seemed enslaved. Blair had always had more important things on her mind. A man would have just held her back.

She could get through this night and this grief without one. She was strong. She was intelligent. And if she could just get back to Cape Refuge and lock herself inside her office at the back of the library, somehow she would be able to figure out who the killer was. Then everything would make sense.

At the funeral home, Blair followed the hearse around to the covered area at the back door. She sat frozen in her car, watching through the windshield as they took the bodies out and carried them in, as carefully as if they were still alive.

She thought about the last time she had come to this place, when Roland Ball died of a heart attack at forty-two, leaving behind a wife and three children.

"What do you say to somebody who's going through a thing like this?" she had asked her parents as they walked across the parking lot for the visitation.

"You just hug them," her mother had said. "Tell them you're sorry. Scripture sometimes helps, but that's better for after the funeral, when you can write it down so they can look at it when they're ready."

"What good does Scripture do?" Blair asked. "Seems a little shallow, to bombard hurting people with platitudes when they're at their lowest point."

Her father, who had been walking a few steps ahead, stopped midstep and turned to face her. "Blair, you know better than that. Scripture is not platitudes. It's life."

"Not for Roland Ball."

"You're wrong about that too, darlin'. He does have life. His wife'll see him again."

"And what if you're wrong?"

"Oh, Blair," her mother had said with genuine despair in her eyes.

Her father got that look in his eyes that she had seen so many times, when he witnessed to a lonely dockworker or an aimless ex-con. It was easy for her to understand why people responded to him so as those soft, doleful eyes fixed on her. "The better question, Blair, is what if *you're* wrong?"

She wasn't wrong, she thought now as she watched them close the door to the hearse. If there was a God, he would have rescued her parents from the evil that defeated them today.

The driver of the hearse saw her car and started toward her. She rolled her window down.

"Ma'am, is there anything I can do for you?"

"No," she said. "I . . . I'm coming in . . . just as soon as I get back with some clothes. Please . . . don't touch my mother."

He leaned down and set his arm on her window. "Ma'am, we have to touch her."

"Don't . . . dress her, I mean." She swallowed, wondering why the words came so hard. "She's very modest. She hates it when people see her dressing. Even in department stores, she makes me stand in front of the dressing room door and hold it shut. But it's okay. I can do it."

"Ma'am, the medical examiner needs access to them. Let us take care of things. There's enough for you to do."

She stared through her windshield, and focused on an azalea bush at the edge of the parking lot. The pink blooms had all wilted. Someone needed to pinch them off, so that new ones could grow back. She didn't know why people left wilted blooms.

She looked back up at the man. "I told you," she said, her voice louder now. "I don't want you to touch her. What about that don't you understand?"

"Ma'am, you're upset." He spoke like one would speak to a rabid tiger, circling and growling, waiting to pounce. "Maybe you'd like to come in and sit down, and I can explain the process to you."

"I told you, I have to get her some clothes. Him too."

"It's no hurry. You can bring them later today or even tomorrow."

She couldn't understand why the man was so obtuse. Her knuckles whitened as she clutched the steering wheel. "I will bring them today, and I will dress her myself, and if you so much as open a button on her shirt, I will get a lawyer and sue you for everything you're worth!"

He nodded then. "Yes, ma'am. We won't touch her, then. We'll just wait."

"Good." She sat there staring at him for a moment, wondering where she would direct her anger now. She shifted into "drive." "I'll be back."

She didn't wait for his response, just rolled up the window and pulled out of the parking lot.

The drive home seemed longer than it ever had before, and when she finally crossed the bridge to take her back to Cape Refuge, she felt the sudden chilling sense that there was nothing here for her anymore. Still, she navigated her way through her town until she got to the little library. It was on the west side of the island, just north of the dock.

Her home and her library sat side-by-side among pine trees and mimosas, across the street from the water.

Next door, Sally Hanfield's Marine Museum sat, sharing an empty parking lot. She hoped Sally wasn't there . . . she couldn't deal with questions and pity.

She hurried to the library door. She had closed it a little early today so she could make the city council meeting, and she walked in and locked the door behind her. For a moment she stood there, breathing in the scent of the books and the dust.

She shouldn't have come here, she thought. She should have gone to Hanover House to get the clothes. She should have hurried back to the funeral home, as she had said she would, to attend to her mother's body.

She stood frozen, running faces through her mind, wondering who on this island had the potential for murder. Maybe Jonathan had done it. Maybe it was someone else running free on the island waiting to do it again. Maybe it was revenge, or just plain evil.

She stood there a moment, staring into space, while all the questions reeled through her mind like microfiche from the back room. Anguish bled into trembling rage, bubbling up, boiling over, shaking her . . .

Finally, she erupted. She grabbed the edge of the bookshelf in the center of the room—and pulled it over.

The books hit the ground first, and then the wooden structure crashed to the floor. She grabbed another set of books, knocked them off the shelf. One shelf at a time, she pulled the books off, then kicked the shelves over. Rage played out of her in violent form, book after book, shelf after shelf, crashing on the hard floor, wreaking havoc on the little building she kept so carefully. Vintage books, antiques, out-of-print books that no one could ever find anyplace else, all went flying in clouds of dust. Shelf after shelf—books landing open, facedown, pages flapping. Every last one crashed and banged.

It sounded like justice. Like broken dreams. Like flattened hopes.

Like she was murdering that thief, Death, who had robbed her of her parents.

She had to upend every one. Destroy them all. Every last one. Then maybe she could cry.

CHAPTER

14

*T*ammy took off her apron an hour later when her shift ended, freshened up her lipstick, then waved her long groomed fingernails at her boss before heading out. When she got to the parking lot, she looked around for any sign of the young girl who had been in there tonight. She hadn't been able to forget that black eye or the way she cradled her arm. She reminded her of herself when she was that age. She wondered if she'd been beaten by a boyfriend—or worse, her father. She had no doubt the girl had fled for good reason.

She got into her old Ford Escort, started it up, and pulled out into the traffic, but instead of starting home, she took off toward Highway 80, driving slowly and glancing at each side of the road for the girl with the backpack. She looked at her watch. Clarence, her boyfriend, would be expecting her any minute now, hungry and waiting for her to cook supper. But this seemed more important now than maintaining his paunch.

She saw the girl crossing a street up ahead, trudging east as if she thought she could actually walk all the way to Cape Refuge before dark. Carefully, Tammy pulled up to the curb and leaned over the seat to roll down the window.

"You ain't gonna walk all the way, are you, honey?" Tammy asked.

The girl swung around, startled. Then recognition flickered to her eyes. She stepped to the car window and leaned in. "I was going to hitchhike before it got dark."

"Scared, huh? Don't blame you. You never know who'll pick you up. Hop in," Tammy said. "I'll take you myself."

Sadie straightened. "You live on Cape Refuge?"

"No, I live about three blocks from here," Tammy said. "I would walk to work, but your dreadlocks friend has buddies, and sometimes they keep the streets from being all that safe. But I can't abide the thought of you walking all the way or even hitchhiking with strangers. Didn't your mama teach you better than that?"

Sadie slid off her backpack and got in, slumping into the bucket seat.

"I appreciate it, but if this is out of your way, really, I can—"

"Honey, I wouldn't be able to sleep tonight knowing you weren't settled. It'll be just fine. I'll take you across the river and drop you right at the front door of Hanover House, then I can go on my merry way knowing you'll be all right."

Sadie was quiet as they crossed the causeway onto Tybee Island. Tammy hoped Thelma and Wayne Owens were home and that they wouldn't let Sadie down.

"Do you know these people, Thelma and Wayne Owens?" Sadie asked her, as they drew closer to her destination.

"No, not personally," Tammy said, "but my sister lives on Cape Refuge and goes to church with them. I'd take you to her house, but her husband is mean as a snake, and it probably wouldn't be any better than where you came from. And I couldn't take you home with me, 'cause Clarence likes blondes a little too much, and I'd be shooting myself in the foot, if you know what I mean."

The beach came into view, and Sadie's eyes lit up as if she had just rounded a corner into some kind of glittering wonderland. The sun was going down over the horizon, and waves frothed and billowed as they hit against the shore. "It's beautiful," she said. "Just like I pictured it."

"Oh, honey, you should see it in the morning," Tammy said. "It's a right pretty little island, nice place to visit and all that. Not for me, though. Things move slower than I like."

Tammy drove along the beach, then crossed the bridge to Cape Refuge. She slowed the car as she got closer to the bed-and-breakfast, and she pulled onto the long graveled driveway in front of the yellow house with its massive front porch and huge yellow Victorian turret. A frilly little sign in the front yard said "HANOVER HOUSE."

"Well, here you are. This is it, the end of the line."

"It's perfect," Sadie whispered.

Tammy looked around to the side of the house. "Doesn't seem to be any cars here. We might have come at a bad time. 'Course, somebody could be inside. If not, I guess I could take you on back with me—"

"That's okay," Sadie said. "There are rocking chairs on the porch. I'll just sit up there and wait until somebody gets home."

"You're sure now?" Tammy asked.

Sadie nodded. "Thank you, Tammy. I really appreciate what you've done."

Tammy reached into her purse and pulled out a receipt, marked her phone number down on the back of it, then thrust it at the girl. "Now, if you find yourself in a jam, you give me a call, you hear? There might be something I can do."

"Okay," Sadie said with a smile. She took the receipt, then grabbed her backpack and got out. "Thanks again."

She closed the door and started up to the porch. Tammy waited as she knocked on the door, but no one came. Finally, Sadie sat down in one of the rocking chairs and waved that it was all right for her to go on. Tammy felt a little better about herself as she pulled her car out of the graveled driveway and headed back home.

*M*organ found the judge on the soccer field, but she couldn't make herself get out of the car and walk through the spectators who were all probably buzzing about the murders. *"Did you hear that Jonathan Cleary did it? I always said that boy was trouble...."*

Those who had counted him the town hero as a quarterback when he led the high school team to a state championship would swear that they had always known he had violence in him.

Judge Simmons ran along the field, yelling at the teenage boys as they kicked the ball toward the goal. Morgan wondered if Nancy had reached him yet. If she had, why hadn't he already gone to the police station?

Someone knocked on her window. She jumped. It was Hattie Brumfield, motioning for her to roll her window down. Morgan did and looked up with dull eyes.

"Darlin', I'm so sorry about your folks," she said. "How did it happen? They know who did it?"

That lump of emotion blocked her throat. "No." She swallowed and drew in a deep breath. "Hattie ... would you please . . . go tell the judge I need to speak to him? I just can't get out of this car and . . . walk through all those people."

"Well, of course I will. But, honey, how did they die? Were they shot or beaten . . . ?"

"Hattie, please." She opened her car door. "Never mind, I'll do it myself."

"No, no, honey. I'll do it. Just get back in."

Slowly, Morgan got back into the car. "Hattie, it's real important. Please. I need to talk to him right now."

"I'm going." The woman left the car and waddled down to the soccer field.

Morgan watched her approach the coach, and he turned back, looking for her. Hattie pointed toward her car, and several heads turned her way. She absently locked her door, as if that would protect her from their curiosity.

Finally, the judge barked a few more orders at the team, then headed toward the car.

He was sweating when he reached her, and his gray ponytail looked as if it hadn't been washed in days. "Hey, Morgan. Nancy came by and told me you needed to talk. I was gon' call you soon as the game was over. You okay?"

She didn't want to answer that question. "Randy, I know you're aware of . . . what happened to . . . my parents. Cade arrested Jonathan. I need for you to do something. Set bail or whatever . . . so I can get him out."

"Why Jonathan?"

"Someone took his speargun and . . . killed them. . . . " She stopped and took a deep breath. "That's all. Circumstantial evidence. Please, Randy . . ."

He straightened and set his hands on his hips. "I'll go right down to the station, but I can't promise anything."

"Why not?" she asked. "You're the judge! You can promise whatever you want."

"I don't like to interfere with Cade's investigations. If Jonathan owned the murder weapon—"

"He is not a murderer!"

"I'll see what I can do, Morgan."

She started her car and jerked it in reverse. "I'll see you at the station."

"No, Morgan. You don't need to be there while I'm reviewing the case."

"Reviewing the case?" she asked. "Randy, the case is about two hours old, and you probably heard through the grapevine everything Cade knows about it. What's to review?"

"I have to take Cade's opinion under advisement. I can't just let people out on the street because their wives don't want them in jail."

"They were *my* parents! Why would I want him released if I thought for a minute that he did it?"

"Go home, Morgan. Take care of yourself. I'll have Cade call you when I've finished." He started back to the game, dismissing the discussion.

Morgan tried to pull herself together. What was she going to do? She thought of going home, walking into that big house with her parents' things everywhere, right where they had left them. And the tenants ... and the friends who would start coming by, meaning well ...

She couldn't go home just yet. She needed to be with Blair, who understood the storm in her heart and needed shelter from it too.

She saw Blair's car parked on the gravel parking lot in front of the library next to her house. She got out and went to the library door. It was locked, so she knocked and waited. Blair didn't come, so she knocked again, harder this time. Still no answer. She stood there, bewildered by the peaceful serenity of the shade trees and the blooming crepe myrtle and the sound of the water washing against the river wall just across the street. You would never know someone had been murdered just a couple of miles from here, that her family had been destroyed, that nothing would ever be the same again.

She heard something crash inside and ran to the front window to peer in through the glass. The shelves were on the floor and there were books everywhere. Alarms went off in her head. She ran around to the back of the building, feeling for the brick that Blair kept there with a key underneath. She scraped her fingers trying to pull it off, then found the key and bolted back to the door.

By the time she got the door open another shelf was flying over and books were catapulting down. She looked around for the culprit, for anyone who might be hurting her sister, when she saw Blair reach for the next bookshelf and pull it over. The books flew out and the shelf smashed to the ground.

"Blair!" she shouted, and Blair spun around. Her face was raging red and wet, and her eyes had a wild, desperate look. The scars on the right side of her face were crimson.

"Blair, stop it!" Morgan ran to her as Blair reached for the next shelf. She pulled her away and pushed her against the wall where she couldn't do further harm.

"Let go of me," Blair cried. "Let go of me *now!*"

"You're going to hurt yourself," Morgan cried. "You need to calm down."

"Who did it, Morgan?" Blair screamed. "Who murdered them?"

"I don't know."

"They won't get away with it." She started to weep and put her arms around Morgan, and they held each other for a long time, standing against the wall, surrounded by books lying open and facedown beneath heavy bookshelves.

"How can you not suspect everybody on the face of this island?" she cried. "How can you walk into that bed-and-breakfast and look in anybody's eye and not suspect them? They shot them in the *throats*, Morgan! Mama and Pop must have looked the killer in the eye and feared for their lives. One of them saw the other one die! The horror they must have felt!"

Morgan couldn't speak. She just clung to her sister and cried, hating where this day had brought them, hating the uncertainty, hating what lay ahead. "What are we going to do?" she asked.

"That's easy," Blair said. "We're going to find the killers. And when we do, I'm going to kill them myself.

CHAPTER

16

An hour later, Morgan paced Blair's office, clutching her cordless phone to her ear. She had finally gotten the judge on the telephone at the police station, but he wasn't cooperating. "What do you mean, you can't release him?" she asked him.

"I'm sorry, Morgan. But Cade had good reason to arrest him, and for a murder case like this, I think it's appropriate to keep him in custody. If I were you, I'd get a lawyer as soon as possible."

Morgan clung to the phone, speechless, then finally set it back in its cradle without another word. She stepped back into the library with its toppled shelves and books scattered like debris from some kind of explosion. Blair still sat on the floor among the fallout. "I've got to get a lawyer," Morgan told her in a dull voice. "I don't even know where to look."

"What about the lawyers who were advising Mama and Pop about Hanover House?" Blair's voice was quiet and without inflection. "We could use them."

"Are they criminal lawyers?" Morgan asked. The words seemed to stick in her throat. It was absurd that she needed a criminal lawyer for her husband.

"No, they're not criminal, but maybe they could recommend somebody."

Morgan called the law firm but got a recorded message that they were closed for the day. She hung up and rubbed her face. "Guess I'll have to wait until morning."

"You can stay with me tonight," Blair said. "I've got the guest room, and I don't think either of us should be alone."

Morgan just looked at her. "You have a queen size, don't you?"

"Yeah," Blair whispered.

"I'm too scared to sleep alone in the guest room. They're out there somewhere, Blair, laughing because the keystone cops in this town have the wrong guy locked up."

Blair swallowed. "Yeah, we can share."

"Just like when we were kids," Morgan managed to get out. "We would sleep together, all huddled up. Two peas in a pod, Mama called us."

Blair stared off into the air, as if she saw something there that Morgan couldn't see. "I have to go back to the funeral home. I have to get Mama out of those clothes, and Pop—"

"Blair, let them do that. That's what they do."

"No, *I'm* doing it. You don't have to come."

"Good," Morgan said, "because I'm not. I can't."

Blair got off of the floor and looked helplessly around her. "I'd better get going."

"Don't go, Blair. Just tonight, let's stay together, okay? I don't want to be alone, even for a little while, and I can't go with you. . . . Please, you're not thinking clearly."

"Someone in the family has to do it, Morgan."

"No, they don't. That's what the funeral home is for."

"Mama is modest! She doesn't want—"

"She's not there, Blair!" Morgan cut in. "She's not in that funeral home, and she's not in those bloody clothes! It's not her!"

Blair stared at her as if she were the enemy—as if those words exposed her.

"Then who is it?" Blair demanded.

"It's her shell," Morgan said. "Mama is somewhere else, and she doesn't care what clothes she's wearing or who sees her. Neither does Pop. They would want us to huddle together and get through this, Blair, and not torture ourselves with things that don't even matter."

Blair stared again, helplessness and hopelessness tightening her face. "It's something I can do. I need to do it."

"No, you don't. You want something to do? Then stay here. Get through the night. Wake up and help me with all the details tomorrow."

"I told them I'd come," she said quietly.

"I'll call them. I'll tell them to go ahead and do what they need to do. Blair, you know Mama wouldn't want you torturing yourself." She reached out a tentative hand and touched her sister's arm. "Come on, Blair. Stay here, okay? We'll just leave this mess and go over to your house where we can think."

Blair's eyes had no luster as she kicked some of the books aside and made a path to the door.

Blair saw Melba Jefferson the moment she stepped outside, and almost turned back. Her mother's best friend stood at her door with tears streaming down her face, and she clutched a casserole dish in her chubby hands. When she saw them, she set it down on the hood of her car and pulled them both into a fat embrace.

"Oh, you poor things!" she wailed. "It's just so awful."

Wiping her tears, she went back to her trunk and pulled out several more casseroles that she had made. Blair wondered if she kept a freezerful of the things, and took them out to thaw when someone died.

"Now just tell me what you need me to do," Melba said, her voice wavering. "I can answer your phone, or clean up your house. Or I can just sit here all day tomorrow while you take care of the arrangements. I'm available. I want you to know that."

Blair wanted to tell her that she preferred to have her sit at her own house and leave them alone, but Morgan piped in, "I just can't think of anything right now, Melba. But we appreciate it."

"If you're not hungry, it'll keep," the woman said. "You'll need it after the funeral." Her voice broke off again and she swallowed. Her ample chest heaved with grief. "I could go to the funeral home with you tomorrow," she said. "You know your mama and daddy wouldn't want anything fancy. They weren't like that. But sometimes in our grief we overextend ourselves, choose coffins that we can't quite afford."

Blair lifted her chin. "We can afford to bury our parents, Melba."

"Of course you can, honey. I'm just saying, don't you get talked into anything. Now if you need me to go, I've had plenty experience with this sort of thing."

"You've had parents who were murdered?" Blair asked. Morgan squeezed her arm to silence her.

"Why, no, I've never had a murder. Just death, that's all. The older you get, the more you deal with death, you know. They weren't just your parents. They were my good friends. I don't know what I'll do without Thelma." She turned back toward the car, as if she didn't know whether to stay or go.

Morgan shot Blair a scathing look and touched Melba's back. The woman turned around, and Morgan pulled her into a hug and held her there just like her mother would have done.

"Oh, darlin'. You've got Thelma's heart," Melba said. "You always have."

Blair had heard that before. Morgan was the one with the heart. But she didn't care. She wasn't out to impress any of the socialites of Cape Refuge. She didn't even care about those who attended church with her parents. They had nothing to do with her, she thought. As far as she was concerned, Melba was among those who stared at her when she was a little girl and clicked her tongue and said what a shame it was that such a pretty girl would be so terribly marred. She had caught Melba's own son shuddering once, sitting next to her in class. It was his way of showing off for his buddies, but Blair had never forgotten it.

"You take care now, Blair," Melba said before Blair walked inside. "I'm going to be praying for you whether you like it or not."

The warm breeze whispered from the Atlantic and ruffled Sadie's hair as she sat on the porch at Hanover House. She could see the beach across the street and the waves rolling in, and her heart soared at the idea that she had actually made it here. Jack would never find her.

A van pulled up into the driveway, and she got to her feet slowly, suddenly nervous at the prospect of meeting these people face-to-face. What if they weren't like Tammy said? What if they were impatient and angry? What if they insisted on calling the police and reporting her as a runaway?

But it wasn't an old couple that got out of the car. Instead, it was a young man of about twenty, with sandy blond hair a little too long and wire-rimmed glasses. He got out of the driver's side and went around to the back, pulled out a big wreath with flowers all over it, and carried it up across the yard. Sadie stepped to the post and met him as he came up the porch steps.

"Hey," she said, awkwardly. "Do you live here?"

The young man shook his head. "No, I just work for the florist. My boss told me to stop by here and put this wreath on the door."

Sadie backed away. "Oh, okay."

He found the nail that was, no doubt, there to hold the Christmas wreath and gently placed it on the door.

"I'm Matt," he said, reaching out to shake her hand.

She took it. "Sadie," she said. "What's the wreath for?"

"Don't you know?" he asked, frowning. "About Thelma and Wayne?"

Sadie had had bad news many times in her life, and it was always preceded by a tightening in her chest, a closing of her throat, a headache starting behind her eyes. She felt all of that now.

"No. What about them?"

"You haven't heard about them being murdered?"

Sadie felt suddenly dizzy, and she stepped back against the post, reached out for it to steady her. "They were murdered?"

"Found dead," he said, "just this afternoon."

She groped back to the rocking chair and sat down. "I was waiting for them. I didn't know."

"I'm really sorry," he said. "They were nice folks. Real nice folks."

That was it, she thought. There went her chance of finding shelter and safety. Thelma and Wayne Owens, the two people in the area who could have helped her, were no longer here.

"Are you all right?" Matt asked.

She nodded absently.

"Your arm, I mean? And that bruise on your face. What happened?"

She got up and slipped the backpack over her good arm. "I've got to go," she said.

He stood there on the porch, then followed her down the steps, but before he could catch up to her, she had crossed the street and was headed out across the sand.

"Nice to meet you," he shouted. She didn't turn back, and after a moment she heard him driving away.

She tried to calm herself, tried to tell herself not to panic. She would be all right. She had pictured it this way, anyway—sleeping on the sand at night under the stars, the warm breeze blowing across her body, the sound of the ocean lulling her to sleep. It looked like the safest place in the world, she thought. If she could get the murders out of her mind, she could sleep here and find the public showers in the morning where the beachcombers washed off. Maybe she could come across a bar of soap and wash her hair, then head out looking for a job.

She stood on the edge of the beach and saw the condominiums and hotel rooms five stories deep for as far as she could see. There were rooms everywhere, empty beds, linens, fresh and clean, but she didn't need them, she thought. She was here and she wasn't afraid.

At least, not yet.

She walked along the beach, carrying her backpack on her shoulder, looking for an inconspicuous place where she could lay her head. She walked until darkness began to fall over the water and the few remaining beachcombers had gone in. Then she found a place between two decks, pulled out a light jacket that she had brought, and slipped it on. The pain in her arm tormented her, and she examined it for a moment, realizing it was turning black and blue, that the bones still didn't quite meet. It throbbed all the way up to her shoulder, but she couldn't get medical help just yet, she thought. She didn't have the money. And besides, whoever treated her would want to know where she had come from, how the accident had happened. She would have to think of a story first, but not now. Now she just needed to sleep.

She made herself a little nest in the sand between the two decks and lay down, then covering herself with a shirt from her backpack, she fell into a light sleep to the sound of the ocean and the wind.

18

$\mathcal{B}$illy Caldwell's nervous radio call was broadcast on every police scanner in Chatham County. "Chief, I found Gus Hampton."

"Where is he?" Cade asked.

"In the Owens's boathouse, about a mile down from Hanover House. His truck's parked out front. Want me to go in?"

"No," Cade said. "Just wait there for backup. But if you hear him starting the boat, go in. We can't let him get away."

Cade cut off the radio and began barking orders to the dispatcher. "Call the other three patrol cars and have them meet me there. No one's to act until I get there."

He heard her dispatching the other three officers, who were all out beating the bushes for leads. Cade ran out to his car, turned on his blue light, and headed for the southern tip of the island.

They had been looking for Gus since the bodies were found. His boss had sworn that he'd been at work until a little after six, probably an hour after the murders, and that he hadn't left all day. He had been there when Gus heard about the killings and said he had been visibly upset. Then Gus had rushed out.

Relief flooded through Cade as he flew across the island, traffic separating to the sides of the road to let him through. Maybe this was the break they needed. Maybe it would clear Jonathan.

The boathouse was a mile north of the bed-and-breakfast, not visible from the street. The woods were thick there, maple trees and mimosa, loblolly pines and sassafras, standing sentry at the dirt road that led down to the water.

Cade pulled in and saw that the other three cars had beaten him here. They had stopped near the entrance, not wanting to alert Gus that they were there. He saw Billy with his weapon drawn, standing near the door of the boathouse. Cade signaled the others to follow him, and he ran quietly down the side path.

They reached the boathouse, a simple wooden building with only three walls. Inside, Wayne Owens kept his small fishing boat, which he allowed his tenants to use as they wished. Cade had been there before. It held only the boat, a couple of toolboxes, some bait and tackle, and his fishing rods.

He stood to the side of the door and drew his own gun and listened hard. There seemed to be no movement inside.

He turned back to the others and signaled for two of them to go to the water side of the building, made sure they were ready, then he put his hand on the doorknob.

He threw the door open and lurched inside.

Gus, crouched on the floor at the corner of the building, sucked in a breath and held out his hand. "Don't shoot, mon. It's just me."

Cade could see that the man had been crying. His eyes were red and his face was wet.

"It's just me, mon."

"Gus, I need for you to get to your feet, and if you're carrying a weapon, drop it right now."

"You crazy, mon?" he asked, getting up. "I ain't got a weapon. What you think? That I'm the killer?"

"Turn around," Cade ordered. "Put your hands over your head."

Gus did as he was told and turned facing the wall. The other officers came in as Cade frisked him. He wasn't armed.

"Gus, what were you doing here?"

"I was trying to get off by myself," he said. "To think things through . . . to pray . . . I didn't want to be around nobody."

"Gus, I'm gonna have to take you in for questioning about the murders of Thelma and Wayne Owens."

"Who did it, mon?" he asked, beginning to sob. He turned around to Cade, his black face twisted in anguish. "Who would *do* that kind of evil? Who would do it?"

"That's what we're trying to find out."

"Am I under arrest? Do you suspect me?"

"We just want to ask you some questions," he said. "You're not under arrest."

"I'll answer whatever I can, mon. I want that killer found. I want to look him in the eye and ask him why he done this."

The man looked like a linebacker for the NFL, but he was as compliant as a kitten as Cade walked him back to the car.

They questioned Gus for a little over an hour, but his alibi was clear. He'd been at work when the murders were committed, and his boss had been there with him. There was no evidence at all that he had committed the crimes.

It wasn't until Cade released Gus that he realized how much he had wanted him to be guilty. Then he could have released Jonathan.

But as it stood, he had a serious problem.

And so did his best friend.

*I*t didn't really matter what size Blair's bed was, because she couldn't sleep anyway. Blair got up and wandered through the house, feeling dazed and light-headed. She wondered why she had knocked over all the shelves in the library, how she would ever put it all back together. She hoped the mayor didn't pay her a visit there in the next couple of days. She might lose her job. Then again, he'd probably understand. She was surprised at herself, surprised to think that she would lose control of her emotions that way and snap like some raging kid throwing a temper tantrum. She would have thought she was stronger than that.

Her head ached, so she went to the bathroom, opened the medicine cabinet, and found a bottle of Tylenol. She poured some into her hand, then caught her reflection in the mirror. As she often did, she held her hand up in front of her scars, imagining what she might look like if she didn't have them. She could have won beauty pageants, she thought. She could have been homecoming queen. She would probably be married by now, have babies.

Thank goodness those weren't things she wanted.

She threw the Tylenol into her mouth, filled her cupped hand with water, and washed them down. Finally, she went back to her bed and lay down next to Morgan. But sleep would not come.

On the outskirts of sleep's netherworld, Morgan sank into a dream of flames dancing around her, someone pulling on her hand. She felt the heat of it on her face, on her arms, on her legs, her bare feet. She heard the sound of her feet running, running, running away, looking back over her shoulder at the flames dancing and prancing around. And then she saw someone coming through—a little girl, wreathed by the flames. She pulled away and took off running toward the child, but hands grabbed her and wrestled her back.

She saw that the little girl was Blair, and the flames were closing in.

She caught her breath and sat up straight in bed, pulling herself out of the quicksand of that dream. She looked over at her sister, saw that her eyes were closed and she was lying still. Blair wasn't three years old anymore, but twenty-five. But there were scars on that face, scars that she didn't think had been put there by a grease fire in the kitchen, as her parents had always maintained. It was a much bigger fire, she thought. She had dreamed about it too often for it not to be real.

Why would her parents have lied about such things?

The truth was there somewhere in the recesses of Morgan's memory, but she couldn't quite get to it.

She got out of bed and wandered around the house, hoping that Jonathan was all right, that someone guarded him at the jail, someone reliable who wouldn't let anybody in. She reeled through the possibilities of killers in her mind.

There was Gus Hampton. She wondered if the police had found him yet. The idea of him killing her parents seemed ludicrous to her. Instead, he was probably grieving like the rest of them.

And then there was Rick Morrison, the gentle, tormented man who'd come to Hanover House to get his bearings after a tragedy had hit his family. A tragedy much like this one.

She went into the living room, curled up on the couch, and tried to pray. She was thankful that Jesus interceded for the saints. Sometimes she couldn't find the words to pray herself. How did one pray when something so hideous and violent preyed on her mind? How did one find that peaceful, joyful feeling that came with salvation when Satan had been so victorious?

Where had God been when her parents were fighting for their lives? Where had their guardian angel messed up? Why hadn't Jesus interceded for them at the moment when they had needed deliverance? She fought the anger welling up inside her at her Lord, for she knew it was irreverent and disrespectful. But she couldn't fight those feelings coursing through her, making her anxious and sick.

"Eat something," a voice in her head seemed to tell her. Maybe she would feel better, she thought. Maybe then she wouldn't feel so queasy, and she could sleep and wake up rested enough to do the business she had to do tomorrow.

She looked in the refrigerator and found the casserole that Melba had brought. She got a spoon and dipped out one scoop, put it into her mouth, and forced herself to swallow it. It went down smooth and tasteless. It didn't settle her stomach or her heart. Nothing was settled, she thought.

She walked around her sister's house, feeling the oppression of some dark force weighing down on her, crushing the breath out of her, keeping her from sleep or rest or peace, reminding her of violent, horrible things like flames dancing around her sister, spears flying into her parents, bars hovering around her husband.

She went to the couch and curled up on it, her knees at her chest, dropped her forehead, and wept hard, knowing that tomorrow, somehow, she would have to get hold of herself. There was too much to be done, and only the two of them to do it.

CHAPTER

20

*M*orning dawned with a stark brightness that contrasted the grief in Cade's soul. But he didn't have time to grieve. He arrived early at the station but, instead of going in, walked across the street to the sand and the beach. He needed to breathe the sea air, to experience the morning when it felt so much like midnight.

He walked to the hard, wet sand and stood there a moment, looking out over the clear sky. Seagulls swooped and squalled, attending to the business God had given them. He needed to do the same.

In this same bright morning, with the sea pounding against the shore, the sun shining with blinding brightness, and the sky clear and blue, a brutal killer lurked. As temperamental as Jonathan could be, he didn't fit that description.

But if he didn't do it, then who killed Thelma and Wayne?

Cade turned around and scanned the homes and condos and rooms along the beach. Something caught his eye between two decks side by side. Someone sleeping in the sand.

Probably a drunk who forgot where he lived, he thought. He trudged across the sand to the two decks with just three or four feet between them, ready to wake the drunk and make him move on.

But instead he saw a girl, scrawny and bruised, sound asleep, with a backpack for her pillow and one shirt as her cover. Her eye was black and swollen, and she held her mangled arm close against her.

He thought of waking her and sending her on her way, but she looked so young. She was probably a runaway and needed to be reported. She also needed medical help.

He bent over her and shook her. Her eyes shot open. She squinted in the sunlight and quickly sat up.

"It's against the law to sleep on the beach," he said. "Can I see some ID?"

She clutched her arm, as if it gave her intense pain, and looked around, disoriented. "I—didn't know it was against the law. I won't do it again."

He held out his hand and repeated the question. "Can I see some ID, please?"

Looking helpless, she got up and dusted the sand off of her clothes and her hair. She put the strap of her backpack in her teeth and with one hand dug into it as if looking for her wallet. She kept the other hand bent against her ribs.

"Oh, no," she said. "My wallet. It's gone. It had my driver's license. It must have been stolen."

He had heard that before. "What's your name?" he asked.

"Sadie," she said. "Sadie—Smith."

He grinned. "Smith, huh? That's convenient. How old are you?"

"Eighteen," she said.

"You're not eighteen. You're not a day older than fifteen."

"I am," she said. "I swear."

He saw the despair on her face and felt sorry for her. He stepped closer, touched her arm. "Let me see that."

Carefully she pulled off the windbreaker she was wearing. He winced at her disfigured arm.

"How'd you get hurt?"

"Fell down some stairs," she said.

"It looks broken. You need to see a doctor."

"Well—I don't have much money. I was going to look for a job and a place to live today, and then I plan to see one."

He frowned. He wondered if someone was looking for her, frantic that she wasn't at home in her bed. The wind whipped up, blowing her hair, disheveled and tangled. She pulled it down from its haphazard ponytail and combed her fingers through it.

"Where are you from, Sadie?"

She hesitated a moment. Clearly, she wasn't used to lying. "Birmingham. I just moved here yesterday."

"Moved here, huh? You got a U-haul somewhere or did you just 'move' that backpack?"

She looked down at the sand. "I was going to stay at that Hanover place—but when I got there I found out the people who ran it were killed. I didn't know what else to do."

He stared at her for a moment, wondering if such a coincidence was even possible, or if she knew something about the murders. "Come with me," he said.

She looked frightened and backed away. "No, I didn't mean to do anything wrong. Please."

"I just need to talk to you at the station across the street."

"Am I arrested?" she asked. "Just 'cause I didn't have a place to stay?"

"No," he said. "Get your stuff and come on."

She turned back and grabbed the shirt that had served as a makeshift blanket, stuffed it and the windbreaker into her backpack, and trudged across the sand.

As they crossed the street, he watched the way she cradled her arm. Fell down the stairs? Likely story. She had obviously been in a struggle, with that eye and arm. Had it been with Thelma and Wayne? Had she been the one who stole the speargun? If she knew how to use it, and stood close enough, it was possible . . .

And here she was sleeping on the beach, thinking she was hidden between the decks of two condominiums.... Her story didn't add up, and he was almost certain she had lied about her name and age.

He got her into the small interview room with another cop to witness, then asked her if he could search her backpack.

"Sure," she said, and handed it over.

There wasn't much there—just one shirt, a few school supplies, her wallet. "Thought you said you'd lost this."

"Oh," she said. "It must have been under something."

He opened it, and didn't find a driver's license. "No ID," he said.

She just looked at him.

That had been no big surprise. He had run her name through his database, but found no match for Sadie Smith. She fit the description of a dozen missing persons, but that proved nothing.

"Tell me how you knew Thelma and Wayne."

"I didn't know them," she said. Her eyes were big and round, blue as the sky today. But one of them was swollen almost shut.

"Then how were you going to stay with them?"

"A waitress at a diner in Savannah told me they might take me in. I didn't know they were dead."

"What time did you come into town yesterday?"

"I don't know," she said. "Maybe seven. It was still light out."

"How'd you get here?"

"Tammy, the waitress, brought me. I don't know her last name. She was nice. She said Thelma and Wayne were good about helping people with no place to go. She dropped me there, and I waited on the porch for somebody to get home. Then a florist guy came with a wreath ..." She dropped her eyes to her arm, and her voice trailed off to a whisper. "He told me."

He leaned back in his chair and rubbed his face. He hadn't slept since they had found the bodies, and he was dog tired.

Her story sounded true. He thought about what Thelma and Wayne would have done for this girl, how Thelma would have embraced her and brought her into the House, seen to her wounds, and taken care of her needs. He wondered if he should call Blair and Morgan, but then he thought better of it. They had too much on their minds. They didn't need the burden of a teenage runaway. But he couldn't just send her back out on the street, and he wasn't too anxious to throw her back to the person who had beaten her up.

He stood up. "Come with me," he said.

"Where?" she asked.

"I'm taking you to the doctor."

"I don't have any money. I can't—"

"I'll pay for it," Cade said, "but you can't just walk around with a broken arm. You need medical attention. Thelma and Wayne would have done that for you."

She was quiet as she followed him out to his car, and when he opened the passenger door on the front seat, she slipped in. He started the car, and she looked over at him.

"Are you going to arrest me after he fixes my arm?"

"I don't know what I'm going to do with you," he said, "but I can't very well send you back out there to fend for yourself."

"It's better than being in jail," she said. "I swore I'd never go to jail. And I meant it. I didn't mean to break the law. I won't do it again."

He wondered why a child her age would swear she would never go to jail. Girls dreamed about being movie stars, models, mothers. Jail didn't cross the average kid's mind.

"I can get a job," she said. "I can find a place to live."

"Let's just take care of one thing at a time," he said. He drove a couple of blocks, then pulled into the driveway of an old Victorian house, painted purple. A sign out front said, "Cape Refuge Medical Clinic."

"Doc Spencer is a good man. He'll fix you up."

She looked pale as she got out of the car and followed him in.

Dr. Spencer was a kind old man who looked like somebody's grandfather. In the waiting room, he had one whole wall filled with pictures of babies he had delivered and children he had treated. In the examining room, he had a model of a skeletal backbone, and a Norman Rockwell print of a goofy boy getting a shot.

He was gentle with Sadie's arm, though any pressure at all felt like a knife stabbing into it. "The X-rays show that it's broken in two places," he said. "I'm going to have to set it and put a cast on it." He took off his glasses and rubbed his eyes. "Tell me, honey. How'd it really happen?"

She decided to stick to her story. "I just lost my balance and fell down some stairs."

He breathed a disbelieving laugh. "Your legs don't look bruised."

She knew she shouldn't have let the nurse talk her into putting on that gown. "I don't know—I—"

"When a young girl like you turns up on this island, sleeping on the beach, with breaks and bruises—I can't help thinking that she might be a runaway who was abused at home."

She swallowed and looked down.

"You *were* beaten up, weren't you?"

She blinked back the tears stinging her eyes. "Okay," she said. "But that doesn't mean I'm a runaway. I'm eighteen. I can go anywhere I want."

"Who beat you up? Your boyfriend? Your father?"

"I don't have either," she said.

"Your mother?"

"No. . . ."

He started to clean his glasses with the edge of his lab coat, then shoved them back on. "Whoever it was, they need to be locked up. They don't need to get away with this."

Sadie looked at the ceiling, trying not to let those tears fall. Jack always got away with it. She had called the police before, but he had threatened to hurt Caleb if she told them what had happened.

"I just want to start a new life," she whispered. "This place looks like a dream I had once. If I could just start over here."

The old man patted her shoulder and offered her a compassionate smile. "Well, let me get that arm cast, and you can get on with starting over."

The funeral director in Savannah was good at his job. His soft, gentle manner suggested that he grieved over their parents too. But Morgan knew he had never met them.

"Will you be having two services, or just one for both of them?" he asked in that cautious, soft voice.

"Just one," Morgan said, and Blair nodded agreement.

"And who would you like to preach at the funeral service?"

Morgan looked at Blair. Their father was the preacher of their little church. "I don't know," she said. "I hadn't thought about it."

"Who preaches at the funeral of the preacher?" Blair said in that weary monotone she had used all day.

"Well, you could choose a member of the congregation, or a preacher from a nearby church, or someone from your past. Or we could provide a preacher—"

"No," Blair cut in. "A lot of people loved our father. We don't need to get a stranger."

Morgan was having trouble swallowing. "That—that man who ran that shelter in town. You know, where Pop went to help out. He brought some of those people home," Morgan said. "Yes, maybe he would do it. His name was Frank. Frank Jordan, I think. It was the Gateway Missions in Savannah."

"I'll contact him for you," the man said. "Now, would you like to have the service here or somewhere on Cape Refuge?"

"At our warehouse, where we had church," Morgan said.

"No." Blair's mouth trembled. "Morgan, that's where they were killed. There's still blood on the floor." Her voice broke. "I don't want it there."

Morgan looked down at her hands in her lap. She wished that Jonathan was here or that they had brought Melba. They needed someone objective to help with the million decisions to be made.

"There's also the problem of seating," the man said. "It's very likely that a lot of people will turn out for this. Probably way too many to fit into a warehouse."

"All right," Morgan said. "Maybe the Calvary Baptist Church would let us use their building."

"I'll take care of it," he said and jotted that in his notebook. "Now, about visitation. When would you like to hold the viewing?"

"I don't want a viewing," Blair said. "I don't want people gawking at my mother and father."

"Then we could close the caskets and simply have a visitation."

"No," Blair said. "I don't want to see people and talk to them and answer their inane questions and hear their empty platitudes. The funeral's enough."

"But, Miss Owens, most families find the visitation to be comforting. People can come by and tell you what your parents meant to them."

"I know what my parents meant to them," she said.

He looked at Morgan, as if hoping she would reason with her sister. But Blair's logic made sense to her. "Just the funeral," she said.

"And the burial, of course," he said. "Would you like to bury them at our cemetery?"

Blair leaned back in her chair and looked up at the ceiling. Morgan knew she was fighting tears. She still hadn't seen her cry.

She wished she were that strong. Her tears hadn't stopped since yesterday.

"I know this is difficult," the man prompted.

Finally, Blair answered. "I don't want them in the ground."

Morgan took her hand. "Blair, they're not in those bodies. It doesn't matter where we bury them."

"I can't do it. Maybe we should bury them at sea. They loved the sea. We could take a boat out and have a small, private service out on the ocean."

Morgan considered that for a moment. "I think they would have liked that."

"Then you'll want them cremated," he said, jotting on his notepad.

"No, we certainly do not," Blair said. "Can't we have a sea burial with caskets?"

"Of course we can," he said. "We'll have to get permission, but it shouldn't be a problem."

"Then we'll do that," Blair told the man. "We can use Jonathan's boat and have a private burial at sea."

"But won't your parents' friends want to come? Your church members? The people of the community? There's comfort in closure...."

"The people can worry about their own closure," Blair said, her voice too loud. "I don't have the energy to do it for them."

Later, as Blair drove home, physically exhausted and mentally drained, Morgan gazed out the window. "Did we do the right things?" she asked.

"We did the best we could," Blair said.

Morgan sighed. "There are still so many decisions to be made. The music, the eulogy—I wish Jonathan was here."

"Maybe they'll let him out in time for the funeral."

Silence lay heavily over them as they drove home. Morgan leaned her head against the window and sniffed and wiped tears. After a while, she said, "I've got to start thinking of them in heaven. Pop's hearing restored, his arthritis gone, Mama's laughter like music in Jesus' ears."

Blair wanted, more than ever, to believe in an afterlife. If heaven was real, were they singing praise songs and running through meadows? Were they reunited with that AIDS patient they had harbored at Hanover House, or Sam, the man in the last stages of cancer when he had come?

She wished she could believe she would see them again. But her mind wouldn't allow herself to believe. Yesterday was the end of them, and that was all there was to it.

If she could only make herself say good-bye.

CHAPTER

*T*he cast itched, and Sadie's arm ached. Gritty sand had worked its way into the cast, and it coated her clothes and her skin. Hot sun lasered down on her with blistering intensity, but she couldn't seem to escape it.

She had spent the afternoon walking along the beach, picking up change left by sunbathers. A quarter here, a nickel there. Once, she had found a dollar rolled up inside a paper cup. She managed to collect a little over ten dollars, half of which she spent on a hot dog and drink. Strength seeped back into her muscles and bones with every bite, but dread overwhelmed her. Night would fall soon, and she still hadn't found a job or a place to stay.

And who in their right mind would hire a girl who hadn't bathed in days, who looked as if she had been in a fight and lost, who didn't have a toothbrush or clean clothes or a hairbrush?

Back home in Atlanta, there were homeless people all over the streets, sleeping in doorways, begging on the curbs, walking the sidewalks, looking for cans or change or handouts. She had walked down those streets with fear and distaste, thinking there was something wrong with people like that. Why don't they just get a job and a place to live like everyone else, she had often thought. If they spent half as much time looking for legitimate work as they spent begging or digging through trash cans, they'd have nice homes and plenty of food.

Now she knew better. She was one of them, a homeless stray hunting for nickels and pennies. She had often guessed what she would do in their position, how she would rise above her circumstances, how she would never allow herself to get that low.

But she had been proven wrong.

Weary, she sat in the sand and watched a group of children playing in the surf. The waves were too tall for them, and she worried that they had gone out too far. She searched for their parents, saw that the mother was on her feet, yelling for them to come back.

The ocean's response was to slap more waves on the shoreline, its loud roar mocking the lone voice of the mother. But the children came back, jumping and challenging those waves, laughing and splashing.

Overhead, a gull squawked in a flat, off-key note. Behind her, someone played a radio too loudly, a vulgar, angry rap song.

Her first sight of the beach, just yesterday, had filled her with such hope, as if nothing bad could ever happen in a place like that. Now it seemed violent and unforgiving, threatening her hope and weakening her resolve. She longed to get away and find a place without sand where she could sleep tonight.

She tried to get her thoughts in order. First, she needed a bath. She needed to wash her hair and get presentable. Then she needed to wash her clothes. Once that was done, she might be able to get someone to hire her. If it was in a food place—a fast-food restaurant, maybe—at least she might be able to get her meals for free. If it was in a hotel, she might be able to get them to let her rent a room.

She turned around and looked at the motel just off the beach. Rooms faced the water, and maids moved with their carts along the rail of the upper floors. She could be one of them, she thought, if she could only convince the manager that her broken arm wouldn't hinder her work. Maybe she could do that work in the daytime and get something else at night.

Armed with purpose, she got up and walked to the concrete sidewalk that led around the pool to the stairs. She went up one flight and looked along the walkway that led in front of the doors. A maid was coming out of a room to drop dirty towels into her cart.

"Excuse me," Sadie said.

The Latino woman had her hair pulled back in a ponytail. She wore a crisp gray uniform, with a white apron. "Yes?" she asked.

"I'm looking for a job," Sadie said. "I wondered who I could talk to about working here."

The woman grabbed a stack of white towels to put into the rooms, and Sadie eyed the cart. A bucket of shampoo bottles, soaps, hand lotions were piled there. "My boss, she on the third floor, behind vending machines," the woman said in a thick Mexican accent. "She not hiring, though."

"She's not?" Sadie asked. "Why not?"

"She have all she need," she said.

"Okay," Sadie said. "I'll try somewhere else." She started to walk away, then stopped and turned back. "Uh . . . would it be possible . . . I mean . . . would you mind . . ." She cleared her throat. "I was wondering if I could take one of these bars of soap and a shampoo? I could really use a bath."

The woman eyed her for a moment, then finally gave her the ones in her hand. "That's all I can give," she said. "I get in trouble."

"Sure, of course. Thank you." Sadie unzipped her backpack and stuffed the items down into it. Now, if she could just find a place to shower.

She went back down the stairs but stopped before descending completely. Her eyes scanned the beach, looking for a shower. There was one near the pool of this very hotel, meant for washing off sand. There were probably others, she thought. She could wash her hair there, and scrub the sand off of her skin.

But then what would she wear?

Her eyes fell on a girl strolling down to the beach, wearing a breezy, pale blue sundress. Her blonde hair flew in the breeze behind her, and her skin was bronze, as if she came here daily to soak up the rays. She looked like a homecoming queen, Sadie thought with admiration. Like a cheerleader or a lifeguard.

She probably had a pink bedroom with flowered wallpaper and a mother who waited up for her at night. She probably talked on the phone for hours each day, went to movies, had boyfriends.

She watched the girl drop a towel onto the sand. Then she shed that dress, revealing a bikini beneath it. She kicked off her sandals, left them there with the dress on the towel, and headed for the water.

Sadie's heart quickened. If she had a dress like that, she knew she could get a job. It would be easy. With her hair washed and those clothes, she would look so much more respectable. That girl probably had twenty others like it in her closet. She probably had a pair of shoes for every outfit.

She hurried down the stairs and out across the sand, intent on taking the girl's clothes while she was in the water. She had never stolen before, so her hands trembled and her heart raced, but she told herself there was no other way. She just wanted a job, a place to stay, food to eat.

Basic things. Wasn't it all right to steal for basic things?

She reached the sand, and her step slowed as she watched the girl get doused by a wave. She stood there, sweeping her hair back.

She had sworn she would never wind up in jail like her mother. Not for anything, she had told herself. It was easy to avoid. All she had to do was keep the law.

But that dress was what she needed, and those sandals that hadn't yet been covered with sand. She would look pretty in them, clean, respectable. Not at all like a runaway.

Her mouth went dry, and her legs grew weak. The girl dove into a wave, came up on the other side, and swam out toward the next one.

There was plenty of time, she thought, and no one was looking. But if they were—if someone saw her—that police chief might have to arrest her, and he would shake his head and say he might have known, that nothing good could come from a girl sleeping on the beach. . . .

She reached the clothes, stood over them, and watched the girl swimming further. The clothes lay in a wad at Sadie's feet. She could swoop them up, stuff them in her bag, walk on, as if nothing had happened. She could just reach down . . .

Her body froze, and she thought of her mother in jail, warning her never to break the law. *Don't wind up like me, Sadie. You're better than that.*

Her resolve suddenly melted like chocolate in the sun.

She would have to find another way.

As if she feared being caught in her intentions, she turned and ran down the beach, away from the dress and the shoes, away from the girl who probably dominated the pages of her high school yearbook, away from the eyes that might have seen her, had she succumbed.

And as she ran, she began to cry, for she didn't know what to do next.

CHAPTER

They held the funeral service two days later in the Calvary Baptist Church on the island. Jonathan was not allowed to leave jail, so Morgan and Blair clung together, alone on the front row of the church. The city council sat near the front like government dignitaries, as if no one remembered that, just three nights ago, they had been trying to ruin those for whom they mourned today. But the congregation of their warehouse church, and most of the town of Cape Refuge, turned out and sang praise songs exactly the way Thelma and Wayne would have directed them.

Morgan closed her eyes and sent her mind on a mission to pull up every Scripture verse she knew to get her through this moment.

Absent from the body, present with the Lord.
We do not grieve as those who have no hope.
Precious in the sight of the Lord is the death
of his saints.

Her mind captured one after another, like lifelines keeping her from sinking into the muck of despair.

She had Blair's hand in hers and thought how cold it was. Her sister's face was pale and expressionless, a blank slate for fertile imaginations who would gossip that Blair had not cried at her own parents' funeral. But they hadn't seen her in the library that night.

The preacher addressed the two of them as if they were the only two in the room, with sweet stories about her parents that made the crowd chuckle nostalgically.

But Morgan couldn't laugh. She wanted to leap up and scream out that they could come here and wipe a tear or two, tell a funny story, laugh, change the subject, network, gossip, catch up, then go home and sit down to eat with their families. Their lives would go on. It was too cruel.

She had often wished that God offered us each one chance to turn back time, one chance to do things over. She would have wasted hers years ago, when she dyed her brown, curly hair blonde and it came out orange, or when her tenth-grade boyfriend broke her heart. Or if she had made it to the age of twenty-eight without using it, would she know how far back to turn the clock to prevent her parents' murders? Would one day do it? Two days? A week? Or had it started years ago, when they began their ministry and started taking risks for the Lord?

God was merciful for not giving us that time-turning option, she supposed. She wasn't wise enough to use it well.

The very act of sitting in this building with this sniffing crowd indicated her acceptance of their deaths. But she did not accept it. Her heart lashed out now with the same screaming, crashing fury that Blair had shown in the library. Only no one knew it.

She quenched her loud, heartbroken, raging grief in quiet nods and weak smiles, as if there wasn't a hole burning right through her center.

We do not grieve as those who have no hope.

If hers was the grief of hope, then she knew that her sister's grief was even more consuming. Blair had no hope.

She squeezed her sister's hand more tightly, trying to warm its icy chill.

But Blair sat stiff, like a statue, vacant and blank and pale, except for the crimson color of her scar.

Blair came back to herself about a mile from shore, as Jonathan's boat took them out to bury the bodies at sea. They had only invited a handful of people to join them—the preacher conducting the funeral, Jay Riley to pilot the boat, and a few of Thelma and Wayne's closest friends.

They rode out for two hours into the deeper ocean, then had another short service. The men Morgan had chosen as pallbearers lowered the coffins over the side of the boat. The friends and loved ones who had been granted the honor of coming out with them came by Blair and Morgan and paid their respects in turn.

When it was finally the crusty boat pilot's turn, he took off his hat and held it over his heart. "I'm sorry for your pain," he said awkwardly.

Morgan took his hand and thanked him. Blair thought he smelled like fish, and she wondered if he hadn't bothered to wear clean clothes for the funeral.

But the boat, itself, had a rank fish odor. Morgan had gotten some friends to wash the deck and clean up the boat before they used it, but the smell was impossible to get rid of.

Jay came to Blair next and took her hand. "Your parents were good people," he said.

He sounded like he was reading a script, and the thought made Blair angry. She'd rather he said nothing at all.

"Ironic, ain't it?" he said to both of them.

"What is?" Morgan asked.

"That we'd take Jonathan's boat out to bury his victims."

Morgan's mouth fell open, but that scar on Blair's face reddened instantly. "Jay," she said. "why don't you just go back and drive the boat, since that's the only reason you were invited to come?"

He looked shocked at her outburst, then shaking his head, as if he didn't know what had set her off, he went back to the helm.

Later, as she and Morgan sat side by side in the back of the boat, Morgan looked over at her. "Everybody thinks he did it."

"They ought to have sensitivity training for people like that before they allow them to walk around in public," Blair said.

Morgan started to laugh quietly, and finally Blair joined. They leaned against each other until that tired laughter played down.

"I'm sorry I thought he did it at first," Blair said. "I know Jonathan didn't kill anybody."

"Thank you," Morgan said, her eyes growing serious again.

"We're going to get him out of there," Blair said. "And we're going to find who did this."

"I know we are," Morgan whispered.

As they pulled back up to the dock, their faces sobered again. "I've got a lot to do tonight," Blair whispered. "I've got to put the library back together."

Morgan was quiet for a moment as the dock grew closer. "You're not going to have to do it alone," she said. "I'll be there to help you."

Blair looked over at her and registered the statement. Somehow it seemed right that her sister would be there beside her, picking up the pieces, putting them all back together. Quietly, she accepted that as the trip to bury their parents came to an end.

*T*he visitation room at the Cape Refuge jail was combined with the kitchenette where the officers heated up their honey buns in the mornings. One of the rookie officers stood near the refrigerator, guarding Jonathan and Morgan as they visited. Her eyes were red and puffy, and she looked like she hadn't slept in days.

"J.J., could we have a little privacy?" Jonathan asked.

The young man shook his head. "Sorry, Jonathan. Can't do it. Cade told me I had to guard you."

"Well, you can guard me, but couldn't you put on some headphones or something? I mean, I'm entitled to a little conversation with my wife."

J.J. Clyde, an officer who had played defensive tackle for Cape Refuge High just a year ago, thought it over, then went over to his locker and pulled out his headphones and his Walkman.

"I'm going to put these on," he said, "but you won't know when I've turned down the volume. I'm going to be listening in and out."

Jonathan rolled his eyes. "Okay, J.J."

J.J. put on the headphones and went back to the refrigerator as if he considered raiding it.

Jonathan focused on Morgan. "Are you okay?"

"It was hard without you."

"It was hard not being there," he said. "My own in-laws. I couldn't even go to their funeral. That beats everything. I can't believe how stupid this police department is."

"Jonathan." Morgan's word cut into his, silencing him. He glanced up at J.J. whose hand gravitated to the Walkman as if he was about to turn it down and tune in to their conversation.

"You don't need to make them mad," she whispered. "It's already bad enough."

"Arraignment is tomorrow," Jonathan said. "If I'm arraigned, they'll probably move me to Chatham County Detention Center."

"No!" She sat up straighter. "Jonathan, they can't put you there."

"It's gonna be okay," he said. "I'm not afraid of jail, baby. I've ministered there with your pop enough to know what it's like. I never wanted to be one of them, but I'll survive it until this is all straightened out."

"But how can we get it straightened out when everybody's focusing on you?" She rubbed her eyes. She hadn't even bothered to wear makeup today. She had barely managed to shower and get dressed for the funeral. Melba had gone to get her clothes from the house, because she couldn't manage to face it just yet. "If I'd only asked who they were meeting . . ."

"They must have written down something," Jonathan said. "Your pop wrote everything on those little index cards he kept in his pockets."

"The police have everything that was on him."

"Maybe he left some on his desk at the house. There's got to be something there. Cade will get phone records, and find out who he talked to that day. Maybe there are some papers or something.

Maybe they have some information about Gus Hampton that could prove he did it. I can't believe they let that guy go."

Morgan sat straighter as a sense of purpose filled her. "I need to go look to see what I can find."

"No, not you," he said. "I don't want you there with Gus Hampton in the house. Cade will look. He's probably already searched the place by now."

"But they obviously didn't find anything," she said. "It might be the only way to get you out of here, Jonathan."

He touched her face and looked hard into her eyes. "Look at me, and listen hard. I don't want you anywhere near that place, do you understand me? I want you safe. Let Cade do the investigation."

She swallowed, not certain she could make that promise. His face softened, and he scooted his chair closer to hers, hugged her, and kissed the top of her head.

She closed her eyes and soaked in the feel and smell of him. "They feeding you okay?" she asked.

"Let's just say they're feeding me."

"Are you eating?" she asked.

"Yes, don't worry about me, baby. Just take care of yourself." He cupped her chin, made her look up at him with her wet eyes. "You're the prettiest girl I've ever known," he said.

She smiled, knowing it wasn't true. But it was true to him.

"Don't you be alone," he said. "I don't want you to be an open target for whoever it is walking around out there."

She closed her eyes. "Jonathan, you're scaring me."

"Good," he said. "I mean to scare you. We don't know who it is or what they want. But you and Blair, you stick together, okay? You'll be okay if you're with her."

"Jonathan, I'm not some weak little spineless creature. I can be strong too."

"I know you can, honey," he said, "but Blair can be a barracuda."

"She's real upset, you know," Morgan said. "She tore up the library out of pure rage. I promised to help her put it back together tonight."

"As long as you're together," he said. "And don't stay at Hanover House. I don't trust anybody there anymore."

"I know," she said. "I won't."

They heard footsteps on the building floor, then Cade came to the door and peered in like a teacher checking on one of his students. "J.J., what're you doing?"

J.J. jumped and pulled off his headphones. "Just listening to the news, Chief," he said. "I thought maybe it would give us a clue."

Cade looked disgusted. "You need a clue all right, but you're not going to get it from the news. Now pull off those headphones and get back to work."

He shot Morgan an apologetic look. "Sorry, Morgan, but I'm going to have to ask you to leave now. Your visitation time is over."

"It's not like anybody's keeping track," Jonathan said. "You're the boss around here last time I looked."

"We have rules," Cade said, "and I abide by them, just like I expect you to."

"I never expected to abide from this side of the bars," Jonathan muttered. He got up and bent over and gave Morgan a kiss.

Cade waited respectfully until she let him go, then he led Jonathan back to the jail cell.

Morgan didn't wait to say good-bye to Cade or anyone else in the station. She just headed out to her car, determined to find Blair so they could clean up the library, then head over to Hanover House to search their parents' things.

CHAPTER

*M*organ was full of plans and purpose by the time she found Blair at the library. They hadn't been there since the other night when Blair had torn the place up.

Blair stood in the middle of the room, surveying the damage. She had a blank look on her face as she stood in profile, the pale, pretty side of her face closest to Morgan.

"You okay?" Morgan asked.

"Yeah," Blair said absently. "Just wondering whatever possessed me to do this."

"I told you I'd help you clean it up. But I want you to do something else first."

Blair turned around. "What?"

"I want you to go with me to the house. I want to look through Mama and Pop's things for clues."

Blair frowned. "But you know the police have already done that. Wouldn't they have found something if there was something to find?"

"Maybe," Morgan said, picking up a book and smoothing out the pages with her hand. "Maybe not.

There may be something that would ring a bell for us but not for them. Besides, Cade's shorthanded for the investigation. They might not have done a thorough job." She looked around at the floor, wondering where to start. Blair didn't seem to know, either. "I was thinking that maybe we could go over there now, then clean this up when we get back."

"I guess we could," Blair said. "Hanover House is ours now. I guess we have to decide what to do. Maybe we should just give everybody notice and close the place down."

"No," Morgan said. "Mama and Pop fought too hard to keep it open."

"Well, we can't just keep it going to spite the city council. It's more than you can handle by yourself."

"But where will they go? No one on the island would take Gus, what with all these rumors. Rick isn't ready to leave yet. He's still not over the death of his wife and daughter. And Mrs. Hern is just in the beginning stages of Alzheimer's. She relied so on Mama."

"Still," Blair said, "I have a full-time job. I can't help with it."

"Yeah," Morgan said. "You've got your hands full with this mess."

Blair looked helplessly around her again. "Do you have any idea how heavy these bookshelves are?"

"I think I'm going to find out."

Blair stepped over some books. "Let's just go. It'll still be here when we get back."

The home in which Blair had spent most of her childhood years looked different as she pulled into the driveway. A wreath hung on the mailbox, offering grim notice of their bereavement. She looked up at the front door and saw another, larger wreath hung on the door in the place reserved for her mother's handmade Christmas wreath.

"We're going to need to write some thank-you notes," Morgan said softly. "The funeral director said they were bringing all the flowers here."

"Why didn't you tell him we don't want them? He should have thrown them away."

"That would have been rude," Morgan said. "Besides, some people sent pots of flowers that I want to plant in the yard. Kind of a memorial garden for them."

Blair's gaze drifted to the yellow Victorian house. White rocking chairs and a swing adorned the front porch. Full-bodied ferns spilled over hanging baskets at intervals along the eaves, and green azalea bushes lined the front lawn, a breathtaking addition to the groomed yard when they were in bloom each spring. Petunias of pink, white, and yellow filled the beds in front of the azaleas.

That was their memorial garden, she thought. Her mother's love shone in every blossom, in every carefully chosen color, in every placement, and her father's care gave them a healthy, hydrated look. He had watered them every morning after returning from Crickets. Sometimes he pulled up a lawn chair and sat down and prayed right out loud, as if God was in a chair next to him as he fed the garden.

"There shouldn't be flowers in bloom," Blair whispered under her breath. "When people you love die, it seems like every flower in the world ought to just die with them."

"It's nice that they don't," Morgan said.

Blair sat there a moment, staring up at the house. Fresh new anger surged through her.

Someone inside could be responsible for their deaths, or someone who had once passed through. Maybe the city council members' concerns had been prophetic. And there she'd been, spouting off at that microphone, defending the house and its tenants while her parents bled to death.

Morgan got out of the car. Blair followed her up to the front porch steps, climbed them one at a time. Morgan opened the front door. The parlor was empty. It was dark except for the Tiffany lamp in each corner, and the piano light that illuminated the sheet music for "It Is Well with My Soul."

So many times, her father had told the story of the man who had written that song. His four children had drowned in a storm at sea, all of them, and his wife sent a telegram home to him. "Saved alone," it said. Later, the man had sailed to that very spot where his children had lost their lives and, standing on the deck of the ship, had penned the song.

Blair didn't know where he got his peace or how he had managed to speak, let alone sing, those words. Her chest tightened in resentment at his misguided faith.

It was not well with her soul, and it never would be.

Someone had brought the mail in and left it in a stack on the coffee table. Condolence cards and notes had already begun coming, and she wondered if people really expected them to read all of them and answer.

Almost reverent in her silence, Morgan went into the kitchen. Blair went with her. Through the back window to the screened porch, Blair saw Mrs. Hern, the old woman who had moved there after serving three years in prison for embezzlement. She sat slumped in front of an easel propped at the corner of the porch, her back to them.

Blair didn't want to see anyone, for the thought of making small talk seemed worse to her than the empty silence of the house. But Morgan opened the door and stepped out. Mrs. Hern turned around, her unbound gray hair swinging around her shoulders and sticking to her wet face. She had been crying for hours, it was clear. Her nose was so red and her eyes so swollen that Blair had to look away.

"Oh, Mrs. Hern." Morgan took the old woman into her arms.

The woman's frail body shook as she clung to Morgan. "I know she was your mama and all," she wept, "but I sure loved her."

"I know," Morgan whispered. "I know."

Blair looked away from the two clutched together, trying not to get pulled into that maelstrom of despair again. Her grief had a different manifestation that she didn't quite understand. It came up in rage, like a cracking, furious storm, rather than a soft drizzle. She had to fight it.

She stepped over to the painting, trying to get her mind off of Mrs. Hern's grief.

There were clouds everywhere, and in the center of the canvas was an unfinished white horse and someone riding it.

When Morgan finally let Mrs. Hern go, the woman turned her tormented face to Blair. "You're not going to close the house down, are you?" she asked, taking Blair's hand.

Blair didn't pull away. "We don't know, Mrs. Hern."

"Please, you can't," she said. "I don't know what I'll do. There's no place else I can stay. They'll put me in a nursing home, only I'm not that far gone yet. My memory goes sometimes, but I think the medication's helping. I don't know how much longer they'll let me work at Goodfellow's because I've been making too many mistakes lately. Thelma told me she wouldn't throw me out if I couldn't pay, that I could help around here to earn my keep."

"I know," Morgan said. "She told me all that. You don't have to worry. We're not going to run you off. When we make a decision, we'll make sure you're taken care of."

Blair wished Morgan wouldn't make such promises. Hoping to change the subject, she looked back into the house. "Where is everybody?"

"Gus is up in his room playing his guitar," Mrs. Hern said, "and I think Rick is across the street at the beach. He likes to go over there by himself and think. Lana and Harry both left. They checked out after the funeral when the police told them they could leave."

"The police questioned them?" Blair asked.

"Oh, yes," Mrs. Hern said. "They questioned all of us here."

"Then they've been through Mama and Pop's things?"

"Seems like they did," she said. "They went upstairs while we were being questioned in the front room." She let Blair go and took Morgan's hand. "I know you don't feel like doing what you usually do around here," she said, "but I wanted you to know that I learned a lot from Thelma. She taught me how to cook some of her best recipes, and I'd been helping her clean up. I can take care of the place if you want until you feel like coming back. I know with Jonathan in jail and all, you've got a lot on your plate."

The woman hadn't even remembered to brush her hair this morning, Blair thought. How could she take care of the house?

"Feels like I ought to do something, the way Thelma and Wayne took care of me." Mrs. Hern burst into tears again and turned back to her painting.

Morgan stroked the old woman's hair. Blair almost envied her sister. This was the strongest she had seen her since they had learned of the murders. Leave it to Morgan to find strength in reaching out to others.

"I was just painting that verse in Thessalonians," Mrs. Hern said. "The one about the Lord coming back from heaven for us."

"First Thessalonians 4:16," Morgan said softly. "Pop's favorite verse: 'For the Lord himself will come down from heaven, with a loud command, with the voice of the archangel and with the trumpet call of God, and the dead in Christ will rise first. After that, we who are still alive and are left will be caught up together with them in the clouds to meet the Lord in the air. And so we will be with the Lord forever.'"

Blair let those words float like a balloon in her mind, bouncing gently off the sides, never quite settling in. She had heard her parents quote it many times. She could probably have quoted it herself.

It made sense that Mrs. Hern would want to be reminded of it now. It did offer comfort. If it was true, then there would be a reunion someday. She wished she could believe it.

She didn't want to think about the crude, amateur painting anymore or the words it represented, so she went back into the house and started up the staircase.

She heard the sound of a guitar playing in one of the rooms, and saw that Gus's door was open. She stood frozen on the stairs, listening, thinking, trying to sort through the things she knew about the man—the *20/20* report, the mayor's accusations, Jonathan's concerns . . .

She heard Morgan's footsteps behind her. When she reached the second floor, she looked inside and saw the big black man sitting on his bed with his red bandana tied around his head. He stopped playing the moment he saw her.

"Blair," he said in his throaty Jamaican accent. "Ah, Morgan." He set down the guitar and came to hug them. Blair was stiff, and she could see that Morgan was cooler with him than she was with Mrs. Hern.

"I'm so sorry," he said in that deep bass. "Who would kill those kind people?"

"We don't know," Blair whispered.

"I know what you be thinking," he said. "I know you are suspicious right now, with all this talk about me. But I tell you, I would never hurt Thelma and Wayne."

Neither of them said a word, and Blair tried to process his statement in her mind. Would a guilty person broach the subject head on or avoid it completely?

He went back to his guitar. "I was just playing 'How Great Thou Art.' Wayne taught me. I played it in the church two weeks ago. You remember that, Morgan?"

She nodded and looked at her feet.

"'Praise the Lord,' Wayne always be saying. So I'm tryin'. Wish I'd known about it in the prison. Instead o' cursin', I coulda been prayin'. You know how I came to be here, don't you, Miss Blair?"

Blair shook her head. "No, Gus. Tell me."

He strummed a few chords. "I just got my release from the prison, and I had no place to go, mon, absolutely no place. Rescue mission took me in and let me sleep there at night. And Wayne and Thelma would come there and do Bible studies with us. After the rescue mission told me I'd been there too long, I had to move on and make room for somebody else, Wayne let me come to stay here and got me a job. Best mon who ever lived."

Blair let her eyes wander around the room while he spoke. It was neat, and he had only a few personal items on the dresser. Some pocket change, the keys to the house and his truck, his billfold.

"The police interviewed me, and let me go. I was at work all that day. I know Jonathan didn't do it, either, Miss Morgan. He wouldn't do that to them."

"No, he wouldn't."

Blair only stared at him, running every expression on his face through her mental lie detector. Did his body language suggest he was telling the truth? Was he hiding something?

She couldn't say for sure.

They left him alone in his room, and Morgan crossed the hall to her parents' doorway. The room was just as they had left it. Everything was neat and in its place, freshly dusted and fluffed. The bedroom was the most lived-in room of the house, and the least elaborate. Her mother's things graced the tables and stand, and family pictures hung in collections on the walls.

Blair went in, but Morgan froze in the doorway. "I can't do this," she said. "I can't go in there and rifle through their things. I'm not ready for this yet."

"Neither am I," Blair said. "But I haven't been ready for much of what's happened in the last few days."

"Maybe Jonathan's right. Maybe we shouldn't have come."

"We're here," Blair said. "Let's just get what we need and take it back to my house."

Morgan took a tentative step into the room. "I feel like I'm invading their privacy."

"We are. But they're not in a position to care." The words came out on a cruel note. She didn't know where that flip tone came from.

She bent down and looked under the bed. She pulled out the boxes in which her parents archived their most important papers. "Let's take these," she said.

"Okay," Morgan said. "And we can take the file cabinet downstairs, if the police haven't already taken it for evidence."

"Do you know where the key to the file cabinet is?"

"She kept it in her jewelry box," Morgan said. She crossed the room slowly, anguish on her face, and went into the closet where her mother's modest jewelry box lay. She opened it, found the key.

"Okay," Blair said, "help me carry the boxes down."

"We could get Gus to help," Morgan said.

"Leave the tenants out of this. It's just us."

Blair grabbed one box, and Morgan took the other.

When they had loaded the car, Blair saw Rick—the other tenant—sitting in the sand across the street, watching the ocean. "There's Rick," she said as a warm breeze picked up and whispered through the trees, blowing her hair against her mouth. She pushed it back. Morgan came up beside her. Her long curls bounced in the breeze.

"He does that a lot," she said. "Just sits out there staring out at the waves. Mama said it's how he grieves."

Blair had heard the story from her mother about how he had lost his wife and daughter in a drunk-driving accident and how he had come here seeking refuge while he tried to endure the pain.

"I'm going to run back in and get a few things together to bring back to your house," Morgan said. "I'll be right back."

Blair waited at the car, watching Rick as the waves lapped up close to his feet. He was a suspect too, as far as she was concerned. She needed to talk to him, read his face. She needed to see if he grieved over her parents.

She crossed the street, and her feet rocked across the sand as she walked toward where he sat. The waves hit hard against the shore. A storm was probably blowing in, she thought. It was appropriate—more so than the bright sunshine that mocked her pain. She wanted thunder and lightning, howling wind, dark skies.

She walked up behind Rick and set her hand on his shoulder. He jumped and almost knocked his chair over.

"Blair!" he said. "You scared me."

"Sorry."

He sat back in his chair, trying to steady his breathing. He looked pale, tired, just like the rest of them, and his eyes looked raw and red.

"I was waiting for Morgan," she said. "I thought I'd come over and speak."

He leaned forward, his elbows on his knees. He was familiar with grief, she thought, and knew what not to say. "I like to come out here sometimes," he said. "There's something healing about sitting here and listening to the waves, knowing that God is still in control even when it seems like he's not." His voice faded out and he swallowed and got to his feet. He was a head taller than she and looked down at her with sorrowful eyes. "I'm going to miss your parents," he said. "I'm going to miss them real bad."

Blair turned the scarred side of her face away and gazed out over the water. A schooner was coming in, slowly making its way to the shore. There had been times in her life when she had sat on this beach herself and watched those boats come and go, wondering what it would be like to be on your way to some distant country, not knowing when or if you would return. She had dreamed of sailing away. But she never had, simply because the scars would have gone with her. And wherever she wound up, they would still be the ball and chain that held her to her past. And thwarted her future.

"I've been sitting here for a couple of hours," he said, "watching for that boat to come in. I didn't see it until just now."

He slapped his hands against his thighs, then let them hang limply to his sides. "I thought I was healing; I thought I was coming to terms with what happened to my family." His voice blended with the sound of the wind and the waves. "Now I have to grieve over the people who were helping me heal. Sometimes you just wonder how many more people are going to have to go before God thinks you've had enough."

Blair swallowed and kept her eyes on that boat.

"I'm sorry, Blair," he said.

She shook her head. "Don't be. It's okay. I feel the same way."

The water began reaching farther as the tide rose. She backed up so it wouldn't rush around her feet. "Sometimes I feel like somebody's just walloped me in the stomach and I can't catch my breath," she said.

"That's it," he said. "That's exactly it. I can't catch my breath. I haven't caught it yet from what happened a year ago."

He sat back down in the chair and dropped his face into his hands. Slowly he rubbed them down his face and looked up at her.

"How do you do it, Blair? How do you not cry? I saw you at the funeral service today. Your eyes were dry."

That boat looked so peaceful, floating toward home. But behind it, dark clouds closed in, moving faster than the boat. "Crying doesn't do much good," she said.

She didn't want to tell him that if she ever got started, her tears might never stop. "I have to go," she said. She started back across the sand.

"Blair." Rick's voice stopped her. She turned back. He had stood up again, taken a few steps toward her. "Yeah?"

"I hope they find them. Whoever did that to your parents, I hope they find them soon."

"Me too," she said.

"You know what your mama would tell you right now?" he asked. "She would tell you to cling to the Lord with all your might. And she would tell you to forgive."

Blair's hair whipped into her face. "That's a tall order when you don't know who to forgive."

"It's a tall order even when you do."

She knew he was talking about his family and the drunk who had killed them. For the first time she felt something of the pull that Morgan had toward the tenants, a little connection of understanding, an affinity that she hadn't expected to feel.

"Your mother wouldn't say it was easy," he said, "but you know she'd say it."

"Yeah," Blair said, "she'd say it, all right."

She met his eyes for a moment, saw the genuine grief pulling at his face, rimming his eyes. Finally, she turned away and hurried across the street where her sister waited.

CHAPTER 27

Sadie had gathered enough change to buy a toothbrush and some toothpaste, so she went into Goodfellow's Grocery and closed her eyes in pleasure at the rush of cool air conditioning. Though she had bathed daily at the outdoor showers, she still felt sticky and sandy. She had washed her clothes in the swimming pool at one of the hotels last night, but they still smelled of perspiration.

She had slept in a boat bobbing in the water near the dock, curled up on the floor so no one would see her. It was comfortable, and she had found a life jacket for a pillow, and a tarp with which to cover herself. The act of surviving had become a full-time job, the only one she could get.

She found the toothbrushes and chose the cheapest one, grabbed a small tube of toothpaste, and counted out her change. There was enough, she thought with gratitude.

She headed for the front and waited in the short line. The people in front of her had obviously been on the beach all day. Like her, they looked sandy and sweaty, and their clothes were rumpled and damp.

Maybe people would think she was a sun-drenched tourist instead of a homeless runaway.

She got to the front of the line and set the items down.

"You find everything all right?" the checkout girl asked.

"Yes," she said, trying to smile. "It sure is hot out there."

"Yep," the girl said. "Humidity's like five hundred percent." She rang the toothbrush and toothpaste up. "That'll be two dollars, thirty-six cents."

Sadie counted out her change, dropped it into her hand. "You wouldn't have any openings here, would you? I sure could use a job."

The girl shrugged. "Sometimes they do. You could ask over there. The guy with the mustache. He owns the place."

"Mr. Goodfellow?" Sadie asked with a smirk.

The girl laughed. "No, Mr. Jenkins." She lowered her voice. "And he's not that good a fellow, either."

Sadie thanked her and headed for the man. He was surveying his stock of soup, and she came up behind him and cleared her throat.

He turned around.

"Excuse me," she said. "I know I look awful. I've been on the beach all day. But I was wondering if you had any job openings. I'm a real hard worker, and I really need the money."

He looked down at her cast. "You live around here?"

"I'm new in town," she said. "I was in a car accident a couple of days ago. Great way to start a vacation, you know? Anyway, I like it so much that I wanted to try to stay. I graduated last month, so I can really go anywhere I want. . . ."

She stopped, realizing she was saying too much. Lies were best told in bits and pieces, not with long explanations.

"You can fill out an application," he said. "If anything comes up, I could call you."

"Okay," she said. "Only, I'm not sure where I'll be staying, so I'll just check back every day. Will that be okay?"

He shrugged like he didn't much care. "Fine." He got her an application. "Just leave it with the cashier when you're done."

She filled it out, lying about her home address, her age, her school. Then she left it with the girl at the front. Brimming with hope, she left the store. Maybe he would hire her. It would be a nice place to work. She could make friends with the cashier, buy the food she needed, and stay in air conditioning.

She crossed the busy road and went back down to the beach to walk along the shoreline. When she reached the end of the sand, she walked further, up along the river side of the island. She crossed through the yard of a house on the water and saw a boat-house at the end of a drive.

It looked like a little house, with a front door and a roof, but only three walls. A boat probably floated inside it, she thought. It would be safer to sleep in a boat that was docked in a boathouse. She would be out of the wind and the sand and the morning dew, and no one would be as likely to find her there.

The idea blossomed in her mind as she walked further, looking for one that wasn't so close to a house. There were several, scattered out along the river, but most were too visible.

Finally, she came upon one situated in a woodsy area, with nothing but a dirt road leading to it. She tested the doorknob, but it was locked, so she took off her shoes and dropped her backpack and slipped into the water. She swam to the opening of the little house. Just as she thought, a boat sat there in the opening of the boathouse floor, and around it was enough room to walk, and various items hung on the walls.

She pulled up onto the floor and looked around. Yes, this place was lonely enough to keep her hidden tonight, and it wasn't likely that anyone would want to take the boat out tonight. Tomorrow morning, she would leave early, then come back when it was dark again.

It was an answer, she thought, until she could get a job and find a better place.

Things were starting to look up.

CHAPTER

28

Morgan was quiet as they drove back across the island with their parents' boxes and file cabinet in the car. Blair seemed pensive too, lost in her own thoughts.

A massive magnolia tree blocked the view of Blair's house, the library, and the marine museum, as they came up the street.

As the place came into view, they saw police cars filling the library's parking lot. Morgan's heart jolted. "Oh, no," she whispered. "What now?"

Blair pulled haphazardly into the gravel parking lot and jumped out of her car. Cade came to the open door of the library.

"What is it, Cade?" she asked.

"Someone's broken into the library and vandalized the place," he said. "The mayor came looking for you, and he used his key to get in. It's a mess in there. We're dusting for prints."

Morgan touched Blair's back and saw that her facial scars flamed with shame. She started to speak up for Blair, but her sister lifted her chin defiantly. "I did it," Blair said.

Cade frowned. "Did what?"

"I'm the one who made the mess. I was—a little angry the other night," she said. "I kind of took it out on the books. I was going to put them back together before anybody saw it. I didn't think it would hurt for the library to be closed for a couple of days. Didn't count on the mayor using his key."

Cade stared at her in stunned silence. Finally, he said, "You did *that?* Shelves on the floor, books everywhere, tables knocked over?"

"Yes," she said. "I was just coming home to put it all back together. I'm sorry, okay? I was upset."

He gave her a long, contemplative look, and she turned her scars away from him.

"Okay," Cade said quietly. "It's no problem. One less crime to solve."

He stepped back to let her in. Melba stood among the books, her massive chest heaving. "Oh, honey, you're not safe anywhere around here," she cried. "They've come into the library and ransacked it—"

"It's okay, Melba," Cade cut in. "We know who's been in the library. Case solved."

Joe McCormick turned from where he was dusting. "Solved? Cade, what's going on?"

Cade motioned him into Blair's office at the back, muttered a few words, then they both came back out.

"Well, aren't you going to tell us who did it?" Melba demanded. "Don't we have a right to know? This could be the same person who killed Thelma and Wayne!"

"It was me," Blair cut in. "Cade's being polite. He doesn't want to embarrass me, but I'm the one who did it, Melba."

"Did what, honey?"

Blair was getting angry again, and the smooth side of her face was coloring to match the scar. "I'm the one who knocked the books over, okay? My parents were murdered that day. I was having a little trouble coping."

"Oh, honey." Melba brought her hand to her chest. "And here we thought you weren't—"

"Weren't what?" Blair asked. "You thought I wasn't grieving for my parents because I didn't cry out in the open where everybody could see and gossip about my tears like they were some kind of cheap entertainment? Is that what you thought?"

Horrified at Blair's outburst, Morgan touched Melba's shoulder. "Oh, Melba, she doesn't mean it. It's just been a really hard week."

The woman drew in a breath, raising her big chest. "Well, you don't have to tell me that now, honey. I understand completely. Just don't you worry another little bit about it."

"I came with Blair tonight to help her start putting things back together," Morgan said. "The library will be good as new before you know it. As organized as Blair usually keeps things, I'd say she has a right to blow a fuse every now and then."

Blair met Cade's somber eyes across the room. "I need to go call the mayor," he said. "You going to be all right?"

"Of course," she snapped. "I'll be fine."

Cade looked over at Morgan. "You'll stay with her?"

"I'm not leaving," Morgan said.

The exchange set Blair off again. "Don't talk about me like I'm unstable. I don't plan to destroy any more public property."

He looked wounded. "No, Blair," he said, "that wasn't what I was thinking at all. I just don't like to see you hurting."

Blair bent over and started snatching books off the floor. "Find someone else to feel sorry for, Cade."

Cade just watched her for a moment. Finally, he and Joe headed for the door.

Melba kissed Morgan, leaving a pink lipstick smear on her cheek. She touched Blair's hair and looked tearfully into her face. Blair moved away and grabbed another book.

When they were alone, Blair stooped down and began stacking books. "I can't blame the mayor for jumping to conclusions," she said with a sigh. "Wonder why he would use his key to get in? He's never done that before."

"Probably saw the mess through the window and got worried," Morgan said.

Blair lifted her stack and set them on a table. "I don't know what came over me. It's going to take us days to put everything back together." She bent over and picked up a rare, ancient book she had bought at an auction with her own money. "What am I saying? Days? It took me *years* to get it as organized as it was in the first place."

"Well, I'll work as long as it takes," Morgan said.

"What about going through Mama and Pop's things?"

"I don't think I'm up to it right now," Morgan said. "It's like rubbing alcohol into a wound. This kind of physical work is just what I need." She went to the top of one of the toppled bookshelves. "Give me a hand with this."

Blair got the other side, and with great effort, they managed to get it standing again.

They worked for twenty minutes trying to get the next one up, when they heard another car pull up.

"What now?" Morgan asked.

Blair went to the window. "It's Cade again."

Morgan looked out over her shoulder. Cade was getting out of his car, wearing blue jeans and a T-shirt with the sleeves cut off. "What does he want?"

Blair went to the door and flung it open. "What?"

"I thought I'd come help out," he said. "I knew you'd need some muscle to get these shelves back up."

Suddenly speechless, Blair turned to Morgan.

"I think we can do it ourselves," Morgan said. "Maybe you need to get on back to the jail and keep an eye on your prisoner."

"The prisoner's in good hands," he said. "I got a few minutes to spare."

"Well, maybe you should be out looking for whoever killed our parents," Morgan said. "The real murderer."

He looked down at Blair. "Do you want help or not, Blair?"

She turned back to the bookshelves lying like dominos across the floor. "I guess we could use his help," Blair said to Morgan. She glanced at Cade. "I appreciate it."

"No problem," he said, then he clomped back across the wooden floor to the bookshelf furthest in the back, the one on the top of the domino pile, and pulled it upright. When he had gotten the third set of shelves up, they heard another set of wheels on the gravel outside.

"Now what?" Morgan mumbled.

Blair went to the door and looked out. Melba and several ladies were getting out of the car.

"It's the cavalry," Cade said. "I asked Melba to get some people together to help with this."

Blair gave Cade a belligerent look. "They're not bringing food are they? We don't have any place to put it."

"No, they're not bringing food," Cade said with a grin. "They're just bringing a few more hands to help."

Melba came in, wearing stretch pants and a big floppy T-shirt. The other ladies were dressed for work, as well. "I couldn't get the whole auxiliary," she said, "but I did get ten of us."

Blair grunted. "Melba, it really isn't necessary. . . ."

"It certainly is," Melba said. "There's no reason you and Morgan should have to do this all by yourself." She stepped into the building and smiled at Cade. "And I see our police chief is already hard at work. Don't you worry about a thing," Melba said. "With thirteen of us working, we'll get it all done tonight. Might even get the place vacuumed and dusted too."

Morgan saw that Blair was about to object again. They both wanted to do it alone, quietly, without people trying to make them feel better. But it was impossible. "I can't argue with that," Blair said finally. "I appreciate it."

The ladies came in one by one with their condolences and hugs, and Blair and Morgan accepted them as each one started to work.

*A*fter several hours, the shelves were standing, the books were stacked, and the ladies went home. Cade lingered behind, as if there might be some last-minute lifting for him to do. He didn't want to leave as long as he could make anything easier for them.

Morgan had remained distant from him and avoided speaking to him, but Blair seemed moved by the help he had brought.

"Looks like maybe I can open again tomorrow," she said. "That'll be good . . . getting back to work."

Cade leaned against the wall, crossing his arms as he looked down at her. "Tomorrow? Don't you think that's too soon?"

"No, the sooner, the better," she said. "Besides, I'll be here, anyway, at my computer. Figuring out who killed my parents."

"Blair, come on. Let me take care of this."

"You're *not* taking care of it, Cade," she whispered, glancing back at Morgan who was still dusting in the back.

"You've got the wrong guy." She started to walk away, but he touched her arm, stopping her.

"If Jonathan didn't do it, then we're going to find who did," he said.

"Well, I'm going to help you," Blair told him. "If there's anything I can do, it's research. I can find anything you want to know faster than anybody you know can do it."

"I'm sure that's true, Blair, but it could get dangerous. If Jonathan is not the guy, then somebody else is. I don't want you walking into any traps. And I'll tell you something. I'm sure not anxious to investigate another homicide."

He realized instantly that the words had been insensitive. Her face went pale.

"You're not going to talk me out of it, Cade," she said quietly. "I'm going to find out who killed my parents if it's the last thing I do. This killer has met his match."

He looked down at her, pensive. She had pretty, thoughtful eyes, the same color as the water off of Cayman Island. It was the only place he had ever seen that exact color. Her eyelashes were long and always looked a little wet. She was prettier than Morgan, he had always thought. Only she would never believe it.

As he gazed down at her, her hand came up to cover the scar on her face. It always did. He had never looked seriously at her when she didn't raise her hand up to scratch an itch just under her eye.

"Well, just do me one favor," Cade said. "If you find anything, let me have a look. It might help."

"Will you do the same?" she asked.

"No."

"I didn't think so. Cade, I'm not interested in sharing information with you if you won't share it with me."

"Well, are you interested in catching the killer?" he asked.

"Of course I am. Aren't you?"

"My point," he said, "is that it could happen faster if we share information."

"My point too."

"Yeah, but I'm an official. I am the police chief of Cape Refuge."

"And I'm the official librarian," she said.

"I don't want you and your sister playing detective and getting into trouble. We have a police force in this town. We can do this."

Blair looked up at him, her gaze sinking deep. "I know you loved them, Cade. They were your friends, even your mentors. They meant a lot of things to a lot of people. But they were *my* parents."

He swallowed and looked at his feet. "I know."

"And you know me," she said. "You know what I do. I look things up. I chase things down. I get the facts."

"I always said you should have been a detective."

"I prefer to chase my facts down on the computer or the telephone."

"Well, just don't fool yourself into thinking you're safe," Cade said, "that nobody's watching or listening or reading. Because you and Morgan could be pretty vulnerable right now."

"Funny. That's what Jonathan told her."

"Well, he's right," Cade said. "I'm going to have my men patrol your house a lot more than usual. You two need to stay together, and you need to watch your backs. Call me if anything happens. If you hear a noise in the night, if a dog barks that you're not used to hearing, if the wind even blows too hard, you call me. You hear?"

Blair looked up at him. "I hear."

"But will you do it?" Cade asked.

She thought about that for a moment. "Of course I will. I don't have a death wish."

"Middle of the night, two in the morning—I don't care," Cade said. "I'm there in minutes."

She looked up at him, met his eyes. "You talk real scary for a man who thought he had the crime solved," she said. "If you're so sure we're in danger, why is Jonathan still behind bars?"

"I'm covering all my bases," he said.

Blair just stared at him. "I do have a .22 in my closet. By Georgia law, I can carry it in my purse, since I have a license. I've never really felt the need to carry it, but maybe I should start."

"As long as you use it for self-defense," Cade said, "and don't go off half-cocked, taking the law into your own hands."

"Who me?" Blair asked.

Cade sighed. He stood straighter and caught Morgan's eye in the back of the library. "See you later, Morgan," he called back.

She only turned away. He wondered if Morgan would ever speak to him again, but he couldn't worry about that now. He had a job to do, and he needed to get back to the station and do it.

CHAPTER

Morgan was seething when Blair came to the back room. "We could have put the library back together ourselves," she muttered. "We didn't need his help. Coming in here like he's still a football star, his arms all pumped up . . ."

"Well, we got it. And now it's done. I'm glad it's behind us."

"He arrested my husband," she said. "On the worst day of my life he took my husband away from me."

"He's just trying to do his job."

"It's not his job to arrest innocent private citizens in their moments of grief."

"He means well, Morgan." Blair realized the irony of the role reversal. She couldn't remember when she had ever defended anyone to Morgan. She was usually the fault-finder.

Morgan swept the last of the dust into a pan, dumped it, then dusted her hands off. "Well, at least it's done. I'm ready to go through Mama and Pop's things."

They carried the boxes into Blair's office and set them on her desk. "I figured out a way to do this," Blair said as Morgan sank into a chair. "I was thinking that the first thing we need to do is get information on the tenants at Hanover House. I can be doing that on the computer while you start digging through the files."

Morgan reached into the box and withdrew a stack of papers. Her face betrayed her fatigue and dread as she began flipping through them.

"The first thing I'm going to need is some information about the tenants," Blair said, tapping the keys. "I need full names if I can get them, social security numbers, birth dates. Do you see a tenant file in there where Mama might have kept up with this stuff?"

Morgan pulled a file out and looked through the contents. "Yeah, this might be it." She took it over to Blair's table and pulled up a chair. "Here's some stuff about Gus."

"Perfect." Blair took the sheets out of the file and entered the information onto the database that she used. Then she entered Rick Morrison's.

Before she had gotten it all entered, the computer chimed, telling her that Gus's profile was already complete. Quickly, she pressed *print* and waited as the pages came off of her printer.

"Okay, look at this," she said. "His rap sheet. Looks bad."

"Well, we knew he had a past," Morgan said. "That's no surprise."

"But he's a three-time convicted felon," Blair said. "He served more time in prison than he's been out of it. Car theft, drug dealing. There's one here for beating his girlfriend back in the eighties. Armed robbery was just the latest."

"Let me see that," Morgan said, snatching the paper out of her hand. "Spent ten years just for the armed robbery," she said. "Paroled six months ago. No surprise there." Morgan scanned the rest of the list, then handed it back to Blair. "Okay, so he abused his girlfriend, stole cars, committed armed robbery. It doesn't say he killed anybody. And he's changed."

Blair flashed a look at her. "What is it with you and this guy? I've just shown you that he has a terrible history of criminal behavior. And you're trying to tell me that since he hasn't been in jail for murder, then he couldn't be a killer?"

"No, that's not what I'm saying," Morgan told her. "I just can't see it. I know Gus. I've been there since he moved in. When he first came to Cape Refuge he was really confused and quiet. He was the most depressed and troubled man I'd ever seen in my life. And I've seen Mama and Pop turn him around. I've seen how they ministered to him, and he's slowly changed. He does things for other people now. He thinks of the other tenants. He cried at Mama and Pop's funeral service."

"Of course, he cried. If he had anything to do with it, maybe he was feeling remorse over it. Or maybe he's just a good actor."

"I just don't think he did it," Morgan said.

"Well, your own husband thinks he did."

Morgan got to her feet and crossed the room, looked out the window. It had started to drizzle, and the sky was darkening with the promise of more. "You keep flipping sides, you know that, Blair? It makes me dizzy just to be around you. Yesterday you thought Jonathan might have done it, and today you're telling me to listen to him because he's right about Gus."

"Okay, I admit it," Blair said. "Everything's a little confusing right now."

Morgan turned back from the window. "I'm not saying that we should just give up the possibility that Gus could have done it. I think everybody's got to be a suspect. And if you show me any viable evidence that he did, I'll believe you. But until then, I'd rather think the best of him."

It was clear that fatigue, grief, fear, and hunger were all combining to take its toll on Morgan. "Look," Blair said, "I know that you've spent an awful lot of your life trying to get Mama and Pop's approval, and that you look at everybody like they have some kind of halo around them, but when your parents have been murdered, it's okay to think badly of people."

"What do you mean, I was always trying to get their approval? So were you. That's what daughters do."

"Yeah, but I didn't make it my life's work."

Morgan turned on her. "I did *not* make it my life's work. If you think that, you don't know me at all. I just wanted to be like her."

"Well, you succeeded," Blair said, beginning to type again. "At least one of us did."

Though Blair kept her eyes on the screen, she could feel Morgan's anger as she stood over her. "Why do you do this?" Morgan asked. "All I'm doing is digging through these files to find the information that *you* think we need."

"And *you* don't think we need it?"

"What is wrong with you?" Morgan demanded. "I'm here with you for comfort, for security, and for my own sanity, but I'm beginning to wonder if it's a safe place."

That sent Blair's own anger up a notch, and she set her mouth and typed faster. "Another one of Mama's words," she said. "*Safe place.* She and Pop made a safe place for everybody in the world. Everybody but—" She stopped before the word was out of her mouth.

"Everybody but who?" Morgan asked. "*You?*" She said the word as if she couldn't believe it, and Blair wished she hadn't even started this. She kept typing, harder, faster.

"They always provided a safe place for you, Blair."

Blair shoved her keyboard away and got up, facing her sister. "It wasn't safe for me, okay? Cape Refuge—the haven for everybody in the world who needed a safe place—was not a safe place for me."

Morgan's voice was as loud as Blair's now. "Why wasn't it, Blair? Because of the scar?"

"I don't want to talk about it," Blair said. She started to sit back down, but Morgan grabbed her arm and turned her around. "Mama and Pop offered you a lot of safe places. You just chose not to take them. And it's not fair for you to have so much contempt toward me just because I did."

"I don't have contempt for you, Morgan," she said. "I'm just speaking my mind. I'm sorry if it hurts you."

"Oh, give me a break." One of Morgan's tears spilled over her lashes and raced down her cheek. "You're not sorry, Blair. It's your intention to hurt me, and I'm not sure why." She sighed and sank back into the chair next to the file cabinet. "I'm sorry I mentioned the scars."

Blair breathed a mirthless laugh and plunked back into the chair. "I know I have scars, Morgan. I can handle your mentioning them."

"No, you can't. Every insecurity in your life, every regret, every disappointment, goes back to those scars."

Blair didn't say a word, for her anger was rapidly escalating into fury. "Don't psychoanalyze me, Morgan. I'm not one of your projects."

Morgan set her arms on the file cabinet and dropped her face into them. "This is crazy. We're supposed to be supporting each other, and instead we're tearing each other down. I hate this. If I had anyplace to go, I'd leave right now. But I need you, and you need me. We're kind of stuck together for a while, until this murder is solved. We need to get along. But when this is over, Blair, I'm going to do everything in my power to make a safe place for you."

Blair was desperate to change the subject. "While you make it for Gus Hampton?"

"When you work in Hanover House every day like I do, and you see the people and get to know them as your friends, it's not easy to think of them as killers, okay? I've heard their stories, Blair. They've shared their hearts with me. I've sung with them in church and praised God, and I've watched them change."

"Hasn't Jonathan?" Blair asked. "If he's watched them change right along with you, then why wasn't he so keen on Gus?"

"You know Jonathan's temper," she said. "Gus made him mad. He saw me comforting Gus when he had just shared something really personal with me, about how he felt like he was never good enough for Christ, and how forgiveness seemed like something he could never quite have. And I gave him a hug. It was spontaneous, Blair. It didn't mean anything except that I was a

Christian sister who loved him and cared about him. And Jonathan walked in and went ballistic."

"Why wasn't he mad at you?" Blair asked.

"He was at first, until he understood the way I felt about it, that I hadn't done anything wrong. I was trying to comfort a friend. But then he started thinking that Gus had ill motives."

"Why didn't you tell me this before?"

"Tell you what? You knew what Jonathan thought. Gus didn't do anything wrong." She flipped idly through the files. "But that's when Jonathan decided he wanted him out of our house. That's all there is to that story. But in my mind, Blair, Gus Hampton is the same man I've watched grow over the last few months. He has the same past now that he had when he came to Cape Refuge. It's just that we weren't all privy to it. But Mama and Pop were. You mark my word. People told Mama and Pop things that they didn't tell ordinary people. They shared their lives and their hearts with them. I want to be like that, Blair. I like people, and I can love them. I can empathize with them; I can relate to what they're thinking. Mama always said it was a gift, but you act like it's a curse."

"It's not a curse," Blair said, typing again. "I never meant it was a curse. At least not your curse."

"Then who does it curse?" Morgan asked. "You, Blair? Does it curse you?"

The keys clicked at record speed. "I'm not like you, Morgan. I've never been like you."

"Of course you're not," Morgan said. "You'd go nuts. You'd pull your hair out. You're not supposed to be like me."

"But you're the one most like Mama. You're the one people love."

"That's because I'm out there," Morgan said. "I'm not hiding away in a library trying to keep anybody from ever getting close to me." Morgan's voice broke, and she dropped her forehead against her palm. "Oh, Blair, I miss them so much. I miss Mama's hug every day. Have you thought about that, Blair? Both of us, we had her hug every single day of our lives. I wake up in the middle of the night and just hunger for it."

Blair stopped clicking and just stared at the screen.

"And I miss Pop," Morgan said. "I miss the way his jaw felt at the end of the day, like sandpaper—and that twinkle in his eye. Whenever he looked at you, you just felt it going into you, warming you up somewhere deep. I miss his corny jokes. I miss how much he loved us."

Blair set her hands on her desk. She didn't want to cry, not here, not now, not in front of Morgan while they were fighting. But it took a valiant effort not to.

"And I miss Jonathan," Morgan said. "I miss my husband because I need him now. And there he is, locked up behind bars for something he didn't even do. All I have is you."

Blair turned and started to say something cryptic about how she was sorry to be the last resort, but Morgan beat her to it.

"And here you are, taking potshots at me like I'm the one who kept you from having a safe place."

"That's not what I meant," Blair said.

"I know what you meant," Morgan bit out. "It's the same thing you've meant for years, that I follow my emotions. You're too smart to have any. But maybe sometimes my heart clears things up for my head, Blair. Have you ever thought of that? Maybe it makes me see things a little clearer than you do."

"And maybe it blinds you," Blair said.

Morgan wilted and leaned against the cabinet. Blair hated seeing her cry. She thought of crossing the room and pulling her sister into her arms just the way her mother would have done. Maybe it would have made up for the lack of hugs they had gotten lately. But it would be too hard to be that soft, and it might lead to Blair's breaking down. She couldn't take that chance.

"Maybe it makes me wise," Morgan said.

Blair couldn't entertain that possibility, but she was weary of the fight. "Maybe it does. And maybe if we put our strengths together, we can get through this. And maybe, if we leave our emotions out of it, we can figure out who did this."

"I can't," Morgan said. "I can't leave my emotions out of anything."

"Well, I'm asking you to try. I'm asking you to give me your brain instead of your heart and see people through a filter of facts."

Morgan sniffed and wiped her eyes again. "All right, Blair. I'll make a deal with you. I'll give you my head with as little emotion as possible, if you'll give me a hug every day like Mama did."

Blair just looked at her as if that was an uneven swap. It would cost her so much, and she wasn't sure she had the deposits to cover it. But she saw no way out.

She got up and pulled her sister into a hug. They clung to each other for a long moment, Morgan weeping into her shoulder, wetting her hair and her shirt. Blair's mind started down a path of no return, a path toward the emotions taunting and luring her, daring her to step over the line.

Finally, she let go and stepped back. "We have work to do, Morgan," she said. "We need to get to it."

Morgan went back to the files she was working on. It took Blair a moment to gather her wits, but finally she went back to the computer to see if there had been any rap sheets sent on Rick Morrison and Mrs. Hern, or the Andersons, who had left right after the murders. There was nothing on Rick, since he had had no arrests. Mrs. Hern's one conviction for embezzlement came up, and the Andersons each had several convictions for drug dealing.

"What's this?"

Blair looked down at Morgan and saw her puzzling over a paper in her hand.

"Looks like a death certificate," Morgan said. "Only you'll never believe whose name is on it."

Blair leaned over to see. "Whose?"

Morgan pointed to the name. "Richard Morrison."

Blair's mouth came open, and she gaped at her sister. "What does this mean?"

Morgan shook her head. "I don't know. Maybe it's Rick's father."

"But why would Mama and Pop have it?" Blair took the certificate out of Morgan's hand. "Let's think this through," she said.

"Mama and Pop have a tenant named Rick Morrison who claims his wife and daughter were killed in a drunk-driving accident. He's steeped with grief so he comes to Cape Refuge. Now how do you explain Mama and Pop having a death certificate with his name on it? Okay, so it could be his father. Or someone else with the same name. But why?"

"Maybe it's fake," Morgan said.

Blair went back to the computer. "That would be pretty easy to check out." She banged on the keys, found the public records that could tell her who had died and when. "Unless this person died in the last few weeks, it should be listed."

Morgan came to look over her shoulder as the answer came up on the screen. Four Rick Morrisons emerged with various middle names. Blair clicked down each one until she came to the one that matched the death certificate.

"He was a real guy, Morgan," Blair said. "Died at the age of fifty-eight."

Morgan frowned. "Can you find out things like where he went to high school, where he lived, what he died of? We need a picture."

"I'll try," Blair said. "Just give me a few minutes."

*B*lair and Morgan spent the entire night looking for information about the Richard Morrison who had died. They had compiled a dossier on the dead man, including a picture that looked nothing like their tenant. Now, mentally and physically exhausted, they vowed to finish it before they laid their heads down to sleep.

Just after six-thirty in the morning, they drove to Hanover House, intent on getting in Rick's room and finding what they could.

"What if he's still there?" Blair asked as they pulled into the driveway.

Morgan shook her head. "He's an early riser. He walks on the beach every morning. He does that every day before he showers for work."

"We can go in with a vacuum cleaner," Blair said, "and pretend we're vacuuming. Maybe something's lying around."

"He's pretty neat," Morgan said. "Makes up his bed every morning, picks up after himself. But maybe there'll be something. Do you even know what you're looking for?"

"If I see his wallet left out I'm going to dig through for his driver's license, credit cards, anything. Maybe a checkbook or some of his mail."

"This feels wrong, somehow," Morgan said. "Mama was always real respectful of their privacy."

"It's not snooping," Blair said. "It's an investigation. It could save people's lives and might get your husband out of jail."

Morgan knew it was true. "Okay, so which do you want to do, make breakfast or vacuum?" Morgan asked.

Blair looked at her like she was crazy. "I don't intend to do either."

"Well, you have to do one or the other," Morgan said. "I mean, if we walk in there after not being here for days and start vacuuming, it's going to look awfully suspicious. Besides, it's a bed-and-breakfast. We're supposed to provide breakfast."

Blair grunted. "I think they understand why they haven't been given breakfast. Besides, they have full run of the kitchen. They can get anything they want."

"I was just thinking that if we acted like things were normal, that we had come to make them breakfast, that would get Mrs. Hern and Gus out of their rooms, so they wouldn't see what you were doing."

Blair sighed. "Well, okay, but you'll have to cook."

"All right. But that means you have to be the one to go into his room."

"That's fine," Blair said. "Let me at it."

A while later, Blair smelled the scent of scrambled eggs and bacon and her mother's favorite biscuits downstairs while she vacuumed the upstairs hall. The smell brought back a mourning so deep that it bypassed tears entirely.

So did the house. She vacuumed around and under things, trying not to let the images bring back a flood of emotions—but it was hard to fight them off.

When Rick finally opened the door, and yelled "Good morning" over the noise of the vacuum cleaner, she watched him head down the stairs. This was her chance, she thought. She vacuumed her way into his room, her eyes darting back and forth at the personal objects he had out.

A Swiss army knife, a couple of keys on a key chain, his wallet—

She grabbed it up and started going through it, looking for some kind of identification. There were no credit cards, no driver's license, nothing with his name on it. She looked through the billfold for a receipt—anything . . .

The vacuum cleaner shut off, and Blair swung around.

Rick stood at the door, looking at her with somber eyes. "I didn't want to scare you, so I turned it off."

She swallowed and dropped the wallet. "You didn't scare me."

He bent down and picked it up, keeping his eyes on her. "Need a loan?" he asked.

Her mind reeled for an explanation. "Of course not," she said. "I was just dusting that table and it fell off." She knew it was a lame explanation, and that he had seen her rifling through it. "I'm sorry. I was looking to see if you had pictures of your wife and daughter."

That seemed to satisfy him, and the suspicion on his face quickly melted away. He went to the bed table and picked up two framed pictures. "Here they are."

Right out in the open, she thought. She gazed down at them, feigning interest. "They were beautiful," she said.

He looked genuinely mournful as he set them back down. When he turned back to her, she saw a glimmer of tears in his eyes. "Well, thanks for vacuuming in here."

"Sure."

He shoved his wallet into his back pocket. "I'm going walking. I always stop by Crickets for coffee. You want to come?"

"No," she said quickly. "Too much to do."

"Okay. See you later."

She turned the vacuum cleaner back on and watched him go down the stairs. When she was sure he was gone, she wilted on his bed. That had been too close. She would have to be more careful.

She looked around again. His trash can had recently been emptied, his bed had been made. The only thing out of place was a lone water glass sitting beside his bed, next to the pictures. *Fingerprints,* she thought. Maybe she could take them to Cade and have him run them down to discover who he really was. She held it with two fingers, careful not to smear the prints, then pulled the vacuum cleaner out of the room and headed down the stairs.

She could hear voices in the kitchen and knew that Gus and Mrs. Hern were there, helping with breakfast and reminiscing about Thelma and Wayne, but she headed out to the car, set the glass carefully on the floorboard, and drove off.

Morgan would wonder where she had gone, but she couldn't stop now. She headed to the police station. It was only seven-thirty; she hoped Cade had made it in by now.

Carefully carrying the glass, she pushed through the door and crossed the room to Cade's office. He sat at his desk, studying something on his computer with a cup of coffee in his hand. He looked as if he had been going without sleep too.

Blair didn't knock. She just bolted in and leaned over his desk. "I want you to get the fingerprints off this glass," she said. "I want you to tell me whose they are."

He looked down at the glass. "Where'd you get that?"

She reached into her pocket and pulled out the death certificate with Rick Morrison's name on it and slapped it down in front of him. "One of my parents' tenants, Rick Morrison. It's his glass. And last night as we were going through my parents' . . . ," she hesitated, avoiding the words "file cabinet." She didn't want to give him the idea to confiscate it. "We were going through some of their things, and we found this."

He looked at it. "A death certificate."

"With his name on it. Only he doesn't look that dead to me. He also doesn't look fifty-eight years old."

Cade sat back hard in his chair. "Interesting . . ."

"I found out that the Richard Morrison of the death certificate had a heart attack, had three grown daughters, two married, and worked as a banker in Atlanta. He left behind a wife who's already remarried."

"And the one staying at Hanover House claims to be here after losing his wife and child in a drunk-driving accident." He nodded, as if this was pertinent information. "We'll run the prints on the glass, Blair. I'll let you know what we find out."

Blair straightened. "Will you, Cade? You promise?"

"I said I would, didn't I? I always keep my word."

That had to be good enough for Blair. She followed him out of his office. "Do it quickly, Cade. Don't waste any time. If this guy's a murderer, we need to know. Morgan's served the guy breakfast this morning."

"I'm aware of the urgency. I'll take care of it, Blair."

Feeling as if she had left her firstborn in the hands of a stranger, she hurried back to Hanover House to tell her sister.

CHAPTER

32

*D*ebilitating fatigue was setting in by the time Blair got back to Hanover House. "Where did you go?" Morgan asked, keeping her voice low.

"The police station. I had to talk to Cade." They glanced back at Mrs. Hern, knowing she could hear every word. Morgan held her hand up to silence Blair, and Blair nodded that she would wait until later.

When the kitchen was as clean as Thelma would have left it, they got back into the car. "Rick came in while I was going through his wallet," Blair said.

"Oh, no. I thought he went out to walk."

"He needed his wallet for Crickets. I told him I was looking for a picture of his wife and daughter," Blair said. "The fact that there were two framed pictures next to his bed didn't help my story. But I guess he bought it."

"Oh, thank goodness. I wouldn't have thought of that. I probably would have broken down and spilled my guts and told him I was looking for his identification."

"There wasn't any. But when he left, I found a glass, and I figured it had fingerprints. I didn't really know what to do with it. I mean, when police take evidence from a crime scene, they usually have a paper sack to put it in, and I didn't have anything. I knew if I came in the kitchen I would call attention to myself, so I just got in the car and took it over to Cade's office."

"Was he interested?" Morgan asked.

"Yeah, he was real interested. I showed him the death certificate. He's going to run the prints and get back to us."

"Okay, that's good," Morgan said. "Did you see Jonathan while you were there?"

"No, I didn't take the time to."

"Maybe they'll decide Rick is the prime suspect, and let Jonathan out today," Morgan said.

Blair looked at her with tired eyes. "Why are you so much more willing to have it be Rick Morrison than Gus Hampton?"

Morgan shrugged. "We didn't find a death certificate for Gus. It's made me real suspicious. When does Cade think he'll have the prints identified?"

"I don't know," she said. "I didn't ask. But I know he'll get it as fast as he can. I'm thinking sometime this morning. Meanwhile, we can go back home and lie down, maybe get a couple of hours' sleep before we hear from him."

"And then I'll go see Jonathan."

Blair was quiet as they got back to the house. She wanted Morgan to think she was settling down to sleep, but she merely waited in her bedroom until she knew that Morgan was sleeping, and then she got up and sneaked through the door. As tired as she was, she couldn't turn things off just yet.

There had been many nights in her life when she had stayed awake all night researching a topic that interested her, then spent the next day following up on the things she had learned. How could anyone sleep when they were waiting for the fingerprints of the person who may have killed her parents?

She went into the kitchen and called Cade. When he came to the phone she said simply, "Anything yet?"

"Blair?" he asked.

"Yes. Have you gotten the fingerprint report?"

"Not yet," he said. "I'm still working on it. I told you I'd call you as soon as I have something."

She sighed. "All right. How long do you think it will be?"

"Two or three hours," he said. "Not before that. I dusted the prints and sent them in, and now the computer has to do a search through every fingerprint on file. It takes a while. Why don't you get some sleep? You didn't look like you had had any."

"Neither did you," she said.

"I'll call you, I promise."

She hung up and sat for a moment, staring at the telephone. She should sleep or eat, she realized, but her mind was still racing, and she had no appetite. The normal body functions like sleeping or eating or crying seemed like weaknesses she couldn't entertain.

But she wasn't sure what to do with herself.

Finally, she stepped out the front door and stood in the shade of the warm breeze coming from the water. The sun was already bright in the sky, and though it was only eight-thirty, it was already hot and humid. The trees around the house whispered and rustled, and birds squawked and cooed overhead. She slid her hands into her jeans pockets and crossed the street to the water's edge.

It was low tide. She could walk way out into the place where, later today, the water would be knee deep. She looked to her right and saw the dock about a mile up the road, right next to the building where worship and murder happened under the same roof. The beach was no more than four miles around, and from where she stood, she could see this side of the Cape clearly. In front of her and to the left was the Wassaw Sound. Across it was Cabbage Island, a marshy place full of marine animals and rabid raccoons that wreaked havoc on the island pets.

The ocean sounds calmed her nerves, made her feel that maybe there was some peace in the world. Desperate to soak up more of that peace, she started walking the island's perimeter, back toward Hanover House.

The wind picked up her hair and feathered it across her face. She pulled it back and slipped it behind her ears, then pulled it out again, trying to make it cover her scar. As she walked, a plan began to form in her mind. It wasn't much after nine. Most of the establishments on the island didn't open until nine. She would hide and watch both Gus and Rick as they left for work. Even though they had cars, both men worked within walking distance of the house. Maybe she would have the opportunity to see what Rick did in the mornings.

She reached the part of the beach across from Hanover House and stepped back behind a magnolia tree near the street. Rick Morrison was already taking his garbage out to the street. She watched as he closed the garbage can carefully, then went back for a few more bags. She wished she had her car with her so she could grab those bags and go through the trash to see if she could find any clues.

When he had finished, he dusted off his hands and started across the street toward her. She let him get a safe distance ahead, then she followed. He didn't go far, just walked along the shore for about a mile or so, to the dock near where her parents had been killed, past the church warehouse and to the Madison Boat Shop, where he worked.

He didn't go right in but went to the boardwalk skirting the bay side of the island, and he stood there, quiet and mysterious, his hands in his pockets, his face somber. She didn't know what she hoped to see in him. A nervous twitch maybe, or a gun packed beneath his shirt. Maybe a bloodstain on his clothes. But she saw nothing except a man who seemed as pensive and troubled as she.

She watched until he went in. Then she turned around and started back. Her eyes strayed to the few people already on the beach. The lifeguards were distributing the chairs they rented in neat little rows on the sand. City workers picked up trash left behind from the night before. A few residents walked at the water's edge, getting their morning exercise.

She gasped as her gaze collided with Gus Hampton's. He stood among the trees near the street, watching her. The big, ebony-colored man was smoking a cigarette, taking long, deep drags, then flicking the ashes to his side.

A chill ran through her, and she quickly looked away and moved closer to the water, and headed home. What had Gus seen? she wondered. Had he realized she was watching Rick Morrison? Or had he been following her for some other reason?

She hurried into her house, locked the door, and stood there for a moment, trying to catch her breath. Finally, she went to the closet that held her gun, got it out, and loaded it. From now on she would have it handy, she thought. From now on, she would be ready.

*B*lair finally gave in to sleep shortly after noon. Since Morgan had gone to visit Jonathan, Blair slept with the gun clutched in her hand.

The sound of knocking awoke her. From the stupor of deep sleep, she looked at the clock. It was nine in the evening. She hadn't meant to sleep that long, but her body needed the rest after the events of the last few days. Darkness was invading the room, and Blair reached for the lamp.

When the knocking started again, she grabbed her gun, slipped it into her pocket, and stumbled to the front door. With groggy eyes, she looked to see who it was. She couldn't make the visitor out in the darkness. She leaned against the door. "Who is it?"

"Rick," the voice said from the other side. "Rick Morrison."

Blair caught her breath and her hand closed over the gun again. What did he want? She knew better than to let him in here alone. She wondered if he realized she had taken the glass from his room and given it to Cade to dust for fingerprints, or if he'd come to ask her about why she was snooping in his room.

She took a moment to compose herself. "Just a minute," she said through the door. She pulled the gun out and reassured herself that it was loaded. Her hands trembled. She was glad she had pockets. She had to act normal. If he hadn't heard that they suspected him, then maybe they could keep him from bolting and running before Cade had enough evidence to arrest him.

She took a deep breath, put her hand on the knob. Slowly she opened the door. "What can I do for you, Rick?" she asked.

He made no attempt to walk in but seemed to linger back, as if he knew his presence might have caused her consternation.

"Sorry to bother you, Blair. I know things can't be easy for you right now, but I wondered if we could talk. I have some things I need to tell you, things you need to know."

Curiosity mushroomed inside her like a nuclear explosion, and she found herself anxious for the fallout. She stepped out into the night and pulled the door shut behind her. "Let's talk out here," she said.

"That's fine, Blair. You don't have any business letting some strange man into your house, anyway, when you're alone."

She swallowed and wondered how he knew she was alone. The fact that Morgan's car was gone had probably clued him. She kept her hand on the gun in her pocket and went to a porch swing hanging from an arbor between her house and the library. She sat at the right end, leaving the other for him. Slowly, he sat down, his solid weight making the chains creak.

The sound of the surf combined with the calls of the insects chirping in the trees. Wind stirred her hair and rustled her wrinkled clothes. She wiped the sweaty palm of her free hand across her blue jeans and swallowed hard as she looked across the street toward the ocean rolling up onto the shore with foamy moonlit eagerness. She remembered just yesterday, looking out at the beach with him as he talked about grief.

She had felt such an affinity with him then, as he talked of his own grief. Had it been an act? Was he playing her?

"Your parents taught me more than I ever knew about God," Rick said, setting his elbows on his knees and folding his hands between them. "Mostly, they taught me about his love. But I got to tell you, I'm having a hard time with why he had to take them."

"I don't believe in God," Blair said.

"Then what do you believe in?"

If he had asked the pointed question a week ago, she would have proclaimed a belief in herself. She would have said that she believed there was a direct correlation between her effort and her results. She would have said that she believed in the basic goodness of man, and the determination of man's spirit. She would have said that she believed in science and mathematics, with their facts and their certainty, and the tangible manifestation of all they represented.

But now she couldn't say any of those things. Nothing was certain, least of all her own autonomy. The facts were hazy, at best, and the goodness of man was seriously in question.

The truth was that the murders had derailed her entire belief system, but she didn't want to share that with him.

He waited. "You must believe in something, Blair. I didn't believe when I first came to Cape Refuge. Your father told me that by not believing in anything, I was choosing to believe in something. He said that all people believe in a god—whether it's the god of hopelessness or the god of circumstances or the god of ourselves or the god of some other person. It took me a long time to figure out what my god was. I finally realized that I was believing in the god of hatred, the one that seemed to feed the thoughts I had toward the drunk driver who killed my family. I couldn't get that hatred or that desire to destroy him out of my mind. But it was only destroying me."

He leaned back hard on the swing. "That hatred robbed me of my memories. It robbed me of my peace, because I couldn't stop going through the if-only's in my mind. If only Karen hadn't been coming to meet me that day. If only I'd left work early and picked them up myself. If only I'd told her I loved her that morning. If only I'd had one last hug from Katie. *If only* . . . The two most hateful words in life."

Those same two words had played like a mantra in her mind for the last few days, over and over and over, tormenting her.

"Your father showed me that if-only's deny the power of the one true God. He said God was in control when that drunk driver ran over the median and head-on into their car. He was in control when I came so close to putting a gun to my head. He was in control when I heard about a place called Cape Refuge."

He shifted on the swing, put his arm on the back and looked at her for a long time until she had no choice but to return his gaze. He didn't have the look of a killer. He looked like a father and a husband. He looked like a grieving man with blue, bloodshot eyes and pink rims around them, and the way he always stared off into the ocean, as if there were some answers there ... or maybe some joy coming up just over the horizon, if only he watched long enough. There was something about their common feelings and the way he stared at her now that made her wish he was genuine.

But she hadn't forgotten that death certificate with his name on it. "You said you had something to tell me," she said. "Was that it?"

He rubbed his eyes roughly with his fingers, then looked back across to the ocean again, and cleared his throat. "No," he said. "It's about my name."

Her eyes flashed back to his. "Your name?"

"Yeah," he said, "my *real* name."

Blair's hand clamped over that gun. "What do you mean?"

"I know that's why you were going through my wallet this morning, Blair. You found out somehow that I'm not really Rick Morrison."

She slowly got to her feet, and put some distance between them. Her hand was slick over the gun in her pocket.

"I know what you're thinking," he said. "You're thinking that if I'm not who I say I am, then maybe I should be a suspect. Right?"

"Well, the thought had crossed my mind."

"But it's not like that," he said. "Rick Morrison was a friend of mine who died. I borrowed his identity. I had this mountain of debts back in Atlanta, and when my wife and daughter died, I was such a basket case I couldn't fulfill any of my responsibilities. That mountain of debt just kept growing and growing. I tried to function, Blair. I really did. I got up every day and I went to work and I sat there and tried. But my head wasn't in it. I was grieving. My whole life had changed and nothing mattered anymore."

Blair stared down at him as the wind brushed her hair across the scar on her cheek. The story seemed real. The expressions on his face left no clues that he was feeding her a lie. It even made sense.

"And then my friend died," he said. "His kids were grown and off on their own, and no one knew where his wife was, so no one really cared, and I started thinking about getting away from it all, from all the things that reminded me of my family. I just had to get away and I didn't want to do it hounded by bill collectors. In my twisted thinking back then, I started to believe that, if I took his name, I could *be* someone else for a while."

"And what's your real name?" Blair asked.

"Richard Dugan," he said. "I've always been called Rick. It's only the last name that's different. That's why it was so easy."

She kept her eyes on his face. "Did my parents know about this?"

"Yes, they did," Rick said. "I told them at the very beginning. When a tenant comes to Cape Refuge, Thelma and Wayne have quite an orientation. They don't want any lies and they don't want any surprises. After I was here for a couple of weeks and had a job under that name, your father found some discrepancies in my story. He told me to either be straight with him or pack up and leave. So I told them the truth and gave them a copy of Rick Morrison's death certificate. As far as I know, they checked out my story and decided to let me go ahead using Morrison, just so I wouldn't wind up losing my job. I expected to have problems with the Social Security Administration soon, since I was using his social security number to get paid. It was getting really complicated and tangled, but they agreed to let me work it out. They had a lot of compassion, your folks did. They really wanted to help. I was at a place in my life where I felt so numb and paralyzed that I just wanted to escape everything, including me. If I could have stepped out of my own skin, I would have."

The moon was rising, casting its own light over the trees and the ground and the swing where he sat. The light caught the edge of his eye, and she could see a tear glistening there. Yes, she did understand that desire to escape. She had felt that way many times.

"I miss Thelma and Wayne," he said, and his voice broke. He touched his finger to his eyebrow and began to cry. Slowly she let go of the gun.

"I guess it was selfish," he said. "I just needed to get it off my chest. I just wanted to explain. I thought maybe you'd understand."

"Thank you," she whispered. "I appreciate your coming and telling me this. I did need to know."

Rick swallowed and raked his hands through his hair. "Jonathan Cleary did not kill Thelma and Wayne."

Blair nodded. "Try telling that to Cade."

"I can't imagine anybody doing that to them," he said.

She thought back to this morning, and the way Gus had watched her as she watched Rick. But before she could bring it up, she saw headlights coming up the street. Her sister's car pulled onto the gravel driveway. Cade was right behind her in a squad car. Blair stiffened as Cade's headlights illuminated her and Rick.

Morgan got out. Her face was pale as she looked at Blair, as if asking if she was in trouble.

Cade wasn't so discreet. "What are you doing here?" he asked Rick.

"I was talking to Blair," Rick said. He met Morgan's eyes. "How's Jonathan?"

Morgan looked too shaken to speak, but she managed to get out, "He's fine."

"He didn't do it, Cade," Rick said. "You've got the wrong guy."

"So I've been told," Cade said.

Rick looked at Blair again, then down at his feet. "I think I'll go now."

"Okay," Blair said. "Thanks for explaining."

He nodded as if it was no problem, then got back into his car. As he pulled away, Blair went into action. "Cade, why didn't you call me back about those fingerprints?"

"Because I told Morgan. I thought she'd pass it on. Either Rick's never been arrested or the prints just weren't clear enough."

"I think it's the first," she said. "He told me why he changed his name." She related his story almost verbatim.

"And you believed him?" Morgan asked.

"You would have too," Blair said, "if you'd heard his confession."

"And why would he make it?" Cade asked. "What did he have to gain?"

"He figured out that we already knew," Blair said.

"So you still believe the story about his family?" Morgan asked.

"I do. It rings true, Morgan. The look on his face, the tears in his eyes, the things he says, they all ring true."

Cade started back to his car. "I'm going back to the station to run a check on Richard Dugan."

"Let me know as soon as you come up with something," Blair said.

He opened his car door and stood there before getting in, looking over the door at her. "You need to be more careful, Blair," he said. "Things could have gone bad just then."

"I didn't let him in the house," Blair said. "I went outside to talk to him." She pulled the pistol out of her pocket. "I had this the whole time, Cade. I'm not stupid."

"Well, I hope you're not naive, either. All it takes is a nice genuine-sounding, tear-jerking story to get you to let your guard down. We don't know enough about him, Blair." He let his eyes roam the trees around her property. "Why didn't he come to me with the story? If he knew he'd been caught, why wouldn't he come straight to the police?"

Blair shrugged. "Maybe he wasn't sure we'd told you. Why get himself into legal trouble if he didn't have to?"

"Maybe he knew we'd have the capacity to check that story out, and he didn't want to go that far with it," Cade said. "And maybe even tonight, he had some other purpose up his sleeve. Maybe my showing up thwarted things a little."

She couldn't help being a little disturbed. "Cade, something kind of weird happened this morning. After I took the glass to you, Morgan and I came back here, and I went for a walk. I saw Rick leaving for work, and I followed him at a distance. When I turned back, I saw that Gus was following *me,* standing back in the trees and watching. It gave me the creeps."

Cade stepped away from the car and slammed the door. "Blair, why didn't you tell me that?"

"Because it wasn't like anything *happened.* I wasn't sure it meant anything."

"Everything means something."

"Well, I've told you now."

Morgan, who had been nursing her own thoughts, couldn't stay quiet any longer. "Cade, if you're so doggone sure that the killer is still out there, then why do you have Jonathan locked up?"

"Because there's still more evidence against him than anybody else. But I'm not betting your lives on it, okay? I *want* Jonathan to be innocent. I want to find out somebody else did it. But if that's what happened, then the killer is still roaming around. I need every bit of information you have, when you get it, so that I can do my job effectively. Got it?"

Blair nodded. "Got it. I'm sorry I didn't tell you, Cade. I was exhausted and upset and real focused on those fingerprints. And then I fell asleep and the day got by me."

He softened a little, and she realized that he could use a few hours of sleep himself. There were dark circles under his eyes, and his face seemed to have aged in the last few days. He gazed down at her, emotions battling on his face. "Well, you needed the sleep," he said. "You need to take care of yourself."

Something about the worried look in his eyes and the gentle entreaty warmed her. She met his eyes and realized that his presence made her feel safe.

She was losing it, she thought. In the space of an hour, she had allowed two different men to move her. She was too vulnerable, too unguarded. Even with a pistol in her pocket, she was exposed.

She hated that feeling.

Finally, he got into his car, started the engine, and rolled his window halfway down. "Let me see you go into that house and lock the door before I leave, Blair."

She lifted her chin. "I'm a big girl, Cade. I've been taking care of myself for a long time."

"So did your parents," he said. "Like I told you before, I don't want any more crime scenes involving people I care about. Get in the house."

She didn't argue. She slipped the gun back into her pocket and followed her sister into the house. When the door was closed and locked, she heard his car pulling away.

CHAPTER

*C*ade didn't like the feeling in his gut as he pulled out onto the street between Blair's house and the water. The sight of Rick in the dark with Blair had set alarms off in his head. He wished he could hang around a little longer, maybe go inside, check out the locks, test the windows, see to it that they knew what to do in an emergency. But Morgan was still nursing her anger at him and had been cool about his even following her home from the station tonight.

And Blair seemed disturbingly defensive about the man she had begged him to check out that morning.

The trees made a canopy across the road, blocking out the light of the moon. He drove slowly, his headlights illuminating his path.

A shadow crossed the road up ahead. He flipped on his brights and tried to follow it. Had it been a deer crossing the road? No, it was tall. The size of a man.

He pulled his car over and got his flashlight, shone it into the woods. He saw the back of a man retreating through the trees. "Stop! Police!" he yelled.

But the man seemed to run faster into a cluster of magnolias and cedars, disappearing in the brush. Cade drew his weapon and sprinted after him, as he called for backup on the radio clipped to his shoulder.

He shone his flashlight through the woods, listening for the sound of those retreating feet, but he heard nothing. He tried to think where the woods would take him. If he could get cars to the other side, maybe they would get him as he emerged. He radioed his orders to the other four cars on duty and shone the light back and forth across the trees. There were too many places to hide and too many directions to run.

Cade's mind reeled with possibilities. Had Rick come back to linger outside Blair's home, hoping to catch them unaware?

Was it Gus, hoping to finish the work he had started with Thelma and Wayne?

Or was it someone else—a dockworker, a tourist, a resident with a beef against the family?

Realizing that he wasn't going to catch anyone with a head start in the black of night, he backtracked to his car. Already, two other officers had joined him on the street. Bruce Allen met him, his flashlight zigzagging its spotlight across the trees.

"See anything?" Cade asked him.

"No, Chief," Bruce said. "Didn't see a thing. You sure you saw somebody?"

"Positive." He glanced back at Billy, who was out of breath with excitement. "You?"

"Not a thing, Chief."

He radioed the other cars. No one had seen anyone emerging from the woods. Either he had gotten out before they arrived or he was still in there.

"All right," he said. "Bruce, I want you to do me a favor and just hang around here tonight. I'm a little uneasy about Morgan and Blair being alone. Just keep an eye on things, will you?"

"Sure thing, Chief."

Cade got back into his car, pulled back onto the street. Quickly, he drove the perimeter of the island to Hanover House.

No lights were on in the house, nor were any vehicles in the driveway, neither Gus Hampton's truck nor Rick's car.

He drove around town through parking lots of bars and past Goodfellow's looking for either of the two vehicles. Finally, he found the truck parked at Barracuda's, the town's most popular bar. He put his hand on the hood to see if it was warm. It was, but that didn't necessarily prove that Gus had driven it in the last few minutes.

He strode inside, where a live band played sixties tunes at an earsplitting volume. The air was heavy with the smell of liquor and cigarette smoke. His uniform called attention to him, and people turned and looked, whispered and pointed. He could feel the tension falling over the room as he searched the faces for Gus.

He saw him sitting at a table near the front, wearing jeans and a tight white T-shirt, and that trademark red bandana on his head. He smoked a cigarette as he tapped his feet to the music. Cade knew he would have noticed if the man running away from him tonight had been wearing a red bandana and a white shirt, but he supposed that Gus could have changed if he had really wanted to create an alibi. There was mud caked on the sides of his shoes, as if he could have been recently strolling through the woods or running away from someone who was after him. He was sweating, but so were many of those in the warm, stagnant air.

Cade went to the end of the bar, and motioned the bartender toward him.

"Hey, Cade. Don't usually see you here." The bartender was a short, heavyset man, with white-bleached hair.

"Sam, how long has Gus Hampton been here tonight?" he asked, pointing to the big Jamaican.

Sam looked across the room. "Didn't even know he was here," he said. "Might as well not be, for all I care, since all he drinks is water when he comes. Sits up there at the front of the room and listens to the bands, but doesn't contribute one thing to the running of this bar."

"So he just got here?"

"I'm not saying that," Sam said. "Just that I hadn't noticed him before now. Why? Is he involved in the murders? I heard you had Jonathan Cleary—"

Cade left him in the middle of his question and crossed the room to Gus. The song ended just as he reached him, and quiet settled over the room. He knew that everyone in the place had their eyes on him. He tapped on Gus's shoulder. The big black man turned around and looked surprised.

"Yeah, mon?"

"I need to talk to you outside, Gus," he said.

Gus looked around and saw that all eyes were on him. He put his cigarette out and got up.

"You got the curiosity up now," Gus said. "Why you need to talk to me again?"

"Outside, I said."

Gus acquiesced and started through the crowd to the door. He led Cade out of the bar and into the fresher air. "What is it, mon? Something else happen?"

Cade looked over his shoulder and saw that several of the bar's patrons had come to the door and were peering out.

"We can't talk here," he said. "Just leave your truck and ride with me to the station."

"Okay, mon. I got nothin' to hide."

Gus got willingly into the front passenger seat, as if to let anyone watching know that he wasn't under arrest. Then he adjusted the red bandana on his head, as Cade drove to the station.

Cade made Gus wait in the interview room while he touched base with each of the cars prowling the island and waited for the court reporter to show up.

Melinda Jane arrived in her bathrobe, with rollers in her hair. Though he had asked her to hurry, he had expected her to get dressed first. He hoped he could conduct a serious interview with her sitting there like that, but he had no choice.

When he had finished the preliminaries, he dove right in. "Gus, tell me about the dirt on your shoes."

"Dirt on my shoes?" Gus asked. He looked down at his feet. "What dirt?"

"There's dirt on your shoes, Gus. It's not on the path between Hanover House and where you work, and it's not sand from the beach. Where did you go to get dirt on your shoes?"

"I like walkin', mon."

"How long have you been at Barracuda's tonight?"

Gus shrugged. "Hour or so. Friend o' mine be playin' the bongos."

Cade had already sent an officer back to the bar to find someone who knew how long Gus had been there.

"Where were you before that?"

"At Hanover House. Why, mon? What's happened?"

"Were you, at any time tonight, in the woods near the library?"

"No," Gus said. "Why I be walkin' around in the woods at night?" He sat straighter. "That be near Blair's house. Nothin' happened to her did it, mon?"

"No, she's fine."

"You know it ain't me you need, mon," Gus told him, leaning his big elbows on the table. "I got nothin' to hide. But Rick . . . he got the secrets."

Cade stood back against the wall, frowning down at the man, and remembered what Blair had said about Gus watching her that morning. He had so many reasons to suspect him, yet no evidence, and you couldn't arrest a person for watching someone in a public place, or even for having dirt on his shoes.

There was a knock on the door, and McCormick stuck his head in. "Chief, can I speak to you a minute?"

"Sure," Cade said. He started to the door, but Melinda Jane jumped up.

"I'm coming too," she said.

He gave her a questioning look as he closed the door.

"Well, you didn't think I was going to stay in that room with a potential killer while you and Joe huddle, did you?"

McCormick looked down at her robe and hair rollers. "What in the world—"

"I was in bed," she announced, thrusting out her chin. "Cade said he needed me right away, so here I came."

McCormick grinned and turned back to Cade. "Mrs. Hern says that Gus had been with her at the House until just an hour or so ago. And the band members are friends of Gus, and they confirmed that he had been there an hour."

"Any word on Rick?"

"Still haven't been able to run him down," McCormick said.

"Well, now that's odd," Melinda Jane said, patting her rollers. "Don't you think that's odd?"

Cade shot her a look. "What's odd?"

"That he's missing," she said. "Looks to me like he must be guilty if he'd run off like that."

Cade couldn't believe a woman dressed for bed was advising him.

"Melinda Jane, leave the police business to us."

He went back into the room, and Melinda Jane took her seat. "I'm going to let you go, Gus," Cade said, "but I don't want you to leave town. I might need to ask you some more questions."

Gus opened his palms. "No problem, mon. I got no place to go."

Cade got one of the officers to drive Gus back to the bar. Cade went to his office and leaned back in his chair, wishing he could go home and catch a few hours of sleep. But he couldn't leave until Rick had been found.

He spent the evening on the phone and his computer, working to get information on Richard Dugan. There were no arrests, no convictions in the man's past. His fingerprints hadn't even been registered. For all he could tell, Rick had been a devoted father and husband until the day a drunk driver changed everything. He had even managed to find a picture of Rick Dugan from a newspaper article about the deaths of the wife and daughter. It matched the man who was staying at Hanover House.

But if he was who he said he was and had no ill motives in visiting Blair—then who had been in the woods?

It was midnight when they finally found Rick, pulling back into the driveway of Hanover House. They had brought him in, and Cade had gotten Melinda Jane to come back. This time she had taken the time to get dressed, but she still had a head full of rollers.

Cade was in no mood to beat around the bush as he faced the man who had disrupted his night. "I want to know where you went when you left Blair's house tonight," he said.

"I drove to Savannah and caught a movie," he said. He pulled the torn ticket stub out of his pocket. "Here's proof. Why? Did something happen? Are Blair and Morgan all right?"

"They're fine," Cade said. Rick's shoes were clean, and he was still wearing the clothes he had been wearing earlier. He looked down at the ticket's showtime, and mentally calculated the time it would have taken to go straight from Blair's to the theater. They didn't normally sell tickets much after the show had begun.

"Tell me about your name," he said.

Rick looked down at his hands. "I imagine Blair has already told you. That's what this is really all about."

"I want to hear it from you."

"All right. I'm not really Rick Morrison. My name is Rick Dugan. Rick Morrison is dead."

Melinda Jane gasped and began coughing. The rollers in her hair wobbled.

Cade waited until she could breathe again. "Why did you feel the need to go to Blair to explain that tonight? Why didn't you come to me?"

"Because I'm not stupid. I didn't want to get into any kind of trouble for stealing someone's identity. But I knew Blair knew, so I wanted to explain. I knew I'd have to account for it someday, but I was hoping to put that off as long as possible."

"I find it hard to believe that Thelma and Wayne would have covered for you, knowing you were breaking the law."

"I didn't use it to get credit or money or anything. I just used his social security number to get a job. If I hadn't, my creditors probably would have found me and garnished my wages."

"Why didn't you file bankruptcy?"

"Because that would have involved getting a lawyer, paperwork, money. I didn't have the presence of mind or the energy to do any of that. I didn't care if I dropped dead, so why would I care if my credit was ruined? I just wanted to be someone else." He closed his eyes and rubbed his face hard. "I don't want you to get the wrong idea about Thelma and Wayne. They kept a close eye on things to make sure I didn't use that name for any personal gain. They wanted me to tell my boss what I'd done, but they didn't force it. They just waited for me to do the right thing."

"Was there some kind of confrontation over it? An ultimatum?"

"No, not really."

"They didn't tell you to confess what you'd done or else?"

"Look, if you're trying to use this to pin their deaths on me, you're crazy. I didn't kill them."

Melinda Jane's fingers tapped wildly on the keys of her stenotype machine.

"But I'll do whatever I can to help you find who did. That is, if you don't lock me up."

Cade tried to think. Fatigue set its claws into his brain. Rick's story sounded convincing, but he couldn't ignore the fact that he had broken the law. He wasn't ready to let Rick go back out on the street until he had at least checked a few more things.

"I'm going to have to arrest you for identity theft," Cade said.

"What? But I didn't hurt anyone."

"It's against the law," he said.

"So you're putting me in jail?"

"Yes. You have the right to remain silent . . ."

Rick moaned as Cade read him his rights, then opted to call a lawyer. Even as he locked Rick into the cell next to Jonathan, he knew that the judge would probably set bail the next day. He couldn't prove that Rick was guilty of any kind of violent crime, so he couldn't hold him longer.

But at least the man was off the streets tonight.

CHAPTER

36

*S*adie's hopes for the next day were shot down when the manager of Goodfellow's had told her that she needn't come back asking for a job. He wasn't going to hire her. He hadn't given a reason, but she knew it had to do with the dirty clothes she was still wearing, the broken arm, and the bruises. She looked a little too rough, despite her efforts not to.

And though she had applied at every establishment along the four-mile stretch of beach, no one else had offered a job either. As a result, she hadn't eaten all day. She scraped together just enough for a stale sandwich at a convenience store, which she scarfed down on the way back to the boathouse.

She had left the boathouse door unlocked so she could come back in without getting wet. She went in, took off her shoes, sat on the floor at the open end of the structure, and hung her feet in the water. She zipped open the backpack and pulled out her picture of little Caleb, so small and trusting, and she prayed that he was all right.

She should have waited until she could take him with her, she thought. She should never have left him.

She wiped the tears on her face, and wondered if she should go back for him. Maybe Jack's wrath was worth it.

Her body was heavy with exhaustion, so she got into the boat. Lying down on the cushioned bench seat at the back of the boat, she fell into a deep sleep.

Morgan's despair loomed heavy, like a fog from which she could not escape. Her visit with Jonathan had simply tangled her in more frustration, grief, and loneliness. There was no pastor to counsel with, no clergy from her church who could minister to her in this dark time. Her father was the pastor, her mother the most attentive counselor. And they were both gone.

She longed to sit in the warehouse church that meant so much to her parents, but their blood still stained the floor, and the police had sealed it off. She longed to stare up at the pulpit where her father used to stand, Christ's ambassador to the lost and wounded who wandered here from the jails or the sea or the highways leading to this place.

She didn't want to go to Hanover House, where Mrs. Hern would need gentle attention. She didn't have it to give right now. And she didn't want to answer all the questions about why Rick had been arrested last night.

And she didn't want to be around Blair right now. She needed quiet, a few moments alone with God.

So she drove to the boathouse down the road from Hanover House. As she pulled onto the dirt road, she saw the building standing idle and alone among the trees and bushes at the edge of the river. The perfect place to sit and pray, the perfect place to get her bearings.

She went in and stood for a moment in the place where they had found Gus after the murders. The air was damp and muggy, and a fish scent blew in from the water. She breathed in the scent of cedar that reminded her of her father and tried to picture him stooped over his tackle box, puttering before going out to fish.

She wiped the tears on her face and stepped further inside. If she could just sit down here for a moment, soak in the scent and the familiar air of her father's life, maybe he would come back to her. But as she stepped across the floor, something in the boat caught her eye.

Morgan screamed.

The teenage girl in the boat sprang up. "I'm sorry!" she shouted.

Morgan grabbed a paddle hanging on the wall and held it like a weapon. "Who are you?"

"Sadie," the girl said. She stood up, and Morgan saw her casted arm and the bruises on her face. "I was just sleeping. I didn't have any place to go."

"What are you doing here?"

"I found it a couple of days ago," she said. "I've been trying to get a job, but no one will hire me, and the police won't let me sleep on the beach. It was the first boathouse I saw that wasn't next to a house. I just needed a place for a couple of days."

Morgan slowly lowered the paddle.

"Please don't call the police," Sadie said.

"Why would you sleep here?" Morgan asked, her heart still racing. "Where'd you come from?"

"West," the girl evaded.

"You a runaway?"

"No," the girl said too quickly. "I'm eighteen. I came here because it seemed like a wonderful place. Just the name—Cape Refuge. I thought it would be a nice place to live. But I can't find a job, and I don't have any money."

Morgan knew the girl was lying, that she couldn't be a day over fifteen, sixteen at the most. "How'd you get here?"

"I rode the Greyhound to Savannah," she said, "and there was this waitress in a diner, and she told me about Hanover House here and the nice people who owned it, Thelma and Wayne Owens, only I didn't know they were dead. And she brought me here and dropped me off thinking they would give me a place to stay."

Morgan gaped at her for a moment. "Thelma and Wayne were my parents."

Sadie brought her hand to her mouth. "Oh, I'm so sorry. I didn't know." She got out of the boat, grabbed her backpack, shoved her empty sandwich bag into it. "I'm leaving. Please, don't be mad. I won't come here again. I'm sorry I scared you, and I'm sorry I came in when I wasn't supposed to."

"Where'll you go?" Morgan asked.

"I don't know," she said. "I'm sure I'll find a job before long, and maybe then I can get an apartment on the beach—I've always dreamed of living on the beach."

The girl sounded like Dorothy dreaming of what lay over the rainbow. She was clueless about the price of beachfront property and had no resources of her own. She might get a job with hourly wages, but until she had a deposit for an apartment, no one was going to lease her a place.

For the first time, Morgan realized what her parents had felt each time they discovered a stray soul looking for refuge.

But she told herself the danger wasn't worth it. She didn't know this girl or anything about her. She was sure she had lied about her age. And she was certainly a runaway.

But she couldn't escape the fact that she needed a place to sleep, a roof over her head. There was a killer on the loose, and this child could be perfect prey for him. She couldn't send her back out there alone.

She set the paddle back on its hook and touched the girl's shoulder. "Look, you did scare me, but a lot of things are happening around here that I can't explain. I'm still upset about my parents' murders, and I'm a little on edge. But your waitress friend was right. My parents wouldn't have turned you away—and I won't either."

The girl looked so small and wounded, so innocent with her wispy blonde hair stringing around her face. "I'll be okay. Really."

"I know you will," she said. "You seem like a very enterprising young lady, very independent. But it would help you a lot if you had a place to lay your head tonight, and I have that big old house."

The girl's eyes filled with tears and hope, and she stepped toward Morgan. "You mean it? I could stay there?"

"I'm not promising it's safe right now," Morgan said. "There are other tenants there. Two of them are ex-cons, and the third one is in jail right now for identity theft. We don't know who killed my parents. But you could lock your door. It's better than sleeping out here. And meanwhile, there would be a place to take a bath and eat. I could loan you some clothes, so you'd have a better chance getting a job." She regarded her broken arm and the big bruise beneath her eye. "Or you could even just hang low for a while, let yourself heal before you start beating the bushes."

The girl's face reddened and twisted as she began to cry. "I'll pay you," she said. "Even for the time when I don't have a job— I'll pay you back as soon as I have money. I don't expect this for free."

"It's okay," Morgan said. "We have a whole list of donors who contribute to the Hanover House ministry. It makes it possible for us to take people in without pay until they get on their feet."

She took Sadie's backpack, slipped it over her own shoulder. "Come on," she said. "It's probably time you got settled. We have an empty room on the beach side of the house. I think you'll like it."

The girl couldn't stop crying as Morgan put her arm around her and escorted her out.

*A*s Sadie showered upstairs, Morgan called Blair at the library to tell her about the girl. Blair went ballistic and told her she was coming over to talk some sense into her. She pulled into the driveway moments later, her face full of indignation.

"What are you thinking?" she asked in a loud whisper when she found Morgan in the kitchen. "We don't even know if we should be keeping the tenants we have, and you're bringing new ones in?"

"You would have done the same thing," Morgan said. "She was sleeping in the boathouse. She has a broken arm and this big bruise under her eye. What did you want me to do, send her back to the people who did that to her?"

"She's not your problem," Blair said. "She's not *our* problem."

Morgan checked the oven, where she had pork chops baking.

Blair grabbed her arm and stopped her. "Morgan, we have to find her another place to stay. We have to tell her to leave."

Morgan swung around and leveled her gaze on her. "Mama and Pop would have done just what I did, Blair."

"Maybe that's why they're dead!" Blair said. "And if we've learned anything from it—"

"I learned more from their lives than I did from their deaths, Blair," Morgan threw back. "I learned that sometimes it's important to do the right thing, even if there's uncertainty."

Blair paced across the room, rubbing her temples. "I don't understand this treacherous compassion you have, just like they had. I guess it's a religious thing, something you feel you have to do to score points with God."

"It's not about scoring points," Morgan said. "We rescue others because God rescued us. We're grounded enough in reality to know that we could be floundering, just like them."

"Reality?" Blair asked. "There's no reality involved here, Morgan. You think you'll bring Mama and Pop back somehow by taking in lost souls like they did. But it's not going to happen. You're just going to have a lot more stress on you, a lot more responsibility."

"I can handle it," Morgan said.

"Well, can you handle moving back into this house? Because you can't bring a teenage girl home and leave her alone here. You have to stay and watch over her."

"The doors have locks on them. And Rick's in jail."

"Didn't you hear?" Blair asked. "The judge set bail this afternoon. He's already out. He'll be coming back here."

"I thought you didn't think he did it!" Morgan said. "You're the one who was all friendly with him last night."

"I *don't* think he did it," she said. "But Gus might have. *Whoever* did it is still out there."

"All right, then, you've made your point. We could bring her to your house to stay with us—"

"No!" Blair cried. "I'm not entertaining some teenage kid!"

"Then I'll have to stay here," Morgan said, picking up a dish towel and rubbing a wet spot on the counter. "And you too because I don't want you alone at your house."

"This is crazy, Morgan!"

"Go up and meet her," Morgan challenged. "See if you could have turned her away. You might think you could, Blair, but I don't think you're that cold."

"Well, that's great, Morgan," Blair said, her lips compressed. "I'm cold just because I think clearly while you think with your emotions."

"Sometimes emotions matter!" Morgan said. "They're not all just whims, you know. Sometimes your heart tells you the truth."

"And sometimes it doesn't. It didn't that day Mama and Pop were murdered. Whatever they had done that day, whoever they had seen, it did them in. And it doesn't matter how good they felt or how emotional, they're still just as dead."

Morgan started to cry, and she flung down the dish towel. "I just want their legacy to be worth it," she said. "I don't want it to end right here. I want some of it to stay!"

"Pass it on," Blair said. "There are other people who can love stray people. If Hanover House doesn't get closed down, we can find somebody else who will want to run it."

"Maybe we don't need to," Morgan said. "Maybe I can do it."

"Yeah, if you don't wind up dead yourself. And if you think Jonathan's going to sit by and allow it, even from jail, you're cracked."

"He'll get over it," she said. "He'll understand as soon as he meets her. He couldn't turn her away either. That's why I married him, because of the compassionate man he is."

Blair pulled out a chair and dropped into it. "All right, Morgan. I can see I can't talk you out of letting the girl stay. But will you at least honor *your* husband's wishes and stay with me tonight? You don't need to sleep in this house, and I won't."

Morgan leaned against the cabinets and crossed her arms. "All right," she said. "I'll ask Mrs. Hern to look after Sadie—if she can remember to—and I'll make sure she locks her door. After I take care of a few things around here I'll go on over," she said.

"You promise?" Blair told her. "You won't get all warm and fuzzy and decide to stay here, will you?"

"No," Morgan said. "I won't. I just want to make sure Sadie's settled."

Moaning, Blair left the house, muttering under her breath about her sister's lethal compassion, and the complications this girl had just added to their lives.

*B*lair left her car at Hanover House and crossed the street to the beach. She needed to walk, to get the anxiety and frustration out of her mind. She needed fresh air and a moment to think.

She walked around to the river side of the island, past her own house, and farther up to the dock where her parents had been murdered. The front door of the warehouse was sealed with crime-scene tape. She walked around to the pier where she had waited as they had searched the building and photographed their bodies. She sat down on the boardwalk, her legs crossed Indian style as she looked between the slats to the water beneath her.

Despite the heat, a chill ran through her. Looking across the water, she saw Jonathan's boat docked in its place. It was a good day for sailing. A schooner moved out from the dock, making its way toward the sound. Another was coming in, slowly drifting home. She knew some of them brought back sweet secrets of faraway places. Others would move on forever out of her sight, taking their secrets with them.

She wondered if any of those secrets had to do with murder.

She looked at the side door of the warehouse. It too was locked, but it didn't have any crime-scene tape across it. She pulled her keys out of her pocket and found the one her parents had given her long ago. She studied the door and wondered if she had the strength to go in and see the blood still on the floor.

She wanted to go in, not because it was the place of her parents' death, but because it was the place of their life.

Slowly, wearily, she got up and unlocked the door.

The building was as they had left it only four days ago, with its donated pews and the makeshift pulpit her father had put together. It smelled of mold and cedar and the faint scent of fish brought in by travelers and seamen who had sought out her parents for help with their sagging spirits.

She stepped across the room, to the stain on the floor where her parents had bled to death. She forced herself to look down at it, but that tornado of emotion whirled up in her again. Queasy, she went to the other side of the room and slipped onto the back pew.

She sat there quietly, wishing she had come to more of their services and watched as her father led in the singing, his deep bass voice ringing with authority and enthusiasm over the crowd, and her mother skittering here and there, greeting everyone who came in with hugs and encouragement.

She hadn't shared much of it with them. More than once her mother had cornered her and tried to talk her into coming. "But I don't believe what you believe," Blair had said. "It doesn't even make any sense to me."

Thelma had looked at her with genuine pain in her eyes. "How could you have grown up in our home and feel that way? Didn't you see all the ways God worked in our lives?"

"He works differently in mine," Blair said. Her hand came up and touched that scar on her cheek. Everything in her life had been filtered through that mangled scar. She didn't see the blessings they saw, for they were not always blessings to her, and she couldn't understand their reason for faith.

But now, as she sat in the pew and looked up at the pulpit from which her father had preached, she couldn't help wishing that she believed.

The front door opened, and she swung around, startled.

Cade stood in the doorway, squinting in as his eyes adjusted to the dim light.

"Cade," she said, catching her breath. "You scared me."

"Someone from Crickets called and said they saw you coming in here. It's still a crime scene, Blair. You shouldn't be here."

She sighed. "You know I'm not going to disturb anything. I just wanted to sit here for a minute." She pulled the pistol out of her pocket. "I've still got my friend with me. You don't have to worry."

He was quiet as he walked down the aisle and sat down next to her. "I know you want to be alone, Blair," he said, "but if you don't mind my saying so, there's got to be a better place."

"I didn't come here enough when they were alive," she said carefully. "I guess I just thought . . . that there would be some answers here."

He looked around at the dim building, its shadows speaking of death instead of life. She knew he wasn't going to leave, not until she came with him, but she wasn't ready to go. She just sat there, her eyes trained on that pulpit, trying to picture her father, his bright eyes laughing and full of life. She had never expected to see them shut in death.

"They changed lives here, Blair," he said softly. "There are people all over the world who've come through here."

"So I've been told."

"Some day when we get to heaven, you're going to see your pop surrounded by all kinds of people who are there because of him."

"I wish I could believe in heaven," she said. "You have no idea how I wish that."

Cade looked at her, and she was glad her scar was on the other side. "You can believe, Blair."

She shook her head. "It's not that easy for me," she said. "I need more evidence, more facts. I don't do well on faith alone."

"Your parents' whole lives were a testimony to Christ. *They* were the evidence."

"But they're dead," she said in a flat voice, "and now none of it really matters, does it? None of the hard work or the love they showed. None of the people they took into their home or the lives they sheltered. *They* weren't blessed or sheltered or protected. They were murdered."

"I see things differently," Cade said. "I knew them to be a couple that is still bearing fruit. Their faith multiplied into lots of other people, and it's still multiplying because those people are out there helping other people. They *were* blessed. You know, if you could sit down with your father and talk to him about this now, that's what he would tell you."

"My father would tell me a lot of things," she said. "But he could never adequately explain to me how God's control works with man's free will. Is God some kind of divine terrorist who uses homicidal maniacs to carry out his will? Or did that person wrench control from God in the time it took for him to get the speargun and shoot them? Was God sleeping when my parents were murdered? Or did he *cause* their murders? And if he did, then why should I pay homage to him? Why should I do anything for him? If there really is a God like that, it wouldn't matter whether I worshiped him or not. It didn't matter that my parents spent their lives serving him."

She hadn't meant to say so much, but her words were fueled by days of thought.

"I don't have all the answers, Blair," Cade whispered. "But your father taught me that God is not a 'divine terrorist.' He's a loving father, with purposes we don't even have the capacity to understand."

She breathed a bitter laugh. "There is no purpose in my parents' murder."

"Not from your vantage point," he said. "You may never see the purpose in it. But I bet they already know the good that will be done through it. Life is such a short little blip on God's timetable. He has all eternity to show them how the plan worked."

It was as if Cade parroted her father's exact thoughts, as if Wayne himself had sent him here to say these things to her.

But she didn't want to hear them. "How convenient, to believe that," she said. "To look at evil and decide that it's somehow good."

"That's not what I said."

"For me to decide to look at this as no big deal," she said, "as just another mysterious part of God's plan, would be the ultimate betrayal. I've earned my anger, and if I ever find out who killed my parents, you can bet that I've earned the right to get my revenge. How could *anyone* see any good in this? My parents were so convinced of a sovereign God. So this sovereign God *planned* to cut my parents off when they were doing so much good for so many people? I never could believe their stories, and I believe them even less now."

Cade shifted on the pew to face her. "What do you mean, their stories? Your parents never told a lie in their lives."

"Yes, they did," she said. "They told lies. Some intentional, some not." She tapped on the scar on her face. "This is the biggest one."

Cade only stared at her.

"They told me I was burned in a grease fire when I was three. But they wouldn't talk about it beyond that. So I'm left wondering why there's so much secrecy attached to a grease fire. It was a lie. But I don't know why they told it."

"What do you think happened?" Cade asked.

"I have no idea," she said, "just like I have no idea what happened to cause their murders. I may just have to add it to that long list of questions I have that I'll never have answers to."

She expected Cade to turn away, to act awkwardly, as if he hadn't noticed the scars. She didn't know why she had shared these things with him. She usually kept the terrible secrets of her heart wrapped up, never to be opened.

But Cade didn't turn away. Instead, he looked harder at her, his eyes cutting deep.

She hated herself for mentioning the scar. She didn't want to be vulnerable, not here with him, when he was sitting so close and looking at her with those eyes that used to make her nervous when she was fourteen. She had had a crush on him then, but she had countered it by acting as if she couldn't stand him, the jock who wouldn't have given her the time of day.

She wouldn't have him feeling sorry for her now. She thought of getting up and walking out, saying something rude and cryptic, something that shifted his focus off of her face.

But she felt tears rising in her throat, her nose, stinging behind her eyes. One move, one turn of her head, and her control would shatter, she was sure.

Cade touched her shoulder. "Hey," he whispered. "Look at me."

She forced herself to meet his eyes.

Slowly, his hand moved up her neck, into her hair . . .

She swallowed, but didn't allow herself to look away.

With the featherlight touch of his thumb, he stroked her scarred cheek.

No one had ever touched it before, no one besides her mother or father. Even Morgan had never intruded on that private part of her.

She felt herself recoiling, knowing it was blood red and testifying to the heart slamming out its cries that this was her scar and no one else's, and he couldn't just reach out and touch it like it didn't repulse him. He couldn't sit here and pretend—

"I know the scar bothers you, Blair," he whispered, stilling her thoughts. "And I know it's caused you a lot of pain. But I don't really see it anymore."

Her eyes misted, so she closed them, holding back those tears. But the hard protective shell over her heart seemed to melt, and one tear escaped, tracing its way down the crusted, blistery skin. He wiped that tear with a sweet, gentle pressure that made her heart break.

"I've known you for so long, Blair," he whispered, "that all I see when I look at you—is the prettiest girl on Cape Refuge. I don't see scars anymore. I know what you *really* look like."

She felt exposed, undressed, as if he could see things about her that she didn't want revealed. Slowly, she slipped back out of his touch.

He kept his hand suspended in the air.

She tried to say something logical, meaningful, something that would make light of what had just happened, but there weren't words like that inside her right now.

Finally, she blurted the only thing that came to her mind. "You really know how to kick a girl when she's down."

She could see that he wasn't fooled. "Blair—"

"I have to go." She launched out of her seat and crossed the floor, her heels pounding with vengeful purpose. She left Cade there and pushed through the hard wooden door.

As she quickly walked away, she told herself she could not look back. What had just happened had no meaning to her, and she would not think of it again.

CHAPTER

*A*fter Morgan had gotten Sadie fed and settled, and had made sure she was locked in her room, Morgan kept her word and headed back to Blair's house to spend the night. Though Blair's car was still at Hanover House, she wasn't there. Morgan figured she had gone for a walk, so she used her key to get in.

Quiet had become a friend to her, a comfort during these painful days. She had no heart or stomach for the radio or television, and even conversation with her sister could be an unwelcome intrusion. She lay down on the couch, closed her eyes, and slipped into a light sleep.

Some time later, she woke with a start. The house had grown dark as night fell over the island. She turned on a lamp and listened for the sound that had awakened her. Something scratched on the side window of the house. She lifted her head and looked toward it. The blinds were drawn, so she couldn't see out. She heard it again, so she got up and started toward the window.

The noise got louder, a scratch, scratch, scratching, like someone was cutting through the screen.

An animal? she wondered. Perhaps a bird tearing it, or some kind of rodent? She reached for the blinds and was about to pull them back when the glass broke. She jumped back and screamed.

Her mind reeled, and she grabbed the antique hutch that Blair kept near the window. She pulled it with all her might, shoved it in front of the window to keep the intruder from crawling through. Then she dove for the telephone.

Frantically, she dialed the number for the police department—but the line was dead.

She stumbled into the kitchen, groped for the silverware drawer, and pulled out a butcher knife. Holding the knife in her teeth, she turned the kitchen table on its side and pushed it against the back door. Then, with Herculean strength she didn't know she had, she slid the kitchen island against it.

She wasn't a strong person. Jonathan and her father had always done the heavy lifting in the family, but adrenaline surged through her as she ran around from window to window, grabbing the piano and shoving as hard as she could until it rolled against the front door. She backed away, and held the knife as she frantically scanned her fortress for a breach.

She heard a noise at the back door. He was trying to come through.

"Get away from here!" she screamed. "The police are on their way. I have a cell phone!" She knew that if the man outside was an islander, he would know that most cell phones couldn't get a signal here.

Her screams only seemed to make him try harder to get into the house. Terror pumped through her veins. She knew Blair had a gun somewhere in the house, but she didn't know where she kept it.

She heard a back window breaking, heard the scraping back of the cedar chest she had shoved against it on its side.

He was coming.

She stumbled and fell as she ran to Blair's bedroom, got up and groped for the closet door. She backed up into the corner of it and hunched down, clutching that knife in her hands, determined to use it.

Suddenly, she knew some of the terror her parents must have experienced in those last moments before their death.

As she crouched there, she prayed that Blair would not be the one to find her dead.

CHAPTER

*B*lair didn't go right home. She walked down the beach, trying to shake off the feelings that had come over her. Night was falling over the water, and the lights of Cape Refuge were coming on. She walked faster and faster back to Hanover House where she had left her car, hoping her speed and her determination would slow the surging of her blood and the racing of her heart. She hoped the blood pumping through her brain would purge her mind of the thoughts of Cade sitting next to her and seeing through the scars. There was too much pain that came on the heels of hope. She had enough pain in her life.

She got to her car, and stared at her windshield until her emotions were under control. Finally, she started home.

Morgan's car was parked in her driveway, and for a moment she wished she hadn't insisted that her sister spend the night there. She needed to be alone to think.

She went to the door and unlocked it, but it wouldn't open more than an inch. Something blocked it. She shoved harder. "Morgan!" she cried. "Morgan, let me in!"

There was no answer, so she rang the bell and banged on the door. "Morgan!" she cried. "Open the door! It's me." When there was no answer, she went to the window.

The screen was cut, and someone had broken the window. She called for her sister again, but no one came. Beginning to panic, she ran around to the back of the house, unlocked the back door. It too was barricaded.

Frantic, she went back to the broken window, knocked more of the glass out, then shoved the cabinet in front of it until she was able to climb through.

"Morgan!" She hit the floor and turned on the light. "Where are you?"

She sucked in a breath as she saw the furniture shoved against the windows and doors, a feeble effort to create a fortress. Panic rose like acid in her throat, and she clutched her gun and dashed for the bedroom.

Something moved in the closet, so she threw the door open. Morgan crouched in the corner, a knife clutched in both hands.

"Morgan!" she cried, and Morgan looked up and began to wail.

"He was coming in," she cried, still clutching the knife. "He broke out the glass, and the back door, and he was coming around . . ."

She was shivering in terror, and Blair took the knife out of her hand and pulled Morgan out of the closet.

"The phone line . . . I couldn't call . . ."

"I've got a gun," Blair said. "I can protect us. We need to get Cade."

Morgan's eyes darted from window to window. "We can't go out there."

"My car must have scared him," she said. "Come on. We'll go outside together. We'll get in the car and go to the police."

Morgan clung to her and followed. Blair shoved the piano away from the front door and held Morgan with one arm as she clutched the gun with the other.

They flew to her car and tore out of her parking lot. Within minutes they were at the police station.

Cade was standing at the door to his office when Blair and Morgan rushed inside.

"Somebody tried to break into the house," Blair cried. "They cut the phone lines. I found Morgan in the closet with a knife."

Cade didn't waste any time. "Dispatch all four cars to 214 River Road!" he shouted to the dispatcher. "Stay here," he ordered Blair. "Don't go *anywhere.*"

Cade rushed to his car and headed toward her house with his lights flashing. Then adrenaline and wrath beat through his head as he walked around the house and saw how close Morgan and Blair had come to death. The intruder had believed they were both at home, and he had been intent on getting to them.

"I got something," McCormick called from the other end of the garden.

Cade crossed the yard and looked over his shoulder. A red bandana lay in the dirt.

"Gus Hampton always wears a red bandana," McCormick said.

Cade didn't answer. "Bag this evidence," he told Joe, then he turned to Billy Caldwell and Alex Johnson. "Both of you, follow me over to Hanover House to arrest Gus Hampton. If he's not there, we're gonna tear up this island 'til we find him."

Leaving two officers to help McCormick, Cade and a convoy of police cars flew down River Road toward Hanover House.

CHAPTER

*I*t didn't surprise Cade to find that Gus's truck wasn't parked at Hanover House. He was probably cowering somewhere or scheming to go back to Blair's and finish the job.

Cade's urgent knock shook the house, and he heard footsteps. A woman's voice called, "Who is it?"

"Chief Cade. Open up."

The door slowly opened, and Cade saw the girl he had found on the beach. "What are you doing here?" he asked.

She was startled. "Morgan invited me," she said. "I haven't done anything wrong. She brought me here, and—"

"Don't worry," he said. "I'm not here for you. I'm looking for Gus Hampton."

"I don't know Gus," she said. "I just got here a little while ago. Mrs. Hern is the only one here."

He stepped inside, his eyes darting across the room. "I need to speak to Mrs. Hern, then."

"She's in the kitchen."

Cade found the woman standing at the sink. When she looked up at him, her face lit up.

"Hello."

He knew the woman had probably forgotten his name. "Mrs. Hern, I'm looking for Gus Hampton. Do you know where he is?"

"I can't say," she said, "but he could be over at ... uh ... that place on the dock. He likes to go there for supper sometimes. You know the place ..."

"Crickets?"

"Yes, that's it. He likes that place."

"Mrs. Hern, when's the last time you saw him?"

"Well, uh ... this morning, I guess. Why? What's wrong?"

"Blair's house was broken into tonight."

"You think it was Gus?" she asked. "Oh my, Gus wouldn't do that."

"I just want to ask him a few questions," he said. "But take my advice and lock your doors tonight, just to be on the safe side."

He could see the fear on Sadie's face as she inched back to the stairs as if she was ready to hide in her room and lock the door even now.

He got back into the squad car and crossed town to the warehouse where he had sat with Blair a little over an hour before. The parking lot at Crickets was full, and he could hear music from inside. Life went on, even though the murder was just a few days old—not more than a few dozen yards from this place. No time to mourn during tourist season, he supposed.

Followed by the officers who had met him there, he went into the restaurant and looked around the bar. He stood there a moment, scanning the smoke-blanketed tables and the faces of diners and drinkers. Finally, he saw a man with his back to him sitting alone at a corner table reading the paper. He had a red bandana tied on his head. He had expected Gus to be without it, with his bald head shining. But he supposed Gus had more than one.

Cade turned to the officers who had come in with him. "Caldwell, go check with the bartender and waiters to see how long he's been here. Johnson, come with me."

Caldwell headed through the people to the bar, and Cade started toward Gus. He ignored the greetings of those who called out to him and kept his eyes instead on the man who may have just broken into Blair's house.

Gus looked up. "You again, mon?"

"I need to talk to you," Cade said through tight lips. "Come with me. *Now.* If you do it quietly and peacefully, I won't arrest you here."

"Arrest me?" Gus asked. "For what?"

"Are you going to come with me or not?" Cade asked.

Gus stood up. He was a good six inches taller than Cade and had at least fifty pounds on him, but Cade was angry enough to tear him limb from limb. "Mon, nothing's changed since the last time."

"In the car, pal."

Gus looked around uncomfortably, then decided to do as he was told. He stalked out of the building, closely flanked by Cade and Alex Johnson.

He got into the passenger seat of Cade's car and propped his elbow on the window. "I be sitting here minding my own business, mon. You making me look bad."

"We can talk about it at the station," Cade said.

As he drove back across town, Cade told himself that he wasn't going to let this man back on the streets tonight. Even if he didn't have the hard evidence he needed, he would lock Gus up and make sure that Blair and Morgan were safe for the rest of the night.

CHAPTER

I was set up, mon." Gus Hampton paced across the interview room, a fine sweat shining on his brown skin. "I never even been near Blair's house."

"Okay, let's just go with your story that you weren't the one who tried to break into Blair's house. Where exactly were you?"

"I be at work, mon. Then I went straight to Crickets."

Cade looked hard at the man. He wanted nothing more than to beat the truth out of him. He pictured him sawing through Blair's screen, breaking the glass, cutting the phone line, going from window to window in a murderous attempt to get at her and Morgan.

The justice system wasn't enough for people like that, he thought. He needed something more brutal.

Knowing his mind was taking him down the wrong path, he got up and stalked to the door. "McCormick!" he shouted.

Joe came to the door. "Yeah, Chief?"

Cade stepped out into the hall. "Help me out here, man, before I hurt this guy."

McCormick nodded. "Glad to."

"He claims he was at work, went straight to Crickets, never been to Blair's house in his life."

McCormick went in and dropped into the seat next to Melinda Jane. He leaned up on the table, looking at Gus with hard, weary eyes. "Gus, take off your shoes. There were footprints near the windows. Big ones."

Gus took his boots off and plopped them on the table. "Check them out, mon." He set his jaw and peered at Cade. "If that was my do-rag you found, it was planted there to make me look guilty. Rick's the *bandooloo*."

"He's the what?" Cade asked, irritated.

"The trickster, mon. He's dishonest, that Rick Morrison."

Cade didn't bother to confirm Gus's statement with what he'd learned about Rick.

"Ask him about the money he be stealing from his boss man," Gus said. "Even better, ask them. He be walking around all misty-eyed and mourning. 'Tom drunk but Tom no fool.'"

"What?" McCormick asked. "Who in the blazes is Tom?"

"It is a Jamaican expression, mon," Gus said. "Meaning things are not what they seem."

"Speak English, Gus, and we'll move along a lot faster." Cade got up and set both hands on the windowsill. He could hear Melinda Jane's fingers clacking on her stenotype machine.

"So tell me what you know about the thefts," McCormick said.

"What I know is that Rick Morrison stole money from his boss man," Gus said. "Check it out. You'll see, mon."

"How do you know that?" McCormick asked.

"I listen good," Gus said. "It's not that hard in Hanover House. You hear things and you put them together."

"And what did you hear?"

"That Rick stole money from his boss man, but he gave it back before they caught him."

"Oh," McCormick said without belief. "So there wouldn't be any evidence at all? No stolen money, no angry employer, no nothing? What does that prove?"

"That he is not an honest man. He has secrets. And if he be involved in this terrible thing, maybe he be trying to make me look like the one. He could have got my bandana out of my room. Or found it after I dropped it somewhere."

When they had finished questioning him, they let Melinda Jane go, and Cade stepped out with McCormick. "I want to lock him up," Cade said. "Too many things point to him. But you've got to get me more hard evidence or the judge will let him out tomorrow. What about the boots?"

McCormick turned them over and studied the soles. "These weren't the shoes used in the break-in attempt. The footprints weren't this big."

"So he changed shoes. Get a warrant to search his room. Call the judge at home."

"Will do."

"So what do we have? A bandana that may not be his, the fact that the argument between Jonathan and the Owens was over him, his access to the speargun, the fact that his shoes were muddy last night when I saw someone running in the woods near Blair's house . . ."

"But we have statements from his coworkers and the folks who saw him at Crickets. Basically, we have nothing to base an arrest on," McCormick said.

"But everything to base an arrest on. I'm locking him up. It's my job to keep the community safe, and there's no way I'm letting him back out there tonight."

He went back in and read Gus his rights. The big man took his arrest with a moan of resignation and allowed himself to be escorted to the jail cells.

As Cade walked Gus past Jonathan's cell, Jonathan came to the bars.

"What's going on?" Jonathan asked.

"You're going to have company," Cade said.

"What did he do?"

Cade didn't answer.

"I asked you, what did he do?" he yelled.

"He's a suspect in an attempted burglary," Cade said. He knew he would find out tomorrow as soon as Morgan visited him, but he wasn't going to get it out of him tonight.

"Whose attempted burglary?" Jonathan demanded.

Cade ignored him.

"Who did you rob, Gus Hampton?" Jonathan yelled as Cade locked him into the cell next to Jonathan's. "Did it have anything to do with my wife?"

"I did not do it, mon."

Jonathan rammed his hand into the cell bar. "Is my wife hurt? Cade, you let me out of here!"

Cade turned back to Jonathon with resignation. His friend was too scared for his wife to accept Cade's evasion.

"She's fine, Jonathan. Just a little shaken up. Somebody tried to break into Blair's house, but they didn't get to either of them." He started to walk out, but Jonathan wouldn't be silenced.

"You're going to leave me in here with him? Man, if he did it, doesn't that clear me?"

"Not yet," Cade said. "Just hold tight, Jonathan."

CHAPTER

*T*he next morning, Morgan tried desperately to keep busy. She paced the second floor of Hanover House, going from room to room and straightening up. The police had searched Gus's room but hadn't seemed to find anything.

She shivered at the thought of him being the one trying to get into Blair's house, so relentless in his efforts. She had no doubt that he would have been brutal if he had gotten in.

The bandana had convinced her that Gus was the culprit and that Jonathan had been right about him all along. She was glad Cade had him locked up.

Today might be the day that her husband was set free.

When she couldn't find anything else to do, she drifted to the door that hadn't been opened since she and Blair had taken the files out of the room and closed it behind them. She touched the knob, turned it, and stepped into her parents' room.

The fresh, clean scent of her mother's shampoo and father's shaving cream drifted on the air, and her heart swelled. She ran her hand along the bedspread, trying to picture them lying there and watching the news before turning in. How many times had she seen them like that?

She pulled the comforter back, took her father's pillow, and buried her face in it. It smelled of salt air and sea breeze, second-hand cigarette smoke from Crickets, and the slightest hint of after-shave—the unique combination of scents that she would always associate with him. She wondered if, later, when all the linens had been washed and the room had been cleared of their things, she would ever smell that scent again.

She climbed onto the bed and curled up, clutching the pillow against her chest. She felt as if she lived in a dream, one with no logical order, that made no sense. But it was no dream.

After crying for a while, she pulled herself off the bed and made it up, hiding any evidence that she had climbed onto it like a child onto a parent's lap. She went to her mother's closet and looked around at all the things stacked so neatly there. There were shoes in one corner in orderly rows on a shelf unit her father had built. On one side hung the dresses and pantsuits her mother had worn. She touched them each with reverence, feeling the fabric and the softness, picturing the way they had hung on her mother.

She looked up onto the shelves of the closet and saw an old teddy bear stuffed into the corner. It had been Blair's when she was a child, and she remembered her sister clutching that stuffed animal with all her might after skin graft surgeries that had left her weak and in pain. She had thought the teddy bear was lost. It had never occurred to her that her parents had kept it.

She went out and got a chair from the bedroom, pulled it into the closet, and stood on it carefully. She reached for the teddy bear. As she pulled it, some papers rustled beneath it. She stretched to look over the shelf and saw that the papers were in a shallow box and the teddy bear sat on it. She pulled the box out with it and got down.

She got down. Sitting on the edge of the bed, she held the teddy bear. Maybe it would give Blair comfort, she thought.

In the box there were letters from family members she had never met, people her parents had rarely spoken of. She skimmed the first one, saw nothing of importance, then turned to the second and third. Clutching the teddy bear, she tried to fathom why her parents had saved these letters over the years, what significance they might have had to be kept tucked in a box at the corner of their closet.

And then she came to one addressed to the little South Carolina town where she had been born.

Dear Thelma and Wayne,

I've thought long and hard about writing this letter to you. It's always easier to put the blinders on and keep quiet about the sins you see in the lives of loved ones, but you have those two children involved, and as their grandmother, I can't help telling you that one day your lifestyle is going to catch up with you and fall back on your children. You can't live a life of deceit and think that God will bless it. Now I know you don't believe in God, not because you weren't taught to, Thelma, but because you want to rebel as hard as you can against what your family embraced. But in your heart I know you know better. I won't lie to the police for you anymore. But I will pray for you, and mostly I'll pray for those little girls who don't deserve parents on the wrong side of the law.

You have a choice to make, Thelma and Wayne, a choice about how to spend your lives, a choice about how your girls will grow up. You've spun them into a dangerous web of lies and schemes, and the thought of it makes me ashamed and afraid. Turn back now before it's too late, before your children suffer, before you wind up in jail and someone else has to raise them. They don't deserve that. You know it's true.

And it was signed simply, "Mama."

Morgan slowly got to her feet, clutching the paper in her hand. She felt as if a hand had reached in and grabbed her heart, squeezing it so tightly that the blood would not beat through.

Her parents on the wrong side of the law? She looked back at the date of the letter and saw that she was only four at the time. That couldn't be, she thought. Not her parents. Always upstanding, model citizens, always willing to help others. How could her grandmother have thought that her parents were doing anything wrong? Yet, here it was, and her parents had kept it for all these years. Her grandmother had died two years later.

She heard Sadie coming out of the bathroom and crossing the hall, and she tried to pull herself together. Quickly she folded the letter up and stuck it in her pocket, clutched the teddy bear tighter, and went to the door.

"Sadie, do you need anything?" Her voice quivered as she spoke.

"No, thank you," she said. "It felt so good to sleep so late. I needed it."

"Good. Just make yourself comfortable. If you get hungry, you're welcome to eat anything in the kitchen." The words came out of her mouth by rote, almost amazing her because she didn't feel like being helpful or generous. Instead, she felt like finding a dark place and weeping again for the double loss she felt now. The loss of her parents' lives—and even worse, the possible loss of her image of them.

She stumbled downstairs to the telephone in the kitchen and dialed Blair's number.

"Hello?"

"Blair." Morgan's voice was soft, breathless. "I found something in Mama's closet. I want you to come over here. Meet me across the street on the beach."

Then without saying anything to anybody, she stumbled out of the house and off the porch, clutching the teddy bear to her chest and the letter in her fist. She crossed the street, out onto the sand and to the edge of the water. One of the chairs her father had built and put out there for the guests was damp with the spray of water. Without drying it off, she sat down and studied the letter again, then put it back into her pocket.

The wind whipped through her hair, slapping it into her face, and she shoved it back and wiped the tears from her eyes. After a while she heard Blair's car pull up into the driveway. Her sister came over, her loose dress flapping against her body in the wind.

Blair saw the teddy bear at once, and her step slowed. "Where'd you find that?" she asked quietly.

Morgan tried to swallow back the knot in her throat. "In Mama and Pop's closet."

Blair reached down and took it, looked at it almost objectively, for a moment, like someone analyzing a piece of evidence. Then she sat down in the chair next to Morgan and slowly pulled the teddy bear against her. "I've wondered where this was. I think about it every now and then."

"They kept it for you," she said. "I guess they knew that you'd need it again."

Blair looked out on the water, her eyes fragile and shadowed.

"There's something else." Morgan pulled the letter out of her pocket again, slowly unfolded it. "It's a letter from Grandma."

"Which one?" Blair asked.

"Grandma Simpson. It's to Mama and Pop. Back when I was about four and you were one."

Blair took the letter out of her hand. "Why did they keep it all these years?"

"Read it," she said. "You'll see."

Morgan watched as Blair's eyes scanned over the letter. At first they were objective, as they had been when she had taken the teddy bear. Then they changed to surprise, then to astonishment, and then to a deep sadness. She brought those grieving eyes back up to her sister.

"Mama and Pop—on the wrong side of the law? That's just not possible. I can't even picture it."

"There are other letters in that box," Morgan said. "I haven't gone through them all. I saw a few of them. They were pretty benign. But it was almost like Mama and Pop kept them because they were some kind of connection with their family. And think about it, Blair. All these years we've never really known any of them. It was like they cut them off years ago. And this letter kind of tells us why."

"Our parents have never broken the law," Blair said, brooking no debate.

"But they haven't always been Christians, Blair," Morgan said. "What if there's something about their past that we don't know, something that happened before they changed?"

"People don't change *that* much," Blair said. "I know you believe in that new creature thing, but I don't. We're talking about inherent personality traits. Our parents have never had that kind of deceit or scheming in them. Maybe Grandma had it all wrong. Maybe she just misunderstood."

"Mama used to grieve every year on her mother's birthday," Morgan whispered. "One time I caught her crying, and she said she missed her, that they'd had a fight before she died and she never had a chance to reconcile."

Blair looked back down at the letter. "Well, it shouldn't be that hard to check out. I mean, there are other family members we could call."

"But you have to wonder how much they knew."

"If our parents were con artists or something, people in the family would talk."

Morgan pulled her feet up on the chair with her and hugged her knees. "Do you think this has anything to do with their murders?"

"It couldn't possibly. This was twenty-four years ago. They've done too much good since then. But I'm still going to check it out. I'm going to find out what Grandma thought, anyway. There must be cousins, nieces and nephews, people who heard something. And then there would be police reports and a rap sheet on them if they'd ever been arrested." Her eyes drifted back out across the water as if the words "rap sheet" associated with her parents didn't quite fit. "This is all absurd, you know," she said. "Our parents never broke a law in their lives."

"But we don't know that much about them before we moved here," Morgan whispered.

Blair's hand came up to cover the scar on her face, as if that was the most critical evidence of all that her parents had a secret past. She looked back down at the letter again as if somewhere embedded in the message there might be an answer about the scars she had carried most of her life.

"I'm going to get to the bottom of this, Morgan," she said. "Trust me. If there's something to know, we're going to know it."

Morgan sighed. "I don't know if I feel right about that. Maybe we're just supposed to let our memory of them rest as it is. It doesn't seem that respectful digging into their past, looking for things they obviously didn't want us to know. And if they did have some kind of criminal past, I'm not sure I want anyone else finding out about it either. If we get on the phone with relatives and start asking questions, it might stir up a hornets' nest."

"We need to know," Blair said. "I need to know. And when we get to the bottom of this, then we'll decide what to do. Agreed?"

Morgan looked out over the water as a sense of dread crushed down on her. She knew she couldn't talk her sister out of this. It was a quest that she needed to embark upon, and Morgan had no right to stand in her way. "All right," she said finally. "Agreed."

CHAPTER

*T*he Madison Boat Shop stood on the coastal side of the highway. Cars zoomed by just yards from its front porch. Behind the shop was a dock where four boats sat in various stages of disrepair. Everyone in the area who had a boat that needed working on brought it here.

And it was where Rick Dugan worked.

Gus's words about the money being stolen from the boat shop had nagged at Cade since he had arrested him, and now he stepped into the shop and looked around, breathing in the scent of lacquer and wood stain. He saw Rick out on the back deck sweeping, and he stepped across the wooden floor and into the smaller room toward the back of the building. He found Gerald Madison at his desk with a pile of paperwork spread out in front of him.

"Hey, Gerald. How's it going?" Cade said.

The old man looked up and rubbed his mustache. He was always rubbing his mustache as if it itched, and Cade didn't know why he didn't just shave the thing off. The man looked as ragged as a homeless man, even though he was probably one of the richest men in town. Cade always wanted to point him to the nearest barbershop.

"How's it going, Cade?" he said. "Hear you been busy the last few days."

Cade shook Gerald's hand and took the seat across from the cluttered desk. A big picture window at the back of the office drew his gaze, and he looked out on the boats that some of the employees worked on.

"Hear you already arrested two people about the killings," Gerald said. "Do you know yet why they did it?"

Cade shrugged. "I can't think why anybody would do a thing like that. But I had a couple of questions to ask you."

The man stiffened and leaned forward on his desk. "Fire away."

"I heard a rumor," he said. "A rumor that you had a theft recently, that a good bit of money was stolen, but that you didn't report it."

Gerald's mouth fell open. "Now who told you a thing like that?"

"Doesn't matter," Cade said. "Is it true or isn't it?"

"Don't matter now," Gerald said. "The money was returned. There was never a need to file a report."

"Returned?" Cade asked. "How much money are we talking about?"

"Ten thousand."

Cade whistled under his breath. "Ten thousand dollars? What, was it in the cash register?"

"No," Gerald said. "It was embezzled."

"Embezzled?"

"That's right," he said. "I discovered it in the bookkeeping."

"Then you must know who did it," Cade said.

Gerald's eyes shot to Rick out on the deck, and Cade didn't miss it. "I have a few people who have access to my books. Maybe I trusted them a little too much. But the bottom line is it was returned."

"Did the thief confess?" Cade asked.

"No, never did. Still not sure who did it." He sighed and leaned back, picked up a cigar, and lit it. "I have a few ideas, but since he turned honest, I don't see no reason to press the issue."

"So you're still trusting him with the books?"

"I didn't say that," Gerald said. "But I figure everybody has temptation now and then. Long as their conscience turns them around, I reckon it's all right."

Cade got up and strolled to the window, looked out at Rick working. The rumor was that he had good carpentry skills that had translated well to this business. But he'd asked Rick once what he did before coming to Cape Refuge. Rick had said he was an accountant.

"Tell me about Rick Morrison," he said.

Gerald got quiet. Cade turned around and saw the closed look on his face. "If you think Rick Morrison had anything to do with Thelma and Wayne's murder, you're wrong. He's a decent man."

"You sure of that?" Cade asked.

"I'm a good judge of character," Gerald said. "Yeah, I'm sure of it."

Cade held his eyes for a moment too long. "Is he the one who stole the money?"

Gerald looked away. "I told you I don't know who stole the money. All I know is somebody put it back, and I can't very well go firing people when I don't have any evidence, especially when no real harm was done."

"You should have filed a police report," Cade said. "It could happen again."

"I don't think it will," Gerald said. "Besides, like I said, I'm taking over the books. It's about to kill me," he said. "But I'm doing it."

Instead of going back to his car, Cade walked out the back door and down the deck steps. He watched Rick Morrison work on the boat for a while, then strolled along until he got near the pier and the warehouse where Thelma and Wayne had been found. A family sat fishing for crabs from the pier just outside the warehouse. He watched as a tawny-haired boy slowly pulled up his line. A crab was wrapped around the chicken neck he used for bait. He scooped the crab up with his scoop net, examined it, saw it was a female, and threw it back in, holding out for a male with more meat. The kid's little sister laughed, her sound lilting across the wind.

Cade stood there a moment, listening to the sound of a sand-hill crane flying overhead and the gentle roar of the surf.

He walked back up to his squad car, got in, and sat behind the wheel. He wondered if either of the two men he had behind bars at the station really had anything to do with the killings, or if Rick Dugan out there on that boat was the culprit. He wondered if Rick had, indeed, stolen the ten thousand dollars and put it back. And he wondered how Gus really knew about it.

He started his car and pulled back onto the highway, made his way around the island back to the station. He had a lot of work to do tonight, he thought, but he was going to get answers before this day was over.

CHAPTER 45

*T*he letter from her grandmother about her parents' lifestyle plagued Blair into the night, and finally when she had given up on sleep, she got dressed and went next door to the library. She used her key to get in, then locked the door behind her, nervous about who might be lurking in the shadows. She kept her gun hidden in the pocket of her skirt, her hand curled around it. Then she went to the computer.

What lifestyle was her grandmother complaining about? And did it have anything to do with the scars on Blair's face? All she knew was that her parents had come from Charleston and that the burns had happened when she was three and Morgan was six. Her parents had never wanted to discuss it or dwell on those years. There were no pictures of that time, no fond memories, no traditions from that time etched in their family's consciousness.

She pulled up a file she had scanned into her computer a year or so ago, when she had ordered copies of her medical records from all the hospitals who had treated her.

She read back over the list of her injuries at age three. She had been burned in a house fire, it said, and had suffered third-degree burns on twenty percent of her body. The scars were still there, despite surgery after surgery, multiple skin grafts, new scars to fix old ones.

She checked the date of her injuries, jotted it down, then went to a database at a Charleston newspaper and pulled up its archives. If there had been a house fire in which a child had been injured, it would have likely been in the newspaper, Blair thought.

Quickly, she did a search of the newspapers in Charleston, searching for any articles with her name. Her heart pounded as she watched the bar move across the screen, and the hourglass telling her to wait. She didn't realize she had been holding her breath until the newspaper article loomed up on the screen. She saw the title: "THREE-YEAR-OLD INJURED IN HOUSE FIRE." She clicked it and waited as the small article filled her screen.

> *Three-year-old Blair Nicole Owens suffered multiple second- and third-degree burns in a house fire Tuesday. Officials said that the child was rescued from a second-story bedroom. Her parents, who had discovered the fire and gotten the family out earlier, were not aware that the child had run back in to rescue a pet cat. The child was transferred by helicopter to the Anderson Burn Center where she is listed in critical condition.*
>
> *The cause of the fire is yet unknown, but arson is suspected, according to fire department sources.*

Blair sat back hard in her chair. Arson? If it had been a simple grease fire, why would they suspect arson? And from the sound of things, it had been so much more than a small grease fire. It had been a raging house fire. Why had her parents failed to tell her that?

Her hands trembled as she bookmarked that page. She turned off the computer and paced around the room, her shoes clicking on the wooden floor. Wouldn't Morgan have remembered a blazing house fire and Blair going back for the cat? Why wouldn't she have told her?

Her heart sped with aerobic force, and she closed her hand around that gun again and headed out of the library, locking the door behind her.

The clock on a shelf in her living room said 3:00 A.M., but time had little meaning to her now. She found Morgan sleeping deeply in Blair's bed, just where she had left her. She flicked on the light. "Morgan, get up."

Morgan squinted up at her. "What is it?"

"We have to talk. About the fire."

Morgan pulled her feet out of bed and sat up, squinting her eyes at the light. "What fire?"

"The one that did this to me," she said, pointing to her scars.

Morgan blinked and got up, staring at her sister. "Blair, I don't remember much about it."

"You were six!" Blair shouted. "You remember who your first-grade teacher was! Don't tell me you don't remember a fire that almost destroyed your sister. I found a newspaper article, and it said I had run back in to get the cat and that arson was the suspected cause—"

Morgan slowly sank back onto the edge of the bed. "The dreams," she whispered. "I have dreams at night of you running through flames . . . screaming . . . I have vague memories of you in the hospital and everybody thinking you were going to die. I remember holding your teddy bear, and Mama and Pop pacing the floor. But I just don't remember the fire." She stared at her sister as her mind reeled. "Why wouldn't I remember it if I was there?"

The look of genuine despair on Morgan's face convinced Blair that she was telling the truth.

"Maybe I blocked it out somehow," Morgan said. "I do remember having a cat, though. She must have died in the fire."

Blair pushed off from the wall. "Why did they say it was just a grease fire? Why didn't they tell me it was arson? Why was it they never wanted to talk about it?"

"Could it have anything to do with the letter we found from Grandma?"

"No," Blair said. "That letter was dated before the fire. But there are so many secrets, Morgan. Why? And now their murders . . . and more secrets."

Morgan took her hand. "These things happened twenty-something years apart, Blair. I doubt if the murders had anything to do with their past, don't you?"

"I don't know what anything has to do with anything," Blair said. "All I know is that I can't crack the code of my past, and nobody else seems to be able to either. There was only that one article that came up when I typed my name in. And it had so little information."

"Maybe you can talk to Cade. Maybe he has other resources."

She thought about that. "Maybe so. But he's got an awful lot on his plate already." Blair suddenly felt exhausted, as if the energy had bled out of her. But she didn't want to sleep. "I'm going to go to Hanover House," she said. "I want to see what else Mama and Pop have in their closet."

Morgan got up and grabbed the jeans she had laid over a chair. "I'll come with you."

"No, you don't have to. You need to sleep."

"Then why did you wake me up?"

Blair saw that Morgan was smiling. "I'm sorry. I was just a little upset."

"It's okay. I'm awake now. Let's go."

Everyone at Hanover House slept, so Morgan and Blair went in quietly and climbed the stairs. They closed themselves inside their parents' room. Then Blair went into her parents' closet where her teddy bear and the letters had been discovered.

Morgan brought a chair in, and Blair stepped up onto it and looked around at the top shelf. She found three shallow boxes full of papers. Some of them were just bills that her father had kept over the years in case of an IRS audit or dispute over the donations that kept the house running. Another was a box of papers on past tenants, and she flipped through and saw that none of the more recent ones was even represented there. The other was full of Bible studies and notes taken at church and at Christian meetings, useless things as far as Blair was concerned, but Morgan grabbed hold of the box as if it was a treasure she hadn't expected to find.

Morgan placed it on the middle of the bed and climbed up next to it. She pulled out her father's notes on the book of Romans, his extensive study on the book of Revelation, his *Experiencing God* book, several Precept courses—

Blair sorted through the papers, her eyes scanning her father's handwritten notes. She picked up one of the books and flipped through, and saw his notes jotted on every page. In a section on forgiveness, her father had written extensive notes on a chart entitled "Things He Forgave Me For." She looked down at the list, curious at the sins that had plagued her father.

Number one knocked the breath out of her.

"Morgan, look at this."

Morgan scooted across the bed and looked at the chart. "'Causing Blair's burns'?" She brought her astonished eyes up to Blair's. "How did he cause them? It was a house fire. You ran in to get the cat."

"There's more," Blair said. "He wrote, 'Because of my own choices, my little girl will suffer with scars for the rest of her life. She almost died. But even as she lives, each time I look at her face I realize what a wretch I was, how selfish and self-centered, how greedy. And even though Christ has forgiven me, I don't think I'll ever forgive myself. Her burns stand as a constant reminder of the enormity of the debt that was paid for me when Christ died on the cross. And knowing the cost of that, how could I ever deny anyone else forgiveness? I only hope that if Blair ever finds out, she'll forgive me too.'"

Blair set the book down as if it had burned her, and locked her gaze on her sister.

"How could it be his fault?" Morgan asked. "What could he have done?"

"I don't know," Blair said. "Do you think he started the fire? Maybe he was smoking in bed or something."

"Pop never smoked."

"But it had to be something. Maybe this story about me running back in for the cat wasn't true. Maybe he didn't really rescue me."

"He would never have forgotten you," Morgan said. "You know better than that. Pop loved us. I remember every time you had a surgery, he'd stay at the hospital with you around the clock, pacing the room and making sure the nurses didn't come in and disturb you when you finally slept, making sure your medicine was given on time, that you didn't have any unnecessary pain. He doted on you, Blair. I was even jealous a few times."

"Then how could he blame himself for this?"

"I don't know," Morgan said, "but maybe that's why he kept it secret. Maybe he didn't want you to know his part in it."

When they had exhausted the possibilities, they both crawled up in their parents' bed. Morgan fell off to sleep, but Blair only lay there, breathing in the scent of her father, resting in the sweet memory of his love for her and wondering how in the world he had almost killed her.

CHAPTER

The stolen money at the Boat Shop plagued Cade all night, and he couldn't help thinking that, somehow, it tied in to the murders of Thelma and Wayne Owens. The night had not been a good one for Cade. He had lain awake trying to put together Jonathan's part in the killings, Gus's, or even Rick's. He went to the police station before the sun had even risen and sat behind his desk trying to figure out what he had missed, whether he should let Jonathan and Gus go, whether he should bring Rick in for questioning.

But he didn't have to wonder any more, when Rick Dugan showed up to talk to him.

"I heard you were at the Boat Shop yesterday asking about me," Rick said, taking a seat across from Cade's desk. "I thought maybe you'd like to ask me those questions face-to-face."

Cade rubbed his jaw wearily. "Tell the truth, I was about to come question you."

"Then I saved you a trip," Rick said. "Is it about the murders?"

Cade didn't know if he wanted to go that far just yet. He leaned on his desk. "It was actually about some money that was stolen from the Boat Shop a couple of weeks ago. You know anything about that?"

Rick's eyes shot to the side, a sure sign of guilt in Cade's book. "Yeah, I remember. Gerald told us that the money was missing and that he was going to report it to the police. But before he did, a deposit for that exact amount showed up in his account. So he never reported it."

"Don't you find that odd?" Cade asked. "I mean that somebody who apparently worked for him would have stolen money and then returned it?"

"Well, if it was returned, then the person turned out not to be dishonest, after all. I guess he figures there's no point."

"Apparently that's exactly what he feels," Cade said. He watched the man try to get comfortable in his seat, and he thought of Blair sitting outside talking to him that night so quietly and intimately. A surge of resentment had washed through him at the sight of it. He hadn't trusted Rick Dugan since.

"Look," Rick said. "I know that every little thing matters when you're investigating a homicide. But it's not the theft of Gerald Madison's money or my name change that really bothers you. You want to know if I killed Thelma and Wayne, and I've told you that I didn't. I could never do that. I was at work until four that afternoon," he said. "The whole crew saw me."

"So somebody was with you every minute?"

He shrugged. "Well, I can't promise that. Sometimes we get to working on a section of the boat by ourselves. I mean, we don't work right on top of each other, if that's what you mean."

"Then it's possible that your every moment wasn't accounted for?"

"It was accounted for," he said. "And for all I know, somebody did see me every minute. I'm just telling you that I don't always work side by side with somebody else. I'm not on a chain gang. And after work, I started to go home, but then I decided to go by the Owens's boathouse and take the boat out. I fished until about six."

The same boathouse he'd found Gus in hours later, Cade thought.

"Thelma and Wayne Owens were the most decent people I've ever met in my life," Rick went on. "I don't know what I would have done without them. When I brought the boat back that day, I stopped by Crickets to get a bite, and I heard about the murders there." His voice broke and his eyes filled. "If I ever get my hands on the pitiful soul that killed them, I might just commit the first violent act of my life."

He drew in a breath and went on. "I went by Cricket's for lunch too that day. Got a hot dog. I don't remember seeing anybody at the warehouse when I passed. No cars, nothing. I keep thinking that I should have gone home or stopped by the warehouse instead of going to the boathouse. Maybe I could have stopped the killer. Maybe I could have changed things somehow."

When he had finished questioning him, Cade walked him out to his car and leaned in the window. He glanced around at the contents inside and saw a Delta Airlines envelope stuck in the visor pocket.

"Look, I'm more than willing to answer any questions you have," Rick said. "I'm in enough trouble for the name thing. I have to go to court about that next month. That's why I came by here today. I don't want anymore secrets, and I don't want to worry if you're going to come break my door down in the middle of the night and arrest me like you did Gus and Jonathan."

"I didn't break anybody's door down," Cade said.

"I'm just saying I'll answer whatever you want to know."

"Then tell me about that airline ticket."

Rick looked up at the ticket in his visor pocket, slipped it out, and handed it to Cade.

"I've been planning a visit to see my mother. She's in a nursing home in Atlanta," he said. "She has advanced Alzheimer's. She doesn't know whether I'm there or not, but I feel like I need to go see her. And while I was there, I was going to pay off some debts to clear the slate." He looked down at the steering wheel. "I've also been struggling with how to forgive the guy that killed my wife and child. Thelma and Wayne kept telling me that until

I forgave, I was never going to heal. They were the ones who encouraged me to go back."

"Well, I'd rather you didn't leave town right now," Cade said. "I might want to question you again."

"Fine," he said. "Look at the tickets. They don't even have a date on them. They're open-ended. Thelma and Wayne bought them for me."

"Thelma and Wayne?"

"Yeah. They also provided the money to pay off the debts. You can look in their bank account. They wrote the check right to me."

Cade frowned. "For how much?"

Rick looked reluctant to tell him the amount, but finally the words came out. "Ten thousand dollars."

That familiar alarm blared in Cade's head. "Thelma and Wayne gave you ten thousand dollars?"

Rick's eyes misted over, and he swallowed. "They were good people."

"Where did they get ten thousand dollars?"

"They said they had it in savings. For all I know, they may have borrowed it."

"Is that why the Boat Shop's stolen money turned back up, because Thelma and Wayne gave you the money and you didn't need it?"

For a long moment, Rick stared at him, his eyes dull, as if he struggled with whether to offer the truth or a lie. "If there's no police report and no money is missing, then there wasn't a crime committed, was there?"

Cade stared at him. "Let's just say the crime was undone. I'm thinking somebody's conscience got to them."

"Well, if that's so," Rick said, "then they wouldn't be much threat as far as murders were concerned, would they?"

"Maybe," Cade said. "Maybe not."

Rick started his car. The engine hummed to life, clicking and moaning. "You know where to find me if you have any more questions," Rick said. "And you know, you really ought to let

Jonathan and Gus go. Neither one of them has murder in them.
I'm not telling you how to do your job or anything, but let's get
real. I've lived with both of them, and they're not killers."

Cade took a step back as the car pulled out of the parking lot
and watched the man drive out of sight.

CHAPTER

47

*C*ade's phone call to Hanover House woke Blair up. It was late, past time for her to open the library, but he was glad she had gotten some sleep. "Sorry to wake you, Blair," he said. "I called your place first. I figured you were there. I need to go to Hanover House and look in your parents' office."

"What are you looking for, Cade?" she asked in a hoarse voice.

"Their checkbook," he said. "I want to know where Thelma and Wayne spent their money. I need to account for every penny."

"Why?"

"It's part of the investigation, Blair," he said. "Do you know where their bankbook is?"

"Yes," she said. "We'll be waiting."

Cade and McCormick got to Hanover House and knocked, but there wasn't an answer right away. He figured Blair and

Morgan were still getting dressed. It had only been a few minutes since he woke her up.

He slid his hands into his pockets and looked out at the water across the street. So much had happened since he had sat in that warehouse with Blair and touched her scars. Life seemed to have sped into fast-forward ever since.

You really know how to kick a girl when she's down.

The words clanged through his heart, a stark accusation. He hadn't meant to hurt her. They had just been sitting there alone, and he had felt so close to her. He shared her grief, her anger, her confusion.

He had only wanted to touch her. And he had meant what he said. He didn't see those scars anymore.

But she did, and her perception of herself was cruelly filtered through him.

The door finally opened, and Blair leaned out. "Come on in, guys." He could see that she hadn't gotten much sleep last night. Her eyes were puffy and red and so were Morgan's.

"Why do you need their checkbook?" Blair asked as she followed them into the office.

"I need to check the deposits. And I want to look through their other papers."

Morgan came down the stairs and followed them into the house. She led them into the room off the kitchen that their parents had used as an office. "It's just like they left it," Morgan whispered.

Cade saw the checkbook sitting on their desk, and he picked it up and thumbed through. "Where are their bank statements?"

"I don't know," Morgan said. "We have their file cabinet at Blair's house. I didn't see them in there." She opened a small cabinet in a hutch on her father's desk. Several notebooks were lined up there. "Here," she said. "I think they kept them in one of these."

Cade took a notebook and began flipping through the pages.

Blair came up beside him, her puffy eyes pleading. "Cade, please, take the bank statements, but leave the other papers where they are. I need them."

"What for?"

Blair looked at McCormick as if she didn't want to answer in front of him. Cade didn't want to make her. "Come here," he said. He took her arm and escorted her out to the sunporch at the back of the kitchen. The smell of oil paint filled the room, and a half-finished painting sat on an easel in the corner.

Blair looked up at him, and he could see the pain in her eyes. He hated that pain, and wished he could exorcise it from her heart.

"Tell me, Blair," he whispered.

She swallowed and looked out at the shed in the back of their yard, where her father used to putter. "I was looking into what caused my scar," she said. "There's some secret in my parents' past, some way my father was involved with what happened to me. Last night I found some notes he'd written. He said he'd caused my scars, but he didn't say how. And I found out that it was a raging house fire, not some little grease fire like they said, and the police thought it was arson. I have so many questions. I haven't finished going through all their papers yet, but I need to, Cade." Her eyes shone with her plea. "If I find anything that will be of interest to you, I'll give it to you, I promise. You know I'm trying to find who the killer is too."

"I need to go through them first," Cade said quietly. "Don't worry. If I find out anything about your past, I'll let you know. Besides, now that I know you're looking, maybe I can do a little snooping around on my own. I have a few resources you don't have."

She turned back to the glass door into the house. "Not many."

He knew that was true. With her library skills and command of the Internet, Blair was usually able to come up with information as fast as he could.

"Promise you'll tell me if you run across anything?" she asked.

"Promise," he told her.

"And do you swear that you won't mess up the files? I don't want anybody but you going through them, Cade. You get a bunch of hands on them, there's no telling what's going to become of that information, and it might have some link to my parents' past."

"You have my word," he said.

She sighed with resignation. "All right, take them," she said. "I'm trusting you, Cade. And I hope you'll hurry because I need them back as soon as possible."

"If I don't find anything vital in there, I'll give them back to you," he said. "But if I do, I'm going to have to hold it as evidence."

She didn't like it, he could tell, but he could see the trust in her eyes. That made his work a little less difficult as he went back to riffle through her parents' things.

CHAPTER

*B*lair was in no mood to take the phone call that came that afternoon from East Coast Properties, Inc., the company who had approached Thelma and Wayne weeks ago about selling Hanover House.

The caller identified himself as James Clark. "I'd like to make an appointment with you and your sister," he said. "I'd like to discuss the possibility of my company purchasing your property."

"It's still not for sale," Blair said, though she knew they should listen to the offer.

"We're prepared to offer you fair market value. There's no harm in discussing it with us. We'll come there, if you'd like."

Blair's eyes were tired from staring at the computer screen for so many hours as she tried to get more information about her parents. She swiveled her chair around and rubbed her eyes roughly.

She supposed he was right. There *was* no harm in listening. They could always say no. But in case money got tight or Hanover House became too much of a burden for Morgan to handle alone, it would be good to know what their options were.

"All right," she said. "We'll meet you at Hanover House at seven tonight. I'll make sure my sister is there."

James Clark was a tall man in a thousand-dollar suit. His pitch to buy the house was more persuasive than Blair had expected.

The offer was generous, too generous to ignore. But Morgan sat quietly through the whole conversation, her lips compressed with distaste.

When Clark left, Morgan started up the stairs without a word.

"Where are you going?" Blair asked. "Aren't we even going to talk about this?"

Morgan turned around at the top of the stairs. "Blair, this is my home," she said. "It's where we spent most of our childhood. It was our parents' dream. We have no business selling it."

"Morgan, the city council may not even let us keep it open. Contributions from our donors are bound to drop as they hear about the murders. And if it's not making money, the property taxes will do us in. Besides, who will run it?"

"I can," Morgan said.

"How can you say that?" Blair asked. "It took four people to run it before. Mama and Pop and you and Jonathan. And who knows when Jonathan is going to get out? It's just you now. And I don't want to help, Morgan. I don't want to take this on."

"You don't have to," Morgan said. "It's not going to be your problem."

She disappeared across the top floor, and Blair followed her up. Morgan had gone into their parents' room. So Blair rushed behind her. "It's my problem just knowing it's here," she said, "just knowing it's something that we own and that we can't manage."

Morgan sat down on the edge of the bed and ran her hand over the bedspread that her mother had made. "Jonathan and

I will manage it. He'll get out and come home, and we'll manage it."

"Jonathan will want us to sell it," Blair said. "You know he will."

Morgan wiped the tear rolling down her cheek. "Why would you say that?"

"Because he's been wanting the two of you to get a home of your own since you got married. He's done nothing but complain about this place. Just ask him."

"All right, I will," she said. "When I visit him tonight I'll ask him." Her eyes glimmered with tears as she stood up again. "I love this place."

"But let's face it," Blair said. "We're trying to solve their murder. We're trying to deal with the stress of what's happened in our lives. Keeping this place up is going to be a major burden, not to mention the questionable character of some of the tenants who come here. I mean, Sadie alone is going to drain you. And then there's Gus, if he gets out of jail. Mrs. Hern will be a handful before long. And Rick Whatever-His-Name-Is."

"I can do it," Morgan bit out.

"They're offering an awful lot of money," Blair said. "Think about it. We wouldn't have to fight city council anymore. We wouldn't have to deal with these tenants and all the questions flying through town. We could start over and try to put this awful thing behind us. We could invest the money and live off of it. And you and Jonathan could have your own place and start a family."

"We could have a family here."

"All right, just ask him. That's all I ask," Blair said.

"I said I would."

"Just see what he wants to do," Blair said. "But if he agrees with me, we'll sell it, right?"

Morgan looked down at her feet, struggling with the emotions on her face. "I don't know," she said. "All I'm promising to do is ask him."

CHAPTER

"Let's do it, Morgan," Jonathan told her when she visited him later that day. "Come on, we could get our own little place, maybe right on the beach, and not have the burden of always taking care of other people. We can't do what your parents did. I can't."

Tears filled her eyes, and her mouth trembled with the effort of holding them back. She didn't want him to know how disappointed she was in his answer.

"Think about it. Do you want to be a mother to everybody in town at your age, to every transient who comes up on a boat, to every prisoner released with no place to go?"

"Somebody has to do it," Morgan said.

"No, somebody doesn't," Jonathan threw back. "Your parents did it and it was wonderful. They filled a need. But they were *called* to fill that need, Morgan, and we weren't. You can't inherit a ministry and expect to be as passionate and adept at it as the people who left it to you. And whether you like it or not, the bed-and-breakfast is a ministry. It was their ministry. But not ours. There are other things we can do."

"But what about the tenants?"

"Well, Gus is here," Jonathan said. "He'll be in prison for the rest of his life, I hope."

"But there's Rick and Mrs. Hern, and now Sadie."

"Then give them notice," he said. "Give them time to find a place to live, and then we can sell."

"What if they can't find a place?"

Tears rolled down her cheek, and he wiped them, tipping her face up to his. "Of course they can find a place," he said. "There's real estate all over town, people renting places out. We're not the only game in town."

"We're the only ones who take in the refugees," she said.

"The what?" he asked.

"Mama used to say we took in spiritual refugees. That's what they are, you know."

He pressed his forehead against hers. "You have a sweet heart, baby. That's why I love you. I know God's going to use it somehow, but it doesn't have to be at Hanover House."

"Is it just the money?" she asked. "Is that what means so much to you?"

He leaned back. "That was a low blow," he said. "I just want a fresh start with you, Morgan. I'm being accused of your parents' murders. There will be people in this town who'll always think I did it. I'm not sure how it's going to be, living in that house without them—the shadow of their murders hanging over us like that. And I've never been comfortable with you being around what you call the 'refugees.' Call me overprotective, but that's what husbands are for."

She dropped her face in her hands. "I'll think about it," she said, "and I'll pray about it. It's just so hard. Too many changes all at once. And you're still in here. I thought you'd be out by now."

"I'm going to get out soon," he said. "As soon as Cade comes to his senses."

She got up, and he pulled her into a crushing embrace. Alex Johnson, the cop guarding them, turned his back to give them some privacy.

"I miss you," she whispered.

"Me too," he said. "It's going to be all right, okay?"

"I know."

"We're going to find who killed your parents. Beyond a shadow of a doubt, and they're going to be punished, and we're going to get our lives back to normal."

She nodded, trying to believe.

She wept all the way back to Hanover House, then ran inside, hoping to avoid any of the tenants until she got to her room. But Sadie was sitting at the top of the stairs.

"Hi, Morgan," the girl said brightly.

"Hi, Sadie."

Sadie's face changed as she saw the tears. "I was waiting for you, but if you're not in the mood—"

"What is it?"

"Nothing."

"Come on, it's okay."

"Well, you had some apples in the refrigerator. I was just wondering if I could have one."

"Of course you can. You can have anything you want in the kitchen. I told you that."

"But I don't want to take advantage," Sadie said. "I mean, it is a bed-and-breakfast, and this is a snack."

"The guests have full run of the kitchen, all the time." Through the blur of her tears, she regarded the bruise around Sadie's eye. It was healing to a yellow hue, and her arm, in its cast, still hung in a sling. The girl had been no trouble since she had come. She picked up after herself, helped Mrs. Hern, and kept quiet. "You can have all the apples you want."

"Thank you," Sadie said. She stood up and looked awkwardly at Morgan, as if she didn't know what to do next. "I'm still looking for a job, but when I get one, I promise to pay you back for all this."

"Don't worry about it," she said. "Just go eat."

The girl ran down the stairs.

Morgan was emotionally drained by the time she closed herself into her room. She lay on her bed, staring at the ceiling and wondering what she would do if they sold this place. What would it be like to have a home of her own with Jonathan, knowing she could never come here again and walk through these halls and into her parents' room?

The phone on her bedside table rang. She picked it up. "Hello."

"What did he say?" It was Blair's voice, soft and familiar.

Those tears assaulted her again. "He wants to sell," she said. "But I have to pray about this, Blair. I'm just not ready."

"Morgan, Mama and Pop wouldn't want you saddled with this."

"Have you and Jonathan been comparing notes or something? Mama and Pop loved these people. They would be proud if I followed in their footsteps."

"Of course they would," Blair said, "but they'd never ask you to. They wouldn't expect it of you. I don't want to spend the rest of my life taking care of people just because they did, and I don't think you do either. And your husband sure doesn't."

She closed her eyes and wished for sleep. "He thinks he might get out tomorrow, maybe the next day."

"That's great," Blair said, "but I guarantee you, he's not going to want to come back to that house. That money could help with a lot of things, Morgan."

"What would Sadie do?" she asked. "And Mrs. Hern?"

"Sadie'll find someone else to help her, just like she did this time. And so will Mrs. Hern. Maybe a nursing home—"

"I'm *not* putting her in a nursing home! She's a long way from needing that!"

"All right, then. We can help her find a place. I'm not suggesting we throw her out on the street."

Morgan closed her eyes. "What's the hurry?"

"Well, they might withdraw the offer," she said. "I mean, come on. It's a good offer. I say we go ahead and sign on the dotted line while we still can."

Morgan rubbed her forehead. It was beginning to ache. "I can't commit to this," she said. "I have to pray about it. You have to let me do that."

And with that she hung up the phone, no longer interested in what her sister had to say.

CHAPTER

50

ate that night, Jonathan lay on his cot, staring at the jail's stained ceiling tiles where a leak had come through. He had hoped to get out that day, but Cade still seemed intent on keeping him locked up. Even with Gus in the cell next to him, Cade's resolve hadn't weakened.

The anguished look on Morgan's face when he told her to sell Hanover House had haunted him since she left. He wondered if he was doing the right thing to ask her to sell. Was it selfish, or was he really thinking of her?

The thoughts kept him from sleep, and he wished he had the luxury of a telephone so he could call and check on her. He hadn't meant to give her something new to grieve over. She had already lost her parents, had practically lost her husband, and now he wanted her to lose her house too?

He wished he could see her again tonight and undo the damage he had done.

The silence was getting to him, and he wished he had a radio or a television to watch, something to get his mind off of his thoughts. But there was only Gus, and he had avoided talking to him since they put him in the cell next to him. The man had mostly slept since he had been here, and he hadn't seemed interested in conversation either.

But now, in the quiet of the night, he heard a soft sound.

"Amazing grace, how sweet the sound . . ."

It was Gus, singing quietly in his bed. He looked over at him in the darkness, saw him lying there on his back, staring at the same ceiling tiles. He listened as the man got to the end of the verse, and quiet settled back over the room.

"Do you mind?" he asked out loud, his voice echoing over the room. "I'm trying to sleep in here."

"Sorry," Gus said in that deep Jamaican accent. "I just be trying to pull a Peter. You know, when they sang in the jail and the walls fell down?"

Jonathan let that sink in for a moment.

"I always liked the mon Peter," Gus said. "He be saying the wrong thing, all the time, like me."

And like me, Jonathan thought, though he didn't want to engage with the man.

"And then there was Paul, killed all them Christians. God forgave him that."

Jonathan wondered if he had killed Thelma and Wayne, if his conscience was bothering him now, if he was consoling himself with the memory of forgiveness for a similar crime.

Soon he heard Gus singing again, quietly, in the night. Jonathan fell asleep to the sound of "Amazing Grace."

CHAPTER

*C*ade sat at the computer in his den that night, a yellow light illuminating the place where he worked. He had done a search on Gus Hampton in an attempt to find out what he could about the ex-convict he held in his jail cell, and now he tried to put the pieces together.

But as hard as he tried to concentrate, he couldn't get his conversation with Blair today out of his mind.

Abandoning his work, he decided to do a search through his databases for Blair's name. One article came up. He scanned its contents, about a house fire and the injuries sustained by the little girl who lived there. This was, no doubt, the article Blair had already found.

He typed in "Wayne Owens" and another article emerged. The article was titled "Man Arrested for Insurance Fraud." Frowning, he clicked it and read as it filled the screen.

> *Wayne Owens, 28, was arrested today follow-*
> *ing an investigation into the fire that consumed*

his house and injured his three-year-old daughter. The charge was insurance fraud. A spokesman for the district attorney's office cited evidence that Owens and his wife, Thelma, allegedly plotted to set fire to their house in order to collect the insurance money. Owens made no comment as the police arrested him.

Cade felt as if a fist had just belted him in the gut, and he sat staring at the screen. Wayne Owens, arrested for arson? Had he really caused the fire that did that to Blair?

He looked at the phone and thought of calling her, but he wasn't sure there was any purpose in sharing this with her. Did she need to know that her recently murdered father had been arrested for setting their own house on fire? Was there any purpose in telling her that her own father had caused her injuries?

Yes, there was a purpose, he thought. He had promised Blair he would tell her whatever he learned. He intended to keep that promise.

He picked up the phone and dialed her number.

"Hello." She sounded groggy, and he knew he had awakened her again.

"Blair, it's me, Cade."

"Cade?" she asked.

"Yeah. Sorry I woke you, but I just found something I thought you'd want to know."

"About my folks?" she asked.

"Yes," he said. "I did a search for your father's name in the Charleston newspaper, and an article came up about his being arrested for insurance fraud."

There was a long pause. "I never thought to do a search on his or Mama's name. I only entered mine. Give me the date of the article," she said. "I want to see it."

He read it out to her.

"Thank you, Cade," she whispered. "I've got to go."

She hung up, and Cade sat holding the phone, despising himself for bringing her more pain, and wishing he could rush to her side to help her through this. But he knew she wouldn't accept his help. This was something Blair would insist on dealing with alone.

Blair got to the computer as quickly as she could, and within moments had the Website with that article: "Man Arrested for Insurance Fraud."

Blair read the article, her heart beating against her chest. She sat there, stunned, for a moment, then forced herself into gear and found another article. Then she scanned the next article and the next until she had enough pieces to discern the whole story.

Her father had served time in jail. He had served several months, then their family had moved to Georgia.

Had *they* been refugees coming to Hanover House for shelter and safety from staring eyes and pointing fingers? Had Thelma and Wayne been trying to escape a rap sheet that told too much?

She got up and moved away from the computer, staring at the screen as if it radiated danger. This was too bizarre to fathom. It couldn't be possible. Her parents had never done a deceitful thing in their lives. They had always been in ministry. They had been helping people as far back as she could remember.

Blair took the chair across the room and sat in it with her knees pulled up, her arms hugging them to her chest as she stared at the screen. It couldn't be true. They were all lies.

After a moment she got up and forced herself back to the computer, quickly printed out the articles, then snatched them from her printer. Morgan had to see these, she thought. She had to help her discern what was truth and what was not. Morgan would know.

She ran back across the gravel to her house, the articles gripped in her fist.

Morgan sat upright in bed at the sound of the door opening, and she saw Blair's silhouette in the light of the hall lamp.

"Morgan, I've got to talk to you," Blair said.

Morgan reached for the lamp and squinted up at her. "Blair, I don't want to talk about selling the House anymore. I told you—"

"It's not that," Blair said. She came and sat on the bed and laid the articles out. "I've found out about Pop and Mama."

"What are these?"

"They're articles that fill in the blanks," she said. "Mama and Pop started the fire to collect insurance money."

"No." Morgan's word cut through the night, and she got out of bed and stood staring down at her sister. "If it says that in those articles, then they're lying."

Blair's eyes glowed with intensity, anger, sorrow. "Think," Blair said. "Think back when we were kids. Was there ever a time when Pop was gone for months at a time? A time when he could have been in jail?"

"*Jail?*" Morgan asked. "Blair, you've got to be kidding. Our father?"

"It says here he was arrested for insurance fraud. And then in this article," she flipped through the pages and found the one she needed, "it says that Pop was sentenced to a year. And then later on I found this little clip that tells that he was released early for some reason or another."

"Let me see that," Morgan snatched the articles out of her hand. "This can't be. I would remember."

"How?" Blair asked. "You don't even remember the fire. Morgan, don't you see? They lied to me about the grease fire because they didn't want us to know they had done such a terrible thing and that it resulted in these scars. And they didn't want us to know that Pop had served time, that when we came here *we* were the refugees and that the Hanovers had taken us in."

"It's not possible," Morgan said, "and you know it. It's just not."

"Do you remember Pop ever disappearing for a few months, when you might have been given some explanation about where he was?"

Morgan sat down and racked her brain. "I remember you in the hospital. You were there for months. I remember the surgeries, and Mama cried and paced the floors back and forth, back and forth. I remember you coming home and Mama being so glad . . ."

"So where was Pop?"

Morgan looked up at her, and her voice fell to a whisper. "I remember him coming home from a long trip, my being shy about seeing him again. I remember him picking me up and swinging me around."

"Then he was gone a long time."

"I remember him putting me down and looking up at the upstairs window and seeing you looking out. He burst into tears, then ran up the stairs to see you. He was careful picking you up, but he held his face against yours . . ."

"He'd been in jail, Morgan," Blair said. "He served time. The article says they were both charged, only Mama got off."

Morgan closed her eyes against the truth and ground her teeth together. "Stop this," she said, flinging the articles down. "I want you to stop looking for dirt on our parents. They haven't done anything wrong. They were murdered, and it wasn't because of some fire twenty-two years ago."

"That wasn't just 'some fire,'" Blair blurted. "It was my face."

"Pop would have never done anything to hurt you, and you know that."

"But he did," Blair said.

"Something's wrong here," she said. "This just isn't right. I don't believe any of it."

"Then I'll get more evidence." Blair started out of the room.

"And what'll you do then?" Morgan asked. "Are you going to be glad that our parents are dead?"

Blair turned back from the open door and leveled her dejected gaze on her sister. "I'll never be glad they're dead. I just want to know the truth, Morgan. And that's been real hard to come by."

She closed the door and hurried back to the library.

*M*organ got to Hanover House early. In a fog of depression, she made breakfast for Rick, Mrs. Hern, and Sadie. When the dishes were washed and put away, she sat down at the kitchen table, staring at her coffee.

"Do I look all right?" Sadie asked from the doorway.

Morgan looked up at her. The girl had washed and ironed her clothes—a pair of khakis and a bright pink shirt that Morgan had given her.

"You look fine. Why?"

"I'm going to look for a job," she said. "I'm not coming home until I get one."

Morgan smiled and got up. She pulled herself out of her mood and gave the girl a more critical look. "I think we could do something to cover that black eye, Sadie," she said. "A little makeup would do wonders."

Sadie shrugged. "I didn't bring any."

Morgan turned her toward the stairs. "Let's go to my room and see what we can do."

They went into Morgan's room, full of Jonathan's things, exactly where he had left them. Morgan ushered Sadie to a small makeup table in the bathroom. Around the sink were Jonathan's razor and shaving cream, a bottle of aftershave, some Lava soap.

"I heard about your husband," Sadie said. "I'm really sorry."

Morgan nodded. "I'm hoping he'll get out today. It's absurd, their keeping him in there." She pulled out the drawer in the table and got a small jar of foundation. "I think this might be close to your color." She got a sponge pad and began applying the makeup to the bruised area of Sadie's face. "Let me know if it hurts," Morgan whispered.

"It doesn't hurt," Sadie said. "I really appreciate this."

Morgan smiled. "It's fun. I haven't played makeup in a long time. My sister never wanted to when I was young. She hated mirrors."

Sadie was quiet.

"Sadie, did a boyfriend do this to you?"

Sadie seemed to struggle for an answer. "I was in a wreck."

"Really." It was a statement, not a question. She stopped dabbing and regarded the girl who had so many secrets. "It looks great. You can't even see it."

Sadie looked in the mirror, surprised at the change. "Wow."

"How about a little blush?"

"Okay."

She applied the makeup with a deft hand. "You're a pretty girl, Sadie. I have a feeling you don't know that."

Sadie looked embarrassed. "Thank you."

"When you apply for jobs, tell them to call me if they need a reference. I'll put in a good word for you."

"I will," she said.

When the girl had gone, Morgan decided to pray. It had been difficult the last few times she had tried. Anger and despair over what God had allowed to happen to her parents had paralyzed

CHAPTER

*W*ith the clothes Sadie had borrowed from Morgan, her hair clean and brushed, and her bruises carefully covered, Sadie had her hopes up that someone would give her a job. She walked down Ocean Boulevard, going from establishment to establishment. Commercial businesses crowded both sides of the road, tourist traps with colorful, useless products to sell.

She stopped at a hotel half a mile down the beach and inquired if they were hiring. She was politely but firmly told there were no positions open. She crossed the busy street to a gift shop where several tourists milled around. Swallowing back her tension, she approached the counter.

A tall woman, who resembled Popeye's Olive Oyl, stood beside the cash register, arranging a point-of-purchase display.

"Excuse me. Are you the manager?"

The woman looked up at her with her big eyes. Her voice lilted as she said, "Well, yes, I am. The owner, actually, if that makes any difference."

Sadie liked the sound of her voice and the kindness in those big eyes. "I'm looking for a job," she said. "I'm a hard worker. I'm staying at Hanover House, and Morgan Cleary can vouch for me."

"Oh, honey, I'm so sorry about Thelma and Wayne," the woman said. "Terrible, terrible thing." She sighed heavily, then seemed to shake her thoughts back to the question. "I'm afraid I can't afford to hire anyone. I run this place by myself. Where you from?"

Sadie stood straighter and lied. "Hilton Head."

"Hilton Head?" the woman asked, giving her a surprised once-over. "You don't look like anybody from Hilton Head."

She didn't know what that meant, but she didn't appreciate it.

"Are you an ex-prisoner?"

Sadie frowned. "No. I've never been to jail, and I never will."

"So how'd you break your arm?"

"I was in a wreck," she lied again. "I just came here because it seemed like a wonderful place."

"Oh, it is. I didn't mean to offend you. It's just that you don't look like an ex-con either."

She didn't know what ex-cons looked like. She thought of sweet Mrs. Hern. Would anyone have guessed that she had served time? And would her mother come out of prison someday with a tainted, used-up look that told people where she'd been?

"I'm sorry to bother you." She started back to the front door, but the woman stopped her.

"You know, there's an opening over at the paper."

Her eyes widened. "The newspaper?" she asked.

"Yep. Nancy Simmons was telling me yesterday she was looking for someone who could help her put the paper together. Her assistant had a baby and quit. Doesn't pay a lot, just a little over minimum wage, but it's something."

Sadie wanted to kiss her. "It sounds perfect. Can you tell me where the office is?"

After getting directions and being sent on her way, Sadie had more of a bounce to her step. When she arrived at the little house with the *Cape Refuge News* sign out front, she stepped onto the porch and knocked. There was no answer. She tested the door-knob and found the door was open. She stepped inside.

"Hello?" She waited a moment and heard machinery in the back, no doubt cranking out the latest issue. They probably hadn't heard her. She stepped tentatively inside, looking around at the little desk at the front and the cluttered office off the hallway. Then she stepped to the archway at the back of the house and peered inside.

"Hello," she called again. This time she caught the attention of a woman standing behind the machinery.

"I didn't hear you come in," the woman yelled over the noise as she came around the machine. "Can I help you?"

"The lady down the street at the gift shop told me that you were looking for someone," she said. "To hire, I mean. I'm look-ing for a job."

The woman led her back out of the room and closed the door as she surveyed Sadie's broken arm. "Don't know how much help you'd be with a broken arm."

"It's okay," Sadie said. "I'm right-handed, so it doesn't affect most of what I do. I'm pretty good with just one hand."

"You new in town?"

"Yes, ma'am," she said. "I'm staying at Hanover House."

"Ah," the woman said, nodding her head knowingly.

Sadie wondered if she was thinking the same thing that the woman at the store had. Maybe she shouldn't have told her where she lived.

"Hanover House, huh? So Morgan and Blair are taking care of you?"

"Mostly Morgan," she said. "I haven't seen Blair much."

The woman shook her head. "Horrible thing that happened to their parents. Who'd have ever thought?" She clicked her tongue, as if she wasn't all that sorry. "Do you have any experi-ence in the newspaper business?"

Sadie wished she could tell her that she had worked on the high school paper as she had wanted to, but the day applications were due she had been in the hospital with a broken jawbone.

"No, ma'am, but I learn real fast."

The woman assessed her again with that critical eye of hers. When Sadie expected her to show her the door, she said, "You can start tomorrow."

Sadie caught her breath. "Really? You're giving me a job?"

"You'll have to work hard," the woman said, passing her in the hall and heading to her office. Sadie followed. She searched her desk for something, then turned to the file cabinet and pulled out some papers. "Here's an application. Fill it out and bring it back tomorrow. And here's a Social Security form and a few other things. The job mostly consists of running errands and helping me with the layout. If you can write, sometimes I might even have you write an article or two."

Sadie's eyes lit up. It was too much to believe. "It sounds wonderful."

She started out of the room with the papers in her hands, when the woman caught her by her good arm and turned her back around.

"How old are you, anyway?"

"Eighteen," she lied.

The woman stared at her for a moment. "You don't have anything shady in your past, do you, 'cause my husband's the judge of this town, and it wouldn't do for me to have any shady characters from Hanover House working for me."

Sadie frowned. "No, ma'am. Nothing."

"So you just blew into town one day, and they took you in at Hanover House?"

"It wasn't like that exactly," Sadie said. "I've always thought it would be nice to live at the beach. As soon as I graduated from high school I headed out. They said I could stay at Hanover House until I got on my feet. So I'm trying to get on my feet."

"All right," the woman said brusquely. "Be here at eight tomorrow ready to work. When are you getting the cast off?"

"Another month or so," Sadie said.

"Well, I guess it's all right," the woman said. "We'll just work around it."

Sadie wanted to dance and turn a cartwheel as she headed back to Hanover House, but she didn't want the reputation of a crazy reprobate before she started her new job as a newspaperwoman.

CHAPTER

54

*T*he next morning, Morgan scrambled eggs for the Hanover House guests with one hand as she filled glasses with orange juice with the other. When the phone rang, she grabbed it up and held it to her shoulder.

"Morgan, it's Cade."

She froze, bracing herself for news about Jonathan. "What is it?"

"I've been going through your parents' bank statements," he said, "and I have their canceled checks. And there's one here for ten thousand dollars, and the notation on the memo says, 'Paid debt RM.' Did they mention this to you?"

She turned from the stove and gave her full attention to the phone. "No. Where would they get ten thousand dollars?"

"It came from their savings account," Cade said. "And RM is Rick Morrison. He told me they'd given it to him to pay off some debts. I'm not sure I'm buying that story."

"I don't know anything about it, Cade. They never said a word to me."

"All right," he said. "Thanks."

"Cade?" Morgan clutched the phone. "When are you releasing Jonathan?"

"I have no plans to do that, Morgan."

"Come on, Cade. You suspect Gus, and you suspect Rick— you know Jonathan didn't do it. Let him go!"

"I still have more evidence on him than anybody else. He owned the murder weapon."

"Well, then why are you holding Gus?" she asked. "You can't have two suspects for the same crime, unless they were working together, and you know that wasn't possible. Jonathan didn't even like Gus."

"I'm holding Gus for possible breaking and entering into Blair's house. Two different crimes."

"But you know that break-in was related to the murders."

"Morgan, I can't talk about this with you right now."

"Cade, I *need* my husband. He has no business being locked up in a jail cell."

"I'm keeping him until I'm satisfied that he's innocent," Cade said, "and I'm not completely satisfied yet."

Morgan slammed down the phone and pressed her forehead against it. She was soul-weary of this whole thing. The mystery of her parents' murders, Jonathan's incarceration, Blair's anger, her parents' past . . . Smoke rose up from the pan and she swung around. She had burned the eggs.

When the doorbell rang, she felt like screaming, "What now?" She moved the pan off the burner, then wearily went to the door. Melba Jefferson stood there holding a steaming casserole.

"I know I'm early, honey," she said, "but I wanted to get this to you so you could feed the guests for breakfast if you wanted."

Morgan's eyes rounded with relief. "A breakfast casserole," she said. "Melba, you're a treasure. Come in. I had just burned breakfast."

The woman bustled into the kitchen behind her. Morgan turned on the stove's fan to suck the smoke out of the room.

"I need coffee," she said. She poured them each a cup and urged Melba to sit down.

"So why are you up so early?" Morgan asked.

Melba shrugged. "I didn't sleep good last night. I was thinking about Thelma and Wayne." Her voice broke and she reached for a handkerchief in her pocket and dabbed at her eyes. "I'm sorry. I don't mean to get you going too. I know you're having worse trouble than I am."

Morgan sank down across from her and reached out to hold her hand. "Melba, you've known my parents a long time, haven't you?"

"Since the day they came to Cape Refuge," she said.

"Tell me about that," she said, her eyes riveted on the woman. "I mean, what were they like then?"

"Well, they were just the sweetest people I've ever known. Precious through and through."

"Really?" Morgan asked. "I mean, were they Christians then?"

"The genuine article," Melba said.

Morgan sat back in her chair, trying to decide whether to be honest with Melba in hopes of getting some information—or just trying to pump more out of her. She finally chose honesty.

"Melba, Blair and I ran across some information that was very disturbing to us. It had to do with my father being in jail. Do you know anything about that?"

Melba didn't look surprised. She dabbed at her eyes again. "Oh, honey, I promised your mother I'd never say a word. . . ."

"Then she confided in you?"

"Well, of course she did," Melba said. "She was my best friend."

"Melba, it would mean a lot to us if you could tell us whatever you know. Our imaginations are running wild. All we know is that Pop was accused of starting the fire that burned Blair— and that he wound up in jail for it."

"Oh, they didn't want you to know that," Melba cried. "What am I going to do now? I can't betray their confidence."

"You don't have to. We already know it. I just want you to clarify a few things."

Melba gave a sigh of resignation. "They changed, you know. Your father changed when he was in prison. There was a Christian group that came there and ministered to them. He accepted the Lord, then led your mother to Christ. They came here to start their lives over clean, where nobody knew them and they could work for the Lord unhindered. The Hanovers, who owned this place at that time, took them in right here in this house. And they started that seaman's ministry down on the dock, and then their prison ministry, and it was such a success. And then the church. Why, your parents hit the ground running as Christians and never looked back."

"Melba, did my father go to prison for insurance fraud?"

Melba looked down at her hands, as if trying to decide whether to tell her the truth. "Yes, but you know he changed. You know that in your heart."

"Did he start the fire that gave my sister her scars?"

Melba's face twisted. "Oh, honey, that plagued him till the day he died. God forgave him, but he never forgave himself for that. It was the defining moment in his life. The thing that brought him to his knees and made him realize that he had to change."

Morgan wilted. Blair was right. The newspaper articles were real. She looked around, trying to find something to do with her hands, something to keep her busy and get her mind off of this horror. Her parents putting her family in harm's way, almost killing Blair, altering her life.

She didn't want to break down in front of Melba, so she breathed in a cleansing breath. "Jonathan and Blair want to sell Hanover House."

The woman expelled a heavy sigh, then dabbed at her eyes again. "I kind of thought you would. It's a lot to handle, even for someone as young and energetic as you."

"I don't feel young or energetic right now," Morgan said. "I feel empty and numb, like I've been beaten up and shot with morphine or something. I don't want to be in this position. And I don't want to sell."

Melba looked around at the big, homey kitchen. "This was your folks' dream. They loved it so. It was a miracle when the Hanovers left it to them."

The woman got up and stuffed her handkerchief back into her pocket. "Well, I'd better be getting on now. I've got things I have to do." Morgan could hear the emotion still quaking in her voice. "You take care now, you hear? And let me know if there's anything I can do to help you."

Then pulling that handkerchief back out of her pocket, she headed out to her car.

CHAPTER

55

*C*ade needed a break. He wasn't sleeping well, and the workload that greeted him each morning kept him keyed up and worn out. Today, he got up with the sun, put his kayak into the river, and paddled out through the Wassaw Sound. He reached the Atlantic as the sun rose and warmed his bare shoulders.

The act of stroking, front to back, front to back, riding up over the waves, worked some of the tension out of his muscles. He drifted farther out, where the only sounds were rushing waves and birds swooping down for their morning meal. He paddled until the waves calmed, until he was floating alone on the current.

Questions swirled through his mind as he drifted. Did he really need to keep Jonathan locked up? What did Gus know about the money the Owens had given Rick? Why had Thelma and Wayne withheld the truth from Blair?

Why had Blair been so offended when he had touched her scars and told her she was the prettiest girl on the island?

You really know how to kick a girl when she's down.

He wished he could set her free from the prison of her life—the slavery to her philosophies, her beliefs about herself, her lack of belief about the God he believed in. Blair was the toughest woman he knew, but he wasn't fooled by that toughness. It was a cover. Like those scars were a cover for the beauty behind them, her toughness hid the soft heart inside. The heart that hurt. The heart that feared.

He knew these thoughts weren't helping him, so he turned the kayak around and paddled back the way he had come. He moved more easily this time, as the current took him in. When he got back to the river, it was only seven, so he put the boat up, showered, and got to the station by eight.

He got Gus out of his cell and took him into the interview room. "I want to ask you something, Gus," he said. "You knew about the money that Thelma and Wayne gave Rick. How did you know?"

"I overheard. The walls are thin at Hanover House. My room be next to his."

"Did they give him the money voluntarily, or was there some manipulation involved?"

"It was their idea," he said.

"Why would they do that?"

The big black man looked down at his feet and rubbed his eyes roughly. When he looked up at him again, Cade saw that his eyes were red with tears. "They told him that Christ paid for his sins, and the least *they* could do was pay for his debts." He swallowed back the emotion in his throat. "That be when I really came to Christ."

"I thought you were a Christian before they brought you here."

"Me too, mon. But I knew it up here." He tapped his temple. "That day they gave Rick the money, I got it down here." He put his hand over his heart.

Cade didn't say anything. He didn't want to believe Gus had been transformed by the same Holy Spirit that had changed his own life.

"So you heard all this firsthand?"

"Yeah, mon," he said. "They never knew. Too bad it didn't change Rick."

"What makes you say that?"

"He set me up, mon. Took my do-rag while I showered, then left it for you to find. He be your mon, not me."

When Cade had locked him back in his cell, he saw Jonathan sitting beneath the one lightbulb in the room, studying his Bible as if seeing it for the first time. Cade stood at the cell door, watching for a moment. Jonathan never looked up to see him. Finally, Cade went back out to his desk. He dropped his face into his hands and rubbed hard, wishing he knew what to do.

There Jonathan was, studying his Bible while sitting in a jail cell for murder—and another possible suspect sitting in the next cell, talking about how Christ had changed his life. He went to church with both men, believed the same things they seemed to believe.

But he had a job to do. So shaking those personal feelings out of his head, he went back to his office.

CHAPTER

56

*S*adie started her job at the *Cape Refuge News* that day. Morgan loaned her a blazer to wear with her khakis, so she felt mature and professional. Judge Randy Simmons, her boss's husband, was at the paper when she arrived that morning. He was a good-looking man who had a long gray ponytail, and wore jeans and tennis shoes even though he was on his way to the office. Sadie tried to picture him making serious decisions about people's lives. The judge who had sentenced her mother was a stern-looking older man with a bald head and an angry scowl on his face. Nothing like this old hippie who reminded Nancy to order the new T-shirts for the soccer team he coached.

Nancy Simmons, Sadie's boss, was a driven, ambitious woman who took her job seriously. She and the two writer/photographers who worked for her ran from telephone to file cabinet, from the grand opening of the new souvenir shop to the police station—with stops at the office in between. Nancy kept Sadie hopping with a list of things to do, but Sadie met the challenges head-on. She loved the pace of the office, the deadlines they were trying to meet before going to press, the drama of fielding new stories, and deciding what to tell their readers.

The first copies of tomorrow's edition were coming off the press as Sadie prepared to leave. Nancy tossed her a copy. "A memento of your first day's work," she said. "Congratulations."

Sadie clutched the newspaper against her chest as she walked back to Hanover House. As she passed the establishments that had refused to give her jobs, she held her head higher. She was gainfully employed now. She could support herself. And her fear that Jack would hunt her down and drag her back was diminishing. Things were working in her favor now, and she felt she could do anything.

Maybe someday she could even go back and get Caleb.

Hope burgeoned inside her, and she pictured herself playing on the beach with him as he started to walk, teaching him to float in the water, signing him up for a "Water Babies" class at the Y. Now that her feet were on surer ground, she dared to dream of security for the baby too.

She reached Hanover House and trotted up the stairs to the porch, slipped in through the screen door, and found Blair, Morgan, and Mrs. Hern in the kitchen.

"Hi," she said brightly.

Morgan looked up at her and smiled, like she was genuinely glad to see her. "Sadie, how was your first day at work?"

"Fantastic," Sadie said. "I did everything. I proofed articles, filed, and even took information for articles over the phone. It was fun. And look at this." She tossed the newspaper down on the kitchen table. "My first issue."

"Tomorrow's paper?" Blair asked.

Morgan smiled as she looked down at the headline, but her smile quickly crashed. The glass she was holding slipped out of her hand and shattered on the floor. "Blair, look!"

Blair grabbed the paper. "Convicted Killer Living at Hanover House."

"It's Rick," Morgan said, starting to cry. "Look at that picture."

"A mug shot," Blair said. She brought her eyes up to her sister. "I thought there were no arrests. I looked under both names. There was nothing."

Sadie's hands were shaking as she pulled out a chair and sat down. She shouldn't have brought the paper home, she thought. She couldn't believe she had been so stupid, so insensitive. But she hadn't even noticed the headline. She had just been so excited about the feel of the paper in her hands and the knowledge that she'd had a small part in it.

"Read the article," Morgan said. "What does it say?"

"'Rick Morrison is not who he says he is,'" Blair read. "'In fact, sources tell us that is not even his real name. The supposedly grieving man living at Hanover House, the place where ex-cons and criminals like to live, is really Rick Dugan.'"

"Ex-cons and criminals?" Morgan asked. "Give me a break!"

"'But according to police, Rick Dugan is not a suspect in the murders of Thelma and Wayne Owens. Two other residents of that home are, and they are currently in police custody. But should Rick Dugan be free to roam around Cape Refuge at will?

"'*Cape Refuge News* has recently uncovered information that Rick Dugan is already a convicted killer, who has been serving time at Angola for the murder of Rick Morrison. He escaped while on a work detail last year, and has never been apprehended.'"

"This can't be right," Blair said. "Cade would have told me."

"Mama and Pop would have known," Morgan said. "They would have checked out his story. They knew about the name change."

"Where did Nancy get this information?" Blair turned to Sadie. "Sadie, do you know who her sources were?"

"No, ma'am," Sadie said. "I didn't even know she was working on this story. We were working on things about the Tybee Beach Bums Parade and a groundbreaking for a new hotel and a grand opening for a new souvenir shop near the pier."

Blair slapped the paper down and stood up. "Well, there's only one thing to do. I'm going to ask him how much of this is true. And I'm going to ask him about the money Mama and Pop gave him. Something's not adding up here, Morgan."

She headed up the stairs, and Morgan followed.

"I shouldn't have brought that home," Sadie told Mrs. Hern. "It was stupid. I should have looked at it first."

"It's all right, dear," Mrs. Hern said, peering up the stairs. "Let's just stay down here and let them handle it."

Sadie was glad to do that, for she didn't want to be in the middle of a confrontation with a killer.

Blair got to the top of the stairs and felt for the gun in her pocket. She stormed across the floor to Rick's room and banged on it.

"Rick? Rick, it's Blair. I need to talk to you." Her voice left no room for debate.

But there was no answer.

"Rick, open the door!" she said. When there was still no answer, she turned the knob and saw that it was unlocked. She pulled the gun out of her pocket and slowly pushed the door open.

The room was spotless, and the bed was made up. His family picture still sat on the bed table, next to his clock and a notepad.

He had scrawled a note there.

"What does it say?" Morgan asked.

"It says, 'Dear Morgan, I know I'm not supposed to leave town with the investigation going on, but I just found out my mother's in the hospital, and I have to go see her. I'll be back when I can. Rick.'"

The scar on her face burned as she turned back to Morgan. "He's gone," she said.

Morgan tried to think. "Maybe he knew the article was coming out. It shouldn't be that hard to verify that his mother is in the hospital."

"I don't think she is," Blair said. "I think he dreaded being exposed and skipped town."

"You don't think he's the killer, do you?" Morgan asked. "All this time, living in this house? Acting all grief-stricken about his wife and child?"

"It sure does look suspicious," Blair said. "He got ten thousand dollars out of Mama and Pop. Maybe they found out about his background, so he killed them."

"Why would he leave us a note if he was running from the law?"

"To throw us off. To give him a head start."

Morgan brought a trembling hand to her forehead, and her eyes darted back and forth across the room as she tried to sort through the evidence. "That does it," she said. "I'm going to the police station. I'm going to tell them that Rick left and make them let my husband go."

*M*organ and Blair flew to the police station, and Morgan shivered with determination and anxiety as she marched into Cade's office and dropped the newspaper down in front of him.

"I thought you were looking into this," she said. "I thought you said you hadn't found an arrest record on Rick."

Cade picked up the newspaper and frowned as he skimmed the article. "I hadn't," he said. "They didn't get this information from me."

"Well, it's too late to do anything about it because Rick—whatever his name is—has already left town."

Cade stood up. "How do you know that?"

"Because he left us a note that he was going to visit his mother in the hospital. He's gone."

Cade pushed past them into the squad room. "Livvie," he said to the dispatcher. "Put out an all points bulletin for Rick Dugan, alias Rick Morrison. Six feet tall, blond hair, 175 pounds. Driving a white Honda Civic, '95 or '96 model."

"You have to let Jonathan out," Morgan said. "It's madness to keep him in here when you know he's not the killer. Rick has money that my parents gave him for no explicable reason. He had access to the speargun. Mama and Pop may have discovered he was a fugitive and threatened to turn him in. You have all the evidence you need. Now this is coming out, and he's disappeared. Instead of sitting here twiddling your thumbs—"

"I'm not twiddling my thumbs," Cade said over her ranting.

"—you should be out looking for him, tracking him down, and bringing him in, putting him in the cell where my husband is right now." She slammed her hand down on the table. "Let Jonathan out, Cade!"

"No, Morgan," he yelled back. "The district attorney is working on it now and the judge doesn't want to release him."

She wanted to scream, break a chair over Cade's head, make him listen to her. She had never felt such rabid rage before. "Well, I want to see him. Now!" she cried. "Let me see my husband!"

Blair touched her arm to calm her, but she jerked away.

Cade nodded to J.J. Clyde, sitting behind a desk. J.J. got up and escorted her to the back. She knew she was in no shape to feign strength for Jonathan today. He would have to take her as she was—shaken, frightened, and as angry as she had ever been in her life.

Cade was visibly shaken as he turned back to Blair.

"I know how it looks, like I've got some grudge against Jonathan and I'm trying to get even. But it's nothing like that. If I had it my way, I'd let him out. But I don't."

"Get real, Cade," Blair said. "If you told Randy Simmons that his own wife's article pointed to the killer, you know he would let Jonathan out."

"Maybe he will," Cade said. "But unless he does, I have to keep him here."

His face softened as he looked down at her. "Sit down, Blair," he said. "You look pale."

Slowly, she did. Her mind raced with the new facts whirling around looking for a place to fit. She remembered the night she had sat outside with Rick, and he had explained his past to her. She had foolishly believed every word. She had even defended him to Morgan and Cade.

"They'll catch him," he said. "They'll bring him back."

She swallowed and set her chin on her palm. "I got to tell you. He was good. He sure had me going," she said. "I thought he was a decent man. I liked him. I should have known it was an act."

Cade stared at her for a long moment, the concern in his eyes making her want to run away.

Finally, he slid his hands into his pockets and jingled his keys. "We're going to catch Rick Dugan and bring him in. You have to know, though, that I didn't discover the same information about him that was in the paper. I'll have to find out what their sources were and why it didn't come up on my search. Mine didn't show any past convictions, nothing out of the ordinary, except for his changed name. He explained that. I did find evidence of his wife and daughter being killed. Everything I found went right along with his story. He even told me about the money."

"Yeah, well, he explained a lot of things to me too," Blair said. "Apparently none of them were true."

She couldn't sit there and do nothing, she thought. She had to get home and do her own computer search, see what had failed in her attempts to learn about him. She wanted to see his police record for herself. She got up. "Tell Morgan that I've decided to walk home."

Not waiting for Cade's response, she took off across the parking lot and across the busy street to the beach.

CHAPTER

*C*ade double-checked his databases that night and the next morning, trying to find the information Nancy Simmons had cited in her article, but he could verify none of it. Angola had no one by the name of Rick Dugan who had escaped. He couldn't even find evidence that Rick Morrison had been murdered. His sources said that the man had died of a heart attack, just as Rick alleged.

The paper's sources were wrong.

He was about to pay Nancy Simmons a visit, when he got a phone call. The city council had scheduled an emergency meeting for that night. They wanted to discuss Hanover House in light of the news that day.

"Here we go," he whispered under his breath. They were going to use this article to put a scare into the people of Cape Refuge so they would want to close Hanover House. He hoped Morgan and Blair were strong enough to withstand it.

He headed over to the newspaper and found Sadie sitting at the front desk. She looked well groomed and energetic, like any other teenager on the island. Morgan had done wonders with her.

"Chief Cade," she said, coming to attention. "Is something wrong?"

He smiled at her and tipped his hat. "No, Sadie. Everything's fine. I just came to ask Nancy something."

She seemed relieved and wilted back into her chair. "Oh, good. I thought I was in trouble again."

He smiled and glanced around the desk that she had made her own. She had brought some fresh flowers from Morgan's garden and put them in a Coke bottle; a framed picture sat on the corner of the desk. It was a snapshot of a baby.

"Nancy's in the back," she said, "in the printing room. Want me to show you?"

"I know where it is." As he headed to the back, the sound of the printers grew louder. From the hallway, he saw Nancy standing in the hot room.

"Nancy," he said, "I need to talk to you."

She looked up. A thin film of perspiration covered her face. "Now, Cade? I'm kind of busy."

"It's police business," he said.

She sighed as if she wasn't impressed and stepped out of the room. "Okay," she said, leading him into her cluttered office. "What is it?"

He cleaned a few papers off of a chair and sat down. "That article in the paper this morning. I want to know where you got that information."

"What? About the beauty pageant?" she asked.

He didn't find that amusing. "You know very well what I'm talking about."

"Oh. Rick Morrison," she said with a grin. "Yes, the killer. Must be frustrating when the local paper solves the murder before you do."

"Where did you get the information about him being a convict?"

"I have my sources," she said. "I can't reveal them."

"Well, does it matter to you if they're false? I checked with the prison you mentioned and they've never had a Rick Dugan there. I ran that picture through my database and it didn't come up. I've even run his fingerprints through my database, and from the looks of things, he's never even been arrested."

She didn't seem too concerned. "Well, I can double-check it."

"That's it?" he asked. "You're not upset that you slandered a citizen who's done nothing wrong? That you cast fear into the hearts of the islanders, and that the city council has new ammunition to close Hanover House down? They've called a meeting tonight to discuss it."

"Really?" She grabbed the pencil from behind her ear and starting to take a note. "What time is that meeting? Where?"

"It's at the City Hall where it always is," he said, "at seven. Surely your 'sources' could tell you that."

"Look, I'm busy," she said, getting to her feet. "If you don't have anything else to say—"

He stood, appalled at her attitude. "You're not the least bit worried that the front page article in your paper today might be a bunch of lies?"

"I'm upset about it, okay?" she said. "I'm going to check with my sources. I'm going to find out what's going on."

"You need to ask your husband about slander and libel," he said.

She rolled her eyes.

"Show some judgment in your reporting, Nancy, or I'll make sure that every resident of Cape Refuge knows that they can't trust the *Cape Refuge News* anymore. You'll be out of business in two weeks. And when I find Rick Dugan, I'm going to encourage him to sue you for so much that you won't be able to keep it running anyway."

She gaped up at him. "What do you want from me, Cade?"

"A retraction would be nice. Something that tells the townspeople that you lied about this story, that you created a panic unnecessarily."

"Okay," she said. "I'll print it right underneath the article about how Rick Dugan extorted money from Thelma and Wayne before their deaths, how he skipped town the day my article came out, how he's still at large, how our pitiful police force wasn't able to catch up with him yet—"

"You're walking on thin ice, Nancy."

"Fine," she said. "Arrest me. See how long my husband leaves me locked up."

Cade's jaw popped. "If I could lock you up even for an hour, Nancy, it'd be worth it."

As he stormed out into the hall, he heard Sadie talking on the telephone. He stopped and tried to calm himself, taking a deep breath. Sadie's voice was low, as if she didn't want anyone to hear. "Atlanta, please. Miss Tina's Day Care?"

He looked up at her from his place in the hall. There was a pause as she got the number and dialed. "Uh, yes. I just want to check on Caleb Caruso," she said. "He's in Miss Jane's room. Nine months. Could you check on him for me? Tell her it's Sadie calling." Her voice broke, and he saw the tears on her face.

"I just want to know that he's all right," she said into the phone, "that he's not sick or anything, that maybe he doesn't have any bruises or cuts. Yes. So—has he been there every day?"

He saw her listening, her eyes intense as she took in every word.

"You're sure? I appreciate that. No, that's all right. Thank you." She hung up the phone and dropped her face into her hands.

Cade stepped out of the hall. "You okay?" he asked.

She wiped her face quickly. "Sure. I was just working on a story for Nancy."

"A story," he said. "It didn't sound like a story."

"I know," she said. "It's kind of silly. I get all emotional over nothing."

"She has you writing stories?" he asked. "How long have you been here, a couple of days?"

She straightened and lifted her chin. "I'm a good writer. I made straight A's in English."

"Journalism major?" he asked.

She shook her head. "No. But Nancy didn't ask for that."

"Yeah, she doesn't have real high standards, does she? You didn't by any chance write the article on Rick Dugan, did you?"

"No, of course not."

He knew she hadn't, but he was still angry. He nodded to Nancy's office. "Keep an eye on her, Sadie. She's ruthless."

Sadie looked at him as if she didn't know what he was talking about.

Sighing, he went back to his car and told himself that he needed to do some digging into the girl's past. She was calling about a baby named Caleb Caruso. Maybe he was her own child. Maybe her name was really Caruso too.

As soon as he had a moment to breathe, he would see what he could find out.

*J*onathan sat up late in his cell, studying his Bible with a zeal he hadn't had many times in his life. He had convinced Cade not to turn off the light yet, and Gus hadn't made any protest. He read with a new hungriness, searching for something, though he didn't know what. Finally, he heard Gus moving around in the cell next to him.

"Hey, mon," Gus said through the bars.

Jonathan looked up at him. "What?"

"We both be Christians, mon, am I right?"

"I know I am," Jonathan said.

"Well, I guess you don't be trusting that I am. I was thinking maybe we could pray together. "

Jonathan turned back to his Bible and stared down at the page. Had someone he considered an enemy really asked him to pray with him? The thought sent a cold chill through him. Then, suddenly, he was ashamed of himself. He set the Bible down and put his hands on his knees, staring at the concrete floor. Finally he turned around.

"You want to pray with me?"

"The Bible, it says whenever two or more—"

"Yeah, I know what the Bible says," Jonathan threw back.

"I heard Cade tell you about that city council meeting tonight," he said. "We need to pray on that."

Jonathan only looked at him for a moment. The gulf between them seemed as big as the lake out on his granddaddy's farm. He didn't want to do it, but he was supposed to be the big Christian. And Gus, well, what was he? Jonathan wondered. Another ex-con? A threat to his wife? A beloved man Thelma and Wayne had taken under their wings? Had he been the one to try to break into Blair's house when Morgan was there, or had he really been set up as he claimed?

"What is the harm?" Gus asked. "We both be behind the bars."

Jonathan realized that was true. "All right," he said, "I'll pray with you."

Gus nodded and sat down on the one chair in his cell, folded his hands, and dropped his elbows onto his knees. Jonathan did the same, and they both bowed their heads and closed their eyes. After a few seconds of silence, Jonathan looked up.

"You go first," he said. He wanted to hear Gus pray, wanted to hear if it sounded like Gus was used to talking to God, wanted to hear if his words sounded sincere.

Gus's gruff voice grew soft, and he began to speak in a tone that was reverent and awestruck. "My gracious Father, the God of the universe," he said, then paused for a moment as if catching his breath at the awe inspired by such a statement. "I be amazed at you," he went on.

Jonathan opened his eyes, looked over at Gus, and saw the tears on his face and the struggle he was having to keep his voice steady. A sure knowledge came over him that this man in the cell next to him was no threat at all. His heart was sincere. He was, indeed, a brother.

Jonathan closed his eyes and bowed his head in earnest this time, joining his heart with Gus's in prayer.

*T*he standing-room-only crowd at City Hall that night made Blair feel like a movie star whom people had come to gawk at. It was a minidrama, she thought. The daughters of the murder victims having their property snatched out from under them. Adrenaline rushed through her as she prepared for the fight.

"I don't care if we're going to sell the place," she whispered to Morgan. "I'm not going to honor them with that announcement tonight. It's the principle of the thing. They have no right to do this."

Morgan touched her hand. "I wish I knew what Mama and Pop knew that day. They were so confident that they were going to win. They had some information, they said. I wish they'd told me what it was."

"Well, if it was important, we'd have found it by now."

Morgan looked around uncomfortably. "Blair, why don't you let me do the talking?"

"Oh, no," she said. "It's me they're going to contend with. They're counting on our not having the strength to fight. I resent their tactics, and I won't let them get away with it."

The mayor hammered his gavel and drew the microphone too close to his mouth. It produced instant feedback, and people moaned and yelled for someone to fix it. It was like the opening bell in a boxing match, only she didn't intend to shake hands.

"This meeting will come to order," the mayor said. He had dressed up for the occasion in a Hawaiian tourist shirt and a pair of khakis with sandals on his feet. At least Sarah Williford hadn't worn her bathing suit to the meeting, Blair thought.

"As everyone knows," the mayor began, "we're here to discuss Hanover House and the fact that polls show that seventy percent of the citizens on Cape Refuge want to see it closed down."

"Give me a break!" Blair sprang up and pushed through the crowd to the microphone. "Don't give us that stuff about polls," she said. "You know good and well this island doesn't have a pollster. What did you do, go out on the beach and ask random people? Did any of them happen to *live* here?"

She didn't get the cheers that she got the last time she had done this, the night her parents were murdered. The townspeople were scared now and weren't on her side anymore.

"Blair and Morgan, first of all, let me offer my greatest sympathies in the death of your parents," Fred Hutchins said. "The whole island has felt the loss. It's with great sorrow that we called this meeting tonight."

She didn't have the patience for condolences. "Yeah, I'm sure you cried your eyes out as you were putting on your Hawaiian shirt and rehearsing how you were going to twist the knife. Could we just get on with this?"

The council members looked at each other uncomfortably, then went on. "Very well," Fred Hutchins said. "As you know, we're a little upset about the article on the front page of the paper today. It's about one of your tenants being a convicted killer and a fugitive from the law. Your family has been harboring him. He is a danger to the community."

"Cade told me this afternoon that he can't confirm that anything in that article was true."

"I understand Rick Dugan has left town. Is that true?" the mayor asked.

"He left," Blair told him. "But that certainly doesn't implicate Hanover House in any way. It's not a reason to close it down."

"Blair, we all understand your pain," Sarah said, her saccharine voice carrying without the mike. "We understand about the grief that you and your sister must be going through. Having Jonathan on his way to prison for murder, and then Gus and now Rick—"

"My husband is not going to prison," Morgan said from her seat. "He is not guilty!" She stood up. "Do you hear yourselves? You just named three people you think committed these murders. What do you think it was, some kind of killing club?"

"Might have been," the mayor said. "As a matter of fact, there's been quite a bit of speculation that's just what Hanover House is."

"Why are you out to get us?" Morgan demanded. "What do you want?"

"I'm not out to get you," he said. "We just want to make Cape Refuge a safe island for everybody."

Blair wasn't going to let that go. "Well, you don't care about making it safe from tourists. You want more of them to come through, not fewer. And you don't know anything about them. They could be from anywhere. It's your *plan* to have strangers roaming this island. And you can thank the *20/20* piece on Hanover House for tourism picking up thirty percent already this summer. At least the tenants at Hanover House work in the community and contribute to it. People get to know them. They're not just phantom convicts roaming around mysteriously."

"They might as well be," the mayor said. "Rumor has it that you're now harboring a teenage runaway."

"She's not a runaway," Morgan shouted. "She says she's eighteen. She can live anywhere she wants to. She came here with a broken arm and a bashed face, and I wasn't going to turn her away."

"Maybe if you did start turning people away you wouldn't be here before us tonight," he said. "We wouldn't have to close you down. But since you refuse to be discriminating about who you keep in that place—"

"That place is my home," Morgan shouted as tears twisted her face. "It's where I live. It's where my parents lived. How dare all of you treat their memory like it was nothing?" She stumbled across the people in her way, and grabbed the microphone in front of her sister. "My parents did something for every one of you, and you know it. They took in people with problems, even some of you. You have no right to stomp dirt into their memory like this. They were coming here to fight for Hanover House the night of their deaths, but they never made it here. And if they had made it, you would have seen a fight like you'd never seen before. Hanover House was their dream and they loved it, and it was the best thing they'd ever done. We have the right to do whatever we want with our own property, and you don't have the right to choose that for us."

Silence fell over the room as Morgan's impassioned speech hung in the air. Under her breath, Blair whispered, "Way to go, Sis."

"Well, we appreciate your plea," Fred said. "Now, we have a few residents who would like to speak."

Blair shot a look around, daring anyone to get up and speak against them. No one did.

"I think you're mistaken, Mayor," she said. "Looks like these fine folks are here to support us."

"I have something to say." Sam Sullivan got up at the middle of the room, and slid his hands into his pockets. "Mayor, Council Members. . . ."

"Would you mind going to the microphone, please?" Fred asked.

Blair relinquished it to him but didn't sit down. If he was going to trash Hanover House, then he was going to do it standing right beside her.

"Uh . . . Mayor, Council Members . . . I just want to say that ever since Wayne and Thelma's death, I've been afraid to leave my family alone. I don't want my children playing outside. I want to go back to the life we knew before this tragedy. And I think we can do that if Hanover House no longer harbors criminals."

"Hanover House never harbored criminals," Blair said. "And as for wanting to go back to the way things were before the tragedy, you don't know the half of it, Sam. But the fact is that closing Hanover House won't solve anything. We're still going to need a police force because there are still going to be people who come and go with evil intentions. But Hanover House is one of the good things about this island." It had gotten hard to talk around the lump in her throat, so she forced it down and forged on. "Most of you know I'm not a religious person. But I've got to tell you, I do believe in good and evil. Hanover House is a light in this town. It's a beacon and a symbol of all that Cape Refuge should be. A symbol of all it can be. If you shut Hanover House down, then what hope do any of us have?"

She met Morgan's eyes and saw the tears on her face. She fought valiantly to keep her own emotions at bay. "We're a community of kind, warm, caring people. That's what our name represents. Sadie, the teenager who is staying at Hanover House, told us she chose Cape Refuge because the name sounded inviting. It sounded like a pleasant, beautiful place. And she found that it was. Hanover House drew her here because some stranger in a café in Savannah told her that she wouldn't be turned away. Don't you want to live in a place that opens its arms to people like Sadie, instead of a place that shuts them out?"

Hattie Brumfield, who sat near her, got up and waddled to the microphone. "I just have to say that Blair makes a good point, but I feel that we can be a sweet, warm, inviting town without Hanover House. In fact, we might be more inviting if we didn't have the reputation that Hanover House brings us."

Blair rolled her eyes. "What reputation? You've never had a problem with Hanover House until the 20/20 special came out. It's always been known as a good place, not a breeding ground for killers."

"Then explain what's happened with that Rick fellow," Hattie said in her deep drawl. "There he is, a fugitive convict who's already killed once, and now he's disappeared. He could be anywhere, and all because your parents, rest their souls, invited him here."

"I told you, the article is probably a lie. We haven't been able to confirm it."

"Well, Nancy couldn't print it if it wasn't true," she said. "Could you, Nancy?"

Nancy, who sat taking notes on the front row of chairs, said, "We're in the process of confirming the story, but I can tell you that I do trust my source."

"Your imagination is your source, and you know it!" Blair bit out. "Since when has anyone put any stock into what she writes? She makes a hobby of misquoting everybody on this council, and you're telling me that she prints truth? *She's* the one who ought to be shut down!"

Fred banged his gavel. "That's enough, Blair. I think we've heard enough. It's time we took a vote."

She didn't sit down, just crossed her arms and watched as the council members settled in to cast their votes.

Fred got his pen and pad, as if he wouldn't be able to add the five votes up in his head. "To give thirty days' notice to close down Hanover House, vote yes. To keep it open, vote no. Sarah Williford, what is your vote?"

"Yes," Sarah said.

He made the notation. "George O'Neill?"

"Yes."

"You're kidding me!" Blair shouted. "George?"

George looked down at his hands.

"Harold Delaney?" the mayor said.

The man leaned forward to the microphone. "I have to vote yes." He shrugged. "Sorry, Blair."

"Cowards," Blair said. "That's what you all are."

"Ron Helms?"

Helms raised his hand. "Count me as a yes."

"And finally, Ken Adams?"

"Yes, I believe so."

"I can't believe you people! You're not worthy to serve this island! I'll spend every cent I have campaigning against each one of you!"

"Please, Blair," the mayor said. "Don't make me call the police to escort you out."

"Why don't you do that?" Blair asked. "Call Cade to escort me out. He'll probably love reliving the whole thing. I'll just wait right here."

She had called his bluff, and the mayor just sighed. "As you know," he said, "I only vote in the event of a tie if one of the council members is absent—but since we have a unanimous vote to shut down Hanover House, my vote will not be needed."

"We'll get a lawyer," Blair said in a flat voice. "We'll get a *team* of lawyers. We're going to fight this with every resource we have."

"You'll wind up paying more than Hanover House is even worth," the mayor said.

"It would be worth every penny," Blair told him and tore out of the room with Morgan behind her.

The wind was whipping hard from the east as she stepped outside, and she swung around to her sister. "We'll sell that bed-and-breakfast over my dead body. Those people are not going to decide what we do with our own property. And they *won't* tell us who we can have in our home."

Morgan was silent as Blair got behind the wheel and drove them back to Hanover House.

CHAPTER

61

Cade and McCormick spent half the night going over the evidence they had on both of their prisoners and trying to figure out where Rick fit in. They had located the nursing home where Rick's mother lived and learned that she was indeed in the hospital with a case of pneumonia. They called the Sheriff's Department in Atlanta and asked them to post a man near her room, to catch Rick if he happened to show up there.

It was too much of a coincidence that he had left town to visit her on the very day the article had come out. And why hadn't he been found yet? Every police force in Georgia was looking for him.

Cade slept for three hours, then got up and showered. Feeling weary to the bone, he called the DA and went over the evidence with him.

"I'm holding them for two different crimes," he said. "Gus for breaking and entering, and Jonathan for murder. But I haven't been able to build a very strong case against either one of them. In fact, if you took what I've got to a jury, they'd both be acquitted."

The DA agreed. "The speargun was big, but a good defense attorney could refute that with the evidence of the shed being broken into. And it looks like his alibi holds. What's your gut feeling about Gus?"

"I don't know," Cade said. "I was absolutely sure that he was the one who'd broken into Blair's. So far, the bandana is the only evidence we've got, but I'd like to keep him in custody. I don't want to take any chances. But I feel sure that we're barking up the wrong tree with Jonathan."

The DA thought for a moment, then let out a heavy sigh. "The more I look into it, the less of a case I have. I'll go along with Jonathan Cleary's release."

Cade headed to the judge's office, a brand-new sprawling building overlooking the water on the north side of the island. The office buzzed with activity. Judge Randy Simmons had many enterprises other than law. Cade tried to catch the secretary's attention as she flitted from room to room, delivering memos and picking up mail.

"Whatcha need, Cade?" she asked as she hurried past him.

"I need to see the judge."

"I'll tell him you're here." But she headed to the back of the offices, instead of to the judge's office.

Irritated, Cade went to the judge's door and knocked, then pushed it open. Randy had his feet propped up on his desk, holding the phone with his shoulder. He wore Reeboks, faded jeans, and an Atlanta Braves baseball cap. Randy gestured for him to sit.

Cade remained standing.

After a moment, Randy got off the phone and dropped his feet to the floor. "It's a madhouse around here today. Want a Coke or something?"

Cade shook his head. "Has the DA called you about Jonathan Cleary?"

"Yeah," Randy said. "I can't do much about it if he doesn't want to press the issue, but I sure don't want him leaving town."

"I think we can trust him."

"Right," the judge said. "We can trust him—just like we could trust Rick Dugan, who I hear has fled and can't be located."

"You know, your wife's article didn't wash. I checked and Rick Dugan has no prison record. Where she got her information I have no idea, but it was slanderous and inflammatory."

"You sound like a defense attorney now," Randy said, propping his feet back up. "Whose side are you on?"

Cade didn't honor that with an answer.

"If you're wrong, and we let Jonathan out, he could kill again."

"I wouldn't recommend releasing him if I thought he did it. I'm convinced now that he didn't. Enough's been done to the Owens family. I'd like to undo some of it."

"You're telling me. That house must be cursed. Two of them murdered, and three of them suspects. It's a good thing they're closing the place down. Nothing good can come out of Hanover House."

Cade didn't want to get into an argument right now. "So do I let him out?"

Randy rubbed his jaw, as if giving it deep consideration. "So you have people out looking for Rick Morrison or Dugan or whatever his name is?"

"Yes," Cade said. "We have some leads. I think we'll have him by day's end."

The judge sighed heavily, then stretched and got up. "I'm not going to make a decision right now, Cade. I'll get back to you."

Cade had to be satisfied with that, but by the time he got back to the police station there was already a call for him from the judge. He picked up the phone and dialed the number, waited until the call was routed to the judge.

"Randy," he said, "did you call?"

"Yeah. Go ahead and release Jonathan."

Cade was surprised. "All right."

"Just send the paperwork over so I can sign it. I have to leave at three for soccer practice."

"I'll be there as soon as I can," Cade said.

*S*o how does a Jamaican wind up in Georgia?" Jonathan's question didn't offend Gus at all. They had been talking for hours, enough for Jonathan to realize the man wasn't touchy about his past.

"The drug smuggling," Gus said. "I came here with a crateload of cocaine, and they didn't let me leave."

"You got caught then?"

"Served ten years, mon."

"But I thought you were in for armed robbery."

"Got out, couldn't find a job, and didn't have the money to get home to Jamaica. A friend from jail decided we could get fast money at a convenience store. Got us some guns, and we went in the place waving them around. Got fast money, mon, then fast jail time. Another five years."

"So when did you meet Thelma and Wayne?"

"When I got out, I had no place to go. So I stayed at the Gateway shelter in Savannah. Wayne came there, and he preached to us. I had a lot of questions, mon. Down in

Jamaica, I was a Rastafarian. We followed the teaching of the mon Haile Selassie."

"Who?"

"An Ethiopian emperor. He dead now, mon. But that was my religion, and this Christianity was hard for me. Wayne helped me with it, then invited me to come to Hanover House. He told me I could stay there if I would read the Bible and study with him every day. That I did. I owe my life to them."

Jonathan heard the catch in the big man's voice and saw the tears he wiped away in his eyes. He doubted tears were commonplace for the man. He did seem to love Thelma and Wayne. And he really did love Christ.

It was so hard to fathom that this hardened ex-con, who looked like he could break Jonathan in half, had the same hope, the same spirit.

He heard footsteps, and Cade appeared. "Okay, Jonathan. Your charges were dropped. You're free."

Jonathan got up and gaped at him. "You kidding?"

"Nope," Cade said as he opened the cell doors. "You want to stay?"

"No!" Jonathan grinned. "I'm going, I'm going."

Gus stood up and looked at him through the bars. "Good for you, mon. Good for you."

Jonathan gave him a high five as he hurried out of the cell.

CHAPTER

63

"Jonathan's been released!" Morgan shrieked at Mrs. Hern, dancing her around in a circle. Then she grabbed her purse and headed out.

"Call Blair and tell her I'm going to pick him up!"

Morgan sped to the police station. Leaving the car running in the lot, she dashed in. Jonathan was waiting in the front room, looking as victorious as he had after leading his team to the State Championship. She threw her arms around him, and he picked her up and swung her around.

"I can't believe it," she squealed. "You're coming home! Thank you, Cade! Thank you, thank you!"

Cade smiled as if he hadn't expected to be the hero in all this. He just stood back and grinned as they rushed out of the station.

Morgan hopped into the passenger seat, and Jonathan drove. "Free, at last," he said. "I thought I might be looking at a long sentence. Things weren't looking good."

He pulled her against him, and they drove home, clinging together like teenagers who couldn't stand to be apart.

His mood changed as they pulled into the driveway of Hanover House, the first time he had seen it since the murders. For a moment, he sat behind the wheel, staring at the yellow house. "It won't be right without them," he whispered.

Morgan shook her head, and her eyes glimmered with tears. "It isn't."

"But we're going to be all right," Jonathan said. "I'm home now."

CHAPTER

*A*fter a few hours at home, Jonathan craved the sunshine and salt air. While Morgan scurried around the kitchen, making all his favorite dishes, he walked to the dock to check on his boat. The sun burned its welcome on his face, and the smell of the sea made him long to get back to work . . . that is, if he still had any. Being a murder suspect wasn't exactly good for business.

His shirt stuck to his skin as he stood on the deck of his schooner, recalling his last words to Thelma and Wayne. He would give anything to erase the memory of his angry accusations that morning. Why hadn't he just sat down and had breakfast with them? Why hadn't he accepted their explanations about Gus? Why hadn't he enjoyed them a little while longer?

He got off the boat and stood on the pier, looking at the warehouse where they had worshiped and died. He pulled his keys out of his pocket, found the one to the warehouse. He went in the side door.

The bloodstain was still on the floor, and as he stood over it, he remembered what their bodies had looked like lying there limp and empty.

Did that memory ruin the church they had worked so hard to build? Did the blood taint it somehow? Could the Holy Spirit still work here?

He sat down on the old secondhand pew that he and Morgan occupied on Sundays. He looked up at the pulpit and realized that he would never see Wayne behind it again. What would become of their seamen's ministry and the church? Where would the congregation go? He couldn't bear the thought of the church closing down. And all those new, struggling Christians with no one to disciple them.

It was Wayne's calling, Wayne's vocation, Wayne's church . . .

His thoughts screeched to a halt, as if the Lord had thrown up a roadblock. It wasn't Wayne's church—it was Christ's. And the Holy Spirit could still work here.

He started to pray for direction for the church, for guidance for the people, for a preacher who could keep it going. Suddenly he got a glimpse of himself standing at the pulpit, preaching to a crowded room.

No way, he thought. He wasn't preacher material. It had never even crossed his mind.

He wasn't called like Wayne was. He wasn't ordained, anointed. . . .

And yet he saw the need and heard the Lord's voice clearly telling him that the church wasn't finished. Somehow, he had to keep it going.

Maybe he could clean the spot up tomorrow, he thought. Maybe he could get the church ready for Sunday. Maybe he could find some kind soul to preach. In honor of Thelma and Wayne, someone would come. And he couldn't imagine their regular church members staying away.

But as his mind struggled with the concept, his heart swelled. "I miss you, Thelma and Wayne," he whispered. "I'm sorry I was a jerk."

He knew they would have forgiven him, probably had even before they died. And as the relief of that flooded through his mind, he realized that he had someone to forgive, as well.

His oldest, closest friend, who had arrested him for something he hadn't done. Cade, who had done his job despite his personal feelings.

He could do that, he thought. He could forgive Cade. He had no other options.

He got up and walked to the pulpit, stood where Wayne used to stand, and touched the order of worship Morgan had typed for them the Sunday before they died. Thelma had sat at the piano, playing her old favorite hymns.

No one could ever replace them. Their shoes were too big to fill.

But they would have church this Sunday, and the Sunday after that, and the Sunday after that.

He took a deep breath, wiped his face on his sleeve, and left the building with new purpose—one that felt strangely like a calling.

ade rose before dawn, feeling as bone-weary as he had when he had gone to bed. Questions and clues whirled in his head, keeping him from the deep, restoring sleep he needed. There was too much to do.

Before the sun came up, he had made the decision to go to Atlanta. He couldn't keep Rick's airline tickets out of his mind. He had already checked with the airlines and learned that the ticket had not been used. Why would an innocent man disappear on the day that lies were published about him? Wouldn't he stay and fight? Set the record straight?

Cade had learned that Rick's mother did not have pneumonia, though his boss confirmed that Rick had gotten a phone call the day he left, telling him she was hospitalized. Had Rick lied about the call, or had someone else lied to *him*?

He had never shown up to visit his mother in the hospital. They were still watching the nursing home in case Rick showed up there.

Rick's disappearance created suspicion that Cade might not have had otherwise. His all-points bulletin had turned up nothing, and he wasn't sure he could trust the Atlanta PD to be diligent enough to catch Rick. He had to search for Rick by himself. Going to Atlanta would be a start.

But Rick wasn't the only reason to head for Atlanta. Cade couldn't get Sadie's phone call off his mind. She had called an Atlanta day care, Miss Tina's, to ask about a nine-month-old named Caleb Caruso. With that information, he knew he could fill in a lot of blanks about the girl.

One way or another, he would come back from Atlanta with information he sorely needed.

By the time he ended the four-hour trip to Atlanta, McCormick had called him with the name of the nursing home where Rick's mother lived. After arriving in the city, it took Cade another hour to navigate the traffic and find it. He wore jeans and a golf shirt, a baseball cap and sunglasses so that Rick wouldn't recognize him.

He found the home, a one-story building in an L shape, with a sign out front that said "Treasure Oaks Rest Home." He went in and approached the woman behind the nurse's desk. She had a powdered donut in her hand and a telephone at her ear.

Cade waited for her to get off the phone but quickly realized she was gabbing with a friend, and it could be a long wait.

"Excuse me," he said.

She turned around as if seeing him for the first time. "Hold on," she said to the phone, then to Cade, "Yeah?"

"I understand you have a resident here named Marilyn Dugan. Could you tell me what room she's in?"

The nurse dusted the powdered sugar off of her hands. "Yeah, room 432."

Cade waited for her to point him in the right direction, but she went back to her phone conversation instead. "Which way is it?" he asked, annoyed.

She looked at him as if his last question had pushed her over the edge. "It's that way, okay? The number's on the door."

He flashed his police badge and leaned on the counter. "I need to ask you a few questions. You might want to call your friend back later."

The woman looked insulted but picked the phone back up. "Sue, I'll call you back." She turned back to Cade. "Police, huh? Marilyn do something wrong?"

"Could you tell me if she's had any visitors lately?"

She set her hands on her hips and sighed. "Marilyn hasn't had visitors since her son moved away a few months ago."

"Are you sure?"

"You calling me a liar?"

Cade wondered if the woman was married. She must be a delight to come home to. "No, I'm not calling you a liar," he said patiently. "I was actually looking for someone who may have visited her in the last couple of days. But if a fine upstanding woman like yourself says no one's come, then I'll just talk to Marilyn myself."

"Good luck," she said, then added, "she thinks she's living in 1955."

Cade left the nursing home fifteen minutes later, no closer to finding Rick than he had been before. He got into his car and sat there, staring at the wheel.

Rick's mother was not an old woman. In her late fifties, perhaps. Early sixties at the most. He had expected someone old, in her last days of life. Alzheimer's had gotten her early.

"Samuel," she said when she first caught sight of him. Her face lit up like a little girl's, and she sprang up and threw her arms around him. "Samuel, you're almost late for pictures. Where's your suit?"

He felt as if he had stepped into someone else's life. "I'm not Samuel, ma'am," he said. "You have me mixed up with someone else."

She stepped back then, and her face went slack. "I thought we were dancing. I got you a boutonniere."

He felt sorry for her and thought of pretending to be Samuel just to light her face back up. "Ma'am, my name is Matthew Cade. I'm looking for your son, Rick. Has he been here?"

She sank into her chair, her eyes growing vacant. Just when he thought she might answer, she began to sing, in a soft, haunting voice ... "Where have all the flowers gone, long time passing ..."

"Ma'am," he said softly. He pulled a chair up next to her and leaned in close. "I need to find your son."

She stopped singing and smiled again. Her hand came up to stroke his cheek. "You're as handsome as ever, Samuel."

He knew then that he wasn't going to get through to her. Her life was somewhere in the past, in a world that couldn't be penetrated by police investigations or her own son's trouble.

He had been glad to get out of there.

He decided to wait a while, in case Rick Dugan showed up. Rick had laid low a couple of days, but eventually Cade knew he would come to check on his mother. With his car hidden among the others in the parking lot, Cade sat and waited.

CHAPTER

Cade waited until late that night, until the
lights began going off in the nursing home. Then he
returned early the next morning and waited some more.
Rick Dugan never showed up. Realizing his trip had been
for nothing, he decided to see what he could find out
about Sadie.

He looked up the number of Miss Tina's Day Care,
got the address, then made his way through town. He
found it easily, then sat out in his car for a moment, bracing himself for what he might discover inside. Was there
an abandoned child who needed her?

He went inside and found the children all lying on
little cots and in their baby beds. It was naptime, and soft
lullaby music played over the intercom.

One of the teachers got up and started toward him.
"May I help you?" she asked in a voice just above a
whisper.

"Yes," he said, flashing his badge. "Is there someplace we can talk?"

She nodded to an office and led him inside. He closed the door quietly, hoping not to wake the children. These teachers probably needed this break.

"I'm Matthew Cade from the police department," he said, not bothering to clarify that he was from Cape Refuge, not Atlanta. If Sadie was in trouble, he didn't want to lead a trail to her.

"Yes, officer, what can I do for you?"

"I understand you have a child here by the name of Caruso. Caleb, I think it is?"

"Yes," she said. "I wondered if something was up—with his mother in jail and all those calls from his sister."

Cade leaned forward. "His *sister*?"

"Yes," she said. "Sadie keeps calling to make sure he's all right."

"So—who does the baby live with?"

"His father, poor child. The rumor is that Sadie ran away. Is that why you're here?"

"No one's reported her missing," he evaded. "How can I reach her father?"

"Oh, he's not *her* father. He's her mother's boyfriend—or he *was* before she went to jail. A real scary guy, if you ask me. No wonder Sadie ran away."

He let those words sink in for a moment. Her broken arm and the bruises on her face bore witness to that fact. "Do you know how old Sadie is?"

"Sixteen. Sweetest kid in the world. I hope nothing happened to her. On the other hand, she's probably better off now. I feared for her, living with that man. Poor little Caleb. Shame she didn't take him with her."

Cade took his pad out of his pocket. "Could you tell me his name?"

"I don't know his first name. Last name is Dent. I can give you an address, since you're the police. Caleb's mama registered him, but it's the same address."

Cade wrote the address down, then looked up at the woman again. "Why is his mother in jail?"

"Some kind of drug charge. And she seemed like such a nice person. Nearly broke Sadie's heart. I know, because Sadie used to pick Caleb up every day." She looked down at her desk. "Caleb. That's a Bible name, you know."

Cade nodded.

"It's a good name for that baby. As scary as the father is, I'd say he's going to have to be very strong and courageous."

Cade got to his feet. "Can I see the baby?"

"Oh, he's not here today. Sick, I guess. Didn't come in."

Cade had a lot to think about as he made his way back to the nursing home and checked at the front desk to see if Rick had been by. He hadn't.

He went by the Atlanta Police Department to see if a missing-persons report had been filed on Sadie. Either no one had noticed her missing or no one cared.

Then he found the street where Dent lived and counted off the house numbers until he was sure he had the right one. He pulled into the driveway of the old house with peeling paint and a leaning foundation. As he walked up the cracked sidewalk, he saw that the second step on the porch had caved in. Carefully, he stepped over it.

He heard a baby crying through the door and something crashed. The baby's cries hit a higher octave.

He knocked. When no one answered, he rang the bell and knocked again, harder this time. Finally, he heard footsteps bounding across the floor, and the door jerked open.

Through the screen he smelled the alcohol breath of the man standing before him with a week-old growth of beard and a baseball cap on backwards. Scraggly, dirty auburn hair stuck out beneath it.

"Yeah?" the man barked.

Cade knew better than to tip his hand about Sadie's where-abouts. "I was looking for Mrs. Caruso," he said. "I'm with the school board."

"Sheila ain't here," he said, talking loud over the sound of the baby's cries. "She's in jail."

"Oh," Cade said. "And where is she being held?"

He gave him the name of the prison. "So is this about Sadie?"

"Yes. We're checking on her truancy," he said.

"I didn't know they came after tenth graders. I thought you could drop out any time you wanted to."

"We like to have our paperwork in order," Cade said.

The man stepped out on the porch and spat. He wasn't wearing a shirt, and his hairy chest covered a tattoo that was indiscernible. "Well, I ain't signing nothing," he said. "That girl's nothing but trouble. I ain't even related to her except through that kid in there." He nodded toward the door.

The baby kept screaming, anguished, gut-wrenching cries. "Do you need to go get the baby?"

"Naw, he squawks whether I'm holding him or not," he said.

"Where is Sadie?" he asked. "I need to talk to her."

"She ain't here right now," he said. "Girl runs wild."

"Do you know when she'll be back?"

"Got me."

"When's the last time you saw her?"

The man squinted at him, as if he'd asked one question too many. "What difference does that make to you?"

"Just trying to get a clue where I might find her."

The man studied him through his bloodshot eyes for a moment, then shook his head. "I got a baby to tend to," he said.

Before Cade could answer, the man slammed the door. He heard him bounding back across the house as the baby continued to scream.

Cade's heart was heavy as he headed back out to his car. Something had to be done about that child. It wouldn't take a rocket scientist to see that the man was an unfit parent. But first he needed to talk to the mother.

That would shed a lot of light on Sadie's and Caleb's situations.

CHAPTER

67

Sadie's mother, Sheila Caruso, was in the jail in downtown Atlanta. Cade found it easily.

She came to the visiting room wearing a baggy brown jumpsuit. Her brownish-blonde hair was pulled back in a rubber band. He could see Sadie in her face and knew she had once been pretty.

She eyed him suspiciously through the glass, then picked up the telephone that opened their communication.

"Who are you?" she asked.

"Mrs. Caruso, I'm Matthew Cade," he said. "I'm police chief in Cape Refuge, and I wanted to ask you some questions about your daughter, Sadie."

The woman burst into tears and leaned forward, her eyes fixed on his. "Leave her alone, won't you?" she said. "I know she's run away, but please let her go. Wherever she is, she's better off."

Cade hadn't expected that. He waited for more.

"She wasn't safe in Atlanta," she cried. "And neither is Caleb. If you're concerned about any laws being broken, then go get my baby out of that house, get him away from Jack. He'd be better off with almost anybody. Just, please, don't leave him with him."

"Mrs. Caruso, if he's his father, then—"

Her eyes grew hard, more determined. Though she looked young—no more than thirty-five, perhaps—her skin was lined and tired. "You take children away from parents all the time. You can do this. I'm telling you, he'll hurt the baby. He may even kill him like he tried to kill Sadie."

"Mrs. Caruso, if he's abusive, why hasn't anyone reported him to Human Services?"

"I have, but nothing's been done," she said. "They think I'm saying it for spite, but I told them Sadie'd had a broken jaw and a concussion and two broken ribs. There are doctors who can vouch for it, X-rays, but they won't do anything. Sadie came here with her arm all bashed in and her face swollen, and I told her to get on a bus and go as far as it would take her. That's why she left. So you might as well not be looking for her. She's going to be all right. She's got a good head on her shoulders and she's been through tough times. She practically raised herself, when I was doing drugs, and she took care of me—"

She collapsed in sobs, and Cade felt as though he had intruded on her private sorrow. All he could do was hold that phone and avert his eyes. He looked at a spot on the ledge of the glass until she could speak again.

"She's run away before, but he goes after her, chases her down, and drags her back. I'm going to be in here for five years, at least. I want both my kids in one piece when I get out. 'Til then, there's nothing I can do except beg. Please, I don't know why you're here, but please get my baby out of that house."

"I'll do what I can," he said. "Meanwhile, I can tell you that Sadie's safe, her arm's in a cast, and she just started a new job. She has a nice place to live and people watching over her.

Her face twisted, and she touched the glass. "Thank you," she said.

Cade could only nod, for his throat was too tight to say another word.

The best Cade could do was report possible abuses to Human Services before he left Atlanta. It was clear that they were overworked and understaffed and had a long list of abuses to look into. He tried to convince them to move little Caleb to the top of their list, but he wasn't sure that they would.

As he drove back to Cape Refuge, everything kept running through his mind. He hoped the baby would survive the father's abuse, and he didn't know what to do about Sadie. No missing-persons report had ever been filed, and technically, she wasn't a runaway since her mother had sent her away. He needed to pray over this a while before he took any action. And while he was at it, he would pray for little Caleb, and for the mother who seemed so remorseful and helpless as she sat in prison.

Cade went straight to Hanover House as soon as he got back to Cape Refuge. He found Morgan, Jonathan, and Blair in their parents' office, trying to figure out how they could hold onto the house if the city forced them to evict their tenants.

Blair noticed the somber look on Cade's face. "Cade, what's wrong? Has something happened?"

He shook his head. "No, I was just in Atlanta for the past couple of days trying to find some leads on Rick."

"And?" she asked.

"Didn't find anything. But I came here to talk to Sadie. She home?"

Morgan looked up at him. "Upstairs. Want me to get her?"

"If you don't mind."

Blair got up and came closer, searching his face. "Cade, what is it? Has she done something wrong?"

"No. I just . . . I found out where she's from." As Sadie came down the stairs, he stepped out of the office into the living room. Blair followed.

Sadie stopped at the bottom and stared at him with big, worried eyes. It was clear she thought she had been found out, that she would be arrested and sent back to Jack.

"It's okay, Sadie," Morgan said. She took her hand and pulled her down to the couch, sat next to her with her arm around her. Blair sat on the other side, staring at Cade as she waited. Jonathan kept standing.

Cade sat down and fixed his eyes on the girl. "I was in Atlanta today, Sadie."

She leaned back hard on the couch, as if she knew what was coming.

"I met your stepfather."

"He's *not* my stepfather," she said. "He was my mother's boyfriend. That's all." Her face twisted as she started to cry. "Why'd you go there? I haven't done anything wrong. I've been getting along with people, and I've got a job. I'm earning money. I'm going to be able to support myself and take care of everything."

"Sadie, you're sixteen," Cade said.

Morgan didn't look surprised.

"You don't understand," Sadie said.

"I understand more than you think," Cade cut in. "I told you, I met Jack. I saw what kind of man he is, and I can see what drove you away."

She sprang up off of the couch and cut across the room. "He's the devil himself, that's what kind of man he is," she said. "My mama let him move in because she was lonely and he gave her drugs. That's not the first dumb thing she's ever done."

Morgan went to her. "But isn't she worried about you?" she asked. "I mean, your mother must be crazy wondering where you are."

"My mother's in jail."

Morgan caught her breath and looked at Cade.

"I met her too," Cade said.

Sadie's face changed, and she stepped toward him. "You met my mom? You went to the jail?"

"Yes," he said, "and the fact is, she begged me not to tell where you are. She said to let you stay here, that you were better off."

"She's right," Sadie said. "I may be sixteen, but I'm old enough to know when I'm in danger." She took another step toward him and breathed in a sob. "Did you see Caleb, my baby brother? Is he all right?"

"I talked to his day-care teacher," Cade said. "She said he seemed all right."

"But did you *see* him?"

"No," he said. "I heard him crying in the house, though."

"I've got to get him out of there," Sadie said. "He won't be safe. Jack's a crazy man. He has a methamphetamine lab, and he's a drug dealer. He gets high and comes home with all these lunatics for friends. And when Caleb cries, he just goes berserk."

She knelt beside Cade's chair, looking up at him with beseeching eyes. "Please. Isn't there something you can do to get him out of there?"

"Your mother asked me the same thing." He touched her shoulder and looked into those big eyes. "I'll do what I can, Sadie," he said. "I can't promise anything. This is way out of my jurisdiction. But I do think you're all right staying here. No missing-persons report has been filed. Your mother knows where you are, and she gave her permission—so technically, you're not a runaway."

Her face twisted. "You didn't tell *him* where I am, did you?"

"No," he said. "You don't have to worry about that."

"He's smart. A lot smarter than he looks. Every other time I've run away, he's found me."

"You don't have to worry," Cade said.

Sadie stood back up, and Morgan touched her face. "Honey, is he the one who beat you up?"

She nodded. "I should have brought Caleb with me. He beat me and threw me out of the house, and I slept in a car that night. The next morning I hitchhiked to visit my mom, and she told me to get on a bus, not to go back home for anything. But I shouldn't have left Caleb that way. He doesn't have anybody to protect him."

"How old is he?" Blair asked.

"Nine months. That's all. He's so little, so helpless. He cries all the time unless I'm there. He misses Mom. And now he misses me."

"We'll get him out of there, won't we, Cade?" Blair asked.

Cade nodded. "I reported him to HRS before I left town. Hopefully, they'll remove the child." He looked at the broken girl. "I'll follow up on it, Sadie. I won't let you or your brother fall through the cracks."

"Thank you," she whispered.

As he left the house, his heart broke for the desperate girl and for the baby whose cries would haunt him tonight.

CHAPTER

69

*T*hat night, Morgan lay curled up next to Jonathan, her head on his chest. She could tell he had something on his mind, but these days so many things weighed both of them down. "What's wrong, Jonathan?" she asked quietly.

"Nothing," he said. "I was just thinking." His voice was a deep, thoughtful rumble. "The other day when I went to the dock to check my rig, I went into the warehouse. I just sat there and thought what a shame to let the church fold, and all those people who would have to go somewhere else to worship."

"I know," Morgan said. "It seems like all of Mama and Pop's work was for nothing. It's all just disappearing."

"It doesn't have to be that way," Jonathan said.

"What do you mean?"

He sat up. "Morgan, I sat there, looking at that pulpit, and had this overwhelming sense that we need to keep the church going, and that you and I are the ones who are going to do that. And since then, I've been praying and thinking and planning . . . and I'm just wondering how you would feel . . . about us having services starting Sunday."

She thought about going back into that building, trying to forget the sight of her parents lying there in their own blood. . . . "I don't know," she whispered. "Who would preach?"

"At first I thought we should try to get a guest preacher, but I realized our members need someone familiar, someone who suffers with them, someone who grieves as they grieve. And all of a sudden, I felt as if I had a whole lot to say to them. I thought I could speak the first Sunday. After that, we could get guest preachers until we found the right person."

She sat up and hugged her knees. "I could play piano just like Mama did. I never had the confidence to do it before, but I think I could do it now."

"If we got the word out, let the congregation know, we could open up this Sunday," he said. "I think I could be ready. Being in jail gave me a lot of time to think. I could make it a memorial service for your folks. I think a lot of people would come, and then I could tell them about Jesus and why Thelma and Wayne are the only ones not grieving over their deaths. I could tell them what death looks like from the other side. The celebration, the joy, the rewards . . ."

That pain that had hidden in her chest for the past several days swelled and blocked her throat. She couldn't speak.

"They'll come if they don't think of me as a killer," he said.

She swallowed back her pain. "That's their problem. Our job is to carry on and trust God with the hearts of the people. Just like Mama and Pop always did."

He drew her into a tight hug, and she clung to him with all her might. Those she loved were so easily snatched away.

"I've felt so frustrated lately," she whispered. "About the unsolved murders, about the things I found out about Mama and Pop's past, about Blair's scars, about you and Gus and Rick. And Sadie's constantly on my mind. She's just so young. She needs an anchor. A family. People she can count on."

"I think she's found it," Jonathan said. He stroked his wife's cheek with gentle fingertips. "I see so much of your mother in you. The way you've taken over the care of this house. The way you've mothered Sadie."

"She's a good kid," she whispered. "I wish I knew how to keep her from ever going back to that man."

Jonathan stared at the air for a long moment, then finally whispered, "Maybe there is."

"What?" Morgan asked.

"If her mother's so adamant about her not going back there, maybe she'd sign papers to let us have legal custody."

Morgan got up and looked down at him. "Jonathan, do you mean it?"

"Well, sure. That way, when the tenants have to move out, she won't have to go."

"It'd solve so many problems for her. But let's not tell her until we know it'll work out. She's had enough disappointment." She reached up to kiss him. "It's so good to have you home," she said. "You're the problem solver around here."

"Yeah," he said. "If only I could solve the murders."

Jonathan answered when East Coast Properties called the next morning. They demanded to know if Blair and Morgan had made a decision yet. "We're keeping the place," he said. "But we appreciate the offer."

"Mr. Cleary, perhaps your wife didn't convey our generous offer to you. It's cash, full market value. We're prepared to offer more if necessary...."

"Sorry," he said. "We're not interested."

The man sounded stunned. "Mr. Cleary, it's come to our attention that you're being ordered to close the place down. How do you suppose that you can afford to hold onto the house and pay the substantial taxes on the property, when you can no longer accept the donations and rents that keep it afloat?"

"That would be our problem, not yours," Jonathan said. "Please don't call here again."

He took great pleasure in hanging up in the man's ear!

A few hours later Morgan was served with papers from the city's legal department. She scanned the document and handed it to Jonathan.

He quickly read over it. "Another threat to close us down in . . . twenty-seven days."

"It's not a threat, Jonathan. They're going to do it."

"They can't take our property," he said. "All they can do is tell us we can't do business, and even that's debatable. We're going to see a lawyer as soon as we can get an appointment."

Morgan grabbed the phone. "I'm calling Blair."

When she had told her sister what had just happened, Blair wasn't surprised that the papers had been served. "I've got an idea," she said. "We're about to start a propaganda war. We're going to change the tide of public opinion. Just leave it to me."

Sadie had a hard time concentrating on work that day. Her conversation with Chief Cade played through her mind. He had made promises, but she didn't know if she could trust him. He seemed kind, but others had seemed kind before. They hadn't been able to help her or her little brother.

She sat at the computer on her desk, searching the Net for some statistics Nancy needed, when Blair burst through the door.

"Sadie, where's Nancy?"

"Back in her office." She got up. "I'll get her."

"No, I'll get her myself." Blair whizzed past her and reached the door before Sadie did. Nancy looked up, surprised. "I need your help, Nancy," she said.

The woman sat at her cluttered desk, digging through a pile as if searching for something. "Blair, you've got a lot of nerve. After what you said about me at the city council meeting, you have the gall to ask for my help?"

Blair sighed. "Nancy, after all the things you've written in the past few months about Hanover House, you have a lot of nerve being insulted."

Nancy set her chin on her palm. "What do you want?"

"I want to give you a story. News, Nancy. The real kind. The city council just served us papers. I need some publicity. You could do an article on this. You know it's big news and the townspeople would want to know."

"Of course," she said, pulling a pencil from behind her ear. "Sit down."

Blair looked suspicious, as if she knew better than to think Nancy could turn on a dime.

"I could write it!" Sadie said from the doorway. "I mean, living there and all, I could do a good job."

"Sure you could," Nancy said. "Come on in and sit down, Sadie." She pulled a legal pad out from one of the stacks. "Here, take notes."

Pride swelled in Sadie's heart, but her stomach tightened. She hadn't expected it to be quite that easy.

Blair wasn't buying it, either. "Come on, Nancy. I was thinking you could probably devote a whole issue to it. Think of it. You could interview people who've stayed there over the years, do a piece about Joe and Miranda Hanover, interview people in the community about their feelings about the House. . . . No offense, Sadie, but I had a substantial article in mind."

"I can't give it a whole issue," Nancy said. "Sadie can write it up, and if it's any good, I'll run it."

Her noncommittal attitude worried Sadie as she followed Blair back to the front. "Do a good job, Sadie. Hanover House depends on it, and we're not gonna get a lot of help from Nancy. Fax me the article when you're finished with it, and I'll proof it for you."

Sadie felt as if the fate of the beloved home rested on her shoulders. She hoped they were strong enough to carry it.

She spent the rest of the day in a nervous flurry. She went to Hanover House and listened as Morgan gave her a quick rundown of the history of the house, complete with newspaper clippings and pictures of Joe and Miranda Hanover. She had Blair explain in detail what the city council was doing, then she rushed to Crickets and interviewed the few midday diners about their thoughts on the home.

She went back to the office and typed up the article, then faxed it to Blair at the library.

When Blair called five minutes later to say, "It looks great, Sadie. You got talent, kid," Sadie wanted to dance and leap and let out a loud cheerleader whoop, but she had to act old enough to be a newspaper reporter. She took the article in to Nancy's office.

Nancy was laying out the day's edition, and Sadie saw with disappointment that the front page was already full.

"I finished the article," she said. "I hope you like it. I can make any changes you want."

Nancy took it and devoted three seconds to reading it over. Then she tossed it down. "Good job, Sadie, but I'm not going to put it in."

"What? Why not?" Sadie picked it back up, feeling like a failure. "I can redo it. Maybe I just rushed too much. . . ."

"No," Nancy said. "I've just given it more thought today, and I've decided it's not newsworthy."

"But . . . it's Hanover House. People had nice things to say about it. I got a lot of good quotes. . . ." Her voice trailed off. Nancy wasn't even listening.

"Maybe tomorrow's issue, then?" Sadie asked.

"No, not tomorrow either," Nancy said. "The community's tired of hearing about Hanover House."

Blair was waiting at Hanover House when Sadie got home from work that day. The girl came in, a sheen of perspiration on her face. She was flushed, angry, and shaken.

"How'd it go, Sadie? What page did she give the article?"

"She isn't putting it in. She has no intentions of publishing it."

"What?" Blair asked. "Are you sure?"

"She said it wasn't newsworthy."

Blair slammed her hand down on the counter. "Not newsworthy? And the article on the pros and cons of the post office being closed on Wednesday afternoons *is*? She ran a whole series on whether World's Finest Chocolate was a better school fundraiser than popcorn! Last week there was a front-page article about that thirteen-year-old who got her hair cut for the first time. Give me a break!"

"Did you ask her why she didn't think it was newsworthy?" Morgan asked.

"I tried, but she told me the community is just sick of hearing about it."

Blair shot Morgan a look. "That's the most absurd thing I've ever heard. If this isn't news, I don't know what is. Has the whole world gone crazy?"

"Not the whole world," Morgan said. "Just Cape Refuge." She crossed her arms, and looked at the girl. "Sadie, do you think you can get that article back tomorrow?"

"Sure," she said. "I kept a copy."

"We could buy an ad for the paper and put it in that."

"Contribute money to that rag?" Blair asked. "I don't think so. Let's just print it up ourselves and pass it out all over town."

"We can send a copy to East Coast Properties," Morgan said. "Just a few hours before we got served yesterday, they called and demanded an answer. Even raised the offer. Jonathan told them no."

"What did they do?" Blair asked. "Call the mayor and get him to serve us so we'd change our minds?"

"Do you think someone pressured Nancy into not publishing the article?" Morgan asked.

"Could be. But if that's the case, we're about to show them that it didn't keep us quiet. Before the end of the week, we'll make sure everyone on the island knows what's happening to Hanover House."

*T*he more she thought about it, the more suspicious Blair became. Things seemed too coincidental. First, the call from East Coast Properties, then the serving of the papers just hours later, and now Nancy's refusal to run an article about the closing of the island's most revered landmark. . . .

She went back to the library and turned on her computer. Her fingernails drummed on the table as she waited for it to boot up. She clicked in "Copernic," the search engine that had access to eighty databases. She typed in "East Coast Properties, Inc.," and watched as the bars traveled across the screen.

The search didn't come up with anything she could use, so she logged onto the public-records database she was able to access.

While the database searched for East Coast Properties, she went to the bathroom for a glass of water. She turned on the faucet and stuck the glass under it, but her mind drifted back to the company, to those papers, to Sadie's article, to Nancy's refusal.

Something wasn't right.

The water ran over the glass, wetting her arm, and she pulled it back and dried off her hand.

Her computer bell rang, so she rushed back into her tiny office. A few things had come up, so she quickly clicked the first.

East Coast Properties was owned by another company called Georgia Estates. She did a quick search to see who owned Georgia Estates.

Her heart jolted when she realized it was owned by Savannah Enterprises. She saw the pattern forming as she did the search on Savannah Enterprises. It was the classic modus operandi of dummy corporations set up for tax shelters or money laundering.

One company owned by another and another and another in a never ending trail that led nowhere.

But Savannah Enterprises did own quite a bit of property on Cape Refuge—three souvenir shops down by the beach and the Green Eggs and Ham Breakfast Nook near the Pier. They also owned three hotels along Ocean Boulevard, some condominiums on the north side of the island, and various houses and convenience stores that she knew had been bulldozed for parking lots. So what did they want with Hanover House?

She sat back in her chair and stared at the screen.

Who was really behind East Coast Properties, and what did they want with her family home? Did they want to tear it down to build a parking lot, or did they plan to turn it into condos? Or did they hope to remodel it and turn it into a high-priced bed-and-breakfast that only wealthy tourists could afford?

And was it a coincidence that the city council's harassment and the offer had come at roughly the same time?

She couldn't say for sure. Not yet. But she was determined to find out.

Cade leaned against the wall in the back corridor of the Municipal Court building, waiting for the judge to come out of the courtroom. He had timed it so that he wouldn't have long to wait—Randy Simmons never held court after three o'clock.

Randy was already unzipping his robe as he burst out the door. He wore a pair of baggy shorts underneath. "How's it going, Cade?" Randy asked him.

"Pretty good. Can I talk to you in private?"

"Sure." The judge led him back to his chambers, which consisted of a small office just barely big enough to hold a desk and a couple of chairs. Since Cape Refuge wasn't big enough to have court every day, he did most of his work at his law firm.

He took off his robe, tossed it over a chair.

Cade chuckled. "I see you're still taking the office of judge as reverently as always."

Randy sat down behind his desk and propped his flip-flopped feet on it. "If you had to listen to a hundred people whining about speeding tickets and bad checks, you'd want to be comfortable too."

"I guess you're right."

"So, what's on your mind?" the judge asked. "Have you found that Rick Dugan character?"

"No, not yet," he said. "We're still looking for him. It's strange that we haven't found him. I have APBs in every county in Georgia and most of Alabama and Mississippi too. But that's not why I'm here."

Cade got up and slid his hands into his pockets. "Sadie . . . the girl who's working for your wife—I found out she's a teen runaway, but when I went to check on her family, I learned that her mother's in jail, and she's been living with the mother's boyfriend. Name's Jack Dent. He's a drug dealer and abusive— which is why she came here so beaten up. She begged me not to send her back to him, and her mother did too. Morgan and Jonathan Cleary want to take temporary custody of her, with the mother's permission."

The judge dropped his feet and scooted his chair closer to the desk. "You'd have to get the proper papers drawn up, then have the mother sign them. It's no hill for a climber. I could draw the papers up in my lawyer hat if you want me to."

Cade nodded. "I would like to get this taken care of as soon as possible."

"Tell Morgan to call me, and we'll get the papers drawn up this week."

"Meanwhile," Cade said, "can you give me some kind of court order to keep her here?"

"I can't do that," Randy said. "It's not my beat. But drawing up the papers and getting the mama to sign them should be enough."

Cade had to be satisfied with that. He shook the man's hand. "Well, thanks. I appreciate it. I'll get details to you so you can draw them up. I'll take them to the mother myself."

Randy dropped his feet. "Sounds good. So how are Morgan and Blair? I heard Hanover House is being shut down. Any word on where they'll go?"

Cade frowned. "They're not going anywhere, and they plan to fight this."

Randy breathed a laugh. "That's crazy. They ought to just sell the thing and get it behind them."

"I understand they've had offers," Cade told him, "but I don't think they want to sell. Looks like they're going to dig in—and Sadie's one of the big reasons."

"What's she got to do with it?" Randy asked.

"Well, if Hanover House is closed down, they have to ask all their tenants to leave."

"They could get another place, take her with them."

"But they're real attached to that place, you know. They grew up there. Their parents were so invested in it. All this has happened kind of fast, and they're just not ready." Cade moved his chair out of the way so he could get to the door. "Thanks a lot, Randy. I'll get in touch with you."

"Yeah," Randy said, behind him.

Cade was hopeful that they had an answer for Sadie as he went back to the station.

Jonathan couldn't help being amazed at the number of people who turned out for the memorial service for Thelma and Wayne Owens. Many had come to the funeral, he understood, but now that their grief had taken root, they needed more of a good-bye to their friends. Some were gawkers, and others just came for the gossip value. But most came because they had loved the vibrant couple who had been such a part of the island's life.

Jonathan was nervous and found himself perspiring more than he had ever done when he had come to this church before. He had them open all the doors, and as they began to sing the praise songs that Thelma and Wayne would have led, he felt a calm wash over him, reminding him that it wasn't about how good he was as a preacher or how well he filled Wayne's shoes. It was about reaching people, changing hearts for Christ just as they had always done. That is what Wayne would have wanted.

As their songs rose to the sky and spread out to the street, stragglers began coming in from the dock, seamen who had just come to shore, and customers from Cricket's who heard the sound of praise. They all stood at the doorways, peeking inside. Morgan smiled as her mother would have done and played the chords of the praise songs that Jonathan led.

When they stopped singing, Jonathan began to preach about the two lives that had been so beautifully dedicated to the Lord, about the work and the place where they had invested their lives, and he told where they were and what their legacy was to the people of this community. And then he told why. As he did, he realized that the inadequacies of his own speech were overshadowed by the Holy Spirit as it worked in the hearts of those who listened.

Blair sipped her coffee at the picnic-style table in Cricket's, watching through the screen window as people crowded into the doorways of the warehouse. She had not been able to make herself go. She didn't want to hear testimonies about her parents and their life's work for the God who had allowed them to be murdered.

She could hear the singing, the sweet peaceful sounds of praise for a God that so many seemed to believe in. She watched as people from the restaurant got up and gravitated toward the music. Whether it was curiosity or religion that drew them, she wasn't sure. All she knew was that it wasn't for her. She knew her sister would be disappointed, that others would wonder where she was. But they would just have to understand.

"Gonna miss the service," Charlie said from behind the bar as he wiped the counter.

Blair stared into her cup. "I was at the funeral service," she said. "I don't need to say good-bye again."

The screen door to Cricket's bounced, and Cade walked in, looked around, and caught her eyes. He was wearing a sport coat and khaki pants, a white shirt that contrasted nicely with his tan. She propped her chin on her fist and looked out at the water.

She heard his footsteps approaching on the wooden floor.

"Mind if I sit with you?" he asked.

"Sure."

He slid across from her, his eyes silently resting on her. "I thought I'd see you there," he said finally. "Somebody said you were over here. Thought I'd see if you're okay."

"I'm fine," she said. "I'm just not into church. Never was. You know that."

"It's no big surprise, but this *is* a memorial service for your folks."

"As I was telling Charlie, I've been there and done that."

"And then there's that minute possibility that you might learn something."

"Doubt it." She brought her cup to her mouth.

He just gazed at her, those eyes seeing far too much. She turned her face again, hiding the scars.

"So tell me what you're thinking about while you watch those people fill that little building."

"I'm thinking that I'm tired of this town, Cade," she whispered. "That I don't know why I stayed here all these years."

"I sometimes ask myself the same thing," he said, "but I think the island gets under your skin, in your blood. We couldn't leave if we wanted to." He shifted his body and looked back toward the warehouse. "Look at that, Blair. Those are your friends. Your parents' friends. They love your family and what it represents. Those are the ones who make up the real Cape Refuge. Not that city council. That's why you can't ever leave."

"Think again," Blair said. "I'm thinking about doing just that." She met his eyes and saw the concern on his face.

"You'd miss the ocean," he said, "the sound and the smell. You'd miss the sand and the sunshine."

"There are other beach towns," she said, "but I was thinking of going to the mountains. Colorado, maybe. I want to live where there's snow."

His eyes were as serious as she had ever seen them. "There are people here who'd miss you, Blair."

She smiled. "Who? My sister has Jonathan, and all those people she hovers over. They probably wouldn't even notice I was gone."

"You'd miss her."

"Yeah, well, everything's a trade-off."

He reached across the table, took her cup out of her hands, sipped it. There was something strangely intimate about that, and Blair questioned the warm feeling it gave her.

He set the cup down and put her hands around it, pressed his over them. "And then there's me. I would miss you, Blair."

She knew her scars were probably blood red again, so she turned back to the window. "That's nice, Cade. But soon enough you're going to meet one of these blonde tourists breezing through town, fall in love, marry her, and have tanned little children running around crabbing on the beach."

He grinned. "Or you could," he said. "There are plenty of tanned *men* breezing through town."

She smiled a sad smile. "Not going to happen," she said, "not to me."

She dug into her purse, pulled out two dollars, and set them on the table. "You better get back to the service, before somebody misses you and turns you in to the spiritual police."

He smiled and slid out of the booth. "You won't run off to Colorado without letting me know, will you?"

She sighed. "Don't worry. I'm not planning to leave in the next few days. Too much is unsettled. I fight to win."

She started past him to the door, but he caught her arm and stopped her. She turned around and looked up at him. "Are you okay?" he asked in a low voice. "I mean, really okay?"

She felt exposed, and she didn't like it. "I'm fine," she said. Then before he could say anything else, she pulled out of his grasp and headed back to Hanover House.

CHAPTER

74

*M*organ found Blair lying in their parents' bedroom at Hanover House, curled up on the bed, clutching both of her parents' pillows.

"We missed you at the service," she said.

Blair sat up as if she didn't want to be seen that way. "I saw that it was a big crowd. I'm glad it went well."

Morgan came in and closed the door behind her. "Jonathan was wonderful," she said. "He did a good job. And Wilson Riley offered to preach next Sunday. He's a retired preacher, you know. He wants to do it."

Blair breathed a laugh. "No one can fill Pop's shoes. You know that."

Morgan sat on the bed and pulled her feet up beneath her. "What's the matter, Blair?"

"Nothing. I'm just a little amazed at how easy it is for you."

"What's easy?"

"Just moving on," Blair said, "picking up and filling Pop's shoes. Mama's too."

"All I did was go to a church service," Morgan said.

Blair pulled herself off the bed. "I'm sorry. I didn't mean to snap." She fiddled with something on the bed table, then turned around and looked at her sister. "I think I've changed my mind about selling Hanover House."

Morgan grunted. "Why? I thought we had decided that we wouldn't. I thought we were going to fight it, stand firm, and not let the city council intimidate us."

Blair's eyes were misty as she turned back around. "But I'm tired, Morgan," she said, and the weariness was apparent in every word. "I need help moving on."

"How would it help?" Morgan asked. "Selling our home and everything that belonged to Mama and Pop—how in the world could that help?"

"I could use the money," Blair said.

Morgan's mouth fell open. "For what?"

"To move out of this place, to start over someplace else where no one knows me."

"How'll that help?" Morgan cried. "Why would anybody want to go where no one knows them?"

"Because they could start over," Blair said. "There'd be hope for a future."

"You have hope here. You were happy before all this. You never wanted to move before."

"I've always wanted to move," Blair said, "but I never did because they were here, and it would have broken their hearts. But now it's easier. I want to do it, Morgan. I want to sell this house."

"Well, I don't! Mama and Pop would have wanted us to keep going. The church service, Hanover House, they were all tools to Mama and Pop to help them reach people, and I want to do that too. I have it in me and so does Jonathan. We can do it. It can be my mission field just like it was theirs."

Blair ground her teeth together. "Don't you tell me you feel called."

"That's exactly what I feel."

"Oh, please!" Blair shouted. "You make me want to throw up. Why is it that every time a Christian gets a bee in his bonnet they say they feel 'called'?"

"Because it's true."

"It's not true," Blair said. "It's just another manipulative technique that ends the conversation. If you feel 'called,' then nobody can argue with it. But you know what? I don't believe, so it doesn't work with me."

"So you don't believe," Morgan said, smearing a tear across her face. "Mama and Pop couldn't change that, and I haven't been able to change that. But you don't have to mock my beliefs. I do feel a calling and so did Mama and Pop."

"That's right," Blair shouted. "They felt that calling to serve God. They gave him their lives. They served him night and day. And look how protected they were! Look how blessed! They were *murdered,* Morgan! Where was he when they were screaming for their lives? Where is he now, when that killer is still out there, walking around free and laughing because he got away with it?"

Morgan sank back down. "There'll come a time when God's wrath will come down on the person who did this, Blair. When God's anger over Mama and Pop's deaths is avenged."

"How do you know that?"

"Because it says so in the Bible, and I believe it." She wiped her tears and tried to find the words. "Blair, we live in a violent, dark world. It wasn't the way God wanted it in the beginning."

"Oh, right," Blair said. "The fallen nature. Adam and Eve sinned, so our parents had to be murdered. Makes sense to me."

Morgan looked helpless. "Blair, I ask the same questions. Where was God? Why did he let this happen? And I don't know the answers. But I know that our parents are in heaven because Jesus shed his blood so that this world wouldn't be imprisoned to sin anymore. The person who did this will have to face God one day. His knees will bow and his tongue will confess that Jesus Christ is Lord. And he's going to pay for what he did."

"By going to hell? So let me get this straight," Blair said. "Because I don't believe, I'll be in hell with the same person who killed our parents?"

Morgan slammed her fist into the mattress. "Oh, Blair, God never wanted you to go to hell. We were all headed there, anyway. Jesus died on the cross to save us from that. He died to save you too. He probably mourns every day because you haven't reached out and taken the life preserver he's thrown out to you. You'd rather drown in your confusion, in all your unanswered questions, in all the pain you carry around."

"And *you'd* rather drown in your faith."

"Faith doesn't make you drown, Blair. It makes you walk on the water. It makes you go on when life doesn't make sense, when it isn't fair, when horrible things happen. It reminds you that you're not alone. That Someone is there with you, carrying that burden that's so crushing that you can't even stand up straight."

Blair only shook her head and wiped the tears on her face. "I can carry my own burdens."

Then she left the room, ran down the stairs, and out the front door. Morgan just curled up in the same place her sister had been, and wept into her father's pillow.

CHAPTER

*B*lair crossed the street and headed along the beach, her feet digging into the powdery sand. She tried to flee from her rage at the God she didn't believe in, tried to escape the cares that crushed her, just as Morgan had described. But there was no escape. They went with her, wrapping around her throat and constricting it, keeping her from being able to swallow or breathe. Where had they come from, these tears? They came in a torrent streaming down her face, stinging her eyes, dripping from the bottom of her chin. She walked faster and faster as that anguish poured out of her.

She passed the South Beach Pier, where tourists lay as limp as the towels beneath them. She glanced up to the pier, hoping no one she knew would see her in this condition. No one even noticed her.

She walked faster, the angry wind whipping through her hair. Black clouds blew up from the east, threatening furious storms that would slow the island down. She welcomed that storm, longed for the lightning and the claps of thunder, the sound of pouring rain on her roof. It would feel like justice.

She kept walking until she ran out of beach; then she took to the grass and the occasional sidewalk and the packed dirt, walking from pier to pier around the cape.

She had meant what she said about leaving Cape Refuge. Somehow, she would make it happen. She could sell her half of Hanover House to Morgan and take off to Colorado. She could find a research job or a librarian's position there, rent a little apartment overlooking the mountains, soak up the peace and the newness of the place, and put the past, with all its questions and maddening answers, behind her.

She trudged along the river wall, through backyards, and around boathouses. A few residents waved at her and asked how she was doing, but she just waved and walked on.

She rounded the northern tip of the island, only a mile across the river from Tybee Island. The back of the Simmons's house came into view, and she saw the judge and Nancy sitting out beside their pool. A red-haired man, dressed in a Miller Light T-shirt and jeans, sat with them, deep in conversation.

She didn't want Nancy to catch her with tears on her face and drill her with a million insincere questions, and she wasn't up for a fight about the article Nancy hadn't printed. So Blair chose, instead, to turn around and head back the way she had come, before they even saw her.

She'd be glad to put people like Nancy in her rearview mirror, she thought—along with their arrogant opinions and lethal tongues and complete lack of regard for the things that made this island great.

Her house would sell quickly, as property on Cape Refuge always did. She would make enough to get started. She'd call a realtor tomorrow, she thought. She wouldn't let Morgan convince her to stay. And she wouldn't let Cade's soft, knowing gaze change her mind either.

Her mind was made up, but as she walked the perimeter of the island, she realized that, no matter how fast she walked or how far she went, Cape Refuge was still with her.

She wondered if she could ever really escape it.

Sadie's first paycheck came the next day. It was such a thrill that she didn't know what to do first. When she left the office that afternoon she hurried through the rain down to the bank a block away and cashed the check. With her money tucked into her pocket, she hurried back to Hanover House, anxious to pay the rent and show them that she could indeed earn her keep.

Soaking wet and almost running by the time she got to the front yard, like a child with a straight-A report card, she bounced up the steps and across the porch.

"Morgan, you won't believe it!" she cried as she burst into the kitchen. It was empty. She went through the rest of the downstairs rooms, searching for someone to tell, then looked outside and realized that Morgan's car was gone. She would have to wait.

She heard movement upstairs, a door closing, footsteps across the floor . . .

She ran up the stairs, turned the corner—and stopped cold.

It was Jack.

The man who had beaten her leaned against the wall, smoking a cigarette and watching the shock on her face.

"Surprise," he said in that voice heavy with evil.

She screamed and started to run down the stairs, but he was on her in seconds. He knocked her legs out from under her, and she tumbled down, her cast breaking as it hit against the stairs.

She managed to get up before he was on her again, but he grabbed her and knocked her to the ground. His fist cracked across her cheek, producing a bloody gash, but she got her feet under her again and ran. She stumbled out the back door and took off into the trees, knowing he was behind her. She could hear him panting and calling her name.

"Thought you could hide, did you?" he was saying. "Thought you could report me to HRS and get away with it? You can't hide from me, Sadie. You ain't smart enough."

But she *was* smart enough to get away. She had walked this way too many times and she knew which routes might lose him. She ran for her life, through yards and behind houses, into the heart of Cape Refuge, running, running until she thought she had lost him. Because if he ever did catch her, she knew this time he would kill her. There was no mistaking it.

Her breath sounded amplified in her ears, and her heart beat rudderlike against her chest. She stopped and hid in a cluster of wet bushes in someone's yard and waited there as rain drizzled down and the moments ticked by. She listened for him, smelled for him, but when he never made a move, she knew she had lost him. Finally, she made her way to a convenience store with a pay phone. She thought of calling the police, but she'd never had good luck with them before. Morgan wasn't home. So she called information, got Blair's number, dropped in some more coins, and dialed.

Lightning shocked overhead, making her jump, and she put her back to the wall and clutched the phone tight as she waited, watching for him to come upon her and finish the job. Blair's phone rang once, twice, a third time.

"Please answer!" she whispered.

The voice mail picked up.

"I'm not home right now," Blair's voice said, "but if you'd like to leave a message, wait for the beep."

She waited for the beep, then in a breathless, panicked, high-pitched voice said, "Blair, I went home, and Jack was there waiting for me, trying to kill me, and he chased me, and I got away, but he'll find me." She stopped on a shivery sob and brushed her wet hair back from her eyes. "I don't know where Morgan is, so I'm going to Nancy's to see if I can hide there so he can't find me. Please, when you get this, come get me there. I'm so scared."

She hung up the phone, then took off walking to the judge's house, praying that Nancy would take her in.

The light on Blair's machine was blinking when Blair got home from the library. She didn't want to talk to anybody. She had spent the day secluded in the back room. Because of the storm, hardly anyone had come in, and those who had were not interested in conversation.

Still, she pushed the button and went into the kitchen as she listened.

The tape beeped. "Blair, it's Morgan. Call me, please."

Blair got a can of Diet Coke from the refrigerator and poured it into a glass. The tape beeped again. Sadie's high-pitched, panicked voice fired across the line: *"Blair, I went home, and Jack was there waiting for me, trying to kill me, and he chased me, and I got away, but he'll find me . . ."*

The glass slipped from Blair's hand and shattered on the tile.

"I don't know where Morgan is, so I'm going to Nancy's to see if I can hide there so he can't find me. Please, when you get this, come get me there. I'm so scared."

Blair crunched the glass under her shoes and reached the phone. She dialed the police station and waited as the call was routed to Cade. "Cade, Sadie's in trouble," she blurted. "She left me a hysterical message that Jack is in town, that he broke into Hanover House and was waiting for her. She's hurt."

"Jack? The mother's boyfriend?"

"Yes. Cade, you've got to catch him before he kills her. She said she was going to Nancy's because he wouldn't look for her there."

"I'm on it, Blair," he said. "I'll get back to you."

77

Limping and clutching her broken arm against her body, Sadie made her way to the northern tip of the island where the Simmons lived. She rang the bell, then banged urgently on the front door. After a moment, Nancy opened it. "Sadie, what happened?"

"He's here," Sadie cried, stumbling in. "Jack's after me." She closed the door behind her, and looked out the window.

"Jack who?" Nancy's voice was laced with irritation.

"*Jack!* My mother's boyfriend. He tracked me down. I can't ever get away from him! Please, can I stay here, just until they catch him?"

"Of course you can," Nancy said.

"We have to call the police," Sadie cried, running from window to window to check the locks.

"Sadie, calm down," Nancy said. "Let's clean that cut—"

Sadie was wet and cold, shivering so badly that she could hardly stand. "They have to find him before he tracks me here. They have to catch him ..."

"Sadie, stop!" Nancy turned her from the window and looked her in the face. "You're bleeding, and your cast is messed up. One thing at a time."

"The police," Sadie cried. "Please, the police . . ."

Nancy walked her into the bathroom and made her sit down. Sadie hugged herself and wished for a blanket. Her clothes were wet, and she couldn't stop shaking.

Her eyes shot to the window, and she wondered if it was locked. He could break the glass and come in after her.

"Here," Nancy said, pouring two pills into her hand. "It'll help."

"No!" Sadie squealed. "The police—"

"Take these, Sadie," Nancy insisted, filling a glass with water. She thrust the pills into her trembling hands. "They'll help the pain and calm you down."

Sadie took the pills, and Nancy came at her with a cotton ball and alcohol.

"You need stitches," she said. "And your arm—we need to get you to the hospital."

"No," Sadie cried. "I can't go out. He's waiting for me. He wants to kill me."

"Okay," Nancy said. "Let's just stop the bleeding, and we'll call the police."

Sadie felt the fight draining out of her. "Yes," she whispered. "Tell them . . . he's after me . . . little Caleb . . ."

Nancy walked her to the guest room and turned on a lamp. There were family pictures, plants, a clock that ticked too loudly . . . and windows. "Lie down and rest now," Nancy said, "and I'll call the police. Just keep this towel pressed against your face to stop the bleeding."

"The window," Sadie said. Her voice was weak. Her body felt as if she had strapped weights to her limbs.

"It's locked," Nancy assured her. "Now you just rest here. I'll get the police."

Sadie lay down and pulled her knees to her chest, pressing the towel to her face. She was still wet and so cold but too tired

to pull the blanket over her. . . . She thought of little Caleb, screaming out his pain and anguish with no one there to help him. Where
was he? What had Jack done with Caleb?

The rain's patter against the panes of glass soothed her,
lulling her mercifully into sleep. She felt as though she had fallen
into a deep pool, her limbs moving slowly around her. She floated
that way as her fear lifted and her body warmed. . . .

The door to the room opened so hard that it banged against the
wall, shocking her out of that warm pool. She sat up, her body
still heavy, her eyes trying to focus.

Jack stood in the doorway. "I told you you can't hide from me."

She opened her mouth to scream, but he slapped his hand
across it. She tried to fight as he lifted her, but she was so tired.
Nancy would stop him, she thought, the police would come. . . .
But no one was there as he carried her through the house.

He got her out into the closed garage, and she saw that his
car was sitting there, sheltered from the view of neighbors. He
threw her in and got in behind her, forcing her down to the floorboard. She tried to get up, but the debilitating fatigue kept her
down. Somehow, he had gotten the remote that opened the
garage, and the door slid open.

He pulled out of the garage, and Sadie wondered where
Nancy and the judge were and why they weren't helping . . . how
Jack had gotten into their garage and their house . . . whether they
were all right . . .

Something hard whacked across her skull . . .

. . . and everything went black.

CHAPTER

*N*ancy was waiting when Cade and Cald-well arrived. Randy rushed home as well, with his baseball cap on backwards and a Dr Pepper in his hand.

"Where is she?" Cade asked as Nancy let them in.

"Asleep in the back. She was hysterical, so I gave her some codeine to calm her and help with the pain." She started leading them up the hall.

"She all right?"

"She's got a cut on her cheek. Bruised and limping. And he may have rebroken her arm." She got to the guest room and knocked lightly.

"Sadie," she said as she opened the door.

The room was empty.

"She's not here," Cade said. He met Nancy's eyes.

Nancy rushed out and went up the hall. "Maybe she's in the bathroom."

Cade followed her but Sadie wasn't there. "Cade, she was right here. I cleaned her cut myself. She was panicked and dripping wet."

352

Randy stood at the end of the hall, looking irritated, as if they were making him late for soccer practice.

There was a scuff mark on the wall, like a foot might have kicked it. "Randy, was this here before?"

He gave it a cursory glance. "Before what?"

"Before Sadie got here."

He studied the scuff mark, shrugged. "I couldn't really say."

Cade knew better than that. He had been in this house before for some of the parties that Nancy and Randy threw, and he knew that it was always immaculate and perfectly decorated. Nancy was known for being obsessive about her home, even though her office was cluttered beyond reason. Once he had been at a Christmas party here when a candle had caught a wall hanging on fire. Nancy had put it out and repainted the wall while the party went on around her.

"She probably just took off again," Randy said. "Who can understand a teenager?"

"Have you both been here the whole time?" Cade asked.

"No," Randy said. "I was at the office late. She was already here when I got home."

"Did you leave the house at any time?"

"We were sitting on the covered patio, watching the rain," Nancy said.

Cade gaped at him. "While you were supposed to be guarding Sadie? Why would you leave her alone when she told you someone was trying to kill her?"

"Well, we didn't think he knew where she was," Nancy said. "We thought—"

Cade threw the door open and headed outside. "I'm going to talk to the neighbors."

It didn't take him long to find a witness who had seen Jack's car pull into the judge's garage. It didn't make sense, he thought. The judge had the best security system money could buy. Why hadn't it kept Jack from getting to Sadie, and why hadn't Nancy and Randy heard her fighting?

And how had Jack figured out where Sadie was? Here he was, new to the island, not knowing anybody, and yet he was able to find the house where Sadie just happened to be hiding?

When he got back to the squad car, he called in an all-points bulletin for Jack and Sadie. When he got back to the station, he called Blair to warn her that Sadie was missing and the man was still at large. He told her about the scuff on the wall and the judge's nonchalance.

"This guy Jack's dangerous," he said. "He's about six feet tall, has long red hair, a goatee ..."

"Cade!" she cut in. "I saw him yesterday. I was walking around the island, and he was sitting in the judge's backyard, talking to him and Nancy!"

Cade just stared at a spot on his desk as the words sank in. "If Randy Simmons has been in contact with Jack...." His voice trailed off as he tried to process the thoughts whirling through his mind.

"Why?" she asked. "How would he know about Jack, and what would he have to gain?"

Cade closed his eyes. "I told him about Jack, when I asked him to do the paperwork for Sadie. I also told him that Sadie was one of the reasons you wouldn't let go of Hanover House."

His heart ticked off milliseconds as Blair sat silent. "Cade, you don't think he's the one who—?"

"I'll call you back, Blair," he said, and cut her off.

His mind reeled with the disconnected facts, the fragmented hunches, the threads that ran through every part of these crimes. He needed more to go on, something substantial, before he could pick up the judge. And if he was involved, what about Nancy?

What would have motivated them?

He bolted out of his office. McCormick was on the phone, a look of disbelief on his face. At the sight of Cade, he put his hand over the phone. "You'll never believe what just washed up on the shore over by the South Beach Pier."

Cade braced himself. "Tell me."

"Rick Dugan," he said.

Morgan mothered Sadie's room, smearing her tears with trembling hands. "When's it going to end?" she muttered. "So much violence."

Jonathan tried to calm her with a hug, but she slipped away and straightened the comforter on the girl's bed. "She'll be okay, honey. They'll find her."

"Like they found Rick?" Her voice choked off, and she went to the mirror, where Sadie had a picture of Caleb wedged in the wood frame. What would become of the baby?

Blair stood dry-eyed in the doorway. Morgan could tell her wheels were turning, working through scenarios, solving the crime. "I know the judge is involved," she said.

Morgan took Sadie's pillow off the bed and pulled the loose sham over it. Her gaze drifted out the window, and she searched the street, silently praying that it wasn't too late. . . .

"That article came out in the paper," Blair went on, "full of lies, yet Nancy wouldn't print a retraction, then Rick disappeared, making him look doubly guilty, only to

show up dead. Meanwhile, Jack shows up out of nowhere after
Cade told Randy about him, and he comes straight to where
Sadie's staying, finds her where she's hiding—"

Morgan turned from the window. "Why haven't they found
her yet? It's a tiny island. How hard could it be?"

Jonathan put his hands on her shoulders. "Maybe they're
not on the island," he said. "Maybe they got out before anyone
knew to start looking."

Blair slid her fingers through the roots of her hair. "And that
delay is, once again, traced back to our judge."

"Then what're they waiting for? Why don't they arrest him
and force him to tell them where she is?"

"Cade's working on it. I'm sure he'll get him soon. But he's
also trying to catch up with Jack and Sadie and figure out what
happened to Rick." Blair walked to the window, and she too
looked out. It was still raining. Dark clouds hovered over the water.

She imagined Sadie, soaked and beaten up, terrorized by the
man she feared the most. She wished she believed in prayer.
Instead, she believed in the gun she had in her pocket.

"I need to go home," she said. "I need to use the computer
at the library. I was getting to the bottom of this dummy corpo-
ration thing, all these businesses that owned East Coast Properties,
Incorporated. Maybe with a little more searching, I can find out
who owns what."

"What difference does it make now?" Morgan asked her. "I
don't really care who owns East Coast Properties."

"But it could tie in," Blair said. "I have a hunch."

"You can't go alone," Jonathan said. "It's too dangerous."

"Then come with me," she said. "Please. It's something I
really need to do. Maybe it'll shed some light on all of this."

"All right," Morgan said. "But we have to tell Cade where
we're going in case he finds Sadie."

Within half an hour after getting to the library, Blair had found
what she was looking for—the owners of each of the dummy
corporations.

"Just what I thought," she said. "Randall and Nancy Simmons . . . and look—Fred Hutchins."

"The mayor?" Jonathan asked. "You've got to be kidding."

"So this is why he was so gung ho about closing us down. Between him and Nancy, they got the whole city council inflamed against us."

"Boy, this smells bad," Blair said. "The mayor convincing the City Council to close us down, the judge casting doubt on Gus and Jonathan by keeping them locked up. Rick Dugan dead after Nancy publishes a bunch of lies about him, Sadie kidnapped from their very house—"

"I think I'm gonna be sick," Morgan said through tight lips. "To think that Mama and Pop might have been—murdered over money."

"I bet they knew about all these dummy corporations," Blair whispered. She turned around in her chair. "Morgan, remember that day—how confident they were about the City Council meeting? When I talked to Pop that afternoon, he told me not to worry, that there had been some new developments. Maybe they'd discovered who was behind East Coast Properties and that the city's threat to close them down was only to force them into selling, so the mayor and the judge could get their hands on the property and turn it into some kind of tourist trap. Maybe the judge knew it and wanted to shut them up."

"But what about Jack? Where does he fit into the whole thing?"

"Maybe he's just a pawn."

Jonathan grabbed his keys. "Come on. We're going to find Cade and tell him what we know."

CHAPTER

*T*hey found Cade at the South Beach Pier, where Rick's body had washed up. The rain hammered down as they approached the yellow crime scene tape and asked for Bruce, the police sergeant, to get the chief. Rick's body wasn't visible from where they stood, for a crowd of police blocked the view. If it had been, Blair would have had to turn away. She couldn't bear the sight of another dead body.

Cade's eyes were alive with fire and fury as he crossed the sand toward them.

"What happened to him?" Blair asked.

"He was murdered," Cade whispered. "Neck was broken. He was probably dead before he hit the water."

"Cade, we need to talk," Blair whispered. "I just finished tracing the companies that own East Coast Properties. You'll never guess who's on the list of owners."

"Who?"

"Judge Randy Simmons, his wife, Nancy—and the dear mayor of our town."

"*My uncle?*" Cade asked. He took a step back, turned around to the crowd of cops working the scene, then settled his eyes back on Blair. "It's not possible," he whispered. "My uncle's not a killer."

"They were trying to force the sale through," Blair said. "He was in on it, Cade. I think our parents knew. I think they'd found out and were going to expose them. That's why they wound up dead."

"Blair, it's one thing to carry out a shady business deal, but to kill over it . . . ?"

"Think about it. If it came out that Randy and Nancy Simmons and Fred Hutchins were part owners in the company, people all over the island would put two and two together. They own dozens of places around town, and a lot of them were sold when the owners were at the end of their ropes financially, sometimes due to hassles from the city council. East Coast Properties happens to extend an offer at the right time, and people are so fed up they sell. The judge would lose his bench and be disbarred, no one would ever trust Nancy's paper again, and the mayor would be forced to resign. Not to mention the fact that they'd probably be in trouble with the IRS once all their holdings were exposed."

Cade looked back to the place where Rick's body lay. "So the article about Rick and his subsequent death . . . were just to make Hanover House look even more dangerous. . . ." He closed his eyes. "And I told Randy about Sadie hiding from Jack. I even mentioned that she was one of the reasons you probably wouldn't let go of Hanover House."

"He called him," Morgan said, her face twisting at the danger they had brought upon Sadie. "Randy helped Jack get to her. So help me, if anything happens to her—"

"Can't you just go and arrest Randy?" Jonathan asked. "Right now. Handcuff him and parade him out like you did me?"

"The problem," Cade said, "is he's the one who issues the arrest warrants."

"But there must be somebody you can go to."

"There is," Cade said. "The supervising judge in the county. I can get a warrant from him. But I have to be able to convince him, and right now all we've got is circumstantial evidence and hunches. It's going to take some heavy persuading ... and some time."

"We may not *have* time," Morgan cried. "Cade, you've got to hurry before they kill again."

Cade swallowed and looked back toward the body. When he turned back to them, that fire in his eyes burned brighter. "Okay, you've got to keep this quiet," he said. "If word gets out, it could all slip through our fingers."

"Not a word from us," Blair said. "Just please hurry. Randy may know where Jack went with Sadie. If you can get him to talk, it could save Sadie's life."

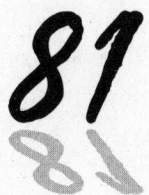

As Blair, Morgan, and Jonathan drove back toward Hanover House, Blair scanned the woods through one car window and the water through the other. They drove past the Crab Shack tourist trap, carefully hidden in the woods on the north side of the island, where the boats made their way up and down the Bull River. They drove past Chutney Creek, where Toothless Joe started his dolphin tours. And they drove past the gate to their own boathouse.

It was open and there were tire tracks in the mud. Blair caught her breath.

"Jonathan, were you at the boathouse today?"

"Not in this rain."

"Then why's the gate open?"

Jonathan met her eyes in the rearview mirror. "You don't think . . ."

"Turn the car around!" Morgan cried.

He made a U-turn on the road, then pulled into the muddy driveway. The boathouse couldn't be seen from the entrance. He stopped the car. "There are clear tracks going in, but it doesn't look like they came back out."

Morgan's face lost all color, and she grabbed her husband's arm. "Jonathan, we've got to get to a phone. We have to call Cade."

"How would Jack know about the boathouse?" Jonathan asked. "Sadie wouldn't tell him."

Blair clutched the gun in her pocket and opened the car door. "Maybe Randy did, as a way to help him stay low until he could get out of town. I'm going down there to find out. Cade said he's driving an old gray Malibu. If it's his car, I'll signal you, and you can go call the police."

"No, Blair!" Jonathan said. "If anybody's going, I am. Get back in the car."

But Blair's mind was made up. She jumped out of the car and took off into the trees before anyone could stop her.

CHAPTER

Blair's feet slipped on the mud. She fell to her knees, got up, and steadied herself on a tree. She searched for footholds, rocks or tree roots or grass.... The storm roared overhead, dripping through the trees.

She trudged on, stepping carefully, her feet sliding and sucking. She pushed through the brush, stepping over decayed logs and straining to see the boathouse through the trees. As the small structure came into view, she saw the Malibu parked in front.

Just as she started to turn back and tell Jonathan and Morgan, a scream ripped through the air—

Sadie!

Something erupted inside her, hot and volcanic. Another murder was taking place, and she was close enough to stop it.

She launched forward, tripping and skidding in the mud. She reached the door and threw it open. Jack stood over Sadie, who was crumpled in a heap at his feet.

He swung around, training his rifle on Blair. She raised her .22.

Sadie raised herself up behind him and flung her body at him as his gun went off. The bullet missed as Blair hit the floor. She kept the gun aimed at him, but she knew she couldn't fire. Sadie was too close . . .

Suddenly, Jack dove for Blair, knocking the breath out of her and grabbing her pistol.

Sadie's screams shrieked through the air, and she got into the boat and hunkered down. Jack put his muddy boot on the scarred side of Blair's neck, holding her down with the barrel of his rifle on her temple.

Blair's mind raced with hot, dizzying images: her parents' bodies on the warehouse floor, Rick dead on the beach, Morgan terrorized in Blair's own home, Sadie on the floor of the boat, abused and beaten . . .

Adrenaline burst through her head, and she told herself she would not die here . . . not like this . . .

She twisted her body, knocking him off balance. The gun fired again as she scrambled into the boat. Sadie grabbed her, trembling. Blair groped around. There were things she could use for a weapon. The anchor . . . where did they keep the anchor . . . ?

But there was no time.

He brought her .22 up . . . aimed . . .

Blair grabbed Sadie, threw her off the end of the boat, and dove in after her. Her face slapped the cold water, but she pulled deep into the emerald darkness, her eyes open and searching for the girl . . .

Sadie's eyes were panicked as she groped toward the top for air, weakly fighting the current. Blair followed her up toward the angry, rain-rocked surface and drew in a deep breath as she came out of the water.

She heard a crack like thunder, and pain shattered through her, thrusting her back under, ripping through her side. She gurgled water, and blood floated up around her as she sank deeper, deeper . . .

She was dying, she thought. Bleeding to death at the hand of a maniac . . .

She sputtered in the water and tried to pull herself up, but the current was too strong, and the strength had been blown out of her . . .

Darkness closed over her as the water marked its claim.

Sadie gasped for air, sputtered to stay at the top, and searched frantically around her for Blair. Jack stood in the bobbing boat, holding that rifle.

She tried to swim, but pain ratcheted through her arm, rendering it useless. Where was Blair? She had to find her.

She went under again, her face stinging in the salt water, and saw the cloud of blood.

She shot out of the water and sucked in air.

The gun fired, and she screamed wretchedly, desperately . . .

Jack splashed into the water.

Sadie blinked the water from her eyes and tried to find him. She saw the blood rippling out from where he'd fallen.

Confusion played in tandem with her fear, and she found it hard to focus, hard to think, hard to tread water—

Then she saw Randy Simmons, standing on the opposite bank with a gun in his hand. The world slowly shifted into clear focus. The judge had shot Jack. He had come to rescue her. He could save Blair, and pull Sadie from the water. It was over, she thought. All over.

She started to swim toward him, her rescuer, her salvation . . .

But he slowly raised his gun again.

After receiving Morgan's frantic phone call, Cade arrived at the boathouse entrance in moments. Morgan was there, standing in the rain near the gate and crying for help.

Jonathan had gone down after Blair, and as Cade, McCormick, and J.J. Clyde fanned out to make their way down to the building, they heard the gunshot rack the air like a thunderclap through the sky.

Cade's world seemed to retreat into slow motion, while his body lunged fast-forward toward the sound of water splashing, someone gasping for breath, a woman crying ...

He reached the door and went in barrel first. Competing images slammed through Cade's brain: Jack in the boat, his rifle aiming, a blood cloud in the water, Sadie sputtering and splashing ...

He raised his gun, but before his finger closed over the trigger, another shot fired, and Jack doubled and splashed into the water.

Again, the world moved slowly, seconds like hours, as Cade sought the source of the bullet. He saw Sadie calling for Blair, jerking in a circle in the angry water, seeing someone on the other side of the river.

His eyes moved up, to the lone figure standing in the trees, the man's gun following Sadie's progress as she swam toward him.

Cade raised his gun with both hands, and muttered a silent, pleading prayer . . .

He fired.

The municipal judge of Cape Refuge dropped to the ground.

Sadie went under, then bobbed back up, screaming out her terror at the horrors unfolding around her, closing in on her, floating near her—

But Cade couldn't see Blair.

"Blair!" he shouted, but he knew without waiting for an answer that one of the circles of blood at the top of the water was hers.

He dove in and swam out past Sadie, came up for a gasp of air, and looked around. Seeing nothing, he dove down again, searching for her, swimming, searching, swimming—

He came up again, and as he did, he saw Jonathan breaking up out of the water, pulling Blair with him.

She didn't gasp for air, didn't fight for release. Her face was white, and even her scars were void of color.

"She's shot," Jonathan yelled.

Cade took her from Jonathan's arms and carried her to the river wall. Sirens blared and horns bleated, but Blair couldn't wait for help.

He laid her down, his heart wildly beating, ticking out escaping seconds. Cade bent over her and pressed his mouth against hers, began pumping air into her lungs. As he did he sent a soul-deep cry up to heaven, pleading with God not to take her yet.

CHAPTER

84

$\mathcal{B}$lair woke to a blur of voices and faces. She began to cough and sputter; then she vomited on the dirt. Her lungs rebelled with a fit of coughing, and a sharp pain webbed out from her side.

"She was shot in the back," someone shouted. "She's lost a lot of blood."

Hands poked and prodded, needles pierced, voices yelled in sounds she couldn't understand.

She felt herself being lifted, rolled, loaded . . .

And numbing fatigue removed her from it all.

H
ours later, Blair woke, groggy in the aftermath of anesthesia. She recognized that she was in a hospital bed with an IV in her arm. Morgan lay in the small space next to her.

"Couldn't you afford a bed of your own?"

Morgan sucked in a breath and lifted her head. Tears filled her eyes, but she started to laugh. "You're awake."

"What'd they do to me?"

"They repaired the hole in your side. Jack almost killed you."

"Is he dead or alive?"

"Dead. The Honorable Judge Randy Simmons shot him. Then Cade shot Randy."

"Randy? Where was he?"

"Across the river," Morgan said. "It was all a setup. He told Jack to hide there with Sadie until he came. He was going to kill them both to get Sadie out of the way because Cade told him we wouldn't sell the house because of her. Jack was his pawn; someone to blame when Sadie wound up dead. He didn't count on you showing up before he could silence both of them."

Blair just stared at Morgan for a moment, taking it all in.

Morgan tipped her head, and grief reddened her face. "He killed Mama and Pop, Blair. Just like you thought."

Blair swallowed. "I hope he's dead, too."

"No. He's alive. Just barely. He's in intensive care, unconscious. They don't know if he'll make it through the night. Cade arrested Nancy and Fred Hutchins a few hours ago. Nancy's confessed to her part as an accessory in exchange for some kind of plea bargain. Fred caved pretty quickly too and spilled his guts to get out of a murder-one charge. Said Randy killed Mama and Pop because they were going to expose him at the city council meeting. Randy broke into the shed and stole the speargun the night before, to set Jonathan up. It almost worked. Jonathan's fight with Mama and Pop that morning only helped Randy's plan along."

Blair closed her eyes as the pain of that information cut through her. As much as she had wanted to know, as hard as she had struggled to solve this crushing mystery, the truth only made her grief twist into bitter, burning anger. "How did he do it?" she asked. "How did he get in and out of the church in broad daylight, without being seen?"

"Came through the water, went in the side door. Fred said that Randy told him he shot Pop first. Mama fell to his side, and Randy had time to reload and shoot her too."

Tears rolled down Blair's face, and Morgan wiped them away. "Unbelievable," Blair said. "The good guys die, and the bad guys live to cheat justice and move on."

"They won't cheat justice," Morgan said. "And Randy may not cheat death. Besides, good guys don't always die." She touched Blair's face and tilted her head as tears rolled down her cheeks. "Sometimes the bullet misses all of the major organs, and the good guy lives to see justice done."

"That a fact?" Blair asked in a weak whisper. "I could've sworn this was going to be that conversation you'd always remember. My last words."

Morgan smiled and wiped another tear. "Well, I have no doubt that you *will* have the last word, in this and almost every other conversation we have. Or you'll try. But I guess I have to remind you that I'm older than you, so according to nature, and probably God, I'm supposed to go first. Sorry, Sis, but that's just the way it's got to be."

"We'll see about that." Blair lay still, looking up at the sister and friend who had always been there for her. She reached for Morgan's hand and squeezed it hard. Morgan leaned down and hugged her, and the two sisters clung together, as grief and relief battled for places in their hearts.

Blair slept for a while, then woke to find her sister, sitting in a chair beside her bed, her Bible open in her lap. "You haven't been quoting scripture to me in my sleep, have you?" she asked weakly. "Trying to give me some kind of subliminal conversion experience?"

Morgan smiled and closed the Bible. "How do you feel?"

"Like I've been drawn and quartered. But hey, I'm tough."

"God was with you in that water, Blair. I know you don't want to admit it, but he was. And he was with Sadie."

"Good," Blair whispered. "I mean, that she's all right. She sure had the deck stacked against her."

"There was no deck, Blair. God was on his throne the whole time." Morgan leaned over her, her eyes wet and sad. "Blair, after you came out of surgery, I was sitting beside you, waiting for you to wake up, wondering if you would. And I thought a lot about what you asked the other day. About where God was when Mama and Pop were screaming for their lives."

Blair closed her eyes. "I don't want to talk about it, Morgan."

"Well, I do," Morgan said. "And since you're too weak to fight me, I'm going to have my say. Earlier today I read again in Genesis about Joseph. His brothers threw him into a pit—"

"I know the story, Morgan," Blair said wearily. "I grew up hearing it just like you. His brothers were jealous, sold him to slave-traders."

"But think about it," Morgan said. "You want to know where God was when tragedy struck our family. He was on the same throne as he was when Joseph was in that pit, screaming and begging for his brothers to let him out. When he was bound and dragged off to Egypt. When he was thrown into jail for something he hadn't done—"

"You're making my point for me, Morgan. Either he's a helpless god watching a world spin out of control, or he's a mean god orchestrating the cruelest kind of pain. If you want to believe in a god like that, Morgan, be my guest."

"You're not thinking, Blair. Think about the suffering Joseph went through. The injustice. The tragedy and loss and heartache. But it was for a purpose. He had to be there, to save his family when there was a famine. He saved a nation, Blair. God put him there for a reason. And he told his brothers that what they had intended for evil, God meant for good."

Blair was getting angry. "So—what? God murdered my parents so I could save a nation? I don't think so, Blair, not from Cape Refuge, Georgia. Tell me what good can come of that."

"Blair, when things looked dark and grim for those first people of Israel, God gave them a savior. When things were dark and grim for Mama and Pop, there was a savior."

"No, there wasn't!" Blair shouted. "He didn't save them!"

Morgan's answer came on a tearful whisper. "Oh, yes, he did, Blair. He saved them, all right. Took them right to heaven. Salvation was there, when evil tried to take them out. Our parents probably died with the name of Jesus on their lips, and when they called him, he came for them. They're with him now."

Blair was too tired to fight. She just let out a long, loud sigh. "It's a comforting thought, Morgan. I'm glad you believe it."

When Cade and Jonathan came in, the conversation ended, but Blair played it through her mind for the rest of the night, dreaming of her parents in heaven, laughing and young, standing at a sea of glass, full of some nameless wonder that no mortal could ever describe.

She woke up angry—at her parents, at her sister, at Matthew Cade, at the mayor, and at Nancy and the judge who had instigated the greatest injustices in her life.

And most especially at the Honorable Judge Randy Simmons, who lay in a hospital bed one floor beneath her . . . probably plotting his defense.

She had sworn that when she learned who had killed her parents, she would kill him herself. She owed that to her parents, she thought. She owed it to herself.

Morgan lay sleeping on the small sofa by the window. Blair sat up, waited to get her balance, then tested her legs. Though pain shot through her side, she was able to stand. Shaking, she pulled off the tape covering her IV needle. Then she pulled the needle out.

She walked barefoot to the door, peered out, and saw that the hall was quiet. Slowly, she walked toward the elevators. She pressed the button for the fourth floor and got off at the intensive care waiting room. People slept in plastic recliners with blankets too short to cover them completely. She wondered if anyone was there waiting for word on Randy.

The double doors of intensive care required a security code, so she waited in the hall until a nurse came out. She caught the door before it swung shut, and she slipped inside. She made her way from one care cubicle to another, careful to avoid the nurses in the center station.

Finally, she saw him. She could see the long gray hair and his tanned face, though the dark circles under his eyes spoke of his battle with death. The floor was cold beneath her bare feet as she went into the room and stood over his bed. Hatred tore at her like a hungry animal as she gazed down at him. He was hooked up to several monitors and had a respirator mask over his mouth. She thought of unplugging it, watching him choke and struggle until the life smothered right out of him.

But she didn't move. She just stood there . . . staring down at the man who had killed her parents . . . hating herself for not grabbing that plug.

"What are you doing here?" The nurse's bold voice startled her, and she swung around.

"I just wanted to talk to him."

"He can't talk to you. He's in a coma," she said.

She let the nurse usher her out of the intensive care unit. Then she stood in the hall, feeling weak and tired and helpless. He would probably die anyway, but her parents would still be gone, and Rick Dugan's death would still be senseless and without purpose.

It was all out of her hands.

She just didn't know whose hands it was in. A benevolent, gentle god with some great purpose, or a cruel, unfeeling god who saw them all as toys to be shuffled around.

But her troubled mind wanted her life to be in someone's hands. The thought of it all being random, hopeless, was more distressing than anything else she had suffered.

Slowly, she made her way back to her room, but any kind of peaceful rest was out of her reach.

CHAPTER

*O*n the day Blair was to be released from the hospital, Sadie and Morgan fussed over her, driving her nuts. Sadie looked worse than she had when she had come to Cape Refuge, but her arm had been re-set and her wounds were healing. She and Morgan chattered like kids as they packed Blair's things. Then the room got quiet as five members of the City Council filed in.

Awkwardly, Sarah Williford said, "Blair, we wanted to come together today to tell you how sorry we are about all that happened . . . with us closing down Hanover House and everything. We were taken in just like you were. Fred was working us hard, trying to convince us it was the right thing to do. And with the murders and the articles coming out in the paper . . ." Her voice trailed off.

"We were caught up in the emotion and fear," one of the others said. "We hope you'll forgive us."

"Truth is," Sarah said, "our phones have been ringing off the hook. Half the town has called us to tell us not to close Hanover House. Folks are fed up with change on this island. That's one change they especially don't want."

Blair met Morgan's eyes, then looked at Sarah again. "I'm a little fuzzy with all the medication and stuff. You'll have to make this real clear for me. Are you saying . . . ?"

"We've rescinded the order to close Hanover House."

As she and Morgan embraced with the thrill of victory, Blair began to wonder if miracles did happen, after all.

That night they got Blair home from the hospital, and Morgan smiled as she apologized to Gus for suspecting him. He wrote her a song on the spot and played it with a reggae beat on his guitar. It actually made Blair smile. Sadie laughed out loud, the first time they had ever heard that, and Gus promised to write her one next.

Later that night, as Morgan lay next to Jonathan in bed, he brought up something that had been on his mind. "Something's got to be done about that baby," he said. "Little Caleb, Sadie's brother."

"I know," she whispered. "They're not going to let Sadie have him. And he can't spend those crucial years going from one foster home to another."

"Unless it was this one."

Morgan sat up in bed and smiled down at him. "Do you really think we could take him?"

"I can't imagine leaving him there."

"But what about his mother? We'd get attached to him, and then she'd get out of prison and want him back."

"She'll need a place to stay when she gets out," Jonathan said. "We could take her too."

Morgan began to laugh and threw her hand over her mouth. "Jonathan, I love you. I really, really love you!"

He grinned and pulled her back down. "This doesn't mean we'll quit trying to have one of our own."

"Of course not," she whispered, and melted into a kiss that tasted like joy.

She knew the dark hours of her suffering had passed and light shone over her now. And in the rays of that sunshine, she thanked God for redeeming the pain and filling her with new hope.

Caleb was not in a foster home. The HRS had no idea where he was. When Jonathan questioned them about reports of child abuse, he learned that they had only interviewed Jack Dent but had never actually removed the baby from the home.

After Sadie thought of several names of people with whom Jack might have left the baby, she, Jonathan, and Morgan took off for Atlanta.

They found Caleb at the home of one of Jack's girl-friends who lived in a trailer park with mounds of garbage festering in a ditch outside. She answered the door with a glazed look in her eyes.

"Stacy, did Jack leave Caleb with you?" Sadie asked.

"You bet he did," the woman said, letting them in. "It's about time somebody got here."

They heard Caleb crying in a back room. Sadie ran through the house and snatched him out of a playpen. The child was dirty, with thick caked snot crusting his nose. "Sadie's here, sweetie," she said, crying as she pressed her face close to his. "Oh, honey, Sadie's here."

His sobs faded into hiccups, and he looked up at her with mournful eyes. She held him tight as he laid his head against her chest.

"Jack said two days," the woman shouted. "Two days, and here it's going on a week. I thought that kid'd never shut up."

She ran and got his diaper bag and the things she had in the refrigerator, threw them into the bag, and thrust them at Morgan. "Take him. Good riddance. And tell Jack Dent that he owes me big for this."

"I'm sorry, Stacy," Morgan said. "But Jack's dead."

The woman gaped up at her, then turned to look at Sadie. "Is that true?"

Sadie nodded. "He was shot . . . trying to kill me."

Stacy was quiet as they gathered the rest of Caleb's things and loaded them into the car.

As Sadie hooked him into the car seat they had brought with them, the child put his thumb in his mouth and looked up at his sister.

"I missed you," Sadie cried softly. "Big time. I'm sorry I left you. I'll never do it again."

He hiccuped another sigh, and she kissed his wet cheek. Morgan leaned over him with tears in her eyes as she saw what a beautiful child he was. "We're so blessed, Sadie," she whispered. "Jesus is watching over us."

"I know," Sadie said. "He's answered my prayers. He saved me from death . . . and from Jack. And he saved Caleb too."

Before they left Atlanta they went by the jail, where Sadie had a brief reunion with her mother. Morgan and Jonathan got to know Caleb in the car, keeping him out of the jail so as not to traumatize him further with the confusing sight of a mother he couldn't touch. Sheila Caruso signed the papers allowing Morgan and Jonathan to take temporary custody until she was out of jail.

She was neither surprised nor saddened to hear of Jack's death.

In fact, no one mourned Jack's death.

No one at all.

CHAPTER

87

*B*ut Rick was mourned for. On the day of his funeral, Blair, Morgan, Cade, Sadie, Gus, and Mrs. Hern were the only ones who attended. As it turned out, he was all that he said he was. He had never killed anyone, and there really was a wife and baby who had died. It seemed that Randy Simmons had set him up because he was convenient, having the most mysterious background of all the tenants at Hanover House.

Cleaning out Rick's room after he was found, Morgan had found Rick's journal. Jonathan read an entry from it as he stood at the pulpit in their warehouse church. It was written on the day that Thelma and Wayne had given him the check for ten thousand dollars.

"'Thelma and Wayne discovered the money,'" Jonathan read. "'And I felt more shame than I'd ever felt in my life. I finally decided I would take the money back, put it right back where I'd found it, and Gerald Madison would never know it was gone. I thought Thelma and Wayne were going to turn me in, anyway, have me arrested, and I figured I deserved it.

"'Instead, they told me they knew about the money, and they handed me a check for ten thousand dollars. Said it would pay my debts in the same way that Christ had paid my spiritual debt. They were more concerned about my soul than they were about justice. It moved me to tears. It moved me to Christ.'"

Jonathan's voice cracked as he read those last words, and he looked up across the meager congregation, saw the tears on his wife's face . . .

. . . and on Blair's.

After the burial, Blair and Morgan sat quietly on a bench at the grave site, staring at the mound of dirt with flowers laid over it. "He's with his family now," Morgan said. "His wife and his daughter. And with Jesus."

"I wish I could believe that," Blair whispered.

"You can," Morgan said. "You know in your heart that it's true."

She struggled with the thought. "Morgan, why did Mama and Pop do the things they did for people? Like giving Rick ten thousand dollars? That was probably their life's savings. There sure wasn't much left in the bank. Why did they feel such a need to provide refuge for the lost and the weak and the despairing? Why did they give people so many chances?"

"Because it had been done for them."

Blair tried to get her mind around the thought of grace being dispensed because grace had redeemed them. But grace was a concept that couldn't be seen or smelled or tasted . . . and as much as she wanted to stand on ground as solid as that beneath Morgan, she still couldn't quite believe.

Morgan hugged her, kissed her on the cheek, then got up and left her alone there to think.

Cade had been watching from the street, hoping for a chance to talk to Blair, but when Morgan had joined her on the bench, he hadn't wanted to intrude on a private moment.

When Morgan left Blair alone, Cade got out of his car. Blair was alone at last. He started down the hill toward her.

She looked up at him.

"Mind if I sit down?" he asked.

She shrugged and nodded, and he took the seat that Morgan had just left. Quiet settled between them. Blair looked past the gravestones to the water beyond, to the sailboats lined up in the harbor. "I'm thinking of leaving Cape Refuge soon," she said. "As soon as I'm well enough."

"I've been thinking about that too," Cade said. "About what it would be like here without you."

She looked over at him, surprised that he had given it any thought at all.

His eyes were misty, serious, as he held her gaze. "I really wish you wouldn't go, Blair."

She swallowed and looked back at the harbor. Something about those words changed things in her mind. She didn't even know why. She couldn't think of a thing to say, so she just sat there staring, and he sat there with her, quietly content in her presence.

For the first time in her life, she didn't analyze the peace that he seemed to radiate like a warm wind. She just borrowed from it—astonished at the way he seemed to fill in the loneliness.

And she wondered if there was really any hurry to leave Cape Refuge. Maybe she would stay for just a while longer.

THE END

AFTERWORD

I don't understand suffering. This past year has been a time of grief for my family and many of my friends, and if I could, I would lift it off us and make it go away. But I can't.

At this writing, I'm grieving over the death of Landon Von Kanel, my daughter's eighteen-year-old friend, who was taken unexpectedly in a car accident. Just two years ago, we buried another of her friends, Anthony Shams, sixteen. Both of these young men had circles of influence that reached far across the globe. Their unique and vibrant personalities, their colorful wit, their big dreams, made them unforgettable and irreplaceable. I daresay that thousands have been impacted by their deaths, many for eternity. But I don't understand why Randy and Cindy, or Deborah and Al had to bury their children.

My friend Rick McMahan died a year ago. He was a mentor and friend to my husband and me. He and his wife, Lynda, were a true brother and sister. I miss seeing him on Wednesday nights after church, leaning on the visitor's booth as he waited for his wife and daughter to come down from youth group. He was the one I always gravitated to, to air my latest complaints about children or parenthood or life. He always seemed so in tune with God, and his wisdom always challenged me. I miss him on Sunday mornings. He and his family used to sit behind us, worshiping the Lord and shedding tears over his goodness and his awesome sovereignty. I miss him on Sunday nights, when we would sit together and worship again, and share stories and laughter and praises afterward. I miss his sense of humor, and his hugs, and the peace that he radiated. I miss the fact that my youngest child will not get to go through his Sunday school class and experience the love he had for the kids to whom he ministered. I miss the way his marriage set an example for the rest of us, of love and protection and nurturing and endurance.

I don't know why God chose to take Rick so early, or why he allowed him to suffer as cancer ravaged his body. I don't know why Lynda and his children, Kerry and Brad, had to say good-bye to their husband and father.

I have also grieved for Stephanie Whitson, another Christian writer, who said good-bye to her husband, Bob, after a long, exhausting struggle with cancer. In his last days, when he could barely sit up, Bob searched through his Bible for reasons that we suffer and wrote it all down. This long list of God's reasons for putting us through adversity has blessed my friend Lynda as she has grieved and suffered over Rick's death. It has also blessed many, many others. And his love and urgency to make others understand the Lord will live on long after him. Bob's teaching and his wisdom will continue to work in the lives of all those he touched. Yet Stephanie has a hole in her life, and she and their children miss him terribly.

And I have grieved for a friend, Patricia Hickman, another Christian writer who is completely sold out to the Lord. She and her husband, Randy, have devoted their lives to planting churches and drawing people into a knowledge of Jesus Christ. Why, then, did God choose to take their beautiful twenty-year-old daughter, Jessi, in another terrible car accident? I have so many questions for the Lord, so many whys as I weep for that loss that can never be replaced. With a daughter almost the same age, who has the same goals and interests as Jessi, I find myself shaken and humbled and slightly frightened by the suddenness of death. And my heart is broken for this dear family.

But I see so much fruit that has sprung up from these deaths and know that entire crops are yet to come. And I can't help remembering that my own salvation was the result of the death of a boy in my school, Ricky Bogan, a fifteen-year-old who died in an accident on the way home from school. Whatever fruit I bear is his fruit too. And despite the sorrow his death produced in me as a fourteen-year-old seeker, I am glad that God used it to bring me to him. I know the Lord well enough to trust that he is doing the same to many others as the result of these deaths.

Psalm 116:15 says, "Precious in the sight of the LORD is the death of his saints." I know this is true, and I also know that Jesus weeps over our losses, and he shares our grief. But he also sees the future, and he sees the whole picture. He knows his purpose in taking Landon and Anthony and Rick and Jessi and Bob. And he's already seen the reunions that are yet to come. Joyful, over-whelming, celebratory reunions.

We cannot control God, and we cannot second-guess him, as much as we'd like to try. Our God has plans and purposes that are far beyond our understanding.

Sometimes those plans and purposes break our hearts.

Sometimes they require sacrifices we never agreed to make.

Sometimes they stop us dead in our tracks, turn us upside down, inside out, and paralyze us with pain.

But his comfort is not far behind. And as we climb up into his lap and weep into his chest, he whispers in our ear, "Shhh. It's okay. I did it for a reason, and some day I'll tell you what it is." He strokes our hair and hugs us tight, and cries with us. "Shhh. Just hang on. It's not that long before you'll see them again. And then you'll be with them for eternity. I promise to see you through this."

Our whys are not answered, but we trust that there is a reason. God is in control, and he loves us through our pain.

As the song says, "Life is hard, but God is good." How precious is that goodness, and how sufficient is his comfort. And how thrilling are his promises of what will happen when he returns for us.

Come quickly, Lord Jesus!

SOUTHERN
STORM

*This book is lovingly
dedicated to the Nazarene.*

ACKNOWLEDGMENTS

I've been writing professionally for over twenty years now and long ago realized that it never gets easier. The truth is, each book is more difficult than the one before it. Fortunately, I have people in my life who help me. I'd like to thank some of them now.

Thanks to my dear friends (and family) of ChiLibris, a group of Christian writers who hold me accountable and constantly challenge me to grow as a writer and as a person. Writing can be a solitary life, but ChiLibris keeps me connected to others with the same passions. I also owe a debt of gratitude to James Scott Bell, lawyer-turned-writer, for answering all of my legal questions with such patience. And again I thank Dr. Harry Kraus Jr., surgeon-turned-writer, for choreographing medical emergencies with me and helping me figure out how to write my way out of them.

A special thank-you to those at Zondervan for their excellent work in getting my books into the stores. I owe more to Dave Lambert, Sue Brower, Lori VandenBosch, Bob Hudson, and the others on the fiction team than I can say.

Thanks also to Greg Johnson, my agent, whom God seemed to drop out of the sky for me eight years ago. He is evidence to me that when I follow God's direction, I can't go wrong.

And finally, thank you to my husband, Ken, for brainstorming with me, encouraging me, and rooting me on when the deadline looms near and my creativity seems dried up. I appreciate your constant reminders that I panic on every book, and it still usually turns out all right.

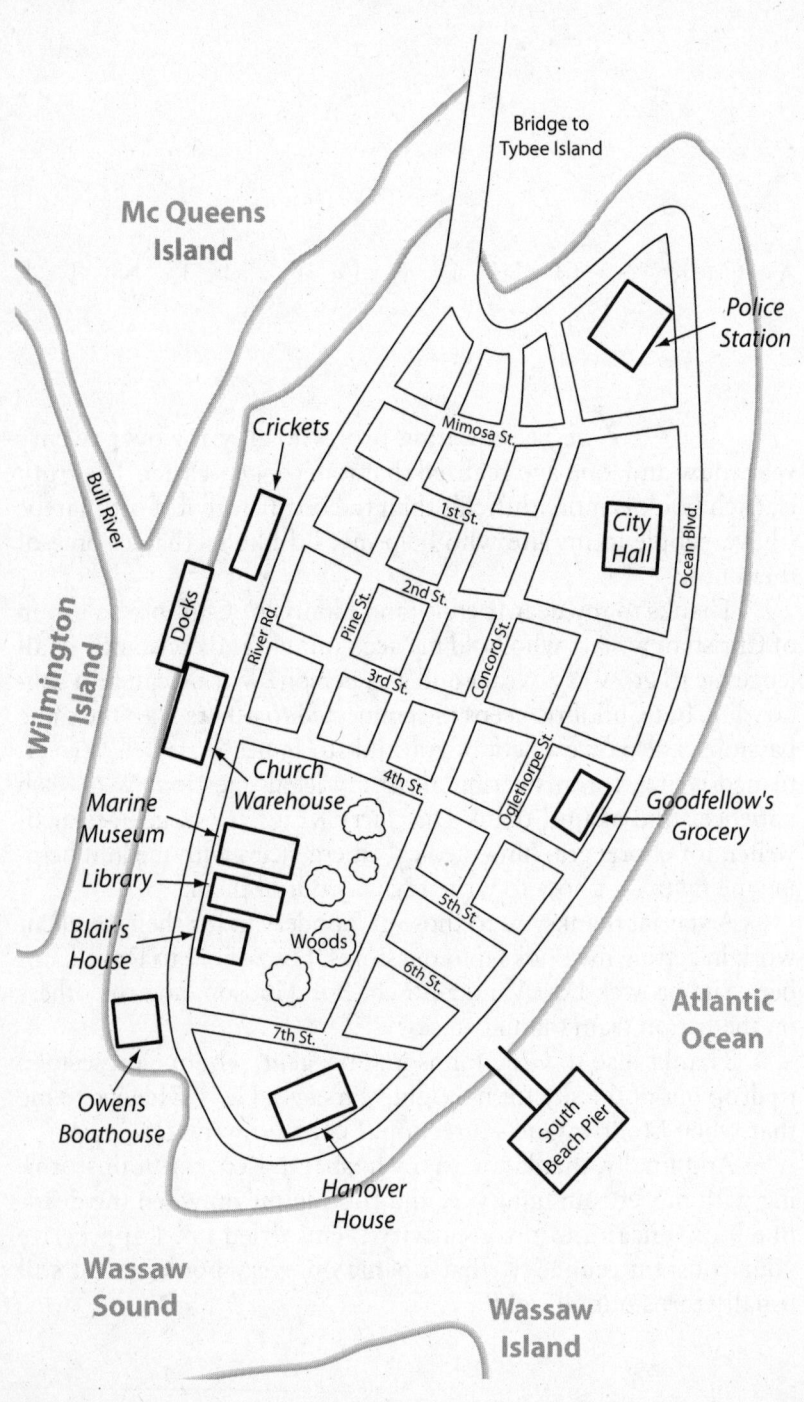

CHAPTER

The Georgia Weather Bureau's prophecy of fifty-mile-per-hour winds had been fulfilled and surpassed, much to Matthew Cade's chagrin. As chief of the small Cape Refuge police force, Cade could do little about the ravages of the storm as it beat across the island toward Savannah. But the safety of the residents was always his concern.

Though it was two in the afternoon, the sky looked as dark as nightfall.

Lightning bolted overhead in a panoramic display of white-hot fingers, grounding on the island and splaying across the angry Atlantic. The thunder cracked in rapid crashes, and rain slatted down at an angle that made umbrellas useless and flooded some of the streets.

Cade strained to see through the windshield of his squad car. The rain pounding on his roof and his wipers slashing across his windshield made it difficult for him to hear the radio crackling on his dashboard. He turned it up.

Fender benders had been reported at three locations on Cape Refuge, and a power line was down near the condos lining the north beach.

If everyone would just stay inside, maybe they could avoid any more problems. But that never happened. On days like this, residents insisted on driving through the storm at the same speeds they used on dry, sunny days. Tornado watchers stood out on their front porches, watching the sky for funnel clouds. And the most reckless among the residents would brave the lightning and drag their surfboards out to the waves, hoping to catch a thrill in the tempest.

Cade and his police force were left to clean up the messes and head off new disasters.

The dispatcher's voice crackled across the radio, and he picked up the mike. "Go ahead, Sal."

"Chief, there's another power line down on a road over at the dock. Somebody's going to get hurt unless you detour that traffic."

Cade sighed. "All right, I'm on my way."

He set the mike back in its holder and turned on his blue lights. Making a U-turn, he headed back around the southern tip of the island, then northbound toward the dock. He couldn't have residents driving over live power lines. He hoped the power company would hurry up and get its trucks out here.

The wipers swiped across his windshield, but the rain pounded too hard to give him much visibility. He strained to see.

Most cars pulled to the side of the road to let him pass. He turned on his siren to alert the others, but three or four kept their course in the lane in front of him.

"Get out of the way!" he yelled, pulling so close to the car in front of him that he knew one touch of its brakes would put him in the front seat with the driver.

Fortunately, the man pulled over. The other cars ahead of him still hadn't heard or seen him, so he moved up behind the next one, his siren still blaring. A block ahead, Cade saw a man standing on the opposite side of the road, seemingly oblivious to the rain pounding down on him. Passing traffic sprayed walls of water up over him, but he just stood there, watching the traffic pass.

The car in front of Cade still didn't move, so he punched his horn. The southbound lane with traffic coming toward him had cleared as drivers pulled off to the shoulder of Ocean Boulevard. He pulled around the car in front of him into the southbound lane and gently accelerated.

The man on the side of the road still stood there, drenched and undaunted. Cade knew that, as he passed, his tires in the water would spray him. Why didn't the man move?

He kept his siren blaring and pushed his horn again as he drove northbound in the southbound lane. He pulled even with the car that had refused to move out of the way and looked across at the driver. The driver looked back, panic evident on his face— a teenager, probably a new driver with no idea how to react. The kid slammed on his brakes.

Cade stepped on his accelerator and turned his eyes ahead again—just in time to see the pedestrian step out in front of him.

Cade yelled and slammed on his brakes. His car slid straight toward the man. . . .

Thunder cracked at the same instant as the impact. The man flew up over the hood and smashed into Cade's windshield, shattering it . . . then, as if he'd bounced, he flew out in front of the car and landed in a heap in the middle of the road. Cade couldn't move for a few seconds, then fumbled for the door handle and managed to get out. The rain flooded over him, and the wind almost knocked him back into the car. He rushed toward the man.

Oh, dear God, what have I done?

He heard yelling and doors slamming as other drivers got out and splashed toward him.

Reaching the man first, Cade knelt in three inches of water. The victim's eyes fluttered open, and his lips moved without sound. Cade grabbed the radio on his shoulder. "Sal, I need an ambulance just half a mile north of the Pier!" He yelled the words to make sure he was heard. "I need it right now! I just ran over a pedestrian!"

"Right away, Chief."

Cade touched the man's head, careful not to move it. Warm blood soaked his hand, but the pelting rain quickly washed it away.

"Can you hear me, buddy?"

The man tried to speak, but Cade couldn't hear him. Thunder crashed again.

He touched the man's throat; his pulse was weak, erratic.

"Hang on! You're gonna be all right. Just hang on." He had to stop the bleeding, so he pressed against the wound at the back of the man's head. But there was so much blood . . . too much . . .

The man tried to rise up, and this time Cade heard his raspy voice. "You have to . . . please . . . out of control . . ."

"Don't move!" What did one do for an open head wound?

He heard sirens blaring, voices calling. Someone opened an umbrella over them in a feeble attempt to shelter the victim from the storm, but the wind turned it inside out. Someone else threw a raincoat over the man. . . .

Lightning flashed, thunder bolted. . . .

"Cade," someone said, "he just ran right out in front of you!"

The blood was coming so fast. The man's pulse weakened. Where was that ambulance?

"I saw him. It was like he was in a trance or something."

"Is he dead, Cade?"

The siren grew closer, and he prayed that people would stay off the road and leave the ambulance a path. It stopped short, and he heard feet running toward him. Paramedics knelt beside the body, and Cade moved back. "Head injury," he yelled over the storm. "He bounced off my windshield."

As the medics worked, Cade backed farther away, his mind racing with the facts.

I've hit a man . . . an innocent man. . . .

He started to whisper rapid-fire prayers for a miracle. The man couldn't die. That was all there was to it. Police cars were meant to keep people from danger, not kill them.

"Call for a Medi-Vac, Cade!" one of the medics cried. "And clear us a path. He's running out of time."

"The helicopter can't fly in this! You'll have to drive him." He helped the paramedics get the man into the ambulance and then directed traffic as the ambulance headed out.

He shook his head, trying to pull himself together. Somebody had to be in charge here. But what did the chief of police do when he was the one who had almost killed a man?

He turned and saw some of his uniformed officers coming toward him.

"J.J., detour traffic," he yelled. "Keep it off of this block until we finish here. Jim, get over to the downed power lines out in front of the dock and divert traffic there. Alex, you take pictures and work the accident. . . ."

"But Cade, are you sure you don't want to work it?"

"I've got to get to the hospital and see if he's all right." His voice broke. "Just write the report and treat me like any other driver who hit a pedestrian. Call my cell phone if you have questions. It should get a signal by the time I reach Savannah." He walked back to his car and got in.

Through the shattered windshield, he saw Alex looking back at him as if he wasn't sure what to do. Then he turned away and began questioning witnesses.

Cade closed his eyes and lowered his head to the steering wheel. *That man could die.*

Why had he stepped out into traffic? He must have seen Cade coming. The squad car lights had been flashing and his siren was on. Even people in cars with radios blaring and air conditioners humming had heard him and gotten out of the way. How could this man have stepped into the path of a speeding police car?

He felt as if a fist had punched a hole in his lungs. He found it hard to breathe, and his head had begun to throb.

He reached for the keys hanging in the ignition, then realized that he couldn't move this car until they'd finished working the scene. Besides, he couldn't drive with a busted windshield.

He got out of the car and started walking through the rain.

"Where are you going, Chief?" Alex asked him.

"To find a ride back to the station so I can get my truck."

"I'll take you, Cade!" Melba Jefferson, a little round woman who attended his church and made it her business to comfort those in need, stood nearby, fighting her umbrella with a distraught look on her face.

"Okay, Melba," he said. "Let's go."

She led him to her car parked on the side of the road. He got into it, and she slid her round body into the driver's side. "Honey, are you all right?"

He shook his head. "It's not about me, Melba. There's a man dying."

She reached into the backseat and got a box of tissue. "Sweetie, your hand's all bloody."

Cade looked at it. The man's blood had stained it, though the rain had begun to wash it away. He pulled out several tissues and wiped the rest of it off.

Melba pulled out onto the street, and Alex directed her so that she could turn around and head back to the station. When they were on their way, she stayed quiet, which Cade appreciated. Clearly, Melba knew when words were appropriate and when they weren't.

She drove him up to the station, pulled into the parking lot. "I'll get some people praying, Cade," she said.

He nodded. "You do that. Thanks for the ride, Melba."

Cade jogged across the gravel parking lot to his truck, jumped inside, and was pulling out onto the street before Melba could get her car turned around.

CHAPTER

"Is this some kind of April Fool's joke?" Blair Owens leaned on the small conference table in the cramped library and tapped her pencil on her palm. "Because if it is, I need to get back to work."

"It ain't no April Fool's joke," Morris Ambrose told her. "That woulda been last Thursday."

She laughed. "You people can't seriously want me to run for mayor. That's insane. It's ludicrous. And I wouldn't go around saying it out loud, Morris, or you might lose your seat on the city council. Folks will start thinking you're showing signs of dementia."

Morris was undaunted. So were the other three who had come with him—Jerry Ann Shepp who ran the Cape Refuge Racquet Club; Matt Pearl, proprietor of the most expensive restaurant in town; and Gerald Madison, who owned Madison Boat Shop.

"Blair, think about it for a minute," Gerald said, wiping the beads of perspiration from above his lip. "The mayor's seat is empty since Fred got thrown in jail. Some real lowlifes are running. Sam Sullivan doesn't have the brains of a shrimp, and Ben Jackson hates big business."

Blair grinned and shook her head. "Gerald, Cape Refuge doesn't have any big business."

"You know what he means!" Jerry Ann piped in. "Blair, he's an electrician and thinks he needs to stick it to every business owner in town. We need somebody with a clear head and a backbone. Somebody honest. Somebody who can't be pushed around."

"Oh, brother." Blair felt the scars on the right side of her face burning. It always happened when she was surprised or embarrassed or, in this case, amazed. She got up and went to the pot of coffee she had brewed for this Sunday afternoon mystery meeting. Glancing out the door into the room stacked with books, she saw that Gray Foster was still studying at one of the reading tables, his nose buried in a book.

She turned back to the group. "This is crazy. Just crazy. I'm not the political type. I hate that kind of stuff. I'd much rather *fight* city hall than *run* it. Besides that, I'm not all that committed to living here since my parents died. One day I might pick up and move. You don't want a mayor who'd do that, do you?"

Matt Pearl, dressed in a designer suit with a black T-shirt underneath, crossed his sockless foot over his knee. "We know you, Blair. If you were elected mayor, you'd stay."

She poured her coffee and took a sip. "See, that's just it, Matt. I couldn't get elected. I've insulted ninety percent of the residents of Cape Refuge at one time or another. No, you've got to find yourself another patsy."

The four of them looked at each other with brooding eyes. "Well, who then? We've got to come up with our own candidate so some rube doesn't take the mayor's seat."

Jerry Ann began to rub her temples. "It's awful, you know. For our town to be without a judge, a mayor, and a newspaper all in one fell swoop."

"That's the way it goes." Blair came back to her seat. "But I'm not the one."

The phone rang, and she excused herself and dashed out into the book room and across to her office to answer it. "Cape Refuge Public Library, may I help you?"

"Blair, it's Morgan."

"Let me call you back, Sis. I've got people here."

"It's important. Did you hear about Cade?"

Blair stiffened. "No, what about him?"

"He hit a pedestrian. The man might die."

Blair caught her breath. "You're kidding."

"Melba Jefferson saw the whole thing. Cade's on his way to the hospital."

Blair shoved her blonde hair back. "Is Cade hurt?"

"I don't think so. Melba didn't mention it. She just said he's pretty torn up about it."

"Okay, I'm closing shop and going to the hospital."

"Come by and get me," Morgan said. "I'll go too."

"Five minutes. Be ready." Blair reached for her keys hanging on a hook on the wall. She hung up and ran back into the conference room. "Meeting's over, guys. Thanks for coming by. I have to run to Savannah."

She herded the four out of the library and turned back to the college student. "Gray, you have to go."

"Let me stay, Blair," he said. "Come on, I'm right in the middle of something. I'll lock up when I leave."

She didn't have time to argue, so she gave in. "All right. But don't leave me a mess to clean up."

"I won't."

She hurried out to her car, hoping the streets weren't too flooded to get through.

Cade was hurting, and she didn't want him to be alone.

Morgan set the phone back in its cradle and took off her apron. At twenty-eight, she was responsible for Hanover House, a bed-and-breakfast that served as a halfway house for the down-and-out instead of a haven for tourists. In an attempt to foster a family atmosphere for the tenants, she cooked a full meal each night and expected everyone to eat together. But tonight, Cade, her husband's best friend, was in trouble. She wished she could reach Jonathan to tell him, but he'd gone to Savannah for his Sunday Bible study at the county jail.

"Sadie, can you watch Caleb and get dinner out when it's done? I've got everything in the oven. It should be ready at six."

Her seventeen-year-old foster daughter bounced baby Caleb on her hip. "Sure, no problem."

Morgan smiled at the young girl she had found hiding in her boathouse just a few months ago. She'd had a broken arm and was desperately hiding from the man who had beaten her. Only later had Morgan learned about Caleb, Sadie's baby brother, still in the man's possession.

Thank goodness that was behind them and Sadie's mother had given Morgan and Jonathan legal guardianship over both of them while she served her prison term. Sadie was more help than responsibility, and seventeen-month-old Caleb was pure joy.

Morgan heard Blair's horn outside, and she pressed a kiss on Caleb's cheek, then Sadie's. "Don't forget dinner. And when Jonathan gets home tell him I went to the hospital with Blair."

"I didn't think we had a hospital on Cape Refuge," Sadie said.

"We don't. They took the man to Savannah." She pulled on her raincoat, grabbed an umbrella, and dashed out the door.

The umbrella did little good. By the time she'd climbed inside Blair's old Volvo, her long hair was soaked. "Look at me," she said with disgust.

"Yeah, look at you." Blair put the car into reverse and, wrenching her neck around, backed out. "You're the only one I know whose hair can take a rainstorm."

Morgan didn't answer. She'd always hated her curls; Blair had always coveted them. "Hey, you might want to cut through the island, since Ocean Boulevard is blocked off at the South Beach Pier."

"I'm on it," Blair said and pulled her car out of the driveway.

CHAPTER

3

*T*he tempest still raged in Savannah as the tropical storm pushed inland. Trees bent like bows in the wind, their leaves and branches reaching west. Water rose on some of the streets, making them impassable, but Blair navigated her way through the detours and reached Seventy-third Street and Candler Hospital at last.

The white building with its black windows loomed up in front of them, and she drove around to the emergency room and pulled up to the door. "Here, I'll let you out and park."

Morgan looked relieved. "Thanks. I'll find Cade. Use my umbrella."

Blair watched as Morgan rushed in. Pulling out of the covered drive, she found a parking place not far from the door. Normally, she wouldn't have used the umbrella, but she didn't like the idea of looking like a wet puppy in front of Cade.

The moment that thought flashed through her mind, she rebuked herself. This wasn't a fashion show, for heaven's sake. She had come to support Cade, not impress him.

Still, she used the umbrella and made a run for it. She made it inside without too much damage, and shaking out the umbrella, she looked around for Morgan or Cade.

Morgan stood at the reception desk. Blair joined her. "What's the story?"

"The man's still alive," Morgan said. "They said Cade is back there, that we could go to him."

Blair followed Morgan through the doors and into the wide antiseptic hall. She saw Cade farther down, sitting outside an examining room, his chair tipped back on two legs. His head leaned back against the wall, and he stared into space with reflective brown eyes. She could see he was troubled.

Something in her chest tightened.

Blair slowed her step as they approached. "Cade?"

Cade turned and dropped the front two legs of his chair. Surprise registered on his face as he got to his feet. "Blair . . . Morgan. What are you doing here?"

Morgan went to hug him. It was natural for her, the Earth Mother. Who *wouldn't* want a hug from her? Blair hung back.

"We heard what happened," Morgan said. "How is he?"

"I don't know. He's in surgery." He looked at Blair and offered a half-smile. "You're wet."

She smiled. "So are you."

He looked down at his wet uniform, then regarded her again. "I can't believe you came here in this storm."

She shrugged. "We couldn't let you go through this alone." Blair sat down in the chair beside him, and he dropped back into his own. His dark hair was still damp and disheveled, and the lines around his eyes gave him the look of a man much older than thirty-three. Those lines were part sun, part laughter, part stress. Today's accident had added at least another ten years.

"Cade, are you all right?" Morgan asked. "Were you hurt at all?"

"No, not me. But this guy's in really bad shape."

His chair went back on two legs again. Blair saw clearly that he was not all right. "I can't believe this happened."

"How *did* it happen, Cade?" Blair asked.

He swallowed and crossed his arms over his chest. "I was trying to hurry over to a downed power line, and I saw him standing on the side of the road, looking straight at me. And then he just stepped out in front of me. I slammed on my brakes, but the car skidded because the road was too wet...." His voice broke off, and she saw the slight tremor in the muscles of his chin.

Blair wished she had a little Earth Mother in her. "Who is he?"

Cade shook his head again. "That's just it. I don't know. He was trying to speak, but he didn't make any sense. The paramedics said he had no identification on him. None. Not even a wallet. Not a penny in his pocket."

"Well, that's not so unusual on Cape Refuge," Blair said. "Tourists leave their stuff in hotel rooms or glove compartments all the time while they go to the beach or sightsee."

Cade's eyes glistened as he stared straight ahead. "He just stood there. People spraying him as they went by. *Why* did he step in front of me?"

"Maybe he was drunk," Blair offered.

"Who knows?" He rubbed his eyes. "I can't notify anybody until we find out who he is. They need consent forms signed, insurance. I don't even know who to call."

His nostrils flared with the effort of holding back tears.

Cade was tough, but he had a sensitive heart. She knew what this was costing him. She wanted to touch his hand, but that kind of gesture didn't come as naturally for her as it did for Morgan.

She looked away, hoping to make him feel less vulnerable.

A door opened near them, and a doctor came out in green scrubs with his mask pulled below his chin. Cade got up and looked at him hopefully.

"Chief Cade?"

Cade nodded. "I've got my men trying to figure out who he is, so we can notify the family and get the insurance—"

"I'm sorry, Chief." The doctor's words cut Cade off, and the rest of his sentence hung in the air. "He didn't make it."

Cade's mouth dropped open, and he looked as though he hadn't heard right. Then understanding dawned. "Oh, no," he whispered.

"We did what we could," the surgeon said, "but he had multiple injuries. A very serious head injury, and the gunshot wound through his torso."

Cade stared at him blankly for a moment. "No, there was no gunshot. Just the impact of the car. He was walking and he came out in front of me—"

The surgeon shook his head. "He was shot, all right. Maybe that's why he stumbled out in front of you."

Blair looked up at Cade and saw the confusion on his face. "You mean, he was already shot, trying to wave down help? And I came along and ran him over?"

The surgeon took off his surgical cap and wadded it in his hand. "I'm sure you tried to avoid it, Chief. But yes, there was probably already an injury. It looks like he was shot at very close range. Possibly a suicide attempt. Maybe he lost his nerve and went for help."

Blair saw the color draining from Cade's face, and for a minute she thought he might just hit the ground. "He might have lived," Cade said. "I might have gotten him help."

Blair forgot her inhibitions and pulled Cade into a hug, and he slumped over her. She felt his body shaking, his breath catching as he tried to calm himself. She touched his damp hair.

"I killed a man . . . a perfectly innocent man whose name I don't even know."

Blair knew he had killed men before in the line of duty, men with guns who were trying to use them, men who were intent on murder.

But this was different. "Cade, it's not your fault."

"Why didn't I stop sooner? Why wasn't I going slower? A man standing there bleeding to death in the rain, and I didn't even see that he was in distress."

"How could you have known?" She would have pulled back then, but he clung so tightly that she kept holding him. Morgan began to rub his back.

The surgeon looked as if he didn't know whether to stay or go. "Chief, given the gunshot, how would you like us to proceed?"

Cade straightened and looked back at him, clearly trying to think. "Well, the gunshot changes everything. I'll call the medical examiner. I'll need to see the body, take pictures, examine his clothes for evidence." He paused, his eyes moving back and forth as he thought through the proper steps. "Just give me a minute, Doc."

Cade watched the doctor head back to the operating rooms. Morgan had tears in her eyes as she touched Cade's face. "Look at me, Cade," she whispered.

Cade looked down at her.

"You know you didn't do it on purpose," she said. "The man was already dying. You can't blame yourself."

Cade raked his hands through his wet black hair. "I killed a man who was in trouble. How are we going to notify his family? There could be a wife, children ...?"

Blair wished she knew what to do. "We'll figure out who he is, Cade."

Cade started to pace. "I need to call the station, tell them to change it from an accident scene to a possible crime scene. We have to figure out where he was walking from, so we can determine if it was suicide or homicide. His car's probably parked at the South Beach Pier, since he seemed to be coming from there. It's raining, so the parking lot wouldn't be full. Maybe we can figure out which car it is and find the weapon...."

Blair wished she could help. "Cade, what can I do?"

"Nothing," he said. "I just need to get busy. Thanks, you two, for coming."

Blair watched him head down the hall.

"Well, I don't guess there's anything else we can do here," Morgan said. "We might as well go."

But Blair just stared in the direction he had gone. "I think I'll stay. Take my car and go on home."

"Why?"

"Because I think after he examines the body he's going to need some support. I want to be here. I'll ride home with him."

Morgan just looked at her for a moment. "Are you sure? It could be hours."

"That's fine. I can wait."

"What about the library?"

"Gray Foster said he'd lock up."

Morgan sighed. "Well, all right. If it goes too long, call me and I'll come back to get you."

As Morgan left her, Blair took the seat Cade had abandoned, and waited.

Two hours later, she watched as the Medical Examiner and some orderlies wheeled the body out to an ambulance for transport to the morgue. Cade and Joe McCormick, his detective who had rushed to the hospital as soon as Cade had called with news of the shooting, walked out behind them.

Blair got up, and as Cade turned around, she saw that he looked pale and defeated. Surprise registered on his face at the sight of her. "You're still here."

She felt a little silly. "I figured you might want some company for the ride home. Morgan took my car."

His eyes softened as he gazed down at her. "I appreciate that, Blair."

The scars on her face felt hot, and she knew they were flaming. She turned her face away and glanced toward where Joe and the medical examiner stood at the exit. "So what do you think? Homicide or suicide?"

"Hard to say," Cade muttered. "All I know is the impact of my car did more damage than the gun shot. He might have made it if—"

"If he hadn't walked out in front of you?" Cade was going to try to shoulder the whole burden of guilt. She couldn't let that happen.

He raked his hands through his rain-styled hair. "Guess we'd better hit the road. I have a ton of work when I get back."

She fell into step beside him. "Have they identified the man yet?"

"No, but we should have something soon. Joe's running his prints through AFIS."

"AFIS?"

"Automated Fingerprint Identification Systems. If the guy's ever been fingerprinted before, we should find a match pretty quickly. But they still haven't found a car or apartment or hotel room yet. The rain isn't helping. His tracks were washed away, so they haven't been able to determine where he came from."

They went through the ER to the overhang just outside the door, and stood there for a moment as Cade stared out at the storm. Blair saw in his eyes that he wasn't hanging back because of the weather. He was still working through the facts, dealing with that dead body he'd just had to examine, trying to make some logical sense of it all.

"I could go get the truck," she said. "Bring it up for you."

Still staring at the rain, he shook his head. "I'm okay. I won't have you getting drenched to keep me from it. I'll get the car and come get you."

"No way." She grabbed his keys out of his hand and started for the truck. But he launched out behind her, reached it before she did, and unlocked her side. She slipped in, soaking wet.

Cade got in on the other side, slammed the door shut, and set his hands on the steering wheel. For a moment he stared out through the blurred windshield, as if gathering his strength for the drive home. The sound of the rain against the roof was punctuated by the thunder cracking at unexpected intervals. "You didn't have to stay all this time, Blair."

She stared straight ahead at the raindrops making quarter-sized circles on the windshield. "I know."

"How'd you hear about the whole thing?"

"Melba's prayer chain."

Cade's face twisted. Blair knew he was thinking that she wasn't a praying woman. "She called you to pray?"

"Of course not. She called Morgan, who told me."

"Oh." Disappointment slackened his face.

Blair knew her lack of faith in the things he believed was like a wall between them, but she refused to masquerade as a believer when she wasn't one.

He backed out of his spot and pulled out into traffic on the busy street beside the hospital. "Maybe I can brainstorm with you on the way back," Blair said, "and help you figure out how to find out the man's identity, in case there's not a match for the prints. You gotta admit I'm a pretty good problem solver."

He considered that a moment. "Guess there's no better person to help me figure it out." He sighed. "You should be a cop."

"Yeah, that'll be the day. I look awful in black."

He smiled then, and Blair felt a small sense of victory.

For a while, he drove through the storm, concentrating on the roads rather than trying to make conversation. He drove too carefully, as if certain that another pedestrian-in-distress would jump out in front of him.

The steady *whish-whish* of the wipers worked itself into Blair's brain as she tried to think of solutions. Finding the man's identity wouldn't make Cade feel any better about what had happened, but at least he wouldn't feel so helpless.

"I'm thinking that you could give a picture of the man to the media and let them get it on the ten o'clock news. By midnight you're sure to have somebody calling with information."

"Where are we going to get a picture, Blair? We can't very well flash shots of the man's dead body on the television screen. I don't want his family to find out that way."

"Yeah, you're right." She thought about that for a moment. "Maybe just a physical description of what he was wearing and what he looked like. Weight, height, eye color ..."

He blew out a long breath. "Maybe someone's already missed him. Maybe they'd call in. Then I could go to their residence and explain what happened."

She shot him a look. "Yourself?"

"Who else?"

"Well, I don't know, but Cade, don't you think you should send someone else?"

She saw the muscles of his jaw flexing. "No. I'm the one who should go."

Silence again. Blair knew there was no use trying to talk Cade out of that. As difficult as it would be for him, he would never ask anyone else to do it.

"It's weird how suddenly life can spin out of control," he said.

She let her eyes settle on him. "Isn't it, though? I've been there, Cade."

His face softened and he looked over at her. "Yeah, I know you have."

She didn't have to say it. The day her parents were murdered had been the worst day of her life. One minute she was standing in a city council meeting with her sleeves rolled up, ready to fight for Hanover House to stay open, and the next she was standing in the room with her parents' dead bodies. Cade had been right there beside her.

"I felt helpless that day too," Cade whispered, as if he'd read her mind.

"You weren't, though. And you're not now."

They drove across the Island Expressway to Tybee Island, wound their way to the mouth of the Savannah River, then crossed the island bridge to Cape Refuge. "My cell phone doesn't work on the island. Let me just stop by the station and see how far they've gotten," he said, "and then I'll take you home."

"Take your time," she said. "In fact, just don't worry about me. I'll call Morgan to pick me up when she gets home."

They rounded Ocean Boulevard at the northern tip of the island, and as they approached the small police station, they saw that the parking lot was full of television vans.

The media had already heard.

Cade groaned. "I don't believe this."

"Keep driving, Cade," Blair said. "Give yourself a minute to think."

Cade passed the station and headed down the island. "They must have heard the police scanner. This is all I need. Now it'll broadcast all over the airwaves."

"But they don't know who the man is, right? So it won't matter."

Cade breathed a laugh. "Right. They'll just tell how the Cape Refuge police chief ran some injured man down. And every family in town whose father isn't home will think it's him."

"Maybe the newscasts will lead someone to identifying the body."

Cade reached the South Beach Pier, where the accident had occurred. The road was clear now. It didn't look as if anything significant had happened here . . . like a man dying for no good reason. The blood had all washed away.

He drove past Hanover House and headed to Blair's house, next to the library. He pulled onto the gravel parking lot in a grove of pine trees and mimosas, and stopped the truck.

She didn't get out. "Cade, are you going to be all right?"

He didn't answer for a moment—just stared through his windshield to the trees beyond her house. "Yeah. Thanks for coming. I really appreciate it."

She was quiet for a moment, racking her brain for the right thing to say.

"Cade, if you need some company when you go tell the family, I'll go with you. I'm not known to be the most sensitive soul in the world, but I know what it feels like to get horrible news about someone you love."

He patted her hand. "Thanks for the offer. I'll let you know."

"And for what it's worth, when you told me about my parents . . ."

He met her eyes, waiting for her to go on.

"Well, you did it right. You'll do this right too."

"Thanks," he said.

She got out and ran through the rain to her front door, but she didn't go in until Cade was out of sight.

*T*he moment Cade pulled into the parking lot of the police station, reporters surrounded him with microphones aimed like grenade launchers.

"Chief Cade, is it true the man you hit is dead?" someone asked him as he got out of the truck.

He slammed the door and didn't answer. Maybe they didn't yet know about the gunshot.

"Did you know the man you killed?"

He trudged through them, wanting to just get inside and get dry. They seemed ravenous, standing out in the lightning and rain, waiting for a morsel of news. "I'm not ready to make a statement yet," he said.

At the front door of the station, which had once been a laundromat, some of the reporters pushed closer to follow him in. "Please wait out here!" He barely had room inside for all the officers on duty. Storm or not, there wasn't room for all these reporters.

"Chief Cade, don't you feel any compulsion to speak to the people about what you did?"

He turned back to the reporter whose face he saw each night at six and eleven. There was something gratifying about seeing him sopping wet now. "No, James, I told you I'm not ready to make a statement."

He went in and stood on the mat just inside the door. Man, he was wet. He'd give anything for a change of clothes. He should have gone by his house and gotten something before coming here.

J.J. Clyde sat at one of the desks talking into a phone, and Cade pointed at the door. "Don't let any of them in, you hear?"

J.J. put his hand over the phone. "I hear, Chief. Any word on who the man is?"

"None," Cade said. "Where's Joe?"

"On the phone in your office. It's been ringing off the hook, people asking questions."

Cade shot a look through the storefront window to the crowd of reporters standing in the elements. He imagined they were just as interested in the storm pummeling the coast as they were in the death. He almost wished for a tornado to get their mind off him.

He went into his office and found Joe, Cade's second-in-command and the town's only detective, sitting in a folding chair near Cade's desk, the phone cord stretched taut. "No, ma'am, I can't comment on the investigation. Yes, ma'am."

Cade saw that Joe, too, was wet. No doubt he'd been out in the storm with the others, looking for the man's car.

"No, no one was in jeopardy at any time. Yes. All right."

He hung up the phone and got to his feet. "It's been a madhouse. Rumors flying all over town. J.J. said we had a few calls speculating on who the man was. Somebody said he was a Hollywood producer renting a cottage over in Eastgate, but they checked and that man is alive and well. Somebody else claimed he was the sprinkler guy putting in a new system over at the Catholic church. But the sprinkler guy is accounted for." He looked at the puddle gathering under Cade's feet. "You really ought to change clothes, Cade."

"Later." Cade ran his hand through his wet hair. "So what are your thoughts on the gunshot?"

"Sure raises the stakes, doesn't it? If it wasn't suicide, then we've got a killer out there."

Cade dropped into his chair. "We can't speculate until we have some evidence. There's got to be a car somewhere. An apartment he was occupying. A condo or hotel room. Something."

"Alex checked the condos in that area," Joe said. "He wasn't a tenant. I was thinking about sending men around to all the hotels on the island, to see if any guests are unaccounted for. It'll take a while."

"Better get started."

"Will do." Joe started for the door. "What about the press?"

"Ignore them. They know about as much as we do right now. Soon they'll be scurrying off to meet deadlines."

"I hear some of them did live remotes for their six o'clock broadcast."

Cade dropped into his chair. "You're kidding."

"Nope. Sorry, Chief. Two birds with one stone, you know. The storm and the accident both in one place. How lucky can they get?"

Cade rubbed his face and watched as Joe disappeared. Could this day get any worse?

When he heard a knock on the door, he looked up with dread. Jonathan Cleary—Morgan's husband and Cade's best friend—stood in the doorway. "Hey, buddy. You okay?"

Cade just looked at him.

"Man, you need a change of clothes."

"Tell me about it."

Jonathan came in and turned the folding chair toward Cade's desk. He sat down. "Morgan told me what happened. Want to talk?"

"I don't even know what to say." Cade slapped his hands on the desk and made himself straighten. "You don't happen to have any new tenants at Hanover House, do you?"

"Not this month, no. And we checked. Everyone's there."

He sat back, rubbing his mouth. "There are hundreds of tourists on the island this time of year. Maybe I need to do what Blair suggested and make a statement to the press, to give them a physical description."

"Morgan told me about the gunshot," Jonathan said. "You gonna tell them?"

Cade looked down at the wood grain on his desk and wondered how long it would be before the press learned of that. Doctors and nurses from the hospital knew, and he'd notified his men as soon as he'd heard. Morgan had told Jonathan. . . . Someone would leak it, and the town would panic.

Cade rubbed his eyes. "I can't believe this happened. A man's life . . ." He sighed. "Jonathan, I know I didn't run the man over on purpose, but maybe I was driving faster than I needed to. Maybe I was negligent by not stopping in time. I saw him standing there. If he was bleeding, I should have seen it."

"From a distance, in a driving rain? Cade, you didn't do anything wrong. You were trying to save lives."

"And I took one instead."

Jonathan shook his head. "No, you didn't, man. The guy stepped out in front of you. I talked to Melba Jefferson myself after Morgan told me. She said she saw the whole thing and that you didn't do anything wrong. The man walked right out in front of you, almost like he meant to. And she didn't know about the gunshot wound, but she would have said if she'd seen him bleeding. It was pouring rain, Cade."

Cade got up and paced across the room, his shoes squeaking on the floor. "He's dead, Jonathan. The man is dead and I killed him." He stepped into the doorway and, through the glass, saw that the press corps was not going away.

He turned back to Jonathan. "I have to go make a statement," he said. "I have to give them a description of the man so they can put it on the news. If I don't, they'll start making up facts."

Jonathan got up. "They're going to attack you with all kinds of questions. Why don't you let someone else do it? Joe McCormick or somebody."

"I don't believe in passing the buck. I can take it." He walked to the door, took in a deep breath.

"Don't you want to put on a dry shirt and comb your hair?" Jonathan asked. "I could go to your house and get you a change of clothes."

"What's the point? I'm going outside anyway."

Jonathan grunted. "Let them in, man. You don't have to do this out in the storm."

"They're not coming in here and disrupting my whole operation. There's not room."

Jonathan groaned. "At least take my umbrella."

Cade took the umbrella and Jonathan touched his shoulder. "What about the gunshot?"

Cade thought that over for a moment. They were going to find out anyway, but if he could hold off just a while longer, maybe he'd find the man's identity and be able to determine whether it was suicide or murder. There was no point in creating a panic about some killer still at large when there might not be any foul play involved. "Think I'll wait," he said. "There's too much we still don't know."

Jonathan opened the door for him, and Cade stepped out and opened the umbrella. The winds had died somewhat. The umbrella might hold, after all.

The press swarmed and Cade took immediate control. "I'd like to make a statement," he yelled over the voices. "Please get back. I have a statement to make."

The reporters got quiet, but they didn't step back. Microphones loomed so close to his face that he felt he might emerge bruised. He hoped the rain didn't electrocute any of them. Trying to ignore them, he spoke.

"This afternoon at 2:00 P.M., a pedestrian was killed on Ocean Boulevard near the South Beach Pier. The man had no identification. I'd like to give you his physical description in hopes that someone who recognizes it can identify him.

"The man was wearing a red plaid short-sleeved shirt, khaki pants, and a pair of Dockers deck shoes. He had blondish-brown hair and brown eyes, was approximately 220 pounds, approximately thirty-five years old, and about six feet tall. If anyone listening to this can identify this man, we would appreciate your calling 555-8327. Thank you."

"Chief Cade, did the impact kill him instantly?"

"No, it didn't," Cade said. "He was alive and speaking right after he was hit and did make it to Candler Hospital in Savannah alive. He died shortly thereafter."

The reporters began shouting out questions, but Cade headed back inside, blocking out the noise. Jonathan ducked back in with him and took the umbrella out of his hands. "Good job, Cade."

Cade sighed and looked back out at them. "Maybe it'll do some good. We've got to get a name."

"We'll be praying for you, man."

Cade stared at his friend for a long moment. "'Preciate it, man. You have no idea how bad I need it."

CHAPTER

*C*ade looked weary and tired when Blair found him at the police station at eleven that night, and from the defeated look on his somber face, she knew he still hadn't been able to identify the man.

"Hey," she said from the doorway of his office, and he looked up at her and smiled.

"Hey. What are you doing out so late?"

"I thought I'd come by and watch the news with you. Jonathan told me you'd made a statement to the press. I see most of them are still out there."

He glanced at his watch. "Yeah, they're doing live broadcasts. Guess it's time, isn't it?"

He had finally changed clothes, and instead of his uniform, he wore a pair of khaki pants and a blue dress shirt with the sleeves rolled up. His face was gray with end-of-day stubble, and his hair seemed to have been unattended since he'd been drenched that afternoon. She felt the urge to push it back off of his forehead.

He got up, stretched, and turned on the television that sat on top of a file cabinet. Turning a chair around for her, he said, "So you think they know about the gunshot yet?"

She sat down and pulled her feet up to the seat. "Probably. But they'd find out sooner or later, Cade."

"I thought we'd have found something by now. But the man seems to have come out of thin air. No match on his fingerprints. No car, no nothing."

"There's something somewhere. Just give it time."

He dropped back down in his own chair, and she saw his fatigue as he leaned his head back. The theme song for the *Channel 3 News* came on, and she glanced back at him. His face had tightened, and she knew he dreaded the report. The camera zoomed in on the anchor who had stood out in front of the station just a short time ago. Covered with makeup and hair mousse, one would never know he'd been standing in torrential rains for most of the night.

"Our top story tonight, another baby kidnapped from a hospital in the southeast."

Blair smiled at Cade. "Well, at least you're not the headliner."

Cade didn't seem comforted by that.

"According to a spokesperson for the Woman's Hospital in Hilton Head, South Carolina, the day-old baby of Sarah and Jack Branning was kidnapped at 1:00 P.M. today. The kidnapper has been identified as a woman dressed as a nurse, with curly blonde hair and black-framed glasses."

"Want something to drink?" he asked, as if trying to divert his own attention.

"We might need vodka." She grinned at him. Cade didn't drink, and the thought that he'd have some sitting around his office was absurd. She'd hoped to get a smile out of him, but his eyes had drifted back to the set.

"This disappearance makes the fifth in as many weeks. The others were taken from hospitals in Florida and Southern Georgia.

"And in other news ..."

Cade's picture flashed up on the screen. "There it is."

"The Cape Refuge chief of police is in the hot seat for running down an injured man on Ocean Boulevard at 3:30 P.M. today."

"Okay," Cade said, "they know he was shot."

"Sources say that Chief Matthew Cade was on his way to direct traffic around a downed power line when he hit an unidentified pedestrian who was bleeding from a gunshot wound to the abdomen. The man was rushed to Candler Hospital in Savannah but later died. Police don't yet know how the man was shot and have been unable to identify him."

The anchor paused, and the video of Cade's press conference filled the screen. *"The man was wearing a red plaid short-sleeved shirt, khaki pants, and a pair of Dockers deck shoes. He had blondish-brown hair and brown eyes, was approximately 220 pounds, approximately thirty-five years old, and about six feet tall ..."*

As he spoke, another picture flashed on the screen—a sketch of the dead man's face.

Cade sprang up. "What in the name of—?"

"Our WSAV-TV News sketch artist was able to make this drawing of the man who was killed. If you know him, please contact us here at Channel 3, or you can call the Cape Refuge Police Department at 555-8327. Chief Cade refused to comment on his part in the man's death, though he did say that the man spoke to him before he died."

Blair dropped her feet. "Cade, is that what the man really looked like?"

"Exactly. What did that reporter do? Go to the morgue to draw the man's face? What if his family sees that? What if they're sitting in the living room wondering why Dad's not home and all of a sudden that stupid sketch pops up on the screen?"

It was just the kind of thing she'd expected from the press. Blair got up and grabbed the phone. "I'll get to the bottom of this right now."

"Who are you calling?"

"A friend at Channel 3. I'm going to find out how they got the picture and how they knew about the gunshot."

Cade changed the channel and watched the tail end of another station's coverage of his impromptu press conference. Relieved, he saw that there was no picture there, but they too had the information about the gunshot. He switched to the third local channel. Again, no picture, but the gunshot dominated the piece.

Blair got the station's recorded greeting, then navigated her way to her friend who worked in the newsroom. She'd worked with him several times when he'd needed research done for a report he was working on. He'd hired her, knowing that she had an uncanny gift for finding facts that no one else could find.

The man answered quickly. "Jason Geddis."

"Yeah, Jason, hi. Blair Owens."

"Yeah, Blair. How's it going?"

"Great. And you?"

"Can't complain."

She met Cade's eyes. He looked as if he wanted to jerk the phone out of her hand and interrogate him himself. "Listen, I was just watching the news and saw the sketch you guys had of the man who died on Cape Refuge . . ."

"Yeah. Pretty good reporting, huh?"

She didn't comment. "The police didn't release a sketch of the man, and there were no media at the scene of the accident, so really, Jason, how did you guys get that?"

Jason laughed. "Well, I'm not saying this was the right thing to do or anything, but our artist went to the morgue. He told them he was sent there to do a sketch of the man to help police identify the body. So they let him in."

Cade turned the volume down on the set and looked over at her, waiting.

"You're kidding me. And they *believed* him?"

"Sure they did. Let him right in. Ethics aside, it was an exclusive, and it might help identify the guy."

Cade set his hands on his hips and stared down at her, waiting.

"So that would be how he knew about the gunshot too, huh?"

"Yep. The person helping him mentioned it."

Blair breathed out a bitter laugh. "Amazing. How do you guys sleep at night?"

He muttered something about sleeping just fine, and she quickly said good-bye. She knew the scar on her face was crimson.

Cade's face was red too. "Tell me, Blair."

She sighed. "He led them to think he was with the police department, and this rube let him right in, gave him access to the body, and listed the injuries."

Cade dropped back into his chair. "Unbelievable."

She watched him for a moment as he leaned his head back and stared at the ceiling. "Cade, maybe it's for the best," she said. "You've got his face out there now. Somebody's bound to call in soon."

"And what if they call Channel 3 instead of me? Is the press going to rush to the family's home and ask them for a statement?"

Blair tried to think of something that would comfort him, but the phone rang, and J.J. rushed into the doorway. "Chief, we've got a lead."

"Already?"

The phone began to buzz again. The viewers were already responding.

Cade picked up the phone. "Chief Cade."

Blair sat and listened as one after another television viewer called in to ask questions or provide leads.

It was going to be a busy night.

CHAPTER

*I*t was after midnight when the phone calls with empty leads stopped coming. Blair still sat in a chair in Cade's office, her feet propped on his desk. Cade's eyes were dry and weary, but fatigue had not drained him of worry. He wished it would.

"I'm going home." Blair dropped her feet and got up. "You ought to do the same. Get some sleep, Cade."

For a moment he just looked at her, his finger rubbing gently across his lips. She was pretty; he'd always thought so. The scars on her face marred only her self-image, as far as he was concerned. They were part of her, the part that spoke of pain behind her tough shell, the part that reminded him how vulnerable she could be.

He wished she was a believer, so that God could heal the inner reaches of those scars.

He wished it for selfish reasons, too.

"I'll go home soon," he said. "Thanks for being here during this. I appreciate your support."

"No problem." She got up and started out.

Cade followed her. He mentally kicked himself for sounding dismissive or impersonal. He really did appreciate it. She had been there at the hospital when he'd needed someone, and tonight as the saga continued, she'd helped so patiently and compassionately.

Yet it always ended so coolly with them, as though some line existed between them that neither would cross.

It had finally stopped raining. He walked her to her car, opened her door, and stood there as she got in. "Be careful," he said.

She smiled up at him. "You too. Go home, Cade."

"I will."

Closing her door, he stepped back and watched her drive away.

The wind was muggy and angry, and he looked at the night sky, wondering how in the world this day had taken such a horrible turn. He slid his hands into his pockets and crossed the quiet street to the beach. His feet left the pavement and began to rock through the sand as he walked to the edge of the water.

The morning sun had come today as it always did, and the tide had risen and fallen. Waves still beat against the shore as if everything was the same. How could he have known when he got up this morning that he was going to kill a man today?

Or would the man have died anyway, from his wound?

He went to the lifeguard's stand, climbed up, and sat in the chair that looked out over the water. The night stars twinkled bright and abundant tonight, reminding him of God's majesty, but he couldn't help questioning God's purpose. He leaned his head back against the wooden slats of the chair. How did one repent for something he had not meant to do? His heart had cried out in contrition ever since the accident occurred. God knew he was sorry, but it didn't make anything right. For all he knew right now, there was a family grieving because they had seen their father and husband's face flashed on the television screen, a poor sketch of a dead man rendered by someone who'd never seen him alive. By morning he expected to know who the man was. But what then?

As he sat in the lifeguard's chair staring up at the sky, he tried to pray. But his supplications to God were a jumble of incoherent fears, concerns, and self-indictments.

He should pray for the wife, the family, if there was one. He should pray for the friends and loved ones who would grieve over this missing man. He should pray that, if it wasn't a suicidal gunshot, the shooter would be found. But he couldn't manage it.

He climbed down to the soft sand and walked down the beach. The surf rumbled loud tonight, hitting hard against the shore. Tourists clamored for rooms in beachfront hotels, but on days like this, when a storm had come and gone and the ocean was restless, they often had trouble sleeping with the roar of the Atlantic in their ears. Tonight the commotion of the waves only mirrored the noise of the voices inside his head—voices that questioned, taunted . . .

Oh, how he wished that his mentor, Wayne Owens, were here to talk to. Blair reminded him a lot of her father. She had his matter-of-fact ways, but without his passion for Christ. She had much advice to give, but few answers. Still, she'd been a comfort to him, and he had to admit that there was no one he'd rather have had by his side tonight.

He turned around and started back to the police station, where his night staff fielded phone calls and chased down leads. He stopped beside the lifeguard's stand again, leaned against it, and looked out over the water.

"Lord, help me." It was the only thing he could manage to pray tonight. Maybe what he had done today had put up a wall between him and God. He hoped not. He could not stand the thought of being isolated like that.

Maybe he just needed to rest.

He went back to the station, got his keys, and headed back out to his truck. Quietly he drove home, hoping that the day would shed some light on the things he needed to know and, thus, change everything.

7

*B*lair had not slept well, and when dawn began to break across the sky and turn the darkness in her room to gray, she got up and decided to check on Cade. She called his house first and waited as the phone rang four times. Finally, his voicemail picked up.

"Hi. You've reached Cade. I'm not at home right now but if you'll leave a message, I'll call you back."

The phone beeped and Blair cleared her throat. "Hey, Cade, it's Blair. I was just checking on you, hoping you're all right. I'll try you at the station." She hung up and dialed the number of the police station.

"Cape Refuge Police Department." The voice was dry and clipped. She recognized it to be Alex's.

"Alex, this is Blair Owens. Can Cade come to the phone?"

"Cade isn't in," Alex said. "He doesn't usually come in until eight."

"Yeah, well, I thought he might have gotten started earlier today. He must have gone to Cricket's."

"Yeah, you'll probably catch him there."

Blair decided that instead of calling, she would just get in her car and drive over to the dock. The little restaurant called Cricket's sat back from the water. It was where fishermen and sailors and those who worked along the beach often had breakfast in the mornings. As she pulled into the parking lot, she saw that Cade's truck was parked there.

She left her car and went inside the structure that looked as if a strong wind might blow it over. One whole wall was made of screens, which let in the ocean breeze, along with the sea air and the rank odor of fish from the boats docked nearby. She stepped in, letting the screen door bounce shut behind her, and looked around at the usual faces. Her parents used to be among them. They had come here each morning for years in hopes of ministering to seamen who were passing through. Their little church was housed in the warehouse just a few yards away.

Blair walked up to the bar and waited for Charlie to notice her.

"Well, if it ain't Marian the Librarian."

"Hey, Charlie. What's going on?"

"Not much," he said. "Same old same-old." He poured her a cup of coffee, shoved it into her hands.

"Have you seen Cade this morning?" she asked.

"Yeah, he was in earlier."

"Where is he? His truck is still here."

"I don't know," he said. "Musta left."

Blair took her coffee and stepped out of the restaurant. She looked up and down the dock, wondering if Cade was nearby. By now, most of the shrimp boats had already gone out, but some of the late-goers were still preparing their rigs for the day's work.

She walked up the dock, saw her brother-in-law, Jonathan, getting his tourist boat ready to take passengers out for a day of saltwater fishing. His nineteen-year-old deckhand helped the passengers board while Jonathan busied himself on the deck.

She waved and called out, "Jonathan, you seen Cade?"

He turned. "I saw him a little while ago coming out of Cricket's," he yelled back. "I figured he was headed to work."

"He's not there and his truck's still parked at Cricket's," she said.

He shrugged. "Then I don't know where he went. Sorry."

As she kept walking, she saw Toothless Joe chomping on his cigar as he prepared for his dolphin tour. Up ahead was Mill Malone, loading his cargo for a trek up the coast. Cade was nowhere to be found.

Giving up, she went back to her car and headed back to the station. Maybe his truck had died in its parking spot, and he had hitched a ride or walked to the station.

But when he still wasn't there, she began to get concerned.

"Where could he be?" she asked Alex. "I mean, if he was out working, wouldn't he have let you know?"

"Usually," Alex said. "But he'll come along shortly. He's a big boy."

"I know he's a big boy," Blair said, "but I'm worried about his state of mind. He's really beating himself up about what happened yesterday."

"Maybe he headed over to Savannah looking for the family."

Now, there was a possibility. "Do you think he knows who it is yet?"

"I don't see how. We got a few calls through the night but they were all lame leads. Didn't take us anywhere."

Blair checked her watch. It was past time for her to open the library. She supposed Cade would turn up eventually, with or without her help. Trying to put him out of her mind, she headed home.

Five hours later, when Blair checked on Cade again, he had still not been in to the police station. No one had heard from him. Several important matters had come up and they had tried to contact him, but he had not answered the cell phone that he used when he went into Savannah. His truck still sat at Cricket's, and no one in town seemed to know where he was.

By that evening, when there was still no trace of him, Blair began to fight a growing sense of dread. Something had happened.

He would not have just disappeared without a trace. She went over to Hanover House and found everyone sitting around the table—the whole brood of them. Mrs. Hern sat with that blank Alzheimer's stare, a dribble of mashed potatoes on her chin. Gus Hampton scarfed down a pork chop with the urgency of a starving man, his elbows digging into the table. Felicia, the big woman who'd just been there a few weeks, seemed to be the only one among them who had any manners, though Blair couldn't imagine where she'd gotten them. She'd been in jail for ten years before coming here, and Blair doubted they emphasized etiquette in the prison cafeteria.

Sadie seemed preoccupied with her baby brother, Caleb, who sat in a high chair between Morgan and Jonathan.

"His truck's been at Cricket's all day long," Blair said, standing over the table.

"Sit down, Blair," Morgan said. "I made plenty."

Blair waved her off. "Not hungry. Jonathan, they haven't even heard from him at the police station."

"At least have a glass of tea," Morgan insisted.

"I don't *want* a glass of tea. Did you even hear what I said, Morgan? Cade is missing!"

Jonathan slid his chair back, and took his plate to the sink. "Calm down, Blair. He's not missing." He rinsed the plate off, then wiped his hands on a towel. "He was just really upset about what happened yesterday. Maybe he just went off by himself to think."

"No way," Blair said. "It's not like him to buck his responsibilities. He would have been out pounding the pavement today trying to find out who this guy was."

Caleb got restless and started trying to stand up in his high chair.

"No, Caleb," Sadie told him across the table. "Sit down. Eat your peas."

When Caleb managed to turn around and got up on his knees, Morgan pulled him out of his high chair. "Well, maybe that's what he's doing. Maybe he just went to find some leads on the man."

"But don't you think it's strange that he wouldn't share those leads with anybody at the police department?" Blair asked. "They haven't heard from him all day long. He hasn't even called to see if they've learned anything."

That got Jonathan's attention. "Weird," he said. "Makes me wonder about that woman."

"What woman?"

He shrugged. "Well, I don't know. He was talking to some woman at Cricket's this morning. It wasn't anybody I knew. I saw him coming out with her."

Cade with a woman? Blair was silent for just a moment. She knew her scars were reddening. "What did she look like, Jonathan?"

"I don't know, mid-thirties, long, big brown hair, kind of petite-looking."

Blair hated petite women, especially the ones with big hair. She wasn't exactly an Amazon herself at five-feet-five, but those tiny little women really got on her nerves. Men loved them, though. She supposed Cade would be no exception. "Why didn't you tell me this when I asked you this morning? I asked you *point-blank* if you had seen Cade."

"And I told you point-blank that I had seen him coming out of Cricket's."

She grunted. "You didn't say anything about a woman."

"Well, I didn't think it was relevant at the time."

Baby laughter came from the living room, then a ball rolled into the kitchen and Caleb came running after it. Jonathan laughed and scooped the ball up, then rolled it back across the floor. Caleb screamed in delight, and Morgan followed him.

But Blair's eyes pinned Jonathan. What was wrong with them? Didn't they understand how serious this was? "I need more specifics, Jonathan. Did he look like he was just talking to her in passing or did she look like somebody he knew? Were they deep in conversation? Were they headed out to *her* car or *his?*"

He rolled his eyes. "Come on, Blair. You know me. I was busy, and I don't have time to sit around watching the movements of every guy that comes out of Cricket's. I had passengers on my boat."

"He's your best friend, Jonathan. Don't tell me you wouldn't be interested if you saw him with a woman."

"Then I guess that means I didn't consider her to be any kind of love interest. He just looked like he was talking to her. He had a real serious look on his face. I saw them walk around Cricket's, but I didn't see what car they got into."

She sighed and turned to Morgan, who had caught Caleb and was handing him a cookie. "We've got to find out who that woman was," she said.

Morgan put the toddler down. "I think so," she agreed. "Someone must know."

Blair grabbed up her keys. "I'm outta here. I'll let you know what I find out."

As Blair went back to her car and pulled away from the family home that had become everyone else's family home, she thought of some petite, big-haired woman with Cade. Had he gone off with her? Did she have anything to do with his disappearance? Frustrated beyond measure, she drove back to Cricket's. His truck still hadn't been moved.

That night, Blair had trouble sleeping again. She tossed and turned, and twice she got up and called Cade's voicemail again. He still was not answering. She lay in bed, wondering what on earth could have happened to him. Who was the woman Jonathan had seen him with? If he was seeing a woman, Blair would have known it. He wouldn't have kept it secret.

Maybe this woman did have something to do with the case. But why would he just vanish like that after meeting with her? Had he been a victim of some kind of foul play?

Did it have anything to do with the man he'd hit?

By morning she called the station again. There'd still been no word from him, and they admitted their concern. She drove over to Cricket's, noting the irony that today the sky was cloudless and blue, and the sun shone so brightly that the water glistened like a bed of diamonds. It felt like it should be storming until Cade turned up.

Cade's truck still sat in the parking lot. She almost ran into her brother-in-law as he came out of the rickety restaurant. "Jonathan!"

"Still looking for Cade?" he asked.

She grabbed his flannel shirt. "Jonathan, he hasn't been heard from since yesterday morning when he was here at Cricket's. Where do you think he could be?"

Jonathan's eyes squinted in the morning sun. "I don't know, but I'm getting a little worried myself."

That was all Blair needed. "Jonathan, let's go to his house. We have to get inside somehow and see if there's a clue."

"We can't break into his house! He's the chief of police. You don't think he'd arrest us? I have firsthand knowledge that Cade puts the law over friendship."

"It wouldn't be like breaking in," she said. "I just want to see if there's anything wrong. He could be dead in there, for all we know."

Jonathan jerked his arm back. "Come on, Blair. He's not dead."

"Well, how do you know? It's not like him to do this. Something has happened!"

Jonathan looked out at his boat. So far no tourists had shown up for his tour, and his deckhand sat in a rusty folded chair, looking like he'd rather be in bed.

He turned back to Blair. "I'll tell you what. I know where Cade keeps a key. We'll go in and see if everything is all right. But we're not going to snoop around through his stuff. He deserves his privacy."

"Fine! That's good enough for me."

He told his deckhand to board any passengers who showed up, then Blair drove him over to Cade's house. She followed Jonathan around to the backyard and waited as he went into a utility room to look for Cade's extra key.

She stood in Cade's backyard and noted that the grass needed cutting. She crossed it and went to his patio, where a green iron table stood with four chairs. One of the chairs sat back away from the table, and a pair of mud-caked work boots stood in it.

She sat down and leaned forward, her eyes scanning the crepe myrtles that weren't yet in bloom, the azalea bushes that were, and the hodgepodge of untended and unidentifiable plants.

Something at her feet startled her, and she looked down to see Cade's big black cat. It looked up at her and let out an urgent meow. "Hey, kitty." She reached down and picked it up. "Come here." Cradling the cat, she began to stroke it.

Jonathan came back out. "Found it."

Blair looked up at him. "I didn't know Cade had a cat."

"Oh, yeah. His name's Oswald."

"After the assassin?"

Jonathan grinned. "No, after the theologian, Oswald Chambers."

The cat purred as she stroked it, then meowed again and jumped down, rushed to the door as Jonathan went toward it.

Jonathan opened the door, revealing the small laundry room, and the cat darted inside and headed straight to his empty bowls on the floor beside the dryer.

"He's hungry," Blair said. "See there? Cade wouldn't leave his cat to starve."

Jonathan scooped some food out of the Cat Chow bag and dropped it into the bowl, and the cat devoured it.

"See? That cat hasn't eaten today."

Jonathan seemed to turn that over in his mind.

As he got the cat some water, Blair stepped into the small kitchen, with its round little table and four chairs, and looked beyond it to the living room she had never been in before. All these years she had considered Cade a close friend. It seemed strange now that she'd never had cause to be in his house.

Jonathan went in and turned the light on. It looked different than she would have imagined, had she ever given Cade's living quarters a thought. The couch and love seat were brown leather, and a beige recliner sat opposite the love seat. A big beige ottoman served as a coffee table and footrest.

The decorating style spoke of masculine comfort, but it was neat.

She walked through the kitchen, saw that nothing seemed out of place. A lone coffee cup sat inside the dishwasher. The coffee pot sat half full and cold.

"Bed's made up," Jonathan called.

Blair went to the bedroom, saw the queen-size bed draped over with a gold and brown comforter that matched the curtains. There was no way to tell if he'd been home since yesterday.

"Man, he's neat," Jonathan said. "We used to really butt heads when we roomed together in college. I don't remember a day when he didn't make up his bed. I went weeks without making up mine. Drove him crazy."

Blair crossed Cade's room and went to the walk-in closet. She turned on the light and stepped inside, trying to determine whether he had packed or left in a hurry. Three suitcases lay on the top shelf.

"Do you think a bachelor would have more than three suitcases?" she asked.

He followed her in. "I doubt it."

"So he didn't pack."

Jonathan shook his head. "No, I wouldn't think so, either. As neat as he is, it seems like there'd be a space on the shelf for a missing suitcase if he'd taken one."

Blair turned back to him. "Okay, so what does that tell us?"

"Well, it tells us that he didn't plan to be going on a long trip. And the fact that he left his truck at Cricket's would sure be an indication that whatever happened wasn't planned."

She turned off the closet light and walked around his bedroom, saw the Bible and another book open on his bed table. It was just like Cade, she thought. In the midst of his worrying— probably after a sleepless night—he had gotten up and read his Bible.

Jonathan picked it up. "Oh, man. Numbers 35. He was reading about the cities of refuge."

"What are those?"

He put the Bible back down. "They were a provision God made for someone who had accidentally killed. There was a death sentence for taking someone's life. The family of the person you killed had the right and obligation to kill you."

"Obligation? Legally?"

"Yes, because God said that bloodguilt polluted the land. But in case the death was an accident, the Lord set up six cities of refuge. Every city in Israel was less than thirty miles from one, and the roads were smooth and well maintained, so someone who'd accidentally killed could get there within hours before the avenger could overtake him. The family of the dead man couldn't avenge the death if he was in a city of refuge. He was safe there until he could stand trial before the congregation."

She looked down at the Numbers passage. "Does Cade consider himself to have bloodguilt?"

"Probably," Jonathan said. "You know Cade. He doesn't let himself off the hook for anything."

"But none of this applies today. That was Old Testament stuff."

"Everything in the Old Testament is a picture of something in the New. Cade knows that. And besides, the city of refuge probably gave him comfort. It probably reminded him that God makes provision for accidents."

"What did he do? Run off to some modern city of refuge?"

Jonathan frowned. "Cape Refuge was practically named for that whole concept. No, Cade wouldn't go off looking for that city. He knows where his real refuge is found."

Jonathan looked at the other book, *My Utmost for His Highest,* and pointed to the author's name at the top of the page it was opened to. "Oswald's namesake."

Blair took the book, careful not to lose Cade's place. Keeping her finger there, she looked just inside the cover. "I thought so." She showed Jonathan the inscription there. "Pop gave him this."

Jonathan swallowed. "I remember."

She opened to the page he'd been reading from. "It's yesterday's reading. Which means he hasn't been home to read today's."

"Not necessarily. But it sure doesn't look like he has." With troubled eyes, he looked around the room and sighed. "Well, I can't say that breaking into his house has enlightened us any."

She went up the hall, looked into the second bedroom where Cade had a desk and computer. It was turned off.

Going back into the living room, she looked down at the phone, saw the light blinking. "He has voice mail. Do you know how to get it?"

"Of course not," Jonathan said. "Besides, it's probably us. I've left at least three messages myself."

She looked down at the caller ID and clicked the arrow key to scroll through his calls. Her own number came up several times, along with that of the police station, Hanover House, and several of the television stations in the area. She scrolled through until she came to a name she didn't recognize.

"William Clark. Do you know who that is?"

Jonathan shook his head. "It's a Savannah number. Probably a reporter."

Frustrated, she abandoned the caller ID. "Where could he be? I can't imagine him vanishing unless something happened."

"Me either," Jonathan said, "but let's not jump to conclusions. There might be a perfectly good explanation for where he is."

"I sure wish he'd let us in on it."

Satisfied that there were no clues here, they took the cat outside, along with its bowls, and locked the door. Blair went back to Cricket's, hoping to get some more information about what Cade had done in there yesterday, whom he had been talking to, where he had gone. She finally hit pay dirt when Creflo King, who owned most of the parking lots in town, told her he had seen Cade talking to a pretty woman yesterday.

Again, Blair bristled. "Who was she, do you know?"

Creflo sucked on the toothpick in his mouth and leaned on the counter. "Never seen her before. Nobody from around here, and she wasn't dressed like a tourist. She had on a dress like she was going to church. I just figured she might have been kin to that man Cade killed, they were talking so serious and all, and Cade had this whipped look on his face like he was about to bust into tears or something."

Now they were getting somewhere. Blair turned that over in her mind. He must have had someone come forward about the body.

"Did he leave here with her?" she asked.

"Oh, yeah, sure did." Creflo took off his cap and scratched at the bald spot on his scraggly head. "In fact, I walked out behind them. He got into a blue PT Cruiser with her and they took off."

Her eyebrows shot up. "He got into her car?"

"That's right."

"You didn't see the license tag, did you?"

"Of course not. It did have a Hertz sticker, though, so the car might have been rented. I didn't see no reason to be suspicious. Cade's a cop. He knows what he's doin'. And he has the right to go off with any woman he wants."

Blair wasn't sure why that statement stung her.

When she realized she had gotten all the information she was going to get out of him, she headed to the police station, and found Joe McCormick sitting at Cade's desk with a pile of reports in front of him. He looked up at her with weary eyes and ran his hand across his closely shaved head. "What you got, Blair?"

"Joe, I talked to Creflo King at Cricket's and he said that he saw Cade getting into a blue PT Cruiser with a woman yesterday morning before he disappeared."

"Yeah, what else is new?" He went back to writing. "I found that out yesterday."

Her mouth fell open. "Well, why didn't you tell me?"

He grunted. "Why should I tell you? You're not a member of this police department. I don't have to share classified information with you."

"Well, why is it classified?" she asked. "Come on! For heaven's sake, I was calling all over the place yesterday trying to find him."

"Well, we didn't know where he was," Joe said, "and we still don't. We don't know who the woman is, and we don't know anything about the blue PT Cruiser or where they went." He dropped his pencil and leaned back, rubbing his eyes. "I'm beginning to get concerned, Blair."

She sat down in front of him, her eyes locked on his face. "Define 'concerned.'"

Joe gave her a smirk. "Concerned, meaning that something's not right. Besides his wanting to find out who he ran over, we might have a murder case on our hands—that man had been shot. Cade would be here working on this case. I mean, it's possible that Cade just took off with a girlfriend, but I just can't see that happening."

"No, me either. Besides, Cade doesn't have a girlfriend."

Joe got up, went to the window. "He was too worried about the identity of the man. He had us all hopping the day of the accident. He wouldn't just vanish the next day."

"So who is the woman?"

"We're trying to find out." He turned back to her. "But there are a lot of unknowns right now. If we could determine the identity of the dead man, then maybe we could figure out who she was."

"Then you think she was connected to the man who was killed?"

"It's just a guess, but it's as good as any other."

When Blair left the station, she sat behind the wheel of her Volvo, trying to think. Joe's concerns only validated her own. Something had, indeed, happened to Cade.

Fear churned in the pit of her stomach. What if he wasn't all right?

She drove home, pulled into the parking lot between her house and the library. She didn't feel like working today, but she supposed she had no choice. She went to the library next door and unlocked it. It felt cold and barren in here today, even though outside it was nearing eighty degrees already.

She thought of the petite woman with the blue PT Cruiser. Was it even possible that she was Cade's girlfriend? That he'd been so traumatized over killing the man, that he'd gone off with her without telling anyone?

No, it wasn't possible, she told herself. That was ludicrous and completely out of character for Cade. She was thinking like Creflo King, not like an intelligent woman who knew Cade well.

Cade was in trouble. But she didn't have a clue how to help him.

At three o'clock that afternoon, Blair's restlessness overcame her, and she decided to go back to the police station to see if there had been any news. As she pulled into the parking lot, she saw Joe burst out of the police station and head to his car.

"Joe," she called through her car window. "Has anything happened?"

He glanced back at her as he got into his unmarked car. "Somebody just reported finding an abandoned car."

"Where?"

"In the woods over by Hampton's Place." He slammed his door and started his car.

Hampton's Place was a condominium complex about a half mile from South Beach, where the man had been killed. Was it his car they had found? Would it have his identification? Would it provide any clues about Cade? Blair turned her car around and followed him.

When they got to the parking lot of Hampton's Place, Joe got out of his car and stalked toward her. "Are you crazy?" He flung her door open. "Following me like that! I'm on police business, Blair. I ought to ticket you."

"After we see the car." Blair got out of her Volvo and, with an air of authority, started toward the man and the other cops waiting for Joe at the edge of the woods.

Joe grabbed her arm. "Blair, I don't want to arrest the town librarian for interfering with an investigation."

Blair looked up at him. "Come on, Joe. Please let me go. I just want to see the car. I won't get in the way."

"You're already in the way!" He turned to the cops who had been the first responders and ordered them to tape off the area before anyone else went near the car. Turning back to Blair, he said, "Don't you cross that tape, Blair Owens. There could be footprints or other evidence and we don't want it trampled."

She didn't answer, just waited until they had taped it off, then walked the perimeter until she could see the car.

Harris James—the man who'd found it—stood under the shade of a pine tree in a wooded area. Blair had known him for years. He was a Cape Refuge native, and he and his family had owned the property on the southern tip of the island for generations.

The red-haired man looked excited as he led them through the trees to the car that had been abandoned there. It was a gray four-wheel drive Passport.

"I was just walking through the woods," he said, "and I ran across this SUV with the driver's door wide open. Look here, there's blood and a gun on the seat. I figured I'd better call the police."

Blair wanted more than anything to duck under the yellow tape and examine the car for herself, but she hung back, listening.

Joe radioed in the tag number, then checked the outside of the door and window for prints, took a few pictures. Blair could see that there was blood on the outer edge of the seat, and splattered on the door.

But if it was suicide, wouldn't he have shot himself in the head? Why would he put the gun to his abdomen? And if he wanted to die and had the energy to walk to the street, he could have just shot himself a second time.

On the other hand, maybe someone had shot him and left him for dead. Maybe they hadn't expected him to be able to go for help.

Blair straightened and looked around, scanning the ground for footprints. The car had been here for two days, and the rain had washed any prints away.

Joe opened the glove box and pulled out the registration. "Car's owned by a William Clark."

William Clark. Where had she heard that before? Blair racked her brain, trying to think. William Clark, William Clark. *The caller ID!* She caught her breath and called out across the tape. "William Clark's name came up on Cade's caller ID this morning."

He pulled back out of the car and regarded her. "What do you mean, it came up?"

She realized she had just incriminated herself, and shrank back. "Well, I sort of used his key. I know where he hides it." *Okay, it was a lie,* she thought. Jonathan had been the one who knew where he had hidden it, but she didn't want to drag him into this. "I just went in to make sure he wasn't lying dead in the house, and I looked at his caller ID, and the one person I didn't recognize was William Clark."

Joe came toward her. "Then someone from the dead man's family must have called him. Only, Cade's number is unlisted. How would they have gotten the number?" He looked back at the vehicle, then turned back to Blair. "What time was that call?"

She shook her head. "I didn't think to get the exact time. I didn't realize the call was significant."

Joe went back to searching the car, and Blair watched. They dusted for prints, took pictures, bagged the floor mats, vacuumed for trace evidence, chalked the location of the gun, all before having a tow truck come get the car to take it to a secure location where they could examine it more thoroughly.

As the tow truck took the vehicle away, Joe looked at Blair. "All right, I've got to go over to Cade's house," he said. "Blair, you come show me where the key is."

Blair was glad she had watched Jonathan put the key back. She followed him over to Cade's house.

Oswald, Cade's cat, nuzzled up to her feet as soon as they got to the backyard, and Blair leaned down and stroked his back.

She got the key out of the utility room, and Joe took them and went in. "Don't touch anything, Blair. I don't know if a crime's even been committed, but just in case, we don't need to disturb any evidence."

She realized with a pang of guilt that she had disturbed quite a bit that morning. So had Jonathan.

She led him straight to the caller ID. He flipped through the callers and came to William Clark.

Joe nodded, his forehead still pleated. "Okay, the call came at five-thirty yesterday morning."

"Five-thirty," she whispered. "What a time to call somebody, especially if you don't know them."

"And if they didn't know him, how did they get his number? Cade's not listed. Most cops aren't."

"Maybe someone at the police station gave it to her."

"No way," he said. "That would never happen. Besides, I checked on the drive over, and no one from that number called the station. In fact, we didn't get any calls after 2:00 A.M. Not until 7:00 this morning."

"So it was someone who already had his number, then," Blair said. "Someone who knows him socially, maybe?"

Joe didn't commit to an answer. "I've ordered a copy of William Clark's driver's license. That'll have his picture. Once we have that, we can decide for sure if he's the man Cade hit, and we can go from there."

She waited as Joe made a search of Cade's home, then finally, he let her put the key back and headed back to the station. Blair followed him as if she belonged there, and when they arrived, Joe didn't stop her. Preoccupied, he hurried into the small building and went straight to the fax machine. Blair stood at the door, waiting to see the DMV photo for herself.

Joe jerked it out of the machine and started to nod. "That's him, all right."

Blair looked at the picture and saw the similarities to the sketch that the artist had drawn. She looked up at Joe. "So what have we got? A man who was shot in his own car, someone from his house calling Cade, Cade disappearing with some woman in a PT Cruiser . . ."

He rubbed his temple. "Maybe the woman in the Cruiser was the one who called Cade from Clark's house." He sighed. "Well, it won't be hard to find out. I have to go there and notify the family."

"I'm coming with you."

Joe looked at her like she was crazy. "Think again. Police business, Blair. You're not a cop. Why do I have to keep reminding you of that?"

"Show me in the police manual where it says that only officers can notify families of tragedies."

Joe shook his head. "Blair—"

"You can't, can you, Joe? You can't because it's not in there. Cade was going to let me go with him because he knew that I could relate to how this family felt getting this kind of news."

Again, a little white lie. Cade had never really committed to letting her go with him. But she knew she could have talked him into it.

"You don't know *what's* in our manual. It sure doesn't say to take the town librarian with us!"

"Come on, Joe. You know you don't want to go by yourself. Maybe if I come it'll soften things up a little. Maybe I can give his wife a hug or help her in some way."

He almost laughed. "No offense, Blair, but that's not your thing."

She threw her chin up. "It could be my thing," she said. "I watched my parents and Morgan do it enough. I can hug, Joe. Come on, I want to see this woman. I want to see what she drives, and I want to see if she has big brown hair and is petite, and I want to ask her if she's the one that came here yesterday to see Cade and if she knows what happened to him."

"And what if she's not?" he yelled. "What if she's just a woman who doesn't know her husband is dead? And we go and tell her and break her heart? Are you prepared for that, Blair? You gonna interrogate her then?"

"I can handle it. Take me with you, Joe!"

He sighed and got up, strolled to the window and looked out. Finally he turned back around. "All right, Blair, but only because I have the feeling I couldn't get rid of you if I wanted to. And Cade thinks a lot of you and trusts your instincts. But you let me do the talking unless you have something worthwhile to add. And when I say it's time to go, we're going. Got that?"

She almost hugged him just to prove she could. "Yep, I got it. You're the boss."

"That'll be the day," he muttered as he started out of Cade's office. "Blair Owens doesn't have a boss."

CHAPTER

*T*hey rode in silence to Savannah and
found the address of the man who had died. The house was
situated in one of the town squares set up by James Edward
Oglethorpe when he'd laid out the city of Savannah in the
eighteenth century. It was an old house across the street
from Washington Park, though it looked as if attempts had
been made to preserve and restore it. The Savannah Historical Society had declared the entire downtown area a
historical landmark so that it couldn't be bulldozed and
made into parking lots. Some of the homes still needed
transformation from eyesores to historical beauties.

The Clark house was painted pink, with white lacy
trim and wrought-iron railing, but parts of the house were
in stages of decay and disrepair. As they pulled into the
driveway of the modest structure, Blair had the feeling that
William Clark may have been working on restoring the
house completely but hadn't quite finished.

Something about that saddened her. She looked up
at the front door, and wondered if someone was already

grieving behind it, or if she and Joe would be breaking the news. She recalled sitting out in Cade's police car the day her parents were murdered, trying to push through the shock. The worst news of her life had attacked her with no warning.

Joe pulled far enough into the driveway to see that the garage attached to the back of the house was closed. Clearly, the update on the house had included the more modern garage than some in the area had.

"I was hoping to see if there was a PT Cruiser here," he said.

Blair just looked at the garage. There was a window there, but she knew she couldn't get away with going to look in it.

Joe started to get out. "Now I'm telling you, I do the talking, you hear?"

"Fine, sure." Blair got out and looked up at the front porch. "Don't worry about me."

They walked up to the front porch, and Blair hung back as Joe raised his hand to knock. "Now, Blair, I mean it," he said in a low voice. "Nothing about Cade or her being in Cape Refuge, at least not until I've had the chance to break the news about her husband."

"And if she already knows?"

His eyes pierced her. "Then you let me do the questioning. Got that?"

She agreed, but only because she had no choice. He knocked again.

She heard footsteps coming to the door, a fumbling with the lock as if it hadn't been opened in some time, and then a woman peaked out from the darkness. She was a blonde instead of the brunette Blair had expected, but she did qualify as "petite."

"Yes? May I help you?" she asked.

"Mrs. Clark?" Joe asked.

"Yes," she said.

"Are you the wife of William Clark?"

"Yes." She opened the door wider. "Do you know where my husband is?"

He shot Blair a look. "Ma'am, I'm Joe McCormick with the Cape Refuge Police Department, and this is Blair Owens."

She half expected him to introduce her as the town librarian, as if that had any bearing at all on anything. But he left it at her name.

"Could we come in for a moment and talk to you?"

The woman studied his badge, then looked up at him with pleading eyes. "You have bad news, don't you?"

When he hesitated, she stepped back from the door and let them in, watching their faces with glistening eyes. Blair's heart ached for the woman. She remembered Cade walking into the City Council meeting on the day of her parents' murder, asking Morgan and her to come outside. She had known there was bad news, though she could never have imagined how bad it was.

They stepped into the dark house that smelled of age. When the woman had closed the door, she turned back to them. "Has something happened to my husband?"

"Ma'am, if we could just sit down for a moment."

The woman ushered them into a parlorlike room and turned on a light. Suddenly Blair was able to see her fully. Her eyes were a light green, and her skin was pale like porcelain, untouched by the sun.

Blair took a seat on a sofa, and Joe sat down next to her.

The woman remained standing. "Willie killed himself, didn't he?"

Joe looked up at her, stricken. "Why would you ask that?"

"Because he said he was going to when he left here that day. We'd had an argument—a stupid, silly argument—and he said he was going to kill himself. He hasn't been home in two days. . . ."

Blair looked at Joe, waiting for him to go on. He set his elbows on his knees and looked down at his hands. "Your husband is dead, Mrs. Clark," he said. "I'm so sorry to be the one to tell you."

She seemed to deflate with the news, and wilted into the chair across from them. Her face twisted as tears reddened her eyes. "I didn't think he'd do it. He'd threatened it before, but he always came back home. We always made up."

Joe swallowed and went on. "Mrs. Clark, Sunday afternoon, during the storm, your husband walked out in front of a police car. He was struck. He died shortly after being taken to the hospital. But they discovered that before the accident he had been shot. We found his car today. The gun was still on the seat."

"Oh, Willie!" Her cry carried over the house, and she fell back with both hands over her face.

"We would have notified you sooner, but we weren't able to identify him until we found the car today."

Blair knew she had to do something to ease the woman's anguish. She got up and went to her. Stooping on the floor in front of her, she pulled the woman into her arms, as Morgan would have done. The woman's body shook with sobs. "I'm so sorry," she whispered. "I know this must be a shock."

"I'd been calling around," she said through her sobs. "Looking everywhere. I even called the hospitals, but they didn't have anyone by his name." She drew in a breath. "Where . . . where is he?"

"He's at the Chatham County Morgue," Joe said in a low voice. "We need for you to go identify the body."

Blair felt the pain of that finality racking through the woman's bones. All her questions about Cade vanished from her mind as Blair felt her grief.

Mrs. Clark pulled back. "I want to go now. I want to see him. Maybe it's not really him."

Blair looked back at Joe.

"All right," he said. "I'll take you over there right now."

"No, I'll drive my own car. I want to be alone."

"But are you sure you're up to driving?" Blair asked gently.

"Yes." She got up and looked around helplessly. "My purse. I'll get my purse."

"We'll follow you over there," Joe said. "I'll go in with you. Be sure to bring some identification."

She looked off, her eyes fixed on a spot on the wall. "It was just a little fight. Nothing to kill yourself over. I thought he was just taking a breather, putting some space between us." She pressed her hand over her mouth. "I'll back my car out and you can follow me over."

Blair followed Joe out, feeling as helpless as she'd ever felt. When they got back into Joe's car, she looked over at him. "Should I go in with her?"

"No. You'll need to wait in the car. I'll go."

"But she may need some comfort. Some support."

"Blair, I really need for you to wait in the car." He started the car and watched the garage door come open. A white Buick Regal pulled out.

"Not a PT Cruiser," he said. "And she wasn't a brunette."

Blair nodded. "But you still need to ask her if she was in Cape Refuge yesterday, or if she called Cade."

The woman pulled out, and Joe led her to the County Morgue.

Joe had been inside the morgue for over half an hour, when Blair finally saw him coming back out. His face looked pale and grim. He got into the car, set his hands on the steering wheel, and stared down at the dashboard.

"It was her husband, all right."

"Is she going to be okay?"

"I guess so. I hope she has some kind of support system."

Blair looked toward the door. "Where is she?"

"She's filling out paperwork. She didn't want me to stay with her." He started his car, and pulled out into traffic.

"So did you ask her about the phone call?"

"Yep. She claims she didn't call him and says she's never been to Cape Refuge in her life."

Blair frowned. "Then how does she explain the phone call?"

He shook his head. "She couldn't. And I checked. No one else lives in that house, and there wasn't anyone there besides her yesterday."

Blair leaned her head back on the headrest. "Weird. That just doesn't add up." She narrowed her eyes, trying to think. "I would have believed her about not being on Cape Refuge, since she doesn't really fit the description, but to lie about the phone call."

"Yeah, it worries me too. She swears up and down that she didn't know about her husband until we told her. That she wouldn't have had any reason to call Cade."

Blair shook her head. "We need a picture of her. We need to show it to the ones who saw the woman yesterday. We have to find out if she was the one they saw with Cade. She could have changed her hair, or had on a wig or something."

"That should be easy enough," Joe said. "I can get a copy of her driver's license when we get back."

CHAPTER

10

*W*hen they were back on Cape Refuge, Blair went into the station with Joe and waited as he ordered the license. While they waited for the picture to be faxed, she stepped into Cade's office.

His chair sat empty—a comfortable executive chair that he'd gotten when the city council had allocated thousands of dollars for themselves rather than fixing the potholes on Ocean Boulevard. Cade was probably the only one who really deserved it.

On his wall hung a matted and framed copy of a newspaper article that had come out about him when he'd solved her parents' murder. Melba Jefferson had given the framed account to him as a gift. Ordinarily, Cade would not have been vain or insensitive enough to put it up, but Melba had brought a hammer and hung it herself. He'd explained it to Blair with sincere apologies, and she'd understood why he'd left it hanging.

His desk held several stacks of files and papers, with a couple of gaudy paperweights on top, which had probably been passed through several of his predecessors.

"Picture's here," Joe said from behind her. "I made you a copy."

She took it and looked down at the image of Ann Clark. Her hair in the picture was just the way she'd worn it today—blonde, thin, and shoulder-length. "I'll take it to show Jonathan."

"I'll take it to Creflo King and the others who saw her," Joe said. "Let me know what Jonathan says."

She hurried over to Hanover House, hoping Jonathan had made it home already. She found him in the kitchen on his back under the sink, working on fixing a leak. He smelled of sweat, saltwater, and fish. He had just come in and hadn't had time to shower or change yet before Morgan had hit him up with the leak.

Blair knelt beside him and thrust the picture at him. "Jonathan, look at this picture. Could this be the woman Cade was with the other day?"

He slid out from under the cabinet and studied the picture. "Well, no. The woman had brown hair, kind of big and frizzy."

"Okay, picture this woman with that hair. It could have been a wig or something."

He looked up at her. "Who is she?"

"She's the wife of the man Cade ran over."

"No kidding?" He got to his feet and leaned back against the counter. "Cade was talking to the wife of the man he killed?"

"I'm asking you," she said. "It may not be her at all. But look at her face, her eyes."

"She had on sunglasses," Jonathan said. "But she did look really pale. I hadn't really thought about it until now, but yeah, it could have been her. You think she had something to do with Cade's disappearance?"

She sighed. "I really don't know. But yes, it's possible." She went to the phone on the kitchen wall and dialed the police station. Alex answered again. "Let me speak to Joe McCormick, please." She waited as Joe picked up.

"McCormick."

"Yeah, Joe? Jonathan says she could be the same woman, only with different hair. What did you find from Creflo?"

"He's here right now," he said. "He remembers her being real pale. Says she had on sunglasses, so he didn't get a good look at her face."

"Sounds like a disguise, like she might not want to be identified later," Blair said. "But could all that crying back at her house have been an act? Could she have known all along about her husband?"

"Maybe. I'm checking rental car places in Savannah, trying to see if any of them has a Cruiser and whether it was rented out yesterday. If she came here with evil intentions against Cade and went to all the trouble of a disguise, then she probably wouldn't have wanted to be seen in her own car. And Creflo mentioned a Hertz sticker."

Blair sat down, clutching the phone. "Evil intentions?"

"Hey, I don't know what happened to Cade, but he's still not here. She's the last person he was seen with."

Morgan came into the room, and Blair looked up at her, then at Jonathan. "I think Cade is in danger, don't you, Joe?" she said into the phone.

"Could be."

"Go search her house. See if there's any clue."

"I was thinking the same thing," he said. "Only I have to convince a judge to give me a search warrant, and there's no clear evidence of a crime being committed."

"Explain to them that the chief of police of Cape Refuge has disappeared. Don't you guys have a brotherhood or something? When a cop is shot, the whole force goes after the perpetrator. Shouldn't it be the same thing for one who's vanished?"

"We'll see," Joe said.

Frustrated, Blair hung up, and she turned to her sister and brother-in-law, who stood staring at her.

"He thinks it was her?" Jonathan asked.

"Sure does."

"What could this woman have done to him?" Jonathan asked. "She's what, five-foot-two, a hundred pounds? It's not like she could overpower him."

Blair felt sick. "Depends on what kind of weapon she had."

"Well, did Joe question her?"

"Not really." Her eyes ached with tears. "It was kind of a touchy thing, you know. I mean, how do you interrogate a woman who's just been told she's a widow?"

"But if she's a suspect in Cade's disappearance," Morgan said, "wouldn't it be appropriate to question her?"

"Well, sure, but we still don't know for sure she is the same woman. Different hair, different car . . ."

Jonathan pushed off from the counter and started toward the stairs. "I'm going to shower and head for the police station."

"What for?" Blair asked.

"I don't know," Jonathan said. "I just want to talk to Joe. Make sure he understands the urgency. Cade's time might be running out."

Blair watched him leave, and Morgan came up behind her and began massaging her shoulders. "Your shoulder muscles are like bricks, Sis."

Blair wasn't listening. "If she lied to us, what could it mean?"

"I hate to think," Morgan whispered.

Blair turned around and looked at her sister. "If anything happens to him . . ." The statement trailed off. If anything happened . . . what? Would she die? Destroy something? Implode?

She thought of that city of refuge passage he'd been reading in his Bible. It was her last clue about where his head had been before he disappeared. What did it mean?

She needed more information.

"Morgan, I need to borrow a Bible."

The delight on Morgan's face almost made her angry. "A Bible? Sure."

"Don't get excited. I just want to do some research on the passage Cade was reading before he vanished. And I need to borrow a concordance."

Morgan quickly led her into the office, as if she feared she would change her mind if she lingered. "Here," she said, thrusting a Bible at her. "It's Pop's Bible. It has his notes."

Blair's throat tightened as she looked down at it.

"And here's the concordance." She dropped it on top of the Bible. "And here, take these commentaries." She pulled three dictionary-sized books out of the shelves and dropped them on the stack.

"We might be getting a little carried away here," Blair said.

Morgan turned around, still a little too happy at the request. "I just want to make sure you have everything you need. You know what you always say, about knowledge being power."

"You're getting your hopes up, Morgan. You think my research is going to lead me to some dramatic conversion. It won't. I just want to get inside Cade's head."

"I know. Just information. That's fine."

But as Morgan pulled out more books, Blair began to wish she'd never asked.

CHAPTER

*B*lair curled up on her couch that night with her father's Bible and read the passage that Cade had been reading the morning he disappeared. Though she'd spent most of her childhood in church and had endured endless hours of Bible teaching from both parents, she couldn't remember ever hearing about the cities of refuge until today.

One would think that it would have been incorporated into some of the town's celebrations, or at least explained in Cape Refuge's written history, since someone who had a part in naming the island clearly had known about Numbers 35. But this wasn't the case.

She tried to imagine what Cade had been thinking when he'd turned to that passage. Had he considered himself guilty of manslaughter, even though the man might have died, anyway, from the gunshot? Was he thinking he had bloodguilt on his hands? That he needed refuge from some unseen Avenger?

She began to read about the Levitical cities and how six were to be set apart.

Then the LORD said to Moses: "Speak to the Israelites and say to them: 'When you cross the Jordan into Canaan, select some towns to be your cities of refuge, to which a person who has killed someone accidentally may flee. They will be places of refuge from the avenger, so that a person accused of murder may not die before he stands trial before the assembly. These six towns you give will be your cities of refuge. Give three on the side of the Jordan and three in Canaan as cities of refuge. These six towns will be a place of refuge for Israelites, aliens and any other people living among them, so that anyone who has killed another accidentally can flee there."

It was interesting, she thought, but had no application to Cade's life today. Even Cape Refuge wasn't a shelter from the legal system. People came there, specifically to Hanover House, to take refuge from their own trials.

She read on, about the distinction between manslaughter and murder. If the killing was proven to be intentional homicide, the avenger—someone from the dead person's family—would have the responsibility of putting him to death.

No death row. No government executioner. Up-close-and-personal revenge. That was what was called for.

But if it was an accident, then the congregation was to let him live in the city of refuge until the death of the high priest.

No complete acquittal. His life was altered for years. She wondered if he had to leave his family, his friends, or if they came with him. Did he have to stay in that place alone, eking out a living among priests and other manslayers?

And what did the high priest's death have to do with anything?

She read further.

"Do not pollute the land where you are. Bloodshed pollutes the land, and atonement cannot be made for the land on which blood has been shed, except by the blood of the one who shed it. Do not defile the land where you live and where I dwell, for I, the LORD, dwell among the Israelites."

Did Cade think he had somehow defiled the land? Or had he already gotten that call before he turned to that passage?

Could it be that he'd heard from Ann Clark and wondered why she wanted to meet with him? Maybe he sensed revenge in her voice.

The passage gave Blair no peace—just more questions that kept her from sleeping.

She rose feeling achy and frustrated the next morning. She headed over to Cricket's and saw that Cade's truck was still there.

Wearily, she went into the place and took a table where someone had left a copy of the *Savannah Morning News*. She picked it up as Charlie brought her a cup of coffee.

"Thanks, Charlie," she said, taking a sip.

He nodded. "Terrible about Cade, ain't it?"

She looked up at him. "What do you mean?"

"The article in the paper," he said. "Don't look good."

She looked down at the front page, and gasped. Her coffee sloshed and spilled.

CAPE REFUGE POLICE CHIEF UNDER SUSPICION.

Charlie grabbed a napkin and blotted up the coffee as Blair began to read.

The disappearance of Cape Refuge's Police Chief Matthew Cade, after running down a pedestrian on Monday, has cast him under a cloud of suspicion, sources said Monday. The dead man, who had been shot before walking into the street, was identified as William Clark yesterday. Chief Cade disappeared after being seen having breakfast with Ann Clark, the wife of the dead man.

Blair almost choked. How could they have put this in the paper? They weren't even sure it was her, and here it was in print for everyone to see?

Creflo King, who breakfasts each morning at a small island diner called Cricket's, said he saw Cade there getting into the car with Clark's wife the morning after he killed Clark. "I didn't know who she was then," King said, "but later the police showed me a picture of her and said that was who she was. Her hair was different, but it was the same woman I saw, all right."

Chief Cade has not been seen or heard from since. *Savannah Morning News* tried to contact Ann Clark, but she did not return our calls.

"Makes you wonder if William Clark's death was an accident, after all," King said. "Sure makes you wonder if this ain't something staged just so they could be together."

Blair screamed and flung the paper across the room. "How could he say that?"

She saw Creflo King sitting at the bar, looking back at her over his shoulder.

"How dare you!" she screamed across the crowd. Everyone got silent, and all eyes turned to her as she erupted out of her seat. "Creflo King, how *dare* you say those things about Cade!"

Creflo shrugged. "Just told the truth."

She picked up the paper she had thrown and waved it in the air. "It was your fifteen minutes of fame, wasn't it? You must feel like a big man now."

Creflo got up. "All I did was answer the questions, Blair."

"You've ruined Cade's reputation," she shouted. "You've made people think he was an adulterer and a murderer! How could you do that to him?"

She started toward him across the wooden floor, and Charlie stepped into her way. "Come on, Blair. Calm down."

"I will not calm down!" She looked around at the astonished faces, most of whom she knew well. "Everybody in this place knows that Cade is a decent, upstanding Christian man. If any of you knew him at all, you'd know how upset he was over the accident that happened the other day. He was beating himself up over it. There's no way he did that on purpose!"

She got to Creflo and grabbed his red plaid collar. Through gritted teeth, she said, "You call that paper right now, and you take back what you said."

"I can't, Blair," he told her. "I told them the truth. I did see him leaving with that woman. Joe told me hisself that it might be William Clark's wife. And he ain't turned up since, so you tell me, where is he?"

"I don't know where he is," she said, "but I can guarantee you he's not in some lover's arms, snickering about how he got her husband out of the way." She shoved him, and he stumbled back against the counter. "You make me sick, you know that? We don't even know for sure if that was Ann Clark, but if it was, she has time to hide all the evidence before the police can search her place. But you got your stinking name in the paper! I could just kill you."

"You hear that, everybody?" Creflo yelled. "Blair Owens just threatened me right in front of God and everybody."

She knew her scar was flaming just the way she hated it, and she slapped her hair back from her face and pointed at him.

"Don't doubt me for a minute, Creflo," she said. "If you open your mouth and even speak the name of Matthew Cade, I will personally come back and deliver on my threat." With that, she stormed out of Cricket's, leaving the gossip and speculation to go on behind her.

Joe McCormick cut through the squad room at the Third Precinct in Savannah. The officer at the front desk had pointed him to the offices in the back, Sergeant Tim Hull's domain. Joe had worked with the detective on a number of overlapping cases in the past and figured he wouldn't have any trouble getting his help now.

But Hull wasn't in his office. Joe stood in the doorway, surveying the clutter of weeks-old coffee cups and empty Diet Coke cans, wadded fast-food bags and ashtrays overflowing with cigarette butts. From the looks of things, one would have thought the occupant of this office was a stuffy old Lou Grant type, but that wasn't true. Hull looked more like Don Johnson from old *Miami Vice* reruns, with his sandy hair and darkly tanned skin, his two-day growth of stubble, his neutral-colored blazers, and his sockless ankles.

He would have fit right in on Cape Refuge, though he looked more like one of the lifeguards on the police department payroll than the cops who protected the island.

Joe looked toward what Hull often called "the war room" and saw the detective standing over a fax machine with a cigarette hanging from his mouth. "Hull!" he called, and the man turned.

Taking the cigarette out and stubbing it in a nearby ashtray, Hull blew out smoke and grinned at his island counterpart. "Well, if it isn't the big man from the small town." He reached out to shake.

"I need to talk to you," Joe said. "It's about our police chief."

Hull pulled a pack of cigarettes out of his pocket and lit another one. "Can't talk now. I'm on my way to the hospital. Another stolen baby, this time right here in Savannah. It hasn't been missing more than an hour. I've got to get over there if this fax machine will hurry up and print out what I need."

Joe regarded the paper rolling through the machine at its own pace, and finally Hull jerked it out. He took his cigarette out and studied the page for a moment. Then he seemed to remember Joe was there. "Walk with me. I'm in a hurry."

Joe matched his step. "I'm trying to get a warrant to question a woman and search a house over at Washington Square. Since it's on your turf, I thought you might want to be involved."

Hull took his cigarette out again and squinted at him through the smoke. "What for?"

"The wife of the pedestrian Cade ran over the other day lives there."

Hull shook his head. "I heard about his disappearance. Is this a lead on where he is?"

Joe nodded. "We think she was the last one seen with Cade the morning he disappeared. And if so, then her weird behavior might implicate her in her husband's shooting. I need to question her and search the house and see if there are any clues as to where Cade might be."

They burst out the front doors of the precinct, and Hull dropped his cigarette and stepped on it. "Good luck trying to convince a judge to give you a warrant to search a bereaved woman's

house, when you can't even be sure a crime has been committed."
He reached his car and unlocked it. "Your chief could have gone
fishing, for all you know. There's no evidence of foul play, if the
papers are right, and he hasn't been gone that long. That's a hard
sell to a judge. And you say she *may* have been the last one seen
with him? You don't know for sure?"

"She called his phone that morning," Joe said. "Witnesses
are pretty sure she's the same woman he was with. And the car
they got into was a rental car that was checked out at the airport
the night before, and returned the next day."

Hull reached his car but didn't get in. "Was she the one who
rented it?"

"Whoever it was apparently used a fake name and ID. We
can't trace it. I'm thinking there might be some revenge involved,
Hull. I know you don't know Cade that well, but he wouldn't up
and disappear like this. I don't want to do any kind of intense
search. I just want to walk through her house, check the bedrooms, the basement, her car. I want to scare her a little in hopes
of her spilling her guts."

Hull put his hands on the roof of his car and shook his head.
"Maybe she did go talk to him, just to look into the eye of the
man who killed her husband."

"She said she didn't. Said she'd never been to Cape Refuge."

"Maybe she chewed him out and wasn't proud of it, so she
lied. That doesn't mean she had anything to do with Cade's disappearance or her husband's shooting."

"All of those things could be true," Joe said. "But I want to
know for sure. If I can get the warrant to search her place, do you
want to go along or not?"

Hull looked across the roof of the car, thinking. Finally, he
opened the car door. "I've got to go, Joe. I have to see about this
missing baby. A woman walks into the mother's hospital room in
a nursing uniform and tells her she needs to take the baby because
the doctor is on the floor and needs to examine it. Half an hour
passes before the mother inquires about when the baby will be
brought back. Turns out the woman who took the baby isn't

employed there. Baby's gone. Now that's a crime, Joe. A real-live, bona fide crime. I realize you don't see many of those on Cape Refuge, so you go looking for crimes where they haven't happened."

Joe just looked at him. "We had a double homicide just a few months ago, Hull. You know that."

"Well, you and I both know that's not what this is. Chief Cade will mosey in in a day or so, claiming to be depressed about running a guy down, with a song and dance about how he needed to get away. Your famous yet amusing city council will be in an uproar, and there will be hearings and meetings for months on whether or not to fire him. You might even get the job."

He got into his car, closed the door, and rolled the window down.

Joe leaned in.

"When I get the warrant, Hull, do you want to search the house with me or not? I can do it alone, but I thought I'd offer you the chance since it's your territory."

Hull sighed and started his car. "Missing baby, Joe. First things first."

Joe stepped back as the car pulled away, and watched the man drive out of sight.

CHAPTER

*H*ull had been right about the judge's reaction to Joe's request for a warrant. He'd claimed there was no proof of a crime even being committed in Cade's case. His only option now was to question her and ask permission for a walk-through of her house. If she didn't grant it, he was out of luck.

Joe had half hoped that Hull would pass on sharing the questioning with him now that there wasn't a warrant, but the truth was that he needed another pair of eyes. He could have brought any of the officers from Cape Refuge with him, but none of them were trained detectives. He didn't have time to give them a cram session on this kind of search.

Hull had agreed to come a little more easily than Joe had expected, but he had known the Savannah detective wouldn't want to be left out. Since the FBI had taken over the baby-kidnapping case, he'd had no reason not to come. He would meet Joe at the house at noon, he said.

Joe pulled up to the front curb of the house at 11:55 in his own unmarked car. The house he'd visited just days ago looked unchanged. Nothing seemed out of the ordinary.

Another unmarked car pulled up behind him, and Joe got out and closed his door quietly. Hull was dressed just as he'd been earlier, in a faded navy blue T-shirt under a tweed sport coat that looked like it had seen better days, a pair of khakis with a dirty hem, and deck shoes with no socks.

"Thanks for coming," Joe said.

"Sure you want to do this, Joe?" Hull took the cigarette out of his mouth and dropped it on the sidewalk.

"I know it'll be unpleasant," Joe said, "but it has to be done."

Joe led him up the front steps to the door and knocked hard. After a moment they heard footsteps again, then Ann Clark opened the door and peeked out.

"Mrs. Clark, I'm Detective McCormick from the Cape Refuge Police Department. I was here yesterday?"

She touched her throat. "Yes?"

"This is Detective Hull from the Savannah PD."

"Nice to meet you," she said.

Her eyes looked swollen and red, as if she'd been crying for days. Joe felt an instant pang of guilt. He hoped he wasn't making a mistake.

"I'm kind of busy right now," she said.

Joe pressed on. "Ma'am, we need to ask you a few questions. Do you mind if we come in?"

By the look on her face, it was clear that she did mind, but she stepped back from the door. She led them to the same parlor where he had broken the news yesterday. Joe took the same sofa, and she sat across from him.

Hull remained standing, looking around as if he was already involved in a search of the place.

Joe looked up at her. "Ma'am, I just had a few questions to ask you."

"I read the article in the paper today." Her voice wavered. "The things they said about me, they weren't even true. I don't know your police chief, Detective. I've never seen him in my life."

"I'm sorry about that article," he said. "It was irresponsible reporting. But witnesses believe it was you they saw on Cape Refuge, and we know for sure that a call was made from this house to Chief Cade's house on Tuesday morning." He leaned his elbows on his knees. "Mrs. Clark, you seemed surprised when we told you your husband had died. Were you?"

She cleared her throat. "Well, it was a shock, as you can imagine."

"But did you know about it already?"

She fidgeted, got up, walked near Detective Hull as if guarding her things from him. "I had seen it on the news the night before."

Joe stared at her. "You saw it on the news? Then why didn't you call us to let us know who he was?"

"I wasn't thinking clearly," she said. "I don't know."

Now Joe was sure she was involved. Why else would she have lied? He got to his feet, and faced her. "Why did you let us think you were hearing it for the first time, Mrs. Clark? Why the act?"

Ann Clark came back to the chair she had been sitting in and stood behind it, fingering the cord across the top seam. "I told you, I wasn't thinking clearly. I heard about it on the news the night before, and I was kind of in denial, hoping you were coming to tell me it was all a mistake, that he was all right. In the hospital maybe, but that he wasn't dead." Her voice broke then, and she crumpled over the chair, bringing her elbows close up to her chest and covering her face with her wrists. "Willie is dead. He shot himself to get away from me. What did you want me to do?"

Hull turned around, and Joe just looked at her. He hated it when women cried. He never knew what to do. Shoving his hands into his pockets, he looked down at his feet. "Mrs. Clark, we're not certain it was suicide. Do you know of any enemies your husband had?"

Her face went crimson. "I told you he'd threatened suicide. Even told me how he would do it! He had a gun and said he was going to shoot himself. He was his own worst enemy."

Joe shot Hull a look. "Mrs. Clark, why didn't you call the police when he threatened suicide?"

She pressed her hand against her forehead. "I told you. I was in denial. I wanted to think it was just another threat. But now that it's done, I see that I should have called someone to stop him." She broke off and muffled her mouth.

Joe decided to switch gears.

"Ma'am, witnesses saw Chief Cade talking to you that morning, then getting into a car with you, and now Chief Cade is missing. Are you sure you don't know anything about that?"

She stiffened again and looked at him, her wet face raging red. "Of course not. I don't know who they saw your police chief with, but it was *not* me."

"We just thought that since Chief Cade was involved in the accident, you might have had reason to want to see him."

Anger tightened her face, and her hand trembled as she touched her throat again. "I've already told you, I've never been to Cape Refuge in my life."

"Ma'am, we have your number on Chief Cade's caller ID. We know someone from this house called him the morning he disappeared."

She seemed to struggle with her answer, then finally, she let out a rough sigh. "I'm sorry, my brain is just so muddled with all this ... I can't think ... I did try to call him. But I didn't speak to him. There was no answer."

Joe was silent for a moment. Her story wasn't adding up. "Why did you try to call him?"

"Because I had seen the news report the night before, and I spent all night just a wreck, not knowing what to do. I didn't sleep at all. I was pacing the floor and praying. And finally, early the next morning, I decided I needed to call him. I don't know what I was hoping, but it didn't matter because I let it ring twice and then I hung up."

"How did you get his number? It's unlisted."

The woman fidgeted again. "I have a friend who works for the phone company."

Joe got out a notepad and pen. "What's that friend's name?"

She seemed cornered. "I don't want to get her in trouble. What does it matter, anyway? I didn't reach him."

Detective Hull finally spoke. "Ma'am, we were wondering if you'd give us permission to walk through your house."

Her face twisted. "Walk through? For what?"

"As I told you," Joe said, "Chief Cade is missing and the witnesses thought they saw him with you."

"And you think he's here?"

For a moment he thought he saw fright cross over her face, and she looked toward the door leading into the dark hall. Something was up, he thought.

Hull clearly noticed it too. "Ma'am, if you don't give us permission, we'll have to get a warrant. In that event, it won't be a walk-through, but a full search of the premises."

She stared up at him, visibly shaken. Joe hoped she didn't know enough law to realize they didn't yet have probable cause for a warrant.

Hull's bluff worked. "Well, go ahead," she said. "I have nothing to hide...."

Hull headed out of the parlor and into the hall. Joe followed. "You take the upstairs," Hull said in a low voice. "I'll take this floor and the basement."

Joe nodded and went upstairs. He began checking the bedrooms, every bathroom, an extra study that he found near the back of the house. He looked in closets, drawers, trash cans, but the garbage bags all looked freshly changed.

He came downstairs and saw Ann standing in the hallway at the bottom of the stairs, looking up at him with worried eyes. "I told you you wouldn't find anything there."

He saw the open basement door. Hull trudged up the steps and stepped back into the hall.

"Nothing there," he said. "Just a lot of dust and mold."

"Of course there's nothing," she said. "What do you think? That I have some man hidden in my house somewhere?"

Joe went into the kitchen, noting how clean the place was. Nothing seemed out of place, and it smelled of Lysol. Wouldn't a woman in mourning at least leave a glass out? How many people would scrub with Lysol until the house reeked of it, when going through something like this?

Not many, unless things just weren't what they seemed.

When they had finally left the house, Hull said I-told-you-so, then headed back to his precinct. Joe went back out to his car and sat behind the wheel for a moment. He hated to go back empty-handed or to tell the rest of the force—or Blair and Jonathan, for that matter—that they had not found anything concerning Cade. Where could he be? The fact that he hadn't found evidence against Ann Clark certainly did not take her off the suspect list. She could have put a bullet through Cade's head and dragged him off to some remote grave in the middle of the woods, though he didn't think she looked strong enough to do such a thing. But one never knew.

A chill went up his spine at the thought that something like that could have happened to Cade. He didn't know what his next move would be, but somehow, he had to find his friend before it was too late.

*S*craping, rattling, darkness . . .

Cade slid out from under a black quicksand sleep and struggled to orient himself. He could not see a thing in the opaque darkness. His head felt as if it had been cracked through the skull. He reached up to touch it and felt a sticky, painful wound. What in the world had happened?

The scraping sounded again, and he tried to sit up. A crack opened in the darkness. Dim light shown through as the silhouette of a woman stepped into the doorway.

He frowned. "Who are you?"

She turned on the light and it flooded the room, blinding him. He squinted and turned his face away from it, then he forced himself to look back at her. The face was familiar, but he couldn't place her.

"Headache?" Her eyes were hard, piercing. "You're lucky you're alive."

"Who are you?" He tried to sit up again, but the pain in his head pulled him back down.

"Think. It'll come back to you."

He tried to think. There had been an accident . . . a man killed . . . a phone call at home . . .

He squinted his eyes at her. Was she the woman he'd met at Cricket's? She looked different, yet the same. Her hair had changed . . .

"Mrs. Clark?" he asked.

She didn't answer him, and he watched as she brought a two-liter bottle and set it down beside his cot.

He raised up as much as he could and looked down at himself. Blood had dried all over the front of his shirt. He touched his head again, found the gash that had bled. "Was I in an accident? I don't remember—"

"No accident," she said, moving back to the door. "It was quite deliberate."

Confused, he tried to focus. He was in a small room, with nothing but the cot he lay on and a commode. It wasn't a hospital—the walls were studs and tarpaper, like in a basement. And he couldn't imagine why he would be here with her.

She had wanted to talk alone and had suggested that they go for a ride in her car so he could show her where the accident happened. He had obliged, recognizing her grief.

That was the last thing he remembered.

"I want to know what he told you," she said.

He looked at her. "What who told me?"

"My husband, before he died. You said in your press conference that he spoke to you. What did he tell you?"

"Nothing . . . I don't know . . . I could barely hear him. He was bleeding to death."

Her teeth came together, and she spoke through them. "The gunshot. What did he say about the gunshot?"

Her curiosity implicated her, and he realized he was in danger. He tried to rise up again. "What did you do, knock me in the head with something?"

"I asked you a question!"

Her face was harder than he remembered, and her eyes were cold. She'd been wearing sunglasses at Cricket's.

"I didn't even know about the gunshot until after he was dead." He tried to get up again. What had happened to his head? "I need to use your phone," he said. "Please ... I need to call the station ..."

She laughed then, a brittle, frigid sound. "You're not calling anyone, and you're not going anywhere. You're staying right here where I put you."

Finally he managed to sit up. "Why? What purpose could that serve?"

"Many purposes."

With great effort, he got up and started toward her.

She took a pistol out of her pocket and leveled it on him. He froze and recognized it to be his own firearm.

"Get back on that bed before I blow your head off."

He knew she meant it. It was clear in her eyes. "Why? What do you want? Is it revenge?"

"Shut up and get back on the cot."

He backed to the bed and slowly lowered himself down. "What are you keeping me here for?"

She didn't answer. She just kept that gun on him as she backed out of the door. He saw that he was in a room inside a basement, and across the room outside his door stood wooden stairs, probably going into her house. She closed the door behind her. He heard it lock and then heard scraping noises as if she pushed furniture against the door. He wondered if anyone was looking for him. Surely people had seen him leaving Cricket's with her. Surely *someone* saw him getting into her car.

But how could she have gotten him here? She wasn't big enough to carry him. He wondered if she had drugged him at Cricket's. He did remember feeling very tired as he'd gotten into her car, but he hadn't slept that well the night before.

His throat felt blistered and parched, and he wondered how much time had passed. He looked down at the water bottle she had brought him, grabbed it, and drank down the water. It went down smooth, wetting the tissue in his throat, hydrating his mouth.

He looked at his watch, squinted to focus on the date. It was April 7. He'd been missing for three whole days?

He felt a lethargy washing over him, making him weak, sleepy, heavy again. He lay back and searched his brain for a plan of escape.

But he was so tired . . .

Then he heard voices. Distant, muffled voices coming from the vent over his head. Somewhere in another room of the house, their voices carried.

Sleep tried to pull him under into a swampy haze, but he fought to stay awake.

". . . told you I should have killed him . . . never wanted to bring him here . . ." It was Ann Clark's angry voice. "He didn't tell him. . . ."

". . . stupid phone call . . . why didn't you think?" a man's voice said. "We can use him. . . ."

". . . too dangerous . . . ," he heard Ann say. "What if they do search again . . . ?"

The sounds became more muddled, confused, and the words blurred and flattened in his head as he drifted deeper. . . .

Just before he went entirely under, he thought he heard a baby cry.

"Lord . . . please . . ." No clearer plea would form in his mind. He couldn't make his thoughts evolve into words, and soon his brain released those thoughts as blackness overtook him again.

CHAPTER

$\mathcal{B}$lair sat on the porch at Hanover House, watching Joe McCormick's car pull away. He had come to update them about the search, and his news—or lack thereof—had left her numb.

She'd had such hopes that the search of Ann Clark's house would lead them to Cade.

Morgan sat down in the rocking chair next to Blair, but didn't rock. Silently, they both stared out at the ocean lapping against the beach across the street.

"He'll be all right," Morgan said. "He has to."

Blair couldn't answer. He wasn't all right. It was a knowledge that came from the deepest part of her heart. Cade was in trouble, and no one was able to help him.

"I have to feed Oswald," she whispered.

Morgan looked over at her. "Cade's cat?"

"Yes," she said, "someone has to feed him."

Morgan touched her arm. "I don't want you over there alone. It could be dangerous. I don't want whatever happened to Cade to happen to you too."

"I'm not going in," she said. "I'll just feed him outside."

"Well, I'll come with you then."

Blair was glad Morgan had offered. As she waited for her to go tell Jonathan, Blair walked to her car and leaned against it, looking out at the beach. How many mornings had she seen Cade out there in his kayak, rowing as the sun shone down on him?

She wondered if, perhaps, he had done that the morning of his disappearance. Maybe he'd gone kayaking again, and had an accident in the water. Maybe he'd drowned ...

Panic rose inside her, and she tried to think whether she'd seen his kayak in his utility room either time she'd gone in for the key. She couldn't remember.

"I'm ready." Morgan hurried down the steps and got into the car.

As they drove across the island to Cade's house, Blair was pensive. The thoughts of all the things that could have happened to Cade stirred new grief in her soul. She hadn't entirely gotten through the grief over her parents; she couldn't imagine dealing with Cade's death too.

He couldn't be dead. He just couldn't.

A tear rolled down her scarred cheek, and she wiped it away.

Morgan noticed. "Jonathan's getting a prayer chain activated," she said quietly. "They'll all be praying for him."

Blair nodded. "Good."

Morgan smiled. "I expected you to come back with something cryptic about sending empty wishes up to the sky."

Blair swallowed. "I have to at least consider the possibility that I could be wrong about prayer. If there's any chance at all that it works, then I want it done for Cade."

Another tear. She smeared it away.

They pulled into Cade's driveway. His truck still wasn't home. It sat where he'd left it.

She got the bag of Cat Chow she'd bought and the jug of water and went around to the backyard. Before looking for the cat, she stepped into the utility room. The kayak hung in its place on the opposite wall.

She wilted with relief. "The kayak's there. I had started to think that maybe he took it out and drowned."

"I hadn't thought of that," Morgan whispered.

The cat meowed and came toward her. Blair bent over and picked him up. "Hey, there, Lee Harvey. How're you doing?"

"Lee Harvey?" Morgan asked with a smile. "I think he named him after Oswald Chambers."

"Whatever." Her relief quickly turned to sorrow, and she realized that this abandoned cat was a symbol of Cade's vanishing. He might not be dead in the ocean, but he could be dead *somewhere*. She felt her mouth trembling, and those tears spilled over again. Slowly, she went to one of the patio chairs and sat down.

Morgan sat down beside her. "Honey, are you all right?"

"No, not really." Blair buried her face in the cat's fur. She could feel Morgan's soft gaze.

"Your interest in Cade is deeper than friendship, isn't it?" she asked softly.

Blair looked up at her. "Why would you ask that?"

"Just a sense I have. I've always thought he was interested in you."

Blair caught her breath. "Interested in me? How do you figure that?"

Morgan took the bag of cat food and tore the top open. "The way he looks at you. You know it and I know it, Blair. You two have gotten close over the last few months, whether you want to admit it or not."

"We've become good *friends,* Morgan. That's all. I'd feel this way if any of my friends suddenly disappeared, so you don't have to make more of it than there is, okay?"

Morgan shrugged. "Okay."

Blair put the cat down, filled his bowls, then sat back down and watched as he ate. "I don't get God."

Morgan just looked at her. "I didn't think you believed in God."

Blair shook her head. "Sometimes I do, sometimes I don't. But if there is one, I don't get why he would let this happen."

"We don't know what happened, Blair. Maybe nothing. Maybe it's all just a misunderstanding. Maybe Cade will come riding back into town with some perfectly good explanation."

Blair shook her head. "You and I both know that's not going to happen."

"Well, don't blame God before you even know what to blame him for. God's the only one who knows for sure where Cade is."

"God and that Clark woman," Blair said.

"You still think she was involved?"

"Joe said she admitted that she called him." Blair closed the cat food and put it into the storage room. "All she had to do was slap on a wig and sunglasses, and show up here intent on doing Cade in."

"But why would she want revenge if it's clear her husband tried to kill himself first? She couldn't blame Cade."

"Maybe she's really the one who shot him. Maybe she thought Cade knew. Or even if it was a suicide, maybe she just needed to blame somebody." Blair knew that was why she'd entertained the possibility of God existing. It was handy, when she needed someone to take the blame for Cade's disappearance.

Pulling herself together, she got up and wiped her tears on her sleeve. "Well, let's go," she said. "I have some computer work to do at the library. I'm going to find out everything I can about Ann Clark today."

CHAPTER

*S*lowly, gradually, Cade emerged from the mire of his unconsciousness and realized that he still lay in the dark basement room. The two-liter bottle he had drunk from earlier lay empty on the concrete floor.

He didn't remember finishing it off. He remembered drinking it while he'd racked his brain for a plan to escape, and then he'd grown so sleepy that he'd hardly been able to think. Had the woman drugged his water?

He squinted up in the direction of that small vent above his head. He'd heard voices coming from it. A man's and a woman's. . . .

He forced himself to sit up and looked around in the darkness. He got up and stumbled drunkenly to the door. He felt a light switch next to it and turned it on.

The bulb at the center of the ceiling cast the place in a yellow glow, revealing exposed studs and tar paper, like a room that had never quite been finished.

He tested the doorknob and found that it was locked. It was a metal door, not something he'd be able to kick through. He banged on it with his fist. He had to get out of here.

But the door would not budge.

Giving up, he leaned back against the wall and tried to think. The room had no windows through which to escape. The vent in the ceiling over his cot was no more than six by eight inches.

He turned to the wall and wondered if he could kick or beat his way through the Sheetrock. He peeled back the tarpaper but saw only cement beneath it.

There was no way to break through.

Weary, he went back to his cot and sank down. It was hot, sweltering, and he was thirsty again. His stomach burned with hunger.

He wondered where his cell phone was. He'd been wearing it the morning he'd met with this woman, even though he couldn't get a signal on the island. He had planned to drive in to Savannah that day to confer with the Savannah police about possible missing person reports.

She must have taken it, along with his gun.

He spotted the tank on the toilet lid and stumbled toward it, lifted it, and slipped it between the cot and the wall. Maybe if she came back, he could use it to knock her off guard, and somehow get the gun out of her hands.

He heard the scraping sound again and knew his banging had alerted her that he was awake.

He waited, every muscle in his body poised in readiness.

Her face was hard as she stepped into the room. She held the gun in one hand and a box of Kentucky Fried Chicken in the other. In her apron pocket, she carried another bottle of water.

"Just so you know," she said, "if you try to escape, I'll kill you."

His fingers closed over the tank lid. "What do you want from me?"

She didn't answer, just thrust the box at him and set the bottled water down on the floor beside the door.

"Go ahead and eat while I'm feeling generous. I don't want you dead just yet."

He needed her to come farther into the room. Just a little closer. . . . "Look, if you think you're going to get ransom for me or something, you're sadly mistaken. I don't even know anybody with money. Not anybody who'd put a dime out for me. Most of my family members are broke."

"It's not ransom we want."

We? Of course. He'd heard another voice through the vent.

"Then what do you want?" he asked. "Revenge?"

He had heard vengeance in her voice that morning she'd called. The idea of meeting with her had worried him, which was why he'd picked a public place.

He had gone to Numbers 35 to read of the cities of refuge, then had prayed that God would be his emotional refuge from a bitter, grieving widow who blamed him for her husband's death. He'd prayed for words to comfort her in her suffering.

But she must have drugged him and brought him here.

"You're our scapegoat," she said. "A distraction."

"Scapegoat? For what?"

She didn't answer, only smiled coldly at him. His hand slid over the toilet lid. He had to make her come closer. Softening his voice, he said, "Look, you seem like a decent person who was motivated by grief and shock when you abducted me. It may have seemed like a good idea at the time. Revenge and all that. Maybe you even planned to kill me. But surely now reality has set in, and you must see that this is crazy."

From some distant part of the house, he thought he heard a baby crying again. She and William must have been new parents. Now the husband and father was dead. No wonder she had snapped.

She stared at him then, her eyes dull and unmoving, as she seemed to process his words. Blocking the tank lid with his body, he started to slide it out of its hiding place.

"I think I have a fever," he said. "I've been having chills, and my head is splitting."

"Your head hurts because you fell down the basement stairs."

"Fell?" he asked. "How?"

"We dropped you."

She said it so coldly that he wondered for a moment if she was a psychopath.

"We?"

"You're making me tired, Chief Cade. I didn't come here for an interrogation. You're the prisoner, remember?"

She wasn't going to come closer. He was going to have to go to her. Pulling the lid behind his back, he scooted to the end of the cot and opened the box of chicken. She still held his gun on him, but he knew that one carefully aimed swing with the tank lid would be enough to knock it out of her hand.

He feigned interest in the chicken, judging her distance from the corner of his eye. If he didn't still feel drugged, he'd be more certain of his chances. But he had no choice but to act now.

She pulled a writing pad and pen from the pocket that had held the bottle and tossed it to his cot. "Here, take that. I want you to write a letter."

"A letter?" he repeated.

"Yes. Address it to Joe, your second-in-command at the Cape Refuge Police Department."

He glared up at her. "What do you want it to say?"

"Copy what I've written on the second page of the pad."

That gun was still on him, but he realized that if he did as she wanted, when he handed it to her, he might have the chance to get the gun.

And just in case his attempt to escape failed, maybe he could plant clues in the letter.

"Write it word for word. No tricks, Chief. I'm warning you. Don't change a thing. Make it look natural."

He read the letter.

Joe,

   Just wanted to touch base with you guys and let you know that I haven't dropped off the face of the earth. I was just a little depressed after the accident, so I decided

*to take some time off. The truth is, I'd been seeing a girl
from Savannah, and we decided to get married.*

*I know it sounds crazy, and I'm going to have a lot
of explaining to do when I get back, but I've never been
happier. Let everyone know that for me, will you?*

*I'll call as soon as I know when I'm coming back.
Meanwhile, I know Cape Refuge is in your good hands.*

He closed his eyes. "They're never gonna believe I got married."

"I've done my homework, Chief. You're an eligible bachelor in your town. Very quiet about your private life. There's a lot of speculation about you. They'll believe it."

Cade wasn't going to argue. If they didn't believe it, maybe they'd realize the letter was fake. The more unbelievable it was, the better.

He started to print.

"No, that won't do," she said. "That's not how you write."

He looked up at her. "How do you know how I write?"

"I've seen your handwriting," she said.

"On what?"

"I told you, I've done my homework." She raised the gun. "Do it right, Chief. Do it right or lose that hand."

He knew she meant it, this desperate, crazy woman. He tore off the paper, and started on the next sheet. *Think. Think!*

He changed his *d*s, looped them bigger than he normally did.

"Try again." She was getting angry now, holding that gun aimed at his forehead. "I'm warning you! I know how you write. This is your last chance, Chief. You're just as good to me dead as alive."

He wiped the sweat dripping into his eyes and tore off the top sheet, and began to write again. He wrote it just as she'd typed it, in his regular handwriting, conscious of that gun pointed at his forehead. It wouldn't be mailed anyway, he thought. He was going to get out of here any minute now.

But just in case, he signed it "Matt Cade." Joe would realize it was a fake as soon as he saw the signature. Cade had never gone by Matt in his life.

He handed the pad back to her, hoping she'd move one step closer. She still hadn't seen the tank lid at his back.

She read over the letter. "Good. That one should do."

He turned the lid sideways, brought it to his side, watched her stick the letter into her pocket. Slowly, he stood up . . .

. . . and swung.

The lid knocked the gun from her hands and sent her reeling back. She screamed as he grabbed her arms and flung her around, picked up the gun, and jabbed it into her ribs.

"Let go of me!" she screamed. "I'm not alone in this house! Let go of me!"

He threw his hand over her mouth and pulled her small body back against him. Keeping the gun in her ribs, he walked her through the door, out into the larger part of the basement. He looked around, saw the empty bookshelves that had been in front of the door. That was the scraping he had heard. Each time she left, she slid them back, so that if anyone came down here they wouldn't know a door was behind them.

He shoved her toward the stairs and forced her up. He still felt dizzy, weak, drugged, but he could do this, he thought. As long as he had the gun. . . .

They were halfway up the stairs . . . when the door at the top creaked open.

Ann flung herself out of his grasp, and Cade raised his gun.

A gunshot blasted him back. Pain cracked through his leg, hurling him back down the stairs, smashing him on the concrete floor. Another shot . . . his body jolted . . .

Voices . . . a man's yelling . . . Ann Clark hysterical . . .

Agony in his leg . . . his side . . .

He felt his arms being lifted over his head, his body being dragged . . . a door closing . . . that scraping sound.

He thought of the wall being bricked up with Edgar Allen Poe evil, someone discovering him forty years from now, nothing but a skeleton in a dark hole.

Blood loss drew him into its mire, and finally, he succumbed to the dark.

CHAPTER

*T*he air conditioner hummed from the large vent overhead, and Sadie shivered and tried to get comfortable in her desk. Her English teacher waxed poetic about the lessons one could learn from Shakespeare, but Sadie's gaze drifted across the room to a cluster of girls, busily engaged in note writing—not on the merits of Shakespeare, but probably on something much more important, like what Sadie had worn to school today.

Never the recipient of those notes, she'd been the subject of a few. She knew that because, after registering their whispers and stolen looks across the room, Sadie had occasionally waited for the class to empty and dug them out of the trash.

The first one that had her name had knocked the wind from her like a shovel swung across her stomach. *Whack!*

It had criticized the shoes she wore, the way she wore her hair, whether it was really blonde or bleached that way. Another gossiped that she was seventeen, two years older than the other tenth graders.

The final blow had come when she'd found one in which they had called her the "tramp daughter of a jailbird."

Whack! Whack!

She had read others, where they'd called her stupid and suggested that she needed to be put back into seventh grade instead of tenth, because she had the education and the brains of a manatee.

She knew they were right. She didn't have a strong background in school. For most of her life, she had yawned through classes and had trouble focusing, since she'd gotten so little sleep at night. Most nights she spent avoiding the men her mother brought home and all the other "friends" who came and went through all hours of the night, vile foulmouthed people with selfish motives, coming to buy drugs and sell them and sometimes even to make them.

School had been a sanctuary to her, but she couldn't say that she'd been able to learn all that much. She had street smarts, her mother had always told her, and that was what really counted. Street smarts had saved her life on many occasions, but she yearned for the other kind of smarts—the kind that made you fit in and seem normal and get ahead in this world.

The bell rang, and Sadie looked up at the teacher. The tall, skinny woman barked out their assignment as the students began filing out the door like evacuees during a bomb threat. Sadie closed her books, loaded them back into her backpack, and followed the students out.

She went to her locker and got the books she would need for the last class of the day. Next to her, the three girls who'd been writing notes babbled about a party that Friday night.

"On South Beach," Crystal Lewis was saying. "My parents are letting me hire a DJ. Everybody'll be there."

Sadie knew that "everybody" didn't include her. The girl giving the party was the one who'd called her a tramp.

Not for the first time, Sadie wished Morgan had allowed her to home-school or work fulltime instead of enrolling here. She could have gotten a job in one of the souvenir shops on the island

and done just fine with the tourists and beach bums. Last summer, when she'd first come to Cape Refuge, she had worked at the *Cape Refuge Journal* and had been proud of the job she'd done. But the paper had closed, and Morgan had insisted on school.

Even the principal knew the story of how she'd shown up here and slept on the beach until Cade had forbidden her, and how she'd then slept in the boathouse that belonged to Hanover House, until Morgan had discovered her and brought her home. And the principal knew—like everyone else—that her mother still served time on drug charges.

She closed her locker and headed up the hall to her class, walking against the flow of rushing students, as if she alone had a class in the other direction. She always felt alone at school, even in a crowd. She sometimes went entire days without anyone in class acknowledging her.

Sighing, she slapped her fine hair back over her shoulder and heard a voice behind her.

"What class do you have next?"

She glanced back and saw Trevor Beal, the star linebacker for the Cape Refuge football team, whom many of those intercepted notes had been about.

"Biology," she said with a nervous, surprised smile. "I hate biology."

"Could be worse." He fell into step beside her. "Could be calculus. That's where I'm going."

She thought of the remedial math class they had put her in and knew that she would never make it through calculus. Not in a million years.

"Hey, listen, I'm going to a party Friday night on the beach. Crystal is giving it. You want to come?"

Sadie stopped in the hall and looked up at him. It was no wonder Crystal Lewis followed him around like a starving puppy. With his black, wavy hair, those movie-star blue eyes, and that athletic build, every girl in the school had tried to get his attention.

She didn't really want to be one of them. "I can't go to that party. I wasn't invited."

He grinned. "If you go as my date, you're invited, okay? Come on, it'll be fun."

She just stared at him. Was he making fun of her? Asking her on a dare? She glanced around, expecting to see a vicious crowd of giggling girls waiting nearby.

But no one watched.

The hall was emptying. The bell would ring any second.

"I don't think so, Trevor."

He looked shattered. "Why not?"

"Because . . ." She didn't want to confess her distrust of anyone here who was nice to her. If she was wrong, she'd seem pitiful, a fate worse than being mocked.

"Come on, Sadie. I really want to get to know you."

She narrowed her eyes. "Why?"

"Why?" he repeated. "Have you looked in the mirror lately?"

Her defenses shattered, and she smiled. He meant it. He wasn't mocking.

She thought of Crystal, her nemesis who had coined the worst phrases about her. It was no secret that she'd had a crush on him all year. If she went out with him, Crystal would declare all-out war.

Sadie pushed her hair behind her ears, then flipped it back out and raked it back with her fingers. She started to say yes, that she would go as his date.

But then reality struck. She couldn't go to that girl's party and risk having her call her the "tramp daughter of a jailbird" out loud in front of everyone. She didn't want people whispering about her, snubbing her, staring at her. What could she be thinking?

"I'd like to, Trevor. I really would, but I don't think I belong at Crystal's party. Maybe some other time." She started to walk away.

Trevor stepped in front of her. "Okay, then we can do something else," he said. "I don't have to go to that party. We could go to Savannah and see a movie, maybe get a bite to eat."

Her eyebrows shot up and her eyes widened. It was too good to be true. "You'd miss the party?"

"Sure. There are millions of parties every weekend. Nothing special about this one." He pushed her hair back, sending a jolt through her. "Besides, it was just an excuse to get you to go out with me. I don't care anything about Crystal's party."

Her heart felt like a dove flapping at her rib cage, ready to soar. "I'd love to go," she said. "It sounds fun."

"Okay, I'll pick you up at six Friday night. Sound okay?"

She bit her bottom lip. "Yeah, sounds great. You know where I live?"

He grinned. "Everybody knows Hanover House."

She watched him lope off to his classroom. Quickly, she headed to her own, ducked inside, and sat at the back. Crystal and her cohorts clustered at the front, their sandaled, red-toenailed feet stretched out in front of them, their moussed hair perfect as it blew under the vent of the air conditioner.

Somehow she didn't feel quite so alone anymore. There was someone in this school who saw value in her. Someone substantial. Someone important.

Maybe things were about to change.

Sadie found Morgan sitting at the desk in the little office off the kitchen. A Bible lay open in front of her, and next to it a stack of checks that had come from the donors who supported the house. On the floor behind her, little Caleb slept soundly on his favorite blankie, his little mouth open. She knelt down beside him and gave him a gentle kiss.

"What you doing?" she asked Morgan in a low voice.

"Just posting these donor checks."

"Any news about Chief Cade?"

Morgan shook her head. "None. They're still looking for him." She put her pen down and reached for Sadie's hand. "How was your day, sweetie?"

Sadie grinned and bit her lip. "Good. Really, really good."

Morgan seemed to notice the excitement on Sadie's face and pulled her into the kitchen so they wouldn't wake Caleb. "Okay, spill it. Something happened." She sat her down at the table and reached for a soda in the refrigerator.

"Something really unbelievable," Sadie said on the edge of a squeal.

Morgan set a plate of cookies down and joined Sadie at the table. "Come on, start talking."

Sadie giggled. Her life at Hanover House seemed like a fantasy, something she had dreamed of at night when she had lain in her bed and heard the sounds of Ozzy Osbourne music coming from her mother's living room, people cackling and doors slamming, and strangers intruding on her private space. She had dreamed of a home where she could go off to school rested and secure, then come home and have a snack waiting for her, someone to ask her how things had been and get excited when she had news. And now she had all that. She had no right to complain about a few smart-aleck girls at school treating her like trash.

"A guy asked me out for Friday night!"

Morgan's eyes reflected her delight. "Sadie, that's great!"

Sadie did a little dance in her seat. "He originally asked me to some party that Crystal Lewis was giving, but I told him no way I was going to one of her parties, not that she'd let me come, anyway."

Morgan touched her hand. "Honey, she'd love you if she got to know you."

"Well, she's not too interested in that. Anyway, I said no, so he's like, 'We don't have to go to the party. We can go to a movie. It was just an excuse to take you out.'" She stopped and covered her mouth and let out another muffled squeal.

Morgan laughed with her. "So who's the boy? Do I know him?"

"A senior named Trevor Beal. The star linebacker on the football team."

Morgan's face changed, and Sadie thought that if smiles could really crash, there'd be lip fallout all over the floor. "Oh. Him."

Sadie didn't like the sound of that. She set her cookie down. "What's the matter?"

Morgan got up and went to the counter. She got a wet sponge and began to wipe it. It was her way. Whenever something disturbed her, she wiped something. "Nothing. It's just that . . . I know his family. They're not very . . . reputable people."

Sadie sat back in her chair. "Well, I'm not very reputable, either, if you ask anybody at my school. What's the matter with them?"

Morgan stopped wiping and turned back to her. "Sadie, Trevor's family has been involved in criminal activities for years. A few years ago his father and uncles were indicted for drug trafficking. During the trial, their major witness wound up dead. No one could ever prove they'd had anything to do with it, but without that witness they couldn't get a conviction, so they got off scot-free. But not before a bunch of evidence came out about their family being one of the biggest suppliers of cocaine in the southeast."

"But Trevor's not a druggie. He's a nice person."

"No, none of them are druggies. They don't *take* drugs—they just sell them. And that's not just a rumor, Sadie—I've heard it from a number of the people we work with at the jail. The drug dealers get their supplies from this family. They're also big loan sharks around this area. And I can't prove it, but I think Trevor is one of the ones who goes around beating people up for not paying on time."

Sadie gaped at her. "No, he wouldn't do that. I mean, he's big and everything, but he wouldn't just beat people up over money."

Morgan sat back down and took her hands. "Sadie, a guy at our church was having financial problems and borrowed from them. He wound up in the hospital with two broken legs. He told the police that Trevor and some other guys did it, but they got off because they had some tight alibis."

"Then he couldn't have done it."

"But it was his own family that backed up his alibi, Sadie. They've been known to lie to protect their own before. They're scary people."

Sadie wanted to cry. Maybe Trevor *was* too good to be true. "Morgan, I'm telling you, he wouldn't do that. You're just listening to gossip. And I thought we were supposed to love everyone. Not just the ones whose parents are perfect."

"Sadie, I have prayed for that family. When Trevor's grandmother died, I took food over there. I've invited them to our church. I would love it if any one of them wanted to come. But dating one of them is another thing altogether."

"But he's the only one who's asked me out! And besides, Jesus hung out with the publicans and the prostitutes. Maybe Trevor's family are just the kind of people Jesus would have spent time with."

Morgan breathed a bitter laugh. "Honey, you don't know how many times I heard my sister say that to my parents, when she wanted to hang around with people who were getting her into trouble. The fact is, Jesus did come to seek and save the lost. But he didn't *leave* them lost. He told them to go and sin no more, and lots of them listened and did just that."

"Well, maybe I could do that for Trevor. Maybe I could lead him to Christ."

Morgan tipped her head and touched Sadie's chin. "Honey, that hardly ever happens in a dating relationship. What happens instead is that the unbeliever changes the believer."

"You don't have much faith in me." Blinking back tears, Sadie wadded her napkin and took it to the waste basket. "He's a good person, Morgan."

"Sadie, as long as I'm your guardian, it's my job to protect you." Morgan sighed. "I know you're excited about this boy asking you out, but I don't feel comfortable letting you go. Please understand. You're a great person, and there will be other guys."

Sadie felt as if the world had been pulled out from under her, just when she was getting her footing. "I was so excited ... I've tried to make friends, but it hasn't happened. And then he came along." She started to cry and hated herself for it. "I've been there for months already, Morgan. Almost a whole school year. I'm older than everyone in my class. I'm a freak. Nobody's noticed what a great person I am. Nobody *cares* what a great person I am.

Nobody even *thinks* I'm a great person. They think I'm the tramp daughter of a jailbird."

Morgan looked as if she'd been slapped. "Did someone say that to you?"

"Yes! It's like some kind of nickname. I hate it there. I didn't want to go in the first place. But now something's happened that makes it bearable, and you're telling me you won't allow it?"

"Honey, like I said, you can be his friend. But you cannot go out with him."

"But you've told me that we're supposed to influence the world around us. Salt and light and all that. How can we be that if we avoid people who need it?"

Morgan was undaunted. "Sadie, we've been over this. You can be salt and light to someone without *dating* them!"

It was the closest she and Morgan had ever come to fighting, and Sadie hated it. But she wasn't ready to back down yet.

She heard Caleb chattering in the office off the kitchen, then he appeared, sleepy-eyed and with the imprint of his blankie on one cheek. "Say-Say," he said and reached up for her. She picked him up and kissed his warm cheek. He saw her tears and touched her wet cheek.

"Here, let me have him." Morgan took the chubby baby. Sadie watched, crying silently, as Morgan poured some apple juice into his sippy cup and took him to his high chair.

When he was settled, Morgan reached for her hand and pulled her back to her chair.

Sadie sat down and looked dully at her.

"Sadie, I'm not trying to ruin your fun. I know how much this means to you."

"Morgan, please don't make me tell him no. I'll look like such a dork. It'll be one more rumor that'll go around about me."

Morgan inclined her head as if Sadie had made her point. "If he's the kind of guy who would start a rumor about you, then why do you say he's so decent? Sadie, you've got to quit worrying what people think of you. You've gotten this far in life without it."

"I've *always* cared what they think," she said. "I just didn't have any control over it before. When I was living in Atlanta with my mom and her boyfriends, I pretty much just rolled with the punches. People thought I was trash at school. And I knew I couldn't ever be anything better, so it didn't really matter." She watched as Caleb bit into a cookie. "But now I'm different, Morgan. I'm with you, and things are better . . . and I feel like I could really be somebody if I just had a chance."

Morgan gazed into her eyes. "You are somebody, Sadie. You're somebody very special. That's why I feel so protective. That's why I don't want you dating Trevor Beal. There'll be other guys, Christian ones."

"And where will I meet them?" she asked. "Our church doesn't exactly have a youth group, since Caleb and I are practically the only ones under twenty-five."

"Well, then we need to work on getting you some fellowship with other Christians your age. Maybe you could join a Christian club at school or start going to Bible study at one of the local churches that does have a youth group."

Sadie sighed. She wasn't getting through to her. Even the Christian kids at school shunned her. She had little hope of friendship with any of them. She pictured the Christian guys having conversations just like this with their parents, only about her. *I don't want you dating that girl. Haven't you heard about her mother?*

The doorbell rang, and welcoming the chance to end this dead-end conversation, she got up. "I'll get it."

As she went to the front door, she heard Morgan talking baby-talk to Caleb, and his laughter filling the room. She opened the door.

A black woman who looked at least ten months pregnant stood there with a suitcase in her hand. "Hi," the woman said. "I'm looking for the Clearys—Morgan or Jonathan. Is this the right place?"

"Sure," Sadie said in a flat voice. "Come in. I'll get Morgan."

The woman waddled in and set her suitcase down. Sadie went back to the kitchen. "Somebody here for you. I'll clean Caleb up."

Still sulking, she got a napkin and wet it and began to wipe the baby's face as Morgan rushed to meet her visitor.

Morgan noticed the suitcase first. "Hello, I'm Morgan," she said.

The woman stuck out her hand. "I'm Karen Miller. I knew your mama and daddy. I was in the jail when they used to come. I got out just a few weeks before they died. When I heard what happened to them, I cried my eyes out."

Morgan gave her a weak smile. "Thank you." She glanced at the suitcase again.

"You're as pretty as your mama said, Morgan. Your mama talked all the time about you and your sister."

Morgan didn't want to talk about her mother. "What brings you here, Karen?"

"Your mama and daddy wanted me to come live here after I got out of jail." She looked around at the room she stood in. "It's just like they described—antique tables, Victorian sofa, plants and baubles every which way you look. I should have come then, but I didn't. I went back to the old neighborhood and my boyfriend. I thought I could make it on my own, but it was hard, going back to all the same temptations. Crack dealers on every corner . . ." Her voice faded off. It was the kind of thing Morgan warned the prisoners about in her own jail ministry. Without a sound strategy, it was difficult for any of them to make it.

"I just kept remembering how your mama tried to convince me to come here. And then I found out the house was still running. I know I haven't filled out the application, and you don't know me from Adam, but I thought you might take me in, anyway. For the sake of my baby."

Morgan regarded the girl's swollen belly. She looked ready to give birth right now. She took the woman's hand. "Come sit down, Karen." She led her to the couch in the parlor. As the young woman got settled, Morgan checked her watch. Jonathan would be home soon. Maybe he could help her with this. They had agreed not to take in anyone who hadn't been through a stringent application process—those who proved they wanted to change their lives, who could commit to hours a day of Bible study, who were willing to get jobs and work and help with the chores. They wanted to do extensive interviews with them to make sure they were sincere in their desire to change, to screen out those who were violent or dishonest, or those who might pose a danger to Caleb or Sadie or anyone else in the house.

But when they showed up at the door like this, with no place else to go, clearly in a bind . . .

"Karen, when is your baby due?"

"Any day now. And I couldn't let it be born at home." Tears sprang to Karen's eyes. "My baby's daddy is a dealer, and he gets mean. . . . It's no place for a baby . . . and it's no place for me. Your mama told us in jail, she said we had to have a plan for when we got out. That we couldn't make it on our own. I came up with my plan too late, but I don't know where else to go. I want to change, Morgan. I want to live a life like you have, one that's clean and good and Christian. God put it in my mind to come here. I know he did. I don't have money or a job or any plan past ringing your bell, but I didn't think you'd turn me away. I have Medicaid, so you don't have to worry about hospital bills, and I'll get a job as soon as I can after the baby comes."

Morgan's heart burst with compassion. Her mother wouldn't have turned her away, she knew, and neither would her father. Jonathan was a little more pragmatic, but even he would have been persuaded by the urgency of Karen's situation.

"I'm a Christian, Morgan. I found Christ in jail. I backslid real bad when I got out." She patted her stomach. "I shouldn't have, but I can't undo it now."

Morgan sighed. "I have to talk to my husband, Karen. If you can't stay here, we'll find another place for you."

There were homes for unwed mothers with no place to go, ministries that took in people like Karen. They would be better for her in the long run, with their parenting classes and their counseling, their day care, and their help finding jobs.

"I promise I won't send you back out into the streets," Morgan said.

The woman looked around. "I don't think there could be a better place than right here. It looks like a dream."

Morgan got up and grabbed the suitcase. "Come with me, and I'll show you a room where you can relax until Jonathan gets home."

The woman beamed through her tears as Morgan led her up the stairs.

Voices yelled above and around him, and Cade squinted his eyes open. Paramedics ran his gurney down a hospital corridor, and Blair hurried beside him, sweating and panting with her blonde hair flapping into her face.

"Hang in there, Cade! We're going to help you."

He felt a jolt as they pushed him through double doors.

Then all at once he saw blue sky and an egret flying and felt the cool breeze in his hair, and he opened his eyes and was flying across the heavens, soaring and sailing through the blue, following his egret until it took a nose-dive and started down ... down ...

He woke with a shock.

There was no egret and no blue sky, no gurney and no hospital, no paramedics and no Blair.

Just Cade lying on the cold concrete floor, sticky in his own blood.

He'd been shot through the left calf, shattering bone and slicing out muscle, and the pain strangled him, nooselike, closing his throat and tearing a moan from deep within him. He forced himself to sit up, and winced at the pain spearing through his right ribs. He'd been shot there too.

Sweating with the pain, he tore his shirt open and stared down at the wound. The bullet had missed his rib, though it had blasted the flesh in its deadly path. It had not missed the bone in his leg, however. The bullet had gone right through him, shattering a hole in his tibia before exiting out the back.

He'd been going up the stairs . . . a gun in Ann Clark's ribs. So who had been at the top of the stairs? Who had shot him? And why hadn't they killed him?

He reached down to his bloody leg and ripped the fabric of his pants, so he could better see his wound. Carefully, he peeled it away from his blood-caked skin.

The sight of it made him dizzy, so he stopped a moment and looked up toward the vent that hummed and blew cold air into the room. He needed to get up. He needed to stop the slow bleed, and figure out a plan of escape.

He tried to rise up, but there was no way he could put weight on his leg.

With his good arm and leg, he managed to pull himself up. His head throbbed, and as he rose up to the mattress a wave of dizziness washed over him again. He grabbed the blanket and ripped off a strip, then used it as a bandage on his leg.

He didn't know what to do for his side.

Lying back, he tried to catch his breath. The only relief was the cool air blowing through that vent on the ceiling just above him.

But he couldn't lie here, wallowing in his weakness. He had to get away.

He knew the life was running out of him, and he didn't have much time left.

20

*S*adie hadn't had the nerve yet to tell Trevor Beal that she couldn't go out with him. She'd tried talking Morgan into it, and when Jonathan came home, she had enlisted his help. But he was too preoccupied with Karen's appearance and Cade's *dis*appearance. Irritably, he'd told her no. She was not to go out with "that boy."

She had to tell him soon, but she hadn't seen him yet today, and she dreaded what he would think of her. How dare she judge him for his parents' reputation? *Do not judge, or you too will be judged.* She pushed through the crowd to her locker, rolled in her combination.

A locker two down from her slammed, making her jump, and she turned to see Crystal glaring at her.

"Is it true that you're going out with Trevor Beal?" the girl snapped at her.

Sadie looked from Crystal to the two friends who waited behind her, spearing her with hateful looks. She wasn't going to discuss this with them. Slamming her own locker, she turned and started away.

"I'm talking to you!" Crystal shouted. "I asked you a question."

Heads were turning, so she stopped and looked back. "Who I go out with is none of your business." She kept her voice low to keep from calling more attention to herself.

"The only reason he's interested in you is that he thinks you're easy. A tramp like you, living at Hanover House, of all places. He knows he can get you to do whatever he wants."

Sadie hadn't expected for Crystal to have a more hurtful comment than "tramp daughter of a jailbird" in her arsenal. *Don't react. Just turn and walk away.* Blinking back the tears threatening her, she turned and started up the hall.

"That's the only reason he'd go out with you," Crystal shouted. Others turned their heads, looking to see who she was referring to. Sadie lifted her chin in the air and held her lips tight.

She hurried into her biology class, tears in her eyes, but she would not cry in front of anyone who would tell that girl and her friends. She bit her lip and pulled out her biology book, opened it to the page they had studied for homework, got out her pen, and held it poised.

Crystal and her friends filed in like Nazis in a prison camp. The teacher sat at the front of the room, a sentinel who kept them quiet. But she couldn't stop the looks the girls shot her—hate-filled, venomous looks.

She kept her head down and her eyes on her book, and when the class finally ended, she dashed out of the room. Trevor Beal was waiting for her.

"So how's it going?" he asked, those blue eyes twinkling, oblivious.

She looked up at him. He *couldn't* be part of a criminal family. He looked so normal.

She shrugged and looked back over her shoulder. Crystal and Company were down the hall, watching with those piercing eyes, their faces twisted with contempt. "I'm okay, I guess."

"So have you thought about what movie you want to see Friday night?"

She drew in a deep breath and decided to get this over with. "Morgan and Jonathan told me I couldn't go."

His face changed, and his cheeks suddenly mottled red. "What do you mean they told you you couldn't? Why?"

"They just didn't approve. It's a long story." She hurried to her locker, knowing the girls were following behind. Pulling her backpack off, she started digging through it.

Trevor took it out of her hand. "Sadie, you're not going to do what they say, are you?"

"I'm sorry. I wanted to go, but I just can't."

He flung the backpack against the locker, startling her.

"It's because of my family, isn't it?" he said.

She looked away.

"Come on, Sadie. Those people you live with are so holier-than-thou that there's probably not a guy in this school they'd let you go out with. They think they're better than everybody. They're the moral police, that's what they are. And you're their prisoner."

"No, I'm not!" She picked her backpack up. "They care about me."

"Then they should let you go. Come on, I'm a nice guy. You shouldn't judge me on the basis of my family any more than I judge you on the basis of yours."

It was as if he had read her mind.

"Come on," he said, leaning toward her. "I want to take you out. I'm not going to drag you to some family dinner or any other place that you don't want to go. I just want to spend time with you. I want to get to know you. Is that wrong?"

She thought of what Crystal had said about his reasons for asking her out. "Are you sure that's all?" she asked. "Because there's talk that you had ulterior motives. So if you think that I'm easy or that—"

"Who told you *that?*" His words slashed across hers.

"It doesn't matter," she said. "It's just a rumor going around, that the only reason you asked me out is that you think I'm easy."

His hand hit the locker again. "Whoever said that is a stinking liar." He leaned down until his face was inches from hers, his blue eyes searching her face. "I don't want anything from you. Come on, Sadie. Give me a chance. I didn't think you'd let somebody's background or their family ruin your opinion of them. I thought you were different."

Sadie thought of Morgan and Jonathan. There had been no gray area in what they'd said to her. She was simply to obey. And why wouldn't she? They'd been nothing but good to her, and all their advice so far had been wise. They cared about her and Caleb, worried about her well-being . . .

But they didn't understand.

She looked into Trevor Beal's blue eyes. His interest made her feel better about herself. She needed that, she thought. If Morgan and Jonathan understood how much, they wouldn't deprive her of this.

"Come on," he whispered. "I won't pick you up at Hanover House if that's a problem. We can meet somewhere and then go off quietly. Nobody has to know. You can tell everybody you broke the date with me, and then Morgan and Jonathan will never have to know. Who could it possibly hurt?"

Sadie closed her eyes and tried to think. "I don't have a car," she said. "I can't meet you anywhere."

"You can walk, can't you? You have feet." He wasn't going to give up easily. That fact sent a warm thrill rushing through her. "What about their boathouse? You could walk down to the boathouse, and I'll pick you up there. Nobody will ever have to know. We'll go to Savannah, eat, see a movie, come home. I'll drop you off a little distance from the house and you can go home."

"Where will I tell them I've been? They'll have to know I'm gone."

He considered that for a moment. "Tell them you're going to the Methodist dance. There really is one Friday night, no kidding. Tell them some girls invited you to come. They'll like that, won't they? They'll buy it."

She grinned. "You've done this before."

He shrugged. "Sue me for being creative."

She laughed then as the bell started to ring. Quickly she grabbed her book out of the locker and shoved it into her backpack. "I've got to go."

He blocked her way. "Not until you say yes."

She grinned up at him. "All right, yes."

"Great," he said. "So Friday night, the boathouse at six. We'll have a blast together. You'll see."

A chill shivered over her, but the thrill that rivaled it made the reservations flee from her mind. It wasn't her fault Morgan and Jonathan were being narrow-minded. She wasn't hurting anyone, after all. Pushing her doubts to the back of her mind, she hurried to her next class, knowing that nothing Crystal or her friends said to her could hurt her now.

CHAPTER

*B*lair's preoccupation with Cade's disappearance worried Morgan almost as much as Cade did.
She had been camped in front of her computer for hours
at a time, forgetting to open the library or closing it at odd
hours of the day as she took off on a hunch that led
nowhere. She hadn't been eating or sleeping, and her face
was pale and distracted, her eyes full of things that only
she could see. The scar on her face burned more brightly
than usual.

"I want you to come to Hanover House for dinner
tonight," Morgan had insisted when Blair finally answered
her phone. "You need to be around people and get your
mind off things."

"I don't want my mind off *things*," Blair said. "Other
people's minds are off *things,* and that's why no one's
found Cade."

"Just come," Morgan said. "You have to eat, and
maybe we can put our heads together and come up with
something."

She had reluctantly agreed to come, but the moment she'd arrived, Morgan knew Blair would rather be any place but here. The house was crowded with the tenants who had just gotten home from work, the television in the den blared, and Caleb cried intermittently as Morgan tried to prepare dinner.

Blair seethed past the den, where Karen, the pregnant woman Jonathan had reluctantly allowed to stay, sat watching a rerun of *Step by Step* at a volume so loud you could have heard it from the second floor.

"Blair," Morgan yelled over the volume, "I'd like for you to meet Karen. Karen, this is my sister ..."

"Nice to meet you," Blair yelled, and turned with disgust to go into the kitchen. Morgan followed her in as Karen mumbled that it was nice to meet her too.

"Karen just showed up yesterday," Morgan said in a low voice when they were out of her earshot. "Mama and Pop led her to Christ when she was in jail. She isn't married, and she finally realized that she couldn't have her baby in the environment she was living in, so—"

"So she came here to get a free ride and leach off you for a while?"

Morgan glanced around, hoping no one had heard. Sadie sat at the table feeding Caleb. She looked up and then hastily looked away. Morgan hoped she hadn't taken the comment wrong.

Out on the sunporch sat Mrs. Hern, rocking blankly. She was having a bad day, and her boss, Mr. Jenkins, had sent her home early from her job at Goodfellow's Grocery. The woman's Alzheimer's wasn't severe enough for a nursing home, but she couldn't live on her own or support herself. The donations that came to the home helped to subsidize her. Thankfully, she hadn't heard Blair's comment, and if she had, she'd have forgotten it so quickly that it would hardly have mattered.

Felicia, the fifty-year-old former bank robber, who was strong as an ox and worked for the town's sanitation department, was out in the backyard pulling weeds. It was one of the household chores on her list this week.

"Blair, keep your voice down, please," Morgan said. "I don't want the tenants to hear you say that kind of thing."

"I'm serious, Morgan. I thought you only took Christians who were committed to studying their Bible and stuff."

Morgan smirked at Blair. "Yes, that's true, although I can't imagine what difference it makes to you."

"I'm just saying that she wouldn't be walking around nine months pregnant and unmarried, if she'd really become a Christian in jail."

Morgan sighed. "She says she backslid. But who am I to judge where she is in her faith?"

"Who are you to judge?" Blair asked. "Are you kidding me? For safety's sake, you *have* to judge. Mama and Pop always judged. They wouldn't let anyone in here unless they were sure they were committed. The whole purpose of having this place is to help them get on their feet and get a good foundation in their faith."

Morgan stared at her sister and wondered if this defense of their work was the beginning of a softening in Blair's heart toward Christianity. It wasn't like her to talk about faith.

"I mean, I don't care whether she's a Christian or not," Blair went on, "since all that seems like nothing more than illusion anyway, but the fact is that it does sometimes change people's behavior. And the ones who come here and commit to changing usually do. I'm just saying that there may not be a commitment to changing her behavior if she's walking around pregnant and unmarried."

"I understand and agree with you, Blair. But the woman is in desperate need. She's going to have that baby any day. I'm trying to get her into one of the unwed mother homes, but until I do, she has to stay here."

Blair still didn't like it, and that fact shone clearly on her face. "Morgan, what are you going to do when she has that baby?"

"Bring it home, I guess," Morgan said.

"How in the world are you going to take care of two babies at once?"

"I won't be taking care of two babies, Blair. She'll be taking care of hers."

"And what if she doesn't? What if she just dumps him on you?"

"She won't." Putting an unmistakable period on the end of that sentence, Morgan went to the oven and pulled out the roast. Its scent wafted over the room.

"Smells good," Sadie said. "Doesn't it smell good, Caleb?"

Blair finally noticed the girl at the table. "Oh, hi, Sadie."

"Hi, Blair."

Blair touched Caleb's head and bent over to kiss his forehead.

"Any news about Cade?" Sadie asked, as if trying to help change the subject.

"No." Blair turned back to Morgan. "Look at you. You're working yourself to death with all these people to feed. It's a bed-and-breakfast, for heaven's sake. You're not obligated to cook supper for an army every night."

"I like cooking supper for them," Morgan said. "They've worked hard all day. Besides, it makes us feel more like a family."

"But you're not a family," Blair said. "Except for Sadie and Caleb, these people are strangers living in your house."

Morgan drew in a deep breath and stirred the pot of beans on the stove. "Come on, Blair. Give it a rest, will you? Mama and Pop did this for years and it never bothered you."

"That's because it's who they were. But you don't have to be Mama's clone just because you feel the need to continue her work."

"I'm not continuing her work. I'm continuing *Christ's* work. End of story. Now will you please put ice in the glasses?"

Blair sighed and went to the cabinet. "Let's see. I don't think you have twenty-five glasses."

Morgan groaned. "There aren't twenty-five people, Blair. There's you, Jonathan, Sadie, Karen, Felicia, Mrs. Hern, Gus, and me. Caleb has his cup. So that's eight."

"Eight," Blair said, pulling the glasses out. "That's almost a baseball team. An army. My twenty-eight-year-old sister is mother to an army."

"I'm not their mother," Morgan said. "What is wrong with you?"

Blair shook her head and jerked the ice drawer out of the freezer. "Nothing. I shouldn't have come. I don't feel like a party."

"It's not going to be a party," Morgan said. "After we eat, we can talk."

"Yeah, after we've spent a couple of hours doing KP."

Sadie wiped Caleb's face and got up from the table. "I'll clean up after supper, Morgan."

Her voice was soft, hurt, and Morgan shot Blair a scathing look. Then she moved to kiss Sadie's cheek. "Thank you, sweetie. We'll all help. Don't mind her. She's just worried about Cade."

Blair didn't seem to appreciate the comment and began firing the ice cubes into the glasses. The front storm door slammed, and Morgan glanced through the living room and saw Jonathan coming in, flanked by Gus. They both looked filthy from the day's work.

Morgan crossed the house and kissed Jonathan. It didn't matter how dirty he looked or the way he smelled after a hot day of salt-water fishing with a boatload of tourists, the sight of him always made her heart jolt. "Go on up and shower. Supper's almost ready. Blair's here."

"Any news about Cade?"

"None yet." She looked up at the Jamaican man standing behind her husband. "Hey, Gus. How was your day?"

"Okay, Miss Morgan. Hot like hades."

Morgan noticed that Karen had suddenly turned the volume down on the television, and the *Step by Step* theme was now a distant melody rather than an amplified, heart-shaking aggravation.

Karen smiled up at Gus. He nodded at her. "You okay, Miss Karen?"

"I'm fine. How are you, Gus?"

"Dirty," he said. "I'll go take a shower now."

He bolted up the stairs, and Karen watched him go.

Morgan got an uneasy feeling.

From Jonathan's expression, she knew he was troubled too.

Jonathan pulled her through the kitchen, greeted Blair and Sadie, and kissed Caleb on the top of his head. "Morgan, I need to talk to you in the office," he said in a low voice.

She followed him into the small room, and he dropped into the chair that used to be her father's.

"Did you see that look Karen gave Gus?"

"Yeah, I thought I saw something there."

"If Karen is interested in Gus," he said, "then it isn't good to have her staying in the house with him. Your parents were always very strict about dating among the tenants."

"I know," she said. Several times they had decided to make it an all male or all female house, but inevitably someone of the opposite sex came along who was desperate for help, and they hadn't had the heart to turn him away.

The few times that there had been attraction between male and female tenants, her father had found another home for one of them immediately.

"So if there's an attraction, we'll make one of them leave. But which one?"

Jonathan began taking off his shoes. "Gus has been here for almost a year. I don't think we should run him out."

"But Karen's in such need, and that poor baby . . ."

"Well, I doubt Gus would return the interest with her nine months' pregnant. But after the baby, it could be a real problem." He got up, hooking his dirty shoes with two fingers.

"I know," she said. "But I had really hoped we could keep her until after the baby comes."

He smiled down at her. "Tell the truth. You just really want a newborn baby in the house, don't you?"

"No, that's not it at all. Caleb has filled my yearning for a baby."

"But a newborn." He pressed a kiss on her lips. "I know you, Morgan."

Something clanked in the kitchen. Morgan glanced out. Blair was almost slamming the glasses onto the table, and Sadie was putting the dishes out. "I have to finish supper," she said. "We'll talk about this later."

Jonathan grabbed her hand. She looked up at him. "Honey, we'll have a baby of our own. I know we will. It's just a matter of time."

How much more time? Morgan wanted to ask. They'd been trying for over a year. "I know," she said, though she didn't know at all. "Go upstairs and get cleaned up now. Supper's almost ready."

Jonathan crossed the kitchen in his sock feet and went upstairs to shower. Morgan went back into the kitchen and found that the table was set.

Sadie had managed to get Blair's mind off Karen and Cade and was chattering about Trevor Beal.

". . . Morgan and Jonathan said no. I understand why and everything. I was just so amazed that he asked."

Morgan tuned in to the conversation as she took the roast beef out of the oven. "You hear that, Blair?" she asked. "She was flattered. Like he's the only guy who wants to ask her out."

"Morgan's right, much as I hate to admit it," Blair said. "You're the kind of girl whose pictures men hang on their gym lockers."

Morgan shot her a look. "Blair!"

"I don't want them hanging my picture up," Sadie said. "I just want one to like me. And one does."

Morgan looked back over her shoulder. "Honey, I know you're disappointed. What did he say when you told him you couldn't go?"

Sadie turned back to Caleb and wiped his face again, even though it didn't need it. "He tried to talk me into going anyway."

Morgan sighed. "I'm so sorry, Sadie. But another guy will come along soon. You'll see."

Sadie fell into silence as she folded the napkins and set them beside each plate.

After the prayer to bless the meal, it seemed as if the group gathered around the big round table erupted into football-stadium chatter with everyone talking at once—everyone, that is, except Blair, who brooded as she picked at her food.

Karen sat on one side of her, and Gus on the other, and they talked over her as if she wasn't there.

"When is the baby supposed to come?" the Jamaican asked Karen.

Blair leaned back so they could see across her. "I'm due Thursday," Karen said.

"You don't look that big."

"Well, thank you, Gus. I feel like the Goodyear blimp."

Blair tried to tune out their conversation and fixed on the one across the table between Morgan and Mrs. Hern.

"Mama called me today and told me she'd painted her house," the old woman said.

Blair knew her mother was dead, but she often relived past days. The house-painting story was one of her favorites. She'd probably repeat it five times before Blair left here tonight.

She glanced at Felicia, the big woman who practically inhaled her food. She ate like a linebacker. Blair hoped the donations this month were enough to cover her meals.

Caleb chomped string beans and mashed potatoes and made an occasional squeal, but Sadie ate quietly, as if lost in her own little world.

The whole situation gave Blair a searing anger. Cade was suffering somewhere, maybe even dead, and life was going on just as it had before he left. She resented it and fought the urge to scream out that they needed to *do* something, that a friend could be dying, and no one cared.

"I was in there for three years, worked out on the road crew," Karen was saying to Gus. "Ate slop most days. Spent all the money I earned on commissary. Snickers and Milky Ways, potato chips and such. Gained about fifty pounds in there. I lost thirty of it when I got out, but then I had to go and get pregnant and gain it all back."

"You look fine to me," Gus said, and Blair shot him a look of pure disgust.

"Would you like to trade places with me?" she asked him loudly.

Silence fell over the table, and Morgan and Jonathan looked up at her.

"Uh, no, Miss Blair. I'm fine right here."

Karen seized the opportunity, though. "I'll trade."

Morgan stiffened. "No, everybody stay where they are, please."

Blair rolled her eyes and wondered when and if the conversation was going to come around to Cade.

"You'll never guess who came to see me at the dock this morning," Jonathan said, taking advantage of the lull in the conversation.

"Who?" Morgan asked.

"Morris Ambrose, Jerry Ann Shepp, Matt Pearl, and Gerald Madison."

Blair looked up. That was the same group who had urged her to run for mayor. "Don't tell me. They want you to run for mayor."

He smiled. "That's right."

Morgan put her hands over her mouth and started to laugh. "Really?"

Blair's eyes glowed. "Are you going to?"

He shrugged. "I don't know. It's kind of crazy, don't you think?"

Morgan grabbed his arm. "I don't think it's crazy at all. We need someone with integrity in that seat. Why *not* you?"

"Well, Sam Sullivan and Ben Jackson are both running, for one thing. I'm not the politician type. And it would cost money. Signs and whatnot. I'm just a fisherman."

"You are not *just* a fisherman," Morgan said. "You're a businessman. You own your fishing tour business *and* Hanover House. You're a part-time preacher too. You're more qualified than Sullivan or Jackson, and you're sure more honest than our former mayor."

He shrugged and cut a piece of roast. "I'll think about it," he said. "I'm not sure yet."

Blair set her fork down. "I think you should do it. Too bad we don't have a newspaper on the island anymore. You could get some free publicity through that."

Sadie laughed suddenly, and everyone looked at her. "If Jonathan was mayor, he would be Blair's boss, wouldn't he?"

Blair gave a half-grin. "Something like that."

"And Cade's boss too," Sadie added.

Blair's grin crashed, and Jonathan's faded. They all looked down at their food.

"Mama called me today to tell me she'd painted her house." Mrs. Hern's sweet voice rose out of the silence. "Lemon yellow. She said the shutters are white. I'm going to see it this weekend, I reckon."

Blair closed her eyes and fought the urge to scream at Mrs. Hern that her mother was dead, and there wasn't a house, lemon yellow or any other color.

But suddenly Karen yelped out and grabbed Blair's arm. "Whoa. This is some contraction!"

Morgan froze. "Is there anything I can do?"

Karen stared down at her food, her hand over her stomach, concentrating on the birth pang.

Blair stiffened. This was all they needed. Cade in trouble, and everyone's attention focused on this woman and her labor. And Karen clutching her like she had something to do with it.

Karen came out of the contraction and let go of Blair's arm. "Man, I didn't expect that. I thought it would come easier at first. My back's been hurting today, but I didn't think anything of it."

Morgan looked flustered. "Do you think it's labor?"

"I don't know," Karen said. "Guess we'll see."

Blair had had enough of the drama of this household. She scraped back her chair and got up. "I have to go." She took her plate to the sink, rinsed it out, then clattered it into the dishwasher. "Thanks for dinner."

Morgan looked distraught. "Don't go, Blair. We were going to talk afterward."

"You won't have time to talk," Blair said. "Let me know if it's a boy or a girl."

With that, she hurried out of the house and back to her car on the gravel driveway, wondering why the woman's contraction had revived the rage in her heart. It was because of Cade, she thought. He was somewhere in trouble, waiting for rescue, certain that of all the friends he had on Cape Refuge, someone would be able to help him.

But no one was giving it much thought because of crazy old ladies and pregnant ex-cons and the mayor's race and Sadie's love life . . .

She should be ashamed of herself for letting those things make her so angry, she thought. Where was her compassion? Her sense of decorum? Her mother would have given her a good tongue-lashing for having so little feeling for the people her sister loved.

But her mother wasn't here, and neither was Cade. So really, there was no one to be her best for. No one who cared whether she was a good, loving person or a bitter spinster. Morgan didn't have time to care.

Her heart swelled with missing Cade, and she remembered not so long ago how they'd sat in the church warehouse after her parents died, and she'd opened her heart to him about what the burn scars had done to her life. . . .

He had touched her scars with gentle fingertips and told her that she was the best looking woman on the island of Cape Refuge, and he didn't even see those scars anymore.

She had fallen apart at that and run out like a scared kid. But she'd never forgotten it.

Where are you, Cade?

The question ached through her heart as she made her way home.

Joe McCormick had never applied for the job of police chief, and he didn't much want it. At twenty-eight, he was just settling into the job of detective. But since cops didn't seem to stay long in Cape Refuge before moving to Savannah to work for a larger force, he was the one with the most seniority and the greatest amount of training.

Even so, he'd never expected to have to step into Cade's shoes at a moment's notice.

He creaked back in Cade's chair and ran his hand over his bald head. It needed shaving, but he hadn't had a minute to put a razor to his face—or his head. The smooth top of his head, where he was naturally bald, contrasted against the dark stubble of the rest of his hair, making him look much older than his age.

Today he felt even older than that.

He clutched the phone to his ear, mentally rehearsing what he wished he could say to the person who'd put him on hold. You wouldn't think it would take an act of

Congress for an investigating officer to get forensics information. The medical examiner who'd examined Clark's body had sent the gunshot residue analysis to the crime lab on Sunday, and he still hadn't gotten the results. Until they knew if Clark had fired the gun on himself, it was difficult to proceed.

Finally, the music that Joe was sure had been designed to drive people insane stopped, and someone answered the phone. "Craig Haughton."

Joe sat up and leaned on the desk. "Yes, Craig, this is Joe McCormick of the Cape Refuge Police Department. I've been waiting almost a week for the results of the GSR test on William Clark. I need that information ASAP."

The man hesitated a moment, as if fumbling through his files. "Yeah, uh . . . I have his file here, but I'm gonna have to call you back."

"No, you don't." Joe had had enough. "I'm trying to conduct a police investigation here, and I need to know if the man's shooting was a suicide attempt or a homicide attempt! You people are supposed to be the forensics geniuses. Just tell me if the man had gunpowder stains on his fingers!"

Silence again, then finally, a loud sigh. "All right, Detective, just a minute." More fumbling. "Okay, the man did not have gunshot residue. Of course, this isn't conclusive. The rain or blood could have washed it off."

Joe leaned back hard in his chair. "All right, fax me that report, will you?"

The man agreed, and Joe hung up. Carefully, he read back over his notes and studied the photographs taken at Clark's car. The fact that Clark had no gunshot residue on his hands only corroborated the conclusions he'd already drawn. The gun had been fired from at least two feet away. From the position of the bloodstains, it appeared that Clark was resisting the shot, backing away, possibly opening the door.

His shirt had a trace of mud stains that hadn't been completely washed away by the rain, as if he'd fallen out on his back.

Those things, coupled with the angle of the bullet hole and, now, the lack of gunpowder residue on the dead man's fingers made Joe suspect that someone in the passenger seat had shot him, then left him for dead. But Clark had lived, and he had gotten up and stumbled through the woods to the busy street beyond them.

So it was a homicide. Someone had been with William Clark when he pulled his car into the woods. Someone had shot him, then vanished.

But who?

His wife?

The gun had been registered to William Clark. So someone had shot him with his own gun, and other than his and his wife's, there were no new prints on either the gun or the car.

Ann Clark was looking guiltier all the time.

And how did Cade fit into this? If the woman had tried to kill him, then the fact that Cade ran into him would not provoke an act of revenge.

But the man had spoken to Cade. He distinctly remembered Cade saying that in the press statement he'd made. He went to the door and called across the squad room, "Somebody get me the video of Cade's press conference the other night."

In a moment, J.J. Clyde loped in with the video. "Want me to pop it in?"

Joe nodded and stared down at his notes. J.J. put the video in and turned the set on.

Joe watched and listened through the statement. Nothing about the man speaking. Then someone asked a question.

"Chief Cade, did the impact kill him instantly?"

Cade shook his head. "No, it didn't. He was alive and speaking right after he was hit, and did make it to Candler Hospital in Savannah alive. He died shortly thereafter."

There it was. Joe stared at the television, running the facts through his mind. So the woman, who had heard the report that night, thought that her husband had spoken to Cade. Could she have wanted to get him out of the way before he identified the killer?

But that was crazy. He was a cop. Of course he would have identified the killer the moment the man told him. For Ann Clark to wait for the next morning, then do him some kind of harm, wouldn't even make sense.

"That it, Joe?" J.J. asked him. "Want me to play it again?"

Joe rubbed his mouth. "No, thanks. That's all I needed."

As J.J. headed out, Georgette, the woman who served as office clerk to the small operation, came in. "Here's your mail, Joe. I'm giving you all of Cade's too, in case there's anything important."

He took the stack of mail and started sorting through, as his mind still worked through the evidence.

And then he froze. In the return address corner on one of the envelopes, he saw the name "Matthew Cade," typed with no address.

He dropped it on his desk, pulled some tweezers out of Cade's drawer, and pulled the letter from its envelope. He grabbed a plastic evidence bag from another drawer and slipped it inside. It might have fingerprints, or some other evidence he could use. Slowly, he began to read through the plastic.

*T*he phone was ringing when Blair got home from Hanover House, and she dove for it. "Hello?"

"Blair, Joe McCormick here."

Blair froze. His voice sounded grim, clipped.

"Do you have something on Cade?"

He was silent for a moment. "Can you come down to the station for a minute? I have something I need to show you. I just got off the phone with Jonathan. I want him to see too."

Blair didn't want to know, yet she forced herself to ask, "What is it, Joe?"

"Just come in, Blair. You're not going to believe this if you don't see it."

For a moment after she hung up, Blair just stared at a spot on her wall. If Cade was dead, would Joe have told her over the phone?

She tried not to panic, but forced herself to move and made it to the station in record time. Jonathan was just pulling in too. She jumped out of the car and crossed to her brother-in-law, who stalked across the parking lot with a grim look on his face. "Jonathan, what's going on? Have they found Cade?"

"He wouldn't say. But I have a bad feeling."

They burst into the station together and found Joe in Cade's office. He sat in Cade's executive chair, slouched back with his legs crossed, his shoulders hunched as he leaned on the armrests.

He looked up at them with weary eyes.

"What is it, Joe?" Blair demanded.

He pointed to a clear bag with a handwritten letter on his desk and turned it around so they could read it. "A letter from Cade. Don't touch it. It might have evidence."

"A letter from Cade?" Jonathan leaned over it, and Blair began to read.

> *Joe,*
>
> *Just wanted to touch base with you guys and let you know that I haven't dropped off the face of the earth. I was just a little depressed after the accident, so I decided to take some time off. The truth is, I'd been seeing a girl from Savannah, and we decided to get married.*
>
> *I know it sounds crazy, and I'm going to have a lot of explaining to do when I get back, but I've never been happier. Let everyone know that for me, will you?*
>
> *I'll call as soon as I know when I'm coming back. Meanwhile, I know Cape Refuge is in your good hands.*
>
> *Matt Cade*

Rage rose like lava inside her, and Blair backed away. "No way," she said. "There's no way. Cade did not write that."

Jonathan stared at the words. "It looks like his handwriting, Blair."

"It's not, though." She looked up at Jonathan as if he'd just betrayed his best friend. "Jonathan, you know Cade better than anybody. Would he just run off with some mystery girlfriend and get married? Is that even possible?"

He sighed. "I wouldn't think so. But at least it would mean he's alive."

She slammed both hands down on the desk. "Then why wouldn't he call?" she yelled. "Why would he write a stupid note like some kind of wimp? He killed a man just a few days ago. He wouldn't just run off and get married! Jonathan, why would he hide a girlfriend from you ... from us? It's not true, that's why!"

"I'm gonna have a handwriting expert analyze the letter, Blair," Joe said. "But I think it's his. I've seen Cade's handwriting a good bit. He has a funny way of making his *d*s. This is it. And his fingerprints are on it."

She couldn't catch her breath, so she sat down and studied the letter again. The paper shook in her hands. She read it over, looking for some sign, some clue, in the words. But there was nothing ... until ...

"His signature!" she said. "Since when has Cade gone by 'Matt'? I've never heard him refer to himself as Matt in his life! He goes by Cade, just Cade. Why would he sign 'Matt,' all of a sudden? Matthew, maybe. That's his official signature. But never 'Matt.'"

Jonathan looked over her shoulder. "She's right."

"Of course I'm right." She bent over the desk. "If someone was holding him, say Ann Clark, she might not know that he only went by 'Cade.' It would be his way of telling us that things about the letter weren't right or true. That he was being forced to write it."

"Maybe the girlfriend—er, wife—calls him Matt," Joe said. "That happens, you know. My brother went by Billy for twenty-five years, and all of a sudden he meets this girl, and he becomes 'Bill.'"

"It's not the same thing!" Blair said. "There are too many things that don't add up! This is a sign—a clue for us. He's letting us know."

"What, Blair?" Joe asked. "What is he letting us know?"

"I don't know," she said, her eyes beginning to sting. "That the letter isn't true. That he's not really married and irresponsible and reckless. That he's not really a different person than we all knew."

Her voice cracked, and she turned away. Could it be true? Could Cade be a different person, someone she thought she knew, but didn't really?

No, her mind couldn't adjust to the new picture. It couldn't be possible.

Tears pushed to her eyes, and she realized that at least the letter did put their fears to rest, that Cade's corpse didn't lie undiscovered in a swamp somewhere.

She looked up at Joe. He needed a shave, both on his face and his head. She knew he hadn't gotten much rest since this whole thing had started. He sighed. "I guess I wanted to believe that Cade's disappearance wasn't connected to Clark's death. That all I had to figure out was who shot him before he walked out in front of Cade's car."

"Shot him? I thought it was suicide."

"Nope, couldn't have been. No gunpowder stains on Clark's fingers, and the gun was fired from a couple of feet away, in the direction of the passenger seat. There was definitely someone in that car with him. But if you're right and Cade didn't mean anything in this note, then what would the shooter have to do with Cade?"

Blair needed to think. She got up, paced back and forth across the room. She looked back at Jonathan, saw that his eyes were fixed on a spot on the back wall, as if he could reach an answer if he stared hard enough.

"Who knows, Joe?" Blair asked. "But I'll guarantee you the shooter *knows* what happened to Cade. If you were going to skip town and get married, would you go park your truck at Cricket's? No. Even if it was some spontaneous crazy last-minute idea, you'd take a minute to take your truck home and leave some food out for your cat. And he was *seen* with Ann Clark!"

"Yep," Joe said. "She's my number one suspect."

Blair backed up against the door's casing. "So are you going to arrest her?"

Joe stiffened. "Not yet. I have some work to do yet, Blair. It doesn't pay to go arresting people before you have enough evidence. I'm going to start with this letter."

"What about fingerprints in the car?"

"Well, her fingerprints were in the car, all right, but that's to be expected. She was his wife. She would have been in that car all the time."

"What about the gun? Were her fingerprints on it?"

"Yes. But again, she was his wife and they owned it."

She looked at Jonathan, saw the deep lines of worry around his eyes. "That woman knows where Cade is. She knows who shot her husband. And they're not going to do anything."

"We are going to do something, Blair," Joe said. "Just not your way and not in your time. We're going to go by the book and get this right."

"Meanwhile, Cade's life is in jeopardy," Jonathan said quietly.

Joe tipped his head. "You think I don't realize that?"

Blair pointed at the letter. "I need a copy of this."

"No, Blair, you can't have one."

"Joe, please. I just want a copy to take home. I won't give it to anybody. You know you can trust me."

He looked up into her face. "Why do you want it, Blair?"

She sighed and looked down at the page. "I don't know. But sometimes if I have something in front of me, I'll get ideas. I might notice something. I just want it so I can look back at it if something comes to me."

He groaned and took the letter into the squad room to the copier, made her the copy. "I don't know why I'm doing this. But Cade put a lot of stock in your brains, so maybe I ought to, too."

She took the copy out of the machine. "Thank you, Joe."

"Yeah, no problem." He shot Jonathan a look. "I'm not making one for you."

Jonathan just nodded. "I'll look at hers if I need to see it again."

Joe stalked back into Cade's office, and Blair looked around at the other cops sitting at their desks, staring up at her. They were practically kids, most of them. How could they be expected to solve a murder and find their missing chief?

She headed for her car, and Jonathan came out behind her. "You okay, Blair?"

She turned back to him. "Yeah. You?"

"He's alive," Jonathan said. "Don't forget that. He's not dead somewhere. He's alive and well enough to write."

"Yeah, I'll try to hold onto that." She stopped at her car and realized she was going to shatter. Any minute now, she'd fly into a million pieces. "I'm telling you, he's in serious trouble. We have to help him, Jonathan."

"I know," he said. "I agree with you. But Joe is our best bet for finding him. Don't give up on him yet."

But as Blair drove home, she realized she *had* all but given up on Joe and Jonathan and anyone else who was looking for Cade. His life was, quite possibly, on the line. And she was the only one she could trust to find him.

W hen she got home, Blair crossed the street to the Bull River and stood on the rock wall, looking out at the water. Any moment now, they would get a phone call. There would be a body lying in the woods, and they would discover that Cade was dead, after all, murdered like her parents.

She sat down on the grass and looked up at the dark sky and the angry constellations above her head. Times like these she desperately needed to believe in something. But a belief system wasn't something you concocted just when you were in need. God wouldn't exist just because she forced herself to believe, any more than Cade would be all right just because she wanted him to be.

Believing in God had to do with a system of convictions, deep faith, things that her parents and her sister and Jonathan had, things that had never come easily to Blair.

She was tired, bone-weary, for she hadn't slept well in days, not since Cade had disappeared. She couldn't think, couldn't eat, for thinking of him somewhere helpless and wounded, praying to the God he believed in that some rescue was imminent. But they were failing him, everyone who loved him and cared for him. Everyone who would hear about that stupid letter and believe it . . .

Tears rolled down her face, and she wiped them away, then got up to walk some more. She had been by his house to check on Oswald at least three times a day. Joe had sealed up the place so evidence couldn't be disturbed, so she hadn't been able to go back in. But it was clear he hadn't been home. His truck still sat at Cricket's as if waiting for its owner to return. Somewhere there had to be a clue, a puzzle piece, that would lead them to wherever he was, but she couldn't help believing that Ann Clark held the mystery to it all.

She walked back to her house, but instead of going in, she got back in the car and pulled out of the gravel driveway. As if her car knew exactly where to go, it headed across the bridge to Tybee Island and up toward Savannah. She navigated her way through the town and back to Washington Square. Her heart pounded with urgent certainty as she stopped directly across the park from Ann Clark's house.

The old Victorian home had an eerie look at night, like a Halloween screen-saver with its haunted windows blinking on and off. Light shone from these windows, stark white in some, a yellow flicker dancing against the curtain in others. The drapes were closed, but Blair watched them for shadows walking by—Ann Clark's or even Cade's.

What if he was there, just on the other side of that wall? What was keeping him from escaping?

Was he bound in some way? Injured? Had she taken him somewhere else?

Or was he honeymooning with his secret bride who called him Matt?

She chased that renegade thought out of her mind. No, Cade was in trouble.

She would find him, no matter what it cost her.

CHAPTER

*M*organ woke during the night and saw that Jonathan wasn't sleeping. He lay on his back with his hands behind his head, staring up at the ceiling.

"Can't sleep?" she asked him softly.

He shook his head. "I just don't know what to do."

Morgan sat up and turned on the lamp. It lit the small room in a yellow glow, illuminating the pictures they'd hung of Caleb and Sadie, a painting Mrs. Hern had done, and a tapestry wall hanging over their bed that Morgan had made herself.

Even though her parents had been gone for several months now, she hadn't had the heart to move into their room. It still sat just as they'd left it on the morning of their death.

But nights like tonight, she wished they had a sitting area with a Bible on the table, rather than a twelve-by-twelve room that could barely contain a bed, dresser, and chest of drawers.

Her shadow moved across the wall as she lay back down and snuggled up to her husband. "You can't do anything, Jonathan," she said. "You just have to wait, let the police do their job."

"He's my best friend," he said, as if that heightened his own responsibility. "What would he do if I was missing?"

"That's different. He's a cop. You're not."

"I don't know what I was thinking, considering a campaign for mayor. I'm completely inadequate. That letter was a cry for help, and here I am in bed." He threw back his covers and sat up.

Morgan got up on her knees and began massaging his shoulders. "You can pray for him, Jonathan. That might be all you can do."

"I've been praying all night."

"Then stop thinking you're not doing anything. God knows where Cade is." She kissed his neck, pressed her face beside his. "And I think you should run for mayor. If you weren't a good candidate, they wouldn't have asked you."

A knock on their door startled them both, and Morgan let him go.

"What now?" Jonathan asked. "It's the middle of the night."

"Maybe it's Karen."

Jonathan went barefoot to the door, wearing his T-shirt and a pair of gym shorts. Morgan got up and pulled on her robe.

Karen stood leaning against the casing, her face covered in sweat and her hand over the lower part of her belly. "I know it's after three, but I think I better go to the hospital."

Morgan crossed the room. "How far apart are the contractions?"

"Five minutes. And they're hard, Morgan."

"Well, then, we'll go. Let us throw some clothes on."

They quickly got dressed and told Sadie they were leaving. Then Jonathan carried Karen's suitcase to the car as Morgan helped her get in. In the grips of a contraction, Karen couldn't get the seat belt on. Morgan slipped into the backseat with her and hooked it. "Hurry, Jonathan!"

Morgan held Karen's hand. "Don't tense up, honey. Try to relax. Breathe."

Jonathan pulled away from Hanover House, quiet as Karen went through that contraction. When she came out of it, they all breathed a collective sigh of relief.

"Hold tight, Karen," he said. "Well be there soon."

It was almost dawn when Karen's labor began to reverse itself. After hours of contractions as close as three minutes apart, their severity began to decrease and slowed to every ten minutes. Exhausted, Karen lay on her side, watching the monitor for the signs of the next contraction.

Morgan sat like a rag doll in the chair next to the bed, staring into space with eyes red from lack of sleep. Her head had begun to throb, and at this pace the road ahead of them looked long.

Jonathan had fallen asleep in a chair across the room, his head back against the wall and his jaw slack.

"Maybe it's a false alarm," Karen said in a voice raspy from groaning. "I'm sorry, Morgan. Really, I am."

"Don't apologize. It isn't your fault." Morgan got up and went to the door, looked out in the hallway for the nurse. "And we're not going home until they can assure me you're not in labor. How long's it been now?"

Karen checked the clock. "Fifteen minutes since the last one. And it was too mild to speak of. It's tapering off. I can't believe it. After all that."

Morgan tried to muster a smile. "Wonder if that says anything about the baby's personality."

"Oh, I know my baby's personality," Karen said. "This baby's a survivor."

The statement came out with such conviction that Jonathan woke. "A survivor?" Morgan asked. "Why do you say that?"

"Because of what we been through." Karen slid off the bed, stood up with her hand on her back.

Morgan's mind was too foggy to follow her. "What have you been through?"

"With my baby's daddy," she said. "See, he had another baby a few weeks ago, with one of his other girls."

Morgan's eyes met Jonathan's. "He has another girlfriend?"

She breathed a bitter laugh. "Not just one. But this one, she was pregnant, and she had her baby three weeks ago. That baby's wishing it'd never been born."

While she spoke, Karen paced the length of the bed, stretching the IV tube with her as she did. "She left her baby with him while she went to work. Went back too early, but she had to make a living, you know? He took this week-old baby with him on his drug deals. Somebody somewhere hurt that baby. When she got it back that night, the little thing had a seizure. She got him to the hospital ... but it was too late. He had a cracked skull, and his brain was swelling. . . ."

A strange sense of anger and injustice soared up inside Morgan's chest. Here she and Jonathan were, so far unable to conceive a child, yet people that careless and irresponsible could have as many as they wanted. "Karen, that's awful," she managed to say.

Karen's eyes filled with tears. "Poor baby's not but three weeks old. And then Jeffrey, that's my baby's daddy, he came to me all mad and upset, breaking things and kicking furniture over, scaring me to death. And I knew I had to get out of there if this baby was gonna be all right. I had to get out of that place, away from him."

Morgan crossed the room and put her arms around the girl. "I'm glad you came to us," she whispered.

Jonathan stayed where he was, but Morgan saw that he, too, was moved. He leaned forward, elbows on knees, his serious eyes fixed on Karen.

"I haven't always lived like this," Karen said. "I was brought up better than to hang with crack dealers. I was walking the straight and narrow until I got with the wrong man. He got me started on crack myself, and next thing I know, I'm hanging with dealers and walking the streets so I can pay for my habit. I got nobody to blame but myself, but I want you to know that I haven't always been like this."

"And you're clean now, Karen," Morgan whispered. "That's what matters."

"That's right. I been clean since I was arrested. Haven't used once since I got out of jail. But it's been hard, when everybody around me was using, and it was like they wanted me to fail, like they wanted to see me back hooked, so I could be just as miserable and ruined as they are. It was just a matter of time if I stayed there, Morgan. Just a matter of time."

"You're right," Morgan said. "That's what we always warn the inmates we work with. We always tell you that you have to remove yourself from that environment."

Karen looked down at her huge, swollen belly. "I want to be a good mama, Morgan. Like you with Caleb. I want to raise my baby to be smart and healthy and never to run around with anybody who'll lead him wrong. I want to raise him to think for himself. I want him to know God, Morgan. I've prayed so many times for that."

Morgan's eyes misted over, and she smiled down at Jonathan. He was smiling back. "I think your prayers are going to be answered, Karen," she said.

Jonathan agreed. "Karen, I know that God sees a willing, obedient heart when he looks at you. I know he sees that you're trying."

Karen hugged Morgan, and the baby kicked. Morgan jumped back. "He kicked me!"

Karen started to laugh, and Morgan pressed her hands over her stomach and waited for more movement. "Come here, Jonathan. You've got to feel this!"

Jonathan had a grin on his face as he came and touched Karen's abdomen. As if on cue, the baby stomped.

Laughter renewed their strength.

When the nurse came in, she smiled with them. "Glad you're all in a good mood, because the doctor told me to send you home."

Karen's smile crashed. "You mean I'll have to go through all this again?"

"I'm sorry," the nurse said. "But you don't want to stay here if it's not real labor." She started to remove the IV.

"Seems like I'm going to be the first woman in history to carry the baby the rest of her life."

The nurse laughed. "They all think that, but it can't be that much longer."

Within the hour, the paperwork had been filled out releasing her. They rode home in sleepy silence, just as the sun began to rise.

Morgan couldn't wait to lie down, but she knew that the tenants would expect breakfast soon. Jonathan had tours booked on his boat, so he wouldn't have the luxury of catching up on his sleep. When Karen had gone up to her room, Jonathan stopped Morgan from going into the kitchen. "Tell you what. I'm going to get a few boxes of donuts. It'll be a treat for everybody, and you won't have to cook."

"Good," she said. "No argument here."

She went up the stairs as he left the house and peeked into Caleb's room. Sadie was already with him, changing his diaper as he sucked on a bottle. "Hey, Sadie." Morgan went to kiss her forehead. The girl's hair was tousled, and she still wore her gown. "Caleb got you up?"

"That's okay," Sadie said. "Have you been at the hospital all night?"

Morgan bent over Caleb and blew a raspberry on his stomach. He squealed with giggles. "Almost all night."

"What did she have?"

Morgan picked Caleb up and grinned back at Sadie. "Nothing yet. False alarm."

Sadie gasped. "All that for nothing?"

"It wasn't Karen's fault. She really was having contractions. They just stopped. That happens sometimes, I understand." She kissed Caleb, and he closed his little arms around her neck and hugged back in a way that sent her heart into meltdown.

"You go get ready for school, Sadie. I'll take over with Caleb."

Sadie stood there a moment, raking her hand through her tangled hair. "Morgan, I need to ask you something."

"Yeah? What?"

"Tomorrow night there's a dance at the Methodist church. Do you think I could go?"

Morgan smiled. "That sounds like fun. Who with?"

"Some girls from school. I don't know them very well, but they invited me. Sharon Zeal and Beth Walker."

Morgan tried to place them, but couldn't. "I guess that would be all right."

Sadie looked a little uncertain. "Okay. Good. I'll go then."

"See? I told you you'd make friends."

Sadie didn't answer her as she left the room. Morgan decided she was just a little groggy. She sat down in the rocker and gave the bottle back to the baby, as a sense of peace fell over her.

Things would work out for Sadie, Caleb was happy and healthy, and Karen's baby would be born into a safe and loving environment.

If only they could find Cade, all would be right with the world.

Blair wasn't surprised when she got the phone call from Joe McCormick at the library the next day.

"Blair, our handwriting expert has confirmed that it was Cade's writing, all right."

Blair picked up her copy. It was dog-eared and wrinkled, for she'd read it so many times, wadded it up, and bitterly thrown it away, then dug it back out of the trash to read it again. "Big surprise, huh?"

"Not to me. But I thought you'd want to know. And we weren't able to get any other fingerprints or fibers from the letter, so it didn't provide any clues."

After thanking him for the information, Blair hung up and let out a frustrated yell that shook the small library. What good was it to know he'd written this letter full of lies if it didn't help them find him?

The front door opened, and anger surged through her. Who would come in here at a time like this? She didn't have time to show them where she kept the cookbooks and help them find a recipe for Mud Bottom Pie.

Storming across the wood floor, she saw that it was Sue Ellen Jargis. "Hey, Blair," she said. "I was just looking for something that would teach me how to speak Italian. You got anything like that?"

Rage erupted inside her. Cade was in trouble, suffering somewhere, maybe dying, and this woman wanted a book on Italian?

"No," she said. "We don't have anything like that."

"But I was told you had a whole section on foreign languages. That maybe you even had tapes. See, we're going to Europe next month."

"You can't learn an entire language in a month, Sue Ellen." She took her arm and escorted her back to the door. "You know what? I just remembered that I need to close early today. Maybe if you come back tomorrow I can help you."

"Closing early?" Sue Ellen stopped at the door, resisting Blair's efforts to evict her. "Well, why? The hours on the door clearly say you're open until six."

"Emergency," Blair said. "Really, I have to close." She got her out the door, then started to close it behind her. "You have a nice day now."

Before the woman could object, she locked the door and leaned against it.

Ann Clark, she thought. Ann Clark was the key to the whole thing. The police might need evidence, probable cause, motive, warrants. But she didn't.

Cade might not have time for red tape.

She hurried back to the office and got the letter again, folded it, and shoved it into her jeans pocket.

She had to get out of this place and think. She had to make a plan.

She got her keys and locked the library behind her.

Outside, she saw the sun glaring down on the water, and she longed to see Cade kayaking by, his tanned skin soaking up the rays of the rising sun. There were days when she'd sat on the shore and watched him without his knowing and dreamed stupid dreams befitting of an adolescent.

But Cade wasn't here, and those stupid dreams left her with a sense of loss so great that her heart felt too weak to contain it. She'd dealt with many things in her life—pain, humiliation, rejection, deceit. But of them all, loss was the hardest to bear. And this particular loss—the might-have-been kind—pierced so deeply within her that she knew no place to turn for relief.

What if Morgan was right, and Cade had harbored interest in her? What if there really was one man on this earth who could see past her scars? Wouldn't it be the height of cruelty for him to be snatched away?

She was selfish, she told herself. This wasn't about her. Cade's vanishing was a tragedy for him, regardless of what it did to her.

She thought of Oswald, probably standing sentinel over his empty bowls, waiting for his master to come home and put the world back on its axis.

For now, she was the only one who would do that for the cat, even if she couldn't do it for Cade or herself.

She drove to Cade's house and went around to the backyard.

Oswald began grumbling and croaking to her in his clipped, agitated meows. "I know, Lee Harvey," she said as she filled his bowls. "The service is lousy around here, huh?" While he ate, she sat down on the patio chair and looked around at the yard. Maybe she'd borrow Jonathan's mower and come cut it tomorrow.

Hugging herself, she scanned the crepe myrtles that weren't yet in bloom, the azalea bushes that were, and the hodgepodge of untended and unidentifiable plants that grew in his yard.

How would anyone expect them to think he was bringing a bride back here with no preparation at all? He would have called someone to come and cut the grass, at least. He would have put up his mud-caked boots that sat in one of the chairs. He would have weeded the garden.

But what if she was giving Cade more credit than he deserved?

What if the letter was true?

She pulled the letter out of her pocket and stared down at it again. The possibility that it was, indeed, true had hung in the

TERRI BLACKSTOCK

back of her mind since she'd first seen it, a distant thought that she dared not entertain. What if Cade did have a secret girlfriend and had run off to marry her to counter his depression? A spontaneous act like that wouldn't have provided for a mowed lawn or a fed cat.

Was Cade even capable of such a thing?

He was a man, wasn't he? She'd had lots of experience with men, though not the kind that most of the women she knew had. Her experience consisted of brush-offs and snubs because of the scars on her face. Men who were attracted to one side of her face while being repulsed by the other.

She had long ago begun to believe that there was something different about Cade. He was not the womanizer that so many of his cohorts were. He wasn't what she called a serial dater. He seemed too serious to spend time with a woman if he couldn't consider her for a wife.

There had been times lately when, like Morgan, she had sensed his affection for her. He'd called her beautiful, asked her to abandon her plan to leave the island, behaved as if he cared. But even then, some part of her knew that he would never consider her seriously. Their worldviews were too different. They didn't have the same core values, the same deep-seated faith.

But the signs were still there. Was she so deluded that she'd manufactured them in her mind?

Maybe there *had* been another woman all along, one he kept secret. He was a private man and wouldn't have wanted his life to be examined under everyone else's microscope.

And it would mean that he was alive and not in danger. Wouldn't it make her feel better to know that?

No, she thought. Somehow, the very idea of that made her want to put Cape Refuge in her rearview mirror and never think of it again.

But the alternative, if the letter was a fake or if he'd been forced to write it, meant that he was suffering, his life in someone else's hands.

It all came down to what she believed about Cade.

She rubbed her unadorned eyes and combed her fingers through her hair, trying to sort out all she knew about him.

He was kind and wise and diligent and thoughtful. His compassion for William Clark would not have allowed him to blow things off and elope. She knew that for a fact. Wasn't that why he'd been reading about bloodguilt and the cities of refuge?

If it turned out she was wrong in proclaiming the letter a fraud, then she'd just have to look like a fool. But if she was right, she had to save Cade's life.

First, she had to use all her resources to learn everything she could find on Ann and William Clark. Then she could decide how to proceed.

She didn't really care what it cost her.

CHAPTER

*T*hat night, as Sadie prepared to go and meet Trevor, guilt almost unraveled her. But it was too late. The plans had been made, and she had to go. If Morgan had been her age, she would have understood. She might have done exactly the same thing if her parents had been unreasonable.

She stood in front of the mirror and tried to see herself from Trevor's eyes.

Have you looked in the mirror lately?

She had inherited her mother's blonde hair and big eyes. She could see that fragile look she'd always seen in her mother—that look that invited men to rescue her. They had rescued her with the drugs of her choice, then turned on her under the strain of those choices.

Sadie hoped her own fragile look didn't attract the same kinds of men.

Was Trevor like the many men who'd come in and out of her mother's life? Wild, dangerous, reckless?

No. She turned from the mirror and banished that thought. Trevor was not like Morgan and Jonathan said. He was decent, sweet . . .

. . . and looked like he belonged in Hollywood.

It would all turn out fine, and Morgan and Jonathan would never know she'd lied.

Caleb had already been bathed and was dressed in his pajamas, taking his bedtime bottle as Morgan rocked him. For so long, Sadie had served as his surrogate mother, and it had been a heavy burden. What a miracle that Morgan had stepped into that role, and now he had two surrogate parents who delighted in him, leaving Sadie to enjoy him as a sister and not his sole protector.

She left them thinking she was walking to the Methodist church for the dance, but instead walked toward the boathouse that Morgan and Jonathan kept for the tenants of Hanover House. It was the place she had discovered months ago when she was a scared runaway with a broken arm. It had been a comfortable place to rest and hide. It had also been a place of terror where bullets had been fired and people had been killed. But now it was a place of redemption, she thought, where Trevor Beal would meet her, and things in her life would begin to turn around.

When she walked up the long dirt road toward the Bull River that fed into the Atlantic, she saw him leaning there against the wooden structure, his arms folded and his feet crossed at the ankles. He looked like one of those renegade guys in a prime-time television show, with his dark hair and his blue eyes and that knowing grin on his face. Her face flushed with pleasure at the sight of him.

"So, you came," he said, pushing off from the wall. "I was afraid you wouldn't."

She smiled. "Me? Why wouldn't I?"

He put his arm around her shoulders and kissed her on the lips, startling her. She hadn't expected that. She had kissed guys before back in Atlanta, greasy motorcycle types with tattoos on their arms and no familiarity with shampoo bottles or soap. They'd been some of the ones who came and went from her house when Jack was manufacturing his crystal meth and raking in the bucks as he made it available. She'd never had a guy kiss her in a chaste way that suggested he had nothing further in mind.

"You look awesome," he said, his face near hers. "Absolutely awesome."

She started to tell him he did too, but her throat seemed to tighten. Taking her hand, he pulled her to his car—a black Firebird that she had often watched driving away from school.

He helped her in. "So you're okay with this?"

She looked up at him, and her fears fled. His eyes were so crystal clear, so honest. "I think I am," she said, "only I feel pretty crummy about lying to them. I told them I was going to the Methodist dance."

"So we'll go." He went around the car and got behind the wheel. "I'll drop you off at the door and you can step inside, buy a ticket if you want to, walk through. Hang out for a minute. Then you can say you were really there."

She thought about that for a moment. That would make her feel less like a liar. "That might help. But I can't be seen there with you."

"I'll wait in the car, and then we'll go out to eat. There's a new restaurant in Savannah that I've been wanting to try. I've heard a lot about it." His voice was a lazy rumble that made her heart flip into a triple-time cadence.

"But we could be seen there too. I really don't want to make Morgan and Jonathan mad. Maybe we ought to stay here, just sit out in the boathouse and look at the water and talk."

Those eyes. She watched them laugh as if he loved the idea. "Sounds good to me. Just the two of us, alone."

She looked away quickly. Maybe that was a mistake—to be alone with him. "Or maybe we could get a hot dog on the beach and go for a walk. Not a date, so I wouldn't really be lying that much."

"And don't forget that Crystal's having her party tonight. We could still go if you wanted."

She laughed bitterly. "Yeah, like I'd really want to go to that."

"All right," he said, "but first things first. We need to eat, and I don't want to buy you a hotdog. You'll think I'm cheap."

Cheap? In his brand-new Firebird that made her feel like Somebody?

"Come on," he said. "We'll go into Savannah and eat at this little place, and we won't call it a date. It'll be just two friends interviewing each other."

"Interviewing?" she asked.

"Yeah. You used to work for the paper, right? Just pretend you're interviewing me and I'm interviewing you."

"We're playing games with words," she said. "Trying to make me feel better about telling lies to people I love."

"Well, we're playing games with words whether we sit at the beach or go out to eat. You're on a date with me, Sadie. Face it. You lied to Morgan and Jonathan, but it was for a good reason."

She didn't like the reality of that, but she wasn't about to back out now. "Okay, let's go eat."

"Then when we get back it'll be getting dark and I'll drop you by the dance. You can go in and make your little appearance and come back to the car. Then we'll go sit on the beach and talk. By then it'll be too dark and nobody will recognize us."

It sounded good to her, so she tried to relax as he started the car and pulled away from the boathouse.

They sat over mozzarella sticks and hamburgers, and Sadie listened to funny stories about Trevor's charades with his teachers in school.

Finally he took her back to Cape Refuge, to the Methodist church. She ran in and paid for a ticket, walked around the rec hall and heard the band, saw the people dancing and having fun, and quickly headed back out to his car.

He drove them to a public parking lot on the side of the beach, and they walked across the sand and sat on a blanket he'd brought, watching the waves hit against the shore. Not too far away they could see the firelight of Crystal's party. The music made its way all the way up to where they were, and she heard the sounds of laughter and people having fun. She looked in that direction and wondered if Trevor wished he were there.

"I heard that Crystal's parents let her have alcohol at her parties," Sadie said.

"Oh, sure," Trevor said. "They're real laid-back. They don't get all hung up over the stuff most parents do."

She didn't know what to think about that. Were Morgan and Jonathan "hung up"? Her own mother sure hadn't been.

"What about yours?" she asked. "Do they let you drink?"

"They let me do what I want," he said. "They trust me."

Somehow she had expected him to say that, and as she turned it over in her mind, it seemed reasonable and healthy.

He put his arm around her so naturally that it was as if they'd been going out for a very long time. It made her feel as if she belonged to someone, as if she had worth and value, as if she wasn't the school outcast whom everyone wanted to avoid.

"So when do you have to be home?"

"Ten. That's when the dance is over."

"All right." He looked over at the party still going on. The music drifted up on the wind.

"You're going to go to the party, aren't you?" she asked.

He shrugged. "Well, why shouldn't I? I mean if you're not going to be with me, I've got to have something to do."

She knew he was right. She couldn't expect him to go home and moon over her. She supposed it was fine. She just hoped word didn't get around that he had been out with her earlier tonight. She hoped she could trust him to keep the secret.

As he walked her back toward Hanover House, she realized how much she dreaded the secret she was keeping. The more people knew about it, the more likely she would be to get into trouble. She didn't want Morgan and Jonathan to be disappointed in her.

He held her hand as they walked back, and finally he stopped across from Hanover House and kissed her on the lips. This time it was a slow, mournful kiss, a kiss that said good-bye . . . but not for long.

"Say you'll go out with me again," he said.

"When?"

"Tomorrow night."

Sighing, she looked up at her house. "I don't think I can come up with another lie for tomorrow night. I'm going to get caught."

He pulled her closer. "It'll be okay," he said. "Just tell them you're going for a walk along the beach. Some friends of mine are having another party tomorrow night. Don't worry, Crystal won't be there. It's mostly friends I know from my boating club. For the most part they're college-aged, so you probably won't even know them."

"I don't know," she said. "The more people that see me with you . . ."

"What do you think, they're going to call Morgan up and say, 'Oh, by the way, I saw Sadie out with Trevor last night'? These are the kind of people who mind their own business."

He tipped her chin up and kissed her again, and she melted in it, washed in a tide of protection, propriety, possession. She liked the way that felt.

"All right," she whispered. "I'll meet you out at the South Beach Pier at eight. How's that sound?"

"Eight? That's too late."

"It has to be late," she said. "I'll tell them that I'm going to my room to read and that I'm turning in early, and then I'll sneak out when they're not looking and I'll meet you, okay?"

He chuckled. "I kind of like this clandestine stuff. Makes me feel real decadent."

Decadent wasn't something she'd ever wanted to be, but she dismissed that thought. "I probably can't stay long. I don't want to make any noise coming back in, and the later I get there, the more locked up everything will be. They have rules."

"All right," he said. "So we'll do whatever you have to do to keep from getting caught. I'll see you tomorrow night."

Sadie floated back into the house. Morgan waited in the den, hemming a skirt that she had on her lap. She had made it for Sadie to wear to church. "Hey," she said as she came in.

"Hey, there!" Morgan sounded oblivious. "How was the dance?"

Sadie had trouble looking her in the eye. "Fine."

"Did you like the band?"

"It was okay."

Morgan stared at her for a moment, and her smile faded. She got up and came to face her, and Sadie wondered if she could see the deceit on her face. "Honey, what's wrong? Did something happen?"

Sadie forced a smile. "No, really. It was fun. I'm just tired."

Morgan looked skeptical. "Then you'll go back to the next one?"

"Maybe." She started up the stairs. "Is Caleb asleep?"

"Yeah, I put him to bed a couple of hours ago."

Sadie stood there awkwardly, knowing that she had guilt written all over her face. "I think I'll go on to bed then," she said.

"Okay, goodnight, honey."

"Goodnight." She didn't look back at the worried expression on Morgan's face as she hurried to her room.

CHAPTER

Cade woke, still locked in the tiny room, with the pain of his bullet wounds radiating through his body. His sheets reeked with the smell of blood, and cold air blew from the vent over his bed. He shivered and tried to sit up.

She had taken out the toilet lid and the commode seat, so he couldn't use them as weapons. He sat up, wincing at the stabbing pain in his side. Slowly, he slid his legs off the edge of his bed. His broken left leg was swollen and bloody, and as he brought it to the floor, the pain exploded.

He imagined his body splitting apart into a million directions, then falling like shrapnel to the concrete floor. He fell back onto the thin mattress.

He was going to die here.

From the foggy depths of his brain he groped for Scripture, something to cling to like a hand, something to remind him that he could make it. He had memorized much Scripture in his life. Wayne Owens had seen to that.

"O LORD, do not . . . do not rebuke me . . . in your anger . . . or discipline me in your wrath. Be merciful to me, LORD, for I am faint; O LORD, . . . heal me, for my bones are in agony. My soul is in anguish."

He had learned that passage from Psalm 6 when he'd made it his business to memorize as many psalms as he could. He'd never expected to need it so much. Every morning, he had met Wayne at Cricket's, and over coffee he would recite the Scripture he'd memorized the day before. Wayne had committed to learning the same passages, and they had recited them together, their eyes transfixed on each other.

Oh, how he missed Wayne.

"How long, O LORD, how long?" His throat was raspy, hoarse, almost too weak to be heard. "Turn, O LORD, and deliver me . . . save me because of your unfailing love. No one remembers you when he is dead. Who praises you from the grave?"

He had often wondered if David understood about heaven, that there was a place of joy and peace where our hearts would overflow. If he had, would he have written those words?

Yes, maybe, Cade thought. Maybe from the depths of his own danger, he had only seen death as being a dreaded end. Cade understood that.

"I am worn out from groaning; all night long I flood my bed with weeping and drench my couch with tears. My eyes grow weak with sorrow; they fail because of all my foes."

Yes, he had foes, though he didn't know what they wanted with him. Whether they would murder him in revenge for the life he had taken, or use him for some other evil intention, he didn't know.

"Away from me, all you who do evil, . . . for the LORD has heard my weeping. . . . The LORD has heard my cry for mercy; . . . the Lord accepts my prayer."

Peace calmed him in the midst of his pain, and he knew that God heard the Scripture he prayed aloud.

"All my enemies will be ashamed and dismayed; . . . they will turn back in sudden disgrace."

Let it be so, Lord, his mind cried out. *Please turn them back in sudden disgrace.*

He wondered who was looking for him. He pictured Blair sitting at her computer day and night, pulling up databases and searching for answers—the armchair detective who should have been a cop herself. Would this be more reason for her to never acknowledge God? Would this be yet more evidence that no one sat on a sovereign throne, governing the universe?

That thought filled him with more despair than his own imprisonment.

He closed his eyes and wondered if she'd seen that sham of a letter he'd been forced to write. Did she believe he'd been hiding some secret girlfriend?

Surely not. Too much had passed between them. She must know that she was the woman he'd been waiting for. Even though he'd never said it, never even acted on it . . . she must know.

He had long ago resolved in his heart not to break God's heart by marrying an unbeliever. That wasn't the kind of life he wanted for himself. How could he become one with a woman whose philosophies and life goals were so radically different from his own?

That meant that he remained a bachelor, biding his time and praying for God to change Blair's heart. So far it hadn't happened. The wait had been long.

But she must sense his feelings for her, and in his heart, he sensed hers too. She wouldn't believe he'd eloped, would she? She'd never buy that.

But if she did have doubts, there was always his signature to clue her in. Blair knew he never went by Matt.

Please, Lord, don't let her believe that letter.

He heard a scraping sound and knew that Ann was coming again. The bookshelves were being moved, the door unlocked. He lay there, defenseless, knowing that he could never make a run for it now.

She came in cautiously, checking to make sure he hadn't found some kind of weapon to waylay her before she could get to him. He wished . . . oh, he wished . . .

"I brought you some water," she said, handing him that two-liter bottle again. It was drugged, he knew. If he drank it, he could be out for days.

"Thank you," he whispered. He set it down on the concrete floor next to the bed.

"Drink it now," she said.

He shook his head. "I'm going to throw up. I'll drink it later."

"You need food."

He could tell from her tone that she had no intentions of bringing him any. Not now.

He looked up at her. "Mrs. Clark, I need a doctor. I've lost a lot of blood, and the bullet shattered the bone in my leg ..."

"No doctor," she said. "That doesn't fit into my plan."

"So what is your plan?" He gritted the words through his clenched teeth. "What are you holding me for? Ransom?"

She laughed then. "One ransom note and they'd be on me in thirty seconds. No, not ransom. I doubt if anyone in Cape Refuge would pay it anyway. They all believe you ran off with a woman. It's all over the news. They're not even looking for you anymore."

Now he really did feel like he was going to throw up. "Then what do you plan to do with me?"

"I plan to kill you." Her tone was matter-of-fact. "But not yet. You're still of some use to me."

She was crazy or evil, or both.

"I didn't kill your husband on purpose. And he was shot first. Maybe you shot him."

Her face was stone cold. "He shot himself."

"I don't think so, judging by where I am right now." He caught his breath, shivered at the pain. He watched with a chill as she left him there on his bloody sheets, locked the door, and scraped the bookshelves back in front of the door.

He forced himself up on his good leg. Pain shot through him as he grabbed the water bottle, unscrewed the top, and dumped its contents into the toilet. Then he put the empty bottle in the tank, where the clean water flowed in, and filled it up. Desperately, he drank a third of it.

Then he hopped back to his bed, his nerve endings screaming out with each jolt, and fell back onto his rancid sheets.

A yellow lamp burned in Blair's office, casting threatening shadows on the walls and ceiling. She checked the clock—2:00 A.M. She'd been at this for hours and had come up with little information. She'd learned that William Clark was a contract lawyer who worked independently. He had no police record and had led an uneventful life up until the day he stepped out in front of Cade's car.

And she'd found next to nothing about Ann.

She sat back in her chair and rubbed her aching forehead. Regardless of her spotless record, Ann Clark knew something about Cade. He could be somewhere in that house. There had to be a bomb shelter the police hadn't seen, a tornado room, something somewhere that they hadn't run across.

The Clarks didn't own any property other than the house at Washington Square. The woman could have him in some vacant structure that she didn't own, of course. A warehouse somewhere or an empty house, or maybe that of a friend who was helping her.

She got up and walked out of the office into the library lit only by a small recessed bulb near the door. The smell of dusty books permeated the room, and her heels clicked on the hardwood floor as she paced, trying to make some sense of it all. What did she have?

Ann Clark had probably been angry about her husband's death and might have sought revenge. It was clear that she had met with Cade on the morning of his disappearance, that he'd gotten into her car, and that he'd never been seen again since.

But that still didn't tell her where he was.

Her stomach sank as if it contained concrete, and her breathing seemed labored and short. The thought that Cade was dead, lying somewhere undiscovered, shot through her. Quickly she shook it away. She couldn't think that way. He had only been gone a few days. He was a strong man, tough and capable, not prone to being bested by a hundred-ten-pound woman.

She went back in and turned off the computer and the lights, locked the door and walked across to her own home. Before going in, she stood out and looked across the street to the water glistening under the moonlight, stars sprinkling without number across its black expanse. Tears came to her eyes, and her heart swelled with emotion. And in her despair, she did something she had rarely done before.

"God, I don't know if you're even there," she whispered, "and if you are, I know you don't have any reason to answer anything *I* ask. But Cade's one of yours. You didn't save my parents, and I don't know why. But save him. Save him, please, if you're really there."

A strong wind blew up from the water, sweeping her hair back from her face and whispering through the leaves on the trees above her. She wiped a tear from her face and felt the hard scaly skin of her burn scars under her fingertips.

It reminded her again of that day Cade had touched her scars, after she'd called God a divine terrorist who enjoyed wreaking havoc on people's lives. Her anger about her scars and the secrets surrounding them had come out that day. Cade had looked at her with puzzlement on his face. Touching her scars with his gentle fingertips, he'd whispered, "I don't even see them anymore."

No one had ever been that intimate with her. Even her parents had avoided touching the scars she was so sensitive about. No one else would have dared do what Cade had done that day. In a lot of ways he had rescued her then, pulled her out of the pit of despair, given her a reason to stay in Cape Refuge and a reason to think she had some value to the people who lived here. She wished she could return the favor now and pull him out of whatever pit he was in.

"Don't let him be dead," she whispered out loud. "Please don't let him be dead."

When she finally went into her house and got ready for bed, she knew she was in for another night of lying awake and filing through the possibilities, dozing off and dreaming of some great Avenger chasing Cade down the road to the City of Refuge.

In her dream, he was overtaken, and left to die outside the city walls, only inches from the gate.

*T*he lies came more easily Saturday night.

Sadie waited until Caleb was bathed and put to bed, the dishes were clean in the kitchen, and all her responsibilities were done. Then she excused herself to go and read herself to sleep. She was very tired, she said. Though Morgan had looked at her with confusion and a little suspicion, she thought she had pulled it off.

She had finally sneaked out the front door, while everyone else was in the kitchen, and headed across the street to the beach and down toward the place where Trevor had told her to meet him.

The sun had set, and the sky at twilight billowed with lavender clouds, waiting for dark. God's handiwork, Sadie thought. Just like she was God's handiwork, inscribed on the palm of his hand.

Guilt surged through her again.

What kind of ungrateful daughter was she, to take the goodness God had shown her through Morgan and Jonathan and throw it back in his face?

She almost turned back, but then she saw him, elbows braced on the rail of the pier, wind teasing through his hair. He was watching her approach with a smile on his face. All thoughts of turning back fled from her mind as he came back down the pier and met her on the sand.

"Hey, gorgeous," he said.

She smiled. "Hey. Am I late?"

"Not too." He kissed her, melting the residue of her guilt. She pulled back, looked up at him, and decided that any trouble this brought her was worth it.

"Come on." He took her hand and pulled her across the sand. "The party doesn't start until after nine," he said. "But we can head on over."

Their shoulders bumped together. "I'm a little nervous."

"Why? A girl like you? You've been to parties before."

She shrugged. "Yeah, but I'm not the same person I was back in Atlanta. And I haven't really been to any in Cape Refuge." The warm breeze flirted with her hair. "I wish we could just skip it."

"But then you wouldn't meet my friends. Come on, Sadie, you can do it. I want to show you off a little."

The idea that anyone considered her something to show off flattered her, and she felt pink warmth climbing her cheeks. He swept her hair behind her ear. Something like an electric shock went through her, jolting her heart. How did that work? she wondered. How could his simple touch make her heart skip beats?

"So you said these aren't your friends from school?" she asked. "Where do you know them from?"

"Here and there," he said. "But some of them are from school. You know how it is. Most of the parties on the island start out with a small list and wind up full of crashers, so there's no telling who might come."

She pictured the kinds of parties her mother used to have. They'd been much the same way. "So they're a real party crowd, huh? Are there any Christians?"

He laughed. "I don't know. If they are, they don't talk about it."

That would be a no, she thought. She slowed her step and looked up at him. "What about you? Do you believe in God?"

He shrugged. "I think there's something up there. I'm not sure what."

She frowned and tried to process that. "What about the Bible? Do you believe in that?"

He laughed again, as if he thought she was cute. "How can I? I'm not going to let some ancient book dictate how I live. No, I don't believe in it. I have my own truth."

For a moment, Sadie walked quietly beside him, battling those guilt feelings ambushing her again. "But Jonathan says that the Bible is the living, active Word of God. How can you know God if you don't know his Word?"

He grinned again. "I don't believe it *is* his word, if he's even there. If there's really a God, he would have more respect for us than to set us up a list of rules. He would want us to be happy and to do what we think is right."

"My mother did what she thought was right, and she let all our lives get messed up. Her boyfriend, Jack, did what he felt was right, and he nearly killed me."

"Come on, Sadie. You don't think they really thought those things were right, do you?"

Darkness was fading over the night sky. "But see, that's the thing. If they don't believe in any system of right or wrong, then who's to say those things were wrong. *I* might think they were wrong, and *you* might think they were wrong. But *they* didn't. They did what they thought was okay . . . for them. But the things that made them happy—drugs and parties and stuff—weren't good for my little brother or me. People need a clear-cut system of right and wrong. And we can't just decide that as we go along."

Even as she spoke, she recognized the hypocrisy in her words. Wasn't that what she was doing? Justifying her sins and making it up as she went along?

Her spirits sank again. He seemed to sense that and stopped walking. Turning her to face him, he whispered, "You're cute when you talk religion."

Before she could muster a retort, he kissed her, a long, disarming kiss that made her forget that guilt again.

When it was time, they walked up the beach until they came to the condo where a party was in progress. Loud music spilled out onto the beach behind it. A bonfire raged in the middle of the sand, and people danced together on one side of it and sat in clusters around the other side. It looked harmless enough.

In the golden light of the bonfire, Trevor introduced her to a few of his friends, then left her alone to go get her a drink. She stood awkwardly among his friends, trying to look accessible and not nervous.

"What in the world are *you* doing here?"

The voice chilled her, and she swung around and saw Crystal Lewis. Her heart crashed.

She lifted her chin. "I came with Trevor."

"Trevor?" The girl's lips curled in contempt. "I thought you said you weren't going out with him."

"I changed my mind." Sadie started to walk away, but the girl grabbed her arm.

"He only wants one thing from you and you know it. Everybody on Cape Refuge has heard about where you came from and what you were like in Atlanta."

"You don't know anything about me," Sadie said.

"Well, we know that a person who grew up with a mother in prison and a stepfather with a crystal meth lab sure doesn't have lily-white morals. And there you live in the Hanover House with a bunch of ex-cons."

Sadie jerked out of her grasp and started to walk around the fire to get away from her, but Crystal followed.

"You don't have any right to be here, you know. Nobody wants you here. Trevor, maybe, but we both know what *he* wants. If you don't deliver, you're going to wind up all by yourself anyway. And if you do deliver, it's going to be all over town because everybody is going to know."

Sadie saw Trevor heading toward her, so she met him halfway. Crystal saw him, too, and fell away.

He brought her a drink. "You okay?"

"You told me Crystal wouldn't be here," she said. "You told me this wouldn't be the friends from school."

"Well, I told you that lots of people crash. Why? What did she say to you?"

"Nothing." She took a drink from the yellow paper cup he'd given her. It had a sweet citrus taste with a bit of a bite. "What is this?"

"Punch. You like it?"

She took another drink. "Yeah, it's not bad."

"Good," he said. "It's some of Brian's special concoction."

She wanted to cry. "It's not alcoholic, is it?"

His grin told her that it was, but he pulled her close again and put his mouth close to hers. "What if it was? You can handle it, Sadie. You're a big girl."

She started to pour the drink out onto the sand, but then she saw Crystal sitting in the firelight, muttering to her friends. They were all watching him hold her.

She didn't want them to see her acting like a prude, so she drank it, telling herself she wouldn't have any more after this one.

But with each gulp of the sweet liquid, her inhibitions fell. She stopped caring what Crystal and her friends thought of her, and she relaxed and danced with Trevor. Not nearly as tense as she'd been earlier, she actually started getting to know his friends and having fun with them. He brought her another drink, and another, and finally she lost count and just surrendered herself to its numbing power.

She would draw the line when she needed to, she thought. But not now. Not yet.

CHAPTER

*T*he sound of knocking cut into Morgan's sleep. Groggy, she sat up and looked through the darkness, hoping it had been a dream.

The knocking came again.

"Tell me no one's knocking at our door," Jonathan muttered.

"I'll get it." Morgan slipped out of bed and cracked the door open. Light from the hall spilled in.

Karen stood there with a distraught look on her face.

"Karen, are you all right?"

"I'm sorry to wake you up again, Morgan, but my water broke. And I'm having labor pains again. I called the doctor and he said I need to get to the hospital."

Morgan's brain came to full attention. "Okay, then we need to hurry." She flicked on the light, and Jonathan threw his arm over his eyes. "Jonathan, wake up! Karen's in labor."

"I heard." He got out of bed, looking disheveled and disoriented. "Just let me get dressed."

557

"Is your bag still packed from the other night?" Morgan asked her.

"Yeah, packed and ready to go."

"Okay. We'll be ready in five minutes and we'll head out."

Morgan ran back into her room and got dressed. "Will you drive us, Jonathan? It's one in the morning."

"Sure." He still wasn't awake enough. She wished they had time to make a pot of coffee. "Wake Sadie up to let her know where we'll be. Just in case we're not home by morning."

Morgan buttoned the last button on her shirt and raced out of the room. She got to Sadie's room, knocked lightly so she wouldn't disturb the other tenants. When there was no answer, she opened the door and leaned inside. "Sadie? Honey, wake up a minute. I have to talk to you."

There was no answer, so Morgan opened the door farther. The lamplight from the hall spilled in, revealing a bed that hadn't been slept in. Sadie wasn't here.

She went back to her own room and found Jonathan brushing his teeth. "Jonathan, Sadie isn't in her room. She hasn't slept in her bed. It's still made up."

"What?" He spat out the toothpaste. "Well, go look downstairs. Maybe she couldn't sleep and is reading or something."

Morgan dashed downstairs and looked in the kitchen. No sign of Sadie. When she wasn't in the parlor or the den, either, she started to get worried.

Karen had already brought her suitcase down and was waiting in the parlor.

"Karen, how long have you been up?"

"I never went to bed," she admitted. "I was having pains, so I just stayed up. I been down here watching TV since you went to bed."

"Have you seen Sadie? Did she come down for anything?"

"No, I haven't seen her at all. I figured she was sleeping."

Jonathan came down the stairs, and Morgan looked up at him. "She's not here, Jonathan. *Where is she?* It's one o'clock in the morning!"

Jonathan looked over her shoulder to Karen. "I don't know, but we'd better hurry."

Morgan turned back to Karen and saw her doubled over with a contraction, and she remembered the urgency of their mission. She ran to the woman's side and stroked her back. "Okay, honey. We're going." She turned back to Jonathan. "Jonathan, someone has to stay here and look for Sadie. I'll go to the hospital, and you call the police or something. She couldn't have just vanished! Something's happened to her."

He followed them to the door. "Do you think she could have snuck out?"

"No way," Morgan said. "That's not like her. She wouldn't have gone out without telling us."

Trying to keep her heart from giving in to the sudden terror that had overtaken her, she walked Karen out to the car. Jonathan followed, scanning the beach across the street for some sign of Sadie.

"Don't worry, Morgan. I'll find her."

"You have to, Jonathan. She could be in danger, like Cade." Tears came to her eyes, and she hugged him quickly. "Oh, Jonathan, find her."

She heard Karen moaning in the passenger seat and quickly ran to the driver's side. As she pulled out of the driveway, she saw Jonathan standing on the front porch, trying to decide what to do.

Just after one in the morning, Trevor suggested they leave the party and walk a little way down the beach to be alone. It sounded good to Sadie, even though she found she couldn't walk in a straight line. He seemed to enjoy steadying her.

She had never laughed so much in her life.

When they'd gotten far enough away from the crowd, he sat down in the sand and pulled her down next to him. She lay back and pillowed her head in the sand.

"You've had fun tonight, haven't you?" he asked her with a grin.

"Yeah, I did." Her words slurred, amusing her. "I love your friends. They're great."

He lay on his side in the sand and looked down at her. "So are you."

"Yeah?" she asked, grinning up at him.

"Yeah." He leaned over and kissed her, long and hard and hungry, and she felt him moving closer, his hands groping where they shouldn't. . . .

Despite her buzz, an alarm went off in her mind.

But she didn't want to heed it. She wanted to let him kiss her just the way he was, wanted to feel that she belonged just a little while longer . . .

Sliding her arms around him, she surrendered fully to that kiss . . .

Jonathan called the police department as soon as Morgan was gone. Jim Henry answered.

"Jim, this is Jonathan Cleary. I have an emergency. Our foster daughter, Sadie, has disappeared."

"Disappeared?" Jim sounded irritated. "What do you mean by 'disappeared'?"

"I mean that she went up to her room to read and go to bed around eight o'clock tonight, and just now we checked and she hadn't even slept in her bed."

"Well, that goin' to bed at eight business shoulda been your first clue. How old is she? Sixteen?"

"Seventeen."

He breathed out a laugh, and Jonathan knew he wasn't taking this seriously. "Jonathan, I know you ain't been doin' this parenting thing that long, but when a seventeen-year-old goes to bed at eight o'clock, you can bet they got somethin' up their sleeve. She ain't disappeared. She's just gone out. You mark my word. She'll come home."

Appalled at the man's dismissive attitude, Jonathan gritted his teeth. "Do I have to call Joe at home, Jim? Because my best friend is missing right now and no one can find him. Now my daughter vanishes. There's a pattern here, man. Sadie would not just sneak out!"

"Hey, you don't have to get all huffy now. First time my nephew snuck out my brother felt the same way, Jonathan, but I'm telling you, she's probably at that party down at the McRae Condominiums. I been gettin' complaint calls from neighbors all night. Went over there myself to check things out, and the place was crawlin' with teenagers. I tried to break it up and get them to turn down the music, but you know how that goes."

Jonathan clutched the phone to his ear. "Sadie wouldn't go there."

"Think again, brother. You'll see. Just give it a little time, and she'll get herself home."

"And what if she doesn't?" he yelled again. "What if she's been kidnapped, too?"

"Any sign of breaking and entering in your house, Jonathan?"

"Well, I haven't looked, really."

"Broke windows? Locks?"

"No, I don't think so."

"Any sign of a struggle?" Jim asked.

Jonathan wanted to ram his fist through the phone. Then they'd have signs of a struggle, all right. "Look, if you're not going to do anything then I'm going down to that party. If she's there, I'll find her!"

"Yeah, that's a good idea. You let me know, you hear?"

Jonathan threw the phone down.

CHAPTER

*T*hat alarm kept clanging in Sadie's head as Trevor's kiss grew deeper. His hands roamed, and she tried to get hold of them and stop them. But he slipped them free and groped some more.

Breaking free of the kiss, she rolled away from him and got up on her knees. "I have to go."

Trevor looked stricken. "Why? Nobody even knows you're gone. It's not like you have a curfew."

"I just have to go." She wobbled to her feet and straightened her blouse.

"Aw, man, I didn't think you were some prude who'd tease me and then turn to ice."

She looked down at him. "Ice? Just because I won't do what you want? And I didn't tease you."

"Right." He got up and dusted the sand off of himself. "Just forget it."

"I will." On the edge of tears, she started walking away from him. He didn't follow.

The ocean whispered against the shore, reminding her that she was small, insignificant, against the world that seemed to converge against her. She remembered another time that she had been on the beach at night, utterly alone. She had been injured and had fled from home. With no place to stay and not a soul here who knew her name, she had slept on this very beach.

That old loneliness welled up inside her again, and she started to cry as she headed home. She should never have come out tonight. She shouldn't have gone to the party. She shouldn't have gotten drunk.

What had she been about to do?

The question resounded through her mind, blustering up on a wind of paranoia. She had damaged her relationship with Morgan, with Jonathan, with God.

She heard Crystal's voice, cold and condemning, as she'd accused Trevor of wanting only one thing from Sadie. And there she'd been, almost willing to give it to him.

She managed to make her way to the part of the beach across from Hanover House, stumbled across the street, and got up to the porch. Realizing that her gait was still unsteady, she took a slow quiet step up, then tripped over the last step and fell facedown on the porch. Putting her finger to her mouth and shushing herself, she got up and fumbled with the front door lock, got it to open, then stepped inside.

Jonathan stood just inside the door, gaping down at her. "Sadie!"

The light came on, shining overhead like a beacon glaring in her eyes. "I . . . I was just out for a walk."

"At one-thirty in the morning?" Jonathan's voice wobbled with anger. "Sadie, where have you been? I called the police, I was so worried about you. I was just about to come out looking for you."

She backed against the wall to steady herself, and Jonathan took her shoulders and stared into her face. "Sadie, you've been drinking."

"No. I wou'nt do that." She wished her words would come out the way she intended them to.

His face was blurry. "I smell it, Sadie. Were you out with that boy?"

Sadie stiffened and tried to pull herself together. She couldn't fade now. She had to convince Jonathan she'd done nothing wrong. "What boy?"

"Trevor Beal. Sadie, were you with him?"

She searched her mind for an answer that would satisfy him, but her brain wasn't operating the way she needed. "I was with a lot of people." There, that ought to do it. She started to the stairs. "I have to go to bed now." Grabbing the banister, she started up.

"Sadie, don't walk away from me when I'm talking to you." She'd never heard his voice that angry before, so she turned back around and sat down on the step. "I asked you where you'd been."

"On the beach," she said. "Thasall, Jonathan. I think I'm gonna be sick. Can we talk about this in the morning?"

Jonathan sighed, and she hoped that meant that he was going to back off and give her a break. He came up the stairs, took her arm, and helped her the rest of the way up. When they reached the second floor, Sadie broke free of him and stumbled into the bathroom, locked it behind her, then bent over the toilet and wretched. Still nauseated, she sat on the floor and waited for it to pass.

CHAPTER

*B*y the time they got to the hospital, Karen's contractions were three minutes apart. There was no question about it. The baby was going to come tonight.

As the nurses prepped Karen and hooked her up to the IV and monitors, Morgan took a moment to find a pay phone in the hall. She called home, and Jonathan answered on the second ring.

"Jonathan, have you found her yet?"

"She's home," he said.

Morgan almost collapsed in relief. "Thank goodness. Where was she?"

A moment of silence followed. "She snuck out, Morgan. She was with Trevor Beal."

Morgan's heart plunged. For a moment, she couldn't speak. "Are you sure, Jonathan?"

"Oh, yeah. I heard it from the horse's mouth. Slurred, though it was."

Morgan froze. Was there really more? Not just the sneaking out? "What do you mean 'slurred'?"

567

"She'd been drinking, Morgan," he said. "She came home drunk."

Morgan backed against the wall and put her hand over her face as she clutched the phone to her ear. "Are you sure?"

"Yes. She could hardly walk, and she reeked of it."

"She knows what chemical abuse and alcohol have done to her family. Why would she do such a thing?"

"We'll have to wait until morning to ask her," he said. "She's not in any shape to discuss it right now."

One of the nurses came out of Karen's room, just up the hall. She had to get in there. "Honey, are you all right?" Morgan asked.

"I just feel like the recipient of a one-two punch right in the gut. But yeah, I'm fine. You be fine too, okay?"

She sighed. "I've got to go. Karen needs me."

She hung up the phone and pressed her forehead against it. Not Sadie. She hadn't rebelled like that. There had to be an explanation. Finally, she went back to Karen's room. The woman lay on her side, her eyes closed as she suffered through another of her contractions. A nurse stood by her, monitoring the strength of it.

"How's she doing?" Morgan asked.

The nurse glanced back at her. "She's already dilated six centimeters, so she's pretty far along. I don't think this is going to take very long. It's too late for an epidural, I'm afraid."

She watched as the numbers on the monitor went down, and Karen began to relax out of her coil. Morgan stepped up to her side and pushed her hair back from her face. "You're gonna be okay, Karen. It's gonna be all right."

Karen looked as if she braced herself for the pain about to come again.

Morgan made herself comfortable on the chair beside Karen's bed, and trying to keep her mind off of Sadie, prepared for a long night.

Not much later, the nurses declared that Karen had dilated enough to go into the delivery room, and the doctor was called.

"Don't leave me," Karen said, squeezing her hand. "I'm scared."

"There's nothing to be scared of." Morgan stroked Karen's damp forehead. "You're participating in a miracle. Soon you'll meet your child."

"Come with me, Morgan. Please, I need somebody with me."

A sense of excitement jolted up inside her at the idea. She would love to see a little baby coming into the world.

"Is it all right?" she asked the nurses who were moving her to a gurney.

"Sure," she said. "You can be her coach."

"I don't know how to coach. I haven't had classes or anything."

"Honey, you just hold her hand and remind her to breathe."

They went into the antiseptic room, bright with fluorescent lights and cold as winter. Morgan wished they could warm it up and lower the lights for the child.

The doctor got there within minutes. After one quick examination, he declared that it was time for Karen to push.

Karen squeezed her eyes shut and clamped her hand on Morgan's, groaning with the effort.

Morgan hung on, wishing there was something more that she could do. She wondered how it would be when she was in Karen's place. Would Jonathan know what to do? Would he want to videotape? Capture the first breath of their child?

She yearned to have the opportunity to find out.

"The baby's crowning," the doctor said as Karen came out of the contraction. "Just a few more minutes."

Karen fell back on her pillow, trying to catch her breath.

"A couple more pushes and we'll be home free."

They adjusted the mirror over the delivery table so that Karen and Morgan could see.

Then the contraction came, and Karen rose up, gritting her teeth and bearing down. Morgan watched the mirror.

The head emerged, covered with wet, black curly hair. "It's coming!" she cried. "Come on, Karen. Keep pushing."

She watched its little shoulders emerge, then its tiny purple body.

Karen gave a final groan as the baby came fully into the world. Then she fell back and began to weep as she caught her first glimpse. "My baby!"

The doctor turned it over, and Morgan saw that it was a boy, and his face was the most beautiful sight she'd ever seen. She burst into tears.

"Oh, Karen, it's a boy. He's so beautiful."

As the doctor suctioned his mouth, the baby began to scream.

Morgan wept as they wiped him off, wrapped him up, and handed him to Karen. The woman took him like a precious gift and brought him close. Morgan touched his tiny little foot as his mother introduced herself.

"Hey, there, Emory," she said in a soft, weepy voice. "Oh, you're a precious thing. Look at you."

Emory. Morgan hadn't thought before to ask Karen if she had a name. She wiped her eyes and breathed in a sob. "He looks like an Emory."

Karen smiled up at her. "Emory, I want you to meet your aunt Morgan." She handed the baby to her.

Carefully, Morgan gathered him into her arms and looked down into eyes that seemed to understand everything he saw. Every maternal hormone she possessed fired within her. She started to laugh through her tears.

What a miracle. What a joy. What a privilege to have witnessed this.

Lord, let it be me sometime soon.

When they had taken away the baby and put Karen back in her room, Morgan's exhaustion caught up with her.

"You go home now, Morgan," Karen said. "It's Sunday and you have church and all. You need to get some rest. I'll be fine here."

Morgan didn't want to leave. What if they brought the baby in, and she had another chance to hold him?

Then she realized that it wasn't her child. Karen needed time alone with her baby. "Are you sure?"

"Sure, I'm sure," she said. "I'll probably sleep until they bring him to me, and then I've requested that they let me keep him in here with me all day."

"Oh." The word came out softly, and she thought that was what she would have done, too. She would have wanted the baby close, so she could be the one meeting all his needs. "Are you sure you're up to that?"

"If I'm not, I can change my mind, but I want my baby with me. They said it was my call."

Morgan didn't blame her. She got up and found her purse. Every bone in her body seemed to weigh twice its usual weight. The night they'd been here for the false alarm had exhausted her enough, and she'd never quite caught up. Now she felt too weary to even walk to the car.

But it had been well worth it. She kissed Karen on the forehead. "You rest now, and I'll come back this afternoon. Call if you need anything."

As she drove home, she realized that motherhood was one of the greatest blessings of all. She hoped Karen realized it.

Why hadn't God chosen to bless her that way?

As quickly as she'd asked the question, she kicked herself. He *had* blessed her, with Caleb and Sadie. But she hadn't been a very good steward of that blessing, if Sadie had come home drunk this morning. She didn't blame God for not trusting her with a baby of her own.

She tried to think like a good mother. There were going to have to be consequences. Sadie needed to understand exactly what she'd done. But how? What would good parents do to teach a teenager to stay on the right path?

When she reached Hanover House, she found Jonathan already up with Caleb, feeding him in the kitchen. Jonathan had already had his shower, and wore his pressed black "preacher" trousers with a white T-shirt.

"What did she have?" he asked with a smile.

"It was a boy," she said. "A beautiful boy. Eight pounds. In perfect health." She dropped her purse on the table and smiled at her husband. "Oh, Jonathan, you should have seen it. The birth was such a miracle, and that beautiful little body slid out, and those arms and legs were kicking and moving, and he let out this scream that told us he was healthy and whole . . ."

He took her hand and pulled her down next to him. "I'm glad you got to see it."

Tears welled in her eyes, and her throat seemed to close up.

"How's Karen?" he asked.

"Exhausted."

"Like you?"

"I think she's a little tireder than I am." She reached for Caleb. "Come here, you." He laughed and reached back, and she pulled him out of the high chair, wiped his face, and kissed his plump cheek. "You hear anything from Sadie this morning?"

"Nope. I'm sure she's zonked out. I was trying to decide whether to wake her up for church."

"Oh, yes," Morgan said. "She's definitely getting up for church."

"Well, she's not going to be in any mood to worship."

"I don't care," Morgan said. "She needs to understand that we go to church in this family. We arrange our Saturday nights so that we'll be in good shape to worship on Sunday morning. And if she chooses to do what she did last night, she'll pay for it in the morning. But we're not letting her off the hook for church."

"Okay," he said. "I'm with you. So you're going too?"

She wilted with Caleb in her lap, and propped her chin on his little head. "I have to if I'm making her. I'll sleep later." She settled her tired eyes on him. "Jonathan, how did this happen?"

"I don't know." He slid his chair back and took Caleb's breakfast bowl to the sink. "I've thought about it all night. Maybe it's just the power of peer pressure. Or loneliness. Maybe we should have let her home-school. Maybe we need to try to understand her side before we start disciplining her for it."

Morgan got up, Caleb on her hip, and poured some orange juice into his cup. "I don't even know how to discipline her. She's seventeen years old. She comes from a background of parties day and night, strangers in and out of her house, druggies, alcoholics. I don't know why she'd want even a taste of that for herself. I'm so mad at her."

"Me too," Jonathan said, "but these are the perils of parenthood. It's gonna be okay. We'll survive it just like every other parent of a teenager."

Morgan finished feeding Caleb as Jonathan got ready for church. Then she headed up the stairs and went to Sadie's door.

The girl lay sound asleep in the middle of her bed, her covers all twisted around her, and one of her pillows on the floor. Her mouth hung open and saliva pooled on the sheet beneath her.

Morgan stood there looking at the girl who seemed so young and so innocent, and she remembered finding her hiding in the boathouse. She had seemed so small and vulnerable then, with her broken arm and her big, frightened eyes.

She'd been through so much since then. The strength of character she'd already shown Morgan and Jonathan couldn't be overridden by one night of teenage rebellion. Still, her behavior couldn't be overlooked.

She set Caleb down on the bed next to his sister, pushed her hair gently back from her face. "Wake up, Sadie. It's time to get up for church."

Sadie stirred, and Caleb began to pat on her bottom, trying to wake her up. She turned over and squinted her eyes open, saw Caleb and smiled. "Hey, Bud," she said. "What are you doing here?"

He laughed aloud and crawled up to her face, planted a kiss on her cheek. Sadie seemed to remember the night before, and she sat up in bed and squinted up at Morgan. "I thought you were at the hospital."

"Karen had her baby," Morgan said. "It was a boy."

"Great. Everything okay?"

"Yeah," Morgan said. "She's resting, so I decided to come home for a little while."

Sadie rubbed her eyes, shoved her hair back from her face. "Morgan, I'm so sorry about last night."

Caleb slid off the bed and toddled to Sadie's dresser.

Sighing, Morgan pulled a chair out from under her desk and sat down facing her. "What happened, Sadie? Talk to me."

Sadie got up and directed Caleb to the blocks she kept on her closet floor. "Trevor just asked me to meet him on the beach, and we went for a walk. It wasn't going to be any big deal. But his friends were having a party, and we went to it, and when we got there Crystal Lewis told me he was only with me for one reason, and I got so tense and upset . . . then he brought me this drink. I was embarrassed to throw it out in front of these people who already hated me, so I drank it. I didn't intend to drink anymore after that, Morgan. I was just going to have that one, and then I was going to find some excuse to leave and go home." She started to cry. "I don't know what happened. That first drink relaxed me so much that I didn't remember what I'd planned to do. When he brought me a second one, I drank it, too. And then there was a third . . ." She wiped the tears from her face. "I lost count after that."

"Sadie, do you understand now why we didn't want you going out with that boy?"

"Not really," Sadie said. "He's nice. He likes me, and he's the only one who does. He's kind of like the gatekeeper, you know? I can make friends through him, and finally become a part of the people on this island."

"You *are* a part of the people on this island. You're a part of our family."

Sadie sat down next to Caleb on the floor. "I know, Morgan. But that's not enough. I need friends my own age."

Morgan shook her head. "But Sadie, when a guy inspires you to lie to your parents and sneak out and get drunk, he's not good for you. And I'm not so sure that Crystal wasn't right about what he wanted."

"He's not like that." But Sadie's denial was weak. "Man, my head hurts. I'm just like my mom. Nursing a hangover and apologizing about the night before . . ."

"You're not like that," Morgan said. "This was a one-time thing. I'll fix you some breakfast and give you some aspirin or something. But you *are* going to church. We're not going to tolerate having you party on Saturday night and then be in no shape to worship the next day. That's not how it works around here."

"I know."

Morgan took Caleb downstairs and, fighting her aching fatigue, began cooking the eggs and bacon she normally cooked on Sunday mornings. After a few minutes, Sadie came down and took her seat at the table.

Jonathan came in and gave her a look. "So how do you feel?"

She shrugged. "Head's killing me."

He sat down beside her. "Sadie, who was at that party last night?"

"Nobody you know."

"How can you say that?" he asked. "I've lived on this island for most of my life. I know everybody here. Were they kids from your school?"

"A few."

"College kids?" Jonathan asked.

"I don't know how old they were."

Morgan shot Jonathan a look. "But they were drinking and they served alcohol to a minor?" he asked.

"They didn't *serve* it to me," she said. "It was just punch. I didn't know—"

"You didn't know it was alcoholic?" Jonathan asked.

"Well, okay, I did know, but—"

Morgan moved the frying pan from the stove. "Sadie, I don't know what to do. I'm new at having a teenager in the house. I don't know whether I'm supposed to ground you or what."

Sadie just looked up at her miserably. "Ground me from what? I never go anywhere."

Morgan knew she had a point.

"I want to do something effective, honey. I want to make sure that you don't make mistakes that will ruin your life. Sadie, you're stronger than that. You have more character. This is not what I'd expect of the girl who got away from Jack Dent and took care of herself on the beach for days with a broken arm."

Sadie sat back in her chair. Morgan saw the pain in her face, and her heart ached for her. She couldn't seem to work up any anger toward her.

Morgan came to the table and leaned over her. "Sadie, I have high hopes for you. I want you to go to college, do something with your life. I pray every night that someday you'll meet a wonderful godly man who will be your husband, that you'll have a family of your own, and that all the things in your past will be redeemed. I pray that for you. But if you start down this path, Sadie, none of that is going to happen."

Sadie started to cry again. "It's not a path. I'm not on a path, Morgan. I just made some mistakes last night. I won't do it again."

Morgan hugged her. When she let her go, she sat down next to her.

Sadie had trouble looking at her. "I'm so ashamed. I never thought I'd do something so stupid. It's like throwing all the good things you've done for me back in your faces, and I didn't mean to do that. I really didn't."

"You don't owe us anything," Jonathan said. "Nothing at all. We took you in because we love you. And we expect you to obey us because you love us."

"It was just one night," Sadie said. "I really won't do it again."

Morgan wiped the tears off of the girl's wet cheek. Then she did what her mother would have done. She got up from the table and, with her spatula, dipped out some scrambled eggs and a couple of pieces of bacon and put them on a plate for Sadie. "Here. Eat this. It'll make you feel better."

"I don't know if I can eat." Sadie looked up at Jonathan. "Are you going to ground me?"

"Honey, I don't know what we're going to do," Jonathan said. "I need some time to pray about this, whether to ground you or take away privileges or what. But just know that whatever comes is because we love you."

"I know." She stared down at her plate and finally pushed it away. "I'll eat something later." She got up and started back up the stairs. "I have to get dressed for church. I'll be down in a minute."

Morgan watched her retreat up the stairs. Finally, she turned back to her husband. "Jonathan, what are we going to do?"

"I don't know. Maybe it's just a phase. Maybe it won't happen again." He got up and pulled her close. "You look so tired. Why don't you stay home from church?"

She sighed. "I thought about it. But I just feel like I need to worship this morning. With Cade missing, and Sadie . . . I'll sleep later before I go back to the hospital."

As Morgan went to get Caleb and herself ready for church, she prayed that this thing with Sadie was an end, and not a beginning.

Cade emerged from a shallow sleep. His throat felt on fire again, so he reached for the empty bottle beside him and looked over at the toilet tank. If he could just get there again, relieve himself, take clean water from the tank ...

He moved his legs over the side of the bed, gritting his teeth against the pain. Without putting his weight on his wounded leg, he stood up. He managed to make his way over, groaning with the pain incited by each movement. He relieved himself, flushed, then dunked the bottle into the tank of clean water and drank some of it.

He leaned against the wall and looked around the room. There must be something he could use to overpower Ann Clark the next time she came in. But it wasn't just her he was dealing with. There was someone else, someone he hadn't seen, the one who had shot him from the top of the stairs. Even if he bested Ann, he'd have to contend with that other person if he tried to get away.

This time they'd kill him for sure.

He couldn't imagine why they hadn't finished the job by now. She had already stated her intention to kill him. But he still had a use to her, she'd said. He was their scapegoat, but for what?

He made his way back to the bed and dropped down on it, exhausted from the short journey across the room. Carefully, he set his leg back on the bed. She hadn't changed his sheets. They were still bloody and smelled of decay.

"Help me, Lord," he whispered. "Please help me."

He had to find something he could use as a weapon. He couldn't just lie here and do nothing. He looked around the room and saw the bare beams against the tar paper in the wall. Maybe he would be able to break one of the beams free. He began to hit on the one closest to his bed with the heel of his hand, trying to loosen it, but it didn't budge, and each effort shot pain through his side, cutting each nerve ending like a scalpel, making him want to scream out in agony. But he had to think . . . he had to stay focused.

He began to quote Psalm 6 again, praying God's Word back to him and trusting from the depth of his heart that the Lord had heard.

CHAPTER

*B*lair yawned as she crossed the Islands Expressway back onto Tybee Island. She had spent the night staked out in her car down from Ann Clark's house but hadn't seen anything that gave her clues about Cade's whereabouts.

Instead of going home when she reached Cape Refuge, she went to Cricket's and pulled into the space next to Cade's truck. It had been parked here for six days now. *Six days!* Where in the world was he?

She got out of the car, opened the passenger door, and slipped into the driver's seat. On the passenger seat she saw a box of breath mints, a small New Testament, and a couple of ATM slips. A windbreaker hung on the hook behind her head. She unhooked it and brought it to her nose, breathing in his scent. It smelled like wind and sea air and the soap he used.

She sat in his driver's seat, clutching the jacket to her chest and staring out the window to the activity on the dock.

Behind her, she heard the singing from the warehouse church her parents had led for years and where Jonathan and Morgan were now presiding, since they hadn't been able to find a permanent preacher. The parking lot was full.

The chorus of "Be Thou My Vision" floated over the wind. It had been one of her mother's favorites. She'd sung it herself dozens of times as a child, sitting on the front pew in that very building with her father preaching and her mother playing piano. Around her, she had always been aware of the misfits and outcasts, those who'd come in from the sea and those who were just passing through. . . .

But it wasn't just those who had no place to go who came to church in that little warehouse. Islanders who could have gone to church anywhere came to worship there and considered it their church home.

Cade was among them. If he were here today, he'd be in that building, sitting on his favorite pew, raising his hands to the Lord he believed in, and worshiping with his whole heart and soul.

She hung his jacket back up and got out of the truck. The breeze blew through her hair as the song continued, and she thought about the prayer she'd breathed the other night in her yard. The prayer for Cade. If there was a God to hear it, she didn't know why he'd pay any heed to her, not when she'd been so blatantly defiant about her parents' religion. She had grown to hate the church and, somewhere during her college years, had decided to stop going.

Now she would give anything to be within those walls, singing that song led by her mother and soaking up the wisdom her father imparted.

That was never to be again.

But the longing was still there, to go into that building where she'd spent so many Sundays of her childhood. She felt that yearning to sit among those people who believed in a God who answered prayers. Maybe if she did, she could get them to understand the urgency of praying for Cade. Maybe then something would break and he would be found.

But she couldn't go in there. It would be hypocrisy, sitting in a church pretending to worship when you didn't believe a word of what you were hearing or singing. Instead, she turned to Cricket's. How many times had she gravitated here on Sunday morning only to sit inside the dirty little restaurant and listen to the music pouring from the windows of the building next door?

She could do it again today, but she didn't want to. She wanted to go to the church.

Maybe she did believe . . . just a little.

Quietly, she crossed the boardwalk and made her way around to the front of the building. Her parents' murder came back to her, their blood on the floor, their bodies lying there while the police investigated the scene.

She stood at the front door before going in, put her hand over her chest, and tried to breathe deeply. There were good memories here too. Mostly good ones, if the truth were known. And if Morgan and Jonathan had been able to clean up the stains of their parents' murder and come back to this building to worship each week, then she should be able to do the same.

The song ended and she waited a moment. She heard Jonathan's voice and knew he must be praying. Then the piano started up again, and they started to sing "The Old Rugged Cross." Finally, she opened the door and stepped inside.

The building was full, nothing like she remembered. From somewhere Jonathan had gotten extra pews and had put them in four rows of five pews each. He'd moved the pulpit that her father used to stand behind, and now it was more in the center of the room. Morgan sat at the piano playing the songs that they had known since they were children. Sadie sat on the second row, holding Caleb.

Jonathan had had the room air-conditioned, and Blair suspected that was why so many of the sailors coming in from the sea filed in here. It probably had nothing to do with worship, she thought. They were just trying to get cool. To her, it seemed like manipulation.

She slipped into a back pew, hoping to be unnoticed, but the moment the song ended and they sat down, Jonathan met her eyes. She saw him look over at Morgan, and Morgan's face erupted into a smile.

Don't get your hopes up, Blair told them with her eyes. *I'm not here to convert.*

But she wasn't sure why she had come. She couldn't have explained it if she had tried, but as Jonathan began to preach she felt an overpowering sense of nostalgia. She would have never figured him for a preacher, yet he had learned well from her father.

She closed her eyes, and tears pinched through her eyelashes at the memory of her parents filling up this room, their spirits and souls so big that everyone who came in felt as if they'd been hugged—whether they really had or not. Oh, she missed those hugs.

She swallowed and looked around at the faces of those who had meant so much to her family. Cade should be here, she thought, sitting on that second row in the middle. He might have gotten up to lead a prayer or pass the plate for the offering.

Jonathan read from the parable about the shepherd leaving his ninety-nine sheep to look for the one. She wondered if God would do that for Cade—or if Jonathan considered *her* the one lost sheep in this group. As her mind worked on the implications of that story, Jonathan closed out the sermon. He led the group in a prayer for Cade's safety, for his health, for him to be found, or for him to return from wherever he'd been. She found hope in that. There was supposed to be power in the prayers of groups. Her parents had quoted the two-or-more Scripture so many times.

Maybe she didn't have to rely on her own meager prayers to reach the ears of God if he really did exist. Maybe he would hear the prayers of these righteous people and deliver Cade from wherever he was.

When the sermon ended, Morgan led them in "Love Lifted Me." Blair didn't sing along. Instead, she slipped out of her pew and out the front door. She could still hear the voices singing the song as she went to her car.

While everyone napped after church, Jonathan paced in the office, a million frustrations whirling through his mind. Another day—and Cade was still missing.

Why wasn't there an all-out hunt for him?

He decided to go to the police station and see what was being done. Then he could decide how he could be involved.

He found Joe sitting at Cade's desk, poring over lab reports, looking even more exhausted than Morgan. "Hey," Jonathan said. "Got a minute?"

Joe nodded and rubbed his eyes. "Come on in."

Jonathan dropped down into the chair across from the desk and set his elbows on his knees. "It's been six days, Joe. What are you doing about Cade?"

"Everything I know to do." Joe leaned back in the chair. "I decided to turn his house into a crime scene. We searched it last night, but I don't think it turned up any leads. Today I'm going to have his truck moved from Cricket's so we can search it more thoroughly."

"Can't you do a full search of Ann Clark's house?"

"I wish. But I've still got to have more evidence to establish probable cause. I've finally got the Savannah Police Department looking for Cade too, but it's taken a few days to convince everybody he's really disappeared. And the letter didn't help. People who don't know him are inclined to think it's real." He rocked forward and set his jaw on his fist.

Jonathan let out a long sigh and shook his head. "What can I do, Joe? I feel like I'm letting him down, just sitting here doing nothing."

"Let the police do it, Jonathan. We have the resources and the training."

"Come on," Jonathan said. "You may be trained, but half the force is under twenty-five. They don't have the experience to solve something like this."

"It's not just us. Cops in other jurisdictions are looking, Jonathan. He's one of our own. We're not going to let it rest."

Jonathan looked down between his feet and stared at a spot on the floor. It was going to take an act of his will to leave it in their hands, he thought. He didn't know if he could do that.

Looking back up, he said, "There's one other thing I wanted to talk to you about."

"Yeah? What?"

"Last night, Sadie, my foster daughter, went to a party on the beach. Mostly teenagers, but alcohol was served. I thought there was a statute against that. I thought we weren't allowed to have parties on the beach after dark. And I want to know why no one was arrested for serving alcohol to a minor. Jim Henry told me last night that he'd been over there, but nothing was done."

Joe looked as if he had more important things to talk about. "Jonathan, I don't know anything about them serving alcohol to minors. We do have statutes, but they're not real enforceable."

"Why not?" Jonathan demanded. "All you have to do is have an officer patrol the beach. It's not that hard."

"It's harder when people have parties in their condos, and they spill out onto the beach. There's not a lot we can do about that. And I don't know, Jim might not have realized there was alcohol there."

"He *told* me there was. Why didn't he break up the party, slap them with fines, take them to jail?"

"Look, I'm sorry your foster daughter got involved in that, but don't dump it on us. We have a lot going on. The last thing I needed last night was a jail full of drunken teenagers and a lot of screaming parents."

Jonathan felt his ears growing hot. He stiffened and looked across the desk. "So you're telling me that you let it go because you don't want the hassle?"

"Hey, I didn't ask to be in charge, Jonathan. I didn't set policy. Alone, I can barely handle the murder investigation and Cade's disappearance, but you want me hovering over the night shift to make sure they crack down on every kid with a beer?"

"So who could change policy and see that you enforce the laws? The mayor?"

Joe moaned. "You know we don't have a mayor."

"No, but we're voting in June. Would you listen to *him*?"

"I'd have to," he said. "He'd be my boss."

"I thought so." Jonathan got to his feet. "Well, we'll just have to see what we can do about that."

When Jonathan got back in his car, he sat behind the wheel, tapping his hand angrily as he looked across the street to the beach where Sadie had gotten drunk last night. Maybe he really should run for mayor. Maybe then he could make sure that the laws already on the books were enforced. If he was mayor, maybe he could make them clean up the beaches so that they were a safer place for families.

As he pulled out of the parking lot and back on to Ocean Boulevard, he began to feel a growing sense of purpose. Had God called him to run for mayor? Was it something he was supposed to do?

He wouldn't tell Morgan until he'd made up his mind for sure. There was still time to talk God out of it.

CHAPTER

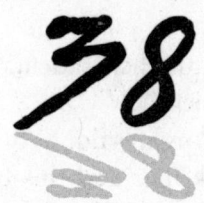

38

*M*organ woke from her nap midafternoon but still felt weary and unrested. She made herself get up, determined to get back to the hospital to check on Karen and the baby.

She went downstairs and found Sadie sitting outside on the back lawn, watching Caleb climbing on his plastic jungle gym.

Sadie looked a little more like herself now. The hangover must have worn off, and there was a little more color to her face. Morgan pushed through the back screen door.

"Sadie, thanks for watching Caleb while I slept. It was a long night."

She smiled up at her but still had trouble meeting her eyes. "I didn't watch him the whole time," she said. "He slept most of the time."

"Good. Then you got some rest too?"

"Yeah, I did."

Morgan went to Caleb and picked him up, deposited him on his little slide, and watched him go down. Caleb hit the dirt, then got on his knees, and crawled through the little tunnel. They could hear him laughing inside.

"I'm going back to the hospital," Morgan said. "I want to check on Karen and see how the baby's doing."

Sadie looked up at her. "Can I go with you, Morgan?"

Morgan was glad she wanted to. "Sure. I'll get Jonathan to keep Caleb."

Sadie got up, and her trademark smile cut across her face. "I love tiny little babies."

"Me too," Morgan said. "You really should see him. He's so sweet. Curly black hair and this full-of-himself voice. It felt so good to hold him. I wish I'd gotten Caleb when he was newborn."

Sadie's smile faded, and she gazed toward her brother. "Boy, I do too."

"I can't wait to bring them home. A newborn in the house."

"Do you think she'll let me hold him today?" Sadie asked.

"I'm sure she will."

Karen couldn't have been happier. There had never been a time in her life when she'd felt such intense love for another human being. She had already managed to nurse without a hitch, and Emory lay cradled in her arms now, sleeping contentedly. His hair was still curly, hours after his birth, and his skin was the most beautiful shade of ebony she had ever seen. Softly, she kissed his plump little cheek.

When a knock sounded on her door, she looked up, hoping to see Morgan. But it was only a nurse. "Hello, Mrs. Miller?"

Keeping her voice low, Karen said, "Yes?"

The woman came farther into the room. "I'm afraid I need to take the baby for a few minutes. The pediatrician is on the floor, and he likes for the babies to be in the nursery so he can examine them."

She didn't want to let him go. "Can't he come in here?"

"No, I'm sorry. But don't worry. I'll bring him right back in just a few minutes."

Sighing, she kissed him again, then handed him to the nurse. The woman's long brown hair almost swept into his face. Karen thought of telling her to tie it back, that it might carry germs.

"Say bye-bye to Mommy," the woman said, then grinned back at Karen. "Get some rest."

Karen nodded and watched them leave. Laying her head back on her pillow, she checked her watch, and hoped that the doctor wouldn't take long.

But a half hour passed, and the nurse didn't come back. Finally, she pressed the buzzer.

"Yes?" a nurse called from the station.

"I was wondering if the doctor was finished with the babies yet. I expected to have mine brought back by now."

There was a long pause. "Isn't your baby in your room with you?"

Karen's chest tightened. "No. A nurse came and took him. She never brought him back!"

She waited for a reply, but none came. Frustrated, she pressed the button again.

Her door flung open and two nurses came in. The alarm on their faces was unmistakable. "Miss Miller, are you sure a nurse took your baby?"

"Positive. She said the doctor was on the floor. . . ."

"Miss Miller, the doctor hasn't been here this morning. None of our nurses told you that."

She stared at them for a moment. "What are you saying? She came right in here and took my baby—"

One of the nurses dashed out of the room. "I'll call the police!"

"The police?" Suddenly it was all clear to Karen. Her baby had been kidnapped, just like those other babies she'd heard about on the news. "No. She was a nurse. She had on a nurse's uniform!"

"Miss Miller, your baby isn't in the nursery. Please—describe the woman to me."

A sense of horror settled over Karen.

Her baby was gone.

CHAPTER

*T*here was a commotion in the hall when
Morgan and Sadie reached Karen's floor. Several police officers stood among a cluster of nurses, as if taking statements.

"What's going on?" Sadie whispered.

Morgan shook her head. "Maybe Karen will know."

She got to Karen's door and heard wailing from the
other side. Without knocking, she pushed the door open.

Karen was on her bare feet, still in her hospital gown,
and two men stood with her. It was clear that she had been
weeping. She turned as Morgan came in. "Oh, Morgan,
thank God you're here!"

Morgan crossed the room and embraced the woman.
"Karen, what is it?"

"My baby! She took my baby."

"Who did?"

"Some woman who looked like a nurse, only no one
here knows her! I waited and waited for her to bring him
back, and when I asked about it, nobody knew who she

was. She had a thirty-minute head start out of the building. They have video of her just walking out with my baby!"

Morgan felt the blood draining from her face. She looked at the two men.

"I'm Detective Hull, Savannah Police Department," one of them said. "This is Officer Coleman."

Morgan introduced herself. "You don't think it's that kidnapper, do you? The one who's taken all those other babies?"

"It looks like it."

"They have to find him!" Karen wailed. "Please, you need to go look for them. She's probably still in her car. Do one of those Amber Alert things, so people will know."

Detective Hull looked as if he was one step ahead of her. "Ma'am, we're putting out an alert as we speak, and we have roadblocks being set up. They're going to be looking for a white woman in green scrubs with long brown hair."

"She was small," Karen said, "not as tall as me, and that long brown hair. If they set up roadblocks they'll see my baby, won't they? How many day-old babies are there out there?" She swung around to Morgan. "He's just a few hours old, Morgan. What if he's not all right?"

Morgan looked back at Sadie. She stood back at the door, listening in horror. Her face was white.

Morgan knew she was remembering her own baby brother, in the grips of evil.

The memory of five other kidnapped babies reeled through Morgan's mind. One in Hilton Head, others in Pensacola and Mobile, the most recent from St. Joseph's here in Savannah.

"We've also called in the FBI," Hull said. "Since the babies have been taken from three different states, they're taking over the case."

"Have they found any of them?" Karen demanded. "Even one?"

"Not yet, ma'am. All of the babies are still missing. But this might just be the case that helps us find the rest of them."

Jonathan came as soon as he'd heard about the baby's kidnapping. When the FBI had finished "sweeping" the hospital and questioning Karen, Jonathan realized there was nothing more he could do. Dismally, he left Morgan with Karen and drove Sadie home.

Sadie was quiet as he drove, her silence broken only by sniffs.

First Cade and now Karen's baby. And all that following the murder of his in-laws just a few months ago. It was as if the world tipped off its axis. . . .

Sadie got a tissue out of the box sitting on the seat and blew her nose. "Jonathan, I'm so sorry I gave you guys more to worry about last night. It all seems so stupid with so many desperate things going on."

"It's okay, Sadie. We'll get over it, as long as it doesn't happen again."

She wiped her face. "That poor little baby. It's just like when Jack had Caleb."

"Maybe not." It was starting to rain, and rivulets of water streamed down his windshield. He turned his wipers on. "I was just trying to think why a person would kidnap a little baby like that. Maybe it wasn't a violent thing, like when an older child gets kidnapped. Maybe it's somebody who's just desperate to have a child of their own. . . ."

Sadie looked at him hopefully. "Somebody like you and Morgan?"

He frowned. Did everyone realize how much he and Morgan wanted a baby? He hadn't told more than a couple of people. "Maybe someone like us, only more desperate."

"That makes me feel a little better," Sadie whispered.

He glanced at her. "Why?"

"Because maybe it's somebody nice. Not somebody like Jack. Maybe it's somebody who loves babies, who'll take care of him. Maybe they won't hurt him, and he'll be found in one piece."

He drove in silence for a while, making her hope into a quiet prayer.

Sadie hadn't been home more than an hour when the phone rang. She answered it quickly, hoping it was news about the baby. "Hanover House."

"Sadie? Good. It's you. I didn't want to get you in trouble."

She recognized Trevor's voice and looked around to see if she would be heard. No one was in the kitchen, and Jonathan sat out on the sunporch with Caleb. She pulled the phone cord into the office. "Trevor?"

"I was going to hang up if anyone else answered."

She drew in a deep breath. "You shouldn't have called. I shouldn't even be talking to you."

"Well, I was worried about you. I just heard about that baby being kidnapped. The news said that the mother lived at Hanover House."

"Yeah. It's Karen, the new tenant."

"I figured you were all freaked out and everything. I wanted to call and see if you were okay."

She raked her hair back from her face and tried to force away those warm fuzzy feelings he always invoked. "I'm fine. But I can't talk. I have to go."

"No, don't do that," he said. "Come on, Sadie. We had something good going between us."

She swallowed and checked the kitchen again. "Look, Trevor, I got caught when I got home last night. I was drunk. I lied to them and deceived them, and then I got drunk. That's not the kind of person I want to be."

"I can understand that."

She thought of the way he'd groped her out on the beach, Crystal's predictions coming true. "I'm so embarrassed by everything that happened—"

"What happened?" he asked. "Nothing happened."

"Something happened, all right. I wasn't so drunk that I don't remember that. Crystal Lewis said you were only with me for one thing. And you pretty much proved her point."

"What did *I* do?"

"What did you do?" she repeated. She looked out and saw Jonathan pushing through the screen door with Caleb on his hip, walking out into the yard. "Let's just say you got a little too aggressive."

"Oh, that," he said, and she heard a chuckle in his voice. "Sadie, I was drunk too. I won't judge you for what you did drunk, if you won't judge me."

That stopped her. She leaned back against the wall, wondering if she was, indeed, being judgmental. She hated that and didn't want to be accused of it.

It was true. He had been drunk. And didn't everyone act out of character when they'd been drinking?

"Look," he said, "if it means that much to you, I'll promise to be nothing but a perfect gentleman from now on. And no more alcohol when I'm with you."

She wanted to believe him, but Morgan's and Jonathan's voices kept playing through her mind. "Why do you even want to go out with me when you could have any girl in the school you want? It doesn't even make sense."

She could hear in his voice that that pleased him. "It's you I want, Sadie. Are you so down on yourself that you can't believe someone would want you?"

"I'm just not your usual type."

He laughed. "That's a good thing. I'm raising my standards, okay? You're the smartest and the best looking and the most interesting."

Those didn't sound like Crystal Lewis's reasons. Maybe he was being straight with her.

"Come on," he said. "Go out with me again. I promise not to take you to any wild parties. I promise. I just want to spend time with you. And you know you need to talk, after all this with the baby."

Confusion settled into her heart. She had promised Jonathan and Morgan that she wouldn't drink again, and she intended to keep that promise. But what would it hurt just to spend a little more time with him?

"I don't want to let Morgan and Jonathan down again. They've made it clear that they don't want me with you."

"So it won't be a date. You'll just go for a walk along the beach and run into me. We'll get a Coke somewhere. It doesn't have to be a big deal. I want to hear about the kidnapping. We'll just talk."

Sadie looked out the door and saw that Jonathan was still in the yard. "I don't know, Trevor. I'm just not sure it's worth all the trouble I could get into."

"Sadie, you're going to have to decide if I'm worth it."

That was just it, she thought. She hadn't decided that.

"When you do, I'll be waiting. Just call me, and I'll meet you anywhere you say."

She listened to him hang up and kept holding the phone to her ear as the dial tone clicked on.

As she hung up, she made her decision. She wasn't going to let Morgan and Jonathan down again, whether Trevor was worth it or not.

CHAPTER

*T*he tenants of Hanover House waited in the living room as Morgan brought Karen home the next day. Silence hung over the room, much like the silence after the days of Thelma and Wayne's murder.

Karen hadn't wanted to leave the hospital. She had fought to stay until her baby was found, as if part of her believed that Emory lay hidden somewhere within that building and would forever be out of her grasp if she left that place.

Several FBI agents had turned their parlor into a communications center, in case the kidnappers made contact. They sat in there now, talking silently as they prepared for any call that might come.

Sadie had made tea and pulled Karen into the kitchen. Gus, Felicia, and Mrs. Hern followed her in, all of them looking as if they wanted to help but didn't know how. Sadie poured her a cup, then hugged the forlorn mother. "Karen, I'm so sorry. I know what it's like to worry about a little baby being in trouble. It's an awful feeling."

Karen nodded silently and wiped her red eyes. "I just don't understand why anybody would want my baby. Why *my* baby? Why not somebody else's? There were so many of them there. Why did they choose my room to come into?"

Morgan had already asked that question. "She seems to be targeting single moms. Maybe it's because there's no dad in the room to stop them."

Karen couldn't drink her tea. She looked weak and bent over, her face gaunt and unhealthy. She hadn't eaten at all since the baby disappeared. Morgan had spent the night at the hospital with her last night, but neither of them had slept.

"Honey, why don't you go up and lie down? Jonathan took your suitcase up."

Karen nodded weakly. "I just want to be alone for a while. You'll call me if anything happens?"

"Of course."

She watched her go up the stairs, then turned back to Gus and Felicia, Mrs. Hern and Sadie.

"What can we do, Miss Morgan?" Felicia asked her.

"Pray," Morgan said. "She's a wreck, and who could blame her?" She sank into a chair, and dropped her face into her hands. "Who ever would have thought we'd have two people close to us missing like this? It's just unbelievable."

And as Morgan started to cry, the tenants who were used to receiving Morgan's comfort did their best to comfort her.

CHAPTER

Cade shivered with fever when Ann Clark came back to him. He'd heard voices from the vent for the last several hours—a man and a woman embroiled in an argument, and a baby's incessant crying. Part of the time he thought he might be dreaming, but now as the sound of the scraping bookshelves pulled him from his sleep, he came fully awake and knew it was real.

The door opened and Ann came in. She had food again—a burger and fries this time—and a Walgreen's bag.

She took one look at him. "You're getting sick. I don't want you to die of those wounds. I have other plans for your death."

He swallowed and sat up. His leg had swollen and was still bloody and black with bruises, and bone stuck through the skin.

She pulled some bandage material and a bottle of alcohol out of the bag.

"Do you have antibiotics?" he asked.

"No," she said. "This'll have to do."

She pulled back the cloth that Cade had already ripped on his pants leg and cringed at the sight of his wound.

She opened the rubbing alcohol and poured it over his leg, letting it run down onto the bloody sheets.

He arched his back with the pain but lay as still as he could, knowing he needed it. She began to clean the dried, congealed blood, then wrapped a bandage around his leg. It was a haphazard job, but it was better than nothing.

He heard the baby crying through the vent again. So did she, and she stopped wrapping and looked up. He saw surprise on her face, as if she hadn't realized sound would carry down here.

"How old is your baby?" he asked.

She looked stunned. "What baby?"

"The baby I keep hearing. I know it must be very painful to lose your husband when your baby is so young."

"That's the television," she said. "I don't have any children."

She kept working, finished wrapping his calf, then moved to the wound on his side and peeled back the cloth.

He could shove her back, try to escape again, but he knew for certain that the mystery person was still in the house, that he would shoot him again from the top of the stairs, that this time he would kill him without a thought. Besides, he couldn't step on his leg, much less run.

The alcohol stung, but he prayed that it would help the wound. He lay still as she taped the bandage to his bloody side.

"I have to change your sheets," she said. "Get up."

He moved with great effort, but managed to pull up and stand on his good leg. She pulled the sheets off his bed, then backed out of the room, her eyes on him, and grabbed a set of clean sheets she had left in the outer part of the basement.

He felt dizzy, nauseated, as he leaned against the wall.

The room smelled less rank now. He was grateful for that.

When she was finished, she stepped back to the door.

"Thank you," he said.

She didn't meet his eyes. "Eat your dinner."

She left him alone then, locked in his vault, and he heard those bookshelves being pushed back in front of the door.

He sat down, propped his leg back up on the mattress, and ate the first meal he'd had in days.

CHAPTER

*T*he parlor at Hanover House had quickly been transformed into command central, from which FBI agents working on the kidnapping case had come and gone since yesterday. They prepared to record any ransom calls that might come in, and each time the phone rang, recording equipment launched and tracing began.

It seemed to Morgan that the whole focus of their lives had shifted to the missing baby. She tried to go about her daily duties without getting in the agents' way, but it was difficult to keep the house running smoothly.

Caleb was on edge, fussy and nervous from the extra traffic in the house, so she tried to keep him upstairs with her as much as she could. She had finally rocked him to sleep and put him down for a nap, when she heard Karen sobbing from her room just down the hall.

Her heart swelled and her throat tightened. She remembered that grief well.

She thought of knocking on Karen's door and trying to comfort her, but the woman had rebuffed her efforts earlier. Inconsolable, she'd told her she just needed to be alone.

The sound of that unquenchable grief was too much to bear, so she went to the closed door of her parents' room, and stepped inside.

The room remained as they'd left it a few months ago, except that her parents' smells had faded. But the quilt folded at the foot of their bed still spoke of love and warmth. She went to her father's side of the bed and ran her hand across the comforter where the mattress dipped.

What would her parents say about all this tragedy?

Their own murder, Cade's disappearance, and now this baby being snatched out of its mother's arms.

It was too much. She curled up on the bed and pulled the quilt up to cover her.

Fresh tears began to seize her, and she let her grief climb to its peak inside her, then spill over onto her parents' comforter.

So many tears had been shed in this very place in the last few months.

She wondered what her parents would say or do about this missing baby and the grieving woman in her room.

She needed to talk to Blair. She needed to tell her about the baby. She needed to cry on her sister's shoulder.

Her parents' phone still sat on the bed table. Still crying, she picked it up and dialed Blair's number. It rang four times, then her voice mail kicked in. "Blair, call me. I have some more bad news. Karen's baby was kidnapped. Please call!"

Where was she? Hadn't she heard about the missing baby on the news yet? Why hadn't she called?

Fear and worry welled up inside her as she hung up. Had she gone back to Savannah to watch Ann Clark's house again? The danger in that, if Ann indeed had something to do with Cade, struck her.

What if something happened to Blair next? What if the phone rang and it was more police with more bad news....

The idea of that sent her over the edge, and she wilted and sobbed into the quilt clutched in her hands.

A light knock sounded on the door, and it opened. Jonathan stepped inside. "Honey, are you all right?"

She nodded and pressed the quilt against her mouth. "She's not home. I tried to call her. . . ."

He came to her side. "Who's not?"

"Blair. Where is she?"

"She's okay. You don't have to worry about her."

"I need to talk to her!" Her voice broke off at its highest pitch. He sat down and pulled her against him.

She clutched his shoulder with one hand and his shirt with the other, and wept like an abandoned child against his chest. He held her quietly as she cried.

"That little baby. That poor little baby. I watched him coming, Jonathan, his little wet head and his scrunched up little shoulders. And he was all purple, and he let out this yell. And I got to hold him. . . ."

"He'll be okay. You'll see."

"But what if he's not? And what if Cade's not? What if they both wind up like Mama and Pop? And where is Blair?"

"Blair is fine. She's a big girl. And we just have to trust that God knows where that baby is, and he knows where Cade is. They're in his hands. We can't do anything for them except pray, and that's plenty. And we can support Karen and be there for her through this."

"She's already had such a hard life. Why her? Why this baby?"

"We'll never know that." He stroked her hair and lay down next to her.

"It's just one more reproach against Hanover House," she said. "People will say that nothing good ever happens to the people here."

He stroked her arm. "I thought maybe I could deter that. I thought I might go to the city council meeting tonight. I was going to skip it this once because of the kidnapping, but I realized that I need to be there more than ever. They'll talk about Cade for sure, and probably something will come up about the baby and Hanover House. I just want to be there. Would you be okay if I went?"

"Sure, go ahead." She pulled a tissue out of the box on her mother's bed table. It was almost empty. She didn't want it to run out.

Dabbing at her nose, she said, "I'll be okay in a minute. I just needed to have a little nervous breakdown. Nothing serious." Getting up, she blew her nose. Jonathan stood and pulled her back into his arms.

"We'll get through all this too, Morgan," he whispered. "We're strong."

She knew it was true, though her fears seemed to have banished whatever strength she had left.

CHAPTER

45

*B*lair didn't check her messages when she got home that morning. She'd been at Washington Square all night, sitting in her car and watching the lights in Ann Clark's house. She had walked around the block to get closer to the house without trespassing, and had lingered on a park bench across the street.

But she had seen nothing. It was as if the woman never came out. She hated to leave this morning, for fear that the woman did go out during the day. But she'd feared falling asleep in her car and calling attention to herself.

She saw the message light blinking on her voice mail, but didn't feel like listening to people calling to ask why the library wasn't open. Instead, she clicked through her caller ID for the police department's number.

But Joe hadn't called her, so he must not have any information about Cade.

She went to her bedroom and shed her clothes, put on a big T-shirt, and climbed into her bed. Her body sank into the mattress, but her mind would not relax.

How could she sleep when Cade was in trouble?

She lay there with her eyes open, and saw her father's Bible lying on her bed table.

She had planned to do more research about the cities of refuge, but she had almost forgotten it as her search for Cade had occupied her mind.

But it was her last link to him. That morning he'd disappeared, he had read of those cities. He'd been consumed with guilt over the man he had killed, and it was clear that he'd longed for a place where his guilt could be justified.

Wearily, she gave up the idea of sleep and sat up. Grabbing the Bible, she turned back to Numbers 35. Her eyes scanned the passage again, and she paid careful attention to the distinctions God had made between murder and unintentional killing.

Beside that passage, her father had written, "Matthew 5:21–22."

She turned to Matthew, and found those verses in red. Jesus had spoken them.

> *You have heard that it was said to the people long ago, "Do not murder, and anyone who murders will be subject to judgment." But I tell you that anyone who is angry with his brother will be subject to judgment. Again, anyone who says to his brother, "Raca," is answerable to the Sanhedrin. But anyone who says, "You fool!" will be in danger of the fire of hell.*

She sat back, staring at those words. This was why she couldn't buy into her parents' theology. How could Jesus assign equal punishment to murderers and those who called someone a fool?

That didn't even make sense. Was Jesus saying that if we were angry with someone, we were like killers? That we were *all* manslayers?

If her anger and hatred toward those who got in her way made her a killer, then Blair would be on death row.

Beside that verse, her father had written, "1 Peter 5:8."

She turned there, and found the verse.

Be self-controlled and alert. Your enemy the devil prowls around like a roaring lion looking for someone to devour.

She frowned and set the Bible down. Why had her father gone from the cities of refuge, to Jesus's words about murder being a heart thing, to the devil waiting to devour?

Her father had left the clues. It was her job to put them together.

She thought of her own anger and hatred and bitterness, feelings that heaped blood-guilt upon her. It was a heavy burden. Who could honestly not hate? Who could not get angry?

By Christ's standards, everyone carried around a heavy load of bloodguilt. Satan was roaming around, trying to catch one of them outside the city walls, hoping to devour them.

But if hatred and anger were the equivalent of killing, and if Satan was like the Avenger, then what was the City of Refuge?

None of it really made much sense. Yet it had been important enough to her father to have it marked up in his Bible. And it had been vital to Cade, who'd been studying it that morning.

Had Ann Clark become Cade's Avenger? And if so, where could Cade run for refuge? Was there any hope for him?

Frustrated, she closed the Bible and got back under her covers. She wouldn't think of those mythical cities again. There weren't answers there. Only more questions, and as hard as she tried to make all the dots connect, they were not going to lead her to Cade.

CHAPTER

46

*T*he weekly City Council meeting was not usually well attended, unless there was a controversy of some sort brewing. Jonathan tried to make every meeting just to ensure that the Council didn't pull anything underhanded. Just months ago they had tried to shut down Hanover House, until evidence surfaced that the mayor had ulterior motives.

Though the members were duly elected by the people of Cape Refuge, Jonathan often wondered if any thought had gone into their placement or if voters simply marked the name of their cousin or neighbor or anyone whose name they recognized, just so they could say they'd voted. Character didn't seem to play a role.

The small city hall stood on Ocean Boulevard across from the beach. Jonathan pulled his car onto the gravel parking lot. The meeting was already in session, so Jonathan went in and slipped into one of the middle rows. The members droned on about whether to put a stop sign at River Road and Third Street.

Jonathan tapped his foot nervously, wishing they'd move ahead.

"Next on the agenda," Art Russell said, "is the matter of the beach cams that Chief Cade has asked to have put up all over the beach." He fanned himself with a paper fan with the face of one of the mayoral candidates on it, and looked around the room. "I see that Cade isn't back from his honeymoon yet, so he isn't here to argue his case."

Jonathan almost leaped out of his shoes. Had they heard about the letter? Did they really believe it?

Doug Shepherd propped his chin like he might fall off to sleep. "If he don't care enough to come to the meeting and tell us why he thinks we need these, Art, then I say we go ahead and vote on it."

Sarah Williford weighed in. "We can put it off till next time. Wouldn't hurt anything."

"But the plain simple truth is that we don't have the money in the budget for no security cameras on the beach," Art said. "And I don't see why we need them, anyway."

Jonathan could see where this was going. They would vote against it tonight, ending any discussion, and when Cade got back he'd find his proposal dead in the water.

"Does anybody have any discussion on this?" Art asked.

Jonathan got up. "I do, Art."

"Step to the microphone, please, Jonathan."

Jonathan knew the mike wasn't necessary when there were no more than a dozen or so people in the room, the Council included. But he stepped up to it, nonetheless.

"First, I'd like to say that I don't know how you people found out about the letter that allegedly came from Cade, but I can tell you that not even the police are taking it seriously. Cade is not on his honeymoon."

"You're entitled to your opinion," Art said. "Now, if that's all—"

"No, it's not all," Jonathan cut in. "Most of you probably know about our tenant whose baby was kidnapped Sunday."

Sarah perked up. "Yes, Jonathan. Have they come any closer to finding it?"

"No," he said. "But one of the strongest pieces of evidence they have is the video of the woman leaving with the baby. There were cameras in the hall, the elevators, and at each door. If they find her, that video will help convict her."

Sarah looked fascinated, as though she'd just been given insider information on the juiciest piece of gossip in town. "Can they see her face in the video?"

Jonathan didn't see any point in feeding her morbid curiosity. "I can't really talk about the case beyond that, Sarah. My point in bringing it up is that cameras on the beaches would be a big deterrent to crime and would help get convictions. They'd help police to enforce the laws already on the books."

"What laws?" Art asked.

Jonathan cleared his throat. "Laws, for instance, about parties on the beaches at night."

"But it's communism, Jonathan," Morris Ambrose, the lone conservative, said. "We don't need to put Big Brother cameras all over this island, infringing on people's privacy."

"Why not?" Jonathan asked. "We have them in hospitals, convenience stores, banks, grocery stores. A lot of towns have them at red lights. They work in cutting down crime."

"Jonathan, we understand your concern for your foster daughter," Doug said. "But just because Sadie got drunk Saturday night don't mean the whole island should be videotaped twenty-four-seven."

Jonathan grabbed the microphone and shot Doug a killer look. "The City Council is not supposed to be a breeding ground for gossip, Doug, and if you want to make one more comment about Sadie, you and I can step outside—"

"All right!" Art hammered the gavel. "Thank you, Jonathan." It was meant to dismiss him, but he kept standing there.

"I guess we will go ahead and vote. We seem to have our minds made up."

"You can't do that." Jonathan's angry voice cut across the room.

The council members looked up at him. "Why not?" Sarah asked.

"Because Cade isn't here. As police chief of this town, he should have the right to make his case."

"He gave up his rights when he skipped town," Doug piped in. "He should have thought about them beach cams before he run off."

"He didn't run off!" Jonathan bit the words out. "That letter was clearly written under coercion. Anyone who knows Cade knows that he would never rush off and get married like that. He would have put a lot of thought and prayer into getting married, and he would have wanted his fiancée to know his friends. He wouldn't have hidden her."

"We'd expect you to think that," Sarah said. "Being his best friend and all. But most everybody believes that Cade is off on his honeymoon, and any day now he'll be back with his new wife. But his whims shouldn't control this body. So if you'll sit down, Jonathan, we're going to go ahead and vote."

Jonathan sat down, gritting his teeth, as every one of the members voted no. He hoped Cade would appreciate his feeble effort to defend the cause. He knew Cade probably had specific crime statistics, stories of crimes that could have been avoided with greater security on the beaches, other towns' success rates.

"Next up," Art said, "is that we have to name an interim police chief in Cade's absence."

"I say we name a permanent chief," Sarah said. "We don't need somebody as irresponsible as that boy running the police force on Cape Refuge."

"Well," Art said, "I think we can deal with that at some point in the future, but for right now, do I hear a motion that we appoint Joe to run things? He's the second-in-command and is already filling in. We'd just be making it official."

"So moved," Doug said.

"Second," Sarah added.

"Any discussion?"

Jonathan got up again. "I have something to say, Art."

Art sighed. "What is it now, Jonathan?"

"First of all, I'd like to point out that Cade hasn't even been gone more than a few days, and if I'm not mistaken, he did have some personal leave that he'd accrued. Except for a couple of days here and there when we've gone diving down in the Keys, Cade hasn't had a real vacation since he took the job. So there's no reason to get all in an uproar over his absence."

"Thank you for your comment," Art said with clear condescension. "Sit down, Jonathan."

His face burned. "No, I'm not finished. I wanted to point out that without a mayor you don't really have the right to make any decisions regarding the chief of police. When the new mayor is elected, *he* will decide who the chief is going to be. So unless you want a real fight, I suggest that you give Cade a chance to be found before you go naming interim chiefs!"

Dismissing him again, Art looked at the other members. "On whether or not to appoint Joe as interim chief, all in favor?"

Everyone on the council said "aye," and none was opposed.

Jonathan sank back down. These people couldn't be reasoned with.

"Next on the agenda," Sarah said. "Sue Ellen Jargis has a complaint about the library."

Jonathan rolled his eyes and watched as Sue Ellen headed for the microphone. Dressed in some kind of designer garb, she seemed to wear every piece in her jewelry box draped around her neck or wrist, or jangling from her ears.

She cleared her throat. "Ladies and gentlemen of the city council," she said in a saccharine voice. "I feel it is my duty to let you know that our town's library is being neglected and mismanaged. I went in there last Friday in the middle of the day, looking for some Italian tapes. My husband and I are going there next month—to Italy, I mean. More specifically, to Rome, Milan, and Vienna."

Jonathan smirked. "Uh, Sue Ellen, Vienna's in Austria, not Italy."

She could have murdered him with her look. "Of course it is. I meant to say Venice. I certainly know the difference between Venice and Vienna." She softened her tone and turned back to the microphone. "Anyway, as I was saying, I went looking for tapes, and Blair Owens practically threw me out the door, telling me she was closing early, even though the sign on the door said that her hours are nine to six. I came back the next day *and* the next, and both times the library was closed."

"Give me a break!" Jonathan said, coming to his feet again. "Sue Ellen, you know darn well that Blair is preoccupied with Cade's disappearance. Everyone on this island ought to be!"

The woman wouldn't be daunted. "Furthermore," she said, talking over him. "Gray Foster, a college student who uses the library a lot, told me she's left him there alone while she traipses off to who-knows-where.

"Now I think that if the city of Cape Refuge is paying Blair Owens to run the library, she should be expected to keep it open at regular hours. I think that woman needs to be fired for neglect and rude treatment of its patrons."

Jonathan had lost his temper at city council meetings before, but until now, he'd never wanted to hurt anyone. "Blair has never given anyone a reason to question her handling of the library before! Not once!"

Art sat back in his expensive chair and crossed one hairy leg over the other. "Very interesting. We appreciate your bringing this to our attention, Sue Ellen. And Jonathan, we appreciate your defense of your sister-in-law. We'll take this matter under advisement."

Jonathan sank back down. "Whatever that means."

When the meeting was over, he stalked back out to his truck and sat behind the wheel as the council members came out. Sarah Williford threw one flip-flopped foot over her Harley and cranked it up, letting the deafening roar of the motor pollute the peace of the town. Morris got into his Jaguar and pulled out. Doug and

Art had ridden together in Doug's pickup. They laughed about stopping by Cricket's for a beer before going home.

Oh, how the town needed a decent mayor, he thought. And so far the mayoral candidates were nothing but more of the same. Nothing would change if either of them got elected.

But if Jonathan were elected . . .

He started dreaming about the changes he would make, the commonsense approach he would use to matters that came up on the city council's agenda. Maybe he could set a new tone, absent the greed and lack of compassion characteristic of these people now.

As he started his truck and headed back to Hanover House, Jonathan made up his mind. He might not win, but he was going to give it a good run for his money.

He only wished the town had a newspaper so he could get the word out.

CHAPTER

*M*organ tried again to call Blair after Jonathan came home from the city council meeting, but there was still no answer.

When her voice mail answered again, Morgan tried to keep her voice level.

"Blair, where are you? By now you must have heard about Karen's baby being kidnapped, and you haven't called. I'm starting to think that you've vanished too. Come on, Blair, help me out here. I need to hear from you."

When she hadn't yet heard from Blair by midnight, she and Jonathan drove to her house. Her car was not out front.

"Okay, that's a good sign," Jonathan said. "When Cade disappeared he left his truck. If Blair took her car, then chances are nothing's happened to her."

Morgan wasn't convinced. "I still want to go in."

They used Morgan's key to unlock the door and cautiously stepped inside.

The living room was dark, a breeding place for shadows. The pale yellow walls did little to brighten the place. Morgan turned on the light and looked around. The room had always looked much more feminine than anyone would have expected of Blair. Morgan and her mother had helped her decorate a couple of years ago, but the choices had been Blair's.

She looked around and saw that some of the sofa cushions were on the floor, as if Blair might have lain down on the couch.

She pictured her sister sitting up late, terrors about Cade at war in her mind.

Jonathan passed her and went into the kitchen. "It's a mess in here," he said. "If she's been home she's been in a hurry."

Morgan stepped into the kitchen and saw a few dishes and cereal boxes sitting out on the counter. Blair had never been the most domestic one in the family, but she did at least do her dishes.

Jonathan left her there and went into the bedroom. "Bed's not made."

Morgan walked back through the living room to Blair's bedroom. She had slept here herself a number of times, mostly after her parents died, when Jonathan was wrongly imprisoned. Even in her grief, Blair had kept it relatively neat, but tonight a week's worth of clothes hung over a chair and several pairs of discarded socks lay on the floor.

"Okay, here we go." Jonathan picked up her alarm clock and pushed the "wake" button. "She must have been home at some point today, because it was set to go off at 2:00 P.M. Looks like it went off and was reset for tomorrow."

"Are you sure?"

"Yeah. If she hadn't turned it off, it would still be buzzing. Now it's set for 2:00 P.M. tomorrow."

Morgan took the clock. "What is she doing?"

Jonathan shook his head. "You don't think she's been staking out the Clark house all night, do you?"

Morgan looked at him. "I'd be willing to bet that's exactly what she's doing."

"Well, at least there's no sign that she's in trouble." He glanced at the Bible that lay on her pillow. "Look at that. Blair has a Bible?"

Morgan picked it up. "It's Pop's. I gave it to her. She was interested in the cities of refuge."

Jonathan nodded. "Because of what Cade's Bible was open to. Well, looks like she's been reading it. Maybe it'll do her some good."

Morgan set the Bible back down and looked around for any-more clues.

"Let's go home," Jonathan said. "Leave her a note telling her we've been here, and threaten her life if she doesn't call you the minute she comes in."

Morgan left her a scathing note, then wearily, they locked the door and went back to the pickup. As they drove home, she wished she'd found something more conclusive. She wanted to talk to Blair, needed to hear her voice.

Silently she prayed that she hadn't met the same fate as Cade and the baby.

CHAPTER

Morgan lay awake for most of the night and got up with Caleb at six in the morning. When the phone rang at eight, she ran to the parlor, where Agent Tavist sat with his recording equipment. He gave the signal, and she picked it up.

"Hello?"

"It's me." Blair's voice was hoarse with fatigue.

Relief washed like warm honey through Morgan's body. She motioned to the agent that it was okay. No kidnapper.

"Blair, where have you been?"

"Looking for Cade."

"Are you crazy?"

"Morgan, what's this about the baby?"

Morgan sighed and glanced at the agent. He was still taping. "He was kidnapped right out of her arms in the hospital, Blair. Don't you listen to the news?"

"Kidnapped? How?"

"A woman impersonating a nurse told Karen the doctor was on the floor and needed to see the baby."

Silence hung between them for a moment. "What is going on?" Blair said finally. "Morgan, I'm so sorry I haven't called. How is Karen?"

"As well as can be expected." She wanted to tell her about the FBI agent and the recording equipment, but it didn't seem like the right thing to do.

"Morgan, are you all right?"

Morgan breathed a laugh. "You know me."

She could tell Blair was crying now. "The two of us are a real pair," Blair said. Silence again, then, "If only Cade were here. I'll bet he could find that baby."

Morgan rubbed her eyes. "Blair, Jonathan went to the City Council meeting last night, and there was a complaint about you."

"What kind of complaint?"

"Sue Ellen Jargis complained that you've been closing the library. You're going to lose your job if you don't watch it."

"Don't worry about it. There's nobody else on this island qualified to run it." She sighed. "I don't want to talk about it right now."

"Okay," Morgan said. "Go get some sleep."

Blair didn't move to hang up. "Morgan?"

"Yeah?"

Another pause, then, "Do you think that Cade ran off and got married?"

Morgan tried to focus her thoughts. "No, Blair. I don't think that."

"Good," she whispered. "I don't either."

Morgan wasn't sure if she heard doubt in Blair's voice. "Blair, please don't kill yourself trying to rescue Cade. I'm worried about you getting into trouble yourself. Getting hurt, maybe killed. If you're right and Ann Clark had something to do with his disappearance, she could be a very dangerous woman."

"I hear you," Blair said.

"And you need to eat. Why don't you come over here for supper?"

"Can't."

Morgan frowned. "You're going to go back to Savannah again?"

"Don't worry about it, Morgan. You do what you have to do to find the baby, and I'll do what I have to do to find Cade."

Morgan didn't like the way that sounded. Tears stung her eyes, and she twisted her face and tried to control her voice. "Be careful, Blair."

"I will."

When Morgan hung up, she stared down at the phone and wept into her hand. "Lord, help us."

"Amen." She looked up and saw Karen standing in the doorway, her eyes swollen and her arms crossed over her fleshy stomach.

Morgan went to her and pulled her into her arms, and Karen fell apart again. "I handed my baby over to a maniac," she whispered. "I let her walk away with him."

Morgan didn't know how to assuage that guilt, so she just clung to her as they both wept out their grief.

CHAPTER

The phone woke Blair up, and she pulled herself out of the fog of her sleep and squinted at the clock. Twelve o'clock ... midnight? No, noon.

She grabbed the phone up. "Hello?"

"Blair, this is Sarah Williford."

Blair fell back onto her pillow. What did the city councilwoman want?

"I can't believe I finally got you on the phone. Where in the world have you been? I've left messages—"

"What is it, Sarah? Cut to the chase."

Sarah paused, as if making note of Blair's abruptness. "We've had some complaints about you keeping the library closed, Blair."

Blair thought of hanging up the phone, but decided that wouldn't be prudent. She sat up in bed, clutching the phone to her ear. It was time to get up anyway. She'd slept for four hours, and that was enough. She had to get back to the Clark house. "Yeah? And?"

"And I wondered if you intend to open the library today?"

"Wasn't planning on it, Sarah."

Sarah gave an indignant grunt. "And may I ask why?"

Blair stiffened. "Sarah, how many times have I done this in the years since I've been running it?"

"Well, I don't know, Blair, but you've done it a lot lately. What am I supposed to tell people who are complaining? We pay you to work there so that people can have access to it. If you're not going to do that, then we're going to have to make other arrangements."

Blair got up then. "You can't fire me, Sarah. You don't have the authority. The mayor has to fire me, and last I looked, we don't have one."

"Think again, Blair. The City Council has the authority to make decisions about the running of this town during the mayor's absence. And I should tell you that we do have an alternative. The Cape Refuge Ladies' Auxiliary has expressed interest in taking on the library as one of their projects. They could run it on shifts, if it comes to that."

Blair thought of ripping the cord out of the wall and flinging the phone across the room. "The Ladies' Auxiliary? So you think they could do a better job?"

"They would keep it open during its regular hours! I don't see what else they'd have to do. The place practically runs itself."

Now Blair was fully awake, and nuclear rage shot through her head. "You know what, Sarah? I think you should do that."

"Do what?"

"Let the Ladies' Auxiliary run it. Because I quit."

Sarah's silence screamed over the line. "Blair, I do suggest that you think this over."

"No," Blair said in a dramatic voice. "Far be it from me to stand in your way when you have a better option. Let the Ladies' Auxiliary run it. I'm sure they'll do a bang-up job."

"Blair, is this about Cade?"

Now Blair was speechless. "What?"

"Is this all about Cade? Jonathan said that you were distracted trying to find him. I don't know why you can't accept, like everyone else, that he's married and on his honeymoon. You're going to feel foolish when he comes back with his new bride, and you've up and quit your job so that you can spend your time obsessing over him."

Trembling now, Blair clutched the phone to her ear and leaned over, as if looking into the woman's face. "And you're going to feel foolish when he's found dead, and we learn that his life could have been saved if someone had done something!"

"Blair, you're not being rational."

"I'm so rational, Sarah, that I'm going over there right now and clean my stuff out of the library. And you better send one of your ladies over right away, because I'm leaving that pup open! Nice talking to you!" With that, she slammed the phone down, then picked it up and slammed it again.

Furiously, she got dressed, then stormed next door to clean her things out of the building that had been like her home for the last four years.

*S*ue Ellen Jargis showed up to "take over" the library just as Blair got the last of her personal things out. Adrenaline had enabled her to do it in record time. Lugging a box of floppy disks and programs that she'd bought herself, Blair bolted past her. "Knock yourself out, Sue Ellen. The key to the building is on the desk. Stay open as long as you want."

Sue Ellen made some kind of protest, but Blair didn't wait to hear it. She marched across the gravel parking lot and threw the boxes just inside her front door. She didn't go in herself, just slammed it and headed to her car.

Spinning out of the gravel, she headed for Hanover House.

She found Jonathan and Morgan sitting on the front porch with Caleb.

Flinging her door shut, she cut across the yard. "Jonathan, run for mayor. We need someone reasonable running this town."

Jonathan got up. "Blair, what's wrong?"

"I lost my job, that's what!"

"Blair!" Morgan handed Caleb to Jonathan. "They fired you?"

"No! They made me mad enough to quit!"

She came up the four porch steps and stood seething in front of them. "The Ladies' Auxiliary is taking over. Sue Ellen Jargis is there as we speak, showing everyone how easy it is to run the library since there's nothing much you have to do. It practically runs itself, according to Sarah Williford. They're going to run it in shifts. Can you believe that?"

Morgan looked exhausted. "Blair, you shouldn't have quit. You should have waited until your head is clearer."

Blair ignored her and turned to Jonathan. "So what's it gonna be, Jonathan? Are you going to run for mayor and rescue this town before the City Council flushes it right down the toilet?"

"Thinking about it," Jonathan said. "But without a newspaper in town, it's hard to get my issues out. I don't have much money for signs and bumper stickers and whatnot. I need a forum."

"You've got me," Blair said, slapping her chest. "I'll personally go door to door for you, giving every citizen of Cape Refuge an earful."

"Why don't *you* run?" Morgan asked wearily. "Wouldn't you love to be the boss of your tormenters? You were asked, weren't you?"

"Yeah, I was asked. But I'm not the type. I'm not photogenic, and everybody knows that politics is eighty percent cosmetic and twenty percent brains. Jonathan has a much better shot."

Jonathan looked at her like he didn't quite know how to take that.

"I'm one of the least popular residents on the island," she went on. "No, Jonathan has a much better shot."

"And when are you going to go door to door, Blair?" Morgan asked. "You'd have to give up your new career as private detective."

"I'd work it in," Blair said. "Don't you worry about that. So, Jonathan, what do you say?"

Jonathan leaned against the post and studied her for a minute. "I'll make a deal with you, now that you're unemployed."

"What?" she asked.

"You start the newspaper back up, and I'll run."

Blair took a step back. "The newspaper? No way. I'd have to buy it from the previous owner. I wouldn't give her one red cent."

"Then start one up on your own. You could do it, Blair."

"With what money?" she asked. "Talk about irrational. I have some savings but not enough to buy all the computers, photography equipment, and printing presses I would need."

"You could get a loan."

Blair almost laughed. Then her bitter amusement faded, and she stared at her brother-in-law. "You're serious about this, aren't you?"

"Yes, I am," he said. "We desperately need a newspaper, and frankly, if I spent a whole day listing possible candidates to run it, I couldn't think of anyone who'd be better at it than you."

For the first time in a long time, Blair found herself speechless.

Morgan filled in the silence. "He's right, Blair. Maybe losing the librarian job is a blessing in disguise. Maybe the Lord's opening another door for you."

"I think it's more likely that *Jonathan* is opening a door for me. Or kicking it down, would be more accurate."

Jonathan's eyes twinkled with the possibilities. "You do it, Blair, and I'll run for mayor," he said. "I'm not asking for special treatment, either. You could cover all the candidates. But as it stands right now, the one with the most signs up wins. Give us a place to air our convictions."

As much as she hated to admit it, Blair was catching his vision. "I could also cover Cade's disappearance and make people understand that he's in trouble. Put to rest all those insane ideas about him being on his honeymoon."

"You could!" Morgan's eyes rounded. "That would do more good than sitting in your car all night."

Blair started pacing, working out the details in her mind. "And I could cover Karen's baby. Maybe help the FBI get some leads. Being part of the media could give me access to things I can't have access to now."

Morgan started to smile. "Do it, Blair. I think you should do it."

Blair looked out across the street, to the beach beyond it. "Who am I kidding? I don't even own a computer now. I have zilch to start with."

"Don't give up before you try," Jonathan said. "Wouldn't you love to show the City Council and the Ladies' Auxiliary that they haven't bested you?"

That did it. "Yes, I would." She turned back to him, grinning. "I'll look into it."

"When?"

"Tomorrow," she said.

Morgan grabbed her arm. "How about today?"

"Can't. I have to be somewhere."

Morgan groaned. "Washington Park. Blair—"

Blair didn't want to hear it. "I have to go," she said. "Thanks for the idea, Jonathan."

"I'm ready when you are," he said.

Her mind reeled with possibilities as she pulled out of the driveway.

CHAPTER

*A*gain, the night had been long. Blair sat across the park from Ann Clark's house, watching every light in every window. The woman never seemed to leave the house. Not once had she seen her car back out of the driveway. She stayed inside that place as if it were a fortress that hid her darkest secrets.

Blair was more certain than ever that it did.

She hated to go home for rest, but as the sun grew higher in the morning sky, she realized that it wouldn't pay to sit here until she fell asleep and have someone notice her. Besides, she doubted the woman would do anything suspicious in broad daylight.

She drove home, fatigue aching through her body. As she pulled into the gravel parking area she shared with the library, she noticed Sue Ellen's car there already, along with a couple of others.

For a moment she sat in her car, staring at that library door. How dare they? She hoped the pages fell out of all the books, that the tapes broke, that the microfiche jammed. She hoped no one on the island brought back another book and that they never collected another dime for their budget.

Anger revived her as she cut across the gravel and went into her house. The phone was ringing, so she picked it up.

"Hello?"

"Yeah. Blair, hi. This is Jason Wheater down at the Island Bank."

She tossed her bag on the table and sank into a chair. "Uh-huh."

"Jonathan called me and said you were interested in buying the *Cape Refuge Journal.*"

Her eyebrows shot up. "He did, did he?"

"Yes. I told him that we recently foreclosed on all the equipment and the building. We own it now. We're about ready to auction it off, but we'd rather sell it."

Blair rubbed her eyes. She couldn't think. "Look, Jason, it's not a real good time, with Cade missing and all. I haven't slept."

"I understand," Jason said. "But if we had a newspaper on this island, maybe it would help to locate Cade. Heaven knows the *Savannah Morning News* isn't talking enough about it, except to cast aspersions on Cade."

The man had done his homework. He knew which buttons to push. "Truth is, Jason, I haven't really given it all that much thought."

"Well, why don't you meet me over there this morning and I can take you through it? You could see what you'd be getting, and maybe we can make a deal. We'd even be willing to do some financing, Blair. We know you're good for it. And you'd probably have a built-in subscription base, so we know there'd be some income."

Blair sighed. She really didn't want to deal with this now, but Jason was right. If she started the paper back up, maybe somebody would read something and come up with a lead that could help them get to Cade. And she had to make a living somehow. Even if Sarah Williford begged her, she had too much pride to take the library back.

Research was her first love. But she could do that from a newspaper office and actually turn her knowledge into something productive for everyone. What could it hurt to look?

"All right, Jason," she said, "I'll meet you over there at four this afternoon."

"Good deal," he said. "I'll see you there."

Blair got a few hours' sleep, then went over to Hanover House before her meeting with Jason Wheater.

There had been no productive leads on the missing baby, and the parlor still looked like a cockpit, with recorders and telephones and tracing equipment piled on one of her mother's antique tables.

Blair went to the kitchen, and saw Morgan on the back porch playing with Caleb.

Morgan heard her and looked in through the window. She motioned for Blair to come out. Blair pushed through the door and dropped into a rocker.

Morgan regarded her for a moment. "You look awful."

"Thanks."

"No, really. You look worse than you did after Mama and Pop died. I'm worried about you."

"Then stop it."

"Blair, you're not going to do Cade any good if you don't take care of yourself."

Close to tears again, Blair got up and went to the screen door. Peering out, she said, "Who cares if I take care of myself? I can sleep when he's found." She turned back. "Any word about the baby?"

"None," Morgan said. "Nobody's getting much sleep these days."

She put Caleb into his Flintstone mobile, and he used his feet to pull himself along.

Blair went to sit back down. "I know Ann Clark knows where Cade is," she said, knowing she was changing the subject, but unable to help herself. "I know that as sure as I've ever known anything in my life."

"Has she done anything that you've seen? Had visitors? Gone anywhere?"

Blair shrugged. "Nothing yet."

Morgan got up as Caleb hit the wall, and turned him back around. "Want some tea? I could use some."

"No, I didn't come over here for tea. I actually came over to ask you if you'd go to the newspaper with me. Jonathan got Jason Wheater to call me. He wants to make a deal."

Morgan grinned. "So you're going?"

"I thought I would. It's gone into foreclosure," she said. "The building, the equipment, everything. The bank owns it now, and they're trying to get rid of it. They've offered to finance it and everything."

Morgan's face changed. "Blair, that's amazing. You're the only one I know who can quit her job in a fit of rage and not suffer for it."

"It's not a done deal yet. I'm meeting him at four. Wanna come?"

Morgan started to laugh. "Sure, I'll come with you."

She heard the inside door closing and Sadie tromping through the house. "Morgan, I'm home!"

"Out here, Sadie," Morgan called.

Blair looked up as Sadie came to the door. "Hi, Blair."

Blair lifted her hand in a silent wave.

Morgan pulled Sadie out. "Sadie, you'll never guess what Blair's doing this afternoon."

"What?"

"She's meeting a banker about buying the *Cape Refuge Journal*."

Sadie sucked in a sharp breath and stared down at Blair. "You're kidding!"

Blair gave her a weak grin. "Nope."

"Oh, my gosh. Can I go with you? I can show you where everything is. I worked there long enough to get real familiar with the place. I can even show you how to use the equipment."

Blair grinned. "That'd be real nice, Sadie. I could use your experience."

Morgan started into the house. "Let me go change Caleb's diaper, and I'll get ready to go. I'll just bring him with us."

Sadie kept staring at Blair, as if it was too good to be true. "Oh, Blair, if you buy the newspaper can I work for you, please? I was a real good employee for Nancy. I can do a good job. I promise."

Blair got to her feet. She'd never been so tired in her life. "I thought Morgan didn't want you to work, Sadie. I thought she wanted you to concentrate on your school."

"But I can do both. I really can. I don't think she'll mind if it's you. And school will be out for the summer in just a few weeks."

"Well, I will need somebody," Blair said, "and it sure couldn't hurt to have somebody who knows the ropes working there, at least part time."

Sadie punched the air and laughed. "Maybe if I work there, Morgan won't make me go back to school next year. I could work for you and home-school at night—"

"Whoa," Blair said. "I haven't even bought the place, and you're dreaming about quitting school?"

"Not quitting. Home-schooling. The ones my age are seniors now. The kids in my class all hate me. This town isn't very forgiving, you know."

"Forgiving?" Blair asked. "What in the world do they have to forgive you for?"

Sadie's delight faded. "My past," she said. "Everybody knows where I came from, what my mother's done, how I was raised. I'll never escape it, no matter where I go."

Blair looked out across the yard. Morgan had done a good job of keeping the flower beds intact, keeping the weeds out, keeping everything growing and beautiful the way her mother had done it. She'd thought she'd done miracles with Sadie too.

But she understood the girl's insecurities. She'd had much the same experience in school because of her scars.

"You know, my parents came here years ago, and they had a lot of baggage too," she said, "a lot of history, a lot of guilt in their lives. Some of that guilt had to do with me."

Sadie nodded. She'd heard the whole story months before.

"But the town came to love them. They did good things, helped a lot of people." Her voice broke off. "They'll love you too, Sadie. They will. One of these days you'll be so at home here that you'll never be able to leave."

"Like you?" Sadie asked.

Blair shrugged. "Truth is, I had every intention of being out of here by now, but things keep making me stay." Her voice trailed off, and she stared at those flowers and thought of Cade.

"And if you buy the paper," Sadie said, "then you'll be obligated to stay, won't you?"

Blair thought about that for a moment. It might be a good reason not to buy the paper. She wasn't sure she wanted to be that committed to staying in town indefinitely, especially if Cade wasn't here.

She got up, feeling a little dizzy. "Well, I guess I'd better get going. You ready?"

"Oh, yeah," Sadie said. "I'm ready, all right."

*B*lair told Jason Wheater that she'd have to give it some more thought. While everything looked intact and seemed to be in working order, she just wasn't sure that buying the paper was what she wanted to do. As Sadie had pointed out, it would give her roots here like a ball and chain, tying her ankle to this island, keeping her from ever escaping.

And escape might be just what she needed.

On the other hand, if she bought the paper, she could have it up and running within a few days, and she could use it to turn the town's attention to Cade. Jason indicated that he'd have no problem getting the bank to finance her loan. If she wanted it, he could have the paperwork ready within a day.

Until she decided, she would proceed as she had been, staking out Ann Clark's house since no one else would.

That night, as darkness settled in, she drove back to Washington Square in Savannah and watched the lights in the Clark house flicker on and off from room to room.

She had sat here night after night for days and had still not seen a thing. No one had come or gone from this place. Ann Clark hadn't left at all.

Discouraged, she had almost decided to go on home and admit that, perhaps, she was wrong about the woman.

But then something changed.

In one of those windows flickering with light—like several carefully placed candles—she saw Ann Clark's silhouette in the curtain.

She wasn't alone.

The silhouette of a man stood facing her for the briefest of moments, then he walked out of the window's frame.

Blair's heart seemed to stop. She hadn't seen anyone arrive at Ann's home. There were no cars in the driveway. Could that be Cade? She got out of her car and rushed across Washington Park, her eyes locked on that window.

There he was again, the same silhouette in that window. The shape of his face did not look like Cade's, and he was shorter, only six or seven inches taller than Ann's five-feet-two. Cade was taller—at least six-feet-two. This man's nose was bigger, his chin more prominent, his hair longer.

So who was it? She hadn't seen anyone come or go from this house.

She crossed the rest of the park, not taking her eyes from that window. Someone rode by on a bicycle, a car passed, she heard voices on the other side of the park.

She crossed the street to Ann's driveway. Did she dare go to that window to peer in and see who the man was? The curtains were closed. She doubted she could even get a look.

Instead, she went up the driveway that turned behind the house and looked in the garage window. Ann's car still sat there.

She pulled back from the window and looked around the yard.

Then she saw it. A motorcycle, parked next to the garage. She put her hand on it, felt that it was warm.

How had anyone ridden this in without her seeing them?

She looked around, wishing she had a flashlight. There were trees separating the Clark house from the house behind her. On another side, between a fence and a hedge, separating her house from the one next to her, she saw a small driveway. There it was, another way out and another way in. She stole across the yard and started down that driveway. It cut between two houses and came out on the adjacent street.

No wonder she hadn't seen Ann or anyone else coming and going.

She checked the motorcycle, saw that it had no tag. Who was on it? She had to know.

Slowly, she walked toward that window where she could still see the shadows of a man and a woman. . . .

*M*organ checked the address she'd hastily jotted down and turned onto the block where Washington Square sat. She had tried to call Blair tonight, hoping she was home figuring out how she could buy the paper. But once again, she had not answered, and Morgan had little doubt where she was.

A sense of dark foreboding had fallen over her at the thought of her sister trying to be a hero. She had to go talk her out of one more night spent in her car, she decided. She had to convince her that her mission was insane.

Knowing that Jonathan would never let her go after Blair, she told him only that she was going to talk to her. He assumed she meant at Blair's house. If he'd known she was circling the block now, looking for Ann Clark's house and Blair's car, he would have thrown his body in front of her car to stop her.

But someone had to look out for Blair.

She found the address and slowed in front of it. There were lights on in the Clark house, clearly indicating that the woman was home.

But Blair's car was nowhere to be seen. She drove around the block, making the square. Maybe Blair wasn't here. Maybe she had gone to a movie or shopping in the mall. Maybe she had been here and left.

But as she turned the corner, her heart plunged. There was Blair's car, strategically parked where she'd have a direct view through the park to Ann Clark's front door.

She pulled in behind it, and as her headlights shone through it, she realized Blair wasn't in it.

Morgan threw her car into park. Where was she? She cut her engine off, got out quickly, and ran to look in Blair's window.

The car was empty. She looked around, hoping to find her sister on a park bench, but Blair was nowhere in sight.

The Clark house. She had to be there.

Swallowing back her fear, Morgan crossed the park, her eyes straining to see through the darkness. Quietly she reached the sidewalk directly across from the house. She scanned the property for any sign of life.

Finally, she saw her, standing just under a window, peering up over the rim.

Someone was going to see her and call the police—or worse! Morgan crossed the yard and bolted toward her sister.

"Blair, what are you doing?" The question came out in a loud whisper.

Blair caught her breath and spun around. "Morgan! You scared me to death!" she whispered harshly. "What are you, crazy?"

Morgan grabbed her hand and led her off of the property and away from the house as fast as she could. Blair came like a child caught misbehaving. When they were on the other side of the park, Morgan finally stopped.

"I've always thought you were a little cracked, Blair," she said, trying to catch her breath, "but now I know it for sure."

"I'm not cracked," Blair said. "Cade is in that house."

Morgan shoved her hair back from her perspiring face. "Did you see him when you were peaking in the window?"

"No," she said, "I didn't see anything. But that doesn't mean he's not there."

"Blair, you're not thinking clearly. You're breaking the law! You can't trespass on people's property and look in their windows, no matter what you think is going on inside!"

"There was a man in there with her, Morgan! I saw his shadow in the curtain. He drove a motorcycle through a back driveway."

Morgan wanted to shake her. "Blair, I don't want to see you get arrested, and I don't want you killed. You're playing with fire here, and you have to stop it. Let the authorities handle it."

"The authorities are doing zilch," Blair said. "Cade is in trouble and nobody cares, nobody but me."

"You're wrong about that."

"Oh, am I? Then you tell me why the police haven't torn this house apart brick by brick looking for Cade? He's in there somewhere. It's a no-brainer. While they're dancing around probable cause, I'm doing something!"

Morgan started to cry. Blair couldn't be reasoned with. Malnutrition and lack of sleep had caught up with her. "Come home, Blair. Please leave this place and come home. You're scaring me to death."

"Oh, stop crying! This isn't about you, Morgan."

"I know it's not about me," she said. "I just feel like I've lost control of everything in my life. Cade, Karen's baby, Sadie, you. You're all in danger, and I have no control."

"You never had control over me in the first place," Blair said, "so get over it. And calm down about Sadie. She hasn't done anything all that awful. She's just being a kid, and she's going to be all right."

"That's beside the point." She straightened and wiped her face. "My sister has been trespassing on private property and stalking a woman who may have nothing to do with Cade's disappearance at all. You're going to wind up in jail, Blair. I want you to come home now."

Blair turned back to the house as if something might have changed since she'd walked away. "I can't go, Morgan. Something's happening in there."

Morgan had had enough. "Blair, don't make me report you to the police myself. I'd rather have you locked up safely than know you're risking your life here."

Blair glared at her. "You wouldn't dare."

"Try me," Morgan said. "I'll drive straight to the police station."

It was clear that Blair knew she meant it. "Morgan, you're bullying me."

"Whatever it takes." Morgan pointed to Blair's car like a mother who'd had enough. "In the car, Blair. I'll follow you home."

When Blair hesitated, Morgan said, "Now!"

Grunting out her frustration, Blair got into her car and slammed the door. Morgan waited as she started the car, then she got into her own. Blair pulled away from the curb, and Morgan followed.

As she followed Blair back down Highway 80 to Tybee Island, she cried out to God. "Blair doesn't have the power to save Cade, Lord. And I don't have the power to save Emory. And Jonathan and I don't have the strength to save Sadie, either. You're our only hope. Please intervene here. Please let all of them be all right."

She wept into her hand as Blair headed for Cape Refuge. "And let Blair be all right too. Lord, she needs to see your power. Please don't let Satan win this battle."

She followed Blair back to her front door, then watched her go in. Wiping her tears, she drove back to Hanover House. But as she went back in, she knew that Blair wouldn't stay home. She'd be back at the Clark house within the hour.

*T*he phone call that came to Hanover House on Thursday morning silenced the household. As she'd done each time it had rung since the baby's disappearance, Morgan picked up the cordless phone and ran into the parlor. Agent Tavist had started his equipment rolling, and he held his arm up in the air, making her wait for a signal.

The phone rang a second time, and Morgan glanced at the Caller ID. There was no name on the screen, just a number.

"It's a cell phone," Tavist said.

It rang a third time and his arm came down. He pointed at her to answer.

"Hello?"

"Put the mother on the phone." The voice had an eerie, split quality, as if someone spoke through a disguising device.

Morgan froze. Her eyes met Tavist's, and he motioned for her to get Karen.

The kidnapper! She turned back to the stairs. *The kidnapper was on the phone!*

She grabbed the banister. "Karen!" she screamed at the top of her lungs. "Karen, telephone! *Hurry!*"

Karen, who had not come out of her room yet this morning, bolted down the stairs, a look of stark terror on her face. "Is it about my baby?"

"I think so!" Morgan thrust the phone at her, then pressed her face close to Karen's so she could hear the call.

"Hello?" Karen's voice trembled with anticipation.

"Leave fifty thousand dollars in locker number 36 at the Trailways Bus Station."

Karen clutched the phone. "When will I get my baby back?"

"Leave the money by 4:00 P.M. tomorrow, and if it's all there, we'll contact you about where you can find him."

The agent gestured for her to keep him talking. "How do I know you'll do what you say?" Karen asked into the phone. "How do I even know my baby is still alive?"

But the phone clicked, and the dial tone hummed behind it.

Karen began to wail, and Morgan took her in her arms and looked at the agent who was still on his phone. "Did you trace it?"

He took off his headphones and looked up at her.

"Did you?"

"Oh, yeah. We traced it, all right. We have SPD on their way to the site right now."

Karen's face blossomed with hope. "Oh, Morgan, they might find my baby!"

But something in the agent's eyes gave Morgan pause. "Maybe so," she said, putting her arm around the woman. "We just have to wait."

They sat huddled together on a love seat in the parlor, their eyes on Tavist as he talked to other field agents. Finally, he finished the call and turned back to them. "Okay, here's what we've got. The phone call was made near the Laurel Grove Cemetery. Police found the phone, but the caller was gone."

Morgan stood up. "So whose phone was it?"

Tavist cleared his throat and looked at his equipment again. Finally, he turned back to her. "Police Chief Matthew Cade."

The world seemed to freeze, and Morgan couldn't move. Her throat constricted, her heart stuttered. . . . "No way in the world," she said. "Not in a million years."

Karen didn't care who it was. "Are they going after him? Are they going to arrest him? They have to find my baby!"

Cade. It couldn't be Cade.

Morgan grabbed the phone. Blair. She needed to talk to Blair. "Who are you calling?" he asked.

"My sister!"

He shook his head. "We need to keep this quiet."

"Please," she said. "I'll just tell her to come over."

He finally agreed, so she dialed Blair's number. Thankfully, she was home.

"Hello?"

"Blair, get over here. It's important. There's something you need to hear."

Silence, then, "He's not dead. Don't tell me he's dead."

"No, that's not it. Something else. Just come over here, Blair."

Morgan hung up. She needed Jonathan, but he was out on the Atlantic with a boat full of fishermen.

Cade's phone? It couldn't be!

Beside her, Karen began to pace. "The ransom. I have to get fifty thousand dollars. I have to pay them so I can get my baby."

Morgan's mind raced frantically. It couldn't be Cade.

Karen kept ranting. "The bus station, he said. Tomorrow by four, locker 36. I have to do it!"

Morgan heard Blair's car on the gravel, heard her slamming her door. She kept holding Karen as Blair bolted into the house.

"What is it?"

Morgan got up. "Blair, we got a ransom call about the baby. It was from Cade's cell phone."

Blair blinked at her. "*What?*"

"I heard the voice," Morgan said. "They were using some kind of disguising device, so the voice was indiscernible."

Blair turned to the busy agent. "I want you to tell me something." Her voice quivered with emotion. "You're a cop. If you decided to commit some horrendous crime, would you really be so stupid as to make a ransom call on your cell phone?"

"I wouldn't. But people don't think."

She gritted her teeth. "Cade would think! It proves that it's not him. Someone is using his cell phone! Don't you see?" She went to his chair and braced her hands on his armrests. "Someone had him write that letter so we wouldn't look for him, and now they're setting him up for kidnapping!"

She rose up and shoved her fingers through her hair. Her scars flamed with excitement. "We never even considered that there was a connection. But there is! If we can find the baby, maybe we can find Cade."

The agent didn't give any indication whether he agreed with Blair's deduction or not. He just got back on the phone.

Frustrated and fearing further smearing of Cade's name, Blair went into the kitchen and called Joe McCormick. He showed up at Hanover House just a few minutes later.

He got a briefing by the agent, then joined Morgan and Blair in the kitchen. "I'm with you, Blair. I don't believe that Cade has anything to do with that kidnapping. Someone used his cell phone, then left it for us to find."

Blair's eyes were frantic as she moved closer to Joe. "Ann Clark is still the key. Maybe she's the one who stole the baby. They didn't have to keep him alive to use his phone. He could already be dead!"

The agent got off the phone and came into the kitchen. "We have an all-points-bulletin out on Chief Matthew Cade, and they're getting a warrant for his arrest."

"A warrant for him, but not for Ann Clark?" Blair shouted. "That's absurd!"

But Morgan saw it another way. "No, it's good," she said. "Blair, at least there will be an all-out hunt for him."

"What about the fifty thousand dollars?" Karen asked. "They demanded that. Said they would give me my baby back if I left it."

Tavist shook his head. "I'm sorry, Miss Miller, but there aren't any lockers at the bus station anymore."

"What? Yes, there are. I've seen them!"

"They took them out after the September eleventh attacks. There was too much risk of someone planting a bomb in them. No, the caller knew that."

Blair gave a bitter laugh. "That call wasn't about ransom at all, but just a way of setting Cade up."

The cop didn't answer. "If they call back, Miss Miller, you demand some proof that they even have the baby, and that he's alive."

Karen moaned and fell against Morgan. "But they already told me what to do. My baby needs me!"

Morgan tried her hardest to comfort the inconsolable mother.

But the look in Blair's eyes frightened her even more than the call itself. She was going to do something stupid, and Morgan knew she couldn't stop her.

*T*he FBI considered Cade a criminal to be caught now, not a missing person who needed to be found. At least, that was the way it appeared to Blair. She sincerely hoped she was wrong.

But at least they had more than Cape Refuge's tiny police force searching for him. With the feds on the hunt, they would surely be able to find him soon.

When she arrived back at Ann Clark's block that night, Blair half-hoped to see a crowd of FBI agents surrounding the place, searching it like the crime scene that it was.

But no one was there. Ann Clark was still free to do as she pleased.

This time Blair parked on the street where the back driveway came out and watched for anyone to come or go.

No one did.

She wondered if Cade and the baby could be in the same place.

She sat there for another grueling night, fighting sleep and
hunger. Early the next morning, when the paperboy began delivering the newspapers to the driveways surrounding the park, Blair
borrowed one and unrolled it. The headline stopped her heart.

SEARCH ON FOR POLICE CHIEF: ALLEGED INVOLVEMENT
IN KIDNAPPING RING.

The reporter told that a ransom call had been made from
Cade's cell phone and that his sudden disappearance two weeks
ago had spurred rumors of his whereabouts. It speculated that his
credentials as a cop may have made it easier for him to get a
female accomplice into the hospital to take the baby.

Furious, she rolled up the newspaper and threw it back
on the driveway she'd taken it from, then headed back to Cape
Refuge.

That was it, she thought. She was going to buy the *Cape
Refuge Journal* if it took every dime she had. She'd call Jason
Wheater tonight and tell him she would offer all of her savings as
a down payment. He would draw up the papers as soon as possible, and she could have it up and running in record time. For the
life of her, she would counter every allegation the *Savannah Morning News* had made about Cade today, and she would show the
inconsistencies in the case and draw attention to the questions that
still plagued her about his disappearance.

It might be the only hope Cade had left.

CHAPTER

Chaos reigned at Hanover House as they waited for the phone to ring again. Though the FBI seemed convinced that the caller had known there weren't lockers at the Trailways station, Karen still hoped that the kidnapper had made a mistake and would call back to correct it.

While they waited, Morgan tried to comfort Karen, but it was almost impossible.

The sound of Karen's anguish all night had been a terrible thing to hear, and Morgan had spent most of the night in earnest prayer. The pall continued to hang over the house as morning gave way to afternoon, and a quivering sense of anticipation preoccupied them all.

In the parlor, the agents worked, taking calls and coordinating the search for Emory and Cade. Nervous and somber at the accusations being leveled against his best friend, Jonathan paced the kitchen with his hands in his pockets.

"I have to get that money and do what they say," Karen cried. "Lockers or not, I have to be there with that money!"

Morgan leaned against the cabinet, trying to think. Gus and Felicia sat on either side of Karen, like allies against the world that conspired against her.

"You all right, Miss Morgan?" Gus's bass voice cut through her thoughts.

"I'm fine, Gus."

"I been thinking," he said. "What if I go with Miss Karen to make the drop? I could protect her from anybody out to hurt her."

Morgan met Jonathan's impatient eyes. "Gus, there are no lockers," Jonathan said, "and we don't have the money. There's not going to be a drop."

"All's we need to do is stand there with a duffel bag, mon. Maybe they'll come."

Karen slapped her hand on the table. "It's something, Morgan. Something more than we're doing now." She looked at her watch. "They said four. It's two-thirty now!"

Felicia put her plump arm around Karen's shoulders. "Miss Morgan, don't you think you could raise the money with some phone calls to church members? I know fifty thousand is a lot, but for the life of a baby . . ."

Morgan had a crick in her neck, and her shoulder muscles felt as if they'd been tied in knots. The "maybes" and "ifs" were starting to make her crazy. "Thanks, Felicia. I'm sure the FBI is considering everything."

"I don't know why you think that," Gus said in a low voice. "They haven't done nothing for Cade, mon. And now they think he did it."

Morgan knew Gus was right.

Tavist came to the kitchen, leaned in. "Miss Miller, can you come in here, please?"

Karen sprang up and grabbed Morgan and Jonathan's hands. "Come with me."

They both followed her into the parlor, where four agents sat around a table. Tavist lowered his voice so the others wouldn't hear. "Miss Miller, we've decided to stake out the Trailways Station in case the kidnappers show up."

"Yes!" Karen turned and started out of the room. "I'll go get ready!"

"Wait." Tavist's voice turned her back. "You're not going."

"But they told *me* to come!" she shouted. "They said for me to bring the money!"

"But you can't make the drop without the lockers. We're just going to have agents watching for them."

"Watching for who? You don't even know what they look like!"

"We know what Matthew Cade looks like, and the woman who took the baby was a white woman of about five-feet-two."

Jonathan snapped. "If you're looking for Cade, Tavist, then you're going to miss the real kidnapper! Cade is not involved!"

"Whoever is involved, our agents are trained. They know what to look for."

"You can't do this!" Karen cried. "I have to be there if they bring my baby."

"Miss Miller, they're not going to wheel a stroller in there and swap with you. Trust us. We have experience with this kind of thing."

Karen wouldn't hear any of it. "But if they don't see me, they might kill my baby. We have to do what they say."

Tavist stepped toward her. "Miss Miller, I know this is hard for you. But what we're doing is in the best interest of the baby. If you hope to get him back, you need to let us call the shots."

As Karen wilted against Morgan, Caleb toddled in, and Sadie ran in behind him. "Sorry, Morgan. I'm trying to keep him out of the way."

Morgan had forgotten the girl was home. Early this morning, when Sadie would have gone to school, she'd convinced Morgan to let her stay home to help with Caleb while the decisions were being made. Morgan had been so distracted she'd agreed.

Letting Karen go, Morgan picked Caleb up and kissed him. "It's okay, Sadie. We need a distraction."

Sadie stood in the doorway and looked at Karen as if the sight of her tears hurt her as well.

"They're risking Emory," Karen said. "By not doing it the way they said, they're risking his life."

"They're trying to save it," Morgan said quietly.

"He'll be all right, Karen," Sadie whispered. "God took care of Caleb. He'll take care of Emory."

"Babies are hurt and killed all the time, Sadie," Karen snapped. "It's a horrible world. Their daddies take them to terrible places, where people hurt them. They're left in hot cars. They're neglected and left to cry for hours and hours and hours. If they survive being babies, they're hurt when they're older."

Morgan shot Sadie a stricken look, then touched Karen's hand. "Karen, I know things are bad right now. But you can't give up hope. And when things are out of your control, you have to realize that there's ultimately only one person who is in control. And that's God."

"Then where was he when Emory was taken?" Her voice broke off and she covered her mouth and wailed. "I've prayed and prayed and prayed. You said prayer works, and I believed you."

Sadie watched her now, waiting for her answer, as if she too needed to hear why it seemed God had not acted.

"Prayer does work. God answers, Karen. You'll see. He could be protecting that baby from harm while he's with strangers. He could be working it out so that the police find the kidnappers. He could be doing a number of things that we can't see."

Karen looked at her skeptically. So did Sadie.

"And even if God doesn't save Emory, we still have to trust him, because he's still good."

Sadie looked as disappointed in her answer as Karen did. "I think I'll go for a walk, if it's all right."

Morgan nodded. "I don't blame you for wanting to get out of here. Go ahead."

Sadie looked close to tears as she went to the door. Morgan wanted to run after her and make sure she was all right.

But the crisis had not yet passed. She would see about Sadie a little bit later.

*T*ension hung in the air at Hanover House, and Sadie was glad to escape it. She crossed the street to the beach and walked the shoreline. The ocean was gentle today, and the sky a cloudless, solid blue. One would never know that people had vanished, babies had been stolen, and good people might really be evil.

She didn't know what to think about Cade now. Did he have it in him to do these kinds of things?

He was the first one she'd met on the island, the one who had taken her to the doctor and paid, himself, to have her arm set. He was the one who'd tried to get Caleb out of Jack Dent's home.

If you couldn't trust him, who could you trust?

Morgan and Jonathan were certain he was victim and not perpetrator, but Sadie wasn't so sure.

She needed to talk to someone who wasn't involved in these tragedies, but every call in or out of the home was being recorded. There was a pay phone on the South

Beach Pier. She thought of calling Trevor—her only real friend—just to talk.

What could a simple phone call hurt?

She checked her watch as she reached the phone. By now, he was probably home from school. Quickly, she thumbed through the phone book for his number.

Inserting her coins, she dialed. Her heart pounded as she waited for him to answer.

"Hello?"

"Trevor? This is Sadie."

"Sadie!" The pleasure in his voice was unmistakable. "Where were you today?"

"Some stuff was going on at Hanover House. Listen, I'm pretty freaked out about Cade and the kidnapping and everything. You want to meet somewhere to talk?"

"Sure," he said. "Tell me where."

"Well, I'm at the South Beach Pier right now. How soon can you come?"

"Give me ten minutes."

Sadie hung up, gratified that he would come so quickly. She walked out to the pier, took her shoes off, and sat on the side.

Evil was everywhere, she supposed. Though she hated to admit it, even Hanover House wasn't immune.

She leaned her forehead against the pier's railing and looked out at the water billowing beneath her. Another storm was headed this way, and the waves rushed the shore with mad urgency, mirroring the restlessness in her soul.

"Wow, you look really bummed."

She looked up. Trevor stood there in a pair of shorts and a Miller Lite T-shirt. "Hey. You made it fast."

He sat down next to her. "I was anxious to see you."

She couldn't be sucked in by his charm. Not this time. "This is not a date," she said. "I'm not lying to anyone about anything. I just needed someone to talk to."

"I'm your man. What's wrong?"

She crossed her arms on the rail and rested her chin on them. "I'm just . . . confused. Wondering if all the things Morgan and Jonathan say are right."

"They're not," he said. "I can tell you that right now."

Sadie knew better than to dismiss them that easily. She thought of Morgan's deep faith in the power of prayer and knew she couldn't talk this out with Trevor. He wouldn't be objective. So she sidestepped it.

"I was just thinking a lot about why some babies are born into perfect, loving homes and others are born into dangerous, evil homes with mean parents. Or why good people who would make great parents sometimes can't have kids."

She knew the argument Jonathan would make about a fallen world giving birth to evil. About Satan being the "prince of this world" and doing as much harm as he could to the most innocent.

"If you ask me," Trevor said, "it all boils down to luck."

Sadie shook her head. "You can't really believe that."

"Sure I do," Trevor said. "And the truth is, some people make their own luck. Like my dad, for instance. He's a self-made man. He doesn't wait for things to happen. He goes out and makes them happen."

Morgan's warnings about Trevor's family chimed through her mind. "But how do other people fit into that? I mean, if it's all luck, and you make your own luck, but you can't control their behavior. . . ."

"Oh, we can control their behavior, all right." He started to laugh.

Sadie looked at him. Was he talking about beating people up when they paid their loans late? "How?" she asked. "How do you control it?"

"You set examples. You give consequences."

"What kind of consequences?"

He grinned and regarded her for a moment. "What are you asking?"

She decided that she had to know the truth. "Trevor, I heard that you work for your father, beating up people who are late with their loans. Is that true?"

He grinned. "Now, do I look like a mean guy?"

"No," she said. "But you are big. You could do that if you wanted."

"Hey, my job in my father's business is to make sure people keep their end of the bargains they make. That's all. Sometimes a little intimidation is required."

She tried to think it through. Intimidation was not the same as violence, was it? And it was a business thing, not meanness. It didn't mean he was not a decent person.

He nuzzled her neck, trying to illicit a smile. "You have terrible ideas about me and my family, don't you?"

"No, I don't. I haven't believed all those rumors."

"You sure? Because it isn't fair, you know."

"I know."

"Then I want you to do something for me. I want you to meet my folks."

Sadie stiffened. "I can't."

"No, just hear me out. I want you to come with me to a wedding. You can meet my folks and find out they're all right."

"A wedding?" she asked. "Who's getting married?"

"A cousin of mine," he said. "And I hate weddings, but I have to go. It won't be so painful if you're there."

Sadie just looked at him. "I don't know. A wedding's a pretty public thing. If I went, Morgan and Jonathan would be sure to find out."

"So go ahead and tell them you're going to a wedding. She lives in Savannah, so they won't know her. Tell them you met her back when you worked for the paper. If they hear we were together, they'll just think we ran into each other."

Sadie knew that Morgan and Jonathan would never want her there. And she had promised not to lie again.

"Come on," he said. "What could happen at a wedding?"

"I'm not afraid to go to a wedding with you," she said. "I just don't want to lie again."

"You gotta admit, the Clearys are not thinking clearly right now. And you're seventeen, Sadie. At some point you've got to start making decisions for yourself."

She sighed. "When is it?"

"Saturday night."

She looked into the wind as it slapped across the water. It lifted her hair from her shoulders and sent it flying around her face. This storm might even be worse than the last one.

His arms slid around her, and he nuzzled her neck again. "Come on, Sadie. Say yes."

It felt so good to have him hold her like that. Morgan and Jonathan were so wrong about him. "I guess I could go."

"All right!" he said. "You've made my day!"

And she could tell he meant it.

Later, as she walked back down the beach and across the street to Hanover House, she told herself that she wasn't really doing anything wrong. She was just going to watch decent people unite themselves in marriage—and she would meet Trevor's family.

What could it hurt, after all?

CHAPTER

58

*C*ade had been drugged again. He didn't know how, since he hadn't drunk the water she'd brought him in days. She must have figured it out and hidden the drug in his food.

Now each of his limbs seemed to weigh a ton, and he couldn't tell how long he'd been out.

Forcing himself, he came to a sitting position, carefully slid his swollen, mangled leg off the side of the bed. Pain racked through him.

Taking his weight with the good leg, he managed to stand. Slowly, he made his way to the toilet and relieved himself.

He went back to the bed, dropped back down. The sheets were clean for the first time in days. She must have come in while he slept and changed his bed. The sick-sweet smell of dried blood was thankfully gone. But his bandages had not been changed, and blood stained them.

His head ached from the original gash that had begun to heal, and the drug's fog blurred his vision and muddled his thoughts.

He pulled himself back up to examine his wounds. His leg had swollen to twice its original size, and blood seeped through his bandage. His side felt raw and infected, and every breath sent pain ripping through him.

He lay there for a while, staring at that vent over his bed. *I'm still here, Lord. You haven't forgotten me, have you?*

God's silence screamed through his heart and settled like panic on his psyche. There had to be a way out. He was a cop, for Pete's sake. How could he let this happen to him?

After a while, he heard the scraping outside the door and knew that Ann Clark had come to check on him. He closed his eyes and pretended to sleep.

He heard her come close to his bed, felt her checking his leg. As she prodded the wound, he forced himself not to react with the pain.

He could grab her, he thought. If she checked the wound on his side, he could grab her wrist, twist it behind her back, and find the gun she always kept in her pocket.

He lay still as she unwound the bandage and then wrapped it again.

Closer, he thought. *Move closer.*

As if obeying him, she moved to his rib cage. Carefully, she lifted his wrist to move his arm.

Cade clamped hers instead. She screamed as he lunged up, twisting her around. Balancing on his one good leg, he got her hand behind her back and groped for her gun.

It was in her pocket, so he plunged his hand in and pulled it out.

"We're gonna do it different this time," he said, breathing hard with the effort of holding her still. "You're going to help me get up those stairs, and you and I are going to be so close that any bullet meant for me will have to take you with it." He shoved the gun into her waist. "Now let's go."

He leaned on her , using her body to keep from stepping on his shatttereed leg, but the effort still caused agony. He managed to get her to the door that led out into the basement.

He stopped there a moment, looked toward the stairs. If someone else was in the house, he waited at the top of those stairs as he had before.

"You shoot me," he yelled, "and she goes too!"

They had no sooner stepped through the door, when something hit him from the side. He hit the floor.

Someone was on him, wrestling his hands back, grabbing his hair. "Want to try that again, pal?"

It was a man's voice, slightly familiar.

Pain cracked though his forehead as the man rammed his head into the concrete, once, twice . . .

Light faded into darkness, and Cade gave up hope.

CHAPTER

59

*S*omeone had to get into that house. As Blair sat on the road behind Ann Clark's property, near the hidden driveway, she decided it would have to be her. So she'd break the law. So she could do jail time for this. It was a small price to pay for saving Cade's life.

Besides, she didn't intend to get caught.

She had worn black for her mission, in hopes of merging into the shadows. As she got out of her car and stole up the driveway, it occurred to her that she should have had something on her head. Her blonde hair was too stark a contrast against the darkness.

The moonlight was brighter than she would have liked, so she stayed close to the trees as she made her way between the houses.

The house on her left was lit up as if on display, and through the window she saw a mother working in the kitchen, her child at the computer in his room.

The house on the other side of the driveway lay dark, but as she stole past it, she thought she heard a door closing. Maybe someone had let his cat out.

Ann Clark's house came into view, and she looked to see if the motorcycle was there. Not tonight. That was good, she thought. If Ann didn't have company, it might be easier for Blair to get inside.

Her heart whammed against her chest wall as she made her way to one of the lighted windows. Slowly, carefully, she rose up to peer inside.

She saw the parlor where she and Joe had sat that day, breaking the news to her about her husband and listening to her lie through her teeth.

No one was there. The window from the room next door flickered, and she moved to it. The curtains were pulled shut, but there was a slit down the center that she was able to see through.

She caught her breath at the sight of Ann Clark sitting at that table, eating a meal and watching the television just beyond it.

Perfect, Blair thought. She could go in on the other side of the house, counting on the noise of the television to keep Ann from hearing. Surely she could find a window or door unlocked. If not, she was prepared to break the glass.

She ran around the house, to the farthest end from the parlor and dining room. The windows were all covered with screens, so she couldn't check the locks without first removing one of the screens.

But she had to do it.

Her hands shook as she pulled her key chain out of her pocket and slid one key under the screen. She wedged it out, got her fingers underneath it and started to slide it out of its brace.

As soon as she had it pulled out enough, she tested the window. It wouldn't budge.

She snapped the screen back into place, then tried the next one. This one was more stubborn and resisted as she tried to pull it out. It rattled as she worked it loose.

The light flew on, and Blair hit the ground.

Ann had heard her. She would call the police.

Blair headed for the trees near the driveway, made her way along the side of it, cut across the neighbor's yard . . .

She heard a siren, and wondered if they could really be coming for her so quickly. She tried to make it to her car.

But it was too late. The headlights of the flashing squad car found her. The car skidded to a halt, and the door swung open. "Freeze!"

She turned and raised her hands, staring at the blaring lights. "Don't shoot," she said weakly.

"That's her, Officer," a man said from the shadows of the neighbor's house. "I saw her sneaking around in my yard."

One of the officers came toward her, threw her across the hood of her car. Her cheekbone slammed against the metal, and she stiffened as hands began to pat her down, looking for a weapon. "I can explain," she said. "I'm a friend of Police Chief Matthew Cade's. I had reason to believe—"

"You have the right to remain silent." The officer's sharp voice cut through her words.

"You're arresting me?" One of the officers kept her face pressed to that hood, and she found it hard to talk. "I told you I could explain!"

But no one was interested in her explanation.

She felt handcuffs snapping on her wrists, and she tried to straighten. "I didn't do anything!"

They pulled her up, and she looked at the man who'd accused her. He stood in the dark yard, wearing nothing but a pair of gym shorts and a T-shirt. It was the yard where she'd heard the door close. He must have seen her stealing down the driveway.

That meant that Ann hadn't called the police. Maybe she hadn't heard Blair's attempt to break in. Maybe she didn't know.

The officer walked her to the backseat of the squad car. "Please. Once you hear what I was doing, you'll understand. If you'll just listen to me."

They shoved her in, then slammed the door shut. She sat back on the seat, hating herself for getting caught. By now, she might have gotten into the house, found Cade, and exposed Ann for what she was.

She looked through the window, saw the neighbors from the lit up house standing on their front lawn. Thankfully, Ann wasn't among them. Maybe she didn't know.

She leaned back on the seat as the car started to move, and wondered how in the world she was going to break this news to Morgan.

CHAPTER

60

The distant, faint sound of a siren startled Cade, and he sat up in bed. Had they figured out he was here? Were they raiding the place even now?

He tried to stand, the shattering pain in his head and leg shooting fireworks through his nerve endings. Dragging it, he pulled himself to the door. With all the strength left in him, he banged on it. "I'm in here! Please ... can anybody hear me? Behind the bookshelves! Please ..."

No one came. Sweat dripped in his eyes as he frantically looked around. If they were upstairs with her and weren't looking for him ...

He banged again. "Hello! Please ... can anybody hear me? This is Matthew Cade! They have me locked in the basement...."

They were coming! He heard urgent scraping, the door being unlocked....

Ann Clark opened the door and leveled her gun on him. "What are you doing?"

Cade almost collapsed. "I heard something . . . the police . . ."

"That wasn't here, you fool," she said. "Get back on the bed."

She waited with that gun as he lowered to the mattress.

"I think one of the neighbors must have had a break-in. Nice try, though. Too bad there was no one here to hear it."

It was too cruel. He was sure they had come. "Mrs. Clark, please. My leg is shattered and badly infected, my head is killing me—"

"Your problems are no concern of mine."

He wasn't ready to give up. "You know they're looking for me," he said. "Somebody's going to come looking. You're not going to get away with this."

"I already have," she said. "You underestimate me." She backed through the door and started to close it. "By the way, they *are* looking for you. You're wanted for kidnapping. You and your new wife."

She closed the door back, and he heard that scraping of the bookshelves again. Kidnapping? Wife? She must mean the letter he'd written. Had they really believed it? And the kidnapping . . . *he* was the one who'd been kidnapped.

Had they pinned some kind of crime on him? Was that why they were holding him?

Disheartened and dejected, he fell back onto the bed, shivering and fighting the crushing pain. He was going to die here, he thought, and no one would be able to help him.

It seemed as if even God had forgotten him.

CHAPTER

*T*he telephone rang near midnight. Morgan bolted upright in bed and lunged for it.

Jonathan caught her hand. "Tavist," he said.

It rang again, and she grabbed her robe and dashed out into the hall.

Karen was already on the stairs. "I'll get it!"

Morgan hurried down as Karen answered. "Hello?" She was breathless, hoarse. Her expression crashed, and she thrust it to Morgan. "It's not them. It's for you."

Morgan took the phone. "It's midnight. Who is it?"

Tears in her eyes, Karen started back up the stairs. "It's your sister."

Morgan frowned and put the phone to her ear. "Blair, do you know what time it is?"

"I'm in trouble." Blair's words were muffled, as if she didn't want to be overheard. "Morgan, you've got to come."

"What?" Morgan asked. "Blair, where are you?"

"I've been arrested, Morgan."

"You've *what?*" She turned to Tavist. He was still taping, but he looked up at her and mouthed "police station."

"You're in *jail?*" She yelled the word out, and Jonathan came hurrying down.

"Who's in jail?"

"Blair!" she said. "What have you done? Tell me you didn't break into that house."

Blair grunted. "I got arrested for trespassing."

Morgan brought her hand to her throat. She would kill her. She would just kill her. "I warned you, Blair. I told you this would happen! What has gotten into you?"

"Could we discuss this later?" Blair asked, her voice strained. "Right now, I could really use your help."

Morgan realized she was trembling. "Blair, are you all right?"

"I'm fine," she said. "Just a little frustrated."

Morgan knew that frustration. "Which jail?"

"Precinct Three on Victory Drive."

Morgan sighed. "I'll hurry, Blair."

Blair breathed a laugh. "Take your time. I'm not going anywhere."

CHAPTER

*B*lair was in no mood to play games with these officers. They had treated her like a common criminal, ignoring her explanations and protests. She'd had enough.

"If you jerks would do your job," she told the arresting officer, "then I wouldn't have had to be out there doing what I was doing. I was trying to save Police Chief Cade of Cape Refuge."

The cop shot her a look. "The one wanted for kidnapping?"

She sprang out of her chair. "He is not a kidnapper! He's been set up, and he's in trouble!"

"What do you have to do with Chief Cade?"

"I'm a good friend of his," she said, throwing her chin up. "If you want to check on me, you can call Detective McCormick who's running the Cape Refuge PD. Anybody there can vouch for me. I'm a decent citizen who's worried about my friend."

"That doesn't give you the right to go prowling through people's yards."

"If you would do it, I wouldn't have to. That's what I'm trying to tell you!"

The cop laughed and shook his head, and went back to typing up his report.

Blair wanted to go for his throat. "You people are amazing! Unbelievable. You're a police department. Don't you care that a crime's being committed?"

"Yes, I do," the man said. "That's why I'm about to lock you behind bars."

She groaned. "Lock me up then, I don't care. But go back there and search her house. I'm telling you, if you want to find him—whether you think he's the kidnapper or not—you'll find him in that house."

"Ma'am, Ann Clark is not a suspect. And that case is in the hands of the FBI now."

She realized she wasn't getting anywhere with him, so she tried to calm down. "But you can still arrest people. You can search houses if you have reason to believe that someone's life is in danger." When the cop kept hunting and pecking at the typewriter, she leaned across the desk and grabbed his wrist. He glared at her.

"Look," she said in a lower voice as she stared into his face. "I know that you don't know Cade or what kind of man he is. But he doesn't have it in him to kidnap a baby. He also doesn't have it in him to run off and get married secretly. He left his car parked at the restaurant he ate at the morning of his disappearance. He hasn't been home since." Her voice broke, but she had him. He was listening, for what that was worth. "He's a good, decent man with a heart. He wouldn't make his friends suffer this way."

"Maybe. Maybe not. Maybe you don't know him as well as you thought you did. People get under stress and they snap."

She slapped her hand on the desk. "He did not snap!"

"Blair."

She turned to see Morgan and Jonathan. Jonathan looked as if he'd just rolled out of bed, and Morgan's curly mane of brown hair had not been brushed. Smudged mascara underlined her eyes.

Blair got up and hugged her. From the way Morgan clung to her, one would think she faced thirty years. "Morgan, meet Officer Gray, who thinks that crimes being committed under the FBI's jurisdiction are no longer of any concern at all to the police department."

Morgan squeezed Blair's arm to silence her. Blair hated that. "Uh, Officer, I'm Morgan Cleary, and this is my husband, Jonathan. Blair has been under a lot of stress, and sometimes she says things—"

The man shot a look at Blair. "Sit down, lady."

Blair had made up her mind to keep standing, but Morgan pulled her down beside her. Since she had the checkbook, Blair acquiesced.

"He's still there, Morgan," she said. "In that house. To know he's there and not be able to do anything—"

"What's her bail?" Morgan cut in.

"None set yet," he said, still typing. "She's going to have to spend the night here and see if the judge sets bail in her arraignment tomorrow."

"No way!" Blair sprang up again. "I am *not* spending the night here."

He grinned. "Think again."

Blair gaped up at Jonathan. "Do something!"

"What?" he asked. "You broke the law and got arrested, just like Morgan told you you would. What do you want us to do?"

"I want you to talk some sense into them. Get me out of here!"

Morgan started to cry. "Blair, you can't throw yourself headlong into jeopardy, then expect me to fix everything for you. I'll bail you out tomorrow. But short of breaking you out of jail, I don't know what else to do."

Blair wasn't going to break down and blubber like some kind of frightened kid, in front of this cop and his buddies. "Okay, then let's get this show on the road. You're locking me up? Do it now. I'm ready for bed."

Morgan's face twisted, and she cupped her hand over her mouth. "Blair, don't make it worse. Come on, please cooperate."

"Hey, I'm cooperating," she bit out. "I'll fill out the forms for him if he wants me to. I'm not afraid of a jail cell."

Officer Gray couldn't stop grinning as he led her out of the squad room.

CHAPTER

*B*y the time they got Blair processed and transferred to the Chatham County Correctional Facility several hours had passed and morning had begun to dawn. Enduring the indignities they put her through, she donned the orange jumpsuit they gave her and surrendered all her personal items.

She would miss her appointment with Jason Wheater this morning to sign all the papers making the newspaper hers. She wondered if the banker would change his mind when they learned she'd been arrested.

She followed a deputy onto the elevator, and they got off on the third floor. Her parents had often talked of the Bible studies they did in this very place, and some of the "graduates" had wound up as tenants at Hanover House. Morgan and Jonathan came twice a week now. She hoped their efforts had done some good and that she wouldn't run into any angry inmates withdrawing from their drugs of choice, wanting to kill anyone who was handy.

They stopped at a room right outside the elevator and handed her a thin mattress, sheets, a blanket, and a bag of government-issued personal items. She stood there with the stack that almost covered her face. "I'm not going to be here long enough to need these."

But the deputy had heard that before. He led her to Pod 312—a circular room with doors to eight cells around it.

She went into the pod with the small metal table in the center of it and considered the pay phone on the wall. She'd been told she could make collect calls, and she thought of calling Morgan or Joe McCormick or Jason Wheater . . . or a lawyer. Would any of them take her collect call from jail?

She shivered in the cold and wondered why they wasted tax-payers' money refrigerating this place. She was glad she'd taken the blanket. Even if she wasn't spending the night, she needed to keep warm.

A voice blared out over the intercom speaker. "Get up, girls. Five A.M. Out of bed!"

Her heart sank. She wasn't ready to meet her cell mates.

She went into her own cell and dropped her mattress on the metal bed frame. She piled the folded blanket and sheets on top of it and set the bag down.

"Who are you?" She turned and saw a woman with pink spiked hair peering in.

Blair refused to cower. Crossing her arms, she walked toward the girl. "I'm Blair Owens." She thought of telling her that she was in here for killing a former cell mate who'd given her a hard time, but she wasn't sure she could pull it off. "And you are?"

"Brandy," the woman said.

Blair reached out to shake her hand, but the girl didn't respond. Blair dropped her hand and went back to her bag. "Don't get used to me, Brandy. I won't be here long. Probably only a couple of hours."

"Yeah, that's what I said two weeks ago." The girl was staring at her scars, so Blair turned away and started putting on her sheets.

"You been in a fire?"

Bristling, Blair looked back at her doorway. Even in a jail cell her disfigurement stood out. "Not lately."

"Then what's wrong with your face?"

Blair didn't need to ask why she was here. Jail was the only safe place for a woman with such social skills. "My scars are none of your business."

The woman enjoyed that. "Oh, you got an attitude, huh? You think you're somebody?"

Blair went to her door and slammed it shut, right in the woman's face. Fortunately, it locked from the inside.

The woman banged on her door, cursed at her, and Blair began to realize her reaction may have been ill-advised. When she did go out to use the bathroom or eat, the woman would likely ambush her. Watching the door, she sat down Indian-style on her bed and waited for the powers-that-be to come for her before she had to meet the rest of her neighbors.

As she sat there, she felt a surge of shame. If it had been Morgan in here, or her mother or father, they would have used the opportunity to minister to these women. They would have seen them as people with souls, needy, impoverished women who'd been dealt bad cards in life and needed a helping hand to get them back on track. Blair just saw them as a threat. The truth was, she feared them, but she wouldn't admit it, not to anyone. She hated admitting it to herself.

Wouldn't Cade have had a good laugh out of this? Blair Owens sitting in jail for trespassing. And if she'd gotten into that house, she'd be in here for breaking and entering. Yeah, he may have enjoyed the irony in it, but he'd be there to get her out. She had no doubt about that.

Morgan, on the other hand, was probably ranting and raving, waxing eloquent to Jonathan about how irresponsible and compulsive Blair was. But Blair couldn't understand why Jonathan and Morgan weren't trying to break into the Clark house to find Cade themselves, no matter the cost. She leaned back on the concrete wall and looked at the ceiling.

"Please let him be alive," she whispered to whatever Force was listening. "Please don't let anything happen to him." But she feared her plea fell on deaf ears—or no ears at all.

The judge released her that morning on a thousand dollars' bond, which Morgan withdrew from Blair's savings account.

"I hope you're happy with yourself," she told Blair as she waited for her personal items. "Now you're unemployed with a prison record, and the money you would have used to buy the paper is down a thousand dollars."

"It doesn't matter. I'm still buying it. Jason will understand that I got in trouble looking for Cade."

When she'd gotten her things, Morgan walked Blair out to her car. She and Jonathan had retrieved it late last night from the scene of the crime. Blair got in and sat behind the wheel.

"Are you going home?" Morgan asked. "Or are you heading back over to Ann Clark's so they can lock you up again?"

Blair looked up at her with dull, weary eyes. "You're not very supportive, you know that?"

Morgan shook her head. "How can I be supportive of you when you're breaking the law? Blair, next time you could get yourself killed."

"Then you do admit that Ann Clark is dangerous?"

"I don't *know* if she's dangerous," Morgan said. "All I know is you've got to stop this!"

Blair looked at a small chip on her windshield. "I've got to figure out a way to get in there that's not illegal." She looked up at her sister. "Help me, Morgan. I'm desperate to get in that house. I know he's in there, and I just have this feeling that if we don't hurry—"

"Oh, my gosh. You aren't seriously trying to make me an accomplice to your madness!"

"No, I'm not. You're not criminal material." She looked at Morgan carefully. "But I was thinking, sitting in that cell this morning. Maybe we could get Ann Clark to invite us in."

Morgan closed her eyes. "I can't believe you're saying this."

"Just listen! Mrs. Clark didn't see me last night. I don't think she knew anything was going on. So . . . suppose we bring her dinner, a casserole or something, and just tell her that we were from the church in Cape Refuge, and we'd heard about her husband and just wanted to come and minister to her?"

Morgan opened her eyes and leveled them on her sister. "Go on."

Blair grinned. "I knew the casserole part would get you. Most people wouldn't turn you away if you come bearing food. And we could be kind of pushy. I mean, if she tries to take the food at the door, we could insist that we get our dishes back. We could go in and start transferring the food into her dishes. If things go well, maybe I could somehow slip away and look around."

"What if she realizes what we're doing? She could get violent or something."

"I could bring my gun," Blair said. "Just in case."

Morgan gasped. "I'm *not* helping if you take a gun. I mean it. Are you hearing me?"

"Fine! I won't. So you'll do it?"

Morgan blew out her frustration. "I have to go with you, or I'm going to be visiting you in jail every Saturday for the next few years. Or at the cemetery."

"We could find him," Blair said. "It could work!"

Morgan looked sick. "All I'm saying is we'll get into the house. What we see after that is up to God. He's just going to have to reveal stuff to us. But I'm not getting you in there so you can play cops and robbers."

Blair grinned. "So when do we do this dastardly deed?"

Morgan rolled her eyes. "I don't know," she said. "Not tonight. We have to rest. We have to think and plan."

"Cade may not *have* another night," Blair said.

Morgan sighed. "Well, I can't tell Jonathan what I'm doing. He'll never let me go."

"So you're going to lie to him?" Blair asked hopefully.

Morgan shook her head. "Yeah, like the wonderful Proverbs 31 woman that I am. I hate that you put me in this position, Blair!"

"It's to save someone's life," Blair whispered. "You know it is. Jonathan will understand."

"I sure hope so." Morgan blew out a long, weary breath. "All right, Blair. We'll go tonight."

Morgan was exhausted by the time she got the casseroles made. All day, she'd dealt with Karen's swings from despair to rage at the plight of her baby. The FBI had been staking out the bus station since yesterday, but nothing had happened and the kidnapper had not called back. And having the FBI agent there twenty-four/seven was beginning to drain her, as well.

It had begun to rain around noon, so Jonathan had to cut his fishing tour short. He came home early and helped with Caleb as Morgan cooked.

"So who is it you're going to see?" he asked as she set the casseroles into a box for her car.

"I don't think you've met her." Morgan couldn't look him in the eye. "She's new on the island, and Blair and I just thought we'd go by and say hello and take her something to eat."

"You know, you could let Melba take this one. You've got a lot going on. It's not like someone's going to think less of you for missing one newcomer."

"I just want her to feel welcome. And the truth is, I need the distraction." She hated lying to him. Several times today she had thought of coming clean and asking Jonathan to come with them. But Ann Clark was more likely to buy their story if it was just two women.

She hoped God and Jonathan would forgive her when the truth came out.

"I've already bathed Caleb," she said, "so he should be ready for bed in a couple of hours. All you have to do is feed him. And Sadie's going out tonight. She's going to a wedding."

Jonathan frowned. "What wedding?"

"Some girl she met when she worked at the paper. I told her she could take my car. I'll ride with Blair."

He got an apple from a bowl on the counter and turned it over in his hand like a baseball.

"You know, we never did ground her," he said. "We should have done something."

Morgan sighed. "A lot's been going on. I haven't had time to think about it. She has so few friends, though. I thought it was nice that she was invited."

He nodded and looked through the kitchen door. The agents were switching shifts, and Tavist was leaving. Morgan was sick of having these people in her house, and they were no closer to finding the baby than they had been the day he was born.

As Morgan waited for Blair on the porch, she prayed that God would forgive her for failing to submit to her husband and lying to him through her teeth. She didn't know what she'd been thinking to agree to such a scheme. It was desperation, she thought, to keep Blair from breaking out a window or shooting her way in. And it might be the only way they were going to find Cade.

But her own deception wasn't so far removed from Sadie's scheme the other night. She hated herself for going along with this.

When Blair pulled into the driveway, Morgan saw that she looked like the perfect church lady. She had worn a dress for the occasion and pulled her hair back in a bun. The scars on her face flamed redder than usual. She got out and took the casseroles, arranged them on the backseat.

"Where's your gun?" Morgan whispered.

"In my house."

Morgan grabbed Blair's purse off the seat and dug through it.

Blair smirked. "Are you going to frisk me, too?"

Morgan wasn't amused. "Should I?"

Laughing, Blair got back into the car. "I swear, Morgan, I left the gun in the house. We're flying without a net. Now, come on."

Morgan got into the car.

"What did Jonathan say?" Blair asked.

Morgan stared straight ahead. "Nothing. He trusts his wife. He thinks I'm going to welcome a new neighbor to Cape Refuge. I can't believe I lied to him."

"Good story, though."

Blair was silent as they crossed the bridge to Tybee Island, then wound their way around the island and up Highway 80 to Savannah. Quiet hung between them as they got to Ann Clark's house and pulled into the driveway.

"All right, Blair, we're going to get in that house, but I want you to promise me you're not going to do anything heroic or dangerous. Do you promise me that? Can I have your word?"

Blair just stared at the door to the house. "I'm not going to do anything dangerous. I'm just going to try to find Cade."

"Blair, I need your word that you're not going to do anything stupid. I'll never forgive you if you get me killed."

"I'm not, okay?" Blair opened the door and got out of the car. Sighing, Morgan got out the casseroles. Blair came around and took one of them.

"So, how do we act?" Blair asked in a low voice. "Bouncy and happy?"

"Just like Mom used to do," Morgan said. "We have to act genuinely friendly and concerned or she's never going to let us in."

"Okay," Blair said. "I can do this."

They walked up to the front steps of the house, rang the doorbell. There was no sound within, none at all.

"She's got to be home," Blair whispered. "She hardly ever leaves." With her elbow she pressed the doorbell again and waited, then finally balanced the casserole on one arm and banged on the front door.

"She's not here," Morgan said finally.

Blair waited another few moments and finally realized that Morgan was right. Either the woman was in there, refusing to answer, or she really wasn't here. She couldn't believe she hadn't been here to follow her.

"Here." She handed Morgan her casserole, weighing her down.

"Where are you going?" Morgan asked.

"Just down the driveway to see if her car is here."

"You can't trespass again, Blair," Morgan whispered harshly. "You'll be locked up forever. If the neighbors see you—"

But Blair kept going. "I just want to see if her car is home."

Morgan headed back to the car, arms laden down with hot casseroles. She managed to get them back in the box without spilling them and watched as Blair walked down to the back of the house and peered into the garage. Finally she shook her head and came back.

"She's really not here. Wouldn't you know it?"

"Then we'll just have to try again later."

Blair groaned and looked back at the house. "It's a great time to go in. If I could just find an open window . . ."

Morgan grabbed her sister. "Blair, so help me, I will throw myself in front of a moving vehicle to stop you. You're not going to do that tonight."

As she pulled out of the driveway, Blair wondered at the wisdom of involving her sister.

*T*he wedding of Trevor's cousin was held at the home of his father's sister, in a terraced English garden that looked like something befitting royalty. Sadie sat through it, holding Trevor's hand and feeling a sense of euphoria that he would want her here with him.

She didn't know anyone here, so her fears that Morgan and Jonathan would find out faded from her mind not long after the wedding began. Only one face in the crowd looked slightly familiar, and she couldn't quite place it.

The small woman had come in alone, and an usher had seated her near some of the family, whom she greeted as if they were close friends.

Where had Sadie seen her before?

She watched the woman as the ceremony began, racking her brain for a name. When it did not come to her, she leaned over to Trevor.

"Who's that woman over there?" she asked.

Trevor shrugged. "Don't know. I think she's a friend of my father's, but I don't know her name."

Sadie tried to forget about her, but her mind couldn't seem to let it go. She thought of finding her at the reception and asking her who she was, but then she feared that she might be a friend of Morgan's. She couldn't risk letting word get back to them.

The reception was set up on the other side of the house, in another garden area. Before sitting down, Trevor took her around to introduce her to some of his family.

She felt like an honored guest, someone of worth, as they hugged her and welcomed her here. This wasn't a crime family, she thought. They were decent, loving people. Morgan and Jonathan were wrong about them.

She felt giddy as she took her place at their table. But he didn't sit down. His eyes were on a man a few yards away, hobbling toward him on crutches. Trevor seemed to change as he approached. A hard look came over his face. "Smart of you to come," he told the man.

The man's hand trembled as he reached out to shake. Trevor took it coldly, staring into his eyes.

"I wouldn't have missed it," the man said. "And I brought the check. Your father has it."

"So you're not as stupid as I thought," Trevor said.

Had she heard right? Had Trevor really said that? She looked up at his hard face, then at the man's. He was clearly intimidated.

"I won't be late again." The man's voice trembled.

"Smart man."

The man crutched away, and as Trevor sat down, a chill fell over her. Had Trevor had anything to do with that man's injury?

She looked over at him, afraid to ask. "How did he get hurt?"

"He got in a fight," Trevor said. "Don't worry about it."

She stared at him for a moment. "He wasn't . . . late for a loan, was he?"

He picked up his glass and brought it to his lips. He said nothing, but the look in his eyes silenced her.

The music started, and she looked down at her plate. A man with a broken leg, obviously afraid of Trevor. . . .

Maybe Morgan was right, after all.

She watched the bride and groom dance the first dance, but her mind raced with images. Trevor cornering the man, beating him until his bones broke. Would he have used his fists or some kind of weapon?

She started to get dizzy, and beads of sweat broke out on her temples.

Trevor noticed. "Are you okay?"

"Uh, yes." She slid her chair back on the grass. "I just need . . . where is the rest room?"

He pointed to the house. "Sure you're okay?"

"Yes. I'll be right back." She took her handbag and started up to the house, but she saw some of the servants inside, and she didn't want to talk to them.

Instead, she walked back to the other garden, where the ceremony had been held. The chairs were still set up, the flowers still beautifully placed.

She saw a path that led from the rose-covered arbor deeper into the garden, so she headed for it, trying to breathe deeply and calm down.

So a man had a broken leg. She was overreacting. She had no evidence that Trevor had anything to do with it—only her suspicions. Then again, he knew what she was thinking, and he hadn't denied it.

She smelled the scent of jasmine as she followed the path, her mind racing. There was nothing wrong with this family. They were nice, decent people, and Trevor was good.

But he had admitted to her that intimidation was sometimes required to make people pay their loans.

She imagined him swinging a bat at the hunkering man, teaching him a lesson about paying his debts.

She felt sick. She couldn't go back yet. She needed a moment to breathe . . . to think . . .

She turned on the path and stopped suddenly.

A man and a woman stood kissing in a grove of trees. Their lips broke off, and she saw the woman she had recognized earlier. "Ann, we've got to stop this," the man whispered. "Someone could see us."

Sadie caught her breath. *Ann?*

Then suddenly, it all came back to her. The DMV photo Blair had of Ann Clark. She had seen it when Blair showed it to Jonathan.

But who was the man?

She backed away, but her foot broke a twig, and the pair turned and saw her.

"Uh . . . excuse me. I was just getting some air . . ."

She saw the man's face. It looked familiar too, but for the life of her, she couldn't place it.

She turned and started away and made her way back to the reception. Trevor looked up at her as she reached the table.

She could hardly breathe, and her hands shook as she groped for her chair.

"You look like you just saw a ghost," Trevor said. "Are you okay?"

"No. I'm sick, Trevor. I need to go home."

"Sick? Just like that?"

"Just like that. You stay. I've got Morgan's car. But I have to get home."

He walked her to her car in silence, as if he didn't believe her story, but she couldn't worry about that now.

As she drove home, her mind raced through the night's images. What was Ann Clark doing with another man, so soon after her husband's death?

Did it mean something, or was it all just coincidence?

And how could she not tell Morgan? It could be important information. But if she told her, she'd have to reveal the fact that she had disobeyed and deceived them again. She'd have to come clean.

If she didn't tell them, they would go on thinking she was repentant and trustworthy. But Cade's life, and Emory's, might depend on her telling them. It might matter to the investigation if, indeed, Ann was involved in Cade's disappearance.

By the time she reached Hanover House, she was in tears. But she had made up her mind.

Morgan and Blair were inside at the kitchen table when she went in. Morgan looked up at her. "Sadie, you're home early. How was the wedding?"

"I lied to you." The confession came quickly, leaving no room for backing down. "The wedding was Trevor Beal's cousin's. I was his date."

Morgan looked as if she'd been slapped. Slowly, she came to her feet. "Sadie—"

"You can do what you want to me later," Sadie said as tears began to roll down her cheeks. "Throw me out, whatever. I deserve it. But the reason I'm telling you is that Ann Clark was there."

Blair sprang up. "Ann Clark?"

"Yes. I didn't recognize her at first. But then I stumbled on her in the garden, kissing a man. And it came to me who she was."

Blair came toward her. "Who was the man, Sadie? Did you know him?"

"No, I don't know him, but I've seen him somewhere before. I don't know where. I've tried to remember."

Morgan still looked shell-shocked. "Could you ask Trevor or someone who was there?"

"No, because no one else saw them together. They were hidden. I heard him call her Ann. He said, 'Ann, we've got to stop this. Someone could see us.'"

Tears rimmed Morgan's eyes. "Did they see you?"

"Yes," she said. "But I just acted like it was no big deal. And it was dark. They probably couldn't see me that well."

Blair's face was tight, and her scars darkened. "Okay, so now we know that Ann Clark has ties to the Beal family and that she's not exactly grieving over her dearly departed husband. If she's involved in this kidnapping scheme, then it's possible that they are too. We have to tell McCormick. We have to tell Tavist."

But Morgan was still staring at Sadie with those tear-filled eyes. "Why did you lie to us again, Sadie?"

Sadie had never hated herself so much. "I don't know. I liked him so much, but Morgan, I think you were right about him. There was a man there with a broken leg, who'd been late paying a loan. I think Trevor had something to do with his injury. I'm so sorry I didn't listen. I don't know what's wrong with me. I know better, but I just follow my emotions like some airheaded idiot. I don't blame you if you want me to leave."

"Leave?" Morgan asked. "Sadie, we're not going to make you leave. You're not a tenant. You're family."

Sadie wanted to die. "But I betrayed you, not just once, Morgan. I did it over and over."

Blair stepped between them. "Can we do this woe-is-me stuff later? We've got a crisis here. And for heaven's sake, Morgan, she did tell us the truth. If she hadn't, we wouldn't have known about Ann Clark. She did the right thing, even if it started out wrong."

Morgan sighed, and pulled Sadie into a hug. "Blair's right. Right now we've got to decide what to do with this information. We have to tell Agent Tavist and Joe."

An hour later, they had informed law enforcement of the information Sadie had brought home, but it seemed to make no difference.

"Even if Ann Clark was having an affair before her husband died, it doesn't prove that she has anything to do with her husband's death, Cade's disappearance, or the infant kidnappings," Tavist said.

Blair wanted to explode. "Are you telling me that her connection to the biggest crime family in the southeast is not important information?"

"That's not what I'm saying. It may play out later, but right now it gets us no closer to finding either one of them."

Law enforcement was going to be of no help at all in this, Blair finally realized. No, she would have to do this herself.

As Morgan walked her out to her car, Blair turned back to her. "I'm going back there tomorrow night. I'm going to get in that house, with or without the casseroles."

She'd expected Morgan to balk and throw a fit, but instead, her sister just nodded. "Pick me up at six. I'll have them ready."

I'm scared." Morgan muttered the words as she got one of the casseroles out of the backseat. She had pictured them doing this at night, but at almost seven in the evening, darkness had not yet fallen.

Blair got the other one. "Stop shaking! She'll get suspicious."

Morgan looked up at the house. "Aren't you scared?"

"Scared for Cade," Blair said. "Just think about him."

Blair had spent the day choreographing their moves. She'd decided that the parlor just inside the front door didn't give her the access she might need to the house. If they got into the kitchen, she knew that Morgan could distract the woman while Blair went farther in.

Morgan followed her to the side door.

"Ready?" Blair whispered.

"I guess so," Morgan said.

"Remember," Blair said. "We're happy southern church ladies. In other words, be yourself."

Blair rang and then held her breath as they waited for the woman. She heard footsteps and saw the curtain being pulled back slightly as Ann Clark peered out to see who was there.

Blair and Morgan smiled like Welcome Wagon ladies.

Slowly, the woman unbolted the lock and cracked the door open. "Yes?"

Blair put on her best Georgia voice. "Mrs. Clark, I don't know if you remember me, but I was here a few days ago when we notified you of your husband's death. Blair Owens?"

Ann stiffened. "Uh-huh."

"This is my sister, Morgan." Morgan's face was white, but she managed to smile.

"Hello, Mrs. Clark," Morgan said. "You've just been on our minds so much lately, that we wanted to come by and offer you a little comfort in your time of grief." She raised the dish. "We brought casseroles."

"They're a little hot," Blair said. "Can we come in and set them down?"

Ann opened the door farther but blocked the entrance. "I'll take them."

She took Blair's from her and set it on the counter next to her, then reached for Morgan's.

Morgan surrendered it willingly and gave Blair a look that said, *What now?*

Blair grabbed the screen and pushed her way in. "Mrs. Clark, I hate to ask this. I hope it doesn't sound rude, but we were hoping we could transfer the food into some of your dishes, because we need ours back."

Ann gaped at her. "The fact is that I'm in the middle of something right now, and I don't have time for company."

"Oh, you go right ahead with what you were doing," Blair said. "We'll take care of everything."

As they'd rehearsed, Morgan came in behind her and went straight to the cabinets. Opening one, she said, "Where do you keep the casserole dishes, Hon? We'll need one about the same size, since I don't want the casserole to look like mush. It's chicken spaghetti, very good, if I do say so myself. And it freezes well. You might want a dish that you can freeze."

Clearly annoyed, Ann opened the right cabinet and pulled out two casserole dishes. "Here."

Blair slipped behind her, and headed into the hall. "May I use your rest room?"

Ann swung around. "I told you, I'm in the middle of something. I'd rather you—"

Something crashed, and Blair looked back. Morgan had dropped Ann's casserole dish, and the glass was all over the floor.

"Oh, Mrs. Clark!" Morgan cried. "I'm so sorry. You must think we're the rudest things, coming in here like this and breaking your dish. I'll just clean every bit of this up. . . ."

Blair seized the opportunity and took off down the hall, looking in each room for some sign of Cade. She saw a closed door and thought it might be the basement. Quickly, she opened it, flicked on the light and started down the stairs.

She heard Ann shouting at her from the kitchen, and Morgan fussing over the broken glass . . .

She looked around, saw the small basement area. There were no doors down here, only pipes and a furnace, and a set of bookshelves against one wall.

The concrete floor in front of one set of the shelves looked scraped, as if the shelves had been repeatedly pulled away.

She wondered what was behind them.

"Miss Owens, the bathroom is not down here!"

Ann Clark stood halfway down the stairs, her eyes aflame, as if she knew what was happening. "I don't want your casseroles. Get out of my house now before I call the police!"

Blair started back up the stairs. "I was just looking for the bathroom."

"You don't know a bathroom from a basement?" Ann said. "Get out of my house."

Blair thought of running for the bookshelves, knocking them over, seeing if there was a door behind them. She tried to think it through.

Then Morgan appeared at the top of the stairs. "Blair, you heard her. We have to go. Now!"

"All right, I'm sorry." Blair started back up the stairs. "I didn't mean to be rude. I've just had a kidney infection, and when I have to go, I have to go, if you know what I mean. I was kind of in a hurry."

She passed Ann on the stairs, felt the murderous hatred in her eyes. She hurried to the kitchen.

Morgan went back to the pile of glass on the floor. "Mrs. Clark, do you have a broom and dustpan anywhere?"

"I'll clean it up," Ann bit out. "I want you both out of my house."

Morgan opened the door. "Look, just keep our dishes. I'm so sorry to be so rude."

Blair hung back, but Morgan grabbed her hand and pulled her out. Ann slammed the door behind them.

Blair swung around. "Morgan, I was there!" she whispered. "Why couldn't you distract her a little longer?"

"She was going to stop you, Blair! I feared for your life! Besides, I had what we needed."

As she spoke, Morgan got into the car. Blair jumped in next to her. "What do you mean, 'what we need'?"

Morgan pulled a ball of gauze out of her pocket. "This. I found it in the trash when I was throwing away some of the glass."

Blair caught her breath and took it from her. A bloody bandage.

"It's Cade's blood, Morgan." Blair hadn't expected the tears that pushed to her eyes. "He may be dead."

"They don't bandage dead people," Morgan said. "But I'm afraid she'll know I took it."

Blair tried to think as she pulled out of the driveway. "She might do something drastic, like moving him. I can't take that chance. We have to watch her and follow her if she leaves. And somehow I have to get back in that house. I think there might be a door in the basement behind the bookshelves. I have to move them and see—"

"No!" Morgan shouted. "Blair, you can't go off half-cocked and start breaking into people's houses, *especially* if they're criminals. We're taking this to the FBI. Maybe if they can confirm that it's his blood, they'll realize that they've been wrong."

"They won't!" Blair said. "They think he's the criminal! If he's not dead already, she could kill him before those Keystone Cops get stirred up enough to do anything about it."

"Blair, so help me, you are not doing this yourself. We'll head for the nearest police precinct for safety and notify Tavist from there."

"Tavist," Blair said bitterly. "You don't seriously think he'll do anything!"

"Blair, so help me, you drive to the police station now or I'll turn you in. I'll tell them what you're planning. At least if they arrest you you'll be safer in jail than breaking into Ann Clark's house."

Blair hit the steering wheel with the heel of her hand. "Morgan, it'll be a waste of time. We don't have time to waste!"

"Do it!" Morgan yelled. "Blair, I mean what I say. Drive to the police station right now!"

"All right," Blair shouted. "But Cade's life is in *your* hands. You'd better be right about this."

CHAPTER

*T*he police station was just as it had been the night of Blair's arrest. She found Officer Gray—who had arrested her—sitting behind his desk, eating pizza from a greasy box.

She made a beeline toward him, and Morgan followed.

"I need to use your phone to call Agent Tavist with the FBI," she said when she reached his desk.

He looked up at her. "What?"

"It's me. Blair Owens, the one you arrested the other night. I was in Ann Clark's house tonight, and we found a bloody bandage. I have reason to believe that it's Chief Matthew Cade's blood. I need to notify the FBI."

He set his pizza slice back in the box and closed it. "Are you confessing to breaking and entering?"

"No!" Blair shouted. "Ann was there. She let us in. Please, I need to use the phone."

He shoved his phone across his desk, and as Blair dialed Hanover House, he got up and headed to the back.

She got Tavist on the phone, told him what had happened. He seemed more worried about what he called her "interference in the investigation" than he did with the bandage. He told her to wait there, while he consulted with his superiors.

Blair hung up and looked at her sister. "I hope you're happy. They're probably not going to do anything. She's probably doing something drastic as we speak!"

"Calm down, Blair. They're not going to ignore this."

Officer Gray came back, followed by a man dressed in a tweed sport coat with a dark T-shirt under it. He crossed the room and shook their hands.

"Ladies, I'm Detective Hull."

Morgan nodded. "I met you at the hospital when the baby was kidnapped."

He stared at her for a moment, as recognition dawned. "Yes, now I remember. You're Miss Miller's friend." He shoved his hands into his pockets. "I just got a call from Agent Tavist, ladies. He wants me to take a statement from you and take a look at that bandage."

Finally, they were getting somewhere. Blair withdrew the bandage from her pocket, and handed it to him.

She would have expected him to handle it with gloves or something, but he took it in two fingers. "Come back to my office," he said. "You can wait for Tavist there and fill me in on how you got this."

Blair and Morgan followed him quickly, assessing the man from the top of his tousled, too-long hair, to the deck shoes he wore without socks. When they got to his office, he went in, dropped into his chair, and lit up a cigarette. "Have a seat," he said.

Blair sat down, and Morgan hesitated, then picked up a wadded coffee cup that lay in her chair. She set it gently on his desk.

"Sorry about that."

Morgan sat down.

He frowned down at the bandage and leaned forward, blew out a stream of smoke.

"Don't you want to bag that or something?" Blair asked. "Seems like your smoke could compromise the evidence."

Cigarette hanging from his mouth, he pulled an evidence bag out of his desk and dropped the bandage in. "So why were you in the Clark house again?"

"We took her some casseroles," Blair said. "She invited us in. My sister broke a dish and was cleaning it up, and that was in the trash can. It's Cade's blood, Detective Hull. I know it is. All you need is to prove it's his, and you'll have probable cause to do a thorough search of her house."

"It doesn't work that way. We can't test it without his own blood samples."

"Look, I'm not stupid," Blair bit out. "I know how DNA works. You could go to his house and get a hair off of his comb. Besides that, he's probably had blood tests, drug tests, and all sorts of stuff for the police department. There must be medical records. You have to start somewhere."

Hull looked down at the bandage soaked with blood. "Of course we'll do those things."

His noncommital attitude sent her over the edge. "What is wrong with you people?"

Morgan sighed. "Blair, calm down."

"It's like you're afraid you're going to solve a crime or something. I don't get it. I thought police officers were supposed to be real sensitive when it came to violence against their own, but you don't even care."

"I do care," he said, "but I was with Detective McCormick the day he questioned her. There's no one being hidden in that house!"

Blair slammed her hand on his desk. "Are you going to do anything or not? Because if you're not, I'll do it myself."

Hull leaned forward, pinning her with his eyes. "And what exactly are you going to do?"

Blair evaded the question. "I know where she's holding Cade. There are bookshelves in that basement, and they look like they've been moved back and forth to hide something behind them."

He took the cigarette out of his mouth and squinted at her through the smoke. "I went in that basement myself. Your chief is not there."

"Are you blind?" Blair yelled. "Did you see the arching scrape marks on the concrete?"

Morgan touched Blair's arm to calm her, but Blair jerked it away.

Hull got up. "Look, I have to check on something. Stay here for a minute. I'll be right back." He took the bandage and headed back into the squad room.

Blair wanted to erupt. "Morgan, we tried it your way. These people are idiots! They're not going to do anything!"

Morgan sighed. "Blair, you have a way of rubbing people the wrong way, putting them instantly on the defensive. Haven't you ever heard that you attract more flies with honey?"

"I don't *have* any honey," Blair bit out, "and I don't have time to attract flies. Cade could be dying."

"Just calm down. We've done what we're supposed to do, and I know that the bandage is going to be enough to get them to act."

"Well, you have more faith in them than I do." Blair got up and looked out into the squad room. Hull was on the phone.

She had to get out of here, she thought. She had to get back there and move those bookshelves. She never should have listened to Morgan. She should have taken her gun with her and forced Ann to lead her to him.

Well, she didn't have her gun, but she could get back in that house somehow and go down into that basement. . . .

She looked around. "Where's the bathroom in this place?"

Morgan shrugged. "You're the one who was locked up here the other day. I don't know."

"I'm going to go find it," Blair said. "I'll be right back."

But instead of finding the bathroom, Blair looked instead for a side exit. Hull was still deep in conversation, so he didn't see her as she slipped out.

She hurried toward her car before Morgan could figure out what she'd done. Cade was in that house, and she was going to get to him tonight if it absolutely killed her.

CHAPTER

68

*F*ifteen minutes passed before Morgan realized that Blair had left the station. She ran out to the parking lot, and saw that Blair's car was gone. Morgan screamed out her rage, then rushed back inside.

"She's gone," she told Hull, "and I know right where she is. She's gone back to Ann Clark's house to handle this by herself!"

Hull was listening now. "She wouldn't be that stupid."

"Oh, yes, she would," Morgan screamed back. "Please! You guys have got to get over there and do something. She's going to get herself killed!"

Hull sprang into action and rushed out. Morgan sat there a moment as fear gripped her.

She needed help. She needed Jonathan.

She picked up Hull's phone and dialed Hanover House. It rang three times, and she knew one of the agents was giving them the signal to answer.

"Hello?"

"Jonathan, I need you."

He paused. "Morgan, what's going on? Why did Blair call Tavist?"

She started to cry. "I'm in Savannah. I'm no better than Sadie. I lied to you, Jonathan, right through my teeth. Not once but twice."

"What about?"

"We weren't going to visit some newcomer to Cape Refuge. We were going to visit Ann Clark because Blair just had to get inside her house to see if Cade was there."

"You didn't. Oh, dear God—"

"Oh, yeah, we did. We found a bloody bandage and brought it to the police department, and then Blair left me sitting here and went right back there by herself. Jonathan, she's going to break back into that woman's house!"

He was breathing heavy. "Morgan, which precinct?"

"Three, on Victory Drive."

"Stay right there. Don't move until I get there. Do you hear me?"

Morgan knew she couldn't talk him out of that. "Hurry, Jonathan."

"Morgan, I'll be there as soon as possible. But don't you leave there!"

"I hear you," she said. "I'll be right here."

*D*arkness had fallen over the city by the time Blair got back to Ann Clark's house. She had not left. Her car was still in the garage, and Blair could see her through the kitchen window, pacing and ranting into the phone.

She hurried to the window she'd tried to break into last night and saw that the screen was still crooked. No one had noticed it.

She worked it loose, careful not to scrape. Then she tried the window.

It slid up.

She froze. Could she do this? Could she climb in without being heard?

Did she have a choice?

Any minute now, Morgan would notice she was gone. The police would come and stop her, further alerting that woman. She had to hurry.

She pushed the window open a few more inches, then managed to pull herself in. The room was dark, but in the lamplight from the hallway, she could see that it was a library. Law books lined the shelves, and a big wooden desk sat in the middle of the room.

She stood silently in the dark, listening for the sound of Ann Clark's voice.

"I can't move him alone! Even if I drug him, it'll take some time for it to take effect, and I can't carry him!"

Blair shuddered. He was here, all right, and she hadn't come a moment too soon.

She tiptoed to the doorway and stopped.

Ann Clark was coming up the hall.

Blair stepped back into the shadows and waited. She heard a door opening, feet going down basement stairs.

Blair stole out of the room and tiptoed to the cellar door. Sweat beaded across her lip as she peered down.

She couldn't see Ann, but she heard a scraping sound.

Slowly, she stepped down the stairs. Ann was pushing the bookshelf away, and just as Blair suspected, there was a door behind it. She watched the woman open the locked door, heard her talking to someone.

A man replied.

Her heart almost leaped from her chest. Cade! He was alive!

She searched around for a weapon that she could use against the woman. Hurrying back up and into the hall, she reached for a vase that sat on a table.

Her trembling hand slipped. The vase toppled over and crashed.

"Who's there?" she heard the woman cry.

"Cade!" Blair screamed. She picked up the broken glass and held it like a weapon. "Cade! Can you hear me?"

She heard his voice, muffled and weak.

A bullet fired past her head, and she dove to the side. Rolling into another room, she searched for something, anything, that she could use.

She found a fireplace tool leaning against a dusty hearth and wielded it like a sword.

She heard the woman searching for her, going from room to room.

Blair knew she would come here next. She held the tool above her head, waited for her to come through the door . . .

Ann was still holding the gun in both hands, her arms stiff as she came through the door. Blair swung the tool and knocked the gun out of her hand.

The woman screamed, and Blair dove for the gun. Before she reached it Ann was on her back, desperately trying to choke her as she reached. . . .

CHAPTER

70

*J*onathan flew behind Agent Tavist's car to Savannah, then detoured to the Third Precinct to pick up Morgan. He ran inside and found her, pacing in front of the glass doors and crying hysterically.

He threw his arms around her.

"I'm so sorry, Jonathan! So sorry!"

"Let's go," he said. He pulled her back out to his truck, and they took off for Ann Clark's house, hoping to stop Blair before she got herself killed.

*F*rom his bed, Cade heard Blair's voice screaming out his name.

Ann had left the door open as she'd dashed out of his room. He heard crashing glass, breaking furniture, Blair's screams ripping through the house.

Cade pulled himself off the bed and lunged for the door. Pain exploded through his body, but he got out into the bigger basement room.

He heard another crash, Ann's cursing, Blair's frantic voice—

He fell at the bottom of the stairs. Sweat covered his face and neck, and he gritted his teeth against the pain. He pulled himself up one step after another, only able to use his good leg.

"Please, Lord, help me," he whispered. "Don't let anything happen to her."

One by one he made his way up the steps, pain bolting through him with each shove of his body upward. He got to the top of the stairs and looked up the hall. Broken things and toppled furniture bore witness to what he had just heard, and he heard more scuffling in a room just off the hallway. Holding onto the wall and gritting his teeth in pain, he managed to drag himself along.

He heard a siren outside, saw headlights through the windows, but he didn't have time to wait for the cops. He reached the doorway.

Ann Clark was on top of Blair, choking the life out of her. Blair's scars were purple, and her eyes were bulging. He saw the gun lying on the floor where Ann had dropped it just out of either of their reach. He kept his eyes on it, moving toward it as pain sliced through his nerve endings, shards of bone piercing tissue and muscle. . . .

He was going to black out. He turned and saw Blair losing the fight.

The gun still lay there. He got himself over it, grabbed it. . . .

They were too close together—and his hands weren't steady. The danger of hitting Blair was too great. But Ann's hands clutched Blair's throat.

His finger closed over the trigger, and he fired.

Ann Clark fell away.

*B*lair screamed as the force of the bullet threw Ann off her. Trying to catch her breath, she twisted and saw Cade leaning in the doorway with the gun in his hand.

"Cade!"

She started to sob at the sight of him. Getting up, she went toward him. He had a two-week growth of beard, and his skin was deathly gray. His pant leg had been cut off at the knee, and she saw his mangled leg with its blood-soaked bandage.

He fell toward her, and she caught him. "Cade!" She'd heard sirens outside. Where were the police? "Help! Somebody help me!"

She heard the kitchen door crashing open as she fell with him, trying to buffer his landing. "Help him!" she cried as they came into view. "He's wounded!"

Paramedics pulled Cade away, and Blair scooted back against the wall, watching, helpless, as they tried to bring him back around. Others ran for Ann Clark, who lay bleeding on her floor.

Blair shivered and rubbed her neck where Ann's fingers had dug into her skin.

"She's dead," one of them said.

Blair looked through her tears at the woman who had done so much evil. If Cade hadn't shot her exactly when he did, Blair would be dead.

She crawled toward him, touched his face. "Can you hear me, Cade?" she asked through her tears.

His eyes fluttered back open, and he focused up at her. "I hear you."

She caught her breath. "Cade ..."

"Are you okay?" His voice was hoarse, raspy. "Did she hurt you?"

The question undid her. "No, it's you who's hurt."

Her tears dropped onto his face, pooled in his stubble.

"Leg's shattered," Cade told her. "Bullet wound. Another one on my right side."

The paramedics were already on it.

"Baby," he said. "Where's the baby?"

She frowned. "What baby?"

"She has a baby. We can't leave it."

Blair looked up and saw Tavist standing in the doorway. "He said she had a baby in the house."

Tavist frowned and looked down at Cade. "Did you see it?"

"No, I heard it crying," he said. "She denied it, but I know what I heard. And she had an accomplice. He's the one who shot me."

But there was no baby in the house.

When they had him on the gurney, she followed them out into the night. Morgan burst through the crowd forming around the house and pulled Blair into a crushing embrace. "He's alive," Blair wept against her hair. "He's alive!"

"So are you."

Morgan held her and wept as they loaded him into the ambulance.

*B*lair felt a lump the size of Kentucky in her throat as she stood in front of the hospital's bathroom mirror, trying to put herself back together. For the past several hours, half of Cape Refuge had waited with her as Cade's surgery lingered on.

Because of the severity of his wounds, he had been taken straight to the operating room when the paramedics brought him in. A metal rod was inserted into his marrow cavity to repair the shattered bone in his tibia. Because it was set internally, a cast was not needed, only bandages dressing the wound.

He was awake now, and Joe had come to tell her that he was asking for her.

But she couldn't let him see her like this. The bruises had surfaced on her neck from where Ann Clark had choked her. Her throat burned and her voice was hoarse. But it was a small price to pay. Her eyes were so tired they looked sunken in, and scratches marred the good side of her face.

Thankfully, Morgan had makeup in her purse and, sensing her insecurity, had thrust the bag at Blair.

She smeared powder over the scratches, then applied a pale pink lipstick, tapped a few dots of it onto her good cheek. Then she dug through Morgan's bag until she found her mascara and some eye shadow.

She did the best she could, given her fatigue, her injuries, and of course, her scars.

But it wasn't good enough.

She stared at her reflection and slowly brought her hand up to cover the right side. Looking at only half of her face, she could almost think herself pretty. But the other side was what mattered most.

Who was she kidding?

Feeling like a fool for trying, she dropped Morgan's makeup back into her bag and walked out into the hall.

Taking in a deep breath, she went to his door, knocked lightly, and pushed inside.

He was lying in bed with his leg elevated, and as she walked toward him, he smiled.

"Hey," she said.

Cade held out a hand for her. "There's my hero lady."

Blair took his hand. His beard was gone, and the sight of him almost brought tears to her eyes. She stood awkwardly beside his bed, making sure the scar side of her face was away from him. "So how are you feeling?"

"Blessed," he said. "The Lord delivered me. And I know you don't believe, Blair, but he used you to do it."

She couldn't seem to comment on that. If she got too vulnerable, she would fall apart completely.

He reached up and touched the bruises on her neck. "She almost killed you," he whispered. His hand lingered there. "Are you sure you're okay?"

She couldn't stop the tears rimming her eyes. "Better than you."

He smiled. "I thought about you a lot while I was in there," he said. "I worried about you."

She breathed a laugh. "Worried about me? Why?"

"Because I thought this would make you even firmer in your resolve not to believe in God."

She just stared at him for a moment. "You were being held captive in a basement with gunshot wounds, waiting for them to kill you . . . and you worried about whether I would ever believe in God?"

He took her hand then and brought it to his heart. "That's right. You're in much more danger because of that than I've ever been, Blair."

She turned away for a moment because she felt too raw, standing here looking at him. She got the chair that was pushed against the window and slid it next to his bed. Slowly she sat down.

"I took care of Oswald for you." She knew it was obvious, but she had to change the subject. "He sends his love."

He grinned. "Bet he's mad."

"He'll get over it."

"Did you go in?"

She nodded. "A couple of times. I saw your Bible. You'd been reading about the cities of refuge, like you were one of those manslayers and you needed an escape from the dead man's Avenger."

He groaned. "I think God led me to that passage that morning kind of as a way of preparing me for what I was about to go through. He wanted to remind me where my refuge was."

"Only you never made it to the city. The Avenger overtook you."

Cade pulled himself up on his elbow and looked into her face. "Actually, I had already made it to the real city of refuge," he said. "And the Avenger *didn't* overtake me."

She frowned and shook her head. "I don't know what you mean."

"I mean that Christ is my refuge, Blair. He was there for me the whole time, protecting me and watching out for me. When I'm in him, the Avenger can't touch me."

"But Ann Clark did touch you. She and her accomplice shot you, Cade. You almost died."

"But I didn't die, because God didn't let you rest until you found me. And even if they had killed me, Blair, I still would have had that refuge in Christ. Evil might be able to destroy my body and change my life, but it can never destroy my soul. Can you understand that, Blair?"

She understood more than she wanted him to know, but she couldn't make herself answer.

"I want you to understand about that refuge, Blair," he said. "You have enough Avengers chasing you. I'd love to see joy in your eyes."

She swallowed the emotion tightening her throat. "You may not believe this, Cade, but I prayed for you."

A poignant smile lit up his face. "You did?"

"I did," she whispered. "And it appears that my prayer was answered."

"What do you know."

She met his eyes, wishing her heart didn't feel so raw and vulnerable. But he seemed vulnerable, too, as he looked back at her.

Hoping to get the subject on safer ground, she said, "Did you know I quit my job?"

His smile faded. "No, Blair. Why?"

"Long story," she said.

He stared at her for a moment. "You're not leaving town, are you?"

"No, I . . . I'm staying, for a while at least. Actually, I'm buying the *Cape Refuge Journal.*"

He caught his breath. "Blair, that's great! You'll be perfect for that. I couldn't think of a better job for you."

"And in my first issue, I'm going to focus on Ann Clark's accomplice. He's still out there, Cade. We have to find him."

"Not 'we,' Blair. The FBI and the police. You've risked your life enough. I want you to stay out of it."

"But Karen's baby is still missing, and that person must know where he is."

"We're going to find him," Cade said. "Trust me on this. That man is not going to get away with what he did to me. And that baby and all the other babies will be found."

"May I quote you in that first issue?"

"Feel free."

She could see he was getting tired, so she got up. "There are others who want to see you. Joe's waiting outside. I guess I should go."

He reached out then and caught her hand. "Thank you for not giving up, Blair."

She smiled. "How could I?"

He reached up and touched her face—the smooth, soft side. His eyes lingered on hers, and she knew what those sappy poets with their love images meant when they talked about hearts melting. . . .

She was like them, helpless in her connection to him.

The thought made her angry. Who did she think she was? Some bikini-clad beauty-pageant queen? Cade could get any woman he wanted. How dare she fantasize that he would want her?

"You never believed that marriage story, did you, Blair?" he asked.

"No, I didn't believe it."

"Good. Because that never would have happened."

She left him there, and went out into the hall. Morgan and Jonathan stood near his door, and as Blair came out, Morgan reached out to hug her. "Is he all right?"

"Perfect," she said. She knew if she stood here, she would fall apart right in front of everyone. "I have to go. I need to be alone. If anyone needs me, I'll be in the chapel."

Morgan's face changed. "Sure, okay."

Blair hoped she could make it to the room before her tears overcame her.

CHAPTER

*T*he chapel was dark except for four electric candles burning on a table at the front of the room, flanking an open Bible. Six small pews filled the room, three on each side of a narrow aisle. Blair slipped into one of the back pews and sat there quietly, staring straight ahead.

"Thank you," she whispered out loud. "I owe you one. I just wanted to tell you that."

She closed her eyes as her tears came forth, dripped off her chin, and wet the front of her shirt.

Where did they come from? Was it gratitude or relief? Or was it the raw, unfettered hope that left her so vulnerable and frightened?

He had looked in her eyes, touched her, and confessed to thinking about her while he was held. . . .

It was too much. The hope birthed by those facts was cruel, painful.

She pulled her feet up to the pew and buried her face in her knees, weeping out all the weariness and dread that had ridden her for the last few days.

What was she to do with these feelings?

Hugging her knees, she looked up at the front of the room again. "I know I've really imposed lately," she whispered. "It's not like you have nothing better to do. But I'm really out on a limb here, thinking these thoughts about Cade and knowing I'll probably be shot down like all the other times in my life. I don't want . . . to want."

She saw a box of Kleenex someone had slipped under the pew in front of her, so she grabbed a tissue out and blew her nose. Drawing in a deep breath, she went on.

"You answered that other prayer, even though I didn't deserve it. If you wouldn't mind helping me out with this, I'd really appreciate it. Whether it's to make me stop caring so much or work it so it comes out the way I wish. . . ."

The very utterance of that desire sent a shiver of fear through her, greater even than the fear when she'd gone in through Ann Clark's window.

"Stupid," she whispered. "I'm so stupid." What could Cade ever see in her?

Maybe he just sensed her own inane feelings and didn't want to hurt her. That would be just like Cade. Being gentle and sweet to keep from making her feel like an idiot.

But had she been obvious about her feelings? Had she even known for sure what her feelings *were*? Denial *was* her middle name, after all. Maybe it wasn't as obvious as she thought.

She grabbed another tissue and blew into it, then another and wiped her face. She had to stop this. Somehow she had to pull herself together.

She thought of what Cade had said to her about her own Avengers and the refuge he thought she needed. Was she just another potential convert, or were his frequent attempts to share his faith the greatest acts of love he knew?

She pictured herself running, running, away from her own Avengers—away from the secrets that had caused her scars, the bitterness that had taken root and grown within her, the grief over her parents' murders, the loneliness and anger.

She saw herself running from those who would destroy her, racing down that smooth road that would take her quickly to safety. She pictured herself reaching that gate where salvation waited. She lingered outside it, wanting that sweet peace the city walls would provide but fearful of crossing that threshold.

Cade had lived within those walls, even though he'd been trapped in the confines of a basement room. He'd called Christ his refuge, and he *had* been rescued.

But her parents had also lived in Christ, and they had suffered a violent end. She believed what Morgan had said all those months ago, about Christ being there to greet them the moment they closed their eyes. They had lived their life in a city called Refuge, and now their home was Refuge, itself.

What peace there must be in knowing that whether you live or die, the Avenger could not overtake you.

"Jesus, I long for that peace," she whispered on a sob. "I'm so tired of running."

She closed her eyes, covered her face, and pictured herself reaching that gate. She raised her hand to knock, preparing to make her case. . . .

But the door flew open, and she stepped inside . . .

And fell into the arms of Refuge Himself.

*B*lair kept her decision to herself. She had been in church enough as a child to know that a public profession was important, but she couldn't do that just yet. How could she trust her own faith? What if this was just a knee-jerk reaction born of her emotional state? What if it didn't hold up under pressure? What if she simply wanted to believe, but didn't really?

She would sort through it all later when things quieted down. But for now she had a paper to write. Jason Wheater had come to the hospital earlier with a briefcase full of papers for her to sign, making the newspaper hers. She had the keys to the building now and didn't intend to waste a moment. There was a kidnapper and a killer still at large. And that baby needed to be found.

She came back to the crowd of friends in the waiting room and located Sadie across the room with Morgan.

Cutting through, she tapped Sadie's shoulder. The girl turned around.

"Sadie, I need your help. Jason gave me the keys to the newspaper office tonight, and I want us to start working."

Sadie caught her breath. "Really?"

Morgan frowned. "But Sadie has school tomorrow. I don't want her up late. And, Blair, you need to rest."

"There's plenty of time for that later," Blair said. "We're going to need to work through the night to get the first issue out. She'll have to miss one day of school because I'll need her tomorrow too."

Sadie's face glowed. "Oh, please, Morgan. Let me do it!"

Morgan sighed. "Okay. I guess one day won't hurt. You take care of her, Blair."

Energized and full of new purpose, Blair led Sadie out of the hospital, ready to right the wrongs done against Cade by finally getting the truth out.

*B*lair and Sadie worked until morning writing the story, with sidebars about the accomplice still at large and the possible connection this person had to the kidnappings of babies across the south.

Blair placed Ann's DMV photo on the front page.

Sadie came up behind her. "I can't believe I was so close to her at that wedding, and all the time she was holding Cade captive. I wonder if the man I saw her with was the accomplice."

Blair nodded. "My guess is that he is. I'm including his description. I'm hoping someone will read it and remember seeing him with her."

She got Sadie busy hunting down articles about the other missing babies, while Blair wrote about the lies perpetrated against Cade while he'd been held.

It was daylight by the time they had most of their first issue laid out, but they still needed a few things.

"We need some quotes from people who were involved in the case, and a few more pictures," Blair said. "I want to interview that detective who walked through Ann's house with Joe. I want to see him squirm when I ask him how he feels knowing he overlooked the clues that Cade was there."

"You think he'll even talk to you?" Sadie asked.

"He'll talk, even if it's to say he won't talk. And you're going to get a picture of him doing it. Then we'll get back here and get this puppy printed and have it on every driveway in town by this afternoon."

It had started to rain, reminding her of that day over two weeks ago when all of this had started. Her windshield wipers swiped across her windshield, making it hard to drive. Exhausted, but driven, Blair and Sadie drove to the Savannah Precinct as the first shift was getting under way.

The sergeant at the front desk was making coffee, and he looked up as he poured the water in. "Help you?"

"I'm Blair Owens," she said, shaking her umbrella out. "I need to speak to Detective Hull, please."

The sergeant pointed to the back. "He's around the corner there."

Blair looked back at Sadie, who carried the digital camera. "Okay, now you take pictures as I'm talking to him. I want his ragged head right on the front page, with a caption that says what a prince of a cop he is."

"I'm on it," Sadie said. "Photojournalist-slash-newspaper-woman."

"Don't say anything. Just let me do all the talking." She spotted him standing at the coffeepot. "There he is now. Just hang back a minute until I get him engaged. Try to get the front of his face." Locking her eyes on the man who had failed so miserably to help Cade's case, Blair headed toward him.

Sadie hung back a few steps behind Blair and watched as she approached the man. She could only see him from behind, but something about him was familiar.

Then he turned, and she knew where she'd seen him before.

The wedding. He'd been the man with Ann Clark, holding her as if they were lovers!

She quickly brought the camera to her face to cover it and began flashing pictures.

Her heart hammered as she heard Blair asking him if he had any comments on why he failed to find Cade when he'd done the original search of Ann Clark's house.

"If I recall, one of Cape Refuge's finest was also searching the house. Why don't you ask him?" he said.

"I have," Blair said. "He told us that you were the one who searched the basement. I can't imagine why you wouldn't have seen the scrape marks on the concrete floor in front of the bookcase. I was there myself, and it was very clear that the shelves had been moved because something was behind them. Why would a trained detective fail to notice that?"

Sadie turned away and pretended to be adjusting her camera. Her hands trembled so badly that she almost dropped it.

What did this mean? If this man was the detective who searched Ann's house, it was no wonder they hadn't found Cade. He must have known. He must have been helping her.

And he had seemed familiar at the wedding because she had seen him before, in Karen's hospital room after the kidnapping.

She couldn't stand here and take the chance of his seeing and recognizing her, so she took off for the exit door. Stepping outside, she waited for Blair just under the overhang. Lightning bolted nearby and thunder cracked behind it.

Panic sent her mind racing. The accomplice was a cop! And if he saw her face, he would remember that she'd seen them.

Frightened, she dashed out into the rain and got into Blair's Volvo.

After a moment, Blair came out, looking for her. "Sadie, what's wrong with you? I asked you to take pictures."

"Blair, it's him!"

Blair got in and stared at her. "Him who?"

"The accomplice. The one I saw Ann Clark with. He's the one!"

"Detective Hull? Are you sure?"

"Positive. Blair, he's the one. He was working with her, helping her, and that's why he didn't find Cade that day."

Blair looked back at the door, and for a moment Sadie feared she would go back in. Then she started the engine and pulled out of her space.

"Okay, we're going to the hospital. We're going to tell Cade and the FBI. If Detective Hull is who we think he is, he's about to have a big surprise."

CHAPTER

77

Joe McCormick sat in Cade's room when Blair reached the hospital. She burst in without knocking, Sadie on her heels. "Cade, you're not going to believe this!"

Cade sat up. "What, Blair?"

She stood over him, breathless. "We know who the accomplice was. Tell them, Sadie."

Cade regarded the girl, who looked as if she'd been up all night. "I went to a wedding with Trevor Beal ... it was his cousin's—"

"Skip ahead," Blair blurted. "He doesn't care about the cousin."

Sadie tried again. "Ann Clark was there. I stumbled on her in the garden. She was with a man, kissing him."

Cade frowned. "Who was it?"

Blair took over. "She didn't know him. But just now, Sadie and I went to Savannah Police Precinct Three to interview Detective Hull for the paper. And the minute Sadie saw him she recognized him."

Cade's mouth fell open, and he looked at Joe. "Hull?"

Joe took a step toward Sadie. "Are you absolutely sure?"

"Positive. They didn't come to the wedding together, but they snuck away together."

Cade's face looked stricken as he stared at Blair. "No way. Hull's too good a detective to do something so stupid."

But Joe didn't seem so sure. He got up and ran his hand over his just-shaved head. "He was the one who searched the basement when we walked through the house, Cade. He made sure I would search the upstairs. If I'd gone down there, I would have seen the scrape marks and looked behind the bookcase. Any cop would have."

The color was draining from Cade's face. "So he missed it. It doesn't mean he was involved."

Blair's eyes flashed with conviction. "Cade, last night when we found your bloody bandage in the trash, we took it to the police. Hull kept it, then stalled like crazy. He was probably calling her, warning her to get you out of there. I heard her on the phone when I broke in. She was saying she couldn't move you herself, even if she drugged you."

Cade shook his head. "You don't know that she was talking to him."

Joe started pacing. "I wondered how Ann got your unlisted home number. A cop could have gotten it for her. And when the first baby was taken from here in Savannah, Hull was the one in charge of the case. He could have been destroying evidence as he pretended to search for it."

"You're jumping to conclusions! So he was having an affair with Ann, that doesn't mean he's guilty of murder and kidnapping!"

Blair gaped at him. "Cade, if Ann was involved in the kidnapping, then he was too. He may even be the one who shot her husband, if she didn't do it herself."

Cade stared down at his bandaged leg. "This can't be. No cop would have shot me."

"A crooked cop might, Cade!" Blair bent down, her face close to his. "Cade, add things up! If he is involved, then maybe he has the baby."

Cade sat for a moment, his eyes transfixed with possibilities. Finally, he threw back the covers. "I've got to get out of here. I've got to tell the FBI. I want to be there when they question him."

"Cade, you can't leave," Blair said. "Your leg . . ."

He gritted his teeth as he moved his leg to the floor. "I'm fine," he grunted. "Just get me some crutches."

"But you need the IV," Blair said. "The antibiotics. . . . Cade, just talk to the FBI on the phone and let them handle it."

"No," he said. "This is personal, Blair. I'm not a spectator in this. Sadie, will you go find someone who can get me a pair of crutches? Tell them I'm leaving. I'll sign whatever I need to, but I'm outta here."

As Sadie left the room, Blair stood in front of him. "Cade, you're the only witness to these crimes. Hull—or whoever Ann's accomplice was—still wants you dead."

Cade wasn't listening. "I'll go straight to the FBI, Blair. I'm not going to compromise the investigation. But I can't stand back on the sidelines and watch. And if Hull was involved, I have to know for sure."

"She's following us, Cade." Joe muttered the statement with dread. "That woman never quits."

Cade looked out Joe's back window. The rain hadn't slowed Blair any. She drove so close behind them that he feared she'd skid and hit them at the next red light. He sighed and turned back around. "Let her follow. They won't let her anywhere close to the house."

They had found out that Agent Tavist was at Ann Clark's house, directing the search for evidence that would lead them to any accomplices and, hopefully, to the babies. He had called ahead and told Tavist he was coming and that he had some information. Tavist had left word that the agents were to let him in.

Joe couldn't get much closer to the house than Blair could since so many cars blocked the driveway. "Just stay here and I'll go in," Cade said.

Joe gave him a worried look. "Sure you can walk on those things in the rain?"

Cade wasn't sure, but he was going to give it his best shot. "I'll be fine." Carefully, he pulled his leg out of the car and pulled himself up on the crutches. There was no way he could carry an umbrella, and he knew the rain would soak his bandages. He would just have to hurry.

Blair got out of her car when she saw him emerge. "Cade, you need help. You could slip."

"I'm okay, Blair. Just wait in the car."

An agent came forward with an umbrella and held it over him as he hobbled up the porch and into the house. He got in and stood on the entrance mat, waiting for Tavist.

The man came through the house and shook Cade's hand. "Good to see you up, Cade. After last night, I didn't expect to see you out of bed for a while."

Cade looked around at the house where he had been held. "I have some information that may or may not be helpful." He told the agent about Hull's involvement with Ann Clark, and Joe's suspicions about his part in the investigation.

"I don't know what it all means," Cade said. "I've known Hull for a long time. I've trusted him. I find it hard to believe he'd be involved in something so criminal. But it has to be looked into."

Tavist drew his eyebrows together and looked down at his feet. "We found some hair on the sheets of her bed. Brown curly hair, doesn't belong to her or her husband."

"Hull has brown curly hair," Cade said. "Shouldn't be hard to compare."

"We've also found plenty of evidence linking her to the kidnappings. She had papers in a safe in her closet with the name of a prominent lawyer in town—Jasper Beal."

Cade gaped at him. The wedding Sadie had gone to. Hadn't it been for one of the Beals? He knew the family well and had investigated them on a number of occasions. Jasper was the only lawyer, and he lived in Savannah.

"Do you think he was the accomplice?"

"Could be. We have a warrant out for his arrest."

Cade couldn't explain the relief he felt. "So if he's the accomplice, then maybe Hull is innocent."

Tavist shook his head. "There may have been more than one accomplice," he said. "We've investigated Beal and his brother on a number of other cases. Typically, he lets others do the dirty work and keeps his distance."

"It was his daughter's wedding where Ann Clark and Hull were seen."

Tavist nodded. "We think he may have been selling the babies to desperate couples who wanted to adopt. There were five substantial deposits into Ann Clark's bank account the last few weeks. Could have been payoffs for delivery of the babies."

Cade drew his eyebrows together. "Five? But there were six. What about the Miller baby?"

Tavist shook his head. "Maybe it hadn't been placed yet."

"Then where is it?"

Tavist looked up at him. "We don't know."

Cade closed his eyes and tried to put it all together. Ann kidnapping the babies, Hull helping her cover the crimes, Beal placing the babies . . .

Was it even possible?

He looked around him at this house where he'd been held like some kind of caged animal. Had Hull stalked through it, scheming to use his name and his handwriting and his cell phone . . . ? Planning his death after the world was sure he'd committed those crimes?

Tavist touched his shoulder. "Go home, Cade. You've earned your rest. Let us do our job. We'll handle it."

Cade studied the man's face. *Would* he handle it? Or would he take too long compiling evidence before he even approached Hull?

He crutched his way back outside. It was still raining, and the morning sky gloomed gray and angry. He stood in the downpour for a moment, his mind racing through his options.

What if Hull wasn't guilty, after all? What if Sadie had made a mistake?

And even if she'd been right, wasn't it possible that Ann Clark had used him to get information about the investigations? Could it be that he was just a pawn too?

Or was Cade simply in denial?

He took one deliberate step after another, holding his bandaged leg up. The bandage was soaked, and he saw that blood was seeping through. It needed to be elevated, but not now.

Cade went to the car and dropped onto the passenger seat, carefully pulled the leg in. It was swelling within the dressings, and pain pulsed through it.

Joe looked over at him. "What's the story?"

Cade stared at the windshield for a moment. "They've found a lot of evidence, but nothing linking her to Hull yet."

Joe tapped on his steering wheel. "They will. Give them time."

"That baby may not have time."

Joe looked over at him. "So now you believe Hull was involved?"

"I still don't know." In the side mirror, he saw Blair getting out of her car, throwing her umbrella up, and hurrying toward his window.

He rolled it down when she reached it.

"What did he say?" she asked. "Does he believe Hull's involved?"

"He doesn't know," Cade said. "But I told him what you told me."

"So are you going back to the hospital?"

Cade looked up at her for a long moment. The truth was, he didn't want to go back. He wanted to go find Hull and look him in the eye.

But Blair couldn't know that.

"Yeah, we're going back," he said. "But you might want to stick around here for a while. They've found some things that do connect Ann to the kidnappings. Just wait and they'll probably make a statement soon."

That satisfied Blair, and he watched as she got back into her car. She would be safe here, he thought, and it would keep her out of trouble for a while.

Joe started the car and backed away from the blockade. "So we're going to the hospital?"

Cade shook his head. "No. I want to go see Hull."

Joe got the car turned around. "You're kidding, right?"

"No. I'm still not sure he did it, Joe. I just want to talk to him."

He picked up Joe's cell phone that lay on the seat and dialed the number of the Cape Refuge Police Department. Georgette, the office clerk, answered on the first ring.

"Hey, Georgette. Cade, here."

Georgette caught her breath. "Oh, Chief Cade, it's so good to hear your voice! We've been so worried about you! How are you feeling?"

"I'm good. Look, would you put Billy Caldwell on the phone for me, please?"

A moment passed and Billy came to the phone. "Hey, Chief! Good to hear from you."

"Yeah, you too. Look, Caldwell, I need your help. I need for you to find out if Detective Hull of Precinct Three in Savannah is on duty today. I need to get in touch with him."

"Sure. Want him to call you if I reach him?"

"No. In fact, I don't want you to reach him. Just find out if he's working, and I'll take it from there. Call me back on McCormick's phone."

He hung up and looked out the window, waiting for Billy to call back.

Joe shook his head. "Cade, you need to let the FBI do this. If you approach him knowing what you know, you may give him a heads-up that the feds are on to him."

"I won't," he said. "Just a friendly visit, that's all. I'm an angry victim who wants to put all the pieces of this thing together. He has some of those pieces, since he worked on the kidnappings *and* questioned Ann Clark with you."

The phone rang and Cade flipped it open. "Yeah?"

"He's not on duty right now, Chief."

Cade sat silent for a moment. What now? If he couldn't just drop into the police precinct to talk to him, he'd have to go to his house.

But would Hull suspect they were onto him?

"Do me another favor, Caldwell. Find his address for me. I'll hold."

He waited as Caldwell went to his computer and started the search.

Joe looked troubled as he navigated his way through traffic. "Cade, you can't seriously be considering going to his house."

Cade's jaw muscles tightened. "I want to see inside his house. Just look around, that's all."

"The feds'll do that."

Cade sat there for a moment, staring through the windshield. "Whoever was working with Ann Clark dragged me into that house and shoved me, unconscious, down the stairs. He conspired with her to plant evidence that I was involved in the kidnappings. He shot me twice when I tried to escape. He slammed my head into concrete." Cade's voice trembled with the last words. "I have to know if he's the one."

"You will know. Just wait."

Cade leaned his head back on the seat. Joe was driving toward the hospital, but Cade decided it didn't matter. He could make him turn around as soon as he made up his mind.

He thought of Hull, if he was guilty, hearing that there was a warrant out for Jasper Beal's arrest. Wouldn't he realize then that the jig was up? That there was no way he'd get away with placing the Miller baby? Wouldn't he see that baby as too much of a liability and want to get rid of it?

Then again, this whole thing could just be a deadend. Sadie thought she had seen him with Ann Clark, but everyone knew that teenage girls sometimes overdramatize things. Maybe she just *thought* it was Hull. That should be easy to find out. All they needed was the guest list from the wedding. If Hull was on it, then Cade would believe it.

Caldwell came back to the phone and gave him the rural address out on Highway 16.

As Cade hung up, he glanced over at Joe. "Turn the car around, Joe. We're going to Highway 16."

Joe groaned. "Cade, this is a mistake. If he's the one, we need to approach him with backup. We need to go by the book. We need a warrant."

"I'm not approaching him as a killer. I'm approaching him as a cop. I just want to talk to him."

Joe was silent as he turned the car around, and Cade stared out the window.

Joe was right. Cade didn't have any business showing up there like this, when the FBI was on the case. He could be jeopardizing the investigation. He could even get himself killed.

Was he going for the sake of that baby or for the sake of his own satisfaction?

Conviction pressed down on him, aching through him with the same intensity as his leg.

But he just wanted to look the man in the eye. He would know. If he saw him and talked with him about the case, he'd be able to tell if he had something to hide.

Hull was probably not even involved, and Cade would see it as soon as he looked the man in the face.

"You don't have to go with me, Joe. I don't blame you if you don't want to be a part of this."

Joe kept driving. "If you're going, I'm going, Cade. I can't let you do this alone."

C H A P T E R

79

*H*ull lived out in a rural area off of Highway 16, outside the city limits east of Savannah, in a house that they almost missed because it was so hard to spot from the road.

"Secluded," Joe said as he pulled onto the man's dirt driveway. "He could do almost anything out here and no one would see him." He glanced at Cade. "Give me the plan."

Cade leaned his head back on the seat. The pain in his leg was wearing him down. "First we get him thinking we're just his colleagues paying a professional visit. When his guard's down, I've got some questions for him."

Joe pulled up the muddy driveway, his wipers arching back and forth across the windshield. Cade set his hands on the dash and peered through the wet glass as the back of the house came into view.

It was an old restored farmhouse that sat on the edge of a small lake, its front facing the water. As they approached, Cade made note of the doors and windows.

The back door opened on a small porch, and there were six windows, all of them shut against the rain. As they followed the dirt driveway around the house, he saw a side door.

They pulled up to the front of the house. A motorcycle was parked under a tree, a blue tarp thrown over it, protecting it from the rain. Next to it sat Hull's Taurus.

Cade got his crutches from the backseat and got out, wincing as he moved across the yard. He almost wished he had a cast to protect his leg from bumps. But with the internal splint, there had been no need for one. It was swelling now, and the bandage had grown too tight. Gritting back the pain, he made his way across the porch. He stood there a moment before ringing the bell.

What was he doing? He shouldn't be here, facing down his tormentor, if indeed that was what Hull was. He didn't even have a weapon. He needed backup, in case Hull figured him out and made a run for it. He needed to wait for the FBI to act.

But he had to look Hull in the eye.

Joe came up on the porch and stood next to him.

"Gonna ring the bell or kick the door in?"

Cade didn't find that amusing.

"Cade, are you sure you want to do this?"

Cade pushed the doorbell. He heard a television inside. He was watching a ball game . . .

But there was something else . . . another sound . . .

A baby crying.

Cade shot Joe a look. "You hear that?"

"Yeah. A baby." Joe reached for his gun, and Cade nodded. Drawing it, Joe stepped to the side of the door. Cade took the other side, in case Hull came out firing.

The door came open, and Joe raised his weapon. Hull jumped back. "Whoa, man! Hold on! What's this about?"

"I came to talk to you, Hull," Cade said. "But when I heard that baby crying, I decided that talking wasn't necessary." He moved close to Hull and began to pat him down. A pistol was holstered on his belt. Cade pulled it out.

"Come on, man. My sister's here with her kid."

Cade turned the gun on Hull. "How about we go into the house and meet your sister, Hull?"

Hull stared at him. "Look, I don't know what this is about, but, man, you've been under a lot of pressure. Probably on pain-killers." He shot Joe a beseeching look. "Man, I don't recommend you go along with this."

"In the house, Hull," Joe said, pushing him back inside.

Clutching that gun, Cade hobbled in behind them.

Hull backed across the living room, deftly avoiding the fur-niture in his way. "Don't shoot," he said, holding his hands up. "You don't want to kill a brother."

Cade looked around at the mess in the place. It reeked of cig-arette smoke, and ashtrays overflowed with butts. Beer bottles and plates with dried food adorned the coffee table.

He saw a closed door and knew the baby was beyond it. "That door," Cade said, motioning with his gun. "Open it slowly. One false move, it'll be your last."

Hull opened the door, and in one swift motion, grabbed up the infant seat sitting on a table just inside the door. The tiny black infant's screams pitched an octave higher.

Hull held the seat like a bucket, clutching its handle as the child squirmed and kicked, unfastened. If he tipped it enough, Cade saw, the baby would spill out.

"Put the baby down, Hull," Cade said.

But Hull kept moving into the room, knowing they wouldn't shoot with the baby so close to him.

Then Hull grabbed a gun out of the carrier and aimed it at Cade.

Sweat dripped into Cade's eyes. One crutch fell, and he put his foot down to steady himself. Pain exploded through him, blur-ring his vision and loosening his grip on the gun he held.

The child's high-pitched screams pierced through the room.

Cade bent down, grabbed his crutch back up, and propped it under his arm. His hand shook as he took aim again.

"Put the baby down, Hull. Put him down, now!"

Hull laughed. "You thought you could beat me, didn't you, Cade? You thought you could hobble in here and save the day."

"Give me the baby, Hull, and you can make a run for it. All I want is the baby."

"Are you kidding me?" Hull's face reflected his strain at the situation he was in. He held the car seat at his side, swinging it back and forth. "This baby is my way out. Remember, they still think you might have been involved, Cade. I'll let them think I found the baby, that you were running with it."

Joe stepped toward him, his gun aimed for Hull's forehead.

"Come one step closer, Joe, and I'll blow your head off," Hull said.

Joe stopped, but kept his gun on him.

"Take me, instead," Cade said. "Give Joe the baby, and I'll go with you. That's what you want, isn't it? Just a hostage?"

But Hull wasn't buying. He backed his way to a door that led out the bedroom onto the back porch. He managed to open it and stepped outside, still swinging the seat. "Stay back," he said, "or I'll kill it."

Cade held his fire, and Joe did the same. Hull took off through the rain, running toward the Taurus. He started the car and sped down the muddy driveway.

Joe shot out into the rain, firing at Hull's tires, but the car sped out of sight. Moving as fast as he could manage, Cade crutched back out to Joe's car and jumped in, jarring his leg as he did. Choking back his agony, he closed the door. Joe took off, radioing an all-points-bulletin for Hull's car. Within seconds, every officer in the area knew that Hull was fleeing with the baby.

But Hull had a radio of his own. "This is Detective Hull," he screamed into the radio. "I am in possession of an African American infant that looks to be a few days old. I found the baby in a warehouse on Highway 16. I am in hot pursuit of a Cape Refuge police car believed to be occupied by Police Chief Matthew Cade and Detective Joe McCormick, both of whom I believe to be connected with these kidnappings."

Cade heard the transmission and grabbed the radio from Joe. "Negative," Cade yelled. "Detective Hull is not pursuing us, we're pursuing *him* southbound down Highway 16. We found the baby in Hull's home at 353 Highway 16. He is armed and threatening to kill the infant. We need backup ASAP."

The car in front of them slowed, and Cade raised his gun.

Suddenly the Taurus made a U-turn. Joe slammed on his brakes and turned around, but Hull's car took a side street and disappeared.

Joe turned down the street. The Taurus was nowhere in sight. "Where'd he go?" Joe yelled.

Suddenly, a bullet fired through the back window.

"He's behind us!" Joe said.

Cade ducked as another bullet fired. He had claimed to be pursuing them, and now he had made it so.

Cade grabbed the radio and told them where they had turned. "We are under fire. Suspect is armed and dangerous and still in possession of the baby!"

They heard sirens turning up the street, coming after them, but it still looked as if Hull was chasing them.

"Cut him off," Cade shouted. "When he stops, I'll fire."

Joe slammed on his brakes. Hull swerved and came around him. Cade tried to take aim, but as long as that car was moving, he couldn't take Hull out. The baby's life was at stake.

Joe followed him, the convoy of police cars right behind them. "Shoot out his tires, Cade!"

Cade fired, but the Taurus was too far ahead of them, zigzagging from lane to lane, out of bullet range.

Other Savannah police began to fall in behind them.

Cade heard another transmission from one of the Savannah cops. "Hull, do you have that baby with you?"

"Yes, I do," Hull said.

"Then pull over immediately. Do you hear me, Hull? Pull your car off the road now."

"Can't do that," Hull radioed back. "I will not put this baby in harm's way."

"Where are you taking it?"

"To safety," he said.

Cade grabbed the mike again. "Hull, prove you're innocent. If you want to bring the baby to safety, pull over now and turn him over."

The radio crackled again, and he heard another voice. "This is FBI Agent Tavist. It's Hull you're after. Do you read me? It's Hull you want, not Cade!"

Suddenly there was a burst of radio exchanges among other officers. Hull made a turn and flew to the Interstate.

"Where is he going?" Joe asked. "He can't possibly think there's an escape."

"He realizes they're not buying his story," Cade said. "Maybe he's headed to the airport."

But then Hull turned on to Chatham Parkway and headed toward the Savannah River.

"He's going to try to get away on the water," Cade shouted.

They followed, sirens blaring and lights flashing, as Hull led them to a dock where two dozen boats were parked on slips out on the water.

He abandoned his car and got out, holding that car seat in one hand and waving his gun in the other. Rain pummeled down on them.

All of the cars came to a halt in a semicircle around him.

Cade got out. "Leave the baby, Hull! You can go, but leave the baby. Just set him down and run."

Panicked, Hull kept holding the screaming baby and, with his gun poised, backed his way down a pier.

He looked from side to side, trying to find a boat he could step into. But none was close enough.

Instead, he ducked into a shed at the end of the pier. Through the window, he began shooting, holding his colleagues at bay.

*B*lair stood in the rain at the Clark house, trying to get a statement from one of the agents who had been searching Ann Clark's house, when the call came over his radio that there was a standoff at the Riverside Pier on the Savannah River and that Detective Hull was holding a baby hostage.

Her heart plunged, and she knew that Cade would be right in the thick of it.

As the agent ran to confer with his colleagues, Blair jumped in her car. Sadie, who had fallen asleep in her seat, jumped awake at the slamming door.

"What is it, Blair?"

"There's a standoff at the River. Hull has the baby."

Sadie straightened. "We're going there?"

"I am. But I'll drop you off at the Wendy's near the dock. I swore to Morgan I'd take care of you."

"Why are you going? You can't help. You should stay away too, Blair."

"I think Cade's there." It was all the reason she needed.

When they reached the Wendy's, Sadie started to get out. "Go in there and pray while you're waiting," she said. "Don't stop until I get back."

Sadie gave her a surprised look. "I sure will. Be careful, Blair."

Sadie got out of the car, and Blair sped away.

At Hanover House, the agents manning the phones had flown into a flurry of activity, but they weren't talking about what was going on. But when the local television station broke into programming to alert the public about the high speed chase that had taken place down the interstate, and the stand-off on the river that had something to do with one of the kidnapped babies, Karen sprang off the couch.

"My baby!" she cried. "They found my baby!"

Morgan stared down at the television. One of the agents stepped into the room, and Morgan looked up at him. "Is it true?"

"Looks like it," he said. "A black infant just a few days old."

"We've got to go there!" Karen shouted. She turned to the agent. "Please, will you take us? We'll stay back until it's safe, but I want to be there for my baby!"

The agent went to confer with his colleague, then came back into the room. "Let's go," he said.

CHAPTER

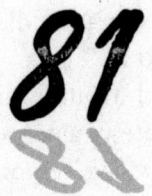

*N*eedles of rain slanted down, thunder cracking and lightning flashing, as if God had had enough.

Hull was still in the building, firing at anything that came near.

The FBI had arrived, and Tavist had taken over. But they were getting nowhere.

Cade sat inside Joe's car, struggling against the agony of his leg. But it was the pain of his own regret that almost did him in.

He never should have gone to Hull's house. If he'd waited for the FBI, they would have surrounded the place before Hull even knew they were there. They might have surprised him and subdued him before he could further endanger the child.

He watched from his car as the agents tried negotiating with Hull through a bullhorn. But the only response from Hull was the occasional gunshot firing from the window.

Someone had to risk going in there to talk to him. But with Hull firing out at anyone who tried, it had become impossible.

Unless . . .

As an idea dawned in Cade's mind, he got his crutches and got out of the car. Making his way through the storm, he got to Agent Tavist's car.

The man was in a huddle with several other agents.

"I want to go in."

Tavist turned around and looked at him. "That's absurd. He'll kill you before you get within thirty feet of him. Our sniper team is on its way. We're going to try to take him through the window."

"I could distract him," Cade said. "We could let him know I'm coming, injured and unarmed. I'm not a threat with these crutches."

Tavist stared at him for a moment. "You could be killed just like that, Cade. It's not worth it."

Rain dripped into Cade's eyes as he looked back at that shed. "It is to me."

Tavist turned back to his men, and Cade waited as they discussed the plan. He heard a van pull up and turned to see a dozen special agents filing out with their rifles.

If they tried to take him out from this distance, they could miss and hit the baby. If he could get in there, maybe he could protect him.

Finally, Agent Tavist turned back around. "Cade, are you sure you want to do this?"

"I'm sure," Cade said.

"All right. We can try it. We'll send you as our negotiator, but all we really want is for you to distract him while our agents move in. If you can, try to stand close to the baby. If we can see you, we won't fire in that direction."

Cade was ready.

Tavist brought the bullhorn to his mouth. Cade hoped Hull could hear him through the storm.

"Detective Hull," Tavist called to him. "We'd like to send someone in to talk to you. Chief Cade is not a threat. He's unarmed. He just wants to hear your demands."

For a moment there was no answer, then finally, Hull yelled out. "Tell him to take off his shirt so I can see if he's armed."

Cade didn't waste a moment. He hobbled on his crutches out in front of the police cars and FBI agents. The rain had already drenched him, but it pounded so hard that he hoped Hull could see him clearly enough. He stood at the end of the pier and, balancing on his crutches, peeled his shirt off and dropped it.

He hoped Hull could see that he had nothing on him, except a bandage over his ribs. His wet sweatpants were plastered to his skin. Anything hidden there would be obvious.

"I'm coming, Hull," Cade said. "We okay with that?"

When there was no answer, he started to move. Slowly, he crutched his way down the pier, one step after another, waiting, almost expecting, for Hull to shoot him dead and finish the job he started in Ann Clark's basement. But he kept going, one step at a time.

Lord, help me do this.

He reached the door of the building. "I'm coming in, Hull," he said. "I just want to talk."

The door came slightly open, and Cade pushed through.

Hull grabbed him and patted him down, each touch of his bandage sending rivets of pain shooting through him.

Satisfied, Hull pulled him in and slammed the door. The old shed smelled of dirt and dead fish, and there was no light except for what little came through the window.

Hull stood in front of him, his gun pointing at him. "Give me your crutches," he said.

Cade balanced on his good leg and handed him the crutches.

The baby seat sat on a shelf behind him. The baby had stopped crying and seemed to be sleeping.

"Start talking," Hull said.

"I came to listen." Cade checked Hull's distance from the window. He wasn't close enough. They would never be able to see him.

"Tell us what you want," Cade said. "The feds are in a negotiating mood."

Hull was sweating, and Cade recognized the terror on his face. He had to show him a way out of this.

"So far, there are no murder charges. We figure Ann killed her husband. And if the babies are found unharmed, then it'll even look better for you."

"The babies were never in danger," Hull said. "Not until you came along, trying to be the hero. Every one of the babies has been adopted out, and this one would have gone to its home tomorrow if you hadn't come along and destroyed everything."

Cade couldn't help the bitter contempt twisting his face. So it was all about money. Kill a man, abduct a cop, rip newborns from their families. He wondered how much they made on each one.

"We had a great setup," Hull said. "Until William went off the deep end. Ann tried to kill him to keep him from talking. You finished the job."

"So," Cade said, "you're not responsible for anyone's death. Get a good lawyer and you could beat this, Hull."

From the corner of his eye, he watched the window. Somehow, he had to get near the baby. "Let me see the baby," he said. "I want to make sure he's still alive."

Hull shook his head. "He's finally sleeping. I can't stand that screaming."

"I won't wake him up," he said. "I can move over there, if you'll give me just one crutch. They want me to let them know if he's okay."

Hull looked out the window, as if weighing Cade's words. Cade saw the confusion on his face.

"If I tell them he's alive, they'll relax a little," Cade said. "Everybody's on edge until they know that. They're liable to do anything."

Hull stared at him for a moment. Finally, he picked the baby carrier up and gave Cade a look. "See? Alive, even though I'm sick to death of it." He set the baby on the floor between them. "And frankly, Chief, I'm sick to death of you too. If I'm going to prison, I might as well make it worth it."

As he spoke, he raised his gun and aimed it between Cade's eyes.

*B*lair pulled into the outer parking lot of the dock where the standoff was taking place. Through her frantically sweeping windshield wipers, she could see the police cars lined up like vicious dogs waiting to attack. Armed officers used their vehicles as barricades as they kept their weapons trained on that building just off the pier, waiting to fire when told.

At the back of the crowd, she saw Joe McCormick pacing back and forth, and she knew without a doubt that Cade was here too.

She got out of her car, leaving her umbrella behind, and ran up to the barricade.

"Ma'am, you can't come any closer," a cop told her.

"I need to speak to Detective McCormick," she said. "The bald guy over there."

The cop went to get him, and Joe hurried over. "Blair, what are you doing here?"

She ignored the question. "Joe, where's Cade?"

Joe looked back toward the pier, though it wasn't visible from where they stood. Finally, he ducked under the barricade and got closer to her. "He's in that shed with Hull and the baby. They sent him in as a negotiator."

Thunder cracked like a gunshot, startling her. Had he said what she thought he said? That Cade was in danger again?

She lunged at him, fists flying. "Why did you let him go? He can't even walk! What's the matter with you?"

Joe caught her fists. "I couldn't stop him, Blair."

"After everything that happened!" she railed. "Hull's going to kill him anyway. Why didn't you just shoot him yourself?"

She collapsed with her hands over her face, wailing out her fear and rage. Finally, Joe reached out for her, straightened her up, and put his arm around her. "Come on, Blair. Let's go back to your car, get you out of this rain."

She didn't care about the rain or the thunder or the gunfire. But she didn't have the strength to fight him.

He walked her back, opened the door, and she got in.

"Wait here," he said. "I'll let you know what's happening."

He closed the door, and she buried her face in her arms on the steering wheel, groaning out her anguished hopelessness.

And then she remembered God. She rose up, sobbing, and looked through that wet windshield to the angry sky above her. She believed that he was there, watching over Cade as he'd done when he was in that basement, fighting for his life. He was Cade's refuge. And he was hers too.

"Don't let him die," she whispered. "Please, God, protect him one more time."

Thunder rumbled, and she touched her windshield, as if reaching through to him. "Please, Jesus." It was real, her belief in the one true God. The one to whom she could run when the Avenger hunted her down. When this was over, no matter how it ended, she would profess his name.

She would make a lousy Christian, she thought. A blackeye to all of Christendom. A huge scar on the face of the church.

But Christ had a thing for scars.

Her crying settled, and her sense of helplessness faded. She was not helpless. She could pray.

It was the most she could do for Cade.

"Nobody has to die." Cade stared into the barrel of that pistol, aiming dead center. "Give me your demands."

"I demand to see you dead."

Cade swallowed. "If you pull that trigger, they'll be on you so fast you won't have time to squeeze it again."

"It'd be worth it," Hull said, "just to see you lying in a bloody heap on this floor."

Cade's eyes locked with his, and he knew in his heart that Hull meant it, that he could kill him in a second without a thought, then go to prison for the rest of his life and think every day of that time that it was worth it.

Suddenly, he saw movement at the window behind Hull. Someone was there.

Cade was close to Hull, and any bullet meant for him could take Cade's head off too.

Hull must have heard movement, and he turned to the window and fired out. The baby began to scream.

Cade grabbed the baby carrier and hit the floor.

Another gunshot ...

And Hull collapsed.

A moment of stark silence followed, and Cade lay there, his body protecting the baby.

The door flew open, and an agent burst in, still holding the gun that had killed the detective.

Cade pulled himself up, biting back his pain. His hands trembled as he scooped the baby out of his seat and brought it to his shoulder. "Shhh," he said. "You're okay. It's gonna be all right."

He grabbed one of the crutches that Hull had taken from him and put it under his right arm, and cradling the baby in his left, he started out of the building. Pain tortured him with each jolt, draining his strength. He stopped and leaned against the building. The baby was getting wet, so he dropped his crutch and bent over him, trying to shield the child from the rain.

And then he heard a woman screaming ...

He searched the crowd through the rain and saw a black woman he'd never seen before, with Morgan behind her, running between the cars, forcing her way out into the parking lot toward him, making her way to the pier.

No one stopped her as she came toward him, running, screaming, "My baby, my baby!"

When she reached him, he handed her the baby. Dizziness swept over him, and he thought he might pass out. He wobbled and tried to steady himself.

He closed his eyes, heard voices screaming, yelling, feet running toward him ...

"Cade, you stupid, reckless idiot! What were you thinking?"

It was Blair's voice, pulling him from his pain. He opened his eyes, and she ran into his arms.

Police surrounded Karen and whisked her off, while others went to the building where Hull lay dead.

Blair began to weep, her body racking with anguish that seemed greater than his. He reached down for her face, tipped her chin up, and pressed his forehead against hers.

"Thank you, Jesus," she whispered. "Oh, thank you, Lord."

It sounded like a prayer. Cade let her words register in his mind, and he pulled back for a moment and gazed down at her. She was more beautiful than he'd ever seen her, with the rain soaking her hair and tears reddening her eyes, and those scars flaming against her pale, smooth skin.

With both hands, he framed her face—the side with the dried-out, crusted-over burn scars, and the soft, silky side—both of which he loved.

Slowly, he lowered his lips to hers and kissed her in the way that he had wanted to for so many years. His heart burst with the joy of it, as she seemed to melt to his touch.

All around them, chaos reigned. Radios crackled, thunder boomed, people yelled and ran past them. But Cade didn't hear any of it. All he knew was the taste and feel of Blair Owens as she surrendered to that same joy.

AFTERWORD

*T*here are times when I read a passage of Scripture, and it goes right over my head. Later, the Lord will direct me to the same passage again, and it's as if one verse is framed in neon and takes on a whole new meaning that applies so perfectly to my life at that moment. I guess that's why we're told that "the word of God is living and active. Sharper than any double-edged sword ..." (Hebrews 4:12).

Recently, that happened to me as I was reading Psalm 84. In the NASB translation, Psalm 84:5 says, "How blessed is the man whose strength is in Thee; In whose heart are the highways to Zion!"

I had been studying about the cities of refuge, and what they mean to us as Christians, so this verse took on special meaning.

And I asked myself if the highways to Zion are in my heart. Do all of my roads take me to Christ? Do all my desires, all my thoughts, all my emotions, all my intentions, point me to him? Have I put obstacles in my own way, roadblocks that make me stumble? Are there potholes I haven't repaired? Do I have detours that take me off that road?

I was further intrigued by the thought that the Lord didn't say that the fastest one to Zion wins or that I had to move down that highway in a certain type of vehicle or that my journey would be compared with anyone else's.

He simply blesses us if our hearts have the highways that take us to him!

I contemplated that for a while, and joyfully understood that the moment I surrendered my life to Christ, those highways were in my heart, already smooth and paved, and all of them took me to Christ. It is my job to keep them clear and well-maintained, to make sure they're not compromised by obstacles or unexpected pitfalls. It's my job to stay on that road. And if I ever do take a detour, with heartfelt repentance I can turn that road back to the highway.

Don't we serve a remarkable Lord, that he would bless us just for looking toward him? That the journey itself is blessed.

My prayer for each of my readers is that you will have the highways to Zion in your heart, and that every single road in your life will move you closer to almighty God, who helps us on our journey and waits with open arms when we arrive!

About the Author

*T*erri Blackstock is an award-winning novelist who has written for several major publishers including Harper-Collins, Dell, Harlequin, and Silhouette. Published under two pseudonyms, her books have sold over 3.5 million copies worldwide.

With her success in secular publishing at its peak, Blackstock had what she calls "a spiritual awakening." A Christian since the age of fourteen, she realized she had not been using her gift as God intended. It was at that point that she recommitted her life to Christ, gave up her secular career, and made the decision to write only books that would point her readers to him.

"I wanted to be able to tell the truth in my stories," she said, "and not just be politically correct. It doesn't matter how many readers I have if I can't tell them what I know about the roots of their problems and the solutions that have literally saved my own life."

Her books are about flawed Christians in crisis and God's provisions for their mistakes and wrong choices. She claims to be extremely qualified to write such books, since she's had years of personal experience.

A native of nowhere, since she was raised in the Air Force, Blackstock makes Mississippi her home. She and her husband are the parents of three children—a blended family which she considers one more of God's provisions.

RIVER'S EDGE

Terri Blackstock

ZONDERVAN

#1 Bestselling Author

Read an excerpt form Book Three of the Cafe Refuge series, *River's Edge*.

CHAPTER

1

*T*he cramps woke Morgan at 3:30 a.m., startling her out of a deep slumber. She'd been immersed in a dream about a little girl on a swing set, her long brown hair flowing on the breeze. She knew without a doubt that the child was the baby she was carrying.

The cramps offered a stark warning, as if her anxiety had shaped into a blunt instrument that bludgeoned her hope.

She sat up, her hand pressed over her flat stomach, and looked at Jonathan, who slept peacefully next to her. Should she wake him to tell him she was cramping, or just be still and wait for it to pass?

She had taken the home pregnancy test yesterday morning, then followed up with a blood test at her doctor's office that afternoon. Jonathan sat in the examining room with her, fidgeting and chattering to pass the time. When the nurse came back with the verdict, he sprang to his feet, muscles all tense, like a tiger tracking a gazelle.

"Before I tell you the results, I need to know if I'm bearing good or bad news."

Jonathan glanced at Morgan, and she knew he was way too close to calling the woman a smart aleck and warning her not to toy with them. "Come on, just tell us."

"But do you want to be pregnant? Is good news a yes or a no?"

Before he could grab the nurse by the shoulders and shake the playfulness out of her, Morgan blurted out, "Yes! More than anything!"

"Are we going to have a baby or not?" Jonathan asked.

"Congratulations!" The word burst out of the nurse's mouth, and Morgan came off the table, flinging herself into his arms, and they yelled like kids as he swung her around.

They agreed not to announce it until today, so they could share that first night of giddy excitement, crushing the secret between them.

They waited until Caleb, their eighteen-month-old foster child, was sound asleep, then went across the street to Hanover House's private stretch of beach. They giggled and danced under the May moonlight, to the music of the waves whooshing and frothing against the shore. When they'd finally gone to bed, they lay awake until close to midnight, wondering if it would be a girl or a boy, and how soon they would be able to see their child on a sonogram. Jonathan held Morgan and whispered about soccer games and ballet, piano lessons and PTA.

Finally, they had both fallen asleep, and now she didn't want to wake him. It was probably nothing. Just something she ate last night. She would have to be more careful now.

But as the moments dragged on the cramping grew worse, and she couldn't ignore it. She folded her arms across her stomach and slid her feet out of bed. She sat up and realized it was worse, even, than she thought. There was blood.

"Oh, no." The words came out loud and unbidden, and Jonathan turned over and looked up at her in the night.

"Baby, what is it?"

She turned on the lamp. "Oh, Jonathan . . ."

He looked at her with an innocent, terrible dread, expecting something, though not clear what. Slowly, he sat up. "What?"

A sob rose in her throat as she pointed to the mattress.

For a moment they both just stared at it, the blood-spot of a dream dying.

Their unformed, barely real, secret baby dying.

Then he jolted out of his stunned stupor and sprang out of bed. "Are you okay?"

"I'm losing it." The words bubbled up in her throat. "Jonathan, I'm losing the baby!"

"We're going to the hospital. Maybe it's not what you think. Maybe they can stop it." He pulled on the jeans hanging over a chair by the bed.

Maybe he was right. Maybe the baby was still there, nestled in its little sac, unscathed by whatever thing had broken loose in her. Or if not, maybe the medical staff could ward off danger, stop the impending doom, give her some magic pill to make it hang on.

She quickly got dressed while Jonathan woke Sadie—their seventeen-year-old foster daughter and Caleb's sister—to tell her of the emergency and ask her to listen for her little brother in case they weren't back when he awoke.

Then Jonathan helped Morgan out to the car as though she were a sick woman who couldn't walk on her own. She tried not to make sudden moves, not to walk too hard, not to cramp so tightly.

But it all seemed out of her control.

"It's okay, baby," Jonathan said as he drove at breakneck speed across the island. "We'll be in Savannah in no time."

Was it already too late? The drive from Cape Refuge to the closest hospital was too far. She cried quietly, staring out the windshield, praying that God would intervene.

"God's going to save her," he muttered as he drove. "He has to."

Morgan's face twisted. "Her . . . you said *her*." She looked over at him and saw the tears on his face. "You think it's a girl?"

He didn't answer. "God, please . . ."

She sobbed as he drove, her hand pressed against her stomach. *What kind of mother am I? I couldn't keep it safe for a day?* Her tears were cold against her face in the breeze of the air-conditioner.

Jonathan's lips moved in some silent monologue—a desperate preacher's prayer of faith and hope—or the angry railing of a seaman who saw terror coming and believed he could head it off with enough threats. His hands clutched the steering wheel, and occasionally he reached over to touch her with fearful reassurance.

Finally, they reached St. Joseph's, and Jonathan pulled up to the emergency room door. He got out and ran to Morgan's side, helped her out. There was blood all over the back of her robe, and some of it had soaked into the seat.

"I need help here!" Jonathan helped her through the sliding glass door. "Please, someone help!"

But Morgan knew there was no help for her baby. It was already too late.

River's Edge
Cape Refuge Series
Terri Blackstock
#1 Bestselling Suspense Author

In Book Three of the #1 bestselling Cape Refuge series, Terri Blackstock weaves another riveting story of blackmail, deceit, and murder. Reconciling themselves to the tragic death of her parents, Morgan and Jonathan Clearly continue to manage Hanover House, a residence for those seeking a new start in life. They are also trying desperately to have a child. When Jonathan is recruited to run for mayor, they are drawn into a gritty campaign that test their faith and ethics.

Ben Jackson seems to have the mayoral election locked up—until his wife's body is found at the bottom of the river. Police Chief Cade investigates Lisa's death and finds the facts of the case don't add up. Lisa's best friend and partner is sure Ben is responsible in some way. Rani Baxter claims Lisa had been receiving mysterious letters written by a woman claiming she had an affair with Ben. Even though Ben swore the letters were a hoax, Blair Owens—in her new job as newspaper reporter—begins searching for the woman who wrote the letters. Could Lisa's death have anything to do with Ben's affair? Was it tied to her decade-long quest to get pregnant? Does the fertitlity clinic she'd been frequenting—the same one she encouraged Morgan to visit—hold any clues? Was this an act of a jealous love? A dangerous client? Or is this all about the elections?

Softcover: 0-310-23594-4

Breaker's Reef

Cape Refuge Series

Terri Blackstock

#1 Bestselling Suspense Author

A famous mystery writer has just moved to Cape Refuge when a teenage girl is found murdered. Sheila Caruso—ex-con, mother to Sadie and Caleb, and resident of Hanover House—is working for the writer when she discovers that a scene in one of his novels matches the crime scene.

When Police Chief Cade and Blair Owens discover a second dead teenager—mirroring a murder in another of the eccentric writer's books—Cade is drawn into a web of trickery and deceit. Evidence turns up in Cade's own truck, and suddenly he becomes the number-one suspect.

Cade tries to clear his name, but when eighteen-year-old Sadie Caruso disappears, tensions mount to a fever pitch. Can Cade find the real killer before Sadie winds up dead? Is the novelist a demented killer, or a hapless victim? And what does Sadie's own mother have to do with the crimes?

Secrets are uncovered, while lessons are learned about the sins of the father being visited upon his children. Will the consequences of Sheila's life be fatal, or is there redemption and mercy for her and her children?

"Chief Matthew Cade rarely considered another line of work, but news of the dead teenage girl made him long for a job as an accountant or electrician—some benign vocation that didn't require him to look into the eyes of grieving parents."

Softcover: 0-310-23595-2

Three ways to keep up on your favorite Zondervan books and authors

Sign up for our *Fiction E-Newsletter*. Every month you'll receive sample excerpts from our books, sneak peeks at upcoming books, and chances to win free books autographed by the author.

You can also sign up for our *Breakfast Club*. Every morning in your email, you'll receive a five-minute snippet from a fiction or nonfiction book. A new book will be featured each week, and by the end of the week you will have sampled two to three chapters of the book.

Zondervan *Author Tracker* is the best way to be notified whenever your favorite Zondervan authors write new books, go on tour, or want to tell you about what's happening in their lives.

Visit *www.zondervan.com* and sign up today!